CULT

Camilla Lackberg is a worldwide bestseller renowned for her brilliant contemporary psychological thrillers. Her books are sold in over 60 countries and have been translated into 43 languages.

www.camillalackberg.com

Henrik Fexeus is one of Sweden's most sought after lecturers and a prize-winning mentalist. He has done astounding psychological experiments on SVT and TV4 and became a household name in 2007, with the debut book *The Art of Reading Minds*. Fexeus's books have won several prizes, sold over 1.5 million copies and are translated into more than 30 languages. Henrik made his debut as an author of fiction in 2017, with YA novel *The Lost*, the first part in his critically acclaimed Final Illusion Trilogy.

www.henrikfexeus.se

Also by Camilla Lackberg

The Ice Princess
The Preacher
The Stonecutter
The Stranger (previously titled *The Gallows Bird*)
The Hidden Child
The Drowning
The Lost Boy
Buried Angels
The Ice Child
The Girl in the Woods
The Gilded Cage
Silver Tears
Trapped

SHORT STORIES
THE SCENT OF ALMONDS & OTHER STORIES

Also by Henrik Fexeus

The Art of Reading Minds
The Art of Social Excellence
Trapped

CULT

CAMILLA LÄCKBERG
& HENRIK FEXEUS

THE INTERNATIONAL BESTSELLERS

Translated from the Swedish by Ian Giles

HarperCollinsPublishers

HarperCollins*Publishers* Ltd
1 London Bridge Street,
London SE1 9GF

www.harpercollins.co.uk

HarperCollins*Publishers*
Macken House, 39/40 Mayor Street Upper,
Dublin 1, D01 C9W8, Ireland

First published by HarperCollins*Publishers* 2023
1

Originally published in 2022 by
Bokförlaget Forum, Sweden, as *Kult*

A catalogue record for this book is available from the British Library

ISBN: 978-0-00-846423-3 (HB)
ISBN: 978-0-00-846424-0 (TPB)

This novel is entirely a work of fiction.
The names, characters and incidents portrayed in it are
the work of the author's imagination. Any resemblance to
actual persons, living or dead, events or localities is
entirely coincidental.

Typeset in Sabon LT Std by Palimpsest Book Production Ltd,
Falkirk, Stirlingshire

Printed and bound in the UK using 100% Renewable
Electricity by CPI Group (UK) Ltd

This book is produced from independently certified FSC™ paper
to ensure responsible forest management.

For more information visit: www.harpercollins.co.uk/green

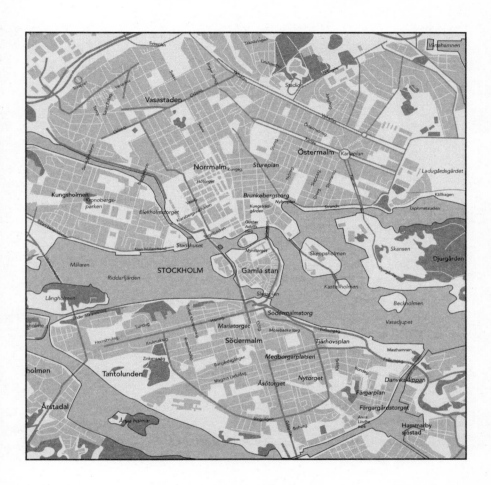

The First Week

1

For what must be the hundredth time, Fredrik checks that nothing is visible through the plastic carrier bag. He doesn't want to spoil the surprise. The summer sun is scorching his face. It must be at least twenty-nine degrees out. Despite the heat, he opts to stroll from his office in Skanstull to Ossian's nursery near Zinkensdamm metro station. It's a Wednesday, but he's still managed to get away from the office a little earlier than usual. No one cares about formal working hours when it's this hot – most of his colleagues are already nursing a cold one in the shade outside a bar somewhere.

The walk only takes around twenty minutes, but he really should have brought a bottle of water, given the heat. His jacket has come off and his shirtsleeves are rolled up. Sweat plasters the shirt to his back. But none of it matters. Today everything is just as it should be.

He checks the bag again. The box containing the Lego Technic kit is so big that it almost protrudes past the carry handles. A McLaren Senna GTR. Ossian's interest in cars remains a mystery: both Fredrik and Josefin border on having an active disinterest in cars. But father and son most definitely share an interest in building Lego.

The age marked on the box is 10+, and Ossian is only five, but Fredrik knows the boy will still work it out without difficulty. He's bright. Sometimes brighter than his old man, Fredrik thinks to himself, before laughing up at the sun. Yes indeedy – this razor-sharp dad who just bought a surprise that entails hours of indoor activity on one of the best days of summer. Oh well. It can't be helped. The weather will probably be fine tomorrow too.

Besides, Ossian has already spent the whole day outside – which is a necessity. When he's not focusing on his Lego, he's climbing the walls at home. Josefin often wonders whether it would be possible to get a diagnosis for their son. Not that they intend to get him examined. Not yet, anyway. Thus far, Ossian's activity levels remain something positive, especially when compared to all those mobile phone kids at nursery who already engross themselves in their parents' iPhones the second they're picked up. Tragic.

Fredrik arrives at Backens nursery and checks his watch. Despite the heat, he's walked there so quickly that he's early. They're probably still up at the Skinnarviksparken.

He hums 'Gangnam Style', Ossian's favourite song right now, as he climbs the hill behind the nursery building. He might as well give in to the urge, Fredrik thinks to himself, smiling. They've even been practising the dance moves together.

On top of the hill there is a large playground and some trees to play among. As far as Ossian is concerned, it's a whole forest. He loves being in the forest.

'Let's dance Gangnam Style!' Fredrik calls out, and kids who barely reach up to his knees look at him in surprise before resuming their games.

The children are wearing yellow bibs emblazoned with the logos of various nursery schools. It's a popular park. The air is filled with screams and laughter. Lego Technic will probably have to wait for another time. Today seems to have been made for hide-and-seek in the trees. There's no rush to get home – Josefin promised to sort out dinner today. He looks around and spots Tom, one of the teachers at Backens.

'Hi!' he says, smiling at Tom, who is in the middle of wiping a thick strand of snot off one of the children.

'Hello,' Tom replies cheerily. 'Guess who got to pick the music for today's movement session?'

'I warned you. You're going to have thirty kids doing the "Gangnam" dance before the week's out. But do you know where the dance genius himself is? I don't see him.'

Tom finishes his wiping and pauses for a moment's thought.

'Check the swings,' he says. 'He sometimes likes to sit there for a while.'

Of course. When Ossian isn't being hyperactive, he loves to

go on the swings. Well, he loves to sit on the swings. It's his sanctuary, where he can think over the big things without being disturbed.

Fredrik walks over to the swings. They're all occupied, but Ossian isn't on any of them. Felicia, one of Ossian's older nursery peers, is leaving. Fredrik catches up with her.

'Hi, Felicia – have you seen Ossian?'

'No, only earlier.'

He frowns. The slight feeling that something is up begins to take over stealthily. He knows it's an irrational feeling, nothing more than an outburst of parental overprotectiveness. It strikes as soon as anything might be wrong, and it doesn't give a damn whether there's any evidence or not. It was probably a great survival instinct in the savannah, but right now it is wholly unwarranted. He knows that, rationally. But it doesn't help. The feeling creeps uncomfortably down his spine like a slightly-too-cold gust of wind. The big box of Lego that previously seemed so exciting is now mostly an encumbrance as he hurries back to Tom.

'He wasn't by the swings either,' he says.

'That's weird.'

Tom looks at a list of kids with checkboxes next to their names.

'He's meant to be . . . actually, hang on. Jenya took the smaller kids back inside. He may have gone with them to go to the loo and then ended up staying there. Sorry. Jenya really should have mentioned that she was taking him with her. But you know what it's like.'

Yes, he does know what it's like. The feeling that something is wrong disappears. He sighs with relief. Tom and Jenya are both good nursery school teachers, but kids also have a will of their own in addition to an unerring ability to not be where you expect them to be. He feels sorry for Tom when he sees how embarrassed he is. Because little kids are not something to be careless with. There are probably parents who would have made a big scene about less.

'Of course,' he says. 'Have a good weekend, Tom. See you Monday!'

5

Fredrik jogs slowly down the hill, heading back towards the nursery school. The door is propped open. He goes inside to the cloakroom where the children's pegs and drawers with their spare clothes are. Ossian's peg is empty. That doesn't really have to mean anything. If Ossian came back to use the toilet, then his jacket might very well be lying in a heap on the bathroom floor. Or, for that matter, it might be back up in the playground, given the heat. Fredrik shouldn't even have put his son in a jacket on a day like this. Silly of him. Ossian must have been boiling.

Fredrik doesn't bother to take off his shoes as he usually would when going inside.

'Ossian?' he shouts, knocking on the first of the two toilet doors. 'Ossian, are you in there?'

Jenya comes walking down the corridor towards him. Behind her, the two-year-olds are hurling finger paint at each other while hooting with equal parts delight and horror.

'Hello, Fredrik,' she says. 'Did you forget something? Ossian's up at the park with Tom.'

The feeling that something is wrong returns so quickly that it almost flattens him. It's no longer a small gust of wind down his spine. Now it's a clenched fist to the stomach.

'He's not at the park,' he says. 'I've just come from there. Tom said he was probably with you.'

'No, he's not in here. Did you check the swings?'

'Yes. I told you. He's not there. Bloody hell.'

He turns on his heel and rushes back outside. It has been known for the odd kid at the nursery to escape. Like Felicia. She managed to make it all the way home once before the staff realized she was missing. Her parents have both felt faintly nauseous about it ever since. Was that a feeling you ever got used to? He hates it.

He runs back up the hill. The damn box of Lego is slapping against his legs. There are kids all over the shop, all of them in the way. He searches desperately among them while also trying to calm down. Nothing will be improved by him panicking. But none of the children is Ossian.

None of them is his son.

Tom's eyes widen when he sees Fredrik returning. He seems to get it right away.

'He must be here,' Fredrik says, dropping the bag so that he can move around the park more swiftly.

Tom asks the nearest children whether any of them have seen Ossian. The playhouses. Ossian might be hiding in the playhouses. Fredrik runs over to them but can already tell from a distance that they're empty. Where else might he . . . Surely he's not in the trees? Not on his own? Surely someone would know if that were the case?

Felicia.

She said she'd seen Ossian earlier.

He runs back to Tom and the other kids. The exertion is scouring his throat as sweat pours from his brow and runs down his back. Felicia is there, building a sandcastle with a bucket. As if nothing out of the ordinary has happened. As if the world isn't about to end. 'Felicia,' he says, making an effort not to sound as wild as he feels inside. 'You said you saw Ossian earlier. When was that?'

'When he was talking to that stupid lady,' she says, without looking up from her construction project.

'That stupid . . .' he says, his throat morphing to sandpaper. 'Was it an old lady?'

Felicia shakes her head resolutely as she pats the castle with a spade.

'Not old,' she said. 'Like my mum. It was just her birthday, so she's thirty-five now.'

He gulps hard. Someone has been here. Someone has been here talking to his child. Someone who wasn't a teacher or parent. A stranger. He crouches beside Felicia, resisting the impulse to shake her.

'Do you know who she was?' he says, struggling not to shout. 'And why was she stupid?'

Felicia looks up from her sandcastle with tears in her eyes. He takes a step backwards to avoid losing his balance. He sees it in her gaze: he already knows full well what has happened. What must never happen. Can never happen.

'I didn't care about her toy cars,' says Felicia. 'Ossian liked them, but I didn't. But I wanted to stroke the puppies too. She said she had them in her car. But I wasn't allowed to come with her. Only Ossian was going to get to see them. Then they went.'

A black hole opens up inside Fredrik and he falls helplessly into it.

2

Mina was standing at the entrance scrutinizing the premises. There weren't many people at the gym at this time of the afternoon. Good. And it was mainly the older crowd. The high school kids, CrossFit ladies and musclemen had already been and gone. At three o'clock on a weekday afternoon, the seniors reigned supreme at the gym. At least for the next hour or so. This was better, since they were far more thorough in wiping down the equipment, removing all trace of both themselves and the sweat monsters who had been here earlier. Not that Mina intended to take any risks. In the pocket of her tracksuit jacket were, as always, thin single-use gloves, two small spray bottles containing disinfectant, microfibre cloths and a resealable bag to deposit them in once they were used.

Today's workout agenda included legs and core. She pulled on her gloves and made for one of the vacant leg machines, where she began to spray every part. She had seen that some people only sprayed the handles. Or worse: just the seat. But other people's dirt and bacteria could end up all over the place. She couldn't wrap her head around people who cut corners.

She folded the cloth, inserted it into the resealable bag and got out a new one. Stepping into the gym was like stepping into a potential nidus. That was why working out in the gym at police headquarters was impossible. She knew exactly which filthy so-and-sos used it. At least here she didn't have to put a face to the filth.

Ideally, she would have preferred to work out wearing a mask, given what was probably circulating in the air in the place. She'd heard that weightlifters often farted and she had difficulty breathing when she thought about all the faecal bacteria circulating through the ventilation system. But a mask would only attract yet more unnecessary attention. On the other hand, maybe she could get a workout mask: one of those ones that people used to hone their respiratory muscles.

'You here to work out or clean? If you're done, I'd like to use the machine.' Mina started and looked up from the backrest that she was in the middle of sanitizing. A white-haired man in his seventies wearing small round glasses was standing before her with a quizzical expression. He was wearing a red top – not gym kit made from something breathable, but simply an ordinary cotton T-shirt. There was a big dark sweat patch on his chest. She shuddered.

'Do you know how unhygienic that cotton T-shirt is?' she said. 'It gets soaked in sweat, then it messes up all the machines. Working out in clothes like that shouldn't be allowed.'

The man looked daggers at her. Then he shook his head and walked away. She was clearly not worth his time. Not that she cared in the slightest. She applied a few more rotations of the cloth before putting it and the gloves into the resealable bag, getting onto the leg machine and adjusting the weight. The man in the red T-shirt was sitting on the pull-down machine with his back to her. Naturally he had a huge sweat patch on his back too. She wrinkled her nose. If the choice were between being liked and being healthy, she knew for sure which one she'd choose. People could keep their bacteria and their approval to themselves.

Mina was used to others thinking she was an alien being. She didn't need them in her life. The whole thing about feeling connected to other people was probably just as big a myth as 'soulmates', 'true love' and all those other unrealistic concepts marketed by Hollywood. The result? Ordinary people were left anxious. There was even research to prove it. She had read that people rated their own relationship and their partner worse after watching a romcom. No real relationship could live up to the fabricated concept of 'eternal love'.

In her own case, she hadn't felt connected to anyone of late. Not in the past either, come to think of it. With the exception of the brief time she had spent with her daughter. But the man she had once lived with was hardly a source of fond memories. No, there had been no 'connection' there. Not with anyone.

Except . . .

With him.

The mentalist.

But that was a long time ago now.

She'd seen an advert for Vincent's new show on Facebook. She'd come so close to buying a ticket. But she'd refrained. She didn't know how she'd react if she saw him on stage. What if he didn't recognize her in the audience?

What if he did?

She frowned. Distance was better. For safety's sake. After all, he hadn't even been in touch. Obviously she understood why. To start with, he had a family. She wouldn't blame his wife if she wondered what on earth he and Mina had been up to almost two years ago. Vincent had said that Maria was prone to powerful jealousy. And events on the island had hardly improved matters. Mina had almost died alongside Vincent. It would be reasonable for Vincent's wife to hate Mina after that. Not that it had been her fault. But she was still a cop.

Besides, she and Vincent had shared something that couldn't be explained to others. Events on Lidö had brought them closer together than before.

At the same time, it was also that connection that had made it so difficult to remain in touch. They'd got so close. Closer than she had been able to handle. So it was better like this. When she was alone, she was in her fort. She was safe. He probably felt the same way.

Still . . .

3

'Remember,' said Vincent, 'that what you're about to see isn't real. This is a demonstration of how to show off your supernatural powers without actually having any. Because, believe me, I really don't have any.'

He raised an eyebrow that formed a silent question mark. About half the audience laughed. But it was a strained laugh. An uncertain laugh. Just the way he wanted it.

Crusellhallen in Linköping was packed to the rafters even though it was midweek: 1,200 people who were either local or had come from other nearby communities to see the Master Mentalist on a Wednesday night. In reality, the audience was rather on the big side for his liking, but his involvement in a murder inquiry almost two years ago had attracted significant media attention. Even if he had not had a public profile beforehand, he would have done afterwards. Not for himself, of course. No one knew who Vincent was. But the Master Mentalist was adored by the media. And the punters. Ticket sales had doubled after the news that he had almost died in a water tank.

However, Umberto had managed to keep the more personal details of Vincent's involvement in the case out of the media. That was frankly the only reason why he still had a career. The public would probably have seen him through very different eyes had they known that he had been the indirect cause of three murders. Of course Vincent was innocent. At least when it came to the murders. But innocence was always a relative concept to the press. So he and his agent had done all they could to conceal Jane's motives and her true identity, which had been aided by Jane and Kenneth vanishing from the face of the earth.

Expressen had briefly tried to dig up the story about his mother, but Umberto had found out and come down on them like a hawk. He'd threatened the paper with being excluded from all future press releases and interviews with the artists that he represented if they went to press. Were they truly prepared to sacrifice their gateway to half the Swedish entertainment business for one grubby story? The answer turned out to be no. Vincent guessed that Umberto's Italian temperament had probably played its part too.

However, the detail that the murderer had spelled out his name using the dates of the murders had managed to find its way into the public domain. The story was too good not to assume a life of its own.

After that, people had started sending in their own mysteries, riddles and puzzles to Vincent, without giving a moment's thought to how insensitive that was. But then again, if people had been easy to understand he would never have resorted to becoming a mentalist.

'What I'm about to do may seem to come from the turn of the last century,' he continued. 'But the same methods are still used to start religions. Not to mention cults.'

The stage was decorated as a late-nineteenth-century drawing room and Vincent wore era-appropriate costume. Two upholstered leather armchairs were angled towards each other. Sitting in one of them was a man who was clearly nervous.

Earlier, Vincent had asked whether anyone in the audience had medical training, or at the very least knew how to take a pulse. The man was one of the people to have raised his hand. He had been completely calm when Vincent had asked him to come up on stage. In fact, he had laughed. But after Vincent had asked him to sign an agreement declaring that the man had no medical or legal liability for what was about to happen, and that Vincent took full responsibility for his actions, the man had become significantly more nervous. And he wasn't the only one – the whole audience was on edge. Vincent loved it. The signed agreement was an easy way to ramp up the drama. Each time he requested a signature, it reminded Vincent that the stunt could actually go wrong for real.

'So, Adrian,' he said, settling down in the empty armchair diagonally across from the man. 'We're going to try and make contact with the other side. With the dead. Do you have any late relatives you'd like to make contact with? I can sense loss in you, but not your grandmother . . . I can feel that she is still alive . . . but perhaps . . . your grandfather? You miss him?'

The man laughed a little nervously and fidgeted.

'Yes, Elsa's alive,' he said. 'But Arvid died ten years back. That's my grandpa.'

It was a trick that any old medium could pull off. Just simple inference. The man appeared to be in his late twenties. This meant his parents ought to be between fifty and sixty years old. And their parents in turn would be eighty to ninety. Since women had a greater life expectancy than men, it was statistically likelier for his grandmother to be alive than his grandfather. In any other setting, Vincent would have been ashamed by his own bluff, especially when he saw how affected the man before him became. But this act was about ensnaring others, gaining their trust and finally their money – which meant all means were on the table.

'Well then, let's try and find Grandpa Arvid,' said Vincent.

He cast his gaze across the audience.

'And yet again, let me remind you that this isn't for real.'

He turned to face Adrian, his expression serious.

'I'm now going to make contact with the other side,' he said. 'But in order to do so, I must first . . . cross over.'

He produced a belt and held it up for all to see. Then he wrapped it around his neck and pulled the end through the buckle to create a noose. He reached out with his left arm towards the man, who was growing paler by the moment.

'Take my pulse,' he said. 'And tap your foot in time with the pulse so that everyone else can hear it.'

The man grabbed him by the wrist and spent a while searching with his index and middle finger until he was satisfied. Then he began to tap the floor rhythmically in time with Vincent's bloodstream. Vincent looked him in the eyes.

'See you when I'm back,' he said. 'Hopefully. Keep tracking my pulse with your foot.'

Then he tightened the belt around his neck and grimaced. He didn't have to fake this bit – it really did hurt. He continued to hold the belt tightly while Adrian rhythmically followed his pulse. After a few seconds, Adrian's tapping began to slow down in pace.

13

Vincent closed his eyes and slumped his head, although he didn't let go of the belt. Adrian made an uncertain foot tap, then he stopped. A murmur of shock and nervousness rippled through the audience. Adrian was still holding him by the wrist, but he was no longer making a sound with his foot. The meaning of that was crystal clear. Vincent no longer had a pulse. He had just strangled himself.

Vincent waited until he heard the sound of people fidgeting in their seats in the stalls. This was the sign that they were beginning to feel scared for real. He slowly began to raise his head, and he let go of the belt. Then he turned towards Adrian and looked at him, his gaze far away.

'Adrian,' he mumbled.

Adrian jumped.

'There is a spirit in this room who goes by the name of Arvid,' Vincent said, his voice groggy. 'Let us be sure that it is truly your grandfather. Ask him something that only you and he know. Perhaps something from when you were little. Arvid says . . . Arvid says he taught you to cycle? Maybe something about that?'

Adrian nodded, clearly confused.

'Ask him where I hit myself,' he said.

Vincent fell silent for a few seconds as if he were listening to a voice that only he could hear.

'You scraped your knee,' he said. 'And you agreed not to tell your mother anything about it. You still have the scar.'

Adrian let go of Vincent's arm, looking visibly shocked. The truth was that most people had a childhood memory of a scraped knee. The rest of what Vincent had said had been nothing more than a downright punt. But memories were vulnerable things. Even if things hadn't gone quite the way Vincent had said, that was now how Adrian remembered them in his head.

'Arvid has a message for you,' Vincent continued. 'He says . . . he says you must persevere and believe in yourself. It will be a success, though it will take a bit longer than you expected. But you must not give up hope. Do you understand what that means?'

Adrian nodded silently.

14

'He's talking about my business,' he said. 'That was the last thing we talked about before he died. I still haven't managed to get it up and running properly.'

'He says he's sorry about what happened. What does he mean by that?'

'We didn't talk much in the final years,' Adrian said quietly. 'We had a row.'

'Yes, he regrets that now. He also says that he loved you then and he still does.'

Tears began to flow down Adrian's cheeks. Vincent had an important point to make in this part of the show, but he really did hate how powerfully it impacted people. All he had done was deliver a series of so-called Barnum statements. Utterances that sounded specific, but which were extremely open to interpretation and applied to most people. The classic trick used by mediums was to let the client work out the meaning of whatever the 'spirits' said by themselves. That way the medium could never be wrong. Anything that didn't add up was simply to be blamed on the client failing to recollect properly.

'Contact is weakening,' he said, his voice strained. 'Do you have anything you want to say before it's too late?'

'Just . . . thank you,' Adrian whispered. 'Thank you.'

Vincent reached out his arm, and his head slumped. He was visibly unconscious. The whole auditorium was dead silent. Adrian hesitantly grasped his wrist and searched with his fingers. After a while, Adrian began to quietly tap his foot. The sound was slow and irregular at first. Then more and more regular, louder, until Vincent's pulse was back to normal.

Vincent opened his eyes. He clutched Adrian's hand, smiling hesitantly. This number was never one to garner mass applause. The audience was always too dazed for that. They were far too unsure of what they had just seen. But he knew that this was something they would talk about for months afterwards.

'Remember,' he said to the audience, using the same words that he had begun with, but this time far more gently.

They were vulnerable now. He had to respect that.

'I can't make contact with spirits. To be honest, I don't think anyone can, since I don't believe spirits exist. On the other hand,

I can make it look like they do – just like mediums, who can be equally compelling. The same psychological and verbal techniques used one hundred and fifty years ago are still in use to give the impression that someone charging a fat hourly rate can make contact with your departed nearest and dearest. As ever: if something seems too good to be true, then it usually is. Thank you for coming this evening.'

He stepped off the stage before they began to clap. He wanted to leave them in a moment of reflection this time.

His neck felt tender. That bloody belt hurt. He needed to be more careful. And he'd also stopped his pulse for far too long today. Contacting the spirits might be fake, but the stopped pulse was very much the real deal – even though he did it using a method other than the belt, and even if he only stopped the pulse in his arm rather than his entire body. The fact that there were techniques to stop the pulse in isolated parts of the body was one of mentalism's best-kept secrets and Vincent hadn't revealed to anyone how he did it. But it didn't matter that it was only his arm. Things could still get really dangerous after thirty seconds. Most often, people would let go as soon as his pulse stopped, but Adrian had hung on, leaving Vincent with no choice. He would be a very happy man when this tour was over. Blocking the body's blood flow this much wasn't good for anyone.

He made for the green room and saw the bottles of mineral water on the table. Three. He clenched his jaw. The sight of three bottles was akin to hearing a dissonant note. He quickly opened the fridge and put out another one, making it four. Only then did his jawline relax. Then he filled a glass with tap water from the sink, sat down on the sofa and exhaled.

The audience were still clapping out there, but he left them alone. It would be all too easy to return, grin broadly and transform their experience into something banal. Instead, he wanted them to hang on to their thoughts.

A minute's rest, then he would change. He was working on no longer lying down on the floor after each performance. Sometimes he was successful. Most often not. He pulled out his mobile. Sains Bergander, Vincent's friend who built illusions and had assisted in the investigation into Tuva's disappearance and the murders, had been in the audience tonight and Vincent was curious to know what he thought about the new production. Sains had indeed texted him. According to the time code, it had been sent at the very moment Vincent had come off stage. But Sains' message would have to wait. There might be others who had been in touch.

One other, to be specific.

Vincent opened his message inbox. Sure enough, there were a few other unread messages awaiting him. But not the one he was looking for. The one from the person who had changed his life when she had become part of it. The one with whom he'd dared to share his innermost self. The one who had vanished from his existence as quickly as she had appeared.

The last time he'd seen her it had been October. Then came winter, spring, summer, autumn, and now another summer. He hadn't spoken to her in more than one and a half years. Going on for two. Not that he'd tried to get in touch, no matter how much he might have liked to; he and Maria had started in couples therapy and he wanted to avoid triggering his wife's jealousy unnecessarily.

They had recently quit therapy since it hadn't helped as much as they had hoped it might. But by then so much time had passed. He didn't want to intrude after such a long silence. She cherished her private life and that was something he had to respect. Even if he missed being a part of it. Of course, there was also no reason for her to get in touch with him. She'd been quite clear about the fact that she could manage on her own. He had no idea what her life might look like now. She might even be married. With a family. Or living abroad.

But he couldn't help it. The first time he'd met her had been after a performance. Since then, he'd looked for her every time he stepped off stage. But his messages told their own story.

Mina hadn't been in touch tonight either.

4

She took off her glasses and smiled at him. Then she crossed one leg over the other and leaned forward in her chair. They were sitting opposite each other without the separation of a table. Initially, Ruben had found this deeply unpleasant. He felt exposed. But he had grown accustomed to it. So much so that he no longer bothered to try and look at her cleavage when she leaned towards him. Not any longer. And Amanda was far from unattractive.

'You mean I'm done?' Ruben said, checking the time.

He'd only been there half an hour. But Amanda seemed ready to draw the meeting to a close.

'I don't think we're ever done,' she said. 'But I don't see any compelling reason why you need to come back here, unless something new happens. Although it's not really for me to decide. How do you feel yourself?'

Ruben looked at Amanda – the psychologist he had been seeing every second Thursday for more than a year. What did he feel? That was one hell of a question. But it didn't annoy him as much now as it had in the beginning.

'What I feel is something we can leave for Freud,' he said. 'If there's one thing I've learned it's that my feelings don't need to be what I think they should be. I no longer choose to act based on my feelings – instead my rational thoughts drive that. Just like I've abstained from sex for six months. No matter how much my feelings would like a shag.'

Amanda raised an eyebrow in an unspoken question.

'No, I haven't been out on the pull at all,' he clarified. 'Like we agreed. That's what I mean. I'm not going to stop that entirely. After all, I am a man in my prime. But it doesn't feel as important now that I realize what need that behaviour was meeting.'

'And what was that need?'

Ruben sighed. They'd got there anyway. To those bloody feelings. 'It gave me a feeling of power to know I could get them. The women. But it also filled a deeper desire for . . .'

He sighed again.

'For closeness,' he said reluctantly. 'Are you happy now?'

Closeness. It wasn't a word he'd ever thought he'd say aloud. It sounded so damn poofy. But even that kind of reaction was a defensive mechanism. That much he'd learned. Jesus. His police mate Gunnar and the other lads in the flying squad would piss their pants if they knew he was seeing a shrink. Gunnar was hewn from Norrland timber – that was what he always said. His solution to every problem was to head into the forest with a couple of beers. The guys would paint his fucking helmet pink if they knew what he told Amanda. He glanced at the clock on the wall again. Half past eight. He ought to have been at police headquarters by now – before anyone started wondering what he got up to some mornings. The usual excuse that he'd had to see a one-night stand off the premises could only be proffered so many times.

One-night stands. Hmm. He barely remembered what to do any longer on that front. He'd obviously tried to proposition Amanda the first time they'd met, running on autopilot. It had not been an unqualified success.

'I think there's only one thing left for me to do,' he said. 'I'd like to see Ellinor.'

'Ruben,' Amanda said, her voice filled with warning. 'Remember what we said about moving on. Ellinor has been hanging around you like a ghost all these years. Your behaviour has been a reaction to that. You have to let go. You won't be done until you've vanquished that ghost.'

'I know. That's why I want to see her. So I can get closure. I promise I'll just go there and say hello. I'll take her down from the pedestal I've put her on. That way, old Ruben won't have any fuel left.'

'That's . . . unusually clear-headed for you,' Amanda said, squinting at him. 'Are you sure?'

'The worst thing that can happen is that you get to bill me for a few more hours of therapy afterwards,' he said, laughing.

But the fact was that he was dead set on it. He was a better Ruben than he had been a year ago. Gunnar could shut his trap.

They both stood up and he shook hands with Amanda. For

the fiftieth time, he resisted the temptation to ask her whether she'd like to go for a drink with him. It was fine to have the idea so long as he didn't act on it. He was still Ruben, after all. Anyway, he had other fish to fry. He'd already found out where Ellinor lived. Just a quick hello. See how she was doing. And a sorry. Then he'd be done.

5

Vincent took a deep breath before he entered the kitchen to make breakfast. His wife Maria had already been in there for an hour or so. He knew the scent that would hit him when he did this would be both overwhelming and intrusive. And he was quite right. A variety of scented candles, potpourri in cloth bags, soaps and air freshener created a wall of smell that enveloped him like a wet blanket.

'Darling, how long are we going to keep all this in the house?' he said, reaching for a mug in the cupboard.

He ended up with one with the slogan: *I'm not immature, you're a shithead*. He filled it with coffee from the machine before sitting down at the kitchen table.

'Don't you remember a single word of what the therapist said?' Maria said from down on the floor. 'About it being important for you to support me in my entrepreneurship?'

His wife didn't even turn from the spot where she was kneeling with her back to him as she carefully packed small ceramic angels into a big box.

'Oh yes, I remember. And you know that I'll support you in whatever you do. This online store you've started is, um, an interesting idea. The only thing is, it might be better if you warehoused your stock in, well . . . a warehouse?'

Maria sighed deeply. She still showed him nothing but her back.

'As Kevin has pointed out, renting warehouse space is

20

expensive,' she said. 'And given the fact that your new show still hasn't covered the costs of production, well, I guess I'll have to take some responsibility and be the family breadwinner.'

Vincent stared at her. This was the most sound argument he'd heard his wife advance in years. Maybe those start-up courses she'd taken hadn't been for nothing after all. Although if he were perfectly honest, he was sick of hearing about the instructor, Kevin, in every second sentence. Vincent knew Maria was a seeker. It was in her nature to find someone to follow. But her most recent guru being a start-up consultant was nevertheless unexpected.

'Responsibility?' Rebecka said as she sauntered into the kitchen. 'This stuff just costs money. Who buys shit like this?' Rebecka's morose expression seemed to have become a permanent fixture on her face. She held up a white wooden sign with a look of disgust and read it aloud. 'Live Laugh Love. I mean, come on. Die Cry Hate, more like.'

'Don't be mean,' said Vincent.

Deep down though, he agreed with his daughter.

'Kevin says I have an incredible instinct for what is commercially viable,' Maria said tartly, glowering at her stepdaughter.

Rebecka ignored her, instead making for the fridge. She opened the door.

'The hell? Aston!'

She yelled towards the living room and received a roar in reply.

'S'UP?!'

'Did you use the last milk on your cereal? And then put the empty carton back in the fridge?'

'IT'S NOT EMPTY! THERE'S DEFINITELY SOME LEFT!'

Aston's voice reverberated between the walls. Rebecka looked pointedly at Vincent while slowly turning the carton upside down. Three languid drops fell to the floor.

'What on earth do you think you're doing?' Maria said, getting to her feet. 'Mop that up.' As she stood up, she dropped the angel that had been in her lap. The figurine smashed into a thousand pieces. The material was clearly leaf-thin.

'Oh no! Look what you did, Rebecka!'

'Me?' the teenager hissed. 'No fucking way was that me. You're the one who's being as clumsy as ever and trying to blame it on me. Bloody typical. It's always got to be my fault. And you, Dad, you never say a word in my defence. You just let her treat me any old how. Fuck's sake! I can't stay here. I'm going to Denis's.'

Vincent opened his mouth to reply but it was too late. Rebecka was already making for the front door.

'Be back by eight!' Maria shouted to her back. 'It's only a Thursday!'

'I'm on my summer holidays!' Rebecka yelled back at her as she grabbed her thin summer jacket off the hook and slammed the door behind her.

'Well, thanks for the help,' said Maria, glowering at him with her arms crossed. 'Make sure you get Aston off to the recreation club. You're already late.'

Vincent closed his mouth again. It was best not to say anything. He still had no clue how to deal with these emotional storms. No matter what he said, he risked being wrong. His new strategy was therefore to remain as quiet as possible.

He rooted through his memory, trying to remember something the couples therapist had said. Something that might help. This was not an altogether easy task since it had been hard to accept help from someone whose profession he knew more about than they did. But Vincent had tried to be humble.

In the beginning, there had been talk of him having therapy on his own too, so that he could process what had happened to his mother when he'd been little – an incident he'd spent forty years repressing. But he'd put his foot down. He didn't dare have someone rifling through his past like that. There was a shadow within him guarding that point much too carefully – there was no one he trusted enough to let in there.

Vincent had wanted the therapy to be some kind of miracle cure where he and Maria were able to reconnect through him beginning to understand the way she thought. Like he had done once upon a time. And through her stopping being jealous every time he was in another town, which was incredibly wearing on them both, given that his job was predicated on travelling. And they had really tried. Maria had most definitely tried.

The therapist had suggested the obvious: the root of the jealousy was in Maria's own lack of self-esteem. And perhaps in the circumstances in which he and Maria had become a couple, when he had left his then wife Ulrika for her little sister Maria.

But Vincent knew it wasn't that simple. There was something else in Maria that neither she nor the therapist were able to put their fingers on, something that reacted by launching an attack as soon as he paid attention to anyone or anything other than the home and his family. He knew that it wasn't really Maria's fault that she reacted the way she did. It was just instinct. The same instinct that meant she was now looking at him as if he were a flying saucer. And as on so many occasions before, he wished he knew what she wanted from him.

It had been so easy in the beginning. Infatuation had made them disregard everything, ignore everyone and everything that was unrelated to their love. He still remembered that feeling. It was still there inside him somewhere. The memory of them finishing each other's sentences, being able to communicate with a look. But it was as if they were losing each other's language with every passing year. As if they understood each other less and less, even though it ought to be the other way around. He didn't want it to be like that. He simply didn't know what he had to do to reach her again. What he should do to find *them*.

It was clear she was waiting for him to say something. Surely he could summon up some small nugget from their therapy sessions? The therapist had suggested that Vincent should always show care to Maria when she was worked up, even if he thought she was being unfair, so that he created a sense of security. That security would in turn give Maria better grounds on which to express her emotions in a more constructive way before they morphed into anger. It didn't generally go well. But trying cost nothing.

'Darling, I can see you're angry,' he said, deliberately making his voice calm and gentle. 'But anger isn't good for your body. You can probably feel that you're tensing your muscles and joints, but your circulation is also slowing down and the natural equilibrium is being disturbed in your nervous system and in cardiovascular and hormonal terms. What's more, your blood pressure is increasing alongside your pulse and testosterone levels, and there's an excess of bile that will end up in parts of the body it shouldn't be in.'

Maria looked at him with raised eyebrows. The therapist's advice seemed to be working.

'When you're angry, it also changes the activity in your brain,' he said. 'Especially in the temporal and frontal lobes. So like I said, it's probably not good for you to get this angry. Maybe you could communicate with Rebecka in a more constructive way?'

He fell silent, venturing a cautious smile. Maria stared at him. Then she pursed her mouth as if she had bitten into a lemon, turned on her heel and left.

6

The joy at being back again made tears prickle behind her eyelids. Julia had never thought it could be possible to long that much to be within the walls of the frankly rather ugly police headquarters in the Kungsholmen neighbourhood of Stockholm. To mark the occasion, the building was hot as a sauna. Apparently, the ventilation system had clapped out just in time for Stockholm's hottest heatwave in living memory. She fanned herself with a sheet of paper and opened the door to the conference room. To her colleagues, this might be a Thursday like any other. But for her, it was heaven.

At least until she had to tell them why they were there.

'Julia!' said a bearded man whose face lit up as she entered. Wide-eyed, she realized it was Peder.

'It's not a hipster beard – it's a dad-beard,' he said with satisfaction when he spotted her look.

'It's a hipster beard, no matter what you claim,' Ruben muttered as he came in on her tail. 'Lucky for us that it's so hot you can't wear that little hat you've been wearing all spring.'

24

Everything seemed to be exactly as she'd left it. But unless she was much mistaken, even Mina and Christer looked relatively pleased to see her.

'Congratulations are in order,' Christer murmured.

The golden retriever Bosse was lying on the floor by his side, panting, in exactly the same spot she'd last seen him six months earlier. But this time the dog was too hot to get up and come to greet her properly. Instead, she got a happy glance and a brief woof.

'Yes, congratulations!' Mina said as she eyed Julia's jacket in horror.

Julia glanced at the point on her left shoulder that Mina's eyes seemed to be glued to and then swore loudly.

'Christ's sake, can't there be one single item of clothing that doesn't have puke all over it?!' She tugged the jacket off and was about to hang it on the back of her chair when she stopped herself with a glance at Mina and instead hung it on a peg over by the door.

'So far, it's only formula coming up,' Peder said with an understanding smile. 'It'll come out no problem. Just wait until it's banana and tinned stroganoff. The only thing that does the trick then is soaking the stains with Vanish. You're best off with the powder – in those pink tubs. And then you have to run a wash at ninety. Preferably with bleach. So you should really only wear white to start with . . .'

'I'll keep that in mind,' said Julia, holding up a placatory hand. 'And a good morning to you all.'

She was fully aware of the Sisyphean tasks associated with a six-month-old baby, thank you very much. She'd cross her bridges of torment from future age phases when the time came.

'Right. It's nice to be back, and it's wonderful to see you all here. Obviously I've been following your work carefully while I was off, and you've done me proud. Mina, a big well done on your leadership during this time. But now I'm glad to be back again and I'm ready and raring to go. Maybe not so rested, but you can't have everything.'

She let out a half-hearted laugh. A part of her wanted to tell them about the infuriating rows that had precipitated her entry

25

through the lobby of police headquarters that day. How they had been the kind of rows that had made her realize that the equal relationship she had thought she had was nothing but an illusion – an illusion that had only made it this far because it hadn't been subjected to the stresses of a child. The arguments that had been hurled at her had been exactly the ones that she'd sighed at when she'd heard them advanced by her friends. She was biologically better suited to caring for a baby. That it was impossible for Torkel to be absent from work – apparently everything would collapse if he was. The company would go under, Sweden's GDP would plummet, the euro would crash, catastrophe would spread around the world and cause the immediate demise of the planet.

But what upset her most was that they'd had a deal. She would take the first six months, he'd take the next six. They'd both applied for parental leave and had it granted. What she hadn't realized was that it had been a show for the masses as far as Torkel was concerned. He'd never thought she really meant for them to share the leave. She could still picture his shocked expression last week when she'd reminded him that she was due back at work this Thursday.

Torkel had apparently thought that she would (quote) 'realize herself that she wanted to stay at home with Harry and that she wouldn't want to go back to work'.

They hadn't spoken to each other in several days.

When she had got ready to leave an hour or so ago, it had been as if a stranger were standing before her, his gaze panic-stricken and furious, his hair standing on end, wittering on about 'attachment' and 'biological heritage' and saying that he 'had to talk to his boss'. In the end, she had simply handed over Harry and quickly exited through the front door. She still hadn't dared to look at her phone.

'Welcome back,' Ruben said, smiling at her like a wolf.

Julia tried to ignore the fact that he seemed to have a hard time taking his eyes off her breasts. She'd stopped breastfeeding a week ago, but her breasts didn't seem to have got the memo. Her B-cups were yet another thing she longed to see again. She'd never really got along with E-cups.

26

'If you're feeling run-down then I've got the best thing to pep you up before we get started,' Peder said cheerily, pulling out his phone.

'Not again,' Mina, Christer and Ruben groaned in unison.

Peder didn't seem to notice. He put his phone in Julia's hand and started a video.

'It's the triplets,' he chortled. 'They're singing along to Anis Don Demina's song in *Mellon*! Aren't they the cutest?'

Julia saw three children in nappies swaying enthusiastically and not in time in front of a large TV. She assumed they were super cute. She was just having a little trouble appreciating it on this day in particular, when the last thing she wanted on her hands were more kids.

'Wait, I'll turn it up,' Peder said. 'They sing too.'

The groans of discontent in the room grew in volume.

'Thanks, I think I get the idea,' she said, handing the phone back. 'Very cute. Anyway. I suggest we make a start. Yesterday afternoon a report came in of an abducted child. A boy called Ossian Walthersson. Five years old. There was a mistake, however, and it didn't get flagged as priority. We only realized first thing this morning.'

'Jesus Christ,' Peder said. 'That's just not on.'

'No, but what's done is done. In any case, the top brass have assigned the case to us, and they want us to make it our top priority.'

Mina nodded and took a long sip of water from a bottle. When she set it down on the table, she seemed to be making an effort to put it as far away from Peder's beard as she could. Bosse noticed it too. He stood up and lumbered over to Mina, his eyes grateful and his tongue lolling.

'Christer!' said Mina. 'If he must be here, then at least keep him watered. If he comes even a centimetre closer to my water bottle, you'll have to buy me a new one.'

'Don't exaggerate,' Christer sighed. 'Dogs' tongues are actually very clean. But it's probably for the best that I put down a water bowl, given how much time we're likely to spend in here. Bosse doesn't like it much either, you know.'

He beckoned to the dog, who looked at Mina with immense

27

reproach before settling down at his master's feet again. Julia wondered whether she ought to explain to Christer that dogs' tongues were not in the slightest bit clean and that they simply had an entirely different bacterial tolerance to humans and that some of those bacteria were downright dangerous. But the tender look that Christer gave Bosse made her refrain.

'I'd forgotten what a madhouse this place can be,' she said. 'Let's focus and get to grips with the work at hand as quickly as we can. Our team will also be assigned a reinforcement – someone who has experience of a similar case. He's from the negotiators . . . er, the negotiation team . . . Honestly, I do wish they'd make their minds up what they're called. But you know who I mean.'

She paused and looked at the surprised expressions in the room.

'Yeah, why is it their department doesn't have a name?' said Peder.

'It's just psychology,' said Julia. 'If they don't have a name then they don't exist. Makes it harder for the crooks to know who they are.'

'Wow,' Peder said, raising his eyebrows.

'But like I said, he's no longer one of them. He's a welcome addition to our small but happy family. He's also already got some thoughts to share with us on the Ossian case and he'll be arriving any moment now.'

'Do we really need more people?' said Mina, frowning.

'You mean to say that we're enough of a handful?' Christer chuckled, nudging his elbow in the air in Mina's direction. He obviously knew his colleague well enough to avoid direct contact. But Julia had anticipated Mina's reaction. Change wasn't something that appealed to Mina Dabiri. Especially not if it entailed new human relationships. But if there was one person whom it might do some good, it was Mina. Since the investigation with Vincent had drawn to a close in the autumn almost two years ago, Julia hadn't seen her speak to anyone else, or about anyone else, except her colleagues. And she guessed that Mina was unlikely to have blossomed socially in the six months Julia had spent on maternity leave. Enlarging Mina's circle of colleagues wouldn't do her any harm.

28

'It's probably something the top brass made up for political reasons,' Christer continued. He scratched Bosse's neck and received a loving glance as his reward. 'Equality and diversity are very in right now. But we've already got two ladies. So I suppose it'll be a gay or an import!'

'Christer!' Peder hissed, looking sternly at his older colleague. 'That's exactly the kind of remark that got you transferred here in the first place. Haven't all those expensive courses the Police Authority sent you on had any impact at all in dragging you out of the Stone Age?'

Christer sighed and scratched Bosse behind one ear.

'Oh, I'm only kidding,' he said awkwardly. 'People get so antsy these days. Anyway, I wasn't making any kind of value judgement with what I said. You would have noticed that if you had taken the same course as me.'

'But certain choices of words have clearly implicit—'

A discreet knock interrupted Peder and made them all look at the door.

'And he has perfect timing,' said Julia, pointing towards the doorway with an outstretched hand. 'Allow me to introduce you to the new member of our team: Adam Balondemu Blom.'

'Impressive pronunciation,' said the man, who strode into the room smiling. 'But Adam Blom will do just fine.'

7

The lady is really, really stupid. She says she has puppies, but she doesn't. But her car is a proper racing car. It looks like the toys she has, but it's a proper big car.

When she came to nursery yesterday, she asked if I wanted to try sitting in the racing car. I said I did. But then we drove off. She said we'd come back and that we were only going away for a minute so that I could see what it was like to ride in the racing car. But we didn't. We didn't go back.

Then I got scared. Really scared.

My tummy felt like when water gets sucked out of the bath and it goes round and round. As if it were being sucked down and down.

I told her that, but she didn't answer.

Then we drove for ages. Now we're at her house. I want to go home to Mum and Dad. I don't want to be here. The lady says 'in a while'. Always 'in a while'. And then she says I have to stop crying.

There are others here too. Other grown-ups. I don't know who any of them are. I'm scared of them. They come and go. They say I can play Roblox on the iPad as much as I want, but I don't want to. It's weird here and it doesn't smell like home.

At night-time, I stare at the ceiling. It's completely dark. There's no light at all.

I call out for Dad. Then Mum. Neither of them come.

'Ossian, you're going to stay here for a little while,' says the lady in the morning. 'Maybe a day or two. Then you'll get to go home.'

They give me food, but it's disgusting and I don't want to eat it. I ask why I have to stay here. But she doesn't answer. No one answers. They just tell me to stop crying. That everything will be fine.

Their voices sound kind. But their eyes aren't kind.

8

Mina surveyed the team's latest addition with curiosity, but she tried to do so discreetly. Not everyone was quite as sensitive. Ruben, for instance, stared openly and without inhibition, with what amounted to a degree of hostility. Mina wasn't surprised by his reaction. Adam Blom was a fine physical specimen, with well-toned biceps and a well-defined six-pack shown off by his tight white T-shirt. She noted with amusement that Ruben sat up straighter and sucked in his stomach.

Personally, the muscular, sculpted body didn't do it for her. She preferred a slim, elegant male body with a confident posture and a physique verging on the sinewy rather than bulging with muscles. Preferably wearing a nice suit and with— Mina came to irritably. Her thoughts really did run off in strange ways on occasion. She forced herself to focus, listening instead to Julia, who was standing by the whiteboard. Julia had a serious expression that indicated she was about to say something important.

'As I said, we're dealing with the investigation into Ossian Walthersson's disappearance.'

'Five years old,' Peder said, his voice sounding pained.

Mina understood why. A missing child was every parent's worst nightmare, and it was impossible not to feel upset about it – even for a hardened police officer. Peder also had young children of his own. And while it had been a long time since she'd had one, it was only too easy to imagine herself in the situation.

'Yes, exactly. Ossian is suspected to have been kidnapped yesterday from his nursery in Södermalm. We'll need to talk to everyone involved as soon as possible. But there are also certain similarities between Ossian's abduction and a previous case. The top brass have asked us to take a closer look.'

Julia turned to the newest member of the team.

'Adam. Maybe you can explain that last bit better?'

He cleared his throat. Julia took her seat and indicated for Adam to take her place at the whiteboard. He stood up and did so. Mina envied the ease with which he seemed to be able to stand before a group of complete strangers who were likely to be sceptical of what he had to say. Personally, she always felt slightly uneasy, even in contexts where she ought to have felt comfortable.

'Firstly, I'd like to tell you a little about myself and where I come from.'

Christer glanced meaningfully at Peder. If he was going to ask whether Adam meant Kenya or the Gambia, Mina would chuck the man out of the room herself. Dog and all.

'I'm from the negotiation team,' Adam said. 'We were involved early on in a case involving a little girl called Lilly Meyer a year back. We had reason to believe that the disappearance was connected to an extremely acrimonious custody dispute between Lilly's parents. The assumption was that someone in the family had taken her, which was why I was brought in – in case we needed to negotiate with her kidnappers.'

'She was the one who was found dead later on, wasn't she?' said Peder, his voice choked.

Mina remembered the case well, even though it had been a whole year since the tragic events in question. The fallout had been terrible. The girl had been found under a tarpaulin on a jetty in the well-heeled Hammarby sjöstad area, a few metres from a well-frequented ice-cream parlour. The media had eaten the detectives on the case alive when it transpired they had been unable to come up with any suspects despite the fact that the child had been identified immediately. The parents had spoken in the press. The case lingered on in the Stockholm police force like an infection. And above all, it remained unsolved.

Bosse seemed to sense Peder's state of mind. The dog crept under the table to Peder's seat and pressed his nose against his knee. With distaste, Mina saw the nose leave a moist patch.

'That's right. Lilly disappeared and was found murdered at the start of the summer. She was found on the Lugnets terrass pier – that's the big one with all the picnic tables in Hammarby sjöstad, right over the water from the harbour at Norra Hammarbyhamnen.'

'Yes, but didn't they conclude that it was related to that custody dispute?' said Ruben in a slightly hostile tone. 'Like you said? So how is it related to our case? And why do we need someone here from Negotiation?'

Mina could see he was still holding in his stomach. It must surely have been very uncomfortable.

'Yes and no. We still haven't identified the killer, and the only description we have is of an elderly couple who were nearby. That was provided to us by a stressed-out nursery school teacher who wasn't paying much attention to them. And sure, suspicions that it might have been someone in the family have remained, and they haven't been ruled out of the inquiry. But . . . I don't think it's to do with the family. Especially not now that we have an almost identical set of circumstances in the case of Ossian's abduction.'

'What do you mean by identical?' said Mina, frowning.

'Abducted from his nursery school by a stranger that no one saw,' Adam said. 'It happens far less often than the supposedly realistic detective shows on TV would have us believe. As a general rule, when someone is abducted in real life it usually turns out to be the work of relatives. Sometimes the plan is to return the child to a home country. Sometimes one parent tries to take the child following a custody dispute. But this? With perpetrators who seem to be unknown to the police and the nursery staff? That's practically unheard of. But now it's happened twice. And the top brass think my knowledge of Lilly's case might be of use to you. We haven't got much time. I can quickly and efficiently share everything I have, both what you can read up on and what can only be read between the lines.'

'I'm in full agreement with management that Adam is a valuable asset to this investigation,' said Julia, fixing her gaze on Ruben. 'So can we move on? Ruben?'

Ruben muttered something inaudible but then nodded.

'Lilly was found after three days, wasn't she?' said Christer, wiping sweat from his brow using his shirtsleeve.

The heat in the meeting room was oppressive. Mina tried to stifle her feelings of discomfort.

'So if Ossian went missing yesterday and it's the same MO, we probably don't have long to find him,' Christer added.

'Wait a moment,' said Peder. 'Do we think it's the same person who has struck again?'

'Right now, we have no reason to believe that,' said Julia, clearing her throat. 'But, as has been noted, the MO is similar. That's why we're working on the assumption that we don't have much time. As it happens, I've been asked to hold a press conference tonight. Prior to that, I want Adam and Ruben to interview Ossian's nursery school staff. Mina and Peder should take Ossian's parents.'

'Can't Adam and Christer take the nursery?' said Ruben, checking the time. 'I've got somewhere to be soon.'

'We need Christer checking the sex offenders register,' said

Julia. 'I want a list of everyone who has been released in the last year. Just to be on the safe side. And Ruben, the last time I checked you were still a police detective. Right now this is your top priority.'

'Sounds like your Tinder dates are going to have to wait,' said Mina.

'The sex offenders register,' Christer sighed. 'Again.'

'I'm not on bloody Tinder,' Ruben snorted. 'Don't need to be. Unlike you, Mina. The spinster who'd rather join a nunnery.'

Mina pulled out her phone and held it in front of Ruben's face. Then she ostentatiously pulled up her app store and downloaded Tinder so that Ruben saw her do it.

'Does that feel better?' she said. 'Has your concern for my well-being been sufficiently placated that you can do your job instead?'

She was going to delete the app the very second the meeting drew to a close.

'Settle down, class,' Julia said loudly. 'Let's get to work. This is serious.'

Adam was standing next to her and looked like he wasn't quite sure where he should go.

'As you can see,' Julia said, turning to him with a sigh, 'we're not necessarily the most . . . disciplined team you'll have worked with. But we're good. Usually.'

'Good thing, that,' said Adam, his tone serious. 'Because as you said . . . we've already lost twenty-four hours and the clock is ticking.'

9

Christer couldn't stand to work in his roasting hot office, opting instead to settle down with his laptop in the open-plan area. He pulled out his phone and stared at the sixty-four black and white squares on the screen. In truth, the game had been over long ago. He was simply struggling to accept the fact.

He'd always considered himself a relatively deft chess player. Not that he'd played all that many games throughout the course of his life. But he felt he ought to be good at it. It seemed to go hand in hand with his taste for whisky, solitude, jazz. Admittedly he was no longer quite as lonely since Bosse had come into his life, but frankly owning a dog was still pretty much in keeping with the persona.

However, his perception of his own chess skills had been transformed the day he had discovered a free chess app. Since then, he had played daily on both his phone and his computer. Almost six months had passed since then, and he was still playing at the beginner level. And he was yet to win a single game. With a sigh he set down his phone. There was no point putting off what he was supposed to be doing.

Mina stopped by and sat down next to him with her own laptop.

'I can help out for a while. Should we make a start?' she said. 'We can't afford to lose any time.'

'Yes, I suppose we should,' he said without enthusiasm. 'The sex offenders register. Yippee.'

He peered listlessly into his mug of coffee. Cold. And it seemed to have been stewed for a little too long. He sighed audibly, which caused Bosse to cock his head to one side in concern.

'Lie down, boy. Dad needs to do some work on the computer. You've got water. And your basket.'

He scratched the dog behind the ears. Satisfied with the attention paid to him, Bosse lay down in the basket after turning around on the spot three times. 'Right then,' said Christer, opening the program. 'Let's see if we can find some slimeballs.'

This kind of work always left him feeling divided. Sitting there hour after hour, scrutinizing page after page, hunting for a needle in a haystack. It was a dispiriting and thankless chore. One they always assigned to him, of all people. Well, fine. This time around Mina was helping out, which was nice of her. But usually he was left to do it on his own.

These days they never invited him to join in chasing the crooks around town. Not that he wanted to. But it might still have been nice to be asked on occasion. Just as a matter of courtesy between colleagues. A small recognition of his experience and his many years spent in a squad car. Granted, it was nice not to have to do it, but still.

'I can check whether anyone was connected to the Lilly case,' Mina said, 'in case we're dealing with a repeat offender. And you can check who is out right now.'

'Sounds good,' he said, beginning to scroll.

Column after column. Scumbag after scumbag. If only the public knew how many awful people there were out there, they'd never leave their homes. And the Sweden's Future political party had conned people into believing that the only danger they needed to be afraid of was called Ahmed or Mohammed. But here he was. Going through row after row of 'Sven Westin', 'Karl-Erik Johansson' and 'Peter Lundberg'. All white as snow. All with a predilection for little kids. And all of them had the kind of appearance that made people say after the fact, 'He was so nice. You would never have thought . . .' Or 'It must have been some kind of misunderstanding. He's always been so good to my children.'

Bosse whined in his sleep and moved his paws as if he were running. Christer wondered what he was chasing. Probably not paedophiles, at any rate. Even if they were what he ought to be chasing. Bloody hell. He hoped that Julia was wrong and that the men and women flitting past on his screen would turn out to have nothing to do with Ossian's disappearance. The world didn't need to get any worse than it already was.

Christer surveyed the other desks. The open-plan office was emptier than usual. Holidays. Many of his colleagues were tipping back the lagers in Sandhamn on a yacht or snapping limestone pillars with their cameras on Gotland or hammering away at the woodwork of a cabin somewhere.

Mina stood up. 'I need coffee,' she said. 'Doesn't matter how hot it is in here. Do you want me to get you one too? I can only help you for a little while longer, then I'm heading off with Peder to see Ossian's parents.'

He nodded grimly. The clock was ticking on them finding Ossian's kidnappers. He could almost hear it. He had many hours' searching ahead of him, scouring the police records for the very sickest of bastards. That definitely called for more caffeine.

10

'Are we really the best people to be doing this?' Peder said, swallowing.

Mina realized that he didn't mean 'we' but 'I'. As in Peder, the man with children. 'If you don't think you can cope then you'll have to stay here,' she said gently. 'I'll do it myself. It's totally fine by me.'

Peder shook his head.

'No, no. It's part of the job. I know that. Let's just get it over with.'

They made their way to one of the police cars in the underground car park, and she let him get into the driver's seat. Driving would give him something to focus on other than what lay ahead of them. To be on the safe side, she directed the topic of conversation on to his children. It was a diversionary manoeuvre that always did the trick. She looked out of the windscreen and allowed her thoughts to wander while Peder chattered away incessantly at her side.

'. . . and then this morning Meja suddenly said "oaty porridge",' he said, apparently in the middle of a story. 'So you can see how intelligent this kid must be. She's two and a half years old and most two-and-a-half-year-olds would just say podge or something, but she manages to say oaty porridge. I really do think we're going to have to enrol her in a school for the specially gifted. I've heard people say that it can be as big a challenge having kids who are specially gifted as it is having kids who present other challenges, but I suppose we'll have to cross that bridge when we come to it. That's what we both think, Anette and me. And then of course there's Majken, who we think has a future in the world of sport. You should see her scrambling up the climbing frame at nursery. I mean, her balance, her strength . . . well, we've got an elite athlete right there. So we've already mentally prepared ourselves for a whole lot of driving her to training sessions and so on. And then there's Molly. She has a real feel for animals. Only the other day she brought home a bird that had hurt its wing, and we both had to settle it down in a shoebox filled with cotton wool, and she kept a vigil over it like a proper little bird mum. Sadly, it died. But that feel for animals . . . it's as if she can talk to them. For real. I reckon we're looking at a future vet in her. Maybe even at Kolmården Wildlife Park or Parken Zoo or somewhere like that, and I think . . .'

Mina looked out of the windscreen again and allowed Peder's enthusiasm to go in one ear and out the other. They passed Stureplan, which was swarming with people wearing expensive sunglasses, elegant clothes, and perfect tans. The terrace outside the main dining room at Sturehof was packed and glasses of rosé wine glittered in the sunshine. She envied them their carefree moment in the sun, and the way they had all the time in the world. As for her, well, here she was with an aching heart on her way to talk to distraught parents who didn't know where their five-year-old was. And time might be running out. The same way it had done for Lilly.

11

Tom the nursery school teacher looked more unhappy than Ruben thought it was possible for a grown man to be. Also sitting in the cramped staffroom at Backens nursery were Tom's colleague Jenya and the nursery manager, Mathilda. With Ruben and Adam too, the room was overcrowded. All the windows were wide open. Not that it seemed to help, Ruben noticed. The sweat on Tom's brow looked like it was dripping down his nose and cheeks.

Ruben tried to gather his thoughts. When Julia had started the morning briefing, he'd already been with Ellinor in his head. Wondering what he was going to say. He'd thought it would be a quick meeting to welcome Julia back and then he'd be able to get in the car and be on his way. Instead, the Ossian case had landed on their desks. Right now, he needed to focus on that. Not the thought that he would soon meet someone who had haunted him for more than a decade. He would have all the time in the world to think about Ellinor later, when this was over. But Ossian needed finding right away. Ossian needed him – Ruben – to do his job.

He pushed Ellinor out of his thoughts and looked at the others who were squashed into the staffroom. But before he had a chance to say anything, Adam began to talk.

'So,' said his new colleague, 'the events of yesterday. How come no one noticed that Ossian was missing?'

Good God. Talk about getting straight to the point. Wasn't Adam supposedly some kind of negotiation whizz? Even Ruben knew that you couldn't open a police interview with an accusation. These people already looked like they thought they were going to prison. He and Adam wouldn't get anything meaningful out of them if they felt pressured. Tom stared at the drawings pinned to one of the walls, where the children appeared to have depicted their teachers with mixed success.

'We're just trying to determine where everyone was when Ossian was abducted,' Ruben said as kindly as he could. Tom looked like he wished the floor would swallow him up. He pulled a tissue out of a box on the table and wiped his eyes.

'There are a lot of kids when we go up to the park,' he said. 'You don't always have eyes on all of them. And the older ones don't need the same degree of supervision as the younger ones. But they know they're not allowed to leave the park without telling us, and we check on them regularly. My not having seen Ossian for a few minutes was nothing out of the ordinary.'

Tom cut himself short and looked at the drawings again. One of them represented a surprisingly detailed male form with a large heart coloured inside. On the man's T-shirt there was a green letter T. In the corner of the drawing it said in straggling but careful script 'opp opp' alongside the artist's signature. Ossian. All of a sudden, a lump formed in Ruben's throat and he had to clear it.

'Their world . . .' Tom said, his voice thick, 'I mean, our world is usually a place of safety.'

'We realize that,' said Adam. 'But the fact remains that you failed in terms of providing that safety and in terms of paying attention.'

What the actual fuck? It was beginning to dawn on Ruben why Adam had been allowed to leave the negotiation team. There were tears pouring down Tom's cheeks.

'Which is perfectly human,' Adam added. 'I'm not passing any judgement on what you say. But you have to realize that this is the attitude you are going to face. Not least from other parents. The more we know about what really happened, the more we can help you to turn others' attitudes into empathy.'

Adam turned away from Tom and looked Mathilda, the manager, in the eye.

'I'm guessing that would be desirable, given how few children have come in to nursery today,' he said.

OK. Maybe Adam wasn't a complete no-hoper. But this was no negotiation. This was a dialogue – something that Adam clearly lacked experience in. Ruben couldn't help feeling smug. Adam could sit there with his six-pack and his one hundred and ninety centimetres of stature, but in the end it was up to him – Ruben – to run the show.

'What we're wondering,' he said, 'is whether you saw or know anything that might help us in our search. For example, do you know who the woman who picked him up is?'

Jenya shook her head. She didn't look anywhere near as sweaty as Tom even though she was wearing a hijab. Ruben resisted the impulse to ask her whether she was insanely hot wearing that head covering. He guessed she'd already been asked that question countless times.

'We've talked to all the kids,' said Jenya. 'They have a surprisingly good grasp of each other's mum and dads, as well as their older siblings. But no one had seen her before.'

Adam stood up and made for the window overlooking the

hill where Ossian had gone missing. He appeared to be ruminating on something. Then he came back and resumed his seat.

'So we're right back where we started,' said Adam. 'Why didn't any of you see her? Given that the kids did? Doesn't that seem a little odd?'

'Are you trying to imply that my staff may have had something to do with this?' Mathilda said, her eyes widening. 'That there's something they're not telling you on purpose? I can vouch for both Tom and Jenya. They're two of the best teachers I've ever worked with. They have my full support. And I'm not sure it's worth continuing this conversation without legal representation if you're going to level accusations at us.'

Ruben held out his hands in a defensive gesture. Nice work. Lawyers. That was all they needed. If Adam was going to keep digging holes this deep for them, Ruben would have to make sure he brought a shovel along in future. Truthfully, he didn't really have any objection to it – he was happy to stand by and watch as Adam tripped himself up. But not when their scant results might tarnish him too.

'No one is accusing anyone of anything. We think she didn't want to be seen,' Ruben said gently. 'So she was waiting for the right opportunity. This didn't happen by chance.'

That seemed to placate Mathilda a little.

'There's one last question,' said Adam. 'There's something that's not adding up for me. It's the idea that he went with her of his own accord. Does Ossian usually turn to strangers?'

'No, but he does to racing cars,' Tom said quietly. 'Lamborghini, Koenigsegg, Porsche. He knows all the makes and models. It doesn't really matter whether they're the real thing or built out of cardboard. So long as they look like they go fast. And they should preferably be red.'

'And this woman had cars, if I've understood correctly,' Adam noted with a nod. 'At least that's what she told Felicia. Cars and puppies. There's no reason for Felicia to have made it up. Of course, there's the question of whether those puppies really existed. Felicia never got to see them.'

'And no one has seen this woman before,' said Ruben, checking his notes. 'Which doesn't necessarily mean she doesn't know Ossian. Has he been behaving at all differently lately? What about his parents, for that matter?'

Tom shook his head.

'There's been nothing out of the ordinary. It was just another summer week like any other. Until . . . until yesterday, that is.'

'Well then,' said Adam, standing up. 'Thank you for your help. I think that's all.'

Mathilda stood up to show them out. Ruben was actually impressed by her. Normally, people were much too docile to dare to take the initiative when the police came calling. But not Mathilda. When it had been called for, she had played the lioness protecting her pride. And she looked pretty nice too. The question was whether she was as dominant between the sheets. Once upon a time he would have been keen to find out. Now he would have to settle for wondering. Thanks to Amanda the bloody psychologist.

'We'll obviously be carrying out our own detailed internal investigation,' said Mathilda, proffering her hand to him. 'But right now you have everything that we know. I would appreciate it if you kept us informed about the search. We recognize our responsibility in this, believe you me.'

Reuben and Adam shook hands with all three of them. Tom's hand was limp and he looked like death. It would probably be some time before he returned to work.

'Nice move there,' said Adam in a low voice as they departed. 'Going for the good cop, bad cop thing. We found out everything they knew fast. Speed is imperative right now.'

Ruben stared at him. Did all negotiators think they were in a movie? As far as Ruben knew, the negotiation team were experts in building personal relationships and getting crooks to confide in them. But Adam had done the opposite. At the same time, Ruben couldn't disagree. They had indeed found out everything they needed to know.

'But next time,' said Adam, 'I want to be good cop.'

Oh lordy. Ruben really would have to remember to bring that shovel.

12

Vincent peered out of the window of the ShowLife Productions office on Strandvägen. The afternoon sun was high in the sky, glittering beautifully on the water outside. But it wasn't the ripple of sunshine on the water that he saw. Instead, he was fully occupied with trying to imagine being launched out of a catapult or worming his way through a room filled with insects. All while wearing close-fitting activewear. Vincent shuddered. The images in his head were anything but appealing.

'Don't be so gauche,' Umberto said from behind him. 'This is going to be good for your brand. We need to show a more . . . human side to you. If at all possible.'

Vincent left the window and sat back down. On this occasion, there was a conspicuous absence of freshly baked biscuits on his agent's desk. It might mean that he and Umberto had once again grown closer and formed a more informal relationship. Or it might mean that Umberto was tiring of him. But the four factory-produced punsch rolls on the table indicated that he wasn't entirely out in the cold.

'But come on . . . *Fortress Prisoners' Flight*? At Fort Boyard?' Vincent said sceptically, taking a punsch roll as soon as he realized that Umberto was about to do the same thing.

That left two rolls on the plate. There had to be some sense of order.

'There must be some other TV show that's more . . . me,' he said. 'If I need to be on television in the first place, that is.'

Umberto sighed and leaned forward, his fingertips touching his chin.

'Vincent, *amico mio*, listen to me. My job is to make sure that as many people as possible buy tickets to your shows and lectures. Because what happens if they don't?'

'You don't make a living,' Vincent said.

'Exactly. But above all, *you* don't make a living. It's pretty simple, really. Basic economics. In order for you to continue supporting yourself on what you do, we need to sell more tickets as our costs increase. And I know we've been cooking with gas for a while now thanks to what happened with Jane. But that interest won't last forever. Which means that more people need to be reminded of and, above all, care about you. Which in turn means you have to be shot out of a cannon on TV every now and then.'

Vincent tried not to give away quite how stressful he found the whole thing. Fort Boyard . . . *Fortress Prisoners' Flight* . . . F P F. The letters in positions 6, 16 and 6 in the alphabet. 6166. When Benjamin had been little, Vincent had bought him a Lego set containing a mixture of pieces. If you were serious about your Lego models when discussing them, as Vincent had often done with Benjamin and latterly with Aston, you always mentioned the article numbers, since there might be several different kits that made similar things. And he was almost certain that Benjamin's box of mixed Legos had borne the article number 6166. Which was naturally nothing more than a random connection between *Fortress Prisoners' Flight* and Lego. On the other hand, the letters L E G O were in positions 12, 5, 7 and 15 in the alphabet. And #125715 was the hexadecimal colour code for moss green. The same shade of green that tinged the water lapping up against Fort Boyard, where they taped the show. At least when the tide was up. It was all connected. If you really wanted it to be.

'Vincent,' Umberto said sharply. 'Where have you gone off to?'

It sounded from his tone of voice as if Umberto had said Vincent's name a few times before he'd heard it.

'Lego,' he replied.

Umberto shook his head. 'You need to do this,' he said.

Vincent nodded slowly, unsure quite how he had even ended up considering the proposal. But Umberto was probably right. He would have to embark on a crash fitness drive. The game show at Fort Boyard would definitely demand more of him physically than he was currently able to deliver. Working out would also be a good way to keep himself busy over the summer, so that his thoughts didn't wander off onto the wrong things.

Like how Mina was doing.

Umberto took one of the two remaining punsch rolls. Vincent sighed. He hadn't wanted to eat the first one he'd picked up, let alone a second. But he had no choice. A solitary punsch roll on the plate was bordering on the obscene. It simply would not do. He picked up the last one and spotted the quiver of a smile at the corners of his agent's mouth. Bloody Umberto. He'd done it on purpose.

'OK, suppose we say yes,' he said. 'To the show. If so, when would they be taping it?'

'In around a month.'

A large piece of arrack-flavoured cake caught in his throat. Around a month. He would have to book a personal trainer this very afternoon.

13

They tell him not to be afraid. That's a weird thing to say. Why shouldn't he be afraid? After all, he doesn't get to see Mum and Dad. And they won't say where his parents are. Perhaps something has happened to them.

Ebba at nursery has a mum who died. Ebba's grandma and grandpa came to pick her up and the teachers said that Ebba had to go home. Her mum had died from something called calcer.

What if Mum and Dad have got calcer?

And died?

Maybe that's why he was picked up at nursery. But why haven't his grandma and grandpa come to pick him up? He curls up on the mattress. It smells weird. Everything smells weird.

He actually stopped sucking his thumb ages ago. He's a big boy. Big boys don't suck their thumbs. Anyway, it can make your teeth wonky if you suck your thumb for too long. That's what Grandma said. But he needs his thumb now.

His body is tired and heavy. He hasn't slept all night. All he's done is think about Mum and Dad and calcer. Far off, he hears voices. But they don't sound like Mum or Dad.

He closes his eyes.

If he sleeps for a while, then maybe they'll be here when he wakes up.

14

The apartment on Bellmansgatan was small but homely. Everything gave away that a child lived here. Among the shoes inside the front door there was a plastic bag containing a sealed Lego kit for a racing car. Toys were strewn all over the hallway. This was clearly an active family. There were drawings stuck to the fridge together with holiday snaps. The remnants of a child's breakfast were still on the kitchen table – dried pieces of cereal in a plastic bowl.

'Sorry about the mess, we're . . .'

Ossian's mother Josefin didn't finish her sentence. Her gaze was distant and Mina guessed that she was on powerful sedatives. But Fredrik, Ossian's father, had a gaze that was clear and steady. A slight tremor in his hand as he pointed to a white set of IKEA sofas was the only thing that gave away the tumult within.

'Come on, sweetheart. Come on.'

He softly touched Josefin's arm and tugged her gently towards the sofa. She followed and practically slumped into the sofa rather than sitting down. She brushed her hand over the upholstery. There was a large stain visible on the light fabric.

'We should have known better than to buy a white couch just as we were about to have a baby. But we thought . . . we thought it would be like in the baby magazines and on TV. A cute, babbling baby who does nothing but sleep. We thought . . . we'd be OK. No problems. Fredrik and I both rode a lot as teenagers and we figured that if you've cared for a capricious horse then a child is no trouble. But then . . . he was born . . .'

46

'Josefin, we don't have to—'

Fredrik laid a hand on her arm but she shook it off as she sobbed.

'He was born and all he did was cry and cry and cry. All the time. Round the clock. He was so angry . . . And I couldn't understand why he was so angry all the time. It was as if he hated the world. Hated us. And I wanted . . . I wished . . . I sometimes wished we'd never had him, that things had stayed the way they were before he was born, that we'd made do with each other. I know you're not allowed to say that. That you're not allowed to regret having kids. But things were so good for us, Fredrik. Don't you remember how good things were?'

She turned her face to her husband, who nodded.

'Josefin, you're in shock. You feel guilty and you're looking for an explanation,' he said. 'Don't. But yes, I remember.'

He tried to lay his hand on her arm again, and this time she let it stay there.

'I remember how hard it was in the beginning,' he said. 'You're right about that. But we got through it. Didn't we? We got through it. Together. He stopped being so angry. He's a happy little boy. We sing and dance to "Gangnam Style" together, right? Sure, he gets angry sometimes, but that's mostly because he's so fulfilled and so focused when he's playing with his Lego. Isn't that right, sweetie?'

Josefin nodded mutely without meeting his gaze.

'Yes. He's happy. But think of all the times in the beginning when I wished he didn't exist. What if karma has stacked up, someone heard me and thought I meant it, and now . . . now it's caught up with us?'

Fredrik's face contorted. He let go of her arm and stared at the white-patterned rug.

'That's not how it is. You know that. And he'll come back. I know it. He'll come back. He's just . . . gone . . . away for a while.'

He looked at his watch. Then he turned to look up at Mina.

'Isn't that right? Don't they basically always come back? It's only been twenty-four hours. Exactly twenty-four hours. Surely he'll be home soon?'

Mina swallowed. She of all people knew that people went missing. And that they didn't come back. But she had disappeared of her own volition. That wasn't the case with Ossian.

'Most people come back after just a few hours,' Mina said. 'Ossian has been gone for twenty-four hours, which is a little longer than normal, but there's no reason not to believe that he'll be found soon. This is our top priority right now.'

She avoided mentioning that the children who returned after a few hours had usually only got lost or gone around to a friend's without saying anything. They weren't abducted by women in cars full of toys. But she could feel the stress from the fact that Ossian still hadn't been found in every cell of her body.

'Tell me about the morning he disappeared,' said Peder, addressing the question to both parents. 'Was there anything that stood out? Perhaps something you saw when dropping him off at nursery? Maybe someone you hadn't seen before nearby?'

'I did the drop-off,' said Josefin as she continued to caress the stain with her hand. 'You know the advert isn't true, right? Their claim that detergents get it all out? I've tested every single product on the market, pre-treating . . . washing with white laundry detergent at ninety. It still won't come out. I think this stain here is chocolate. He was allowed to eat a Kinder egg on the sofa, but he wanted to get at the toy, so he put the chocolate down next to him. Do you remember that, Fredrik? I think it was some little robot that you built out of five parts. He wouldn't stop until . . .'

Her voice trailed off into a void.

'Darling,' said Fredrik, and Mina saw how hard he was fighting to keep it together. 'Darling. Focus. The police want to know whether you saw anything when you were doing the drop-off. Something? Anything at all . . . that might help them find Ossian?'

'Nothing. I saw nothing. Everything was as usual. Parents. Kids. I'm the kind of parent who never learns the other parents' names. Or even knows who belongs to who.'

'Josefin . . .'

Fredrik caressed her arm. She shook herself like a wet dog. 'I'm also the kind of parent who never remembers parent-teacher meetings, or outdoor days, or theme days, or . . . like yesterday morning. He was meant to have his packed lunch with him. But I forgot it. As usual. He liked cold pancakes. Rolled up. If only I'd remembered, it would all have gone differently. If he'd . . .'

Josefin fell silent.

'I'm sorry we can't be of any more assistance,' said Fredrik.

'There is one thing you can do for us,' said Mina. 'With your permission, we'd like to publicize the search for Ossian at a press conference in a few hours' time. The public can often be a great help.' Fredrik looked at his wife, who had gone back to staring at the sofa. She nodded silently.

'We'll do anything,' he said.

He got up and went over to the fridge in the kitchen. He took down a few of the photographs attached to it with colourful magnets.

'Here are some pictures of Ossian,' he said upon his return. 'I assume you want them.' Mina saw how he held up the photos with their backs towards his wife so that she didn't have to see them. Josefin stifled a sob. It contained more sorrow than ought to have been found in a single human being.

'Thank you,' said Peder. 'Remember, this will be shown in the media. It's for a good cause. But you might like to avoid the papers and TV for a few days.'

'One last question,' said Mina. 'There's no one around you that you have the slightest suspicion would want to harm you or Ossian? Or who might want to take him for some reason?'

Fredrik digested the question, but then shook his head vociferously.

'If we'd thought of anything, the smallest thing, anything at all that we thought would be of interest to you then we would have said so. But we're . . . we're completely ordinary. I'm an art director for an ad agency and Josefin is an editor at a publisher's. We're . . . from ordinary backgrounds, ordinary families, our friends are ordinary . . . We have . . . an ordinary life . . . Well, had.'

Mina saw that his composed exterior was breaking apart. She exchanged a glance with Peder, and they stood up.

'We understand,' she said. 'Peder has three three-year-olds and I've got . . .' She stopped herself in the nick of time and paused for breath. She had come close. She could feel Peder's puzzled stare, but she avoided meeting his eyes. 'We'll do everything we can to find Ossian,' she concluded.

Josefin remained on the sofa but looked up at Mina.

'Don't get a white sofa,' she said.

Mina nodded. She deliberately averted her gaze from the child's shoes in the hallway as they exited through the front door.

15

Julia's chest tightened in response to the mere act of approaching the front door of the apartment. Conditioned reflexes were a funny old thing. Taking a deep breath, she pushed down the handle. She could hear Harry crying inside the apartment.

'Hello?'

She made her voice cheerful and light-hearted. No reply. She called out again, but once again got no response. Apart from the loud crying from an incredibly disgruntled baby.

On her way to the bedroom, she passed the kitchen. It looked like a bomb had gone off. Empty baby food jars, dirty plates, banana peel, scrunched-up sheets of kitchen roll, and an infinite number of half-empty mugs of coffee. Interesting . . . When she was at home with Harry, Torkel always sneered at her when he got home from work and the place looked like this. He never missed an opportunity to ask her what she did all day while she was at home.

She carefully pushed open the bedroom door.

Harry was lying in his crib, his face bright red with rage. He was calling upon all the vocal resources he possessed, which were by no means inconsiderable. Torkel was asleep in the adjacent double bed. He was snoring loudly and had lain down on top of the duvet in his clothes.

Julia checked the time and swore. She really hadn't had time to come home, but she urgently needed to change before the press conference. The clothes she was wearing were impregnated with sweat. And she wanted to shower Harry's chubby cheeks with kisses. Torkel's mass explosion of text messages during the day had finally managed to burrow under her skin and give her a guilty conscience. Even though she knew she shouldn't have one.

She picked Harry up. He fell silent as soon as he was in her arms, just as she sensed the reason for his crying. There was an intense smell of poo. She carried him to the changing table in the bathroom. He gurgled when she'd cleaned him up and he reached out towards the figures dangling from a mobile above the table. The Babblers. The colourful figures seemed like pure heroin to babies – they were immensely popular.

'Come on, sweetie. You can hang out while Mummy changes, but then we have to wake Daddy up because Mummy has to go back to work. You know, somewhere else there's another little boy who's probably both scared and sad. And he's waiting impatiently for Mummy to find him.'

Harry gurgled and responded by trying to pull her hair. His small, chubby fists had the unerring ability to catch hold of a couple of strands of hair near the ears where it hurt most, and then to tug with surprising strength.

'Ouch, ouch, ouch! Don't hurt Mummy,' she said, grimacing and carefully prising Harry's fists open.

Julia put him in the baby bouncer chair while she changed. First, a tactical shower – spray deodorant without washing first – and then a fresh shirt and trousers. Now she was ready to keep going for as long as it took.

When she was done, she picked Harry up and buried her face in his pudgy neck, drawing in the scent of his baby skin. He laughed loudly and waved his arms in the air. She felt something inside her dissolve and she felt all warm and fuzzy.

Until now she had managed to keep the two things apart. The disappearance of a child. And her own status as a parent. She had managed to keep Ossian and Harry apart. Now they were blurring together rapidly.

51

Ossian.

Harry.

Ossian.

Harry.

One bigger, one small. Someone's child. Their child. Her child. A missing child. A child here in her arms.

It was for Harry's sake that she had to hurry back to work. The day wasn't over yet. She held him tighter. She felt his soft little hand against her neck. Julia took a deep breath. Then she went into the bedroom. She laid Harry down next to Torkel and shook him gently. Torkel came to with a start and looked around groggily.

'Huh? What? Wha—'

'It's me. I just popped back to get changed. I have to go again. Harry's got a clean nappy, but I think he's starting to get hungry.'

Torkel leapt out of bed and looked at her with savage eyes.

'Go? You're going again? But what about me? I've had him all day. I thought you'd at least be at home this evening. You haven't even bothered to reply to my texts. Look, Julia, this isn't going to work. The office called and I've got a thousand emails and . . .'

Julia hurried out of the bedroom as Torkel's words continued to pelt her back. In her mind's eye she saw Ossian's face.

With Harry's superimposed over it.

She grabbed her bag and headed for the front door. Behind her, she heard Torkel's words continue unrelentingly.

16

The laptop perched on Vincent's knees had an almost full battery. He had made sure to charge it – he didn't want to risk missing anything because the battery suddenly went flat. A clock on the display showed how many minutes and seconds remained until 5 p.m. when the livestream on the police website was due to begin. The press release had only mentioned Julia by name, since she was charged with leading the press conference. Vincent didn't even know whether Mina was still on Julia's team. But he could always hope.

If he was lucky, he might catch sight of her.

If he was lucky.

The shadow within him shifted. It had been there ever since he was little. Since the whole business with his mother. That was when it had taken up residency. But he had learned pretty quickly to keep it in check by doing things like counting objects or seeing how something connected to something else in a pattern. Sometimes it could be difficult to distinguish which patterns were real and which ones he had invented, but that wasn't necessarily important. Like right now . . . He had noticed that his wife had set up a wasp trap using a plastic bottle on the windowsill while he was waiting for the press conference. Wasp: W A S P. Positions number 23, 1, 19 and 16 in the alphabet, the sum of which was 59. He thought about *her*. P C M I N A. Positions 16, 3, 13, 12, 14 and 1. The sum of which was also 59. The important thing was that he kept his logical, analytical mode of thought active. That kept the darker emotions at bay, giving them less space.

In the end, he'd got so good at ignoring the shadow that he had almost stopped thinking about its presence altogether. His family were a great help in that respect. When he had to remember to pack Aston's lunch or he was worrying that Rebecka's friends were all fake, there simply wasn't space for any spiritual darkness. And when he'd met Mina, the darkness inside had disappeared completely. With her, he had felt normal.

But then it had been over.

He and Mina had stopped seeing each other. And the shadow had returned – stronger than before. The actions of his sister had brought it back to life, and this time his family wasn't enough to make it disappear. He wasn't worried that it would take over completely – the darkness had been a part of him for much too long for that. But it was still there as a stowaway. Or a bad friend. One that was beginning to get more vocal.

However, the thought that Mina might appear in the

conference had suppressed the darkness, at least temporarily. The clock on the screen disappeared, to be replaced by a room. In the centre of shot there was a lectern, but no one was standing at it. There was a murmur of voices and the rustle of people fidgeting. Presumably this emanated from the assembled press corps, who must be out of shot. Five microphones were pointing upwards from the lectern in anticipation of the as yet absent speaker. He sighed. Even the police were incapable of achieving order, it seemed. He got out a pen and propped it against his screen to make it look like a sixth microphone.

That was much better.

After another minute, Julia stepped into shot and stood at the lectern. A number of camera flashes went off and then the hubbub died down.

'Thank you all for coming,' she said. 'I'll get straight to the point. Yesterday afternoon sometime between half past three and four o'clock, five-year-old Ossian Walthersson went missing from Backens nursery in the Zinkensdamm area on the island of Södermalm in Stockholm.'

No one else from the team was visible. Vincent had been hoping that he would see Mina so hard that his chest ached when she wasn't there. But perhaps she would appear soon. He needed to calm down.

Ossian.

Begins with O.

Omega in the Greek alphabet. Also the last of the 24 Greek letters, which lent it symbolic significance. According to ancient Christianity, omega entailed the end of everything. Doomsday. And what better way to start it than by kidnapping a child? Vincent realized he was in no way feeling any calmer.

'There is evidence to suggest that Ossian has been abducted,' Julia added. 'In addition to Ossian, we are also looking for a woman in early middle age who is reported to have been at the scene around the relevant time in a car. While we unfortunately lack any further description, she is said to have left in a sports car. She may also have had puppies with her. We don't have any details of their breed.'

She paused and produced a photograph of Ossian. It looked

54

like it had been taken at a theme park. Gröna Lund, perhaps. Ossian had blond curls, long and summery, and he was smiling happily at the camera with half his face buried in a ball of candy floss. Vincent looked up from the screen and glanced across towards Aston's door, behind which his youngest son was playing. It had taken half an hour's hullabaloo to get him to do something on his own. Of course, Aston always preferred his mother over Vincent, but today of all days the conflict had been particularly volatile. But no matter how much they quarrelled, Vincent still loved his son beyond comprehension. He couldn't imagine what it would be like if Aston were to suddenly disappear. The mere thought of it made him feel sick. He couldn't even begin to think what Ossian's parents were going through right now.

'You have all been emailed this picture,' Julia said to the assembled journalists. 'All information about where Ossian may be – as well as this woman – should be provided as a matter of priority. I don't need to stress that this is very urgent.'

The camera flashes began to go off again.

'What do the parents say?' someone off camera called out.

'Ossian's parents are pleading for your help,' said Julia. 'But right now they're too shaken up to face the media, and they request your understanding on that point. However, they have provided a message.'

The photo of Ossian now covered his screen, together with a caption:

This is Ossian. He likes dancing and singing. Ossian is our whole world. Help us bring the singing back to our world.

This was followed by a phone number and various social media handles.

'We're appealing for any and all tips,' Julia said. 'The police can be contacted via Facebook and Instagram. And of course, you can also get in touch by phone or email. We would also appreciate it if members of the press would provide their own contact details when writing about the case. It can sometimes feel easier for people to call *Expressen* rather than the police.'

'Do you have any theories at this stage?' someone shouted.

Julia looked in the direction the question had come from for a long time. The muscles of her face were tensed. Vincent realized that maybe he should offer her a crash course in controlling her body language. That wasn't a bad idea, actually. Offering training to the police. Maybe Mina would come to it too. Not that Mina needed to take a course: her body language had always been a model of clarity worthy of imitation. A memory of the way that Mina moved awoke in his mind's eye and something fluttered inside him. He had to make an effort to suppress the memory. He didn't really want to, but it would be stupid to miss something said at the press conference. Julia seemed to relax a little on screen and her shoulders slumped slightly.

'Honestly, no,' she said, replying to the question posed.

Julia's tone of voice indicated the press conference was at an end. The journalists would have to do most of the job themselves on this occasion. It seemed that Mina wasn't going to put in an appearance. Perhaps it was just as well, because he didn't know how he would have reacted if she had suddenly shown up.

The front door opened and Maria came in. She took off her jacket with a sigh and flopped onto the sofa next to Vincent.

'Don't get me wrong. I'm so incredibly grateful that he wants to take me on,' she said, stretching. 'But I'm totally knackered.'

After Maria's start-up course, Kevin had offered to continue helping her on a one-to-one basis. In all honesty, Vincent had trouble seeing how much more help there was to give. Or receive. After all, it was only an online store selling ceramic angels and bars of soap. It was hardly a competitor to Amazon. He looked at his watch surreptitiously. She'd been gone for three hours.

'Are all these consultations really necessary?' he asked. 'You're meeting pretty much every night. Aston keeps asking after you.'

Vincent regretted it immediately. What he really wanted was to be supportive and generous. Maria needed to have something that was hers and hers alone. Something where she could shine and grow on her own terms. And now she had found it. He got plenty of attention himself through his work. He had an audience, the public, a faceless mass celebrating and praising him. Maria didn't get any of that. If he was soul-searching, he didn't really give her the attention she deserved either. He meant to say something, but remained silent. Without a manual, he was helpless.

17

She inserted the key into the lock and opened the door. The slight resistance offered by the barrel suddenly and unexpectedly reminded Mina of a different flat. For a moment, it was that hallway that she saw before her as she entered, rather than the apartment in Årsta. She tried to push the thought away. Going over her memories was something she had actively sought to avoid over the years. And the lock on her front door had always been a little sticky. So why did it make her think of another time and another life on today of all days? She tried to shake the feeling, but once it had taken hold it wouldn't go easily.

The other flat – the one in Vasastan – had been smaller than this one. But they'd made it work. She and her husband.

And Nathalie.

Nathalie had been little and they'd slept in the same bed – all three of them. The sudden memory hurt so much that she gasped for breath. The favourite blue quilt. Nathalie had been inconsolable every time it had had to go through the wash and she'd been forced to sleep with another one. In the end, they'd bought three identical quilts.

Stop thinking about it. Don't let it in.

She mustn't think about what she had lost. All the things she'd let her addiction ruin and destroy. At the same time, she had been working hard through all her years of AA to forgive herself. She would never have thought that the tablets they'd prescribed after her postpartum surgery would turn into an avalanche – an avalanche that had buried her completely for so many years. Small, white pills that had looked so innocent in the palm of her hand, but which had taken away everything that meant anything to her.

She'd spent far too much time wondering why she of all people had ended up an addict –which defective gene in her had made it happen so quickly. But given her mother's experience, perhaps she shouldn't have been so surprised. They had chosen different drugs but had fallen just as easily. And they had both thrown away just as much. Mina took off her shoes on the doormat in the hallway and spotted a small pebble that had tumbled onto the floor. That was despite her always taking so much care to scrape her shoes down by the main door. She picked up the stone between her thumb and forefinger and quickly cast it out of the door. Then she closed and locked it, went to the bathroom and immediately washed her hands. She'd not only had to handle a dirty key, but also a stone. That necessitated two washes. Then she undressed, binned her underwear and took an ice-cold shower. It had been a long day. Normally she would have taken a hot shower to cleanse the dirt from her body. But the heat in the apartment would have her sweating as soon as she got out of the shower. She tried to delay that by cooling off as much as she could.

All the while, she tried to shut out the memories. But it was hard. Like the Greek restaurant two floors down from the flat in Vasastan. She hadn't been there in fifteen years, but she could still effortlessly summon the scent of olives, garlic and grilled meat.

After she had showered, she opened a new multipack of knickers and a pack of new vests and dressed. Then she went into the living room in her underclothes and sat down on the sofa.

Some days she had no trouble keeping the past at bay, but not always. That was why she didn't want to let anyone in. Not into the apartment, not emotionally. It was already so crowded.

The worst thing was that it had been her choice. It had been she who had abandoned ship. She had thought she was selfless and that her choices had made things better for the others. How could she have been so naive? So egotistical?

She pressed her fingers to her eyes to stop the tears. They brought dirt with them, and she didn't want to have to bathe her cheeks in sanitizer. It had stung unexpectedly the last time she had done it.

She'd been so young. And she hadn't wanted to be like her mother. Then she'd spent years hating her ex-husband for forcing her to choose. But that wasn't true. The only thing he'd done was to make sure she kept her own promise.

And she had. Almost.

Except for the brief encounter she'd had with Nathalie in Kungsträdgården two years ago when she hadn't divulged who she was, she'd kept away. Not made contact. Done nothing more than watch from a distance. But she had spent countless evenings following the small dot on the app connected to the tracker in Nathalie's backpack.

Mina went over to the desk and looked at the photo of her daughter. She opened a drawer and read the message that Vincent had written that summer.

I'm not going to ask. But when you're ready to talk, I'll listen.

PS Sorry about the cube.

She closed the drawer again. *When you're ready to talk.* That was never going to happen.

She went back to the front door and checked it was properly locked. No one could get in.

18

Vincent ached all over. He had another show tonight. Usually, the only things people went to see at the theatre during the Swedish summer were open-air farces, but there had been so much demand for his latest production that they had extended the tour. Umberto was overjoyed by the increased ticket revenue, but Vincent was beginning to regret the summer gambit. Now there were just two weeks to go before he got some rest. He might even take the family on holiday. If he managed to corral the whole family in the house for long enough that they could actually set off somewhere together.

When he emerged into the kitchen, Benjamin was already halfway through his breakfast. He always ate the same thing: two slices of rye toast spread with butter that had to melt before he made them into a sandwich with a slice of ham. A novelty was that Benjamin had recently started drinking coffee. Following Vincent's investment in a capsule-based machine, coffee drinking in the household had increased exponentially.

While Vincent got out two capsules and loaded them into the machine, he glanced towards the old filter coffee maker that had previously always been sputtering away at this time of morning. It was still on the kitchen counter, but it was now shrouded in a fine layer of dust. It felt like something had been lost. Vincent started the machine, muttered a good morning to his eldest son and then set off for Aston's bedroom.

'Breakfast,' he called out, opening the door and popping his head inside.

His ten-year-old groaned and pulled the duvet over his head.

'I don't want to go to the recreation club.'

'Well, who does? But today's a Friday, and tomorrow it's the weekend and you'll be able to sleep for as long as you want. Come and eat now.'

Aston stuck a leg out from under the duvet, as if he were testing the world beyond. Then he withdrew it. 'Three minutes,' said Vincent.

He returned to the kitchen and inserted the second capsule into the machine. Mornings always required a double dose. Anyway, only crazy people used an odd number of capsules.

Maria was setting out bowls on the table.

'You might have made breakfast for everyone,' she muttered to Benjamin.

'Sorry, didn't have time. Got to be standing by when they open.'

'Surely the stock exchange doesn't open until nine?' said Vincent, looking meaningfully at Benjamin. 'Why don't you tell it as it is? You just lack empathy with your family.'

Maria set down her mug of tea on the table with a bang.

'I don't like you day trading,' she said to Benjamin. 'It feels deeply immoral to earn money from speculation. When did you become such a capitalist?'

Vincent refrained from pointing out that Maria had quit her own studies in social work in favour of entrepreneurial training so she could open her own shop. His wife's disdain for Benjamin's hobby was most probably related to the fact that his son was already making a pretty good living. Probably more than Maria would make from her angels, scented candles and plaques emblazoned with words of wisdom for several years.

'Aston, hurry up!' she shouted. 'There's new cereal!'

'No!' Aston shouted in response from his room. That was followed by: 'OK then! Is there jam?'

Aston had dropped his previous breakfast of choice – slices of apple in yogurt – a few months earlier. It had been around the time that he'd stopped eating more or less anything that wasn't based on bread or wheat flour. He was currently following a diet comprising hamburgers, pizzas and hot dogs. Instead of fruit and yogurt, Aston now ate Cheerios. There would usually be a mountain of hoops in his bowl, so precipitous that it risked spilling onto the floor.

Aston came out of his room yawning. He sat down at the table and began to heap a veritable pyramid of circular cereal into his bowl. Maria looked pointedly out of the window.

'Well, as you know, *Fortress Prisoners' Flight* . . .' Vincent said hesitantly.

'Has anyone seen Rebecka?' Maria interjected from the window. 'Is she up?'

His wife obviously hadn't noticed that he'd started to speak. And it was probably just as well. Vincent in tights was perhaps not the best topic of conversation for breakfast.

'She didn't come home last night,' Benjamin said, slurping his coffee. 'Didn't she text Dad about it?'

Vincent, in motion towards Aston's cereal box, stopped mid-movement.

'I didn't receive any text message,' he said.

'Actually, I think you did,' said Benjamin. 'But your phone's still charging so I guess you haven't checked.'

'Is she staying with that Dennis guy?' said Vincent, grabbing the cereal before the box was completely empty.

'Dad!' Aston yelled.

'His name's *Denis*,' Benjamin sighed. 'He's from France. Try to keep up.'

'*Oui, monsieur*,' said Vincent in an exaggerated French accent as he set down the cereal box out of Aston's reach.

He still hadn't got over the fact that his daughter was now seventeen years old and had started doing as she pleased. He'd tried to assert that while she lived under their roof she was subject to their rules, and that this was even enshrined in law, but he suspected she no longer really respected him as the family's authority figure. Which was, perhaps, as things ought to be. Funnily enough, Maria wasn't anywhere near as worried about Rebecka as he was. On the contrary, his wife seemed to appreciate Rebecka spending less time at home.

'*Denis, l'homme mystérieux*,' she said, curling her upper lip and shrugging her shoulders in a stereotypical depiction of a French gesture. 'When will we see him, eh? Does he even exist? *C'est réel?*'

'This is exactly why she doesn't bring him home,' said Benjamin, who sighed as he left the table.

'As long as she's using protection,' Maria said, rinsing her mug at the sink.

Vincent coughed heavily. Maria's prudishness had apparently dissolved for the time being. He made a mental note never to ask his wife what she had done at the age of seventeen.

'Does she need a plaster?' Aston said, his mouth full of Cheerios. Some of the hoops escaped from the corner of his mouth, ending up on the floor.

'No, but Denis does,' said Maria. 'Your father can explain.'

Vincent buried his face in his hands. If it was too early in the morning for *Fortress Prisoners' Flight*, then it was most definitely too early for a discussion on the birds and the bees.

'Anyway, I don't want to go to school,' said Aston, changing the topic to Vincent's relief.

'You're not going to school – you're going to the recreation club,' he said. 'And there's only a few days left. Then you'll be on your summer holidays for real.'

'My God, it's hot already,' said Maria, opening the window. 'And it's not even nine. I'll find some more sun cream for Aston.'

While Maria went to the bathroom, Vincent fetched a dish-cloth to deal with the sticky cereal pieces on the floor. As he bent down and wiped them up, the first beads of sweat for the day dripped from his brow onto his arm. A cool, airy room appeared in his mind's eye. It had pale grey walls, everything was perfectly in order and there was no yogurt on the floor nor potential misunderstandings flying through the air.

Mina's apartment.

He'd only been there twice. And neither occasion had been unproblematic. On the first, Mina had been inconsolable following an encounter with Nathalie. On the second, she'd effectively accused him of murder. But it didn't matter – he still longed for her orderly apartment. His former colleague had no idea what luxury she lived in.

19

She had seen the woman before. Admittedly she couldn't remember where, but the woman was definitely familiar. Nathalie looked over her shoulder. She'd slept over at a friend's and was the only one of the group heading to town this morning. Her other friends had crossed to the platform on the far side.

'Hello.'

Nathalie jumped. The woman had addressed her. She wondered whether to answer or not. She found herself torn by all the admonishments she'd received during her childhood not to talk to strangers, and all the prompts she'd received to be polite to grown-ups. And the woman didn't look at all dangerous. On the contrary. For someone that old, she was beautiful. She was tall, with blond hair she had combed back into a smooth tuft at the nape of her neck. She wore no make-up, but her eyelashes were long and natural, framing her bright blue eyes, while her skin was almost without wrinkles. Nathalie had a hard time guessing how old she was. She generally struggled to guess people's ages. But maybe . . . sixty?

'Hello,' Nathalie replied tentatively, as the metro train pulled into the station.

The woman got on behind her. Nathalie sat down in a vacant set of four seats. The train was fairly empty despite the fact that it was a Friday morning, but the commuters were always conspicuous by their absence in the summertime.

The woman sat down opposite her. Nathalie looked out of the window. It felt weird. The train pulled out of the station and began to pick up speed, the houses outside rushing past ever more quickly. She wiped a few beads of moisture from her brow as she surreptitiously glanced at the woman opposite her. She felt sweaty all over following the short walk to the metro station – the heat was like a wall and the cool train was a welcome respite from the oppressive summer temperature. But the woman looked cool – there were no sweat patches on her white blouse or skirt. The woman caught her eye. Nathalie turned away to look out of the window again in embarrassment. You weren't supposed to stare at strangers. But there was something familiar about her. Nathalie's brain went into overdrive, scouring every nook and cranny of her memories for something that might help her to place the face that seemed so familiar. Slowly but surely, something at the periphery of her brain began to shift – it wanted to emerge from the depths, and it was pushing more and more. It was just out of reach. Every time she tried to grasp the memory it slipped away.

Perhaps the explanation was simple. Perhaps this was someone she had seen on TV, which was why she seemed so strangely familiar in the way that celebrities sometimes did, even though you'd never met them. People would cheerily greet Nathalie's dad while out and about, before looking embarrassed a moment later when they realized that he wasn't someone they knew but merely someone they'd seen on the news.

A chime sounded and the cheerful female voice on the tannoy announced the next stop.

'Gullmarsplan.'

The woman stood up. Nathalie tried not to look at her, but something forced her to pull her gaze away from the window and towards the brightly clothed figure close by. The woman held out a hand to her.

'Nathalie, there's no need for you to be afraid of me,' said the woman softly. 'I'm your grandmother. Do you really not recognize me?'

All the jigsaw pieces fell into place at once. Nathalie had never met her grandmother – not that she remembered, anyway. She hadn't even known that she had one. But she knew what it was she had seen: she'd recognized a part of herself in that kind face. The feeling was overwhelming. It was like meeting a part of herself that she didn't know existed. And that feeling brought with it a conviction of its truth.

This really was her grandmother.

Nathalie looked at the outstretched hand. There was a blue elastic band around the wrist and the reddened skin testified to the fact that it was rather tight. It was hard to feel threatened by an old woman with an elastic band around her wrist.

'Why don't you come with me, dear?' said her grandmother, gesturing invitingly at her with her hand. 'There's something I'd like to show you. I've been waiting so long.'

20

When I wake up I sit down with my back to the wall. That means I can see if anyone is coming to do something mean. Because I don't think they're kind. Even though they gave me ice cream for dinner and said I could watch the Lego Movie however many times I wanted.

I don't believe the mean lady. I don't believe I'm going home. I hate the Lego Movie.

I've been here for ages now. A hundred days. Although I know it's really only been two.

I can hardly cry anymore. I've asked a few times whether Mum and Dad have died of calcer. But they won't say. I just want to go home.

I told them yesterday. I told them to drive me home over and over. Eventually my tummy hurt so much I couldn't say it again.

I'm supposed to be at nursery. I wasn't there yesterday. Or the day before that. We were going to build rockets for our space project. Mine was going to be a Ferrari. And I was going to show them how to dance Gangnam Style. But I didn't get to. And it's all that lady's fault.

A while later, the lady comes back and says there's more ice cream, but I don't reply. I pretend she doesn't exist.

The room doesn't exist.

The stupid grown-ups don't exist.

Nothing exists.

I don't exist.

21

'Good morning, everyone,' said Julia.

Mina waved her hand in a half-hearted reply. Julia was standing by the projector screen at the very front of the room and Mina noticed that she looked exhausted.

'We've received tons of tips following yesterday's press conference,' Julia continued. 'A missing kid always engages people. The tip lines have been red hot. But we can't forget that come this afternoon it will have been forty-eight hours since Ossian went missing. So let's make today count. With each passing hour, our chances of finding him diminish.'

Bosse let out a curt yap. The dog had temporarily abandoned his master and was draped over Peder's feet. It looked uncomfortably warm, but Peder was making no attempt to shift the dog. Mina suspected he didn't dare. Anyone who disturbed Bosse would incur the wrath of Christer. But the shrill sound helped to focus Mina's thoughts.

'The tips are the usual hotch-potch,' said Julia, 'so we'll need to eliminate the crackpots, people out for revenge, pure speculation, and wishful thinking. Ossian has been seen everywhere from Kiruna to Ystad, and we've even had a few sightings in Norway and Denmark. It's going to be like looking for a needle in a haystack as we sort the wheat from the chaff, if you'll tolerate my mixing of metaphors. But it's nothing we haven't handled before. Christer has already made a start on checking which sex offenders are currently at large, and we've got Sara here from Analysis.'

Sara nodded briefly at the group. She'd proven invaluable to them when they'd had to analyse cellular data in the case involving Vincent's sister, and she was a welcome reinforcement in all matters entailing data sifting.

Mina spotted that Ruben seemed to be avoiding looking at Sara. Interesting. He usually checked out women in so much detail that it verged on molestation. She remembered that things had been awkward between the two of them the last time Sara had helped out. Mina couldn't help wondering whether something had happened. Of course it had, given Ruben's involvement. But as it happened, she felt he had toned it down a bit over the last year or so. Sure, there was still plenty of talk there, but there was something about his attitude that had changed.

'Peder, you're a master list-cracker, so I thought I'd put you and Sara on systematically reviewing all the tips that have come in and categorizing them. We need a definite no pile, a maybe pile, and another for promising ones. But be generous in your assessment. We don't want it turning out that a decent tip has ended up in the no pile by mistake. We can't afford to mess up.'

Mina liked Sara. She was a sharp analyst. Peder looked pleased too. He presumably appreciated the chance to work with someone who was as keen to dig up facts as he was. Peder tried to shift his feet, but Bosse whined in his sleep and pressed himself even harder against Peder's legs.

'Ruben, I want you and Christer reviewing whether there's anything you think we should be giving extra attention.'

'Sure thing,' said Ruben, nodding.

'OK,' Julia continued. 'Let's keep at it. Remember that Ossian doesn't fit the pattern for kids who go missing for a long time. Children who are kidnapped are almost always taken by a parent or a supporting relative. The perpetrator is usually a known party. This time, we've got nothing whatsoever to suggest a possible kidnapper. All we have to go on are the similarities to the Lilly Meyer murder. That time, three days passed from the abduction until her body was found. Let's pray that the cases aren't as similar as we think. But we can't afford to take chances. Ossian has been gone for two days. So we have to find him. Today. There's no plan B.'

22

Ruben ran a hand over his face and sighed.

'I still don't understand why there needs to be two of us,' he said.

'Because it makes it twice as fast,' Christer replied. 'Or at least it would if you actually logged on in the first place.'

Ruben had not the slightest inclination to browse the sex offenders register. He was far too restless for that.

The plan had been to pay a visit to Ellinor the day before. That hadn't come off. Of course, he knew that Ellinor could wait and that Ossian couldn't. But something had been triggered in him, and that made it hard to apply the brakes. He needed to be in motion.

'I'll check in with Peder and that Sara woman,' he said, standing up. 'They might have something they want us to check out. I'll get more coffee on the way back.'

Christer looked like he was going to protest, but it was probably the promise of coffee that made him nod instead.

'Julia's not going to be best pleased with you,' he muttered. 'And make sure you get the biggest mugs.'

Ruben headed over to Peder's office and popped his head around the door. Peder was wearing headphones and taking notes from the tip-line recordings, while Sara was reviewing what looked like a stack of printed emails.

'Good thing the two of you are here instead of over at Analysis,' Ruben said, with a smile at Sara.

He'd met her briefly on a few occasions, and each time he'd had the impression she didn't much care for him. He didn't know what he'd done to deserve that, but he was determined that he was going to change it. Sara was good-looking and very curvaceous, even if she was the same age as he was, which meant she was a few years older than the women he usually went for. Albeit that should have been 'gone for' in the past tense – as Amanda would have reminded him. 'I don't know whether I would have survived the walk there in this heat,' he said.

Sara eyed him from head to foot.

'You could do with a bit of exercise,' she said coldly.

What the actual fuck? This heat definitely made people snarky.

'Anything interesting?' he said, curbing his attempt at pleasantness.

Sara handed him a few sheets.

'This is what we want to prioritize right now,' she said. 'Hopefully we'll find more, but most of the tips are pretty implausible. Obviously that doesn't mean they're not true. But we'll start with the credible ones first.'

He leafed through the stack. There were no more than five. Ossian's kidnappers had done a good job of staying invisible. Suddenly he stopped, his eye caught by one of the tips. Someone in Östermalm had heard a child through the wall. The tip was similar to the others, but there was something about the address. Danderydsgatan. Why did he recognize it?

He pulled out his phone and messaged Christer. Search for Danderydsgatan in the sex offenders register and I'll bring the whole pot of coffee, he wrote.

'You do know I'm right here, don't you?' Christer shouted down the corridor. 'You can talk to me like normal.'

Sara laughed as Peder looked up.

'Ruben?' he said in confusion, taking off his headphones. 'Is there something we can do for you?'

'Too late,' Ruben said over his shoulder as he exited the office. 'Lucky you've got help. And thanks, Sara.'

He turned the corner of the corridor heading for the kitchen with the coffee maker just as Julia emerged from her office and passed him going in the other direction. His phone chimed as an incoming text arrived from Christer. *No hits. Any whisky to go with the coffee?* The old man was learning.

Julia had her own phone jammed to her ear and didn't even seem to see him. Her posture revealed that she was not in the best of moods. But that couldn't be helped. Christer's coffee would have to wait.

'Wait a sec, Julia,' he called out, jogging to catch up with her. 'There's something I—'

'You know it should be Up&Go nappies,' Julia hissed into her phone. 'If you want to mess around with cloth nappies then you can wash them yourself.' She hung up and then looked at Ruben.

'Yes?' she said, fanning herself with her hand.

The air in the corridor was completely still.

'Well, I . . . How are you doing by the way? I only saw you from behind, but are you OK?'

Julia squinted at him.

'From behind? If that's innuendo, then it's lost on me.'

'No, I only meant . . . Forget it,' he said. 'I just read one of the tips that came in – from Östermalm. Danderydsgatan. Someone heard a sad child through the wall and thinks their neighbour in the flat next door isn't the type to have kids.'

'Yes, I'm afraid we've had a lot of tips like that,' Julia sighed. 'We've got a lot of parents with young kids and nervous neighbours in this town.'

'Maybe. But there was something about this tip that rang a bell. Christer didn't find anything in the sex offenders register. Yet . . . I can't let go of the address.'

70

Julia looked at him, a well-defined wrinkle of concern visible between her eyebrows. He couldn't help noticing that something seemed to have started leaking under her top. And he'd been making an effort not to look at her boobs.

'Ruben, this isn't like you,' she said. 'Following your intuition like this.'

'I know. But, Julia, I think . . . I think it's right. I can't explain it. Not yet. But I think . . . no, I know this is for real.'

Julia looked at him for a long time.

'OK,' she said. 'You've got an hour to prove it to me. I can't give you any more than that. We've got too many other tips to review.'

An hour. Ruben knew he was right. The only question was how he was going to convince the others without having anything concrete to go on. But he knew he'd heard Danderydsgatan mentioned somewhere before. It had been a long time ago. Years. The memory of it was like a ghost in his subconscious – almost invisible but most definitely there. He had an hour. An hour to work out what it was that might save Ossian.

23

'You needn't have come with me. This is nonsense!' Miriam Blom had protested loudly all the way in the car from Åkersberga, but Adam ignored her. He loved the sound of her voice, even when she was angry. She'd always spoken Swedish with him, ever since he was little, but the melody of her Swahili was still there and brought a tonality to her Swedish that was even more beautiful than her native language.

'You've got better things to do,' she said. 'You've got lots on at work. You can't afford to take time off.'

Adam found a spot in the car park outside the oncology department at the Karolinska Institute. He waited to answer until he had deftly manoeuvred into the slightly-too-small parking space.

'Sit tight, I'll come and help you.'

He quickly moved around the car because he knew that she would otherwise try to get out on her own.

'My God, you're pamby-nambying me.'

'It's namby-pamby.'

'Don't correct your old mother,' she said, cuffing him playfully on the head.

His evasive duck was practised. When he'd been little, it had sometimes been the wooden spoon that emerged if he didn't behave himself. Or one of Miriam's sandals. Back then he hadn't usually managed to duck.

'You should find yourself someone else to pamby-namby,' she said. 'When exactly are you going to get yourself a girl-friend?'

Adam sighed. It was a familiar and by now worn-out subject.

'Now isn't the right time,' he said. 'What with everything at work and—'

'You know it's fine if she's white, don't you?' said his mother. 'Just as long as she's bright as a button. And has nice wide hips so she can give me lots of grandchildren.'

She clung heavily to his arm.

'So that's what it's all about,' he chuckled. 'You don't care one bit about my love life. You just want to be a grandmother.'

'Of course,' she said. 'I want someone I can give far too many sweeties to.'

She had always been a big woman, for as long as Adam could remember. As a little boy, he had loved to crawl into her embrace and be absorbed by her warmth. Miriam had always been safety for him. His hub. The one who grounded him and made him believe the earth was a good place despite everything he saw in the line of duty.

'I already have a woman in my life – you know that,' he said. 'You're right that things are pretty intense at police headquarters at the moment, but they can do without me for an hour or so. But I wouldn't be able to do without you if anything happened.

I promise I'll get straight off to work as soon as I've driven you home.'

'Pfft. I can take a taxi,' said Miriam.

'You can't afford a taxi,' he said. 'You may love your job, but I know what they pay you at the welfare office. I'll wait and drive you home afterwards.'

'A first-rate stubborn child is this one,' Miriam muttered, mopping sweat from her brow with a handkerchief.

'I wonder where I get that from?' said Adam, opening the door to reception. 'You know your grandchildren will be the same.'

He tried not to look at the sign suspended from the ceiling. Department of Oncology. A word he'd never thought about before, but now hated with every fibre of his being.

'We've got an appointment with Dr Stjärngren,' he said at the window.

'Take a seat and we'll let you know when we're ready,' the old woman behind the glass said.

She pointed towards a waiting room behind them.

These kinds of places always made him feel slightly nauseous. He deposited Miriam on a chair and went to fetch them each a plastic cup of water. Thank goodness the waiting room was cool. He could feel the sweat in his armpits beginning to dry. Adam contemplated his mother's face in profile as she greedily downed the cup of water. Once she'd finished it, he took her hand. Miriam glowered at him in surprise and abruptly withdrew the hand. Then she raised it and slapped him across the head again.

'*Simama!*'

'What? Can't a guy show his mother a little love?' He laughed. Miriam snorted.

'You're just making me more worried. *Simama!*'

Adam took her hand again. This time she let him hold it.

24

Mina was sitting next to Christer at his computer, while the faces in the sex offenders register flickered past on the screen. So many monsters, so many people prepared to ruin a child's life just to experience a moment's power themselves. Or sexual gratification. Mina knew she couldn't think about the sex offenders as rational people and that most of them had been assessed as mentally ill and thus not in control of their own actions. As a police officer, she had to relate to them on that basis. But she wasn't altogether opposed to the idea of the death penalty.

Ruben was standing next to her, his arms crossed, while Christer resignedly searched the database again at Ruben's request. He claimed he'd found something. The patches of sweat below Ruben's armpits were uncomfortably distinct despite his crossed arms. Mina shuddered inwardly, and Christer passed him a small battery-powered fan. He'd found a shop selling fans for ten kronor a pop, and judging by the size of the pile in front of him, he must have bought at least fifty.

Then Christer raised a questioning eyebrow at Mina, who shook her head. The last thing she wanted was to waft Ruben's and Christer's sweat particles, which by now were guaranteed to have spread across the whole room in an even layer, into her own face. No matter how hot it was.

Christer reached the end of the database.

'None of the ones living in Stockholm are even close to Danderydsgatan,' he sighed. 'We've already checked this. We've also run the names of everyone living at 12 Danderydsgatan – where the tip came in from – through the police computer. Nothing. How about we start concentrating on some of the other tips instead?'

'No,' Ruben said firmly, shaking his head. 'It's this one. Could the kidnapper have a protected identity? Meaning they wouldn't be in the records?'

'Come on, now you're clutching at straws. The only reason we'd give a paedophile a fresh identity was if his life was in danger. But I can't find any cases like that, and especially not involving a woman. And we know that Ossian was taken by a woman.'

'But that doesn't mean he's still with one,' Ruben countered.

Mina pulled out her phone and cleaned it with a wet wipe. Then she opened Google Maps and searched for Danderydsgatan. When the satellite image appeared, she spun it around until she had a decent understanding of the neighbourhood.

'Have you checked all the tenants at numbers 10 and 14 on Danderydsgatan too?' she asked.

'No, why would we?' said Christer, looking up from the display.

'Because number 12 is in the middle of a row of buildings. Depending on where the flat the tip came from is located, their neighbour might just as well live at number 10 or 14 as at number 12.'

She held up the map on her phone and showed them. Christer sighed and ran the street numbers through the regular address database.

'14 Danderydsgatan,' he said. 'Residents include Mats Palm, Ingrid Börjesson, Gerhard Frisk. The rest are all companies. Any of those names familiar?'

Ruben shook his head.

'And then we've got 10 Danderydsgatan,' Christer continued. 'Not many flats there either. Andreas Wilander, Lenore Silver, Matti . . .'

'Stop!' Ruben exclaimed. 'Her. Lenore. Bloody hell. Have you got a photo of her?'

Christer ran some hasty Google searches.

'Weird,' he said. 'She's got basically no social media presence. She has a Facebook page but it hasn't been updated for five years. The last thing she did was change her profile picture.'

'Five years,' Ruben said, leaning in towards the screen. 'That sounds about right.'

He scrutinized the Facebook profile that Christer had pulled up and pointed to the last photo of Lenore.

'It's her. It bloody well is,' he said. 'New hair colour, new hairstyle, smaller . . . ahem, breasts. But it's her.'

Mina had no idea what Ruben was talking about.

'You know I never forget a face,' he said. 'It's one of my many superpowers. I'm not quite as good with addresses, but you don't forget something like this. At least not if you're me.'

'And what about those of us who aren't you?' Christer said patiently. 'Are you at all inclined to enlighten the ignorant masses about your brilliance?'

'With pleasure. You remember that trafficking bust five years ago? Ten people were charged with unlawful deprivation of liberty and human trafficking. They'd been operating in Stockholm city centre in the midst of neighbours who hadn't noticed a thing.'

Mina remembered the case well. The court had come down hard on the defendants in light of the age of the children being sold, and categorized the case as one of serious human exploitation. The culprits had got prison sentences ranging from four to ten years. Mina would have preferred to see even harsher punishments.

'The guy fingered as the leader of the whole operation was a Mr Kaspar Silver,' said Ruben. 'But his sister testified on his behalf at the trial. She claimed he was completely innocent and that someone else was responsible for all of it. However, she didn't have any names to offer when she was pushed on that point.'

'And it didn't make any difference anyway,' Christer said with a nod. 'Kaspar got the longest sentence of them all.'

'The sister went to ground after the media commotion,' Ruben said, pointing at the screen again. 'Apparently she changed her look and dropped off social media. But she didn't change her appearance enough for me not to recognize her. Meet Lenore. Kaspar Silver's sister. The sister who claimed someone else was responsible for a child-snatching spree. Someone else . . . like her. I reckon Lenore picked up where she left off.'

The fan in Christer's hand suddenly emitted a small bang and ceased functioning. He tossed it onto a pile of others that were already broken.

'I'll notify Julia right away,' said Mina. 'Ruben, you can call the flying squad. We need to get over to 10 Danderydsgatan as soon as we can.'

25

Vincent watched the fish swimming around the aquarium as he folded the yellow paper and tried to remember the instructions. Tonight's show was in Stockholm for a change, so he still had a few hours before he needed to leave the house.

When the children had been smaller, they'd wanted a 'proper' pet, which in their world meant an animal they could stroke. They'd all sworn on their lives that they'd look after the pet themselves, but he knew that their promises would last for all of a week.

So they'd gone with fish. He'd found a species known as central mudminnows, which was a name Aston still seemed to find hilarious for some reason. They quite happily ate from his hand whenever he fed them. Of course, it wasn't the same as petting a dog. But it had to do.

It had surprised everyone – including himself – that Vincent was the member of the family who had really taken to the fish. Some days, it felt as if they were his only friends. Those were the days when the shadow took over. He'd begun to have more days like that. Days that felt as if he were within what the astronomers described as a conical shadow in a celestial body. The location on a planet that was shrouded in eternal darkness and where no light ever reached. The mother of all shadows.

He knew who the mother of his shadow was.

He set aside the folded-up piece of paper and started on the next one. Today was his mother's birthday. But he hadn't told the family. The fewer questions they asked about his background, the better. He added the final folds to the paper and assembled the two parts into the animal they were meant to form. The model was too complicated to be folded using one sheet of paper. Now all that was missing were the dots. Then the origami leopard was finished. He'd made one last year too as a birthday present for his mother, and he intended to do so each year. It was a small tribute to the leopard-skin print dress she had worn on the last birthday they'd celebrated together. The problem was that the leopard also made him think about Jane. Which was a thought he was unwilling to process at this particular moment.

Better to focus on the mudminnows. The *Umbridae* family, as they were known in Latin. Those letters could be used to spell words like Dubai, radium and Burma. But no matter how much he tried, he couldn't find a numeral connection from the letters or anything else meaningful.

He shook his head. Some days, the patterns just wouldn't come. Some days, it was as if it was him and the fish against the whole world. When the house was temporarily empty – as it was now – he would sometimes get it into his head that the family was nothing but a figment of his imagination. That he'd hallucinated them. Not until Rebecka returned home with her ear glued to her phone, or Aston yanked open the front door and ran to the loo still wearing his shoes, was he able to fully relax.

Yet at the same time, when they were at home he had to make an effort to try and meet their expectations of what an OK dad and husband were meant to be. He suspected he left something to be desired.

He poured a little fish food into the palm of his hand.

But with Mina . . .

He'd been himself with Mina.

Back then, he hadn't had to make an effort to be anyone else.

He'd returned to those thoughts many times before, even if he knew doing so wasn't constructive. Because Mina was the past. He had to accept it. Mina was then – not now. She hadn't even been at the press conference the day before. Presumably she had moved on with her life.

But the fact remained that he had felt good, and nothing but good, with Mina.

As the fish tickled his hand, he wondered what to make of that.

26

'Why haven't I met you before? Is it because Dad didn't want me to? Or was it because of you?'

Nathalie looked curiously at the woman who was her grandmother. A grandmother she hadn't known she had. Well, obviously she had realized she must have a grandmother. Just like she'd had a mother. But somehow, she'd assumed that her mother's mother was dead, like her mother. Dad never talked about that part of her family. Not even when she asked. So the most reasonable assumption had been that she had no family left on her mother's side. Perhaps she had chosen to think that. It had been hard enough longing for a mother she barely remembered. There was no room to long for anyone else. But now here she was. With her grandmother. Ines. Which made Nathalie question everything she thought she knew.

'I'll answer all your questions in time,' said the old woman.

'What is this place?' Nathalie said, intrigued.

They had ridden the metro from Gullmarsplan to Slussen and then caught a bus to Värmdö. The city now lay far behind them. As they walked along the narrow lane there was nothing around them but greenery, fields containing sheep and the occasional house.

'This is my home,' said her grandmother.

Nathalie adjusted the strap on her bag, which was diagonally across her chest. The phone in her pocket vibrated. Again. Probably Dad. He'd been calling constantly for more than an hour. She had said she'd come straight home. But she would let him worry. The anger at the fact that she'd had a grandmother this whole time without him saying anything made her clench her jaw. He had been controlling her her whole life. To protect her, he'd said. He had effectively locked her up. And if she went anywhere, she knew that the bodyguards would never be far away. Not that she could always see them. But she knew they were there. And yet Dad had asked so many questions about why she was struggling to make friends. Moron.

When she had chosen to go with her grandmother, she'd fired off a text to him.

With Grandma, she'd written. You know, GRANDMA. Won't be home for dinner.

Then she'd added a middle finger emoji. Her stomach turned a little at the thought of what she'd done. She'd never ever been so openly defiant of her father. Part of her understood why he was so overprotective. It had always been just the two of them. After the accident with Mum, it was no surprise that he'd worked hard to ensure nothing happened to his daughter.

It was only now that she was realizing it hadn't just been the two of them. The whole time she had been longing for a bigger family – for someone who could give her memories of a mother who was little more than a shadow in her consciousness – she'd been there. Her grandmother. Without Dad saying a thing. He could go to hell.

'It's a little way up the hill and then we'll be there.'

Her grandmother pointed at a small hill with a sign at the crest: Epicura.

'What's that? Sounds like a place you have conferences. Is that where you live?'

Nathalie frowned. But she brightened up when they climbed the hill a bit and she saw the building towering ahead of them.

'Wow . . .'

'Yes, it's quite something,' her grandmother said with pride. 'And yes, I live here, although we don't host conferences. We do have courses.'

'What is this place?'

Nathalie felt the sweat running down her back, forming a big wet patch on her T-shirt.

'I'll give you the guided tour and explain. It's easier to show you.'

At the crest of the hill, Nathalie paused to catch her breath. She realized she was panting more than her grandmother, who looked strong and fit for her age.

The building ahead of them sparkled in the sunshine. It was

dazzling white, modern in style, and featured two wings. 'Wow,' she said again. 'Just think if I'd got to spend my summer holidays here instead of with Dad in town.'

Her grandmother smiled. Then she pulled the blue elastic band away from her wrist and let go. When it snapped back against her wrist with a loud smack, she screwed her eyes shut for a split second.

'Doesn't that hurt?' Nathalie said in puzzlement.

'That's kind of the point,' she said. 'I'll explain later. But look around. Do you feel the energy? There's nothing here but positive energy. You can breathe here. Do you feel it?'

Her grandmother closed her eyes and inhaled with her full diaphragm. Nathalie felt a little silly, but for some reason she wanted to please the older woman, so she did the same. When she closed her eyes, everything around her ceased to be. The only thing audible was the sound of her own breathing and the blood pulsing through her veins. The air in her lungs was clean and pure. The wind whispered in the trees.

And she realized something. There were no men with earpieces hiding between the tree trunks. No one was there to take her home. For some reason, the guards hadn't followed her. The only possible explanation was that Dad had asked them to leave her alone. In other words, he must be aware of her grandmother. Of course, she had trouble believing that Dad had that kind of confidence in her grandmother, given that he'd never mentioned her. But there could be no other reason. Not that she cared much what the cause was, if she were honest. The important thing was that the guards were gone. For the first time ever, she was free.

Nathalie felt a hand in hers.

'Come on. I'm going to show you my home.'

Warmth seemed to spread through her body from her grandmother's hand. The phone in her bag began to vibrate again. She ignored it.

27

The flying squad van was parked up on Engelbrektsgatan, a block from Lenore Silver's apartment. There was no need to rouse her suspicions. Especially not when what they had to go on was purely circumstantial. And, of course, there was Ruben's absolute conviction . . . Adam had hoped that Ruben wouldn't come with them in the van. The last time they'd worked together when visiting Ossian's nursery hadn't been entirely easy. At the same time, they needed all the reinforcements they could get. Officers were dispersed across the city. They were following up on as many tips about Ossian's whereabouts as they could.

'Well, well, well. Lenore Silver . . .' Gunnar chuckled.

Ruben had briefly introduced the blokes in the flying squad to Adam and whispered to him that he could expect Gunnar to mention at any second that he was hewn from Norrland timber.

'Damn it, I remember Lenore,' Gunnar said. 'Especially those tits. Thank you very much.'

He held his cupped hands in front of his ribs so no one would be in any doubt as to what he meant. The others in the van shook their heads at their colleague, but their smirks divulged that they didn't object to the image suggested by Gunnar. Adam sighed. Apparently it was the law that there always had to be a Gunnar around.

'But you say they're smaller now, Ruben?' Gunnar continued. 'Fuck, that's a shame. Some people don't know what they have. But maybe she'd like a bit of Norrland wood anyway.' He winked.

'You wouldn't stand a chance with that beer belly,' Ruben countered, patting Gunnar on the tummy. 'But the uniform helps. Believe you me, I know.'

Ruben left the final remark hanging until everyone in the van understood what he was getting at. Adam didn't believe for one moment that Ruben had even been in Lenore's immediate presence, but Gunnar chortled loudly and slapped Ruben on the back.

'I should have known,' he said, laughing. 'You'll get on anything that moves.'

Adam caught Ruben's eye briefly. What Adam saw surprised him. Ruben looked almost tormented. But this was not the time for that kind of conversation – they had a job to do and a ticking clock.

'Pull yourselves together now,' said Adam. 'We need to focus on why we're here. We don't know for sure that Lenore has Ossian – or whether there is anyone else on the scene. We need to clarify the situation before we can act. And we can't afford to take chances, which is why we've got the entire crew here, in case Ossian is on the premises. But we also don't want to scare her off. It's a tough balancing act. Julia has been heading up the operation, but she can't be here right now because she's following up on other leads. So I'll be taking over for the time being.'

A discontented grunt was audible from Gunnar, but Adam ignored it. He couldn't be bothered to contemplate whether the dissatisfaction was based on the colour of his skin or the fact that he'd failed to laugh at the comment about Lenore's breasts. Or perhaps it was because they had a female boss.

'Thanks to Julia, we've already got spotters in civvies across the street,' he said. 'According to the caretaker, the main door onto the street at the front is the only way in and out. There is a door into the courtyard at the back, but that space is surrounded by buildings with no exit to the street. But we've also got eyes there, to be on the safe side.'

'So what's the plan?' said Gunnar. 'We going to storm the place?'

'No. I'm going to go inside and talk to her.'

'What do you mean "talk to her"?' said Ruben. 'You're going to negotiate for Ossian? I know you said you wanted to play good cop next time, but this may not be the best time for that.'

Adam fixed his gaze on Ruben. He didn't need a dick-measuring contest. Not now. Not later either, for that matter.

'I don't negotiate with people like Lenore,' he said curtly. 'But I'm good enough to be able to trick her into thinking I'm someone else so that she lowers her guard. That'll give me a chance to assess the situation in there. If we're mistaken about

83

the apartment we don't want to give the game away that we're on the kidnapper's trail, just in case they happen to be in one of the other apartments. You know this is what I do, right? This is what I do day in, day out as a negotiator and I'm trained for it. But maybe you'd like to have a crack yourself if you think you can do better?'

Something glinted in Ruben's eye and his facial muscles relaxed. Adam had deliberately provoked him, guessing that this was a language Ruben understood. And it seemed that Ruben respected it.

'This is your show,' said Ruben.

Adam nodded. Then he pulled on a top with the logo of the building management company TryggBo Fastigheter embroidered onto the chest, picked up a black folder and pen and stepped into the street. He rounded the corner, moving quickly. The caretaker was waiting for him outside the door to Lenore's stairwell. Once the plainclothes officers in position across the street had indicated that the coast looked clear, the rest of the flying squad approached at a jog in their full kit. The less time they spent out in the open, the better. Once the officers were inside the door, they silently fanned out over the lower stairs. Adam climbed up to the first floor and found Lenore's door right away.

He closed his eyes.

The adrenaline had begun to course through his body. A small dose was great. But too much would mean he couldn't do his job. He took a deep breath through his nostrils and exhaled through his mouth while pretending to check something in his folder in case he was being watched through the peephole in the door.

One more breath.

In through the nostrils, out through the mouth.

Then he rang the doorbell.

Lenore opened the door after seven seconds. That was fairly quick, but not so quick that she would have had time to hide something. Or someone. He recognized her immediately from her Facebook profile. She was barefoot, dressed in shorts and a sleeveless top. Not exactly the attire for a rapid escape. She hadn't been expecting him.

84

Adam flashed her a smile that could melt icebergs.

'Hello,' he said cheerily. 'I'm here from the management company. As you may be aware, we're looking into the water leak up on the third floor.'

He was in no hurry to try and peer into the flat behind her. If he seemed too interested, he might blow his cover. Instead, he looked her in the eye and continued to smile while waiting for her to take the bait. He'd said 'as you may be aware' so that she would automatically think about what he meant by that.

'I don't know anything about that,' Lenore said, frowning.

Her eyes wavered as she paused for thought. This was the opening he'd been waiting for. He continued to maintain eye contact with her, but shifted his gaze by a centimetre or so to the side so that he could see past her. Lenore was standing in a long hallway. At the far end it opened onto the kitchen. He could only see part of it, but he spotted a Smeg toaster and a wall-mounted wine chiller. There was nothing out of the ordinary. Nothing that shouldn't have been there or seemed odd.

He lowered his gaze and pretended to consult his papers, while instead scrutinizing the hall floor for children's shoes. There were three pairs of Jimmy Choo high heels in a row. But nothing to fit a child. He looked up again. He saw a few coats and jackets on the rack at Lenore's side. The adjacent mirror needed a clean. But that was it.

It had all taken no more than three seconds.

And so far there were no signs that a child might be inside the apartment. He needed to get further in.

'Hmm, you were supposed to have been sent an email,' he said. 'But that doesn't matter. There was a major water leak up on the third floor two days ago, and we're now determining what damage has been done to the rest of the building. You'll be able to file a claim with your insurance company based on our report. Do you mind if I pop inside to take a look at your bathroom?'

He tilted his body a few degrees forward. To actually take a step forward would have been too, well, forward.

'It's . . . now's not a good time,' Lenore said, hastily glancing over her shoulder. 'I . . . I was just on my way out.'

Shit. She was beginning to have doubts about him. Or she

was trying to protect something, because he had a hard time believing she was on her way out barefoot. The only question was what she was protecting. Whatever it was, he wasn't going to find out now. He would have to back off completely and give her as much space as he could to extinguish the suspicion visible in her eyes.

'No problem,' he said, flashing her another smile and returning his pen to his pocket. 'We're checking out the whole building today and tomorrow. You'll probably see me coming and going, so give me a shout when it's good for you. But do take a look in the bathroom yourself if you have a moment to spare. Bye for now.' He waved at her and took a step back before she'd even had time to reply. The last thing he saw as she closed the door was the grubby hallway mirror. It was covered in small, oblong-shaped greasy stains. Then the door was shut.

Oblong stains.

Five of them side by side.

At a height of around a metre.

It was as if . . .

As if they'd been made by a child's fingers.

It was far too little to go on.

But then again . . .

What if.

He descended the stairs two steps at a time and gave the signal as soon as he reached the bottom.

28

Her phone chimed to signal the arrival of five new text messages from Torkel. Julia was beginning to seriously toy with the idea of blocking his number. But that kind of thing wasn't on. You couldn't block your husband. The father of your child.

Or could you?

The fact was, he was disturbing her at work. Every time the

number at the centre of that little red circle increased as another message arrived, she was thrown off-kilter. She would start to wonder what he wanted this time and whether it might actually be important. It never was. Torkel's irritating questions robbed her of time and concentration she could not spare. Especially given that the working day was far from over. Maybe the solution was to get another phone with a different number that only Torkel had. A phone she could bury at the bottom of her bag.

As she scrolled through the settings on her mobile, trying to work out how to block a number – merely out of curiosity – the phone rang. It was Adam.

She picked up and listened attentively. Then she asked a question. Then she hung up and quickly made for the open-plan office where Mina, Peder and Christer were working in a row as they followed up on the final tips. It was too hot for any of them to bear confinement in their own offices. But the air in the open-plan space wasn't much better. At least Christer had equipped them all with their own mini battery-operated fans. Even Mina was clutching one, although she was grimacing. She was fanning anywhere but her face.

'How are you all getting on?' Julia asked.

'Not very well,' said Mina, pulling out a wet wipe and using it to sanitize her mouse. 'So far, all the tips have led us to parents with small kids in buildings with thin walls. That's when they've led us anywhere at all, of course. How are you and the flying squad doing?' Mina threw the wet wipe in a bin, where it landed on the summit of a small mountain of them.

'Adam just called,' said Julia. 'They've found a five-year-old child at 10 Danderydsgatan. At Lenore Silver's. And everything indicates that the kid has been held there against its will. I suppose we ought to give Ruben's gut a medal or something.' Mina, Peder and Christer sat stock-still, staring at her.

'Thank God it's all over,' said Peder, looking like he might cry tears of relief. 'We've found him. Now I can finally sleep at night.'

But Julia shook her head.

'That's the thing,' she said. 'They haven't found Ossian. It's a little girl.'

29

'You're home early today. It's only just gone four . . .' said Anette. 'Might this handsome man be hoping for a bit of Friday chill with his better half?'

'I wish I was,' Peder said to his wife, 'but I'm on my way back out of the door.'

He wrapped his arms tightly around Anette, drawing in her scent which was a mixture of her favourite Chloé perfume and . . . fresh baking? He was startled when he saw traces of muffin-making in the kitchen.

'How have you had time to bake already?' he said. 'Surely you only just got back?'

'There was no stopping them,' said Anette. 'They've got some new teacher at nursery who is supernaturally good at baking, so all I had to do was pick up some sprinkles from the shop on the way home.'

'You're a superwoman.' Peder shook his head. 'But I'm going to have to have a word with that teacher about setting the benchmark unreasonably high. Where are the girls?'

'Parked in front of *Winx*.'

'New episodes?'

'No, just the same as usual, but don't tell the triplets that. They're so worried about Bloom being in trouble again.'

'Has she set fire to something?'

Anette gave him a sidelong glance.

'I don't know whether it's sexy or troubling that you know this much about animated children's programmes featuring fairies,' she said.

'I'm going for a combo,' Peder grinned, making for the living room. 'Troublingly sexy!'

He did his best to maintain their playful tone, but he could hear with his own ears that he didn't sound entirely convincing.

He cautiously stepped across the minefield of toys that was the floor. His guilty conscience continued to prick him. Days like this, when he was basically living at work, were tough for Anette to deal with on her own. She had to handle daily life with three two-and-a-half-year-olds as well as doing her job as a high school teacher. He promised himself that he'd let her sleep the whole weekend.

'Daddy!'

Three small voices shrieked in chorus as the triplets leapt off the floor. It was flattering that he could tear them away from Bloom's magical tribulations.

Three pairs of arms wrapped themselves tightly around his neck and he had to gulp to stop himself sobbing. Their warm bodies reminded him why he had to be parted from them. Had Ossian felt this warm when he hugged his parents? Presumably.

'I have to go again soon,' he said, holding them close. 'I just wanted to come home to give my little princesses a hug.'

'Daaaddddyy. We're not princesses. We're fairies! Like in *Winx*!'

'Sorry, Daddy forgot. Of course you are. But it just so happens that I . . . eat fairies!'

He roared and nuzzled them while the triplets yelled in delight. Then something even more dramatic happened to the animated characters on the TV, and the girls threw themselves back onto the floor to glue their eyes to the screen.

He stayed where he was, watching them for a while, then he returned to the kitchen and Anette. All he was going to do was shower, change and then head back in, but he needed to catch his breath for a moment. If only a brief moment. Despite the chaos that usually prevailed in their home, it was always with Anette and the kids that he was able to draw new energy. Energy he needed to cope with the horrors that work sometimes entailed.

'How's the team getting on?'

Anette looked at him from under her fringe as she began to clean up the muffin-making enterprise. It didn't appear to be an altogether easy task. Peder hesitated. Then he told her about the girl they had found that afternoon. Of course it was against the police ethical code of conduct to share details of things that happened in the line of duty, but if he couldn't share with Anette then he would never be able to deal with it. She was his outlet. Sometimes he wondered whether it was unfair to drag her down into his own darkness. But she didn't object. And he really did need it so badly.

'So that means you still don't know where the boy is then?' she said, putting all the messy bowls in the sink and filling them with water and washing-up liquid. 'Did you want one, by the way?'

She pointed to the heap of muffins exuberantly decorated with every colour of the rainbow.

'No thanks, I'll grab something at work,' he said, picking up a cloth to pitch in alongside her.

'Leave it, I'll handle this.'

Anette took the dishcloth from his hand and he didn't protest. Instead, he crossed his arms and leaned against the kitchen counter.

'To answer your question,' he said, 'no, we haven't found him. And time's running out. If it hasn't already, that is.'

'You're doing everything you can. No one could ask for more than that.'

Anette wiped batter and the remnants of icing and sprinkles off the large kitchen island with firm gestures.

'Are we really though?' he said with a sigh. 'I don't know. None of us seem to have a clue what to do or where to look. The only lead we had turned out to be something else entirely. Now we're just fumbling about, and by this time tomorrow it may turn out we were fumbling in completely the wrong places.'

'You're doing everything you can,' Anette repeated. 'And like you said, you did at least find that girl.'

She rinsed the cloth, hung it over the tap, dried her wet hands on a towel and put her arms around him.

'Don't come home too late, sweetie,' she said, burying her face in his neck. 'That Friday chill offer expires at midnight.'

Then she began to sneeze. She raised her head and looked him sternly in the eye.

'And when this is over,' she said, 'we're going to need to have a chat about that beard.'

30

'What a cool place!' Nathalie said, looking around wide-eyed. 'Do you live here?'

They'd entered the main building via the foyer and everywhere she looked there was glass, glass and more glass.

'Yes. I live here.'

'Cool. But don't birds fly into the glass?'

Her grandmother's lips twitched.

'Well, it does happen. But not that often.'

Nathalie nodded. She felt dizzy with everything that had happened in the course of the last couple of hours. She had met her grandmother. She was here at this place in the middle of nowhere. She had broken free from her shackles – at least for a little while.

'Would you like me to show you around?' her grandmother said, looking at her questioningly.

Nathalie nodded eagerly. It was so quiet here. So peaceful. Even though she had seen other people and knew that it wasn't deserted, there was not a sound to be heard. It was as if everyone had learned not to make a racket when moving around. Nor had anyone said anything to her. They had merely nodded and smiled broadly. As if they were the happiest people in the world.

'What do you do here?' she said.

Her grandmother led the way. Nathalie's backpack was starting to feel heavy, and she set it down by a wall before following. This didn't feel like the kind of place where anyone would steal it.

'We work on leadership development. Mostly. Nova – she's our CEO and owner – is a pioneer in the field. She coaches some of the most senior executives in the country. And I can't even tell you how many boards. We also offer courses here on personal development, reducing stress, coping with grief, and even unbrainwashing for people who have been in cults. Nova is one of the few people in Sweden with expertise in that area. She also gets commissioned internationally.'

Nathalie's eyes widened.

'Wow . . . stress and cults. That sounds . . . cool!' was all she could think to say.

Then she felt ashamed for offering such a stereotypical teenage response. She didn't want her grandmother to think she was a total airhead. But she simply couldn't find the words to describe what she was seeing.

This place was unlike anything she had seen before. It was so white, so clean, so . . . transparent. The way the building had been constructed really was a contrast to its verdant surroundings of trees, fields, and flowers.

'It was built in the sixties,' her grandmother said, as if she had read Nathalie's mind. 'By Nova's grandfather. He ran a number of hotels all over Sweden and this was intended to be a conference centre. When he died, Nova inherited the hotel and since then she's put her own mark on it and the business.'

Nathalie stopped in front of a portrait of a man with a big beard and kind eyes.

'Is that him?' she asked.

'Yes, that's Baltzar Wennhagen.'

Her grandmother stood next to her, contemplating the portrait.

'Nova was the apple of his eye. Her father was Baltzar's only child, so she was the sole grandchild. By the way, it was Baltzar who taught her about Epicureanism – the philosophy that underpins everything Nova does.'

'Epi . . . what?'

In her mind, Nathalie was rifling through her school textbooks and all the hours she'd spent in classrooms, but the word didn't ring any bells. She couldn't recall ever having heard it before.

'Come on, let's go into the garden and have a coffee and I'll tell you about it.'

Her grandmother took her hand, and Nathalie was overcome by the impulse to withdraw hers. She wasn't used to being touched. She knew that Dad loved her, but he wasn't the touchy-feely type. That wasn't what she'd grown up with.

She couldn't remember what Mum had been like – Nathalie had only been five when she had died.

But . . . now she would be able to ask her grandmother all about it. About what Mum had been like. Nathalie left her hand in her grandmother's grasp and followed her down a bright corridor that eventually opened onto a big garden. They weren't alone. But the others were almost hard to spot. The difference between life in the city and here couldn't have been greater. People were talking to each other in low voices around her – so low that none of the sounds of nature were drowned out. She heard the wind in the trees, the twittering birds and the bees buzzing around the rose bush against the white wall.

'There are freshly baked biscuits,' her grandmother said. 'Help yourself. Do you drink coffee? Or would you prefer some juice?'

She nodded towards a table where coffee and accompaniments had been laid out.

'Juice, please. And I'd love some biscuits.'

Her grandmother poured a coffee for herself and a glass of juice for Nathalie, and then she sat down at a table and watched Nathalie browsing the biscuit selection. Once she too had taken a seat, her grandmother let her take a couple of bites before she began.

'Nova's grandfather – Baltzar – studied Greek philosophy as a young man and fell for the thing I mentioned earlier. Epicureanism. It's an ancient philosophy that emphasizes the importance of equanimity – peace of mind.'

'Equanimity,' Nathalie said, trying the word for size.

It felt grown-up. And she liked that her grandmother was talking to her like that. As a grown-up. Even if the subject was pretty boring.

'Epicureanism refers to reaching ataraxia – calm in body and soul – by eliminating the fear of death. Another key goal is aponia – the ultimate absence of pain.'

Nathalie took a sip of her juice. It was a sweet and delicious strawberry cordial – it tasted home-made.

'There are four cornerstones to Epicureanism,' her grandmother continued. 'You might regard them as rules for humankind to live by, in order to achieve what we consider our

93

life's goal. Which is, of course, to achieve peace of mind and happiness. The best way of doing so, according to Epicureanism, is to avoid that which causes unrest and anxiety. Politics, for example. But also to live in tranquillity among friends. As we do here. You should also seek out things that provide you with pleasure – but not just short-term satisfaction. It must lead to lasting happiness. The fourth cornerstone of Epicureanism is both the most simple and the most difficult. It says that an absence of pain is the highest good.'

'The absence of pain . . .' Nathalie weighed up these words. 'But what about your elastic band? That hurts, doesn't it?'

Her grandmother nodded. Then she pulled at the band and let go with the same snapping sound as before. She flinched when it struck her wrist, but Nathalie also saw the hint of a smile at the corners of her grandmother's mouth.

'You're quite right,' she said. 'It does hurt. But only for a second. Sometimes we have to subject ourselves to something in order to get away from it. Pain has an important function in life too. And it would be presumptuous of me to think I had already achieved the highest good.'

Nathalie nodded. She didn't understand the half of what her grandmother had said. But she didn't want this moment to end. Her grandmother was so pretty and her voice was so warm. The garden enveloped them with its scents and sounds. And the sugar in the biscuits felt so smooth against her tongue. Everyone was smiling at her with such kind, open eyes.

And no one – absolutely no one – was watching her.

It was probably only a matter of time before Dad showed up to collect her, so she was going to enjoy every second of it until then.

'Grandma,' she said eagerly. 'Can I . . . stay here? Just until tomorrow?'

Her grandmother looked at her with bright blue eyes filled with love. The sun behind her made her light hair shine like a halo. She nodded.

'I'll see what I can do. But if so, you'll have to fend for yourself for a while this evening. You see, Nova and I are going to be on TV.'

31

Mina noticed that Peder wasn't as full of vim as he had been earlier. The tired Peder now sitting at the conference table with his head in his hands was more reminiscent of what he'd been like when the triplets had just been born. He pulled out a can of Nocco and cracked it open with a hiss. This was behaviour she recognized.

Reuben and Adam looked tired too as they stood propped against the wall. The adrenaline from their afternoon raid at Lenore Silver's had clearly begun to drain away. That case was no longer in their in-tray. Another team had taken over the investigation pertaining to the child they had found, while Julia's group remained focused on the continued search for Ossian.

Lying on the table was a big pile of wrapped sandwiches. This was a meagre substitute for dinner, but on the other hand no one seemed all that hungry.

The bags under Julia's eyes were almost like dark bruises, but Mina guessed this wasn't just down to work, given the way her boss had grimly ignored the constant flurry of new texts making her phone light up each time they arrived. Julia had set it to silent, but the notifications were still on. Mina could see that all the messages were arriving from someone whom Julia had named 'That annoying bastard'.

The only one who didn't seem to be tired was Christer. Instead, he looked like a thundercloud as he chewed his way almost frenetically through a sandwich. Bosse was lying at his feet, looking anxiously at his master.

'So, to summarize,' said Julia. 'I want to start by emphasizing that you've done a stand-up job over the last couple of days. You've spun every plate you could and even managed to pull off a raid that recovered an abducted little girl.'

'Do we know who she is?' Adam said, standing a little more upright.

'Not yet,' said Peder with a yawn. 'They're going through

every report from the last two months in both Stockholm and the rest of the country. They've also asked Interpol – she might have been snatched abroad somewhere. They'll find her – it's only a matter of when, not if. Lenore has no chance.'

'Utter scum,' Christer muttered, wiping his mouth. 'Going after kids. I'm raging.'

Bosse gave a brief yap to show that he agreed with his master.

'Good job there, Ruben. With Lenore,' said Julia.

Ruben appeared to be on the verge of firing off one of his smirks only suitable for adult consumption but then he seemed to think better of it. It had clearly been a tiring day for him too.

'Unfortunately, we've got no further in terms of locating Ossian,' said Julia. 'His kidnapper seems to have vanished into thin air.'

'This is unacceptable,' Peder said, setting down the empty can of energy drink on the table. He was speaking much faster than before. 'Tomorrow is Saturday,' he went on. 'By then it will have been three days. If this is the same as the Lilly case . . .'

He didn't need to finish his sentence. Mina knew exactly what he meant, and so did the others. If it was the same as Lilly, then Ossian would turn up dead in the next twenty-four hours if they didn't do something. The only question was what. Mina pulled out a bottle of sanitizer and cleaned her hands. Not that it was necessary; she had only just done it. But she needed to do something. Anything.

'As I've said previously,' said Julia, 'there's nothing to indicate that the cases are related. We're most probably dealing with two different perpetrators. But having said that, there is naturally – theoretically – the possibility that this is a copycat of Lilly's case last summer. We can't rule anything out. So I agree with you, Peder. This is not acceptable. I just don't know what more we can do.'

Mina wondered, as she had done so often in the last year, whether it would have made any difference to have Vincent here. Whether he might have been able to help them. But probably not. They had nothing to base a psychological profile on, there was no connection to illusions, there were no hidden and complex patterns to discover. All they had was a kidnapped child. Whom they had thus far failed to rescue.

'We'll just have to hope that the public have seen something,' Julia concluded. 'They're usually good at that. You've all done what you can for today. There are others in the building who will keep processing the tips as they come in this evening and overnight. There may not be as many now, but we'll still make sure we check every single one. Sara will assist and liaise with me on an ongoing basis. Go home. Try to get some sleep.'

'Just how the hell is that going to work?' Christer muttered. 'I'm going to stay here with Bosse for a little while longer.'

'Me too,' said Peder. 'I can help Sara.'

Julia held out her hands in a gesture of resignation. The strength she normally radiated was gone. Instead, she reminded Mina of a balloon slowly deflating. Another text message notification appeared on Julia's phone.

'For the love of . . .' she said, glowering at the mobile. 'OK. It's up to you. I'm not going to make you go. Who knows – maybe I'll be here for a while too. Peder, get Sara to help you check up on everyone who has been in contact with Lenore Silver. We might get lucky. She might be mixed up in our case after all, businesswoman that she is. Adam, you're most familiar with the Lilly case. Go through all the details of the abduction to see whether you can find anything similar to Ossian's case. Any and all conclusions that can be drawn, on my desk immediately. Mina and Ruben, you go through the interviews with Ossian's parents and the nursery staff again. Look for anything that might be a lead. Christer, triple check whether any of our known sex offenders have suddenly changed their patterns of behaviour in the last few days. I know it's already been done. But do it again. And I'll need you bright-eyed and bushy-tailed first thing in the morning. Peder will just have to issue energy drinks to everyone if that's what it takes. Because we really have no idea what's going to happen tomorrow.'

32

On the wall-mounted TV Tilde de Paula Eby was firing questions at someone who was apparently famous for something or other. Vincent had no idea who it was. Even though he had his own public profile, he had an almost awkwardly poor grasp of other, more famous people. This had caused a number of embarrassing incidents over the years when he had been introduced at various gatherings to people whom it was assumed he knew, but who were in reality complete strangers to him.

Following one particularly cringeworthy occasion when he had mistaken Olympian Kajsa Bergqvist for a set designer he had once worked alongside, Vincent had promised his wife he would start reading the gossip magazines so that he would learn who was who. This undertaking had not been a success. It wasn't that he was uninterested in other people – he simply struggled to raise much enthusiasm for celebrity itself.

He had seen a trailer for this show and spotted that a fellow public speaker was going to be on it. He'd missed it when it was broadcast since he'd been on stage himself, but he'd hit play on catch-up almost as soon as he stepped through the door at home. At any rate, he'd at least recognized her – after all, she was more than just well-known. She was one of those people where all it took was saying her first name to elicit recognition in Sweden.

Tilde de Paula Eby smiled into the camera.

'My next guest on the sofa probably needs no further introduction,' she said, putting Vincent's own thoughts into words. 'Certainly not if you're a user of social media. Or if you've opened a newspaper in the last few years. Nova, welcome to the show! And a warm welcome to Ines Johansson too!'

Two women were sitting on the sofa in the studio. One of them, Nova, had dark brown hair and a visage that the media loved to describe as exotic. This meant that apart from being beautiful, she looked like she might hail from any corner of the world. She was in her forties, but the woman beside her – Ines – looked to be at least twenty years her senior.

The older woman was elegant, her white-blond hair pinned in a neat bun and her skin almost translucent. Vincent had crossed paths with Nova several times in his years on the public-speaking circuit, and it was always interesting to hear what she had to say. But it was Ines who made him catch his breath. Apart from being as pale as a fairy-tale character, she also looked a lot like Mina. The same features, the same eyes. Only older. And fair-haired.

Or perhaps he was just imagining it.

When he looked more closely, the resemblance dissolved as she smoothed her blond hair. He shook his head and felt ashamed. It was lucky that Maria was engrossed in her phone beside him on the sofa so she didn't see him blush. He'd apparently been hoping to see Mina in the press conference the day before more than he'd been willing to admit to himself. So much so that his brain was now showing him Mina as soon as it had the chance, even if it was the face of a much older woman. With the wrong hair colour to boot. A normal brain would probably have done the opposite after almost two years and tried to weaken associations with the policewoman rather than re-inforcing them. He sighed. Twenty months was rather a long time to still have her front and centre in his frontal lobes.

'Let's start with you, Nova,' Tilde said, turning to the dark-haired woman. 'You're a phenomenon on Instagram, not to mention other social media platforms, where you share food for thought and tips on how to live life well through your slickly produced videos. You're a sought-after public speaker and your face is constantly in the papers and on the TV. My notes say that you've been posting new clips weekly for five years. That's . . . well, it's a lot of videos. But you've also got over a million followers. They're tuning in from abroad too – and not only in the west. Three per cent of your followers happen to come from Brazil.'

'A million?' Nova said, smiling. 'Is it that many? Well, if you say so.'

Vincent didn't know Nova personally, but she had always

been pleasant and good at what she did. He'd appreciated her lectures on the occasions he'd heard them. She was a worthy guest on a Friday-night TV chat show. The only thing about Nova that he struggled with was her preference for hugging over shaking hands. Even with people she didn't know.

'But you're not here to talk about your Instagram profile,' said Tilde, raising a book to show it to the camera. 'We're going to talk about this book that you've written: *Epic*. If I've understood correctly, it's the next step in a journey for you – a journey that started when you were a young woman and you were in a car crash?'

Maria looked up from her mobile and nodded at the TV. 'Isn't this all a bit woo-woo?'

Vincent opened his mouth to reply, but quickly closed it again. Maria, with her angels, self-help books and courses, referring to Nova's philosophy of life as 'woo-woo' left him lost for words.

Maria shrugged and looked down at her phone again. She appeared to be reading an article on guerrilla marketing. Obviously it had been sent to her by Kevin. Vincent wasn't sure it was the best strategy for Maria's porcelain figurines, but he wasn't going to interfere. He wanted nothing more than for his wife to succeed in her entrepreneurial endeavours. It was just that he wasn't altogether sure she'd picked the right direction. He saw another text message arrive on her phone display and noted that the sender's name had been updated to read 'Guru Kevin'. A smile flashed across Maria's face. Vincent directed his attention back to the TV programme. He had a feeling in the pit of his stomach, but he forced himself not to let his thoughts wander to where that itch was – instead he focused on the TV.

'And I gather you still suffer from chronic pain in your legs following that car crash,' Tilde de Paula Eby said on screen. 'A crash that not only left you with physical after-effects but also orphaned you.'

Vincent remembered the newspaper headlines, even though it had been such a long time ago. Nova's father – John, if he wasn't mistaken – had owned a large farm that had caught fire one day. All the animals at the farm had burned alive. While fleeing the fire, Nova's father had driven off the road in the family car and died. Nova had been the sole survivor. But the operation she'd undergone in the aftermath hadn't been a success. Nova was condemned to being on strong painkillers for the rest of her life. The story had been recounted many times in the media over the years.

'You know, Tilde, I think we all suffer from chronic pain,' Nova said seriously. 'If not in our bodies then in our souls. But as my dad used to say: everything is suffering; pain purifies. It may sound paradoxical, but sometimes trials are good for us. It means we can then free ourselves from them. And that's where *Epic* comes in. It's not just a book – it's a philosophy and a lifestyle that many people would benefit from applying in their day-to-day. Most of what I write about on social media emanates from it, and now with my book I'm giving everyone the opportunity to make Epicureanism part of their lives.'

'Speaking of pain, what do you do to avoid bitterness towards the doctors who failed when operating on you after the accident?'

'Hamiltonian paths,' Nova said with another smile.

However, there was sorrow visible in her eyes this time.

'It's a mathematical concept,' she clarified when Tilde looked puzzled. 'It refers to a way of moving between points in a geometric shape in such a way that you only visit each point once. I try to live my life the same way. Every time we dwell on something, we visit a point which we have already passed through. And it's completely unnecessary. If the choice is between reliving the past and creating new experiences, it's healthier to opt for the latter.'

Tilde nodded, but a faint crease of her brow gave away that she didn't think what Nova had said was as straightforward as she had made it sound. But no follow-up question came. Vincent guessed that they were running out of time. But thus far, only Nova had spoken.

'It's high time we brought you into the conversation, Ines,' said Tilde, turning to the blonde woman. 'If I've understood correctly, you and Nova have started an organization together?'

'That's right,' Ines said in a deep, full-bodied voice. 'I was

101

originally a student of Nova's, but now we work together. We offer specially designed leadership and management training in Epicureanism. We train people from all over the world. And the content of our courses can be applied to every part of life – not just business.'

'Woo-woo,' Maria said, still glued to her mobile. 'A load of fucking woo-woo.'

Vincent only agreed in part. Epicureanism was an established philosophy – and one that he thought contained a lot of sense. But sometimes it wasn't the philosophy itself that mattered – it was how it was received and interpreted. He had been a guest speaker on enough self-development courses to know that the charged atmosphere could often border on religious fervour, together with the absolute conviction that the participants could change their lives for the better. He also knew that the feeling usually disappeared fifteen minutes after the course reached its end.

That said, he thought Epicureanism was decidedly healthier than many of the home-spun methods and philosophies that modern self-help gurus sold to hungry seekers at great expense. In fact, he thought Epicureanism was almost as sharp as Stoicism. There were far worse things for people to splash their cash on than Nova's book or her courses. She was adroit. And in his view, she was serious, which was not a given in her line of work.

'And we'll have to leave it there, Nova and Ines,' Tilde said, bringing the show to a close. 'As we've already mentioned, Nova's book *Epic* is due out soon – I hear that thousands of copies have been pre-ordered. Happy publication day when it arrives.'

Maria looked up and directed a significant glance at Vincent.

'You see! It is possible to sell more books than you think. If you listened to my advice and wrote something a little more accessible, you'd be a success too. Maybe a detective novel?'

Vincent sighed. Made-up police investigations came pretty far down his list of interests. The real ones were quite enough.

33

Her time today is OK. Her average speed is six and a half minutes per kilometre. Better than yesterday. But on this particular Saturday morning, the heat has eased slightly and there is even a pleasant breeze fanning her as she runs along the shoreline.

Nevertheless, her time is still worse than it was a year ago. The divorce has not only taken its toll on her mind but also her body. Yet another entry on the long list of things he has taken from her.

She's been so fucking stupid. She should have been smarter.

She's demonstrably intelligent, she has an advanced education, an executive role at one of Sweden's leading banks and she usually gets most of the answers right when she watches *Who Wants to Be a Millionaire?* – but she still hadn't got it. Even though all the signs could have been ticked off a checklist of how to figure out whether your husband is cheating on you. Red Porsche, check. New-found interest in working out, check. Toning his hair, check. Late nights at the office, check. New wardrobe, check.

Check, check, check.

Naturally, she observed all this. She wasn't *that* stupid. But she thought it was a midlife crisis and tied it to his fiftieth birthday celebrations.

And in a way, she was right. What she didn't know was that he'd fallen in love with a princess who was a guest at the bash – invited by Sweden's ambassador to Nigeria. It had to be fancy. As always with Rolf.

The thing bothering her most in the wake of it all is that she was prepared to look the other way. Even after the information about the Nigerian princess trickled through to her. But he just looked at her dumbfounded when she magnanimously offered to forgive and forget and move on.

'This is for real,' he said. 'For real!' As if their twenty years together were all pretend. Some kind of waiting room for true love.

She runs past the moored boats on Skeppsholmen. Normally, she has to elbow her way past all the trendy city joggers who have adopted a lap of this leafy island as their morning routine. But with the holidays now well underway, they've all disappeared and been replaced by the odd hollow-eyed tourist dragging their kids around much too early in the morning. The heat has also pitched in to keep the joggers away.

She reaches the southern end of the island, runs past the small bridge across to Kastellholmen and then follows the contours of the island heading north again.

It's not until she reaches the steel hull of the *af Chapman* – a three-masted sailing ship that is now a youth hostel and tourist landmark – that she allows herself to stop. She meant to run all the way without stopping, but she needs a drink. She pulls out her water bottle from the small, lightweight rucksack she always has with her when jogging. Her fingers are stiff and numb, and the lid won't budge. She gives it all she's got, but it still won't open. A man passing by looks at her questioningly, but she avoids his gaze. No bloody way she's going to ask a man for help. For a moment, she considers giving up on the bottle – yet another small setback being dumped on her by life. Sooner or later, something utterly trivial is going to push her over the edge. Like the after-dinner mint in *Monty Python's The Meaning of Life*.

But she's too thirsty to give up. In the end, she manages to open the lid and takes long, grateful gulps of water as she contemplates the large white ship in front of her. She read somewhere that it was built in the late nineteenth century for use in Australia. Instead, it ended up in Stockholm. A youth hostel, she thinks to herself with a snort. Rolf doesn't even know what a youth hostel is. At least she went interrailing to Berlin, back when she was nineteen.

The sun is casting shadows under the gangway connecting her own pathway with the vessel – but it doesn't look as it should. She shades her eyes with her hand and squints. It might be an illusion. Probably is. But it looks like something is wedged

104

against the quayside at the point where the gangway touches the ground. She walks over and positions herself to block out the sun so she can take a better look. A child's shoe.

One of the tourist parents has clearly failed to notice their disgruntled spawn – probably embroiled in a sulk – kicking off their shoe. The thought of it happening has always made her shudder. It had always bothered her, and she and Rolf always scolded their own kids for it when they were young.

She bends down to pull out the shoe. If she leaves it on the pavement, the parents will have a better chance of finding it.

It's stuck. She pulls harder until the shoe comes loose and she grasps it in her hand.

Only then does she spot the small foot and leg protruding from underneath the gangway.

34

Vincent followed the paved footpath winding its way through the garden of remembrance towards the cemetery. He'd gone there early that morning while the rest of the family were still asleep. There was no point getting them out of bed at the crack of dawn when it was the weekend. What was more, the kids were on their summer holidays.

Vincent had petitioned the authorities to have Jane and Kenneth declared dead one year after the events at their farm on the island of Lidön. It wasn't retaliation – rather, it was an attempt to give his sister a graceful ending. She had spent her whole life in hiding; the least he could do was to acknowledge her in death. Admittedly, Jane's body had never been found. But he knew she was no longer alive. Even if he couldn't exactly explain how. He just . . . felt it.

Since they hadn't been found, they weren't officially dead and according to the law a declaration of death could only be made one year after they first went missing. So Vincent had lodged his application a year to the day after he'd seen his sister for the last time. Additionally, it required there to be a 'high degree of probability' that the person in question was dead – which there most certainly was. Even if he hadn't had an overwhelming feeling that they were gone, it was completely unlikely that Jane and Kenneth could have got off the island and remained in hiding for such a long time. No, they had most definitely tumbled into the water and drowned. And even if they had managed to escape, neither Kenneth's nor Jane's health was in a state that would have allowed them to survive in isolation for any length of time. The Swedish Tax Agency had felt differently – at least to begin with. They had decreed that he would have to wait another four years before they could legally declare the couple dead.

Despite the fact that Jane had tried to murder both him and Mina, he'd been disappointed by the news. His sister deserved some certainty. If not in life then at least in death.

Later on, the Swedish Tax Agency had for some reason changed its mind. Jane and Kenneth had been declared dead and it was up to Vincent to deal with all the practicalities.

He reached the tombstones and began to stroll through the rows. His mother was buried in Kvibille in Halland. When she had died, the parish had tried to get hold of Erik – Vincent's father – without success. Eventually, the funeral had been arranged by the local council. But he didn't want to lay Jane to rest in the same grave as their mother. He wanted his sister close. The life that had transformed her and filled her with hatred wasn't something she had asked for. And despite everything that had happened, she was still his sister. So he had opted for the new cemetery at Tyresö church.

He stopped by a stone laid flat to the ground. *Jane Boman and Kenneth Bengtsson*, read the inscription. Year of birth. Year of death. Nothing more than that. Whatever other words he might have added to the stone, they would have been a lie. He bent down and ran his hand over the warm, polished surface. There were four letters in the name *Jane*. That was good. But *Kenneth* had seven. No wonder Vincent had never liked him.

106

A small spider was scuttling about on its eight legs in the engraved J of Jane. Vincent imagined the world from the spider's perspective. Right now, that world comprised a gently undulating ravine offering temporary protection from the scorching sun. But that ravine was also an obstacle – something to escape from. Once it was up and out, the world would transform into a slippery plateau of polished stone. If the spider was brave enough to cross that plateau – without any protection from the elements or predators – the world would soon become a labyrinth of new ravines when it reached the A.

But the spider would have no idea that the shape of the two ravines meant anything – that they were part of a larger pattern. Or that the pattern was a word that represented a person who had once been alive, and thus also represented all that she had experienced and all that she had encountered and influenced. For the spider, there were no such connections. For the spider, there were only temporary changes to its surroundings – changes that it had to adapt to in order to survive. Before promptly forgetting them as the next challenge presented itself.

His knees were beginning to ache, and Vincent stood up. Sometimes he wondered whether his life was like that of the spider. Whether the things he was experiencing were parts of something much bigger – something so big that he would lose his mind if he ever saw what it was.

No wonder people turned to faith or became deeply religious. But he couldn't bring himself to believe in an omniscient being that had created everything and whose master plan encompassed all human actions. There was no need for anything like that to explain reality. Occam's razor, as Benjamin would have put it.

The spider had reached the end of the lettering and was on its way into the grass. Yet another complete change of reality for the tiny creature. Vincent knew what that felt like.

35

Adam stared at the small bare legs protruding from under the gangway. A pair of shorts emblazoned with the Teenage Mutant Ninja Turtles could be glimpsed as the body disappeared into the shadows.

'Those feet can't even be size 12s,' Mina said at his side. 'Without having seen anything else, I'm afraid we've probably found Ossian. This was exactly what shouldn't happen.'

A lump formed in Adam's throat and he averted his gaze. He'd been present when hostage situations had soured. He'd seen up close how innocent people ended up in trouble without his being able to prevent it. Sometimes it had been violent. The legs beneath the gangway were almost peacefully still in comparison.

But they belonged to a child.

He – they – had failed. They hadn't done what they needed to do – they hadn't been quick enough or smart enough. After all their hard work over the last few days, they still hadn't found Ossian's kidnappers in time. And Ossian had paid the price. It was a catastrophic and unforgivable failure.

Forensics were working to document as much as they could of the scene where the body lay. All evidence had to be secured and the medical examiner was still to arrive to take the body temperature and a vitreous fluid sample from the eyes before the corpse was finally placed into a body bag and driven to the National Board of Forensic Medicine.

The crew who transported bodies from crime scenes were, for the most part, odd characters who were eager to be matey with the forensics team. He'd heard plenty of stories about cases where they'd found evidence missed by personnel at the crime scene.

Adam forced his thoughts back to the boy in front of him. The brain's defence mechanisms meant that it wanted to veer off onto something else and away from the dead child on the ground. He took a deep breath and focused, taking in as much of his surroundings as he could. The body wasn't exactly hidden, but it wasn't fully visible either. It had taken an alert jogger on her morning run to find it. She had initially tried to pull the body out, but had then come to her senses when she'd spotted the livor mortis and called the cops. They had already taken a sample of her DNA, given that hers would likely be recovered from the body.

Adam put a hand over his mouth. He simply had no idea how to carry on. He was a negotiator: his expertise lay in talking to armed hostiles, and sometimes dealing with hostage situations and resolving them without anyone coming to harm. But it was always about talking. This was something completely different.

He had no children of his own. Fortunately. Otherwise, he probably couldn't have borne to stand there. But his sister did. A five-year-old. Just like Ossian. They might even have attended the same nursery.

Forensics had cordoned off a large chunk of Skeppsholmen. The last thing they needed were onlookers – or for anyone to post a photo on social media. They began to carefully remove the gangway so they could properly access the body.

Adam recognized Ossian's face right away from the photos provided by his parents. The boy looked like he was asleep. But the skin tone was all wrong. Grey. Stained. And the lower jaw had sagged open. Bloody hell.

'There's something else under here,' said one of the forensic officers, pointing to something next to the body that had until then been concealed by the gangway.

It was a kids' backpack with a My Little Pony image on it. It was as dirty as Ossian.

The bag was almost the worst thing. Adam could convince himself the body was a doll or a prop in a cop show on TV, but that little backpack made it all so much more real. That was where Ossian had kept his water bottle. And his packed lunch when going on trips with the nursery. His own nephew usually took Nutella sandwiches.

The side pockets were probably filled with rocks he'd found to add to the collection that every five-year-old seemed to have.

At the bottom of the bag there was probably a forgotten soft toy hiding away. His nephew had a tatty giraffe. Tears suddenly began to stream uncontrollably down Adam's cheeks. He could no longer bear to see the rucksack and the small body. Instead, he looked out across the water, wiping his cheeks with the back of his hand. The view from Skeppsholmen felt indecently beautiful given the grotesque sight a few metres away. Small boats were pootling across the glittering waves in the morning sun. Across the water lay Stockholm's old town with its green copper roofs and domes.

'This location with the ship and the quay is reminiscent of something,' said Mina. 'I assume you of all people remember how Lilly was found?'

He hadn't noticed her taking up position next to him.

'On a jetty,' he said, nodding. 'I know. This is disconcertingly similar to what happened to her. Too similar. And just like then, we had three days. Three days that we threw away.'

She nodded and followed his gaze across the water.

Ruben appeared on his other side.

'You coming?' said Ruben. 'You and me are going to have a chat with the staff on board. And we're going to rouse the backpackers who spent the night here. Maybe some tourist saw something if they weren't too pissed or too high.'

Adam nodded gratefully. Finally he had a task. He would get to do what he was good at. He would be able to make a difference. Anything was better than just standing there, powerless, watching the world go by.

'We're going to find whoever did this,' Mina said to him before he followed Ruben. 'For Lilly's and Ossian's sakes. And above all, so that it never ever happens again.'

He stopped, his eyes widening, and stared at Mina.

'Do you think it could happen again?'

'I don't really think anything,' she said, mopping her brow with a wet wipe.

The gentle breeze that had been there during the morning was gone and the heat had returned with gusto. He could make out the faint scent of lemon and considered whether to point out that wet wipes actually dried the skin out even more, but he decided to let it alone.

110

'All I know is that this heat drives people crazy,' she said. 'Did you know that an American study showed that all it takes is for the mercury to climb over 29 degrees Celsius for violent crime to increase by almost six per cent?'

Adam glanced at his smartwatch. It indicated an outdoor temperature of 32 degrees.

'And the summer's only just started,' he said.

36

'You all know what's happened,' said Julia.

None of the others replied. All that was audible was the rattling of the air conditioning in the struggle against its own demise and Bosse's quiet whining from where he lay by his new water bowl in the corner. Even Torkel seemed to have the sense to leave her alone. She hadn't received a single text message all morning.

'Ossian was found about two and a half hours ago,' Julia continued. 'We still need to secure a positive ID, but frankly there's no doubt about it. Adam and Ruben are still at Skeppsholmen questioning everyone in the youth hostel on board the *af Chapman* and in the nearby buildings in case anyone saw anything. There are almost a hundred people staying on board, so hopefully we'll get lucky, but we'll have to be quick since people don't usually stay for longer than a night. Mina and Peder visited Ossian's parents on Thursday, so normally it would make sense for them to go back to inform them. But I don't think—'

She broke off and glanced at Peder, who was blinking frantically to keep the tears at bay. She didn't want to subject him to another encounter if she could help it. Perhaps it was unprofessional. But if so, that would just have to be the way it was.

'Christer, can you handle it?' she said. 'Mina still needs to go and see Milda.'

Christer sighed deeply and folded his arms.

'Same old, same old,' he said. 'Whenever there's a death, it ends up in my lap. I don't know whether you guys think I'm best buds with the Grim Reaper or what. But sure thing. Someone has to do the hard work. And I know what you mean. I think it's best if Peder checks out what surveillance there is around the Skeppsholmen area. CCTV and so on.'

She also noted Christer's hasty glance at Peder. Their oldest colleague might be morose, but he had a warm heart when it mattered.

'Exactly what I was going to suggest,' she said. 'I'll get you some extra fancy dry food for Bosse by way of thanks.'

'And a food bowl for him in here?'

'And a food bowl in here,' Julia said.

The air conditioning spluttered particularly loudly before falling silent. Almost immediately she felt a bead of sweat trickle between her breasts. She longed to be at home. And not just so she could take a cold shower. More than anything, she needed to feel close to Harry. To be able to smell his scent in her nostrils and feel his skin against hers. To know that he was alive. That he was OK. Torkel could head out to see some friends or something.

Peder cleared his throat.

'There's just one thing,' he said. 'I assume we're no longer categorizing the similarities with Lilly's case as a coincidence. If so, we need to find out whether the tragic thing that befell Ossian was done by a copycat – possibly after reading about it in the papers. Or whether the acts were actually committed by the same killer. No child in this town will be safe until we can answer those questions.'

Julia nodded.

'Mina – head over to Milda as soon as you can to find out whether she has anything to tell us about Lilly's autopsy,' she said. 'I'll ask her to pull the report for you.'

Peder had opened a door that she had known for several days they were destined to pass through – she just hadn't wanted to acknowledge the possibility that the same person had struck again. The one they'd failed to catch last time. If that was the case, Ossian's death was on their heads.

112

37

Milda Hjort sometimes wondered whether there was a huge set of scales that governed the balance of life. That kept track of it all to ensure things never swung too far one way. That ensured bad luck balanced out against good fortune so that there was never too much of one and not the other. In her case, those scales seemed to function so as to ensure that when one difficult situation in life resolved itself, another took its place.

Her son Conrad had finally exited his rebellious period. He was studying at college, had a girlfriend and seemed – at least as far as she could tell – to have put all the rest of it behind him. Whereupon the scales had tilted again and her brother Adi had got in touch.

'Will you sew her up? I'm done.'

She nodded towards the body lying on the shiny metal before her. Twenty-five years old. Suicide. She had identified the traces of other, failed attempts on the body, but this time it had worked. Hanging. Found by her mother in the family basement. A sight that a mother would never be able to erase from her mind. It would be there forever in her memory bank, together with the first steps, the first lost tooth, the first day at school. All those things that had been life would now forever more be mixed with the memory of death.

And there was Milda, on a sunny Saturday afternoon seemingly without a care in the world, the last person to see the woman before her physical body ceased to be.

Milda pulled off the disposable gloves and threw them away. Her assistant Loke was tasked with carefully sewing up the body where she had made an incision into the torso. She usually preferred to do that part herself, even though it was the assistant's job. But she had too many things rushing around her head right now to really focus, and what was more he was better at stitching. Accuracy was one of Loke's strongest suits as an assistant. Although it might be more fitting to say that he was morbidly pedantic. Milda completed the cleaning ritual before returning to her office in her usual clothes. The heat hit her as she opened the door. At first she recoiled. Then she took a deep breath and stepped inside. The chair was sticky under her buttocks from the moment she sat down, and she looked disconsolately at the wilting pot plants on the windowsill. She felt like they looked.

The call from Adi shouldn't have come as a shock. That it had was the reason why she was furious with herself – more than she was with him. With Adi, it was like the fable about the scorpion that sat on the frog's back to cross the river. The scorpion stung the frog in the middle of the river, which meant they would both drown. When the frog asked why the scorpion had done that, the scorpion merely replied that it was in his nature.

That was exactly what Adi was like. Even when they had been little, her brother had always thought of nothing but his own needs. It was as if he couldn't take in the fact that other people had them. Or rights. Everything was his. None of their parents' attempts to teach Adi about right and wrong, yours and mine, had sunk in at all. So she had undeniably been surprised when he had let her and the kids live in the parental home that they had inherited together after their parents died after her divorce. And that he'd put off extracting his share of the house.

She had convinced herself it was a sign that he too had matured, grown, developed. With the passing of the years, she had avoided questioning the situation and told herself that things would probably always be the way they were. The status quo. The eternal partiality she had for the status quo. But yesterday he had called. Measured, cold. There was rarely any emotion in Adi's voice except when he was angry or offended.

He wanted his share in the house. Now. He'd tried once before, some two years ago. On that occasion she'd received a letter from Adi's 'lawyer'. The ultimatum had been that she had to move, buy Adi out of his share, give up her own half share in Grandpa Mykolas' house when he died. She guessed that he had wanted to stress her out so that she wouldn't think rationally.

Instead, she'd taken the letter to her colleagues at the police. It had seemed wrong for her to sign any agreement relating to her inheritance from Grandpa before he was even dead. And her intuition had been right. Adi had no right to meddle in Mykolas' estate before time. The police had been prepared to file extortion charges if Adi didn't back down. When they then discovered that the so-called lawyer hadn't even graduated and was illegally passing himself off as a lawyer, her brother had disappeared with his tail between his legs.

But Adi had been right about one thing. The house she lived in belonged to them both. He had every right to demand that she bought him out if she intended to keep on living there. Which was exactly what he had done. She had tried to explain that she had no means to buy him out and that she knew he didn't need the money. Adi had made plenty of money his whole life. If he could wait another few years until the kids had moved out, she would really appreciate it. And she had hated how full of pleading her voice had sounded. She'd hated the effect he always had on her – how he made her shrink, made her invisible, made her shift from foot to foot. But before he'd even replied, she'd known what he was going to say. And she had cursed herself for forgetting that she was the frog. While he was the scorpion.

A knock on the door made her jump.

'Come in!' she shouted, but she heard her voice crack and she cleared her throat.

'Am I interrupting?' Mina stuck her head around the door, looking questioning. 'I'd like a chat about Lilly Meyer. And to review the autopsy report.'

Milda shook her head. 'You're not interrupting at all. Welcome to my sauna.'

38

Mina regarded the pot plants in Milda's window with distress. They appeared to be on the brink of perishing in the oppressive heat of the small office, and Milda appeared to be even hotter than she herself was. Mina had read somewhere that sweat was not only the body's way of keeping cool but that it also cleansed it of dirt and waste products. The mere thought made her shudder. She fought the instinct to wrench off her clothes on the spot. She was desperate for a cooling shower. But that couldn't be resolved here in Milda's office.

'I've watered them, but it evaporates quicker than I can pour it,' Milda said glumly, pointing at the wilting plants.

Mina regarded her. Something wasn't quite right. Mina glanced at the chair in front of the desk and considered whether to sit down. But the plastic looked warm and sticky, and bacteria were probably thriving on that shiny surface.

'Here you are – I've already pulled everything you need,' Milda said, opening a drawer. 'Julia called earlier. She said you were all going to be working the rest of the weekend.'

She got out a folder and passed it to Mina, but she first produced a wet wipe and cleaned it.

Mina smiled at her gratefully and opened the folder.

All the information from Lilly's autopsy was neatly printed out and filed.

'You're a rock,' Mina said, and she meant it. 'Don't you ever take time off?'

Milda was usually calm personified. A confident, matter-of-fact, knowledgeable and collected medical examiner. Indeed, collected was probably the word that best described Milda normally. But right now she didn't look collected.

Mina weighed up whether to say anything, but she wasn't quite sure what. They didn't have a relationship that extended into personal life, so she was unsure which words to use.

Suddenly she realized how Vincent must feel. In most contexts and with most people.

'Read through it in peace and quiet,' Milda said. 'I'll be here if you need to ask any questions. But do you really think this is connected to the boy you found?'

'I honestly don't know,' said Mina, pressing the folder to her chest. 'But Adam Blom seems to think so.'

Her top stuck uncomfortably to her breasts. She really did need to find a shower soon. And a change of clothes. There was a moment's silence. Milda's face was overcast, and Mina saw conflict in it, as if she were holding something back. Something that was waiting to explode. Mina opened her mouth. Then she closed it again and made for the door, briefly offering her thanks.

39

He parked on Hornsgatan almost by the square at Mariatorget. There was no need to indicate where he was going by parking the police car right outside. What was more, the short walk up to Bellmansgatan gave him the chance to gather his thoughts.

Christer didn't blame Julia for sending him. Sometimes a policeman needed to be able to switch off his emotions. But a good copper also needed to be able to let them out when they became overwhelming. Which meant that once again it was up to him. At least he didn't have to be the one to bring the news. Uniform and a priest had already been to do that.

He found the right address and pressed the buzzer. The door to the apartment was standing wide open when he reached the right floor. A woman who was presumably Ossian's mother was standing in the doorway with her arms crossed. The posture was aiming for defiant, but her shoulders were drooping.

'I don't see the point of this,' she said. 'It can't be Ossian that you've found – he wouldn't have been on Skeppsholmen.'

'That's just what we want to make sure of,' Christer said gently. 'By the way, we spoke on the phone. My name's Christer. Perhaps you remember?'

There was no colour on Ossian's mother's face – unless you counted the dark rings under her eyes. She probably hadn't slept since the boy had gone missing last Wednesday. And now she was in denial – the first of the five stages of grief. With time, it would slip into the next stage. Anger. That would be when Ossian's parents yelled at him and the rest of the force for not doing their jobs. They might threaten them with legal action – or say that they would take it to the media. Of course, people handled it differently. But regardless of how Fredrik and Josefin expressed their anger, they would be right. Christer would agree with them. The police hadn't done their job. He hadn't done his job. Admittedly, the conditions for finding Ossian in time had been almost impossible, but still . . . They'd done their best, but it hadn't been good enough. Not by a long way.

So far, however, Josefin was still trying to accept the information that she no longer had a son. Some loved ones never got past that stage.

Ossian's father appeared behind his wife.

'Wouldn't it be best if we came with you?' he said. 'That way we can take a look at him and confirm it's not Ossian.'

Christer understood his request. For as long as Fredrik and Josefin hadn't seen Ossian with their own eyes, the thought that it might not be him could linger on. That someone might have made a mistake. And that thought could probably drive someone to madness. But no matter how inhumane it was, he had to ask them to wait.

'You'll get to see him in due course,' he said. 'But right now we have to let forensics do their job.'

There was no need to go into detail about what that entailed. Ossian was about to be autopsied. Their child was going to be cut open. He preferred to keep those thoughts as far away from Josefin and Fredrik as he could. But they seemed to understand. Josefin turned even paler, if that were possible, and buried her face in her hands. She swayed as she stood there in the hallway.

Fredrik put his arms around her, but he barely seemed able to stand himself.

'If Ossian has an e-passport then we'll be able to identify him by his fingerprints,' Christer said. 'Otherwise a toothbrush is fine so that we can take a DNA sample.'

'I'll get his toothbrush,' Fredrik said, sounding almost relieved to have a job to do.

He vanished into the apartment.

'His clothing and backpack are also currently part of the investigation,' Christer said. 'I hope you understand.'

'His backpack?' said Josefin, looking confused. 'Why do you want that?'

She pointed to a yellow child-sized rucksack by the shoes in the hallway. It was a small Fjällräven.

'He was supposed to take a packed lunch on Wednesday when he . . . when he . . .' Josefin's voice died away. 'For once, I remembered to make the packed lunch and put it in his backpack. Then I forgot that instead.'

Christer forced himself not to look at the little bag for any longer than was necessary. A knot formed in his stomach. 'He doesn't have another one?' he asked. 'One with My Little Pony on it?'

Josefin's gaze lingered on the yellow Fjällräven. She seemed to no longer hear him.

'What a peculiar question,' said Fredrik, returning with a small toothbrush in a plastic bag. 'But no. He doesn't have one like that.'

Christer frowned. Ossian had been found with a backpack. But if it wasn't his, then whose was it? Something didn't add up.

40

Milda's office had been extremely hot. But it wasn't one iota cooler at police headquarters – as yet, no one seemed to have shown up to fix the broken ventilation system. They were probably all off for the weekend. The only solution was to escape outside and try and find somewhere with shade that might offer at least a little relief.

With the folder under her arm, Mina stepped out of the main entrance and rounded the corner of the building. She was met by an ocean of cigarette butts on the ground. This was clearly the mustering point for all the secret smokers on the force. The majority of them probably had partners who would swear blind that their soulmate was a non-smoker. It fascinated Mina how little people knew about each other even though they shared their lives. Sometimes, she wondered whether it was even possible to know another person, or whether everyone lived in their own tiny bubble and never fully showed their true selves to anyone. She guessed that Vincent would have had plenty to say on the matter.

It went against the grain to sit down, but it wasn't practical to leaf through the folder while standing up. She pulled her gear out of her bag: wet wipes, antibacterial spray and alcoholic gel. She carefully wiped down the small bench strategically located beside a bin that was full to the brim. She tried to avoid looking at it. A few wasps were buzzing around the bin, but she wasn't afraid of wasps. After all, they were a danger she could see. It was the dangers you couldn't see that scared her.

When she was done, she sat down gingerly and laid the folder next to her on the bench. It was mercifully cool in the shade and a gentle breeze found its way through her thin top, drying the sweat. She took a few deep breaths. Without the oppressive heat, it was as if her lungs and airways were able to open up once again.

With her lungs full of oxygen, she opened the folder. The autopsy report was on top. She had known this would be a difficult task – not even the most hardened detective could remain unmoved by dead children. And Lilly had been just five years old. For once, the cliché of crime fiction had been right. A man out walking his dog had found the body under a tarpaulin.

Mina forced herself to pick up the detailed photographs and lay them out side by side on the bench. The girl had long dark curly hair that spread out like a fan against the shiny metal of the gurney in the autopsy room. She looked peaceful. As if she were asleep.

The cause of death was suffocation – that much she already knew. But the case hadn't been theirs, so she wasn't familiar with the rest of the details. Curious, she picked up the autopsy report and began to read it slowly. She didn't want to risk missing any vital information. In murder inquiries, it was often the very smallest detail that was crucial.

A wasp settled on the centre of the page and she waved it away in irritation. It returned, untroubled by her superiority in size, and settled again. The wasp's courage intrigued her. Most animals had a natural respect for species bigger than themselves. But not wasps. They exhibited a certain degree of hubris, seeming to think that their stingers would make them the victors regardless of their opponents' size. It reminded Mina of certain men she had encountered during her life.

She waved it away yet again. This time the wasp seemed to get the hint and flew over to an ice-cream wrapper in the bin.

Milda's report was, as ever, well structured and easy to understand. It was the information that it contained that was harder to get a grip on. The cause of death was deceptively simple. Suffocation. Hypoxia. The brain was deprived of oxygen until it ceased to function and the body shut down. Mina read on. There was nothing in the airways that might have caused suffocation. Just small remnants of fibres. There was also no water in the lungs, which meant drowning could be ruled out. On the other hand, Milda had noted that there were marks on the lungs – as if the ribs had been pressed against them hard. Mina frowned. What might cause such pressure to the body?

She knew that bodies in deep water could exhibit similar injuries, but once again – there had been no water in the lungs.

What about blows to the body? This had also been ruled out by Milda in the report – Mina saw this as she read on. Blows would have caused bleeding under the skin, which was not present. What about a fall? She had seen a considerable number of bodies that had tumbled from a great height – both intentionally and unintentionally. But in that case, there were usually

121

injuries that weren't localized to just the ribcage, and Milda had quite rightly picked up on this in her report too. Milda indicated pressure to be the most likely cause. She qualified this with a statement to the effect that the pressure could not have been rapid and powerful since that would also have caused bleeding under the skin. Instead, she argued that it must have been even pressure applied to the body for a longer period of time. Mina scratched her scalp thoughtfully. She couldn't make head nor tail of what the cause might be.

Death by pressure?

The time of death was also highly relevant, especially in light of what had happened to Ossian. As Christer had pointed out, Lilly had been missing for almost exactly seventy-two hours from when she disappeared to when her body was found. Milda's assessment was that she had been kept alive throughout and hadn't been subjected to violence. On the contrary, the contents of her stomach demonstrated that the kidnappers had given her plenty of food. Which was something. Lilly had been killed shortly before she was found.

Mina returned to the report. She combined everything she'd been given by Milda with what had emerged from the forensic investigation. Some fibres had been found in the right armpit. According to Forensics, these were the same kind of fibres as those found in the throat. Wool fibres.

The wasp returned – if it was indeed the same one as before. It settled again on the piece of paper that Mina was reading, and her patience was now at an end. She pulled a wet wipe out of her bag, took careful aim and squashed the wasp. She imagined it deploying its stinger blindly inside the wipe – a furious offensive that would ultimately be fruitless. Once again, she thought about men she had known. She unfolded the wipe and examined the wasp. There was no doubt about its cause of death. Crushing. She folded it up again and deposited it in the bin.

After reading the autopsy report, she took out the last materials in the folder: photos of Lilly's clothing and belongings that had been found with her. According to her parents, nothing had been missing and they were the same clothes she'd been wearing when she had disappeared. A few personal treasures from her pockets: a smooth, white stone, a glittery bookmark, a troll-topped pencil with big eyes and a purple eraser that looked like a cat. Mina smiled despite the fact that she could still see the picture of the girl in the autopsy out of the corner of her eye. There was something about a five-year-old's unabashed joy relating to anything that offered a little extra something or was otherwise cute. Glitter, horses, puppies, pink, feathers, flamingos, kittens and sequins. Things that one lost the ability to fully appreciate as an adult. Except when there was a song contest on or a pride march taking place.

She carefully gathered everything back into the order it had come in, closed the folder, stood up and took a deep breath before moving back into the heat. She checked her watch. The day was almost over. She knew more now, but it had only left more question marks – she hadn't found anything that could help them track down either Ossian's or Lilly's murderers. So far, she was groping about blindly in the dark. And all the while a killer was on the loose.

41

Vincent was in his study. Maria had needed to see Kevin again in order to adjust her sales strategy – Vincent had met her at the door on her way out as he returned from the cemetery. Kevin had apparently had some great idea that couldn't wait. Rebecka was at the cinema with Aston, something which just a month ago would have seemed unthinkable. But Aston had suddenly begun to idolize his big sister and Rebecka didn't seem to mind hanging out with her little brother even though he was seven years her junior. Even though she had a boyfriend. It was probably the heat that had sent them a little haywire, but an air-conditioned cinema in the middle of the day sounded like a smart choice.

Benjamin was in his room doing whatever it was that twenty-one-year-olds did when shut up in their bedrooms. Looking for an apartment online perhaps, or so Vincent hoped.

The result was that he had Saturday afternoon all to himself.

Once upon a time, he'd been pretty good at being alone with his thoughts. But not anymore. Not since Jane had brought all the stuff about his mother to the surface. After that experience, he needed to distract himself to keep his thoughts in check. He was afraid of where they would end up if left to roam freely.

He took a Rubik's cube from the bookcase behind the desk and spun it between his fingers. It was the one Mina had given him. He'd tried to solve it before, but the segments were too loose for him to dare to twist them. Yet again, he wondered what she'd done with the cube – it was almost as if it had broken and she had put it back together again. The cube evoked memories that he wasn't ready for. Mina's living room where he'd seen the cube on her desk. Mina inconsolable on the sofa. It cut him to the quick and he realized that his thoughts were heading for exactly the place he was trying to avoid. He opened the desk drawer, intending to put the cube out of sight. His gaze fell on the envelope covered with Santa stickers in the drawer. After a few seconds' hesitation, he picked it up. It was a Christmas card he'd received around two months after his collaboration with the police had come to a close. One of the many home-made mysteries and riddles that the public had sent to him after his involvement in the case had become common knowledge.

Truth be told, he'd amused himself by solving some of them once he'd realized that they weren't fresh death threats. Some of them were pretty rudimentary, while others were decidedly more complicated. Some were completely incomprehensible. Like the Christmas card in his hand. Inside the envelope there was, in addition to the standard card available at the supermarket, which was unsigned, coloured pieces of paper cut into Tetris-style shapes.

He scattered the pieces on the desk and was filled with the same feeling he'd had the first time he saw them. He had immediately felt that this puzzle was different. He couldn't explain it rationally, but the sight of the pieces had filled him with a vague, indefinable anxiety and that feeling was just as powerful this time as it had been before.

There was text on them – a few letters on each piece – and it was obvious that they were supposed to be put together in order to read the message. But the sender had lured him into a trap when he'd first tried to solve it. He smiled to himself. It was a rarity that someone managed to get one over on him, and he appreciated their effort. Because the shapes were reminiscent of Tetris, he had tried to lay them edge-to-edge without any spaces between them. Just like you were supposed to in the game. But the message remained unreadable no matter how he laid out the pieces.

In the end, he had realized that the association with the computer game was a red herring. Not to mention that it didn't actually say in the card that they were Tetris blocks. The well-known shapes and colours had merely led him to assume they were, which he realized had been deliberate. It was a hint that the sender had read about Vincent's magical past. The technique of misdirecting the audience's attention by getting them to focus on the wrong thing was very much the cornerstone of every magic trick.

At the same time, it meant the puzzle had come from someone who had researched him. Which wasn't an altogether comfortable thought. After realizing his mistake, he'd assembled the message in just a few seconds by simply focusing on the text. And there was only one solution.

He picked up the pieces from the table and laid them out the way he had done so many times before. The text that appeared was still incomprehensible. Once assembled, it read *Tim scared deny ageing*. The first time he'd done this, he'd been insulted – he wasn't called Tim and he most certainly wasn't scared of ageing. Then he'd realized that the message was probably a code. The only question was, what kind?

He had tried to search for differences in the handwritten message, but it had been carefully designed so that all the letters were uniform. Which ruled out a Baconian cipher, which usually required two different appearances for letters. He tried a ROT 13 cipher and the more common displacement ciphers where

125

each letter corresponded to another in the alphabet, but those methods rarely resulted in words as complete as those in the message he'd received. The same was true for all other variants where one replaced letters for others.

He went into the living room and put on AES Dana's album *Pollen*. As always, he started by smelling the vinyl record before putting it on the turntable.

The whole family always rolled their eyes at his insistence on using physical media. But hardcover books and vinyl records had their own smells. They were smells that promised adventure and unexpected discoveries. Streaming services might be convenient, but they smelled of absolutely nothing. Just like capsule coffee makers, he understood their practical value. But he felt that something was lost in the experience.

As the first notes emanated from the speakers, he turned up the volume so that he could hear the music from his study. You could say what you liked about the French but they did know their electronic music. Maybe Rebecka was onto something with Denis.

He returned to his desk and once again surveyed the cryptic message. There had to be a deeper level that he hadn't yet uncovered. The only remaining solution was that it was an anagram where the capital letters and punctuation were to be ignored and the letters transposed in order to find the correct message. But with eighteen letters, there were millions of ways to combine them. Without a clue, there was no point in even trying to start.

He sighed and put the pieces back in the envelope again. Of course, it was possible that the puzzle was meaningless. That he'd drastically overestimated its creator. After all, he'd been sent nonsense before. But two things spoke against that possibility. The first was that the initial, instinctive feeling of anxiety that had overcome him had refused to budge.

The second was that a year later, just six months ago, he'd received another Christmas card. Containing new pieces.

42

Mina had nightmares all night without remembering what they had been about. But when she awoke, she was so sweaty that her morning hygiene routine took twice as long as usual. Which meant she was late as she headed for police headquarters. Julia was about to start her briefing. Their tasks for Sunday would depend on what the others had turned up over the course of the day before. Mina hoped that one of them had found a better lead than anything she had managed herself.

When she emerged from the main door into the street outside her building, she came to a halt. A big shiny black car was parked right outside and she immediately realized who it was. Her heart began fluttering like a hummingbird in her breast. Why was he making contact with her? And right now? It was almost as if she had summoned him by thinking about the flat in Vasastan a few days ago. She ran over to the car and yanked open the back door.

'What's happened?'

'Sit,' he said curtly.

With that single word, a deluge of memories washed over her. He had never been generous with words and what he did say always sounded authoritarian and commanding. Which, given his position, she supposed was eminently appropriate. Not even in the beginning when they had lived together and he had just started climbing the career ladder had he sounded different. It was as if his default mode had always been to boss others about.

She got in and sat down after scrutinizing the seat. Glistening and clean. Of course. There were probably people whose sole task was to keep the car in tip-top condition.

'Has something happened?' she repeated, glancing at the driver.

It felt strange to have a complete stranger in the car with them as they spoke, but the man's mirrored sunglasses gave nothing away when she looked at him in the rear-view mirror. He was staring dead ahead. Obviously part of his job was to be both deaf and blind when it was called for.

She turned her gaze to the man sitting next to her in the back seat. Anxiety made her heart race. Why was she sitting here in his not-particularly-discreet car?

He didn't want her in his life. In his and Nathalie's life. She understood that. And accepted it. That was the demand he had made. If she left them, then all ties were to be cut – that was the deal. And that was how it had been for many years now. He didn't approach her; she didn't approach him. Simple. Uncomplicated. Until she'd been found out two summers previously. She hadn't heard anything after that, and she'd been careful to keep her distance. No more surveillance from the platform at Blåsut metro station. No more coffees in the park at Kungsträdgården. But now he was here. All of a sudden.

Right outside her flat.

She focused on a point on the seatback in front of her – a tiny irregularity in the otherwise perfect leather finish.

Breathe.

Breathe.

Then she turned to face him again. He met her gaze. Steadily. But she saw a hint of worry in his clear blue eyes. They were so similar to another pair of eyes. Her chest tightened.

'She's made contact,' he said. 'You were supposed to keep her away.'

Mina didn't have to ask who he meant.

'I haven't spoken to my mother in a long time,' she said.

'Nathalie is with her. Since last Friday. My people obviously saw the initial contact, but I asked them not to intervene.'

Mina thought back to the occasion two summers ago when she hadn't been able to help herself having a prohibited coffee with Nathalie and how the bodyguards had swept her daughter away almost before she'd had time to sit down.

'You clearly had no issues with intervening straight away in the past,' she said.

'I know,' he said. 'But that has led to Nathalie and me having a rather . . . strained relationship. I didn't want to make matters worse unnecessarily. It's not as if I don't know where that farm is, and she's older now than she was . . . then. Anyway. First Nathalie messaged to say she'd met her grandmother. Then I got another message in the evening saying she was going to sleep over. That was last Friday. Since then, she hasn't replied when I call or text. It's now Sunday. Even taking into account teenage obstinacy, there are limits.'

Mina bit her tongue. She had formed the habit of tracking Nathalie via her phone. The little GPS transmitter she had slipped into her daughter's rucksack must have ended up in a compartment that Nathalie didn't use, because its daily movements testified to the fact that Nathalie still hadn't found it. But the Ossian case had consumed all of Mina's time in the last few days – she hadn't checked where Nathalie was since Wednesday morning. And back then she had been at home with her father. Mina was ashamed. If she had been more observant of her own daughter, she would already have known what she was now being told.

'So why don't you pick her up?' she said. 'You know who she's with.'

Mina saw uncertainty writ on his face. She'd seen it before. It had always been for brief moments – so brief that afterwards she had been unsure whether it had even been there. But now it lingered.

'I don't know,' he said. 'Our agreement is no contact. But then again, she is her grandmother. And it's been so many years . . . I don't know what to do.'

The words floated in the silence between them. She glanced towards the rear-view mirror in front and saw the driver still staring dead ahead without even a flicker of expression behind his shades.

She understood the dilemma. Nathalie's father was afraid of the media fallout if it emerged that he'd been keeping his daughter away from her closest relatives.

'I take it you want me to do something?'

He shook his head. He seemed to be searching for the right words. That was one of his main characteristics, Mina thought to herself. He never spoke hastily or unthinkingly. It was one of the things that had got him to where he was today.

129

People passing the car looked at it curiously. It stood out, parked up in front of an ordinary block of flats, and the tinted windows only increased the curiosity as to who was concealed within.

'I want you to talk to your mother,' he said. 'Without Nathalie finding out. Your mother wouldn't listen to me, but she might listen to you. We need to handle this discreetly.'

Mina forced herself to breathe deeply and calm down. Inside, she felt a jumble of emotions. Memories, moments, times she had worked so hard to repress. All the things she had taught herself to live without.

'I'm in the middle of a major investigation,' she said.

'The missing kid,' he said, with a nod. 'I saw the press conference. My sources say you found the boy dead yesterday morning.'

'Good. In that case you understand that I've got other things I need to do right now. I'm not worried about Nathalie.'

His gaze met hers again.

'No, but perhaps you ought to be worried about what she might hear,' he said.

Anxiety took hold of her. Of course he was right. They'd struck a deal. But it was frankly no more stable than a house of cards. Every second that Nathalie spent with her grandmother risked the collapse of that house of cards. And if it did, then it would not only bury Mina but also her daughter.

'I can try,' she said in a low voice.

He held out his hand towards the front seat and the chauffeur passed him a notepad and pen. In that familiar handwriting, he hastily jotted down a few lines, tore the sheet out and handed it to her. The expression of uncertainty appeared to have been vanquished. Now he was collected, controlled, calm.

Mina opened her mouth to say something. There was so much that was unsaid. So much she wanted to ask. But she closed her mouth again and tugged at the handle to open the door. She had opted out of being allowed to ask questions.

As the black car disappeared around the corner, she stood there watching it go. Then she looked at the note in her hand. She pulled out her phone and tapped in the scrawled number. If she didn't do it right away, she would never dare. She was connected to an answering machine. After taking a deep breath, she left a message. Then she returned to the door of her building, mechanically entered the code and climbed the stairs back to her flat. Not until she had firmly closed the door behind her did she permit herself to scream out loud.

43

The Sunday morning sun shone on the rooftops of the terraced houses in Vallentuna. The houses had been brown when he'd lived there, but at some point after he'd left they had all been painted in different colours. Ruben had been planning to visit several days ago, but the search for Ossian had taken priority. Yesterday he had spoken to everyone on the *af Chapman*, as well as the staff at both the National Museum of Fine Arts and the Royal Institute of Art, which were nearby. No one had seen a thing. Obviously. Adam had offered to take the rest of the island on Sunday. If the killer had arrived by boat, then there was a possibility that someone on one of the other boats moored on the island might have noticed. Ruben had said he had an errand to run first, but that he would catch up with him. Now he suddenly wished he had gone straight to Skeppsholmen. No . . . He was going to do this.

The Ossian case had set him off-kilter. He needed to feel like he belonged to something. Or at least that he had done. The camaraderie he shared with Gunnar and the other lads wasn't the same – it was equal parts contest and community. A contest to find out who had the best story to tell. Who had seen the biggest tits over the weekend. Who had got up to the best mischief. Thump on the back, thump on the back. He would trust them blindly if it came down to it, but right now he needed something else.

Ellinor had been easy to find. It transpired she still lived in the house they had shared. He sat inside his vehicle in the car park and contemplated the houses below. The yellow one was Ellinor's. Ruben got out of the car and followed the footpath down towards the row of buildings. Kids were playing in the small park surrounded by the houses.

Kids.

That thought hadn't occurred to him. What if she was married with children? After all, it was a Sunday – the whole family was probably at home. If her husband opened the door then he'd just say he'd got the wrong house.

As he got closer to the yellow house, he spotted a child's bicycle abandoned on the lawn outside. It was as if he had conjured it with his thoughts. And it wasn't one of those learn-how-to-ride-a-bike bikes either. It was bigger than that. Ellinor had had a family for a while. The visit was increasingly feeling like a bad idea, but it was best to get it over and done with. Otherwise he would spend the rest of eternity wondering.

He climbed the front steps and rang the bell. When he heard someone approaching inside, he took a few steps back to ensure he wasn't too close.

It was Ellinor.

'Yes?' The first thing that struck him was how much more beautiful she was than when she had left him. Granted, she'd been quite a beauty then too, but she was now ten years older. Ten years wiser. Ten years more experienced. Another ten years of life. Of being a mother. Of living her own life. Her appearance divulged all this to him in a flash. And it took his breath away. It took her a few seconds to realize who he was. Then she frowned.

'Ruben Höök,' she said. 'What are you doing here?' It wasn't delivered in a tone of voice that said 'how lovely to see you after all these years'. Quite the opposite, in fact. *Get lost before I call my husband.*

'Hi,' he said as gently as he could. 'Sorry to show up like this. I just thought . . . Can we talk?' Someone was moving behind her – he tried to see who it was, but Ellinor positioned herself so that she was blocking the doorway.

'It's nothing, Astrid,' she said. 'I'll be with you in a second.'

He saw on Ellinor's face exactly how much he had once hurt her and how little inclination she had to unpack that.

132

'Astrid?' he said tentatively.

'You have no business here,' she said. 'Get out of here before I call the police.'

He ventured a smile.

'Come on, Ellie,' he said. 'I am the police.'

'You know what I mean. And don't call me that. Please don't come back.'

A small figure suddenly pushed its way to Ellinor's side. 'Hello! My name's Astrid. What's your name?'

'He's leaving right now, Astrid,' Ellinor said curtly. 'Goodbye.' Ellinor shoved the girl backwards and slammed the door right in his face. Then she locked it.

He took a few steps back and stood on the grass, unsure what to do next. But he couldn't just stand there. Neighbours' tongues would wag. Not that he cared about them. But maybe she did.

He began to walk back towards the car. Fuck's sake. Amanda the shrink had been right. This was one of his worst ideas ever. The Ellinor he'd been in love with and shared a home with – the Ellinor he'd betrayed – no longer existed. All that remained were some uncomfortable memories of him. She had moved on. She had a family. It wasn't her fault that he hadn't done the same.

He got into the car and sat there for a few moments before starting the engine. It was weird seeing Ellinor with a child. Ellinor's daughter had her mother's eyes but someone else's mouth. Ellinor had always had soft, plump lips that tasted of salt in the summer when she perspired. He pushed away thoughts of Ellinor's lips. He couldn't afford to drown in memories again.

The girl was called Astrid. Like his grandmother. Ellinor had loved his grandmother and vice versa, and she'd often asked after that lovely fiancée he'd once had. He'd never been able to give her any answers. But he was due to see her in a day's time for their usual Monday coffee. It had been a standing appointment ever since she'd moved to the home which – as luck had it – was just five minutes from work. Tomorrow he would tell her that Ellinor seemed to be doing well and that she had a little girl with the same name as her. She'd be pleased to hear that.

He took a deep breath and pressed the accelerator. Now it was done. Now it was over. Amanda would be proud of him.

44

'There were a number of things that were odd about Lilly's autopsy report,' Mina said on the phone.

Her throat was still hoarse from the screaming.

'But nothing that shed any light on Ossian. I think we'll have to wait for his autopsy for that.'

She heard Julia sigh heavily on the other end of the line.

'Adam and Ruben's interviews haven't given us any leads yet,' said her boss. 'And Peder hasn't found any CCTV cameras along the pavement.'

'What about the bridge to Skeppsholmen? Or on the *af Chapman*? Surely they've got some?'

'There are cameras on the museum building just before the bridge, but they don't have a long range. And if the killer arrived by boat, then they didn't even have to cross the bridge. You'd think that the *af Chapman* would have a camera by its gangway, but they've only got CCTV on board the boat itself. Which leaves us with nothing. I'd hoped you would have more.'

'Not yet. Like I said, the report contained points of interest, but nothing that helps us with Ossian. On the other hand, I think Adam is right that we should take another look at Lilly's case.'

Julia sighed again.

'I'm going to make myself even more unpopular with Peder's wife than I already am by calling him back in,' she said. 'With a little luck, we might be able to get hold of Lilly's mum today. I know the dad is away. But I don't think there's anything else you can do for now. Get in touch if you think of anything. Otherwise I'll see you tomorrow.'

'Of course.'

Mina hung up. The unexpected encounter with Nathalie's father had shaken her up so much that she hadn't gone into the office for Julia's briefing. It had felt as if she were about to crumble, and if that happened, she didn't want it to be at police headquarters. She'd told Julia she had a sore throat and didn't want to pass whatever it was – if it was anything at all – on to anyone else. Given that she'd just screamed herself hoarse, it wasn't a complete lie.

She paced restlessly around the flat. Julia had assigned her tasks she could do from home, but they were already done and did nothing to alleviate the feeling that she was far from the centre of events. Suddenly, the familiar walls no longer felt reassuring. She needed to distract herself. Both Nathalie and Ossian were hovering in her thoughts and preventing her from thinking constructively.

They hadn't found Ossian in time. They just had to accept that. And she had nothing to go on. No matter how much she dwelled on it, it wasn't going to generate any new leads. But it was fortunate that Julia hadn't asked her to come in to police headquarters. She was still too shaken up from the meeting with Nathalie's father.

As if it weren't bad enough to have Ossian's fate running on repeat in her head, her own daughter was with her grandmother. Mina's mother. Ines still hadn't answered the phone, even though the number Nathalie's father had written down for her was guaranteed to be correct. Of course, it would be a straightforward matter to check the GPS tracker to find out where they were and go there under cover of being on duty. But that would hardly improve things. She had no choice but to wait, worrying about what Ines might tell Nathalie. The thought of it quite honestly paralysed her with horror. There were secrets that shouldn't be revealed. Secrets that couldn't be revealed. There was so much that had been built on top of them: without those foundations, everything would come tumbling down. And it would take them all with it. No one would escape unscathed from the chaos that followed. But there was nothing she could do about it right now. Nathalie was with Ines and all she could do was wait.

She wasn't good at waiting. She had already got through the tasks set for her by Julia, and now all she could do was sit there waiting eagerly for fresh instructions.

Ergo, she needed distraction. She pulled out her phone and scrolled through the apps. She had replied to every email and the handful of texts she had received that day. Perhaps there was something else. An important article or . . . She stopped at the sight of a white flame against a red background. Tinder. Curse Ruben. Why had he made her sign up? Well, he hadn't really, if she were perfectly honest. She had downloaded the app just to shut him up. But he wasn't sitting next to her right now. He wasn't forcing her to open it. Yet perhaps it was the perfect, brain-dead distraction. And who said she shouldn't check Tinder? Apparently that was what people did these days. Normal people. And she was no nun. Anyway, the men on the app didn't know she was looking. That made it all a little easier, although not that much. But enough.

She hoped.

She readied herself for what she might see by reading a few online articles on her computer first. They recommended that you post photos with your pets, your friends – or best of all, your family – and photos in which you were doing something active. That was the kind of thing that turned women on, according to the female author. Mina could certainly understand the psychological aspects of showing that a man was caring, empathetic, and had a social life with his own interests.

The only problem was that hundreds of thousands of people had read the same articles as she had. Which surely stripped all photos depicting these themes of any authenticity.

She took a deep breath, sprayed the phone display with sanitizer, opened the app and registered as a user.

The first man to appear was proudly clutching – rather too proudly, Mina felt – a large fish that he had apparently just caught. She hadn't expected that. She didn't quite know how to filter the information. Was the fish intended to be a pet, an activity or a test of strength? Or perhaps a family member? It was presumably meant to symbolize masculinity – the ability to hunt and kill one's own food. The man in the photo was wearing sunglasses, which meant that all she had to go on in terms of his personality was the fish.

And the fact that his hands were bare.

She shuddered.

What woman in full possession of her senses would permit those hands – proudly holding a big, sticky bream – to touch her? Mina felt deeply nauseous at the mere thought of it and was compelled to spray and wipe down the screen yet again. She smelled her fingers. It was almost as if she could make out the smell of fish.

She didn't want to see any more: she swiped left. A quick glance at the next one and then the same movement.

After repeating this some ten times, it became apparent that every man on earth had probably read the same articles as she had. She had lost count of how many photos of man-with-grandfather, man-with-random-pet, man-at-gym and even man-with-cushion she had seen. Not to mention the disproportionate number of men on Tinder who seemed to think that the most attractive way to present themselves was clutching a big fish. Seriously . . . what was it about men and fish? One more big catch and she might have to cleanse her eyes with caustic soda.

Ruben could laugh at her as much as he wanted – she'd had enough.

Suddenly her swiping finger paused. A pair of brown eyes on the screen met her gaze. A man with dark, curly hair pulled back into a loose knot. Not quite a man bun, but almost. Thick stubble on both his cheeks and chin. He was good-looking, but not disturbingly so. He actually looked a little tired. A little . . . earnest. The photo hadn't been taken in a studio – it was a selfie captured when out and about. Not that it was sloppily done – it was still a good picture. But it was unpretentious. In the next picture, he was sitting at a desk with his head propped up on his hands. He wasn't looking into the camera lens – instead he was looking at someone out of shot. White shirt. Rolled-up sleeves. Perhaps the photo had been taken at his place of work. That was it. No gym shots. No fish. She exhaled in relief and read the bio.

'My name's Amir and I'm a lawyer,' he wrote. 'Not got many hobbies or interests because of work. But thought it was time to change that. Maybe we could do it together?'

A lawyer. With no interests. But he looked kind. And unlike the others, he didn't look quite as . . . bloody needy. That was the only description for it that she could summon. She'd show Ruben. She was going to contact Amir. Not that they would actually meet. Because, come on . . . She had Ossian to think about. But that would be a proper slap in the face for Ruben. Never again would he be able to say anything about social phobia or spinsters. She put her index finger to the screen and hesitated for a moment. Then she quickly swiped right before she changed her mind.

45

'I've promised Anette that I'll look after the triplets this afternoon,' Peder said. 'She's going out for a Sunday drink with some girlfriends.'

He and Julia elbowed their way through hordes of tourists who didn't seem to have learned how best to manoeuvre along crowded pavements.

'Let your wife know that she'll have to wait until we've found Ossian's killer,' Julia said sharply.

She regretted it immediately. She had been unnecessarily harsh. It seemed she was still annoyed with Torkel.

'Look, um, sorry,' she said. 'That was a crass thing to say.'

Peder merely nodded.

'Luckily, Lilly's mum lives not far from police headquarters,' she said. 'It shouldn't take that long. You can go home as soon as we're done. Anette should make it to her drinks. Believe you me, I'm the last person who wants to deprive a mother of a little me-time.'

She pulled out her phone and checked her texts. Two new

ones from Torkel had appeared. She dismissed them without reading them.

'Lilly's mum lives at . . . 7 Garvargatan,' she read aloud. 'On the far side of Kungsholms torg. Should be there soon. We'll just have to hope she's in.'

Peder came to a sudden halt in front of a man wearing khaki shorts, sandals and a T-shirt that proudly proclaimed: *I love Hjo.* The man was standing completely still in the middle of the pavement looking confused, and they had to navigate around him.

'Bloody tourists,' Peder muttered into his beard. 'Don't they have the concept of "keep right" in Hjo?'

'Come on, Peder,' Julia said with a wry smile. 'Don't you usually brag that the triplets have given you the patience of a saint? Or is that something reserved for the kids?'

'Hmm, I suppose,' he said. 'I think I'm probably jealous of everyone who doesn't seem to have a care in the world.'

A third text from home appeared on her phone before she had time to put it back in her pocket.

'If I'm late I can always bribe Anette with an Aperol Spritz while she changes,' he said. 'That's a win-win. She's pretty damn sexy when she's drinking in her lingerie.'

'TMI, Peder,' Julia said, hurrying onwards.

Part of her wanted to give him a slap. It was so unfair. She couldn't imagine Torkel bothering to make her so much as a glass of juice if she was about to leave him alone with Harry for the evening. And that would probably be because she had to work. Drinks were a phenomenon that no longer existed in her life. Not on Sundays or any other days. They had disappeared, along with the slightest hint of feeling even a little sexy around Torkel.

'Let's concentrate on Lilly's parents,' she said. 'From what I gather, her mother's still long-term sick. Understandably, Lilly's disappearance hit her hard. But according to what I read about the custody dispute, she may not have been the easiest person to get along with before that. So we'll have to tread carefully.'

Garvargatan turned out to be in shade. They slowed down and enjoyed a brief respite in the cooler temperature before they reached the doorway for number 7. After being buzzed in, they took the lift up to Jenny and Anders Holmgren's apartment. A man of about thirty-five opened the door while using a foot to ward off a chihuahua that was angrily yapping at his feet.

'Hello, I'm Julia Hammarsten. I called earlier,' she said, proffering her hand.

Anders's hand was soft with sweat when it squeezed hers.

'Come in, come in. Don't worry about Mollberg. She's all bark. Thinks she's a German shepherd. Jenny's here – we're in the living room.'

He led the way, Mollberg continuing to nip at his heels. The room they entered was an open-plan kitchen-cum-living room. It was very pleasant. All the windows were open, and if you craned your neck it was possible to glimpse the waters of Riddarfjärden.

'Please sit down. Would you like an iced tea?'

She and Peder nodded gratefully and Anders went over to the kitchen. Lilly's mother was sitting on the sofa. Her gaze was vacant. She was disconcertingly thin and radiated nervousness. One foot was tapping the floor quickly and rhythmically.

'I'm guessing you're here because of that boy who went missing?' she said, lighting a cigarette.

'You weren't going to smoke inside. We agreed.'

Anders turned around as he got ice out of the freezer, a deep furrow forming between his eyebrows. Jenny didn't reply. Instead, she simply took a drag and then slowly exhaled smoke rings into the air.

'That's right,' Peder said, responding to Jenny's question about the boy. 'His name is Ossian Walthersson.'

Jenny took a few more deep drags. Anders clinked the glasses over in the kitchen area.

'We haven't seen each other since the funeral. Did you know that? Me and Mauro. Lilly's dad. But of course you know that. Haven't seen each other, haven't spoken. And why should we? He got what he wanted. He wanted to take my daughter away from me.'

She angrily tapped her cigarette into an ashtray on the table.

'Sweetheart, we've talked about this. You know that Mauro actually wanted her every other week,' Anders said, but he looked like he regretted opening his mouth almost immediately.

'Every other week!' Jenny bawled. 'That's half my daughter's life I was going to miss! *He* was the one who opted out! He chose to abandon his family. Abandon Lilly. For some blonde bimbo!'

'Cecilia's a brunette,' Anders said quietly.

'I swear it was Mauro who killed Lilly,' Jenny continued. 'Him and his fucking psycho family. They would have done anything to stop me having her – to make sure she didn't get her mum. Instead he wanted to play mums and dads with that bimbo bitch! With my kid!'

Julia had seen the court's verdict. It had given serious consideration to not even granting Jenny custody of Lilly every other week. Jenny hadn't been assessed as sufficiently mentally stable to care for her child. The comment had surprised Julia. In custody disputes, the courts basically always took the mother's side – regardless of the situation. Custody disputes were perhaps the only point in society where it sucked to be a man. But the aggressive woman sitting on the sofa left her in no doubt about the validity of the court's reservations.

'There are significant similarities between your daughter's disappearance and Ossian's disappearance last Wednesday,' she said calmly and matter-of-factly. 'That's why we'd like to talk to you again. We're sorry if it opens up old wounds.' She gratefully accepted the glass Anders handed her. Large ice cubes were swimming in golden liquid. It smelled sweet and fresh. She took a sip. Anders clearly knew his thing. Peder had already downed his.

'The police thoroughly investigated all accusations that someone in the family was responsible for Lilly's kidnapping,' Peder said, clearing his throat. 'Including those made by you in court against Mauro. But there was nothing to support—'

'Evidence,' Jenny snorted. 'They wouldn't talk about anything else!'

Anders filled Peder's glass with more iced tea and then took a seat next to his wife. The dog jumped up and laid her head

141

on his lap. It seemed to have accepted the presence of Julia and Peder for the time being. At least it was quiet.

'You know it,' Jenny said to her husband. 'It was red between her legs every single time she came back from Mauro! I took her to see the doctor several times to show them. But doctors these days, I mean . . . they're just so damn terrified of making mistakes. Claimed I'd bought her knickers that were too small and that the marks were from that. Fuck's sake.'

Her long dark hair fell across her face, and Julia reflected that she had probably been beautiful before the bitterness had transformed her face into an angry mask.

'Jenny,' Anders said gently. 'You know that's not true. Mauro's the last person who would hurt Lilly in any way. He loved her as much as you did.'

Jenny stared out of the window and lit another cigarette.

'Today's not a good day,' Anders said, without taking his eyes off his wife.

'There's nothing else you remember about the day she went missing?' Peder said.

Jenny shook her head fiercely.

'I realized straight away that Mauro had picked her up. That he was hiding her somewhere.'

'But the nursery staff said it wasn't her dad who they saw take Lilly,' Julia said firmly. 'They reported that it was an older couple.'

'Mauro is many things,' Jenny hissed back, 'but he's not stupid. Of course he'd never take her himself. He sent someone else. Probably someone from his family. His parents are dead, but some other wrinkly. They're all off their fucking rockers, the lot of them. Total headcases.'

Her voice rose to a falsetto. The dog started and raised her head.

'You know that's not constructive,' said Anders. 'Are you sure you've taken your meds today?'

'Constructive?' said Jenny, imitating his voice in a whiny tone. 'My child is dead and she went through hell before that. I did everything I could to save her from him, from that fucking . . . monster. But . . . she . . . still died . . .'

142

Jenny was shaking with rage. She lit a new cigarette using the butt of the old one and dragged so hard on it that she seemed to be trying to suck out the filter.

'But now we have a new case with another child,' Julia said as slowly and clearly as she could. 'In similar circumstances to Lilly, like I said. Which is why—'

'He thinks he's so fucking clever,' Jenny interjected.

She tapped her temple and rocked back and forth.

'He's probably still worried you're going to bring him in for Lilly. So what does he go and do? Of course . . . he diverts attention away from himself. Away from Lilly. Tries to make you think it's one of those . . .'

She snapped her fingers in the air.

'One of those . . . serial killers.'

'Is that what you think this is?' Anders said, mild-mannered, as he stroked Mollberg's coat.

Peder glanced questioningly at Julia. She discreetly shook her head in return before he answered.

'I'm afraid we can't say much at present,' he said. 'We're exploring all avenues. Which is why we're here.'

Jenny rolled her eyes. She pointed at Peder, jabbing with the cigarette in her hand. The ash on the tip was too long and it fell off, burning the pale carpet. Julia saw Anders's gaze follow the trajectory of the ash and his eyes quiver as it landed. But he said nothing. He just kept stroking Mollberg's coat even more intensely.

'You swallowed all that bullshit he trotted out last time, and you're going to do the same thing again. I know it. Mauro's a devil, but he's bright. I can't fucking talk to you any more right now.' Jenny got up hastily and went out onto the balcony, where she stood with her back to them as the words continued to flow.

'Talk to Mauro. You'll see. That's all I'm saying. Him and his fucking family. Total. Fucking. Headcases.'

Julia and Peder stood up and Anders accompanied them into the hallway without saying anything. When the door closed behind them, they heard Mollberg begin to yap again.

46

'Hello!'

Nathalie was startled. A beautiful dark-haired woman came towards her, beaming. She immediately realized who it was.

'Do you mind if I sit down?'

Nova sat down opposite her without waiting for an answer. Nathalie shrugged. Grandma had left her alone at lunch after someone had come and whispered in her ear. Lunch had been soup served with the most delicious freshly baked bread Nathalie had ever tasted. There was most definitely nothing wrong with the food, even if she wouldn't have turned down a cheeseburger and fries. The portions at Epicura were a little on the small side for her.

People always wanted her grandmother for this and that. In a way, it made her proud. Grandma Ines was clearly a woman of importance. She even got to be on TV. But it also meant that Nathalie occasionally felt a little lost and abandoned. And she still hadn't got answers to all the things she wanted to know. 'Patience,' was all Grandma had said when she asked.

Grandma still hadn't come back, and evening was now approaching. Not that Nathalie had anything against being alone at Epicura. She just wished she'd found something to eat. She had even searched for the biscuits that had been there when they'd arrived the day before yesterday, but they were conspicuous by their absence.

'How are you getting on here?' Nova said, nodding to a woman who came over and set down a cup of tea in front of her.

But no biscuits.

'Does it feel OK, or do you think it's all weird?'

'Bit of both,' Nathalie said, disarmed by her forthrightness.

'I get it,' Nova said. 'We're trying to break patterns and live in a way that we've forgotten in our modern society. I'm sure it must seem strange. But in practice, what we're doing here is actually what's natural.'

'Grandma said it's all from your grandfather.'

'Yes, that's right. My grandfather was a very well-read and intelligent man who didn't shy away from asking the tough questions. I suppose you might say he was searching for the meaning of life – if that doesn't sound too wishy-washy.'

'Honestly, this whole place is pretty wishy-washy.'

Nova laughed outright. It was a warm laugh.

'You know something?' she said. 'You're absolutely spot on. I think this is very wishy-washy. But many have found meaning here. In life. In themselves. In society.'

'Were your parents like your grandfather?'

'My dad was – he was a seeker, just like his own father. Sometimes their paths crossed. Sometimes not. But he was a talented writer, my dad. He was the one who wrote a number of the quotations you can see on the walls around here. He studied Epicureanism side by side with my grandfather for many years. But then he needed to find his own answers. That was a few years before he . . .'

She fell silent and a shadow descended on her face.

'Before he what?'

Nova blinked.

'Before he passed away,' she said. 'Of course, you're too young to know that story. And I think we'll save it for another time.'

'My mother died when I was little too,' Nathalie said glumly.

'How old were you?' Nova asked.

Nathalie hesitated. 'The strange thing is that I don't really know. All Dad says when I ask is that I was little. But I can't have been *that* little. Because I remember her. Or someone. I remember a smell, a feeling; I can see a silhouette in the doorway, I can hear laughter – I remember . . . Or maybe it's just dreams about her that I remember . .' Nathalie cleared her throat. 'So I understand that finding answers thing. It'd be nice to have some. But no one wants to give me any. Not Dad, and not Grandma either. So it's really nice here, but my dad's probably going to get it together and come and pick me up in his big black car whether I like it or not. And I'd at least like to see the animals before that happens.'

She heard the defiant tone in her own voice and immediately

145

regretted it. The last thing she wanted was to sound like a whiny kid. Everyone here had been so nice to her. She could go home anytime she wanted – it was she who had chosen to stay.

Nova rose from the table. Fortunately, she didn't look like she had taken it the wrong way. 'I'm going to have a word with your grandmother,' she said. 'I know she's got something special planned for you. Not even I know what. But of course you can see the animals. Could you give your father a call to let him know you'll be staying a while longer? I've got a meeting in town now, but I'd also like to get to know you a little better.'

Nathalie nodded.

Nova smiled and left her. Nathalie looked at her phone. She already knew she wasn't going to call Dad. Obviously. Best to send a text. But the last one she'd sent hadn't exactly been nice, so she wasn't quite sure how to follow up without making things worse. She sighed and put the phone away. She'd send the text soon. Just not right now. She could stay another day. No problem.

The Second Week

47

Mina stared at the monitor and tried to focus, but her thoughts kept drifting away. She'd struggled to get off to sleep the night before; the encounter with Nathalie's father had stuck with her all day. And it had been even harder to wake up in the morning.

In the lift at police headquarters there was a note pinned up that read:

It's Monday! Time to SHAKE IT UP!

That note was now crumpled up in a ball in Mina's wastepaper basket.

She looked down at her hands, which were trembling slightly. So much time and so much energy had been put into trying to leave the past behind. So many memories hidden in the deepest depths of her brain, memories she had never imagined she would have to revisit. But in some strange way, life kept constantly bringing the past into the present. Seeing Nathalie's father the morning before was all it had taken for the last ten years – more than ten years, she corrected herself – to be erased. In her memories, she was suddenly immersed in everything that had happened back then. Everything she thought she had laid to rest for the remainder of her life. That had been their agreement. And she had paid a high price for it.

She had tried to contact her mother several times the day before, but all she had got was the answerphone each time. It had been hard to think about anything other than what her mother might have revealed to Nathalie. And what she might not have said.

She pulled out her mobile and switched on the GPS tracker so that she could at least watch her daughter at a distance, but the app was struggling to decide where the transmitter was. This had begun to happen more frequently of late. The transmitter was probably running out of battery. After all, it had been in Nathalie's rucksack for a long time.

Her mobile chimed in her hand. It was a message from reception to say she had a visitor. Maybe her mother had done as she'd asked and come anyway? She stopped herself when she saw the unfamiliar name of the visitor. It wasn't her mother. She couldn't help feeling relieved. She wasn't sure whether she was ready for that meeting yet.

She reached for an antiseptic wipe and cleaned her phone. Then she headed for the lifts and went down to reception.

An elegantly dressed woman was waiting for her. Mina only just had time to think that she had never met the woman before when she reached out her arms and quickly drew Mina into an embrace.

'Mina!' she exclaimed. 'What a pleasure it is to finally meet you!'

All the synapses in Mina's brain imploded simultaneously. A thousand thoughts about where the woman had been, whether she'd washed, what she'd touched, whom she'd touched . . . She felt a million germs spreading across her body. The woman who had wrapped herself around her felt like a host who was now transferring all her parasites to Mina, where they would multiply and spread whatever it was they carried. She wanted to tear herself free, but she found herself paralysed and unable to move, unable to say a word.

In the end, the woman took a step back. Mina resisted a strong impulse to rip off her clothes and run naked and screaming down the corridor to the nearest shower.

'I don't think we—' she began falteringly.

'Your mother has told me so much about you!' the woman interrupted, flashing a dazzling smile that appeared well-rehearsed, as if she were accustomed to being photographed.

In spite of her panic, Mina couldn't help reflecting how beautiful the woman was. She had long and luscious dark brown hair that flowed down her back over a cool white silk shirt. Her long slender legs emerged from a matching white silk skirt. Her large blue eyes contrasted startlingly with her olive skin. There was almost no make-up at all, but what little she had applied was perfect. She was eye-catching. And apparently a hugger.

Mina realized one more thing. It was the smile that had done it. She'd been wrong in her initial assumption. She knew full well who the woman was.

'My mother, you said?' Mina said, looking around discreetly in case anyone seemed to have overheard. 'It's probably best you come upstairs with me.'

She admitted the woman through the barriers and showed her over to the lifts.

'Sorry, I thought she might have said I was coming,' the woman said as they were transported to the right floor. 'My name's Nova. I work with your mother. Rather, she works with me. Either way, you and I haven't met before.'

'No, I would have remembered,' said Mina. 'But I know who you are. You gave a talk in my old department a few years back. You talked about your association and about . . . Epson? Was that his name? The philosopher?'

'Epicurus.'

'Hmm. Follow me. We'll go to the meeting room.'

She walked briskly along the corridor – eager to get Nova away from the eyes of curious colleagues.

'I expect you're wondering why I'm here,' said Nova. 'Rather than your mother.'

Mina heard Nova's high heels clattering behind her.

'Yes. Given that it was her I called,' Mina said brusquely before opening the glass door leading to the conference room.

Nova sat down and reached for the pack of wet wipes lying on the table.

'May I? It's so very hot outside.'

Mina nodded. She made a mental note to throw out the packet since Nova had touched it. Not that it mattered – she was already thoroughly infested by whatever it was Nova had brought in with her. She really hated – truly and deeply – people who were huggers.

Nova took a wipe from the packet and ran it across her throat to cool off. Then she wiped her hands with it before screwing it up into a small ball and dunking it into the nearest bin.

'So, what's this about?' Mina said severely. 'Where's my mother? And where's Nathalie?'

This was not a conversation she had time for, and sitting there longing for a sanitizing shower – or full-body sandblasting – made the situation almost excruciating.

'She's told me everything,' Nova said, flashing that smile again. 'About you. About all of you. About Nathalie. You can talk to me instead. Your mother . . . She's in the middle of her developmental curve when it comes to this. She's just come into a granddaughter. She's not ready to talk to you yet.'

Mina felt the anger, the old anger, welling up inside her. It was so strong and caustic that it made her eyes fill with tears.

'I'm not interested in her developmental curve or work or whatever you call it. What I am interested in is Nathalie. And so is her father. I take it you know who he is?'

Nova nodded.

'Yes, I know who Nathalie's father is. You can tell him that there's no cause for concern. But this is a healing process and those can be vulnerable. Things would be much worse for Nathalie now if he or you interfered and interrupted that. As I said, they've only just started.'

'Are you threatening me? Seriously? You do realize you're talking to a police officer, right?'

Nova sighed and shook her head. Then she smiled gently again.

'No matter what you think, your mother is on her own journey right now,' she said evenly. 'She changed her life a long time ago, but there's much from the old days that remains unresolved. Everything is suffering, and pain purifies, as my father used to say. Nathalie is part of that journey. Just like you.'

'Nathalie is a child,' said Mina. 'Do you think it's ethically justifiable for my mother to contact her without her guardian's permission? I'm seconds away from reporting you for kidnapping.'

She forced herself to take a few deep breaths. She couldn't allow herself to get worked up. That would open doors she didn't want to open. Calm. Control. That would keep a door locked.

'Kidnapping,' Nova repeated. 'Ah. I see that the case with the missing child has taken its toll on you. It's quite understandable if you see the world through that lens for some time to come. And perhaps you're right. Maybe a parent should have been contacted. But your mother makes her own choices. I don't control that. I can think what I like about her choices. But things are the way they are, and she is Nathalie's grandmother. There's no compulsion here. They're just getting to know each other. Nathalie is free to come and go as she pleases, but she has said she'd like to stay for a few more days. I'm here to plead with you to make that happen. They need it – both of them do. You're the only one who can persuade Nathalie's father to let her have that chance. I can't make that call. Only you can. I came here because I wanted to look you in the eyes when I said that this is something you have to let happen. Do you think that would be possible?'

Mina hesitated and looked at Nova. She was angry and disappointed with her mother, who had been too much of a coward to come herself. And she quite intensely wanted to dislike the beautiful woman in the cool clothes who didn't appear to be the least bit affected by the heat. Mina suspected the performance with the wet wipe had been for her sake. Nova was just sitting there being . . . unimpeachable. She was getting on Mina's nerves.

At the same time, she had to at least consider the idea that her mother and daughter might be headed for something positive. So what if it hurt a bit too much that she hadn't been included herself? With time that might change. And she did have the GPS tracker. She sighed.

'Let me make one thing clear,' she said. 'I don't give a crap about the stuff people like you get up to. Personal development. Self-help. Healing or voodoo or whatever you call it. It's all just a comfort blanket for people who can't get a grip on their own lives. To my ears, what you're up to sounds no better than a cult.'

She noted with satisfaction that Nova's smile disappeared.

'You have no idea how wrong you are,' said Nova. 'Our

activities at Epicura include deprogramming people who have managed to leave cults. My interest was aroused when one of my course facilitators described their time in the Knutby sect. An early defector. That was before all hell broke loose there. I realized there was a role for us to play. That our philosophy was a good match for bringing ex-sect members back to as normal a state as possible.'

'Or getting them to change cults,' said Mina.

'I'm serious. It's easy to look down on people who join cults. To think they're weak. Gullible. That's vastly over-simplifying things. It's often about attachment. If you grow up with a parent who is hurtful, then that gives you a distorted impression of relationships. You expect to be oppressed. That's something cults are good at exploiting. But it can also be the other way around. A close, secure relationship can mean that you see everyone else as being kind, which means you're defenceless against people with other motives. It's not just cults – you must see this phenomenon on a daily basis in your own work.'

'But surely there aren't any cults in Sweden?' said Mina. 'Apart from Knutby, but that's not—'

'There are between three and four hundred associations in Sweden that can be classified as cults,' Nova interrupted. 'Between thirty and forty of these can be seen as destructive. The police really ought to have a better grasp of this.'

Mina didn't know what to say. She reached for the packet of wet wipes but then withdrew her hand when she remembered that Nova had touched it. Instead, she got a bottle of hand sanitizer out of her pocket.

Nova smiled at her. Again.

'As far as self-help goes, you're a member of Alcoholics Anonymous,' she said. 'Your mother says you've taken the twelve-step programme. Are you saying it didn't help? That you would have managed better on your own?'

Mina frowned. Touché. Nova was right. Admittedly, Mina had almost perished as a result, but she could hardly blame AA for the fact that Kenneth and Jane had happened to find her there. AA had been her salvation – her lifeline for many years. The routine of going there and meeting others facing the same

154

challenges and not having to feel odd or broken but instead being understood. Yes, AA had helped. She wouldn't have managed on her own.

'OK, you win,' Mina said. 'I'll try and talk to Nathalie's father – on one condition. My mother does not have my permission to tell Nathalie everything. Some secrets aren't hers to tell.'

Nova nodded briefly.

'I'll do what I can. And I'm sorry about the hug. I didn't realize it would be bad form given . . . well, your personal preferences.'

Nova glanced at the wet wipes and the bottle of hand sanitizer on the table. Mina sighed. Why couldn't she be a little more normal? Why couldn't she have the same tolerance for dirt that normal people clearly had? On the other hand, they were probably constantly ill. Every last one of them.

'I'm sure you've got a lot to do. I'll show myself out,' Nova said, standing up. 'I'll speak to your mother, and you'll speak to Nathalie's father?'

That was not a conversation that Mina was looking forward to.

'I'll have to escort you downstairs to let you out,' she said. 'You can't get out on your own.'

Granted, this was true, but it also bought her a few minutes' grace before she had to call Nathalie's father. They went down in the lift and Mina tapped Nova back through the barrier.

'There's one more thing,' Mina said, once Nova was on the other side of the barrier. 'Next time I want to see my mother. Not you.'

When Mina returned to the conference room, she slid her sleeve over her hand, picked up the packet of wet wipes and dropped it in the bin. Then she got out her phone. But it wasn't Nathalie's father she was going to call. It was a number she had been waiting almost two years for a reason to call.

48

'Hi Vincent. It's me.'

He froze. He had been counting the seconds, hours, days and eventually months that passed since he had last heard that voice. And now that she was calling, he was suddenly not at all ready for it. He wanted to adjust his clothes and tidy up his hair. Check his breath. All that despite the fact that she couldn't see him and wasn't even in his proximity.

He blinked quickly and his skin tingled.

'Hi Mina,' he said in a low voice, going into his study.

It was best Maria didn't see or hear him. He knew that just like before, he was blushing like a child.

'How are things?' she said.

He could tell from the slightly strained tone that her inquiry was a matter of form. Mina had something else she wanted to talk about.

'Oh, fine thanks. Car's ticking over and I still sleep with my wife once every couple of months,' he said.

'Vincent!'

'I can tell it's something important. Get on with it.'

'OK,' Mina said, sounding a lot more relaxed. 'Could you stop by police headquarters today after lunch? I'd like to talk to you about something, just the two of us.'

Vincent sat down heavily on his desk chair, his throat suddenly dry. Just the two of them. After lunch. There was only an hour to go until then. Granted, he had nothing else on for the rest of the day. Mondays were rarely all that eventful. But . . . today? Now?

Mina's eyes.

He wasn't ready. His heart was pounding as if auditioning to be the drummer in a rock band. He'd been longing and yet trying not to. Trying not to build his hopes up. And then, all of a sudden . . . Today? Mina's eyes.

Now?

'Sure,' he said, making an effort to sound casual. 'I'll need to double-check the calendar, but I think I'm free.'

49

Ruben bought a lunchtime meal deal featuring a sandwich and juice from the cafe around the corner from police headquarters, as he did every Monday. He'd spent the morning transcribing everything he'd noted by hand during interviews over the weekend into the computer. On any other day he would probably have eaten at his desk. But this wasn't any other day – it was a Monday. And Mondays were special. So he ate his sandwich on the go as he strolled over to his grandmother's. It was their own little weekly tradition. He was the only one she had left. And she had always been there for him, ever since he was little. So now it was his turn. The documents about Lilly Meyer could wait forty-five minutes. Ruben swigged the last of the juice on his way through the door. Granny Astrid was waiting for him in her room as usual.

'Hello Granny!'

'Hello, my love!'

As ever, she beamed when she saw him. She turned one side of her face upwards so that he could kiss her wrinkled cheek. She smelled just as she always had done. Freshly washed cotton, lavender and the faint scent of almonds, which he knew emanated from the almond cookies she kept hidden in her nightstand.

'I've brought some goodies with me,' he said, holding up the other bag he'd bought on his way over.

Granny's favourite. Vanilla custard-filled sunshine buns.

'You're fattening me up – I'm putting on so much weight,' she moaned, patting her lean belly.

He smiled at the joke. Granny was nothing but skin and bones, and the two of them both knew she'd never put the weight back on again. But as long as she had an appetite for her secret almond cookies, Ruben remained largely untroubled.

He settled down on the bed next to her. The only other place to sit was a battered armchair in the corner, but he wanted to be close. He wanted to smell her scent, remember all their times together in the little house in Älvsjö and the kitchen where it had always smelled of freshly made pancakes and home-made strawberry jam. He'd spent so many summers and school holidays at his granny's. Just the two of them. Whenever his mother had yet another new bloke she wanted to spend her holiday with, without dragging along some unhinged kid. There'd always been room for him at Granny's.

'Shall I divide it in half for you?'

He pointed questioningly at a bun, but Granny shook her head.

'Life's too short to eat half buns,' she said with a grin.

She still had magnificent, strong teeth. It was something she'd always been proud of. *Not a single cavity,* she used to say, pointing to the perfect row of teeth.

She placed a gnarled, liver-spotted hand on his leg.

'Tell me, Ruben . . . How's life?'

The same question she asked every week when he visited. She never asked about his job, which saved him from having to tell her how dreadful the world could be. Instead, she asked about other things. And every week he told tales about what an interesting and eventful life he led. They both knew he was lying, but she let him.

But today he didn't want to lie. Instead he told her about his visit to Ellinor's. Granny patted him on the leg.

'Well, you know what I think. You were stupid to let that girl get away. She was more than just pretty to look at – she was beautiful on the inside too. But you were young and ignorant. It happens easily to you boys.'

'Yes, I suppose I get that from Dad,' he said, and as always when he was talking about his father, his voice became slightly bitter.

Dad had left him and Mum when Ruben had been little. He'd gone away to a conference and never come back again. He was still alive – Ruben knew that from a Facebook trawl. But neither of them had ever initiated contact with the other.

Granny Astrid didn't reply. She had long ago stopped trying to make excuses for her son. He had made his choice. Instead, she had been given his boy to love.

'Did she seem happy? Ellinor, that is?' Granny said curiously. 'Is she married? Otherwise it might not be too late . . . ?'

Ruben smiled and took a big bite from the sunshine bun. The filling covered his teeth. Just like when he'd been little and eaten sunshine buns at Granny's, half the fun was licking the custard off his teeth with his tongue.

'I don't know whether she's married. Probably. She has kids at any rate. Her daughter came to the door and said hello. And do you know what? Her daughter's called Astrid. You and Ellinor always did get along so well, so I suppose she got the idea for the name from you.'

'Oh gosh, how sweet that would be,' Granny said enthusiastically. 'Was it a little 'un?'

'No, she was probably around ten years old. Super cute girl. She had Ellinor's eyes.'

There was a gleam in Astrid's eyes. She peered at Ruben.

'You don't have a picture, do you? On that face book?'

'You're so inquisitive aren't you,' Ruben laughed, but he took out his phone and began to search.

It wasn't hard to find her. Ellinor was there – still with her maiden name. And her profile was plastered with pictures of her daughter. Ruben clicked on one showing her in a midsummer garland, her eyes joyful and a big smile on her lips.

'Here she is. Don't you think she looks like Ellinor? Although not just her. I don't know who the father is, but she must have some of his features too.'

Ruben frowned as he looked at the photo, his head close to Granny's. Might it be that he knew the father after all? The girl seemed so very familiar. Somehow. A little of the custard from his bun was still stuck to his teeth. He rubbed it away with his index finger and licked the last of the sugar off his finger.

Granny looked at the picture and laughed. Then she stood up slowly and shook her head.

'Ruben, for such an intelligent man, you really are very stupid.'

She laboured over to a brown chiffonier with a white lace cloth on it – one of the few pieces of furniture she'd been allowed to bring with her to the old people's home. The cloth was covered in pictures – mostly framed photos of Ruben at different ages. She perused the frames, then picked one up and limped over to where he was sitting on the bed. She took the photo and held it alongside the picture of the girl.

Ruben's eyes widened. Now he knew why she seemed so familiar.

50

Mina was alone in the meeting room. Since the last time she had met Vincent, the wall in front of her had been filled, cleared and re-filled with pictures, documents and words in illegible handwriting pertaining to other victims. Other destinies. The pictures of the home-made magic illusions were forgotten and filed away. That case felt incredibly distant, as if it had been in another life.

Then, it had ultimately been difficult to see where the investigation ended and Vincent began. It had all turned out to be deeply personal to him, even if they hadn't realized at first. But this time everything was different.

Two children had been murdered.

This was a darkness that it was terrifying to venture into. Not that it was the first time she had seen children come to harm – on the contrary. It was all too common in her work as a police officer. Children who were abused. Children who were exploited. Children living in misery that put a developed society to shame.

But murder. Child murder was not common. That was why the few cases that had been solved were often well-known to the general public. Helén, murdered by Ulf Olsson. Engla, murdered by Anders Eklund. And Bobby, murdered by his stepfather with a little help from his mother. Those cases and others like them were forever etched into the souls of the Swedish people.

The eternal question was *how*. How could someone be capable of such evil?

Mina wasn't sure she wanted to know the answer. The people who committed those kinds of acts were monsters – nothing else. She didn't have to understand them. She just had to find them. But now they were dealing with two deeds carried out the same way. That suggested a possible pattern that she would have preferred not to see.

Mina wondered how Vincent would react when he heard about the case. Not that she was going to ask him for help with it. She had called him for other reasons. But he would obviously ask her what she was working on and she would tell him. And he had a family. He was a father. She didn't think it was possible as a parent to blank out the images of Lilly and Ossian that were in front of her. No matter what he said, she knew that Vincent wasn't as rational and didn't have as much control over his emotions as he pretended to. In the brief time they had known each other, she had caught glimpses of something else. Something that hinted at the direct opposite. She had caught a glimpse of an emotional abyss. Possibly a blackness.

It was hard to put her finger on it – it was like when you saw someone moving out of the corner of your eye. If you turned your gaze in that direction, then they disappeared. That was the way it was with Vincent. She couldn't catch him.

Not that she wanted to catch him. She didn't want to catch anyone. She hadn't been expecting Tinder to proclaim 'It's a match' when she swiped right on Amir. The fact that she'd also contacted him was nothing more than downright cognitive behavioural therapy. But Vincent always eluded her every time she thought she had clearly made out his contours. And now that she hadn't seen him in almost two years, he was blurrier than ever.

Part of her protested volubly against what she had initiated. It was best to keep Vincent out of her life. But another part of

161

her – deeper down – wanted nothing more than to have him close.

And now he was on his way.

The phone on the table buzzed. A notification to remind her that her visitor was due to arrive in a few minutes' time. Mina got up and went to meet the mentalist.

51

He broke out into a sweat as soon as he got into the taxi. And yet he noted that the taxi's air conditioning was set to no more than fifteen degrees. A penguin would have been as happy as Larry in here. But Vincent knew that his sweat was not caused by the heat outside but by nervousness within. The thought of Mina had hatched a whole swarm of butterflies in his stomach.

This would not do. He needed something else to think about. Otherwise he'd be a wreck by the time he arrived. The taxi took the bend up towards Tyresövägen a little too fast and Vincent momentarily pictured Mina having to pay him a visit in hospital instead.

Car accident.

Hadn't someone mentioned a car accident recently? The taxi passed a local bus. On its side there was an advert for headache tablets that pithily read: *Does it hurt?*

Pain.

There had been something about pain, too. Who . . . Of course. *Everything is suffering; pain purifies.* Nova had quoted those words when he'd seen her on TV the Friday before. Nova, who had been in a car accident and lost her father. Her father who'd also been involved in Epicureanism.

That might be a fitting distraction. He pulled out his phone and searched for Epicura's website. It was stylish and modern, featuring a businesslike logo.

He scrolled past a series of videos which all seemed to consist

162

of Nova explaining things and then reached something akin to a philosophical explanation of Epicureanism.

> Epicurus' guideline for the new age is same as for all ages: Allow only the anxiety passing like a comet a star. Fast and imperceptible. Life of stillness is life that purifies. Carefully avoid all kinds of pain and desire nothing, for a life without desire is a life fully freed from suffering, and instead allows you to enjoy great success in attaining Everything
>
> John Wennhagen

John Wennhagen. Nova's father. Vincent had recalled correctly. He guessed the use of the slightly stilted and old-fashioned explanation on the otherwise elegant website was Nova's way of honouring her father. He read the poetic-sounding text twice more without being any the wiser.

'That's us here, sir,' the taxi driver said politely, peering at him in the rear-view mirror.

Vincent realized that the car had been at a standstill for some time. He paid without noting what the meter had stopped on – that was how nervous he was – and got out. The sun was shining straight onto the facade of police headquarters, making it impossible for him to see inside through the large windows. But he knew she was standing inside, somewhere. Waiting for him. He could feel that she was there. Well, naturally he couldn't. The hormone cocktail of serotonin, dopamine, cortisol and adrenaline that Mina's phone call had triggered in him was still playing havoc with his perception of reality. It would be foolish to confuse inner emotions with reality. He didn't even understand himself – despite all his knowledge – why she had such an impact on him. Part of him hoped that he might in turn have the same impact on her.

He usually had scientific explanations for his reasoning, but when he put them together in this case, his emotions overwhelmed them. There was something beyond the explicable when it came to Mina and his feelings for her. And now she was inside. He was about to see her again.

He cleared his throat, which had suddenly gone very dry. He checked his jacket, removing a strand of Maria's hair from the sleeve. He already regretted wearing a suit. Then he went up the stairs to the main entrance and opened the door. Mina was waiting inside.

'Hi,' she said as he entered. 'It's been a while.'

'Hi,' he said, suddenly incapable of continuing.

He had almost forgotten. The black hair, longer than last time even if it still hadn't grown out to the ponytail she'd once had. The dark eyes and the naturally red, plump lips. The white sleeveless top a nod to the summer weather, which he knew would be replaced with a polo neck as soon as the temperature permitted. And the little worry line between her eyebrows. But above all: her eyes. Vincent felt slightly dizzy.

Granted, she was no longer a fictional being on a pedestal – she was a flesh and blood human being once again. But that only made matters worse.

He had thought that his life was carrying on just fine without her. That he'd deposited all the memories in a little mental box and moved on. He realized how wrong he had been. The eyes that were now looking at him searchingly had always been there with him. Every day, behind every thought, they had been there. And now she was here before him, in the flesh.

'How . . . how've you been?' he managed to stutter.

He pointed to the thin white plastic gloves she was wearing.

'Those are new. Has it got worse?'

Brilliant. Moron. That was surely top of the list of things she didn't want to talk about. But Mina just laughed.

'No, no, I've been looking at photographs,' she said. 'I didn't want to leave fingerprints on them. I hope you don't mind coming here? Nice suit, by the way, but you must be far too hot?'

Vincent blushed and took off his jacket. Mina was more right than she knew.

'I think Maria was very pleased to get me out of the house,' he said. 'She's launching an online store and has her hands full with that right now.'

He fell silent. They looked at each other. If only he could know what she was thinking. On the one hand, it felt just like

164

it had done before. On the other hand, not so much. Twenty months was long enough for people to marry, have kids and get divorced. He wasn't the same as he had been then. Mina definitely wouldn't be.

And yet . . .

Mina glanced to one side. Then to the other. It was as if she were looking for something. A thought perhaps, or something to say.

'Well . . . why don't we head up?' she said.

She let him through the familiar barrier and they went up to the meeting room in the lift. He thought he saw a flash in her eyes as they got into the lift – as if she were about to mention another occasion on which they'd been in a lift together, but she said nothing.

'I've been doing my exercises, in case you're wondering,' he said. Then he realized how that might be taken.

'I mean . . . coping with being shut in the lift . . . not that I'm hitting the gym. That'd be a weird thing to say even if it were . . . ah, is this us?'

The lift doors opened and saved him before he could dig the hole any deeper. He coughed heavily and hurried out before Mina saw his face, which by now was surely as red as a crayfish.

In the meeting room, Mina had laid out the pictures and documents in two neat rows and they focused on them. The rows were labelled with names. Lilly and Ossian.

'I saw the press conference about him,' Vincent said, pointing to the picture of Ossian.

'Yes,' she said, nodding. 'Do you know anything about missing children?'

'Only that hundreds of kids go missing every year in Sweden, no more than that.'

'That's right,' she said. 'The media likes to draw attention to how many unaccompanied child migrants go missing, but the truth is that there are even more children from migrant families who go missing. It's a mystery. They're never found again.'

'Trafficking?'

'Often. It's dreadful. But the vast majority of children reported missing usually come back – often within a few hours.'

He pointed to the table. 'So Ossian came back?'

Mina shook her head and frowned. He was unsure what that meant, but suddenly Aston came to mind and a knot formed in his stomach.

'Ossian was found on Saturday morning,' she said quietly. 'He'd been dead a few hours. The same thing happened last summer to Lilly here. Two kids in a year. Statistically speaking, that's extremely unusual. So we're now investigating whether there's a connection.'

He squinted at the pictures on the table. Lilly. Ossian. It really could have been Aston just a few years ago. It became harder to breathe – it was as if the air had been sucked out of the room. He reached for one of the folders on the table, but Mina put her hand on top of it.

'Trust me,' she said. 'You don't want to see the pictures.'

He was still fumbling, unsure how to talk to her. He couldn't find the right way in. He wanted to be careful – he didn't dare assume that everything would be like it had been before. But an investigation would at least give them something neutral to talk about.

'So in what way do you need my help with this?' he said. 'Naturally, I'll assist. I'm already looking forward to the sleepless, slightly horror-stricken nights. In fact, I've sort of missed them.'

He smiled faintly, but Mina only looked confused. And then a little unhappy.

'No, sorry,' she said. 'It's not . . . that is, we don't need you . . . I mean, not for the investigation. There's nothing you could do there. You're probably not even meant to be seeing this. I was just getting my things.'

She picked up a phone and a bunch of keys from the table. The pictures and the folders were left in situ, along with an open laptop – signs that she didn't plan to be away from the room all that long. As they exited, he held the door open for her and did his best not to show his disappointment. He had automatically assumed that the material she had shown him was the reason why he was there. That he was going to be involved in her world again. But the visit was apparently over before it had even begun.

'I needed to talk to you about something else, something . . . private,' Mina said, and Vincent's heart began to pound again.

She stopped, looked him in the eyes and then averted her gaze. Whatever it was, it was clearly not easy to tell him.

'It's about my daughter,' she added. 'She's called Nathalie. I think you once saw her photo on my desk. Could we take a walk?'

52

'Did you enjoy the lecture?'

Nathalie shifted her weight restlessly to her other foot. She didn't want to seem rude, but she hadn't really had the energy to listen to much of what Nova had been talking about in the conference room. It had been nice of Nova to invite her, even though it was really a lecture for corporate clients. But Nathalie had mostly accepted so that she had something to do while waiting for her grandmother. She adjusted one of the straps on her rucksack to avoid giving an answer.

'It's OK. You don't have to say anything,' Nova said with a laugh. 'I get that the topic was chronically boring for a teenager. Especially since you haven't yet gone through much of what hurts in life – the things that mean we are needed.'

'What? You think I'm some spoilt brat who gets everything served to her on a silver platter?' Nathalie hissed.

She regretted it immediately.

'Sorry,' she muttered, trying to keep pace with Nova, who had begun to walk rapidly towards a large building some way behind the main one.

Nathalie had only seen it from a distance so far. She had also seen the horses grazing in the paddock outside. Her father had never let her go riding, even though she had begged and pleaded when she was little. He thought it was expensive, time-consuming, dangerous and elitist. That last criticism was a complete joke, given who he was. Instead, she'd been allowed to have a dwarf hamster. She had christened it Lisa and mourned with a heavy heart when she had found it dead under a heap of straw after just three weeks.

'You'll have to forgive me too. I'm being unfair,' Nova said gently, turning her head towards Nathalie as she continued towards the stables.

'How do you mean?'

Nathalie stumbled over a root sticking out of the ground.

'You've certainly experienced pain. And sorrow. I know you lost your mother. That's something I can relate to.' All Nathalie did was nod. She wasn't used to talking about her mother. No one had ever wanted to talk to her about her mother. Least of all her father.

'And here's Ines!' Nova said cheerily.

Nathalie's grandmother came towards them with her arms outstretched and a big smile on her face. If Nathalie had been upset with her for being absent for a long time, those emotions were gone now. She couldn't help but let herself be embraced and smile just as broadly back at Ines.

'Hello, Nathalie!' said her grandmother. 'Sorry I've been so busy. I hope this is a bit of a consolation prize.'

Nova put a hand on Ines's shoulder and then returned to the main building while Ines led Nathalie onwards. Suddenly, her grandmother came to a halt and Nathalie brightened up when she realized why. Standing in the paddock a little further ahead were six horses, happily munching away on the grass. She felt her heart beat faster. She had always loved horses. They were beautiful, wild, courageous, free. Everything that she wasn't.

'Come on.'

Grandma took her hand and pulled her along until they were almost jogging. The horses raised their heads, sniffed the air and twitched their ears. Then they all turned in Ines and Nathalie's direction and half-cantered over to the fence. They eagerly offered their heads, crowding and butting each other out of the way until Ines had greeted them all by stroking their glossy muzzles.

168

'Would you like to come in?' she said, nodding towards a gate in the fence.

Nathalie's heart was pounding hard inside her ribs. She wasn't used to having horses this close – she had only ever worshipped them from afar. A small pang of fear at their size made her hesitate. Then she nodded eagerly. She trusted Grandma.

'Of course I'm coming in.'

They slipped through the gate and were instantly surrounded by enthusiastic horse faces nuzzling up to them.

'Easy now, easy,' Ines laughed, taking out carrots and chunks of apple from her jacket pockets.

'Here,' she said, handing some to Nathalie. 'Bribes are the best way to make them love you.'

Nathalie began feeding the horses as equitably as she could. One of the horses was smaller than the others, but made up for this with barefaced cheek as he pushed ahead and snatched more of the nibbles just as one of his larger comrades was about to consume them. Nathalie smiled, but it was actually a little scary – they really did seem to have gigantic teeth up close.

'This is Mascot. He's our little bandit.'

Nathalie scratched his nose and the small horse pressed himself affectionately against her. Suddenly all the emotions welled up in her at once. All the tears she had never been able to cry flooded out of her, breaching all dams. And the horses seemed to understand what was happening. They stood around her, pressing their warm bodies and soft noses against her, giving themselves and their assurance to her, letting her feel everything that she had never allowed herself to feel.

She wept tears of loss, of anger, of grief and of frustration. She wept at the unspoken questions and doors that she had never been permitted to open. Questions about her mother. Her grandmother. About who she really was.

Then she felt Ines's arms around her too. It felt strange standing there, enveloped in a fierce embrace from an unfamiliar woman amid a herd of horses. Although no . . . not strange, she decided when Mascot laid his dry muzzle against her cheek. Just the opposite, in fact. It felt as though she had come home.

After what felt like an eternity, Ines loosened her grip.

'Do we have to go back already?' said Nathalie. She wanted to stay with the horses.

'No, we're not going back,' said Ines. 'You and I are moving on.'

Something strange had happened to her voice. The gentle tone that Nathalie had accustomed herself to was gone.

'We're going to a place that only the inner circle visit,' said her grandmother.

She tugged at her blue elastic band and let it snap back against the red marks on her wrist as she looked Nathalie in the eyes.

'Make sure you have all your things. I don't know if you'll be coming back here.'

Despite the heat of summer, despite the love radiating from the horses, Nathalie suddenly felt cold.

53

They strolled through Rålambshov Park. The last time they'd been there it had been blanketed in snow and Vincent had explained the bullet catch to her. Now the sun was shining as if it wanted to scorch the earth. The odd picnic had been laid out in the slightly cooler shade beneath the trees.

They followed the shoreline towards the jetties. Last time, there had been no boats there, but now the hulls were crowding up to the jetties like white leaves on a tree branch. Mina wondered whether Vincent had a boat. It was probably a motor-boat if he did. She had a very hard time imagining him sheeting home and folding up sails. She realized that he still hadn't asked her anything about Nathalie. He was clearly waiting for her to speak. There was so much she wanted to ask him: things that had nothing whatsoever to do with Nathalie. Like why he hadn't been in touch. How he'd been getting on. She wanted to tell him how she'd been doing. But she didn't know where to start.

Instead, she took a deep breath and began to talk about Nathalie before she lost the courage to do even that.

'I was contacted by Nathalie's father yesterday morning,' she said. 'She lives with him on a full-time basis. Neither I nor my mother have any contact with them. But last Friday, my mother contacted Nathalie and she's been with her grandmother since then.'

'And you're telling me this because . . . ?'

'I assume you know who Nova is?' she said.

Vincent raised his eyebrows and nodded.

'Very much so,' he said. 'As a matter of fact, she was on—'

'I met her this morning,' she interrupted. 'My mother lives at a residential training centre that Nova runs. Apparently they work together. Nathalie's there right now. Her father was out of his mind when she disappeared, and I had to try and calm him down. But at the same time, I don't know whether I ought to be worrying myself.'

Vincent suddenly laughed.

Mina frowned. It wasn't quite the reaction she had been anticipating. But at the same time, laughter was good. Far better than the alternative.

'Nova was on TV last Friday,' he said. 'And in the taxi on my way here I was actually reading up on Epicura. Now you're talking about them too. What are the odds of that?'

'Shouldn't the Master Mentalist be able to figure that out?' she said. 'Maybe it's just because this Nova woman seems to be all over the place these days. Whether she's welcome or not.'

'Nathalie's grandmother, you said . . .' Vincent continued. 'At least that means I wasn't seeing things last Friday. I thought there was a resemblance between the two of you, but I assumed it was all my imagination. Your mother's name is Ines, right? She was on TV too.'

There was a warm feeling in Mina's breast. No matter the reason why he hadn't been in touch, he definitely hadn't forgotten her. She had even been on his mind as recently as a couple of days ago.

'So you . . . you think about me when you're watching TV?' she said.

171

Vincent spluttered.

'Well, I . . . uh,' he stammered. 'That sounds very . . . I mean to say, when you put it like that . . . I really didn't mean . . .'

And there he was. The Vincent she remembered. Always afraid to put his foot in it since he had no grasp of what was and wasn't socially acceptable. But who still saw her so clearly.

'Calm down,' she said. 'I was kidding.'

Vincent looked too dumbfounded to answer.

'You used to be on my TV more before the CCTV I installed in your apartment broke,' he said.

'Bloody hell, Vincent! That's very creepy.'

The mentalist looked far too pleased with himself.

'Anyway,' she said. 'My mother. Those kinds of organizations bring me out in hives. Giving courses on personal development at some farm in the countryside – to me that sounds like a cult. I said as much to Nova.'

'And what did she say?'

'That it wasn't a cult. Obviously. But I'm interested in what you have to say. Because I guess you know about her – if nothing else, as a colleague. She's on the lecture circuit just like you. Should I be worried about Nathalie?'

Vincent appeared to pause for thought before he replied. The path followed a sharp bend and led them up towards the big amphitheatre in the park.

'I've bumped into Nova a few times at various lecture events, as you say,' he said. 'She has an interesting and unique angle on things, if you ask me. There are not many lecturing on philosophy these days who do. But I wouldn't say that we're acquaintances. And I know even less about Epicura.'

'OK, but you know how the human psyche functions. Better than anyone else I know. Is this something that's going to do Nathalie good?'

'As far as I know, Epicura are mostly involved in leadership training programmes. And apart from having seemingly declared their leader a guru, they don't fit the model of a classic cult. For starters, they actually engage in deprogramming people from cults. And some self-help is just that. Nathalie is still allowed to mix with others, I hope? She's allowed to go home whenever she wants? And she hasn't started giving away her possessions or aligning all her opinions with what Nova thinks? Does she seem to be under mental stress or otherwise exhausted? Tired and emotionally unstable?'

'How am I supposed to know that? Did you miss the bit where I said she lives with her father on a full-time basis? I've got no idea – we have zero contact. But we're talking about a teenager. Let's assume that tired and emotionally unstable is the default.'

They reached the amphitheatre and Vincent sat down on one of the concrete benches. He opened his bag and took out two bottles of water. He passed her one. She stared at it in her hand. She tried not to think about all the hands that had touched the bottle before it had ended up in Vincent's bag. Putting her mouth around the top of the bottle would be akin to licking the palms of twenty strangers.

Vincent rummaged around in his bag and pulled out a pack of straws. She exhaled in relief. He had remembered.

She gratefully opened the bottle of water, inserted a straw and drank the cool water. She would have preferred to pour it over her face to bring some temporary respite from the sun.

'Like any self-help movement, Epicura is probably rather intense,' Vincent said after taking a big gulp of water. 'But if Nathalie is a seeker, then there are far worse movements for her to end up in. Either Epicureanism will be for her, or she'll get bored of it. I can't see anything in their ideology that's harmful. On the other hand, she is pretty young – mentally, that is – for a movement like that, if you ask me. Your mother probably means well. But it might be worth talking to her. Why not go there? See for yourself.'

'Can't,' she said, looking down into the water bottle. 'Before this weekend, Nathalie didn't even know she had a grandmother. She still doesn't know that she has a mother.'

All of a sudden she felt weak and wanted to lean her head against Vincent's shoulder. She needed his physical support. But she and Vincent hadn't reached that point. Not yet. Maybe they could, though. But not yet. Besides, she didn't know what he made of what she'd just said.

173

Vincent stood up and looked around.

'By the way, there's one thing worth knowing about Nova. She's a hugger. Just so you know,' he said.

'Thanks very much. That information would have been useful to have a few hours ago.'

Sometimes she wondered whether she needed to get a T-shirt printed with the words *Stop! This is my body!* for her to wear when out and about. How on earth could it be so difficult for people to grasp that it wasn't OK to unceremoniously wrap your arms around people? Or even just stand too close?

'I think I still smell of her perfume,' she said.

Vincent leaned in as if he were going to sniff her, but he seemed to think better of it and took a step backwards instead.

'I really like this park,' he said all of a sudden. 'Did you know it was one of the first functionalist parks in Stockholm? It was designed from the very beginning with a focus on how people would actually use it, rather than trying to make it as beautiful as possible. Before long, everyone was drawing their designs that way – so much so that they began to refer to it as the Stockholm style in architectural circles. But Erik Glemme and Holger Blom did it first with this park, back in the 1930s. An outdoor theatre cast in concrete. Paths laid out where the desire lines would have occurred naturally. And completely flat. Look over there.'

'And that's connected to Epicura how?' she said, while looking in the direction he was pointing.

A short distance away, some topless lads were playing a rag-tag football match.

'You couldn't do that if there were loads of trees, bushes or hills in the way,' Vincent said with satisfaction. Apparently the conversation about Epicura was forgotten for the time being. The mentalist had retreated into his own headspace, as he had done so often in the past.

She couldn't help smiling. She remembered this Vincent too. The man who didn't realize that you could have too much information. She watched him without the slightest intention of interrupting.

'Who said parks couldn't be practical?' Vincent added. 'Anyway, there are some crazy statues here.'

'You leapt from Nova to statues via park architecture in ten seconds flat,' she said. 'Just so you know. That must be a record, even by your standards. What statues?'

'Come on.'

Vincent began to head towards the footballers. She had no choice but to follow.

On the grass there was indeed a large bronze statue. It was probably in excess of three metres tall. Yet she hadn't given it a moment's thought until now. She shaded her eyes with her hand to take it all in. It looked like a sharp pair of scissors driven into the ground, with an axe in place of handles. Or, she assumed, a being with two stylised legs and an axe for a head.

'There are more, but this one is my favourite,' said Vincent. 'It's called "Monument to an Axeman". The artist, Eric Grate, seems to have been his own man. He also made a sculpture for the Karolinska Hospital which was so controversial that at first they refused to take it – but it did end up next to the main entrance later on. This one is still an enigma. No one really knows what he was trying to say, but the theory goes that it alludes to a pagan lifestyle. See the phallus in the middle? Some believe the statue is a prayer to the goddess of fertility.'

Vincent looked up towards the axe head and seemed to lose himself in the reflections of the sun in the bronze. Mina could tell that he wasn't finished. But this was a jumble, even for Vincent. She suspected this was all a way of trying to talk about something else. About something he hadn't yet found the right words for. She waited. But nothing came.

'The goddess of fertility, you say?' she said.

Vincent nodded without taking his gaze away from the statue.

'I think Maria's having an affair,' he said.

She didn't know what she'd been expecting to hear, but it definitely hadn't been that.

'With Kevin,' he continued. 'A man who's helping her start her business.'

A brief laugh, almost a yap, escaped from Mina's lips before she could stop it.

'Sorry,' she said. 'Kevin? That sounds like a tennis coach.'

Vincent didn't smile.

'Do you want me to check him out?' she said. 'I don't know what I can do, but—'

'No, definitely not,' Vincent said, locking his gaze to hers. 'I don't want to know a thing. Are we done with the statue?'

Mina nodded and they began to walk through the park again.

'Why don't you want to know?' she said, sipping through her straw.

Vincent shrugged. Despite the scorching heat, she liked walking with him there. She could pretend that they were there for reasons more pleasant than the fact that her house of cards carefully built over the last decade was tumbling down and that Vincent was losing his wife.

'If she's having an affair then it'll result in one of two things,' he said. 'Either it's a springboard out of our relationship and she'll leave me for him. In that case I'll find out about the affair when that happens. Obviously I'll feel betrayed and deceived, but I won't have to feel that way for as long as I would if I'd known about it sooner. There's no need to cross my bridges early if it's going to happen anyway. Or it's that she needs the affair right now for whatever reason, but in the end it'll lead her back to our relationship. In that case it's better that I'm oblivious. The affair might strengthen our relationship from her point of view. But if I know about it then I won't be able to let it go. Which means there's a risk I'll ruin our relationship when it could in fact have been good again.'

They walked on in silence. She couldn't tell whether what Vincent had said was the most sensible thing she'd heard in a long time, or whether he was in fact significantly more emotionally challenged than she had imagined. That she was bad at letting people into her life was one thing. But Vincent sounded as if he wasn't even affected by his wife. Was it really possible to be as rational as he claimed? And if so, where did love fit into it?

'Sorry if I'm sticking my nose into something that's none of my business,' she said. 'But don't you at least want to know whether she's that kind of person? One who might have an affair, I mean?'

They had almost reached the Lilla Västerbron bridge. The

skate park beneath it was full of skateboarders. Wheels were rattling loudly on the concrete and mingling with hip-hop booming from several speakers. They grimaced at each other, turned around and began to walk back towards the corner of the park, where they had entered.

'Do you know what?' said Vincent. 'I think most people are capable of most things. It's all about which point in time we are at. We're not static people. Most of your cells are replaced on a regular basis. Just three weeks ago, you had a completely different layer of skin to the one you have today. Your brain forms new cells every three months. In purely physical terms, you're not the same person today that you were five years ago, or that you will be in a few months' time. It's the same with opinions, values and thoughts. The Mina you are today is capable of things that the Mina of five years ago wouldn't have been able to do.'

Like jumping into a big container filled with minks, she thought to herself. Not that she ever intended to repeat that act of bravado. But she understood his point.

'In all probability, at least one of all the versions of Maria that I'm going to be married to will also be one who is capable of having an affair,' he continued. 'But I've nothing to gain from knowing whether that's the version she is right now. The next version of Maria might not be. Or perhaps she isn't capable of it at present, but the next Maria might be one that chooses to live with someone else. Do you understand? The only thing I can know anything about is the Maria in the here and now. But that's largely not of interest since I'm going to spend the rest of my life with different editions of future Maria.'

'That's quite . . . something,' said Mina. 'So you're sure that all that stuff about you not caring isn't just because it would feel kind of good if she had an affair with Kevin, given what you got up to with your ex-wife Ulrika at the Gondolen restaurant a couple of summers back?'

Vincent paled.

'I really hope that Maria's possible affair is less vengeful than that. But sure. I'm definitely short of brownie points.'

They reached the end of the park and began to walk back towards police headquarters. Mina's water bottle was empty and she threw it into a bin. Maybe she should tell Vincent about Amir, given how honest he'd been about Maria. At the same time, she was nervous at the mere thought of telling him, even though he had no business holding views on it. But she wanted him to know. 'Apropos Mina today not being the same Mina as before,' she said, clearing her throat. 'You won't believe this. But I'm going on a date.'

She felt him stiffen at her side. Only for a moment.

'Who's the lucky person?' he said.

'His name's Amir. He's a lawyer. I don't know much more than that. We chatted and then . . . Well, I don't really know what happened. But we're meeting up.'

It was hotter on the street than it had been down in the park. The heat was bouncing off the walls and the air was shimmering above the asphalt.

'You know the *fovea centralis* – the focal point of the eye?' Vincent said. 'It gathers data from a pretty limited field. So in order to see something like the buildings across the street, your point of focus is constantly shifting. As if it's looking at all the pieces in a jigsaw, one at a time. Then your brain puts the jigsaw together. But your eye won't have had time to see all the pieces, so your brain "colours in" the rest by itself. A lot of what you can see of those buildings is just your brain making the assumption that they look like that.'

Yet again, Vincent's brain had galloped off in a completely unpredictable direction. In a way, she could understand Maria's actions. Kevin was probably a lot easier to talk to. But he was probably a lot duller.

'Did you just change the topic of conversation again?' she said. 'Smooth work, Vincent. Didn't we talk about you doing your socialization exercises?'

'No, obviously I'm talking about your date,' he said. 'You see, when we look at someone's face, it works the same way. The focal point moves in a triangle between the other person's eyes and the tip of their nose in order to take in the whole face. But when we start to get attracted to someone, we also become interested in, erm, there's no nice way of putting this, but . . . swollen, moist body parts. You know . . .'

178

She glanced at the mentalist, who suddenly seemed very interested in some invisible dirt under his fingernails.

'Vincent, are you blushing?'

'Anyway,' he said, clearing his throat. 'The lips happen to be one such body part. Especially if they're as red as yours. Or, well, anyway, if . . . it was Amir, right? If Amir is attracted to you, you'll be able to tell if his gaze starts to move from your eyes down to your mouth instead of your nose. The mouth becomes an erotic, ahem, well—'

'Wow Vincent, way too much information!' she said, taking a step away from him in mock horror. 'Anyway, it's not a date. Not for real. We're meeting at the Museum of Mediterranean and Near Eastern Antiquities. In the daytime.'

They were approaching police headquarters. The pictures of Lilly and Ossian were awaiting her inside. But she wouldn't get anywhere with those. She wished she had stayed in the park with Vincent to talk more about the statues.

Vincent had booked a taxi using an app on his phone and the car was waiting for them outside the main entrance. She watched silently as he opened the nearside back door. No contact at all in almost two years – not even a text message. Now it was as if all those months hadn't existed. As if she and Vincent had always been hanging out. She was pleased he was back. Very, very pleased. Yet at the same time, he was already leaving. He hadn't answered her questions and she needed to get back to work. But she didn't want it to be over. Not yet. She desperately tried to think of a reason to detain him, but nothing came to mind.

'I'll do a bit more looking into Epicura if you like,' he said. 'It can't do any harm. And I think you should probably have a chat with Nathalie one way or another. I'm not exactly sure that their leadership courses are suitable for teenagers. And Mina . . .'

He turned towards her and raised an eyebrow.

'*Fovea centralis*,' he said. 'That's all I'm going to say.'

'Weren't you supposed to be on your way home?' she said, crossing her arms.

Vincent laughed, jumped into the car and closed the door

before the taxi pulled away. She watched the vehicle until it had turned the corner and was gone. A piece of her disappeared with it. She should have asked him to stay. Not for any particular reason.

Just to stay.

But she hadn't. Of course, he was right about Nathalie. If her daughter didn't return from the farm before the weekend, then Mina would go out there and pick her up and risk the wrath of Nathalie's father. If he had a problem with that, then he'd just have to go there himself before she did. After all, Nathalie was on her summer holidays, and Mina trusted her mother enough to leave them alone for another few days. She had other things to think about.

'*Fovea centralis*,' she said to herself with a shiver.

Dates . . . such a bloody stupid invention.

54

The atmosphere in the conference room was no better towards the end of the day than it had been over the weekend. Furthermore, the room was – if it were possible – even hotter.

Mina's thoughts were still revolving around her encounter with Vincent. The feeling it had left in her was both familiar and a little unsettling. She had assumed that he would be the same as before, but he had been the one who had pointed out that all people were in a constant state of flux. Perhaps the new Vincent wasn't someone who understood her as well as the old one had in the past? Perhaps he was someone she didn't really understand? Not that it had felt that way. It had felt just like it had in the past. Almost. She hoped the same was true for him.

'Listen up,' said Julia, fanning herself with her hands. 'I know you're all tired. The weekend has left us all knackered, and I've spent the best part of today keeping the media at arm's length. So far, they're still occupied with the success story about the girl we found last Friday. But they're like bloodhounds that have picked up a scent. And the golden rule of journalism is that everything that is praised must then be criticized. They're building us up to tear us down. It's only a matter of time before they catch wind of the fact that Ossian has been found dead – and that we have no leads to go on. If the media had got their way in the Lilly case, quite a few cops would have been shown the door instantly. Luckily, it's not up to the journos.'

Bosse was eating greedily from a shiny new metal bowl in the corner of the room. Julia had kept her promise. Mina did her best not to watch the way the dog was slopping the food all over the place with his fleshy tongue and the way that strands of fur kept coming loose from his coat and floating through the air. Surely it wouldn't be long before Christer set up a basket in the conference room for the dog to sleep in . . .

'That being said: we can't afford to make any mistakes. This time we're going to find the person or persons responsible. Pending the autopsy report, we need to go over every detail around Lilly Meyer's death again. We'll start with close relatives. They're probably sick of the police, but we've no choice. Peder and I have already spoken to the mother. It was . . . quite an experience. She's sticking to the same story she told at the trial: it was Lilly's father Mauro who killed her. Mina and Ruben, speak to him. He was away over the weekend, but he's due back this evening. Make sure the first thing you do on Tuesday morning is to interview him. Tomorrow, that is.'

'And what about me?' said Christer.

'The sex offenders register,' Julia said quickly. 'No – we need to follow up on the description of Lilly's kidnappers. The elderly couple that someone claims to have seen in proximity to the nursery. That's your task. But after that you're back to checking the database. After all, someone has to.'

Christer had begun to look a little more chipper, but now he returned to his gloomy self.

'I think we need some endorphins in this room,' said Peder. 'So that we can do our jobs better.'

A bright and tinny melody began to play from the phone in his hand.

'This is the triplets singing along to Anis—'

'We know!' Ruben roared, slamming the palm of his hand against the table. 'But Melodifestivalen was five months ago! Five. Whole. Months. We've had that video in our lives ever since. When are you going to pack it in?'

Peder looked down at the table shamefacedly.

'I just wanted to rally the troops,' he said quietly.

'And what an exemplary effort it was,' said Julia. 'Anything that can make our job easier is welcome. Except perhaps those things that actually elevate the stress hormones in here. How about we hold off with the triplets and only break them out when we *really* need them?'

Peder nodded, a little happier.

'Now where was I?' said Julia. 'Oh yes. In addition to taking a closer look at Lilly Meyer, we may also need to expand our horizons when it comes to possible perpetrators. Given that the descriptions of the kidnappers are so different, it's tempting to think that the cases are unrelated. But there are too many similarities for me to believe that. Adam pointed it out from the very beginning, and following Saturday's discovery I'm inclined to agree. The two children are the same age, they were snatched in broad daylight without anyone reacting, they were both missing for seventy-two hours and they were then found dead without any visible injuries to their bodies. That can't be coincidence. But the assumption that there are therefore at least three people behind the two kidnappings gives rise to new questions about who they are and what their motives are. I can't think of another case like this. So we need to find out more. Adam?'

Adam cleared his throat and everyone turned towards him.

'As you may know, there's currently no criminal psychologist based at police headquarters,' he said. 'Not since Jan Bergsvik left us . . .'

'Was let go,' Ruben interjected under cover of a feigned coughing fit.

'. . . chose to resign,' Adam continued, albeit with a hint of a smile on his lips. 'So I've taken the liberty of contacting an expert in extreme behaviour. Because no matter whether we're dealing with the same perpetrators or different ones, I can't classify this behaviour as anything other than extreme. With a little luck, this expert may be able to help us understand how the people we're after are wired. The way they think.'

'Why don't we call Vincent?' Mina said eagerly. 'If we're bringing in an external consultant anyway?'

Adam couldn't just bring in any old person. Not when they could use Vincent.

'Who?' said Adam, looking puzzled.

'Vincent Walder,' said Julia. 'He assisted us on a case some time ago – it transpired that it involved his sister.'

Adam whistled between his teeth.

'Oh *him*. Yes, I remember.'

'To answer your question, Mina,' said Julia, 'Adam has already initiated contact. Why don't we see what this expert can offer us before we go to Walder. Vincent is good, but everything ends up being much more . . . unusual . . . when he's involved.'

Mina nodded but didn't agree one bit. She had let go of Vincent and had regretted it every second since. Besides, he had saved her life. She could hardly say the same thing about whoever it was that Adam had invited.

'What's more, my contact is an expert in group behaviour – especially in extreme forms,' said Adam.

'Group behaviour?' said Peder.

'Yes, this is a new idea,' Adam said, nodding, 'but I want to run it by you. So far, we've been assuming that the murder of Ossian was carried out by the same person who murdered Lilly, or by someone imitating that first killing. A copycat. But I have a third proposal, which would better explain why we have such differing descriptions of the kidnappers while we have murders that are verging on identical in their execution.'

Adam paused and looked at them. The only thing audible was Bosse's panting.

'We may be dealing with an organized group of people,' said Adam. 'I believe our kidnappers know each other.'

No one said anything. It was a terrible thought. And yet, as Adam had said, it was a good explanation.

'As I keep saying,' said Julia, 'we can't rule anything out. And this is undeniably an interesting line of inquiry.'

183

'I just wanted to mention it so that you could ask my expert about that too,' Adam said. 'She's actually been in the media quite a bit lately, so most of you probably already know who she is. I was lucky to catch her when she had a gap in her schedule – she'll be here on Wednesday morning. Her name is Jessica Wennhagen, but she's better known as Nova.'

Mina stared at Adam. It couldn't be possible.

55

Nathalie didn't understand where they were going. Grandma hadn't provided any further explanation. She had merely led Nathalie to a car parked behind the paddock. She had thought the place her grandmother had mentioned would be nearby, but they had been driving for at least half an hour. The man at the wheel was called Karl. He was tall and blond, with a dazzling smile, and he radiated the same calm possessed by everyone else she had encountered at Epicura. It made her jealous.

She wanted to feel that at ease too. She didn't want an over-protective father, a grandmother she hadn't known about and friends who were driven around the bend by what others thought of them.

But surely that Karl guy had troubles in his life or things that irritated him? If he did, it wasn't noticeable from his demeanour. Indeed, despite her hunger, the atmosphere at Epicura had begun to rub off on her. Over the last few days, she had felt calmer and happier than she had in a long time.

'So what's this inner circle you're talking about?' she said to Grandma, who was sitting in the front passenger seat.

Before her grandmother had time to reply, the woman sitting beside Nathalie on the back seat interjected.

'What Nova teaches at Epicura is only the first step,' she said. 'And for the people who visit to participate in her courses, that's enough. But if you really want to understand John Wennhagen's legacy, it takes more than that. Ines is giving you a true gift of love by initiating you now. It usually takes many years to reach the inner circle. I'm Monica, by the way.'

'John Wennhagen?' said Nathalie. 'I don't understand. Wasn't Nova's grandfather called Baltzar?'

Ines turned around in her seat and looked at Nathalie. Her gaze was full of secrets, but also promises. 'John was Nova's father,' she said. 'The only one who really understood. It's him we follow.'

They were driving down a narrow forest track. The trees whipped past, and the rays of the sun flickered uncertainly between the trunks. Further ahead, Nathalie glimpsed a large building. She suddenly realized that no one knew where she was. She had no idea. Not even her father did.

'Everything is suffering; pain purifies,' said her grandmother from the passenger seat, as she snapped the elastic band at her wrist.

'Everything is suffering; pain purifies,' Karl and Monica murmured in unison.

56

'Have you . . . Have you found anything else? About Lilly?' The manager of Nyckelpigan nursery anxiously sought out Christer's gaze. 'Because that's why you're here, right? I know it's been a year, but I thought . . . We haven't given up hope of getting an answer. Or . . . is it about the boy?'

Christer held off answering. That was one of the tough parts of this job – not being able to give the people he met the answers they needed. Lilly's disappearance was still an open wound for the nursery – for all its staff and the children enrolled there. Not to mention the parents. He understood that. No one was untouched. And everyone wanted answers to what had happened. Answers that he still couldn't give them. He just had more questions to ask.

'I'm afraid I can't comment on ongoing investigations,' he said, taking the coward's way out. 'But maybe we could talk somewhere a little more private?'

The stock reply. Stiff, impersonal and keeping a clear distance from whoever he was talking to.

'We'll be fine here. The kids are busy – no one will be able to hear us. And I've got to help keep an eye on things – we need all hands on deck when we're outside.'

The manager was called Johanna, and she kept surveying the child-filled playground outside the nursery with anxious eyes.

'Did the same people who took Lilly take the boy?' she said. 'I can't . . .'

Christer's words trailed off. Bosse was running about like a boisterous puppy among the happy children. Christer had initially tied him up outside, but when the kids had flocked over to the fence a member of staff had asked whether the dog was allowed to come in and say hello. Bosse's joy had known no bounds. He loved everyone, but especially children.

'As I said, I'm eager to talk to the teachers who were working on the day Lilly went missing. Sometimes the memory is a strange thing – for some, it can become clearer with time rather than weaker. We . . . we don't want to leave anything to chance.'

'I'll call them over.' Johanna nodded, standing up from the bench they were sitting on. 'Although we refer to them as educators.'

'Leopold! Aysha!'

A young man and an older woman turned around and came towards them. Their tense body language divulged that they already knew what it was about. In the distance, a child wailed loudly and angrily, grabbed a fistful of sand and threw it in the face of the boy next to them. An educator quickly arrived on the scene to sort things out. The children were already playing nicely with each other again by the time Leopold and Aysha reached Johanna and Christer.

If only things could always be that simple in his world.

186

He greeted them and they sat down on the bench next to him. Johanna excused herself and left them to talk alone.

'Is it about Lilly?' asked the older woman.

'Did the same couple take that boy?' asked the younger man, keeping a watchful eye on the children.

'I can't comment on that,' Christer said for the second time in close succession.

Bosse came over to say a brief hello and Christer scratched him behind the ears before the dog – panting, his tongue hanging from his mouth – ran back to his new friends.

'Your dog is a hit,' said Aysha, her warm brown eyes smiling.

A girl came over to her and Aysha helped her put her sunhat back in place on her head.

'You must be exhausted by this point in the day,' said Christer, contemplating the ocean of children who all seemed to be running in different directions, and at a volume that made his eardrums quail.

'Yes and no. It's intense, but it's fun,' said Leopold, leaning back on the bench.

'What do you remember about the day Lilly disappeared?'

Christer dropped the small talk and got straight to the point. He had no time to lose.

'It was just a normal day. Nothing out of the ordinary. There was nothing that made us sit up and take notice. Both Aysha and me saw the couple passing, but didn't give it a second thought. They looked normal.'

'A completely normal older couple.' She nodded. 'Both had grey hair. His was short, hers was in one of those . . . modish pageboy cuts. If you know what I mean.'

'And glasses,' Leopold added.

A little boy wearing oversized shorts fell face first onto the ground right in front of Christer and began bawling. Leopold quickly reached him and lifted him up to comfort him, brushing the gravel off him and sending the boy off to play when he had calmed down.

'Nothing that stood out?' said Christer.

So far, nothing had come up that he hadn't already read about in the report.

'No, they just looked like . . . any old grandparents. We see plenty of them around here. There was nothing out of the ordinary about them. Nothing at all. And we didn't see the abduction itself. When we couldn't find Lilly, a few of the kids thought they'd seen the man and lady take her. But you know what kids are like.'

'How did you know they meant the same couple you'd seen earlier?'

'The kids described a purple coat,' said Aysha. 'And the woman Leopold and I saw was wearing one. So we assumed it was the same person. It's not a very common colour.'

'And you hadn't seen them before? Not with Lilly, or any of the other children? Or around here in general?'

Both shook their heads.

'Obviously I can't say for certain,' said Leopold, 'but not that I can recall.'

'Same here,' said Aysha.

Christer mused. It had been a long shot. Leopold, Aysha and the rest of the staff had been questioned extensively at the time of the disappearance. As had several of the children.

'OK, I'll get out of your hair,' he said, standing up.

His joints creaked and the summer heat had plastered his trousers to his thighs. He whistled to Bosse, who initially pretended not to hear. But after a few more whistles and a sharp reprimand, the dog reluctantly loped towards him with a column of rowdy children trailing behind him.

'Don't go home, doggie,' said a little girl with blond pigtails wearing a top with a princess in a blizzard of snowflakes on it.

'Sorry, the doggie has to go home, we've got work to do,' said Christer, putting Bosse back on his lead.

At first, the dog refused to budge and four children clung to him, their arms around him. Bosse's eyes were large and pleading.

'No, we have to go now.' Christer tugged at the lead again and this time Bosse reluctantly dragged his paws towards the exit, kids still clinging to his golden fur.

'You'll have to let go of the doggie now – he has to go home,' Christer said awkwardly.

From the corner of his eye, he could see Leopold and Aysha watching him in amusement. He continued to pull at the lead and, once Bosse finally upped his pace, the children were forced to let go. When they got beyond the gate, Bosse turned around longingly for one final look before jumping forlornly into the car.

57

'Mina speaking.' All the display said was *number withheld*. But she had picked up nonetheless in the hope that it wouldn't be who she thought it was.

'It's me,' said a man's voice.

Mina sighed. Of course it was him. Who else would call her in the evening?

'Have you got hold of her?' Nathalie's father continued. 'And what on earth is that sound?'

'The air conditioning. And I've been calling but haven't spoken to her yet.'

'That settles it. It's now Monday evening. She's still not home. I'll send someone to pick her up. This is unacceptable.'

Mina forced herself to take a few deep breaths before answering.

'Please don't do that,' she said, trying to sound more confident than she was.

Just for a moment, it felt like he was there – in her apartment. As if he were penetrating the pure oasis she had created. The apartment was her shield, her defence, her armour. But he could get in anywhere he wanted to. It had always been that way.

He was silent, waiting for her explanation.

What was she supposed to say? That Nathalie had always meant more than the whole world to her? That even when things had been at their worst – when she had been at her sickest – it

189

had been the thought of Nathalie that had made her cope? That their agreement that she would leave the family for Nathalie's sake had almost killed her? She knew that no words would help. She was an adult and responsible for her own actions. But for goodness' sake . . . she had been ill. If only he could at least understand that.

'I know I can't tell you what to do,' she said, lowering her voice. 'Or how you should handle this. I know I gave up that right. But this time you came to me. You asked me for help. So give me some time. I think it might cause a lot of damage if you barge in right now. And Nathalie has the right to ask questions. She has a right to want to know. She needs time. We're the ones who have chosen to conceal the truth – she hasn't chosen to live a lie. So please don't do anything rash. Give me a chance to sort this out first. And even if you don't trust me, perhaps you can trust Nathalie.'

His breathing was heavy at the other end of the line, as it always was when he was engaged in deep thought. She knew he had just drawn up two columns in his head. One for. One against. The heavy breathing revealed how carefully he was weighing them up against each other. It surprised her how well she still knew him. How familiar the unspoken elements still were to her.

'Have it your way,' he said eventually. 'I'll hold off.'

'Thank you.'

Mina slumped back against the sofa cushions in relief.

He was silent. She considered whether to say anything else. Feelings of guilt pressed her to say something – anything. Something that would make him understand. Even if it was too little and much too late. The moment came and went. He hung up.

She frowned at the television and tried to make sense of the programme she'd been watching before her mobile had rung. Not that she could hear what they were saying, given the racket from the two large air conditioning units she'd invested in. One in the living room and one in the bedroom. They blew cold air into the rooms while feeding warm air out through a thick hose she had jammed through a crack in the window. The result was

190

that her apartment was the only place she didn't sweat. She loved it. However, it came at a cost: she could barely hear herself think.

The participants on the show were gallivanting around in couples and smiling nervously at the camera without managing to retain even the slightest shred of her interest. People who had been paired up by experts and only met for the first time at the altar.

Good God. Society's obsessive desire to put people together, two by two. It was too much . . . As if solitariness was an illness that had to be eradicated at all costs – but within a very narrow framework. Was it in the Bible that the universal truth that coupledom was the norm had been established? Had it all begun with Adam and Eve and the animals going aboard Noah's Ark two by two? Nowadays, the ark of the people was called Tinder. An app where people desperately clung to the hope that they wouldn't drown in loneliness. As if it were dangerous.

Yet the story of Adam and Eve also exposed the shortcomings in the logic of being paired up. There was always a snake in paradise. She wondered how many of the couples on TV had managed to stay together until the episode featuring them was broadcast. None of them, she guessed, based on the frosty atmosphere between most of them. Love couldn't be created out of logic. There was no mathematical love code to be cracked. It was one of the few things she knew about love.

She wondered what Vincent would have to say about the matter. A great deal, she thought. Probably explained with the occasional diagram. She so dearly wished they were bringing him in to assist with the case, rather than Nova. Especially considering the situation with Nathalie. Things might get messy. Mina had quite enough Nova in her life already.

They should have gone with Vincent.

She changed the channel to a show with celebrities competing against each other in a quiz. Much better.

Vincent.

He'd managed to get inside too – into her fortress. But that had been different. She had been the one who had let him in. Her choice. And he had understood. He had let her be who she needed to be. It had felt . . . good when Vincent was here. And it had felt good when they had met in the park. Maybe a little too good. Because she knew what could happen. It was better this way. On her own in her fortress. Alone.

To be alone was to be strong.

58

Vincent supported himself against the tree with one hand. In his other, he had a stick he'd found on the ground which he was using to try to scrape mud off his shoe. Given that it hadn't rained in weeks, the summer heat really should have dried the forest out. In fact, it should have been a fire hazard. But Vincent had obviously managed to find what was probably the only marsh left in the region and stepped straight into it.

Luckily, he had chosen a pair of trainers instead of the leather shoes he usually opted for. They would most certainly not have survived. But maybe white trainers hadn't been the best idea.

The plan was to take a morning stroll through the woods to get some fresh air and room to think. Given that he'd made his home more or less in the middle of the forest, he spent outrageously little time in it. But it was never too late to start. Admittedly, he did miss being able to observe other people while in the woods, which was something he could do when walking around town, but there was psychological and biomedical research that showed that being immersed in nature reduced both people's stress hormones and their blood pressure. Nowadays, forest therapy was a thing. And if there was one thing he needed after the events of the day before, it was to calm down. To regain control.

Which was why he was standing here, leaning against the tree, giving the forest a chance. And it really was beautiful. Charming. It was just he couldn't concentrate properly.

Because he had met Mina.

A day ago.

Mina with her black hair, Mina with her gaze that indicated she understood more than she was letting on, Mina who was always on the edge of the world and loved her daughter.

And after all that waiting, she had been the one who had called. She who wanted to talk to him. In retrospect, he was ashamed that he hadn't contacted her. Exactly what had he been thinking? That she would be different? That she wouldn't want to talk to him? He could have called her long ago. He should have called.

Although it had probably been silly to bring up that business with Kevin. That wasn't something Mina needed to concern herself with. But she had confided in him and told him about her family – he had wanted to reciprocate in some way.

And then they had parted ways.

No 'see you soon' or anything like that.

Granted, he had managed to proffer a lame promise to look into Epicura some more, but he didn't expect to find anything. And without anything to say, he had no reason to get in touch. Shit.

He managed to remove the last of the mud from his shoe and straightened up. What on earth was this dark thought loop he'd got stuck in? This would not do. He wasn't going to make the same mistake as last time. Just because they hadn't scheduled an appointment in the diary didn't mean that he couldn't get in touch . . . They were friends, for goodness' sake. And friends called each other. He pulled out his phone and called Mina's number.

As he waited for her to pick up, a squirrel bounded into view and came to a halt when it spotted him. It eyed him up from head to toe – probably trying to decide whether he was a threat or not. Then it plucked up courage, seemed to decide to take its chances and scurried up the tree right next to him, so nervous that it was shaking, just as Vincent's call connected. He knew exactly how the squirrel felt.

59

Mina angled the phone away from Ruben so that he wouldn't see the screen. She'd have preferred he didn't know who was calling.

'Aren't you going to get that?' Ruben said from his position in the driver's seat. 'I'll end up driving into a ditch if it keeps ringing like that. At least put it on silent.'

He pulled into a residential area in Upplands Väsby.

'Wait,' she said, inserting a pair of wiped-down earbuds into her ears before answering. 'Mina speaking.'

She tried to sound as neutral as she could.

'Hi Mina, it's Vincent.'

Silence. It was hard to make it out over the rumble of the road, but she thought she heard the twittering of birds in the background.

'I just wanted . . .' he said, before falling silent again. 'Is everything OK? About the thing that we talked about?'

She was tempted to ask him what he was referring to. That she was in the middle of an investigation going nowhere? Or that Nathalie still hadn't returned from her grandmother and that Mina was still terrified of what she would find out?

Things were most definitely not OK, but they did feel a little better now. Obviously she couldn't say *that*. Not while she had company in the car.

Ruben stopped outside a white terraced house and turned off the engine. Then he looked at Mina, his eyebrows telegraphing a question. She nodded and pointed to her phone.

'I can't really talk right now,' she said. 'We're about to interview a relative. But I'd really like to . . . discuss that more a little later. Can I call you back?'

She hoped Vincent understood why she sounded so formal. That it wasn't about him.

He was silent again for a while. 'I really just wanted to say hello,' he said. It sounded as if he was smiling. 'It was . . . nice

. . . to see you yesterday. And in case you need to google it, there's an S on the end of fovea centralis.'

She coughed as Vincent hung up. Fortunately, Ruben had already got out of the car.

She got out to join him just as Mauro Meyer emerged from the front door of the house.

'Hello there,' he said, shaking their hands. 'I gather you've already spoken to Lilly's mother, so I've a good idea of what she's said about me. But believe me, the only crime I'm guilty of is falling in love with someone else.'

He pushed aside a tricycle in the hallway so that they could come in. The house showed clear signs of being inhabited by a family with young children. There was also a glass-fronted cabinet in the hall filled with plaques and trophies.

'I was very active in my youth,' said Mauro, when he saw what Mina was looking at. 'Everything from riding to fencing. But that was before I met Jenny. She mostly thought I was pretentious. I think she was probably right. Come on, let's go into the back garden.'

He took them straight through the house to the back, where a lovely wooden deck afforded views over the small but well-tended garden. A little boy was splashing about in an inflatable paddling pool beside a heavily pregnant woman who had her feet in a tub of water. Mauro introduced her as his wife Cecilia.

Mina and Ruben sat down in the pleasant shade cast by an awning and accepted the offer of coffee. It had already been prepared and was awaiting them in a thermos. Privately, Mina would have preferred to have something cold.

'Excuse me not coming over to say hello,' Cecilia called out. 'My feet are about ready to explode if I don't cool them down.'

'We've seen it all before,' Ruben said, smiling. 'A colleague of ours had triplets almost three years ago.'

'Good grief, triplets!' Mauro said, horrified, as he sat down with them after fetching a carton of oat milk which he placed on the table. 'How do you survive that?'

'I think he died and became a zombie,' said Ruben. 'But it can't be easy having two so close together either . . .'

Mina found herself staring at Ruben. He was not only being

195

nice, he was talking about children. And it didn't seem in the slightest bit feigned. The fact that Cecilia was sitting right there in her bikini should have had him out of his senses, even if she was pregnant. But he seemed to have barely noticed her. Mina only hoped this wasn't the sign of a nascent illness or anything like that. They needed every hand on deck right now.

'Two?' Mauro chuckled. 'That's only half the pack. We've got another two. Cecilia has a seven-year-old and a five-year-old from before. But they're playing at a neighbour's house right now.'

'Shall we talk about why we're here?' said Mina.

She was beginning to tire of all the kid talk, no matter how well Ruben was forging a connection with Lilly's father and stepmother.

'Well, to be honest we were surprised when you called. What do you want to know?'

Mauro held out his hands and exchanged glances with his wife.

'Two of our colleagues spoke to your ex-wife Jenny yesterday. She still claims you were involved in the death of your daughter.'

'You don't beat about the bush, do you?' said Mauro, taking a sip of coffee. 'But that's right,' he added. 'Jenny has made it her life's work to punish me. Yes, I met Cecilia when I was still married to Jenny. I admit that. I own a construction business and Cecilia was working for me in the office – in fact she still does. But things had been bad between Jenny and me for a long time. She . . . she has her own issues. Which are really nothing to do with me. But it was always easiest just to make me the scapegoat. So in the end I fell in love with Cecilia. And Jenny simply couldn't let me get away with that. So she went for the point where she knew I was most vulnerable. She used our child.'

'She's been making life hell for us since day one,' said Cecilia, stroking her belly. 'She hates Mauro and his family beyond any rhyme or reason.'

'Why your family and not just you?' said Ruben, pouring some oat milk into his mug of coffee.

Mina knew Ruben didn't take his coffee white. Now he was just putting it on.

'We're very close in my family. And none of them ever liked Jenny. They always thought she was a mistake on my part. But they loved Cecilia from the word go, and they may have been a little too open about that. We've got Facebook and Instagram these days . . .'

'The worst part was when she accused him in court.' Cecilia's voice trembled and Mina understood that it was still an open wound.

'Luckily, they didn't believe her. And there was no evidence. Only her claims. And words she tried to put in Lilly's mouth after the fact.'

'I never wanted to take Lilly away from her,' said Mauro. A lock of his black hair had fallen across his brow and he brushed it back. 'I suggested shared custody. One week on, one week off. But for Jenny it's always been all or nothing. And she considered Lilly to be her possession.'

'She's ruining our lives,' Cecilia said resentfully, clenching her fists in her lap.

'I'd like nothing more than to know who took Lilly from us,' Mauro said in a tense voice. 'Because it wasn't me.'

'We don't think it was either,' said Mina. 'And that's what we want to talk to you about. You may have heard that a boy about Lilly's age went missing last week in similar circumstances to Lilly? We're looking into whether there's a connection. Do you really have no idea at all who might have taken her?'

'We said everything we knew last time,' Mauro said, looking down. 'I went to pick her up from nursery. She wasn't there. Three days later . . .'

His dark hair fell back across his forehead.

'And there's no connection between your families? Do you recognize the boys' parents?' Mina showed them a photo of Ossian's parents on her phone and shared their names. Mauro looked at the photo for a long time, but then shook his head slowly.

'No, it doesn't ring a bell. I'm afraid I can't say for sure. I'm basically face blind. But no, offhand, I'd say I don't recognize them at all.'

Mina nodded and showed the photo to Cecilia too. She also

shook her head. Mina returned the phone to her pocket. They were getting nowhere.

'Sweetie, can you get me some more ice?' Cecilia said, turning to her husband, who immediately stood up.

'Of course.'

'No thoughts on who the old couple might have been?' said Ruben.

Cecilia frowned as if she didn't quite understand.

'Ah,' she said. 'No. As far as we know, they weren't even seen near Lilly. Just in proximity to the nursery. They were probably passing by. It's still a mystery who took Mauro's daughter. I could make things easy for myself and say it was probably Jenny, but . . . no. I don't actually think it was her.'

'There were no older relatives involved emotionally or practically in the custody dispute? From Jenny's side? Or your side?' Ruben asked tentatively, but Cecilia merely shook her head.

'No, no, nothing like that. Jenny's parents are dead, and ours . . . Well, they're old and decrepit. Of course, we can give you their contact details if you'd like to check up on that yourselves.'

'I'll take those contact details, thanks,' said Ruben, but Mina's intuition told her that Cecilia was telling the truth.

Bloody hell. Dead ends everywhere they turned. Tomorrow was Wednesday – a whole week since Ossian's disappearance. And they still knew no more than they had done then. In fact, it felt as if they knew less. How could things have wound up like this? They were good detectives. She knew that. And yet they were treading water.

Mauro rummaged in the freezer and returned with a plastic tray of ice cubes. He went over to Cecilia and tapped the reverse of the tray until all the cubes tumbled into the tub with a plop.

'Ooohhh . . . that's so good . . .' she said, closing her eyes with pleasure.

He kissed her on the mouth and caressed her hair. The love between them was obvious. Mina felt a twinge of envy. Mauro would never have to pose with a big fish to get Cecilia's attention. What they had was real.

'We won't disturb you any longer,' she said, rising from her seat abruptly.

She wanted to call Vincent. She needed to hear his voice again without being forced to hang up on him. He was welcome to deliver one of his unnecessarily detailed expositions on a topic no one really wanted to know about.

To be alone wasn't to be strong at all, no matter how much she wished it was.

60

When they returned to police headquarters from Upplands Väsby, Ruben hurried to change into a freshly ironed white shirt he'd brought from home. He had deliberately refrained from shaving that morning, because he knew that his unshaven face gave him a slightly raffish appearance which in combination with his profession made him look . . . well, dangerous and exciting. While he might not actively be on the pull right now, it never did any harm to make a good first impression. And the deal with Amanda the shrink had only covered the fact that he wasn't allowed to pursue others. They hadn't discussed what was allowed if the woman approached him. If he'd happened to nudge the woman in question in the right direction, then that couldn't be helped. It was up to her, really.

His thoughts kept returning to what he had realized while visiting Granny. That Astrid must be his daughter. How on earth was he supposed to process that information?

It had to be pushed aside for the time being – they were due to meet Adam's expert in extreme group behaviour. Nova's arrival was imminent. She was probably used to attention, given her looks – that beautiful, golden complexion that might just as well come from Brazil or Asia or the USA, and that confident but friendly smile. With laughter dimples to boot. The least he could do was try to match her in style.

And hope she didn't remember him.

There had been hundreds of police officers at the lecture

she'd given them a few years ago. The risk that she'd remember him was minimal. Even though he had asked her out twice following the lecture. And then attempted to proposition her in the photocopying room. But that kind of thing was bound to happen to a woman like Nova on a daily basis.

But everything was already going tits up and she wasn't even there yet. While Adam had gone downstairs to collect her from reception, Peder had been busy laying out Danish pastries on the table. You didn't offer a woman like Nova sticky pastries – you offered her a glass of cava. Or possibly sushi balls.

'You'll get vanilla custard in your beard,' he muttered at Peder, sitting down at the table.

Ruben had timed the application of his cologne from Montblanc so that it would have merged perfectly with his natural musk when the meeting began. Until then, he would smell freshly perfumed, which was a classic rookie error. But if there were a delay before she arrived, the scent would have faded. Why was it taking so long? And why was Mina staring at him?

'Can I help you?' he snapped in a whisper that sounded less friendly than he had intended.

Mina flinched.

'I just thought you were looking nervous,' she said. 'Has something happened?'

'Nervous?' he said, aiming for a laugh. 'Me? The last time I was nervous was when I had to ask a one-night stand for ID.'

'Ruben!' Julia said, sharpness in her voice. 'For the umpteenth time, we've talked about . . . Ah! Here you are!'

Adam and Nova entered the room, interrupting the conversation. Splendid timing. Ruben's scent was perfect. And he no longer had to explain himself to Mina. He had spent the best part of a year having to fabricate new hook-up stories for Gunnar and the guys whenever they met in the canteen. He'd become so accustomed to telling tales that they sometimes came automatically, even at the wrong moments. Like now. It was probably only a matter of time before he was exposed. He was running out of material.

Not that Mina seemed to care about him any longer. Her

gaze became thunderous as soon as Nova entered the room. Typical female jealousy. Sure, Mina was good-looking in an austere sort of way. At least when you couldn't see her chapped hands. Still, it was borderline absurd for her to think she could compete with Nova's urbane elegance. Women . . . He sighed to himself and then straightened his back.

'Hello, I'm Julia Hammarsten – I head up this team,' said Julia, proffering her hand to Nova. 'You've already met Adam. The others here are Ruben, Mina, Christer and Peder.'

Ruben smiled at Nova while squinting slightly and nodding almost imperceptibly. It was an old technique that he liked to deploy in interrogation. It got the other person to relax and subconsciously feel that they understood one another – or that they shared something private. Nova nodded back politely before shifting her gaze to Peder and smiling warmly at him. Bloody hell. Apparently his charm was getting rusty. But at any rate, she seemed to recognize him. And once she was no longer looking at him, he could instead appreciatively note that she had unbuttoned the two top buttons of her white blouse. It was too bad that she was wearing a skirt – it was harder to make out the curves of her rear. On the other hand, a skirt left plenty to the imagination. Women in skirts weren't always wearing knickers. Amanda could say whatever she liked – he wasn't banned from thinking.

Nova's smile stiffened as she greeted Mina, who didn't proffer her hand despite being so close by. But then again, she almost never did. She really ought to learn some *savoir faire* and etiquette. Or just wear gloves.

'As Adam has told you, we're working on the disappearance of a little boy called Ossian,' said Julia after Nova had also greeted Christer. 'It's extremely rare for children to be abducted in this way. What's more, this kidnapping is almost completely identical to one that occurred a year ago. So it's our suspicion that there's a connection.'

'How rare is rare?' said Nova, taking a seat at the table.

She ended up across from Ruben. He had no objections to that. Come to that, she was more than welcome to undo another button. Peder pushed the plate of pastries towards her and she took one. Some crumbs were left on her lips as she bit into it, and Ruben took note of the way she licked them off with the tip of her tongue.

Suddenly she stopped herself and stared at Ruben. Her eyes widened slowly. Oh no. She hadn't forgotten after all.

'We've met before,' she said coolly. 'Anyone been helping you to do some photocopying lately?'

Ruben felt his entire face turn hot.

'No, I do it by myself these days,' he said.

Then he heard how that came across.

'I mean, that's not . . .' he said. 'I just . . . erm, we . . . Uh, forget about it.'

His colleagues looked at him in bafflement while Nova's eyes glittered with suppressed laughter. One-nil to her. And why not? He probably deserved it.

'To answer your question, Nova,' said Adam, 'hundreds of children are reported missing every year by anxious parents who don't know what's happened to them. But almost all of them come back after an hour or so. Usually they've gone to a friend's and lost track of time. What's happened in these cases is that a child has actually been abducted and killed – it's one of those crimes that all parents fear but which almost never happens. Almost never.'

'Killed?' said Nova, putting her pastry down on the table with a look of horror.

Julia nodded and then pointed questioningly to the coffee pot. Nova shook her head.

'Lilly Meyer was found last summer on a jetty in Hammarby sjöstad,' Christer said with a sigh. 'Under a tarpaulin. And we found Ossian dead under a gangway on Saturday. Honestly, what a bloody mess.'

'So you'll understand that this stuff is like catnip to the media,' said Ruben. 'For a few days, the TV news will be more like an HBO drama for Joe Bloggs sitting at home on his sofa. And everyone will be relieved that it's not *their* kid.'

Nova looked down.

'The girl who went missing last summer was found dead after seventy-two hours,' said Julia. 'And exactly the same thing

202

happened to Ossian. He was found by the *af Chapman* in Skeppsholmen after he'd been missing for seventy-two hours. We've managed to keep it all secret from the media so far, but they're likely to get wind of it at any moment. The similarity in execution may just be a coincidence. But we might also be dealing with the same person.'

Nova stared at her.

'Sorry,' she said, 'but what's my role here? I'm struggling to see how I can help – no matter how much I might want to. I don't know anything about . . . murderers.'

'The kidnapping method is identical,' Adam explained. 'But the people responsible aren't the same. We have descriptions in both cases. Lilly was taken by an older couple. Ossian was abducted by a woman in her thirties. So either Ossian's kidnapper is someone who read about last year's case and copied it. Or . . .'

'. . . or they know each other,' Nova supplemented. 'Which means it's a group of people – albeit a small one – who have no issue performing extreme acts. Now I understand.'

'Yes, and I gather you're an expert in such groups,' said Julia. 'We need to understand how people like this think.'

'The difference between them and us is sometimes smaller than you'd think,' said Nova gently, turning to the team as a whole. 'Over the years, I've built up a lot of experience of extremist groups. I suppose the most common description for them is cults. It began when a woman came to my business – her parents had been trying to break her free from a group with clear cult-like traits for a long time. She came to us reluctantly. But we managed to free her. In fact, she now works for me. And I learned a great deal from that experience. Word spread and we got an increasing number of enquiries. Now it may not be the biggest part of our operation, but it is part of it. Hopefully the knowledge I've built up over the years can help you in your work – in one way or another.'

Ruben wondered whether she was as gentle when she had sex – when that white blouse was fully open. He hoped not. Maybe he ought to ask her whether she wanted to do some photocopying after all. Then he pictured Amanda's angry face in his mind's eye and felt ashamed. But it had only been a thought. And it had actually been more than six months since he had got some. Which was five months and three weeks more than he was accustomed to.

'Anyone can get caught up in an organization or cult and commit acts they would previously never have contemplated,' Nova added. 'All these people are looking for is a context.'

'Like Manson and his "family"?' Christer said thoughtfully.

'Yes, or like the Bride of Christ and her congregation in Knutby. As it happens, I have two of Åsa Waldau's old parishioners with me at Epicura,' said Nova.

'I've heard that Åsa herself is withering away leading a forgotten existence in a tiny village somewhere with her old dad these days,' Christer muttered. 'Quite a long way from the narcissistic dreams of power and gold. Bully for her.'

'Sorry, but how did we make the sudden leap to thinking it's about a cult?' Peder said, scratching his beard. 'Surely that's not the same thing as three madmen who happen to know each other? And surely a cult is religious? Since when have the kidnappings had religious motives?'

'We don't think anything,' said Julia, fanning herself with a plastic folder. 'Right now, we're just exploring all possible leads. But surely you agree that we very rarely see a group of people commit an act like this together with an interval of a year in between? I don't think they're mad. Their actions are too meticulous for that. Which brings us back to Nova's expertise in extreme behaviour.'

'The thing about cults and religion is a common misconception,' said Nova.

Ruben could see that she'd entered unambiguous work mode. The photocopying room was off the cards then.

'A cult can be focused on just about anything,' she continued. 'There are researchers who have shown the similarities between religious cults, political movements and totalitarian ideas as a whole. What unites them are certain, extreme patterns of thought. Sure, there's always a form of worship in a cult. But that could just as well be addressed to the president of the nation as to a god. Donald Trump or fundamentalism. People can be convinced of most things. And if your kidnappers know each other, then I believe they share some form of strong conviction. Otherwise they wouldn't be capable of carrying out such dreadful murders. Is murder the right term?'

Christer nodded grimly and scratched Bosse's neck.

'The murders of Lilly Meyer and Ossian Walthersson,' he said. 'Five years old.'

Bosse whimpered and looked up wide-eyed at his unhappy master.

'It doesn't have to be a religious belief,' Nova said. 'All it needs is a leader strong enough to send out others to abduct children.'

Ruben snorted to himself. *There are researchers who have shown*. She almost sounded like Vincent. Although Nova was most definitely an upgrade on the mentalist. Even if she was directing most of her attention at Peder. Ruben might have underestimated the magic of that hipster beard. But Julia was right that they were dealing with an unusual case and needed to think in unusual ways. If that meant Nova was going to show her face at police headquarters a few more times, then he had nothing against it.

'A leader?' said Julia.

'Yes, when a group of people exhibit extreme behaviour by doing things that are far outside the norms or laws of society, there's almost always a strong leader behind them. Someone who is sufficiently manipulative, powerful or frightening to convince the others.'

'Let's say we *are* dealing with a group like this,' said Julia. 'For the sake of argument. What, in that case, does the execution of the murders tell us about this group? Who are they?'

Nova paused for thought.

'OK,' she said. 'Cults, whether they're political, religious, or something else entirely, like rituals. It's a way of defining the unique movement. And there are most definitely ritualistic aspects to what you've told me. Not to mention purely symbolic elements. Both Lilly and Ossian were missing for three days before being found. As I'm sure you know, three is the most sacred of numbers. Back in Ancient Greece, Pythagoras argued it was the perfect number. It can stand for birth, life and death.

205

Beginning, middle, end. The Holy Trinity in Christianity. In fairy tales, everything happens three times according to the psychological model of introduction, establishment, change. The only problem is that three can mean so many things. It's hard to say exactly what it means here. The location of the bodies is also interesting.'

Ruben sighed. Now she sounded far too much like Vincent. Actually, it was strange that they hadn't asked Vincent for help instead. But maybe mentalists didn't know much about cults. Somehow, it cheered Ruben up that Vincent had some gaps in his databank of information.

'How do you mean?' said Julia.

'Both Lilly and Ossian were found close to water. Had they drowned?'

'No,' said Mina. 'Lilly had been suffocated. Ossian's cause of death is still to be determined. But he was dry when we found him.'

Ruben noticed that this was the first thing Mina had said since the meeting had begun.

'Then why were they by the water?' said Nova. 'Water has incredibly powerful, almost divine, symbolism.'

'So we're looking for water-worshipping fanatics who like the number three,' Mina said acidly. 'That sounds a lot likelier than, oh, I don't know, a paedophile ring or a trafficking operation gone wrong. You know, the kinds of things that happen in the real world.'

Nova shrugged.

'I agree,' she said. 'A cult isn't a particularly likely explanation. But maybe we shouldn't get too hung up on that particular word. Because, however you choose to look at it, both these murders have clear elements of ritual and symbolism. It would be stranger if they weren't connected. And given how different the descriptions of the kidnappers are, I don't think they're the only people involved. An older couple and a younger woman? Someone has brought them together and made them commit these acts.'

'Why can't it be one of the kidnappers who is the leader?' said Mina. 'I don't see why there needs to be any more.'

Nova nodded.

'You're right, of course. It's possible there are only the three of them. But the leader of an extremist group *always* has a plan. To be personally involved in the kidnappings would entail far too much risk of the leader being apprehended, which would upend the plan. That's why I believe there are more of them.'

Nova turned to Julia.

'I don't know anything about police work,' she said. 'But I dare say there's no one in Sweden with as much experience of extremist movements as me. After hearing the facts that you've shared, it's my view that these are ritual acts carried out by a group of people with a hierarchy with a single person at the top. As I said, acts like these require people to hold a strong belief in something bigger than themselves. Of course, there may be altogether different explanations that you are better qualified than me to find. I can only tell you what I see.'

'And we're grateful for that,' said Julia. 'As I'm sure you can imagine, these aren't the sorts of theories we usually encounter. But we need to consider everything.'

'Murderers who like water,' Christer muttered. 'Lucky for us Stockholm is a city of water. It'd be too bad if we came across something that made our work easier instead of harder.'

'I didn't say that water was really important,' said Nova. 'I just wanted to highlight the clearest connections from my own perspective.'

'Any other thoughts, Nova?' Julia said, one eye on the time. 'Otherwise we can wrap this up. I'd be happy to get in touch to follow up with you again another time.'

Nova seemed to pause for thought before then shaking her head. For a moment, her dark hair covered her face. Ruben realized how much he wanted to touch that hair. Good God. This celibacy thing was a bloody stupid idea.

'Well, there is one more thing,' Nova said, as Julia stood up. 'If you are in fact dealing with a cult-driven approach then there's one thing you must remember. It doesn't matter whether you catch and lock up the people who carried out the kidnappings. They're probably ordinary members, and they are always easily replaceable. The only way to stop them is to find the leader I mentioned – the one who ordered . . . the murders. It's him you have to get to.'

'What you're saying is that otherwise this group will carry on until they've fulfilled the plan you mentioned,' Peder muttered. 'Which means we might end up with more dead kids as a result. More families crushed.'

There was silence in the room. Nova looked at Peder for a long time. Ruben could feel his throat tighten. He wasn't going to be the first person to say something.

'I'm afraid you may be right,' said Nova.

61

'Could it be a coincidence?' said Peder, looking at the front door. It had been forced open.

'Anything's possible,' said Adam. 'But let's start from the assumption that it isn't. Are both parents at home?'

He greeted one of the forensics team with a nod as they passed by, heading inside the Waltherssons' apartment at Bellmansgatan.

The alert had come in shortly after their meeting with Nova at police headquarters had drawn to a close. Adam had gone out to buy lunch, and by the time he returned Peder had already left. By the time Adam arrived, Peder had already been inside the flat. Adam had not yet been in.

'Both Josefin and Fredrik are here,' said Peder. 'They discovered the break-in when they got home after visiting Josefin's parents. Isn't losing their son enough?'

'I'd like to talk to them.'

Adam carefully stepped through the door and Peder followed. They both took care where they placed their feet. Admittedly it wasn't a murder scene, but if the break-in had any connection at all to Ossian's death, then they would have to treat it like one and search just as closely. The last thing they wanted was to destroy forensic evidence.

'They're in there,' said Peder, showing Adam the way to the kitchen. 'The kitchen looked untouched, so I thought it was probably best to keep them in there.'

Fredrik half stood up when he saw them, but then sat back down again.

'Is it . . . is it the people who took Ossian that have been here?' he said. 'What do they want from us now?'

His gaze was slightly panicked but it also testified to absolute exhaustion.

Josefin was simply staring vacantly into space, her eyes unfocused. As if nothing else could touch her. As if nothing mattered to her anymore. Adam guessed she was on a lot of medication.

'We don't know yet,' he said. 'But we're going to do a thorough forensic examination of your apartment and secure everything we can find.'

'I don't understand,' said Fredrik. 'We don't have any enemies. There's nothing in our lives or backgrounds that could make someone want to hurt us. I already told you that last time. We thought it was chance that they took Ossian, but in that case, what . . . why . . . how . . .'

Fredrik spluttered the words and failed to complete his sentence. Instead, he buried his face in his hands. Adam pulled out a chair and sat down opposite the couple at the kitchen table. Without asking for permission, Peder went over to the counter and began to make coffee in the machine. Adam nodded approvingly at him. That was the police's best tool: black coffee.

'How long were you gone?' he asked, clasping his hands on the pale tabletop.

It was covered in lines left by felt-tip pens: yellow, red, green. There were small traces of Ossian all over the kitchen. The drawings fixed to the fridge with colourful magnets. A child's plate in the drying rack with a picture of Blixten McQueen on it. An open pack of alphabet biscuits on the side. Adam swallowed hard and averted his gaze.

'We went over to Josefin's parents' last night,' said Fredrik. 'We stayed the night there. I felt that Josefin needed to get away

209

from here. Well, the two of us needed it. Her parents have a house in Täby, so we stayed in their spare room. We got home . . . well, about an hour ago, I suppose.'

'And that was when you saw that the flat had been broken into?'

Adam knew he was asking obvious questions. But when talking to people who were grieving or in shock, or who were agitated, experience had taught him that asking the simple questions had a calming effect. They represented something that could be understood in a world that had been turned upside down.

Peder placed cups of piping hot coffee in front of them all. 'Milk?'

'Yes please, Josefin takes milk in hers,' said Fredrik, caressing his wife's arm.

She continued to stare blankly into space. Peder nodded, made for the fridge and got out an open milk carton after first checking the best-before date. He put it on the table and Fredrik carefully added a dash to Josefin's coffee.

'There we go, darling.'

She made no attempt to touch the cup.

'Well, the door was partially open, so I realized immediately that something was up,' Fredrik said, turning to Adam. 'I was absolutely certain that I'd closed it and locked up when we left. Then I saw the marks by the lock. And obviously as soon as we got into the flat we saw the mess it was in.'

'Have you been able to spot whether anything is missing?' said Peder, sitting down next to Adam.

He sipped his coffee gently.

'A few bits and bobs. Josefin's wedding ring and jewellery. Earrings and a gold bracelet. And a watch that my dad Allan got for one of his big birthdays. Sentimental stuff. Nothing of any great value.'

'OK. We'll need you to write a list of everything you can think of,' said Peder. 'Sometimes you don't notice exactly what's missing until after the fact.'

'We . . . we can't handle this as well,' Fredrik said, groping for Josefin's hand.

It lay limp in his. Her expression didn't even flicker. It was as if she were somewhere else, somewhere entirely different to the reality in which her child no longer existed. Adam hoped that she felt a little better wherever it was that she had gone.

'There doesn't have to be any connection,' he said. 'Believe me, we see our fair share of break-ins in apartments and there's nothing about this that stands out from what we usually see.'

Fredrik nodded but didn't appear to believe him. Frankly, Adam didn't blame him. What were the odds of it being a coincidence?

They heard forensics moving around the flat. It was usually the local scene of crime teams who led investigations like this following a burglary. They were good – they secured all the evidence there was to be secured so that they could investigate the break-in, and they also provided victim support. The general public seemed to think that the police didn't care about break-ins, but that was completely off the mark. The local officers did incredible work – their low clear-up rate was mostly down to the majority of break-ins being perpetrated by professional foreign gangs. But if this break-in might be connected to Ossian, then that called for the full forensic team. Even the smallest piece of evidence might be vital.

Adam stood up. 'If you think of anything, the tiniest detail even, please get in touch,' he said. 'And do make a start on that list of things that are missing. We're only a call away.'

Fredrik nodded. Josefin continued to stare into space.

After exchanging a few words with the team, Adam exited the apartment and took a deep breath. Peder followed in his wake and put a hand on his shoulder.

'It never gets easier.'

'No. Apparently not.' He turned to Peder. 'You know what? I think I could do with seeing that video now. I need something to offset this.'

'Video?'

'Yes, there's a rumour about a video featuring the triplets. And Melodifestivalen.'

'I think that can be arranged,' Peder said with a smile.

He pulled his mobile out of his jacket pocket.

62

The server in the little neighbourhood bar set down yet another beer in front of Ruben and he mumbled his thanks. He had eaten lunch there on his day off since it had opened five years previously. On the days off when he didn't need to eat at his desk because something still needed doing at work, anyway. And with the exception of Mondays when he went to see Granny. There had been a fair share of dinners at the bar too. There seemed to be no point in cooking at home when it was just him. It wasn't that he was no good at it – on the contrary, he was probably a cut above most other men he knew, at least with the grill. It just felt like a waste of time when he was the only one who was going to eat.

At the weekend, he sometimes even ate his breakfast here, partaking of their weekend brunch offering. Especially if he needed to wait for a one-night stand from the night before to vacate his flat. Which meant he hadn't had breakfast out since last winter. But if he were to be honest with both Amanda and himself, he was actually feeling much better than he had done in a long time.

The neighbourhood haunt had become Ruben's second home. Knowing the staff by name, just as they had learned his own routines, was reassuring. For example, they knew he always had a beer before his food, another with his food, and no coffee afterwards. But today he'd requested a second beer before the food had arrived, which had caused Mikael – on serving duties – to linger.

'Are you OK?' he asked.

'Just got a lot to think about,' said Ruben, taking a gulp of beer. 'It'll work itself out.'

'Don't overdo it – y'know it's only a Wednesday . . .' said Mikael with a nod before leaving him in peace.

Just the way he liked it, as Mikael knew. Not too much small talk. It hadn't been a lie either. His world was a bit of a daze at the moment. There was Ossian, for one – what had happened to him was godawful. The sense of failure and, well, sorrow had seeped into every pore of his body. He knew every single detective on the case felt the same. Nothing hit them like dead kids. Nothing. And it suddenly filled him with terror as he realized that he – Ruben Höök – had a daughter. He had known for three days but still hadn't managed to digest it, given everything else going on. Bloody hell. A daughter. Someone who could be lost. He forced away thoughts of that and tried to think about the more practical aspects of the discovery. Like her name.

Astrid.

Astrid Höök.

Not Höök, he corrected himself. She had her mother's surname. Still . . . So what was the next step? Ellinor had been quite clear that he wasn't welcome back. But that was obviously before he'd known he had a daughter.

'Bon appetit.'

Flank steak with fries. The gastronomic highlight of the culinary world, as far as Ruben was concerned. There were a few haricots verts for the sake of appearances, but otherwise it was perfect. He cut into the dark meat but couldn't quite bring himself to concentrate on eating. Instead, he tried to imagine what Astrid must have looked like at different ages. All the ages he had missed.

He pushed the plate away. He wouldn't be able to eat until he had done something. He chuckled drily. Bloody hell, he was acting like a fucking nervous wreck. Maybe he should talk to Amanda about it? She would most definitely be able to help. The fact that he actually considered it a good idea took him by surprise. Gunnar would piss his pants laughing if he could see Ruben now.

No – this would not do. He already knew what Amanda would say. But he disagreed with her. Time to bend or break.

He pulled out his phone, took a screenshot of the picture of Astrid from Ellinor's Facebook page and sent it to Ellinor.

Maybe there's something we should discuss, he wrote.

Then he set the phone to silent and knocked back a big mouthful of beer. Butterflies were cha-cha-ing in his stomach.

He didn't want to know whether Ellinor had replied or what she had said until he had choked the flying bastards with a hefty dose of meat and fries.

He had a kid.

A daughter.

Someone that he wanted to protect from all evils more than anything else in the world.

63

Julia checked her wristwatch in irritation as she jabbed much too hard at the buttons on the TV remote control for the set in the corner of the conference room.

'Is Ruben on his way?' she said.

'He'll be back from lunch in five – he's hurrying as best he can,' said Peder, offering her a cautious thumbs up. According to Peder and Adam, the Waltherssons had been hit by a standard break-in. But that also meant stolen valuables and the emotional violation of their home. Some people got all the bad luck.

Julia nodded and continued to zap between channels, unable to find the one that showed the input from the computer she had hooked up. Rage welled up within her, temporarily directed at the remote since the true target for her fury was diffuse and unreachable. One of the things she was most angry about was the fact that the police had once again leaked like a sieve. They had tried to keep the details of Ossian's death a secret from the public. But as usual, someone had clearly spotted an opportunity to top up their holiday kitty and had tipped off the press corps. She abused the remote even harder, seconds from hurling it against the wall.

'Why don't you give that to me?' said Adam, taking the remote control from her.

He found the right channel immediately and Julia's laptop screen appeared in enlarged form on the television. She was on the *Aftonbladet* website for the live press conference that was due to be broadcast there shortly. A still image of a lectern with two microphones was visible, in addition to a ticker at the bottom of the screen notifying viewers that the broadcast would start at one o'clock. Which was in three minutes' time.

'What's it about?' said Mina, her eyes on the remote control in Adam's hand as if it might yank itself free and attack her at any moment.

Julia wondered whether Mina kept notes of how many people had held the remote since the conference room had been equipped with the new TV three years earlier. Julia knew that was a mean thought. But it didn't seem improbable, since at that moment Mina took a step back from Adam and the remote control.

'Surely you can wait three minutes,' said Julia. 'We know just as little about what they want as you do.'

She heard how irritable her voice sounded. Sleep deprivation, stress at work, stress at home, missing Harry, feelings of inadequacy. It was all close to pushing her over the edge, and the call from the top brass could not have come at a worse time. The leader of Sweden's Future – the political party that was apparently polling at 20 per cent – had called a press conference in relation to the 'child murders'. Ordinarily, the media wouldn't have cared. Ted Hansson would have been left to spew his views on the party's own YouTube channel just like he normally did. But nothing was normal right now. So the media had listened, in the hope that Ted might know something.

Julia, however, had read the press release, which failed to cover what he was going to say – never a good thing where Ted Hansson was concerned. His leadership had never been characterized by anything other than opportunism and self-service. Julia had no doubt that his goal with this TV appearance was to stir up hatred and uncertainty with a hefty dose of mistrust in the police. That was always a popular point-scoring opportunity.

Admittedly, there was nothing in the investigation so far that suggested a connection to immigration or Swedes from foreign backgrounds. But that didn't usually pose any obstacle to Ted

Hansson and his cronies. If Ted's local supermarket put up the price of cheddar, it was the Kurds who were to blame. If the post office failed to deliver a parcel on time it was because they'd brought in extra manpower born in Somalia. Far too many Swedes liked those kinds of simplistic explanations. Julia carefully untensed her jaw which she had unconsciously been gritting as she thought about Ted Hansson.

'I'm here now!' Ruben hooted as he lunged through the door with large sweat patches across his shirt front. 'Has it started?'

He took the chair next to Mina, who quickly moved away from him. They were all hot in the stuffy meeting room, but Ruben was sweating profusely. He also smelled faintly of fries. Julia wished that Christer had bought more of those cheap fans. Surely the force could shoulder the expense of another box or two . . .

'One minute to go,' she said, sitting down to face the television, her expression grim.

The instructions from on high had been clear. No further criticism of the police's work would be tolerated. They needed results. This press conference had transformed dead children into a political issue rather than just a human or legal one. And once politics was involved, she knew that their ongoing work would be disrupted by that more than anything else.

On the television, two people approached the microphones on the lectern. The buzz among the assembled reporters died down. All the major media outlets, as well as plenty of the smaller ones, were in attendance.

The leader of Sweden's Future cleared his throat. It always surprised Julia how much hatred could be encapsulated in such an unassuming visage. Mousy-coloured hair in a nondescript style. Steel-rimmed spectacles, a narrow mouth and a slightly wobbly chin. Ted Hansson's attire was always a variation on a dark suit for more formal occasions or beige chinos and a casual shirt in either blue or white. For this press conference, he'd gone with chinos and a pale blue shirt. No sweat patches, she noted.

Peder gasped aloud. He had presumably just recognized the woman standing beside Ted – a moment after Julia had also realized who it was. Lilly Meyer's mother. Her face was a study in anger. Jenny's whole body looked like it was vibrating as she stood there with Ted's arm protectively wrapped around her shoulders.

Ted Hansson began to talk, removing his arm from Jenny. He liked gesticulating – preferably with clenched fists – in order to emphasize his point. Julia sighed. Why couldn't people see that he was nothing but a clown? Admittedly a dangerous clown, but a clown was a clown, surely?

'Sweden has become a lawless land,' said the leader of Sweden's Future, by way of introduction. 'Crime has skyrocketed while police presence has fallen. Our police are paralysed in the face of the crime that our political predecessors so naively imported to Sweden. To our country. But today isn't about politics. Today I'm not standing here before you as the leader of Sweden's fastest growing party. I stand here before you as a father. Children are going missing. In Sweden. Children are being murdered. In Sweden. And our police force has neither the will nor the means to find the culprits. One year ago, Lilly Meyer was taken from us. As a father, how can I look Lilly's mother in the eye today? If I can't say that Sweden and the police have used every means at their disposal to help her find answers to what happened to her little girl? She's standing here at my side. What do you think I should say?'

Ted turned towards Jenny Holmgren, tears streaming down his face as cameras flashed. The press were eating this up. That picture would be on every front page in the morning. The photoshoot seemed never-ending. As it happened, Julia had known Ted in sixth form. Back then he'd already been known for his party trick – an ability to cry on demand. He didn't care one bit about Jenny or her daughter. But the media were eating out of his hand.

'And Ossian Walthersson's parents,' Ted added, wiping the tears away. 'Fredrik and Josefin. They have a right to both answers and justice. Not incompetence and inaction.'

Ted raised his voice and clenched his fists. It was coming . . .

'We no longer have a Sweden in which our children are safe. We no longer have a Sweden where we can leave our children

217

unattended – not even for a moment. Danger is now lurking just out of sight. And *we* brought it here. From outside. Sweden used to be a bright, beautiful and safe country. But now there is darkness on our streets.'

He paused and waited. Then he stepped aside and allowed Jenny Holmgren to step towards the microphone. Lilly's mother curled her hands at her sides and took a few deep breaths. Julia felt mixed emotions looking at her tense face. On the one hand, she understood the anger and despair that the victims' parents felt. At the same time, she was filled with repugnance for the way that Jenny's grief was being exploited for other ends. All this would result in was the obstruction of police work and the public turning against them just when the public needed to be their foremost allies.

'Fucking moron,' Christer muttered with a gloomy shake of the head. 'Not her. That slimy bastard.'

'He's an elected representative,' Adam said drily, not taking his eyes off the screen. 'The people who voted for him deserve to have him in power for a while. Then they'd probably realize what they'd voted for.'

Lilly's mother spoke.

'One year. One year without my daughter. Without anyone managing to find out who killed her. And now another child has died. And the police are doing nothing!'

'Nothing,' Ruben said, gritting his teeth. 'Exactly. We're doing nothing. We're just sitting here twiddling our thumbs.'

'Shush,' said Julia, as she kept listening.

The press conference continued in a similar vein for another fifteen minutes. A knot formed in her stomach. Ted Hansson spoke again after Jenny, and expressed further concern about 'a Sweden at war with external forces of darkness'. Then he took questions from the assorted journalists. They were far too uncritical for Julia's liking. Ted's tears had done the trick. And it was a good angle. Picking apart the police and writing about their incompetence always sold papers – it was a fact since time immemorial.

'Well, there we have it,' said Adam from behind her as he turned off the TV. 'There's nothing new under the sun.'

218

Julia sat in silence for a moment. Adam was the member of the team who was presumably hardest hit by the volubility of Sweden's Future. She wondered what it did to a person – to constantly hear that you weren't welcome. She realized that it was impossible for her to imagine.

She spun around in her chair so that she was facing the team.

'We all know that what we just heard was bullshit. And no matter what shit we read or hear going forward, we ignore it and do our jobs. In fact, it might be a good idea not to read the papers for a while. Let the top brass handle this. And we'll focus on what we have to do.'

'Sounds like a plan,' said Mina.

Julia nodded.

'Yes. And remember that we're the best at what we do. Don't let anyone make you believe otherwise.'

No one answered, but Adam patted her on the shoulder as he left the room with the others. She stayed in her seat. The mobile in her pocket was vibrating away as the text messages arrived. It had been vibrating throughout the press conference. She had ignored it then, and she intended to keep doing so a while longer. If Torkel hadn't needed to go to hell before, well, he could bloody well do so now.

64

Mina spritzed a little sanitizer onto a paper towel and wiped down the files she had just put on Julia's desk.

'What do you want me to do now?' she said.

'Go home, Mina,' said Julia, picking up one of the folders.

'I can't,' she said. 'We're in the middle of an investigation. And this morning with Nova was a total waste of time. Water and the number three. Is she really Sweden's leading expert in the field? I told you we should have called Vincent. Because even if Nova is some kind of expert on cults, what does she know about connections? That's Vincent's strength. Nova's only speculating and guessing wildly.'

Julia closed the file she had just opened and looked at Mina.

'I found it interesting,' said Julia. 'And the idea that our kidnappers might know each other isn't any worse than any of our other theories. I'm not going to close the door entirely on the idea of an organized group.'

Mina felt unable to answer. She had always thought people like Nova were mostly full of hot air and the meeting had only served to confirm that impression. It didn't matter that Nova might have helped countless individuals.

'You look as tired as I feel,' said Julia. 'If not more so. It's this damn building. And the heat. You know we're doing everything we can. If I ask you to do anything else, there's the risk you'll start making mistakes. And that's worse than doing nothing at all. I only wish I could trade places with you. Anyway, didn't you have something to do this afternoon?'

At lunch, Mina had mentioned in passing that she might be busy later in the day. She hadn't said what with. But it was typical Julia that she had remembered something like that.

Even when she had been talking to Vincent the day before yesterday, it had felt unlikely that she would actually do it. Not that it felt completely impossible. Ruben could say what he liked. Julia needed her here, in position. There was sure to be something more she could do. Something that could keep her there. She ought to call Vincent – she had said she would, but she still hadn't got round to it. But she didn't want to call from police headquarters.

'I'm going to double-check all the people with records that Christer's gone through,' she said.

'Mina,' said Julia, fixing her with her gaze. 'You can't stay here. Go home. Watch a movie. Eat an ice cream. Drink a bottle of wine. Do whatever you were going to do. Or get some sleep. I don't care. But I don't want to see you for at least seven hours. You can't work around the clock – if you do, you'll be worthless to me. Take a few hours and come back with mind and body refreshed.'

Mina sighed. Everything would have been much easier if she

hadn't swiped right on Tinder. And if Amir hadn't replied almost immediately. Now she had no choice. Just one hour to go until the date. Holy shit.

65

Nathalie rummaged through her backpack, even though she knew it was futile. She usually had one or two changes of clean clothes with her in case she ended up sleeping over at a friend's and couldn't be bothered packing. But the clean clothes had long since run out. Karl had given her a change of clothes – the same white T-shirt and linen trousers worn by him, Ines and Monica. They felt cool and comfortable in the heat, but it would be nice to have something that was her own. Not to mention clean underwear. She pulled a Ramones hoodie from her backpack and sniffed it. Skunk.

Her stomach rumbled again. It was kind of them to offer food without asking for anything in return, but the portions were far too small. Her stomach had begun to protest on Saturday and she was now verging on starving. Hunger made it hard to think.

Ines and the others were incredibly considerate, and Nathalie was super grateful that she'd had the chance to get to know her grandma. But it was time to go home. She hadn't been in contact with her father since she'd texted him, but then the battery in her phone had gone flat and obviously there wasn't a single charger to be found in the whole place. But Dad had his own way of finding things out – she knew that. It was probably only a matter of minutes before a black car with tinted windows pulled up to collect her. She could always come back here some other time.

'Are you going somewhere?'

She looked up from her backpack. Karl was leaning against the doorframe.

'Yes, I need to go home,' she said. 'Before Dad loses it. Have you seen my grandma anywhere? I want to say bye to her before I go.'

'Ines went to run an errand,' said Karl. 'She should be back in an hour or so.'

He straightened up and stepped into the dormitory she shared with the others. He was really tall. And pretty good-looking, Nathalie now realized. It was funny, but since they'd been wearing the same clothes, it almost felt as if they were part of the same family.

'Maybe you can help me out with something for the time being,' he said. 'We're rebuilding and I need an extra pair of hands.'

'But . . . I don't know the first thing . . .' she started to say.

She was about to explain that she hadn't made anything since woodwork in middle school, and that even then the result had been highly questionable, but Karl interrupted her with a laugh. The sound was loud and heartfelt, and it would probably have warmed her more than it did had she not been so hungry.

'But I really do need to go home,' she said.

'I assume you've at least seen a picture of how to hold a hammer?' Karl said, as if he hadn't heard her. 'That's good enough. Your dad can wait a little longer.'

He was right, of course. The least she could do was reciprocate their generous hospitality. After all, they were practically family. She put a hand on her stomach to prevent Karl hearing it rumble, and then followed him out of the room.

66

All around her the place was teeming with activity. Mina knew that she could leave the office for a while – work was continuing at a feverish pace and they were all working shifts to cope. That was the way it had to be – she knew that Julia was right. And she didn't object to escaping from the migrating clouds of sweat that her colleagues had been transformed into. But she still struggled to tear herself away, even though she had to leave police headquarters in the next five minutes if she was going to be on time to see Amir.

It was just she couldn't leave quite yet.

She stared at the documents about Lilly and Ossian on her desk as if she could will them to talk. Mina had printed everything she could find. She thought better when she could hold the words, leaf back and forth through the papers, underline, cut out. It was one of the few situations in which she allowed herself to get a little rowdy. John Cleese was right about the fact that people couldn't find their creativity on a screen. And Mina most definitely needed to find *something*. Because nothing made sense.

No matter how she twisted and turned everything, she couldn't get away from the idea that Lilly and Ossian were connected. Though she wasn't prepared to go as far as Nova in her theory on how they were connected. She needed to find something else that tied them together – a connection they had overlooked.

She reviewed the material again.

She also had Ossian's My Little Pony rucksack on her desk. Julia had waved her magic wand and got the National Forensic Centre in Linköping – NFC – to agree to wait for the backpack until after the weekend. It had turned out to be a completely ordinary model that had been bought relatively recently and was completely empty. There was nothing special about it at all.

Except that Christer had said it didn't belong to Ossian. Ossian's parents, Fredrik and Josefin, had said that Ossian didn't have a bag of that description. Christer had then double-checked by sending them a photo of it, but they had never seen it before. Ossian hadn't borrowed it at nursery either – Ruben had called to check with them, but they didn't recognize it. And that was where all leads relating to the bag ended. Forensics had found no DNA or fingerprints on it. Nevertheless, Mina was convinced that someone had left the bag by the body on purpose.

But why?

She looked up at the ceiling as if she might find the solution there. Something was slowly beginning to shift at the back of her mind. It was too imperceptible to even be a thought as yet. But the rucksack reminded her of something. Because hadn't there been something odd about Lilly's case too? A mere trifle that had seemed a little off in the investigation a year ago, but not enough to stop it being forgotten when the custody dispute had come to light.

Mina spread out the photos from Lilly's folder and looked at them for the umpteenth time. She reread the report. When Lilly had been found, her pockets had been filled with toys, tufts of hair and a bookmark. The parents had identified all the items as belonging to Lilly.

Except the bookmark.

It had simply been assumed she'd been given it by some friend at nursery. But what sort of children used bookmarks these days? Mina highly doubted whether a five-year-old even knew what one was. In fact, she didn't think she'd seen a bookmark herself since she'd been to the dentist as a child. Those had been in an orange plastic box and basically all of them had for some reason depicted angels. But the motif didn't matter – the challenge with bookmarks was to find the one with the most glitter on it. The problem was that glitter stuck to your fingers. She shuddered at the memory. She used to bring her bookmarks home in a plastic bag. Then Grandma Ellen would glue them into a special album. Mina would never touch them. In fact, she never even opened the bookmark album for fear of getting glitter on herself. But you had to have the ones with the most glitter. That was the rule.

She pulled out the photograph of the items taken from Lilly's pockets. The troll-topped pencil. The eraser. The stone. The bookmark. They were lined up neatly in a row in front of numeric labels. It wasn't quite possible to tell what Lilly's bookmark depicted, but at least it wasn't glittery.

But . . . something about the bookmark was off.

It was hard to see the details in the photo, but it looked much too . . . flat. A piece of card that had been in a child's pocket ought to be crumpled and a little grubby. Not clean and uncreased.

It was as if someone had put it there after the fact. Just like Ossian's rucksack.

Mina logged on to the DurTvå database and searched for the files on Lilly before pulling up a digital copy of the picture she had on the desk in front of her. She zoomed in on the bookmark as much as she could.

Then she gasped frantically for breath. She looked back to Ossian's backpack. Then back to the bookmark on the screen. Then to the backpack again. No. It couldn't be. The idea was too absurd for words. Surely it was just her brain bolting off and desperately trying to spot a pattern? It was very, very faint. Barely a connection, even. Anyway, it was incomprehensible.

But what if it wasn't? What if the pattern wasn't too faint?

She began to understand how Vincent felt.

Mina ran into the corridor clutching the photograph, making for Christer's office.

67

The black and white squares on the screen seemed to be mocking Christer. He had been on his way to victory this time. So very close. Until his pre-programmed opponent had made a surprising move and put him in check and mate within seconds.

'Christer, have you—' said Mina, suddenly bursting into the office before cutting herself off.

He sighed deeply. Apparently manners and respect were extinct. In his day, people had learned to knock and then ask politely whether they could come in.

'What are you doing?' she said, looking curiously at his computer.

'Humiliating myself,' Christer said, closing the tab containing his chess app. 'Can I help you?'

'Yes. Well, it's this. I've found something strange about Lilly Meyer. Or not that strange. Well, I don't know. Take a look.'

She handed him a photograph. He took it and frowned. At first he thought it was rubbish. But then he realized that it was Lilly's possessions that he was looking at.

'That bookmark – the last thing in the row,' said Mina, pointing to the picture. 'It wasn't Lilly's. Her parents thought she'd got it off someone at nursery. I need to know whether that's true. You're the best one of us at those kinds of conversations. Please would you call the nursery, and also all the parents of children who were in Lilly's group a year ago, to see whether any of them collect bookmarks?'

He put down the photograph with a sigh and stroked his chin. There would be no more chess today. Not for several days to come either, so he assumed.

'You realize how many calls that is, don't you?' he said. 'How many kids go to a nursery? Thirty? Fifty?' He tried to recall a scene in which one of his favourite fictional detectives spent days on end talking about toys with the parents of small children. He failed. Because they didn't do things like that. On the other hand, he suspected the whole lot of them were probably chess grandmasters. He clearly had some way to go until he was Harry Bosch, despite the jazz and Bosse.

'I think the bookmark might be important,' said Mina. 'I can't explain yet – you'll just have to trust me. I've written down the number for the nursery on the back of the photo.'

He sighed yet again, turned it over and saw the phone number.

'You do realize that she might just have found it on the ground?' he said.

'We have to start somewhere.'

Mina began to leave the room, but stopped in the doorway and turned around.

'Thanks, Christer,' she said.

'What are you going to do?'

She waited a second before answering.

'I'm going to call Vincent,' she said.

Mina looked surprised – as if she hadn't known what she was going to say before she said it. Then she smiled a peculiar smile and said the words once again, slowly and emphatically.

'Yes. I'm going to call Vincent. It's high time we brought him in on this, don't you think?'

Christer didn't know what to say.

'There's something I want him to take a look at first thing tomorrow,' she added. 'But now I have to go and . . . Well.'

The smile disappeared from Mina's lips. Christer nodded without really understanding and waved her out of the office. Vincent. Pfft. Whatever it was Mina thought she had found, it would be ten times worse if that mentalist got mixed up in it again. That much was certain.

The only question was which was more humiliating – being beaten at chess by an app or hunting for bookmarks in a nursery. He sighed. Policing wasn't what it once had been.

68

Vincent tried not to think too hard about the phone call he had just finished with Mina. He tried not to be as excited as a child. She wanted him to come in again – on Friday morning – to discuss something to do with the investigation. As far as he was concerned, he could have got in the car right away. But perhaps that might have seemed strange. Additionally, he had a performance later that evening, so he tried to distract himself with other matters.

Like the two envelopes with Santa stickers lying on the desk in front of him.

He thought the Santas had a malicious glint in their eyes. He had already sorted the Tetris-like pieces of paper that had been in the envelopes into two heaps. He knew the messages on them by heart. He absorbed the letters as he uttered them – as if it might fool them into revealing their true meaning. This time he was going to crack it. It would be a good story to tell Mina tomorrow.

Or perhaps not. Something about the puzzles made him want

to keep them to himself for a little while longer. As if they were a private secret.

He had previously tried to combine the pieces into one big puzzle, but it was impossible. All the pieces contained just half or one third of a word, and it was impossible to make any words with them other than the ones he had already found. The only way to compose a text that made sense was to lay each puzzle out on its own. He picked up the pieces and laid them out in the same irregular shapes that he'd assembled many times before.

Tim scared deny ageing.

Maria dinged cygnets.

It hadn't escaped him that the second message contained eighteen letters, just like the first one. Moreover, these were exactly the same letters. The only question was what on earth all of this meant. Was it about the anagrams themselves? Or the number of characters? Or should he focus on the capital letters? Was it nothing more than chance that his wife's name was in one of them, or was it actually significant?

A loud laugh – bordering on affected – was audible from the kitchen. Maria was apparently on the phone with Kevin. She had explained earlier that day that they were about to embark on the next phase. Vincent hoped she was referring to her company rather than their relationship. But he hadn't dared ask.

He rose from his chair and stood at the end of the desk in an attempt to see the pieces of the puzzle from a different perspective. The best challenges people had sent to him that he had managed to solve were lined up on his bookshelf. He was very eager to consign these puzzles to the same place. But the feeling of anxiety in his stomach told him they were somehow different. Behind the unassuming, almost amateurish design of the Tetris pieces there was something else . . . hiding.

Without knowing why, he knew it was important that he understood what it was.

He squinted at the pieces to see whether anything might suggest itself, but the meaning continued to elude him. Tim and Maria were both names. But that surely didn't mean anything. At first he'd thought it was all a code. But what if it wasn't that complicated?

Maybe he'd been crossing the river for water all these months? Perhaps the text was of no interest at all. What if its task was merely to get him to lay out the pieces in a particular configuration – one he wouldn't think of by himself? What if it was the shape that was important after all – but not the one he'd been tricked into creating the first time he'd laid them out like in Tetris?

He carefully moved the two puzzles onto a piece of paper without disturbing their order. Then he took a felt-tip pen and traced the outer contours of the irregular shapes with great care. He suddenly felt elated. He was on the trail of something – he could feel it throughout his body.

Maria let out an even louder laugh in the kitchen. He hadn't heard her laugh like that since they had been newly in love. Things were apparently going well for her company. The anxiety in his stomach shifted again, but as ever he pushed it away.

After the contours, he also filled in the shapes made by the holes between the pieces, but he made sure that no pieces moved. Then he swept the puzzle pieces off the paper and looked at the result.

A number of asymmetrical squares. Nothing.

It still meant nothing. But the feeling that this was something that only he would see remained – alongside that anxiety in his stomach. The anxiety was growing stronger. This time it had nothing to do with Maria and Kevin.

69

Mina took a deep breath. She was strolling through the city centre, trying not to think about what she might just have discovered. Trying not to think about the fact that she was going to see Vincent in the morning, and above all trying not to think about his scent. She was making an effort not to think about Ossian and Lilly, or what would happen if her own mother let the cat out of the bag with Nathalie. She was trying not to think about the fact that her whole world could come tumbling down at any moment. How much would her mother tell? Would she mention the tablets? Or would she make it sound like Mina had simply left? No matter what Ines said, Mina's daughter would probably hate her afterwards. She came to a halt in the middle of the pavement, finding herself paralysed.

No.

She couldn't think about it now.

Instead, she would have to concentrate on having a pleasant afternoon. Nothing else. Very pleasant. And on not judging in advance.

That wasn't an unqualified success.

She tried to tug the corners of her mouth into a stiff smile, changed her mind and then rounded the corner of the building. Amir was waiting for her outside the Museum of Mediterranean and Near Eastern Antiquities. He looked just like his photos on Tinder, which was at least something. She guessed there was often a few years' gap between photos and reality. And not just an age gap, but also weight gaps and hairline gaps. Admittedly, it wasn't something she really cared about, but she didn't like being surprised.

Amir's dark locks were in a loose knot at the back of his neck, just as they had been in his pictures. She was tempted to suggest a hairnet if he was going to keep it that unkempt. His white shirt was ironed but not properly pressed. She eyed it but couldn't see any loose strands of hair. Her shoulders went down a few millimetres.

'Hello! Sorry I'm late,' she said. 'I've come straight from work.'

'Me too,' he said. 'And you've made me look better because I don't have to admit I was a little late too.'

He looked at the entrance to the museum and the hoarding showing the current exhibitions. She didn't really care what was on display inside. She had chosen the museum solely on the grounds that they always had good air conditioning.

Wandering around town and sweating with a stranger was out of the question.

'So, museums huh?' said Amir. 'I was going to buy tickets, but apparently admission is free.'

Mina frowned. She didn't like that he had been planning to pay for her.

'Don't look like that,' he laughed. 'You were late. I just wanted to save a little time.'

She gave him a narrow smile in response. It was true – she had been late and he had come here for her sake. She glanced at the time. She could get back to police headquarters in twenty minutes if needed.

They went in through the entrance and headed for the main exhibition.

'Is this what you're interested in?' said Amir, reading aloud from a sign. 'Cyprus through the ages?'

'Aren't you?' she said.

'Nope. Not in the slightest. But I can be. Like I said on my profile, I need to learn to work less and spend more time on other things. I just didn't realize that the first step in that would be terracotta sculptures.'

The main attraction of the exhibition was a large glass case containing more sculptures in miniature than Mina could count. This was presumably the perfect opportunity to ask one of those questions she'd read in the Tinder articles, like which sculpture do you most identify with, and why? If he said that or asked her which pizza topping she was, she'd be off in a nanosecond.

She glanced at Amir, who had leaned in towards the display case. He really did seem interested in the sculptures on the other side of the glass. Just as long as he wasn't a floorball bro. She already had far too many colleagues on the force who were. No . . . A guy like Amir was probably cooler. Likely as not he played padel.

'But surely you must do something other than work?' she said.

Amir laughed and straightened up. 'Well, sure. I am a lawyer after all. So I'll give you one guess what I do the rest of the time. The clue is that all your prejudices are accurate.'

'Don't tell me that you . . . play golf?'

231

Amir groaned and staggered backwards with his hands to his chest as if he'd been shot while successfully managing to look both embarrassed and ashamed. She couldn't help but smile again.

'Got me on your first go,' he said. 'Truth be told, I've played competitive golf since sixth form. Obviously I didn't know at the time that I was going to become a lawyer. My colleagues play too, but mostly because all the other lawyers do it. As for myself, I wonder whether it's the other way around. Golf made me become a lawyer.'

'Yes, I don't suppose there are many other golf-related jobs,' she said. 'I guess you had no choice. Poor thing.'

He smiled back at her and they continued to stroll through the exhibition. However, she was struggling to concentrate on it while she listened to Amir. Surely this was only because the rest of the exhibition was less impressive than the large display case? That had to be it. Nothing else.

'What about yourself?' he said. 'You're a police officer and you work a lot – just like me. But what else?'

'There's not much more to tell,' she said.

'Oh dear,' he said, stopping, his expression serious. 'We'll have to change that.'

For a second she had no idea how to reply.

'So tell me about golf,' she said hastily, trying to avoid contemplating whether he'd just been flirting with her.

'What do you want to know?' he said, sounding both surprised and a tad amused.

Presumably he usually had an easier time of it on dates.

'Well, it must be pretty mathematical,' she said. 'Calculating the height of your shot versus the distance to the hole and all that. How do you do that? Is there a basic formula, or does it depend on specific physical conditions?'

There was probably an entire science to playing golf, given how many people seemed obsessed with it. Had Vincent been there it wouldn't have surprised her if he'd started drawing vectors on the wall to explain. Not that she thought Vincent had any experience of golf. But he would doubtless know an unnecessary amount about the relevant equations.

232

Amir looked completely baffled.

'Well, I guess I know down to the metre how far I can get with each club,' he said. 'Regardless of whether there's a head-wind, a tailwind, no wind, height difference, etc. But it's not something I consciously calculate – I don't even know what I'd do if I wanted to work it out. I just . . . play. It's something your body learns. It's not something I think about.'

She looked at Amir. He was both kind and considerate – not in a way that was calculating, but seemingly naturally. He was attentive when they talked and wasn't in a rush. He seemed to live a life that was interesting – although not too interesting. He was funny. And he was good-looking. He was one of those unusual men that women not only wanted to have babies with, but then wanted as the father of said babies. And he wasn't the slightest bit interested in unnecessary calculations.

It would never work.

70

'You came! I thought you weren't going to show.'

Mina stifled a yawn behind her hand and sat down at the table at the very back of Ritorno on Odengatan without looking Ines in the eye. It was seven o'clock on Friday morning and they were among the first patrons in the cafe.

Mina had suggested they meet early so that she didn't spend ages being stressed beforehand about whether her mother had anything useful to tell her. Ines hadn't disagreed, even though she must have had to travel a fair distance.

Mina didn't know how to approach Ines. Their relationship had existed in another era when she had been living another life.

Even though Ines hadn't left her family in a physical sense, she had still abandoned them. Ines's alcoholism had meant that Mina had spent more time at Grandma Ellen's than in her own home. When Mina had been fifteen and Ellen had died, Mina had been forced to spend a few years in the house with Ines. Or rather, with the ghost of Ines, given that her mother was almost never at home. And when she was, she was drunk.

Mina had moved out as soon as she could and had sworn never to speak to her mother again. But when Nathalie had been born, Ines had made contact to broker peace. She'd said she was sober, and that she wanted to be a proper grandmother. But then it had been Mina's turn to be stuck in a cycle of addiction – to tablets.

When she had left Nathalie with her father, she had forbidden Ines from making contact with her granddaughter. Mina's daughter didn't need to swap one addict for another.

Since then, Mina had heard from her own mother no more than once a year. Usually around Christmas. But it had been quite a few Christmases since the last time. Mina was no longer the same person – and Ines probably wasn't either. They might have been mother and daughter, but they were also strangers to one another. At least as far as Mina was concerned.

The fact of the matter was that she knew more about Amir, with whom she had spent just two hours the day before, than she did about her own mother. Amir – the man who had been sensitive enough not to suggest they meet again, but who had been unable to help looking like a wounded puppy when she left him outside the museum. She had been very close to saying 'It's not you, it's me,' but there were limits to how much of a cliché she was prepared to be.

'And good morning to you too,' said Ines, interrupting her train of thought. 'This was your favourite cafe when you were little – do you remember? You always used to have . . .'

She snapped her fingers as she looked towards the counter.

Irritation welled up within Mina. She'd been wrong. Ines was no stranger. She was all too familiar and her presence awakened far too many memories. Memories that Mina had put a lot of time into repressing.

'Elephant ears,' she said curtly, returning to the present. 'And I used to come here with Grandma. Not you.'

'Elephant ears,' Ines repeated, clapping her hands. 'That's right. And you're mistaken – we came here together too.'

Mina chose not to respond. She knew full well that selective memory was part of an addict's personality. It was imprinted into her DNA to beautify, enhance and edit where necessary. To make everything better than it had really been, so that she could make it through life herself.

'Would you like something?'

Mina got up to walk over to the counter.

'A cup of tea, please,' said Ines, and Mina nodded. 'Any one is fine.'

Tea. That was new. In Mina's memory, the presence of her mother was intimately associated with bucketloads of coffee. Black. Always taken with a cigarette.

She ordered an Earl Grey for Ines and double espresso for herself. In a paper cup. She glanced at the pastries behind the glass. The cafe still had its elephant-ear palmiers, but she had no idea how long they had been out or how many people had touched them. She abstained. She opened a disposable pack of wet wipes and cleaned the edge of the paper cup before returning to the table. There was no need for Ines to see that.

'I don't have much time,' she said, after she'd sat down. 'We're in the middle of an investigation.'

She found herself trying to hide her chapped red hands and felt the anger welling up inside her. Why should she be ashamed? After all this time? No, she pointedly put her hands on the table in front of her. She fought the impulse to wipe down the tabletop with a fresh wet wipe.

'You wanted to talk about Nathalie,' Ines said softly.

She didn't seem to notice Mina's hands.

'Well, her father is worried. And that's putting it mildly. I won't be able to prevent him from going out there to pick her up forcibly for much longer. And if I'm honest, that's starting to seem like a good idea. You can't just show up like that – out of nowhere. And then keep Nathalie out there . . . in the woods. She'll have been with you for a whole week soon. That doesn't seem at all right.'

Ines laughed heartily. Small laughter lines formed around

her eyes, and Mina noticed reluctantly how beautiful her mother was. And how healthy she looked. Not at all like the last time they had met. She couldn't even remember when that had been.

'I'll say this,' said Ines. 'You've always had a sense of drama. I'm not holding Nathalie anywhere. Goodness gracious, she's hardly in prison. And she's on her summer holidays. What could be better than letting her spend some time in the great outdoors?'

Mina waved her hand irritably. 'Sure, sure, you know what I mean,' she said.

'Yes, I know what you mean. I didn't mean to poke fun.'

Ines became serious. She carefully sipped her piping hot tea.

'I realize you're all worried,' she said. 'But give me and Nathalie a few more days. We're still getting to know each other. And I promise the secret is safe with me. Nathalie has been asking. But I'm only giving her the answers that I can without revealing anything.'

'Are you sure?'

'I'm sure. I know Nathalie would appreciate it if you could keep her father at bay for a little longer. As would I. She's happy, you know. We're happy together.'

'OK,' Mina said reluctantly.

She hadn't been able to bring herself to even sip her coffee. She rose abruptly.

'I've got to go to work now. But I'll do my best to get you a few more days. For Nathalie's sake. But don't let me down. You've got no room left to do that. My whole childhood with you was one big let-down. Every time you chose alcohol over your family was a betrayal. You can't let me down again.'

'I know that,' said Ines in that same gentle tone of voice. It was beginning to get on Mina's nerves.

Mina nodded, turned on her heel and left the cafe. The paper cup remained on the table.

71

'I thought you'd stopped seeing that cop.' Maria glowered at him across an open cardboard box on the kitchen table. She'd been sent proofs of a flyer that was going to be included with all her future orders. *Sign up for the newsletter and get 15 per cent off your next purchase!* Vincent didn't have to ask whose idea it had been.

Rebecka and Aston came in the front door, singing at the tops of their voices and harmonising on 'Radio Ga Ga'.

During the spring, Rebecka had discovered the collected works of Queen. Vincent had been dumbfounded, to say the least. What seventeen-year-old was aware of – let alone cared about – an old band like Queen in the era of boybands filled with plastic Ken types? Not that he was complaining. He loved that the children continued to surprise him. Even if it could sometimes be a little scary. And given quite how enamoured Aston seemed to be with his big sister at the moment, it was no surprise that he'd hopped on the bandwagon. 'Radio Ga Ga' had become his absolute favourite song. Rebecka's acceptance of, and indeed her active encouragement of her little brother, touched Vincent. However, he guessed that the strong ties forged between the siblings would last the month. At most. Then the bickering would return. But right now they were a delight.

Rebecka and Aston fell silent when they caught sight of Maria and Vincent.

'Oops, ice-cold in here,' said Rebecka. 'Come on, Aston, let's go back out. We can get ice cream. It is the summer holidays after all. Or maybe we should get some milk – I think you finished another carton this morning.'

'Wait a second,' said Vincent. 'Rebecka, which week are you and Benjamin supposed to be at your mother's? I know she wanted to change a few of the times over the summer, but I haven't heard anything.'

'Hasn't she texted you?'

Vincent and Ulrika's relationship had been reduced to the bare minimum even before the incident at the Gondolen restaurant two years earlier. After that, they had only communicated by text message, and even then as rarely as they could manage. As the children got older, there were fewer things they needed to discuss, which Vincent suspected was appreciated just as much by Ulrika as it was by him. But it did sometimes lead to confusion about the children's accommodation. When they had divorced, they had opted for every other week, but that had only stuck for a few years. For some time now, the kids had done more or less as they pleased, which oddly enough suited him down to the ground despite his tremendous need for control. Of course, that might be down to the fact that he couldn't even remember when they had last spent any significant time at Ulrika's. He liked them being at home with him, especially when he was travelling a lot. It really brought him back to reality when he came home to the family.

'I thought I'd stay here a few more weeks,' Rebecka said when he merely shook his head in reply. 'It is the summer holidays, after all. Don't know about Benjamin. Isn't it about time he was moving out? I'll take his room. Once you've sterilized the place with a flamethrower. Come on, Aston.'

'You can have milk,' Aston protested. 'I want the biggest ice cream ever.'

Maria stared at the door as Rebecka closed it behind her and her little brother, and then she turned her gaze back to Vincent.

'We were talking about the cop. Don't you remember what the therapist said? We shouldn't do things that are bad for us. And yet here you are, doing it again.'

'But what's . . . OK.'

Vincent bit his tongue. He remembered the therapist's words all too well. He also recalled that the words had been in relation to Maria's jealousy and the way it was damaging their relationship. And as it happened, there had been a period following therapy when Maria's jealousy had abated. He had even dared to hope it might disappear in its entirety.

238

But that had apparently changed as soon as Mina had resurfaced.

'I hadn't spoken to Mina since all that business with Jane,' he said. 'I was as surprised as you when she called on Monday. But she wanted to discuss one of my colleagues. She thought we knew each other – that was why she called. Mina's worried about her daughter, that's all.'

Maria snorted and sealed the box.

'So the fact that your boxer shorts suddenly smell of women's perfume obviously has nothing to do with it?' she said acidly. 'Or the fact that you're seeing her again today?'

'Firstly, that thing about my boxer shorts isn't true,' he said. 'And secondly, it was me who did the laundry this week. So you couldn't possibly have smelled anything on my underwear even if it had been there. But it is true that I'm going to police headquarters shortly. It sounded like they wanted my help with the investigation after all.'

Maria wasn't going to give in – he could see it in her eyes even as he opened his mouth.

'I did wonder why you were so eager to do the laundry,' she said. 'But I suppose it's best to remove the stains and the perfume . . . before I see anything. Did you do her on the desk?'

And with those words, a year's worth of therapy was consigned to history. He knew he shouldn't offer a riposte, but the adrenaline was already coursing through his body and he couldn't help it. The words spilled out of his mouth without him being able to stop them.

'We're not doing anything you're not doing with Kevin,' he said. 'He's messaged you three times in the last fifteen minutes, by the way.'

He turned around and left before Maria had time to reply. He was much too afraid of what she might say.

72

The air conditioning in the lobby of police headquarters usually worked better than the systems in the rest of the building, but even there it was not capable of withstanding the summer heat any longer. The windows were much too large for that. Standing in the lobby was like being under a magnifying glass with the sun on the other side. Mina imagined that the glass was slowly melting in the heat. She was all out of wet wipes. She pulled out a regular tissue from her pocket, mopped her brow and then threw it into the nearest bin in disgust. He could have another minute. Tops.

The second after she'd thought that, a shock of blond hair appeared on the other side of the window.

Vincent stepped inside and signed in at reception.

'Sorry I'm late,' he said as he came over to her by the barriers. 'Maria and I were having a row and . . . Well, actually you don't want to know.'

'If you say so,' she said, letting him in.

It was far too hot to take the stairs, so she led him towards the lift. It had been fine the last time.

'How's it going with . . . what we talked about?' he said cautiously.

'Nathalie's grandmother is suddenly her best friend,' she said. 'Her father doesn't like her being away from home much, but that's his problem. He's the one who has the image to maintain. I'm mostly worried that this is going to end in tears for Nathalie.'

It was more than she had ever said before about Nathalie's father. Vincent seemed keen to ask a question but refrained from doing so. He seemed to have learned a little sensitivity then . . .

'Am I here on official business this time, or not?' was what he said instead.

Maybe it was a flight of fancy on her part, but he almost sounded a little hurt.

'I want to start by saying that it wasn't my idea,' she said. 'I always thought we should have brought you in instead.'

'What wasn't your idea?'

'The others have . . . um, they opted to bring Nova in as some sort of consultant. As if I hadn't had my fill of her.'

Vincent raised his eyebrows.

'But I was doubtful from the start as to how much she could really offer us,' she said. 'And I wasn't any more convinced when she came in. That being said, she's probably right about one thing: there are certain patterns across the two murders. We seem to be dealing with a killer who follows invisible rules. Even if Nova prefers to call them rituals. But we don't need some self-help guru rambling on about group behaviour. We need someone who understands the human psyche and can interpret what the murderer's actions mean. We need a Vincent.'

'I see,' he said. 'Nova is obviously very competent – at least in her own field. Beautiful too. A better face for TV for the investigation, if I may go so far.'

She had to exercise self-control to avoid stopping midstep. Did Vincent think Nova was beautiful? That was something he would have been better off keeping to himself. Not that it made any odds to her, obviously. Not one iota.

'Nova is actually here right now,' she said, getting into the lift. 'Again. She's meeting Julia.'

'It'd be great to say hi to her,' he said, letting Mina select their destination floor.

'We'll see if there's time,' she replied briefly.

She didn't feel like talking. They ascended in silence.

'Look,' he said, just before the lift doors opened. 'It's . . . good to see you again.'

She turned to him and met his gaze. It felt as if she was looking straight into his soul. But she didn't see the Master Mentalist. Instead, she saw all that he was, all that he showed no one else, all that he had dared to let her – and only her – see back then. He was finally really there. She almost lost her composure.

'It's good to see you too, Vincent,' she said in a low voice.

The lift doors opened and they stepped into the corridor. She pointed towards her office.

'I remember where it is,' he said.

'Of course you do,' she said. 'But there's no need to pontificate on the numerical significance of the area of my office, if that's all right with you. We've got other things to discuss.'

'As if I would!' he said, feigning offence.

Mina opened the door to her office. Two fans were positioned on the floor and were whirring away at top speed without managing to produce even a modicum of coolness. The only thing they were doing was swirling all the dust in the room around. She had probably already inhaled the majority of it. But that couldn't be helped. If she opened the window then she'd let in the dirt and pollution from the street outside, which was far worse. Vincent was wearing a short-sleeved shirt instead of a suit this time, but she could see he was sweating just as much as she was.

'You asked whether this is official,' she said, pointing to her desk. 'The truth is that we'll have to wait and see. And that's exactly why you're here. So that we can see.'

This sounded much too authoritarian and far harsher than she had intended.

'Help me, Vincent,' she said, more gently. 'Help me to see. Or tell me whether I'm just imagining it. I need you for this.'

On one half of the desk was Ossian's rucksack, along with the photographs that Josefin and Fredrik had provided and a printed copy of the current investigation file. On the other half of the desk were the enlarged photos of the objects that had been in Lilly's pockets, as well as the accompanying report and pictures. Mina had taken care to set it all out so that no one part drew more focus than any other. There were probably a hundred different pieces of information on the table, and a thousand ways that they could be combined. It would be devastating if she happened to lead Vincent to a specific line of thinking at this stage. He was there because she wanted to see what conclusions he reached by himself.

'Here's what I've got from the two cases I mentioned before,' she said. 'What do you see?'

Vincent went over to the desk and stroked his chin. She

242

might have misheard, but it sounded as if he had sighed with happiness.

'I take it you're asking whether there's a connection. May I?'

'It goes without saying that what you're examining is highly confidential. But you're welcome to handle it all.'

First he studied the portraits of Ossian and Lilly. She supposed he was searching for similarities. He flipped through the reports and then examined the photographs again. This time he appeared to be scrutinizing their clothing.

'Similar abductions, but by different people . . .' he muttered. 'The odds are long. But it's not impossible. Hmm.'

He pointed at the objects.

'This is what they . . . what Ossian and Lilly had with them when they were found?'

She nodded.

'This bookmark,' he said, pointing at the picture. 'It's brand new. Based on the condition of the other things that Lilly had in her pockets, it's unlikely to be hers. And this backpack was apparently not Ossian's, according to the interview with the parents that's in the report. So that was also added after the fact.'

He'd found it right away. Vincent picked up the backpack. He examined the bookmark.

Mina held her breath.

There were seven big-eyed cartoon ponies around the My Little Pony logo. All were colourful and laughing. The one at the front had wings.

Lilly's bookmark was also illustrated, but it was more realistic in its style. It depicted a beach, and rearing up at the water's edge there was an Arabian thoroughbred, the waves breaking dramatically around the beast's hind legs.

'Horses,' he said. 'Both have horses.'

She exhaled. Of all the things he might have said, all the conclusions he might have drawn, he had made the same observation she had. But the information about Lilly had been in the hands of the police for a whole year. She looked at the clock on the wall. It had taken Vincent barely ninety seconds.

'That was my thought too,' she said. 'But is it a pattern?'

243

'Impossible to say,' he said, opening the backpack. 'It's more likely to be a coincidence. Except that the items were added after the fact. What does Nova say about it?'

'About the horses? Nothing. I'm the only one who's spotted it. And now you. Nova has some far-fetched theory about water being symbolically important to the murderer. That and the number three. She believes the killings were carried out by a group with a secret leader.'

'So it's organized?' Vincent said, raising his eyebrows. 'And do you agree?'

He was on her side. She could kiss him. Well, not literally. She had been thinking more metaphorically. Well, not so much a metaphor as . . . No, just that. She frowned. What the hell was wrong with her? She would have to pull herself together before Vincent noticed anything.

'Organized child killings – sounds like something from a cheap paperback novel,' said Vincent. 'Although maybe I'm being cynical. Let's focus on what you and I found instead. We need there to be three similar pieces of information for us to establish that there is a pattern. That goes for both Nova's . . . water theory or whatever it was, and our own horses. We only have two pieces. The same is true for the way the abductions took place. It might well be a coincidence. It's the third point that stabilizes everything. A bit like when you're drawing a line from A to C. To make sure it's straight, you need a point B too – halfway between the other two points.'

'What are you talking about?'

He put down the rucksack and held the photo of the bookmark for a while. Then he put that down too and produced a handkerchief from his pocket. He wiped it across his face to remove the sweat and then returned it to his pocket.

'Don't worry,' he said, catching her expression. 'I'll wash it in chlorine when I get home. Unless, that is, you'd like to deal with it . . . ?'

He began to remove it from his pocket while giving her a knowing look.

'This might be your briefest engagement on a case yet,' she said.

He tucked the handkerchief away again and to her relief she also saw him take a dollop of sanitizer from the bottle on her desk to clean his hands.

'So, Lilly and Ossian,' he said. 'Pattern or not. This is a terrible question, but . . . do we only have the two of them? No other dead children in this period?'

'I think two is far too many as it is,' she said, shaking her head. 'We would have heard if there were any more. Dead children, especially unsolved cases, keep police officers up and down the country on their toes.'

She sat down at the computer and logged in to the DurTvå database. 'I can obviously double-check whether we have any other child murders on the books, but like I said, we would have heard. It hasn't been . . .'

She faltered, staring at the monitor.

'Bloody hell.'

A six-month-old case was staring back at her. She turned the screen to show Vincent.

'There was a dead four-year-old back in the winter,' she said. 'I remember it now – even though we weren't the ones who handled it. But the circumstances were completely different. There was no kidnapping. The child – William Carlsson – was found on Beckholmen. You know, the little island by the theme park at Gröna Lund with the historic shipyard. He was lying in the dry dock – it was as if he'd tumbled in and died from the fall. But there was past violence in the family. The neighbours had reported their concerns about the father, and the body bore the marks of repeated past beatings. The investigating officers were convinced that William hadn't actually fallen into the dry dock, but that it was a clumsy attempt to cover up the abuse he'd been subjected to. The father was remanded on suspicion of murder with immediate effect. It was a pretty open-and-shut case, with no loose ends. It's got nothing to do with Lilly and Ossian. But it is a dead kid.'

Vincent grimaced and leaned over her shoulder to look at the screen. He smelled faintly of spices. It was a scent she hadn't even realized she missed. She couldn't help involuntarily leaning a millimetre or so back, closer to him.

'How sure are the police that it was the father who killed the child?' he asked.

'Very,' she said, pointing to a section of the report on the screen. 'The case reached court in record time. The father is now doing time at Hall prison, and as you can see, he confessed to most of the abuse. The only thing he hasn't admitted to is killing his son. But there is a note about drug abuse. So the question is whether he was high when it happened. It's all pretty awful.'

They read together about William Carlsson, found in nothing but a grey T-shirt and long johns in the middle of a freezing cold winter. There was no backpack – no items out of the ordinary – nothing with or without horses. Just big bruises and a colossal tragedy.

'But you don't know,' said Vincent. 'The father hasn't confessed. And furthermore . . .' He pointed to a photograph of the place where William had been found. There were three dry docks on the small island, but only one of them was in use. William had been found between two of the vessels in the dock. The only thing in the photo that testified to this horrific occurrence was the police tape cordoning off the area between the two boats.

'Close to water again,' said Mina. 'If so, that gives Nova's theory a boost.'

Vincent nodded, although he didn't look at all happy.

'Perhaps,' said Vincent. 'Lucky the dock wasn't filled – you would never have found him otherwise. But I think we should go and take a look. Just because the police didn't find anything at the scene doesn't mean there's nothing to find.'

'Are you saying we don't do our jobs?' she said, slapping him playfully on the arm.

'Not at all. But the forensic specialists who examined the scene had no reason to look for anything unusual. I'm aware that the chance of something still being there, if it was ever there in the first place, is minimal. The police probably drew the right conclusion – William was beaten to death by his father. This is a straw so weak that it'll probably crumble to dust the second we grasp at it. But I think we need to be as sure as we can be that this really isn't connected to Ossian and Lilly. Because if it is . . .'

He didn't finish the sentence, instead taking the handkerchief out of his pocket. After glancing quickly at her, he put it away again.

Mina looked at the screen and suddenly felt chilled, despite the heat.

'We'll have to run it by the team and Julia first,' she said. 'I'll see if I can call a meeting right away. Everyone should be in now.'

'We?' he said, looking at her in surprise.

'Welcome back, Vincent.'

73

The team had grown since Vincent had last encountered them. The new addition, Adam, was tall, his features chiselled and his eyes lively and intelligent. It was as if he'd arrived straight from an American TV show.

'Hi, I'm Vincent,' he said, proffering his hand to Adam.

Adam shook his right hand so firmly that the coffee in the mug in Vincent's left hand spilled over.

'Adam. I've heard a lot about you.'

Three clear pumping movements, eye contact and a ten-degree forward tilt of the upper body. It was a handshake worthy of a gold star. Firm and clear but not dominant. A handshake that said that its giver was in control of the situation and that both parties would work well together. Vincent glanced at the others in the room. Christer and Peder each nodded an appreciative hello to him, in Peder's case now accompanied by a bobbing full beard, while Ruben seemed to greet him by glaring and crossing his arms.

'Ruben, I didn't thank you for what you sent,' he said. 'It meant a lot. Sorry, would you mind holding my coffee while I take off my bag?'

He rapidly handed the mug to Ruben, who automatically

accepted it with a surprised expression. Vincent had counted on Ruben's programmed reflexes to kick in before his brain had time to think about whether he really wanted to hold the mug. Now that he was already holding it, it was too late to decline.

It had actually been about getting Ruben to open his body language by easing those crossed arms, so that he would be more receptive to what Vincent and Mina had to say. And the easiest way to do that was to ask him to hold something.

But Vincent also had actual cause to thank Ruben. Shortly after they had last crossed paths in the month of October almost two years previously, he had received an envelope in the post from Ruben. It had contained the newspaper article about his mother's death – the one that Ruben had presented as evidence, proving that Vincent was involved in the murders they had been investigating. Which he had been – just not in the way they had thought.

I still have no idea who sent this, Ruben had written on a note attached to the sheet of newspaper with a paper clip. *But I don't need it. I don't think anyone else needs to see it again. Burn it or do whatever you like with it.*

Vincent had been touched. But the Ruben who had sent the article didn't seem to be present at this meeting. He merely shrugged in response to Vincent's thanks and handed the coffee back. Everything was, in other words, as normal. Of course, Vincent was unlikely to play a particularly big role in this investigation – after all, they had already brought Nova on board. So he could condone some of their behaviour. But it was probably lucky for the police that they had an Adam for every Ruben on the force.

'Nice to see you again, Vincent,' said Julia. 'I gather you and Mina have had a few thoughts on the current case. Of course, I would have appreciated it if this had gone through the appropriate channels so that I was at least aware that you were back with us again.'

'I didn't know whether it would lead to anything,' Mina said apologetically. 'I wanted to be sure first. And I'm still not. But we want to take a closer look at the William Carlsson case. We thought we'd start with where he was found.'

'The boy beaten to death by his dad last winter?' said Ruben, sitting up a little straighter. 'What's he got to do with it?'

'If I might butt in,' said Adam. 'William's father, Jörgen Carlsson, was indeed convicted of the murder in an unusually swift trial. But if I remember correctly, Jörgen Carlsson never confessed to the actual murder, which was a little strange, given he admitted to everything else without hesitation. I don't know whether he thought he'd do better that way. What's more, and I may have misremembered the details on this, there was a witness early on in the investigation – an old woman who lived in a flat with a view of the playground in front of their building – who claimed she had seen someone other than Jörgen leaving with William. But since Jörgen couldn't account for his whereabouts and the woman's vision left much to be desired, it was written off.'

'In light of Ossian and Lilly, that sounds like a mistake,' said Julia. 'Jörgen Carlsson may have been telling the truth when he said he didn't do it. In which case he's been wrongly convicted.'

Ruben once again folded his arms and looked like he'd eaten something unpleasant.

'Jörgen Carlsson is a first-class, unparalleled bastard who is exactly where he should be,' he snorted.

'Agreed,' said Peder. 'I remember it too. The boy had wounds all over his body in various stages of healing. He'd taken so many beatings in his childhood that it was frankly a miracle he'd survived that long. And from what I understood, his mother had taken her share of beatings too.'

Bosse whimpered and licked Peder's hand – it was as if the dog understood how much it hurt Peder to even think about child abuse.

'In my book, there's no doubt about it that the dad killed the kid,' said Ruben. 'I'd been called out there a few times. Once on Christmas Eve. Fuck me. It was a goddamn bloodbath when we got there. Jörgen had slammed his wife's face against the hob, leaving blood all over the kitchen. And we found William behind the tree with the parcels, baubles and tinsel. I think he must have been about three. No fucking way is Jörgen innocent. He's one of those guys who should be locked up and the key thrown away.'

Silence descended. Vincent fixed his gaze on the only decoration to adorn the room – a large map of Stockholm on the wall opposite him. He tried not to visualize what Ruben had just said. But it was too late. He stared at the old town until his eyes filled with tears as he tried to expunge the memory of the bruises he had seen in the photographs of William's body. A body that was so similar to how Aston's had looked only a few years ago.

Christer cleared his throat.

'I'm with Ruben on this,' he muttered. 'Jörgen Carlsson is a swine. He should never see the light of day again. Luckily for us, what he's confessed to is enough to keep him inside for quite a while yet. And luck's the right word, because Adam's got a point. It's not certain that Jörgen killed his son.'

'Adam and Ruben – I think it's best you speak to William's mother Lovis right away,' said Julia. 'Try to speak to the neighbour who claimed to have seen William abducted and find out just how bad her eyesight is. It would be great if you can do both today. And on Monday you can pay a visit to Hall prison to see Jörgen. I'll get in touch to let them know you're coming.'

Ruben turned to Adam. 'You can forget about good cop this time,' he said. 'Not with that bastard.'

Adam nodded grimly. He appeared to agree. Julia looked at Mina and Vincent.

'I don't know what it is you think you might find,' she said. 'But go and take a look at the scene. Take Peder and his beard along too. If you happen to pass a barber en route, the force will foot the bill. But Vincent . . . while you're here, we've got a woman in custody that I'm keen for you to meet before you go. Her name is Lenore Silver.'

74

'How long have you lived in Sweden?'

Adam sighed deeply to himself. He considered not answering Ruben's question, but realized that small talk was part of life in police cars. He just wished that the question was a different one.

'I was born here.'

'Aha. OK.' Silence.

It was a source of constant surprise to Adam how often that answer left people speechless.

'But what about your parents? Where are they from?' said Ruben.

'Uganda.'

'Aha, Uganda.' Silence again. Then: 'Fuck it. I've got to confess I don't know a thing about Uganda.'

'No, why would you? I don't know much about Uganda either.' Adam felt like rolling his eyes. There was something about Ruben that riled him. Something beyond his stereotypical line of questioning. He had encountered this type of cop on so many previous occasions. A lot of focus on muscles, not so much on brains.

'So when did they escape to here?'

'They didn't escape. My mother came here to take up a professorship. She found out she was pregnant after she arrived, but never wanted anything to do with my father.'

'Jesus,' said Ruben, nodding. 'But haven't you ever wondered about your dad? Haven't you tried to contact him?'

'No – why would I? I trust my mother's judgement. If she didn't think he was worthy to be in my life, then I assume she was justified in that assessment.'

'Ah,' said Ruben, suddenly looking distressed. 'That kind of dad.'

Adam glanced at him briefly, but then shifted his eyes back to the road again. Adam was deeply uninterested in rooting through his colleagues' private lives. Especially Ruben's.

251

The high-rises in Rissne where Lovis lived loomed above them and Adam pulled into the car park. Ruben was still sitting in silence, his face a picture of dejection. Adam checked the address on his mobile. The first door beyond the car park. He looked around and pointed.

'There. That must be the playground where William's parents claim to have last seen him.'

'I still don't believe for a moment that it wasn't his old man that beat him to death,' Ruben muttered.

'I don't intend to argue with you. We have a job to do.'

He could hear just how sharp his tone was. But he was so sick of all these cops who wanted nothing but easy solutions. Reality was rarely easy. It was complicated.

They climbed the three flights of stairs to Lovis's flat. A pushchair containing a sleeping baby stood outside the neighbouring flat. The child stirred in its sleep and whimpered when they knocked on Lovis's door. It took a long time for it to open. But in the end they heard shuffling footsteps inside. A long silence. Hesitation. Then a lock turned and the door opened slowly. But only a crack.

'Yes?'

The voice was hoarse, and Adam could feel the stench of old alcohol hitting him even through the small crack.

'Police. We want to talk about William.'

'Oh, so now you want to talk about William?'

She began to close the door, but Adam stuck his foot into the gap.

'Lovis. For William's sake. Let us in.'

Silence again. Then the door opened. She shuffled ahead of them, further into the flat. It was dark. No light penetrated it: all the windows were covered in black fabric. It smelled bad – a mixture of rubbish, rancid food and cigarette smoke. Behind him, Ruben coughed slightly.

'You can sit there.'

Lovis showed them into the living room and pointed at a shabby couch covered in stains and burn marks. The table in front of it was strewn with overflowing ashtrays and empty bottles that had previously contained wine and spirits. The only

252

adornment to the walls were a few framed photographs. Lovis with William. Jörgen and Lovis together. A child – possibly Lovis – perched on a horse with an expression of pride.

Adam sat down without hesitation but saw from the corner of his eye that Ruben was considering standing. He gave him a look. They were here to interview the mother of a murdered child. They couldn't afford to carry on like the Princess and the Pea. Ruben seemed to catch his drift and sat down on the sofa, although not without grimacing slightly.

'Is it Jörgen? Has something happened to Jörgen? You know, he shouldn't be inside. He didn't kill William.'

Lovis lit a cigarette, her hands trembling, and then took a deep drag from it and glowered at them. Then she pointed her finger at them in agitation.

'That boy! The missing boy! That's why you're here! It's the same person who killed William who took that boy! I told you so! I told you it wasn't Jörgen!'

'We can't say anything at this stage,' said Adam, holding out his hands. 'Except that we're looking into the circumstances around your son's death. So we'd like—'

'Out!'

Lovis glared at them.

'We need to ask . . .'

Adam cleared his throat. The smoke was irritating his windpipe and making his eyes tear up.

'Out!'

Lovis stood up rapidly, sweeping an empty bottle of Smirnoff off the table in her haste. It fell to the floor with a clinking sound and rolled a little way before it stopped.

'I want you to leave. Out!'

Ruben stood up and Adam followed his lead. They might have to come back. But for now it was probably best to let Lovis calm down a little.

When the door had slammed shut behind them, Adam shook off the disappointment. Talking to Lovis hadn't given them much.

They had two visits left to make. The witness. And then Jörgen.

253

75

Mina knew the corridors off by heart, but Vincent looked around curiously as Julia led them to Kronoberg Remand Prison, which was conveniently located in the same building as police headquarters.

'As I said, her name's Lenore Silver,' said Julia. 'We're holding her on suspicion of unlawful deprivation of liberty and human trafficking of minors. So far, she's denied any connection to the Ossian case, as well as the other kids, but there's no harm asking the question again. Well, actually, letting you ask, Vincent.'

Vincent stopped and frowned.

'As I said last time—' he began.

'We know,' Julia interrupted. 'You're not a trained police officer, interrogator or anything like that. You can't assume that kind of responsibility. Believe me when I say that it caused me a lot of grief on more than one occasion the last time you worked for us. But it all worked out in the end. And I just want you to . . . talk to her. You're good at that.'

They arrived at the interview rooms. Anonymous doors with black numbers. It could have been a corridor of offices in any public sector building. But the woman waiting behind one of the doors made Mina's skin crawl every time she saw her. She was everything Mina wasn't. Self-confident. Well dressed. Beautiful. She had long, manicured nails instead of red, chapped fingertips. And she was most probably a psychopath.

'OK, I can give it a try, but I'm not promising anything,' said Vincent. 'And I'll do it my way. Does anyone have a pen?'

Julia handed him one.

The mentalist carefully drew a small dot on one of his cheeks, around a centimetre below his eye.

'What are you doing?' she asked.

'*My way.*'

Julia shook her head. This had clearly already started to go south as far as she was concerned.

254

'Mina, take over,' she said. 'I have to go upstairs to tell the top brass what our next step is. Lenore is waiting in interrogation room 3.'

Julia disappeared down the corridor. Mina felt the sweat exuding from her armpits. It had nothing to do with the person they were about to see – it was just so damn hot.

She took a deep breath and opened the door to reveal Lenore Silver, who, despite the heat and having been in custody for some time, was still managing to look cool, well dressed and freshly made-up. She was sitting on one of the three chairs inside, but the table was missing. Presumably, Julia had arranged for its removal to make it easier for Vincent.

Lenore's smile disappeared when she spotted the mentalist.

'What's he doing here?' she said. 'I've seen him on the telly.'

'Vincent's going to ask you a few questions,' said Mina, sitting down on a chair opposite Lenore. She immediately felt a little better. Not nearly as sweaty. Vincent sat down next to her.

'I'm not answering nothing,' said Lenore, crossing her arms. 'Not without my lawyer. I've been in here since last Friday. That's a week ago, right? You can't hold me for much longer.'

'That's true,' said Mina. 'But, Lenore, we've identified the girl we found in your home. We know she comes from a family of recent arrivals who live in Midsommarkransen. We know you were planning to sell her – just like you did five years ago. You've already been named by others who want to get lighter sentences.'

The last bit was a lie – there was no one else. They knew no more than who the girl was, and the case was now being handled by other detectives. But Mina's gamble seemed to pay off, given how hard Lenore squeezed her arms with her hands.

'There's not a single lawyer willing to touch you with a barge-pole,' Mina added. 'Of course, you'll be assigned one by the state. But I have a hard time believing that they'll want to assign you the sharpest tool in the box. This is a chance for you to show your willingness to cooperate. And believe me, you need to.'

Lenore sat up straighter on the chair, her hands on her lap.

'So what does he want to know?' she said.

'It's more of a little game,' said Vincent with a smile. 'I'll say a word and when you hear it, say the first thing that comes to mind. Don't think too much. The important thing is that it's the first thing you think of. No matter how strange it might be. Can we test it out?'

Lenore sighed and nodded.

'OK,' said Vincent. 'Let's begin. Horse.'

'Saddle,' said Lenore, fixing her gaze on Vincent.

'Water,' Vincent said.

'Thirsty.'

'Children.'

'Other people's.' Lenore crossed her arms again, her eyes remaining locked with those of the mentalist.

'Death.'

'Life.'

'Ossian.'

'Ireland.'

'Lilly.'

'Wedding.'

Vincent raised an eyebrow.

'There's a bridalwear shop in town called that,' said Lenore.

'Planning on getting married?' said Mina.

'None of your business. Are we done?'

'Nearly,' said Vincent. 'William.'

'Spetz.'

'To kill.'

'TV series.'

'Thanks, that's great,' said Vincent, standing up. 'We're done here. Thanks for taking the time to talk to us.'

He offered his hand and Lenore took it automatically. Vincent suddenly inserted his left hand under her wrist and then released his grip with his right hand. The result was that her arm was resting on his hand in mid-air. He swayed his hand gently, making her arm move back and forth as he pointed to the dot he'd drawn onto his face.

Mina watched in fascination.

'Lenore, look at this spot,' he said in a completely different tone to before.

Vincent's voice was soft but simultaneously commanding.

Mina had difficulty not looking at his cheek too. The situation was so peculiar that she obeyed the instruction simply because it was something she understood. Which she guessed was the whole point.

Lenore's gaze began to cloud over. She seemed unaware of her arm.

'And while you watch it,' Vincent continued, 'do you notice how your thoughts are becoming as unfocused as your gaze, just like that, and the less focus you have, the less you need to think about. Instead you can just allow yourself to flow into the thoughts – it's like a big, friendly sea drawing you down . . . and you're allowing yourself to be drawn into those reassuring depths . . . now.'

He let go of Lenore's arm, which fell straight down. Lenore's head also fell forward. Mina saw that she had closed her eyes.

'Great, keep going,' said Vincent, placing his hand on Lenore's neck to ensure she remained tilted forward. 'Sink even lower, to where you're safe and it feels good. Are you there?'

Lenore nodded slowly. Mina didn't really believe in hypnosis, but whatever it was Vincent had done to Lenore, she really did seem to be hypnotized. It probably wasn't even allowed, but Mina suspected that Julia had been hoping for something like this when she had approved Vincent's help.

'Now I'm going to ask you the same questions again,' said Vincent. 'And this time I want you to answer whatever it is you find down there in your innermost self. OK?'

Lenore nodded again. The only thing audible in the room was the creak of the chair as Vincent sat down in front of Lenore.

'Horse,' he said.

'Cock.'

Lenore's voice was clear – it wasn't anything like how Mina thought hypnotized people would sound. But it was very clear that Lenore was currently somewhere else. Mina didn't think she was faking it.

'Water,' said Vincent.

'Drown.'

'Ossian.'

'Ocean.'

Vincent glanced at Mina. She nodded at him to continue.

'Children.'

'Money.'

'Death.'

'Me.'

'Lilly.'

'White lilies.'

'William.'

'The will.'

'To kill.'

'Nightmares.'

Vincent grabbed Lenore's hand again and pulled it straight out from her body. When he let go, it remained in mid-air.

'As you feel your arm slowly sinking,' he said, 'you can allow yourself to sink even deeper into your thoughts.'

The arm began to slowly move down. The self-confident woman was gone – Lenore's expression was more reminiscent of that of a child.

'And when the hand reaches your lap, open the door to the place where you keep your dreams.'

The hand landed in Lenore's lap and she frowned.

'I want to ask you something about the last thing you said,' said Vincent. 'Do you mean that you get nightmares from killing, or that you have nightmares about killing someone?'

'The second one,' said Lenore.

Her voice was now much darker and huskier. As if it was emanating from deep in her throat.

'Although when I do that it stops being a nightmare. The darkness ends.'

'Do you kill what you find in the darkness?'

'Yes.'

'Lenore, what's in the darkness?'

'Ulf. My uncle.'

Vincent paused and looked at Mina. He looked deeply unhappy.

'I'm going to count down from five to one,' he told Lenore. 'Start swimming back to the surface on five. Back to us. On four, you can start to feel refreshed and restored. On three, you can choose to remember whatever you want about what we discussed, but may forget anything you don't want to remember. On two, take a deep breath, and on one open your eyes again.'

Lenore opened her eyes and looked around in confusion.

'What was that?' she said. 'What were we just talking about?'

'Nothing,' said Vincent, standing up again. 'I was thanking you for your time. We'll get out of your hair. One last thing, though: where does the Lion King sleep?'

Lenore looked even more confused.

'What? What do you mean?'

He left the room, giving Mina no choice but to follow. Lenore watched them go in astonishment as Mina closed the door.

'The Lion King?' said Mina once they were in the corridor.

'If you want to create memory loss following hypnosis,' said Vincent, 'it's important to provide the brain with a distraction afterwards so that it doesn't start dwelling on what just happened.'

'So what did you find out?'

'Didn't you hear?' he said, looking at her in surprise. 'Obviously I was a little puzzled at first when she associated water with drowning and then Ossian with ocean. I thought it might be a lead. But I think that was purely linguistic association. As in, the words sound the same. We had already discussed water, so it's hardly surprising that she was still there in her next thought. And Lilly and William gave no connection of that kind whatsoever. Nor when I mentioned horses. I don't think she has anything to do with our dead children.'

Mina nodded. That had been her conclusion too. But it had still been worth a try.

'But,' said Vincent, stopping, 'Lenore primarily sees children as a way to earn money. So I would imagine that she has a serious empathy disorder. It might be a physiological defect in the brain – such as a dysfunction in the amygdala or damage to the synapses between the frontal lobes and the hippocampus. But if you ask me, it's a psychological defence mechanism. White lilies? Lenore has a fixation on death. She was abused by her uncle when she was little. *That* Ulf. Of course she's suppressed it, but he's created a lot of the woman inside that space. It might be a good idea to have a psychologist speak to her.'

Mina stared at Vincent. Beyond the names of the children, he had asked Lenore about just five words. No more. And yet they now knew more about Lenore Silver than they had found out from almost a week's worth of interrogation.

'I have one question,' she said. 'Then we need to get Peder and head to Beckholmen. But I won't be able to let go of it otherwise. Where *does* the Lion King sleep?'

The corners of Vincent's mouth twitched.

'In a Simba bed,' he said.

Then he howled as she punched his shoulder.

76

Nathalie gathered up the tools she had used and walked slowly to the shed with them. She was so incredibly tired. The hammer had to be put back in its place, as did the saw. Order was important to Karl.

A few more members of the inner circle had joined them – all wearing the same white clothes – and they had worked very hard together on the renovation. The white clothes were completely impractical. Every day after work they were covered in dirt. Especially the time she had to clear up the remains of the building a little way off that had burnt down. She had asked what the building had been before, but had received nothing but silence in return.

Nathalie stretched to relax her muscles. Working with her body created a sense of satisfaction that was new to her. But she wasn't really fit yet – she lacked the muscle power and stamina expected of her, which meant the mere act of closing the shed door was an exertion by this time.

Monica and Karl had set her and the others to work in the mornings and then they had just carried on all day. The result was that she had got so tired she could have fallen asleep standing up. She probably would have done too, had she not been so hungry. At the same time, the atmosphere in the group was great – she most definitely wasn't going to be the first to complain. But this had turned into a rather different summer holiday than expected.

She followed the others into the building that had been her home of late. She still hadn't learned their names, even though there weren't that many of them. But the white clothes and the constant smiles made them look surprisingly alike. She directed her feet towards the dormitory, her eyelids heavy. It would be wonderful to lie down on the camp bed that had been hers lately. And she really ought to get in touch with Dad. After all, he hadn't heard from her since . . .

She came to a halt.

Just when had that been? The days were merging together. She tried to count on her fingers how long it had been since she and Ines had met on the metro. A week? Two? Thinking about it made her head hurt – she needed to rest first. But then . . . then she'd get in touch.

She just needed to charge her phone first. Wherever was she going to find a charger . . . ?

'Nathalie? Nathalie, where are you going?'

She was so close. The bed was only a few metres away. But she could tell from her grandmother's voice that she wanted something in particular. She turned around, saw her grand-mother and was startled. Like Nathalie, Ines wore white, but her T-shirt and trousers had been replaced with a long robe. There was a green ribbon draped over her shoulders.

'What's happening?' was the best Nathalie could muster.

'It's time for you to begin to understand the meaning of John's words,' said Ines. 'Come with me.'

Grandma took her hand and led her towards the room where they usually ate. Nathalie was too tired to protest. The tables they usually sat at had been pushed up against the walls and a long plank of wood supported by trestles ran down the room. The others in the group were standing shoulder to shoulder, hands resting on the plank. Ines directed Nathalie to stand with the others. She stood at the end of the plank next to Karl, while Ines assumed a position at the far end.

'Everything is suffering; pain purifies,' said Ines.

'Everything is suffering; pain purifies,' the group replied.

'You all carry pain of different kinds,' Ines said. 'Pain that helps you to see the world clearly. We have a newcomer among us today. My granddaughter Nathalie. Her pain is spiritual rather than physical, but it is nonetheless real. Today we welcome Nathalie among us and remind ourselves that we are not afraid of pain. Instead, it brings us clarity.'

Ines produced a riding crop and approached the person standing closest to her – a silver-haired man in his sixties. The man tensed his whole body.

'Everything is suffering; pain purifies,' said her grandmother.

'Everything is suffering; pain purifies,' the man replied quietly.

The whip whistled through the air and struck the wood, the sound echoing as Ines hit the man's fingers. He shuddered as if he had been electrocuted but remained fixed to the spot with his hands on the plank. An angry red line appeared immediately on his fingers and the man's eyes filled with tears. Nathalie tried to understand. Were they being punished? No, it didn't feel like it. Her grandmother didn't look angry. On the contrary, the room was filled with an almost-religious sense of reverence. The man frowned in concentration. Then a small smile played across his lips. He nodded at Ines, who moved on to the next person.

'Everything is suffering; pain purifies,' she said, raising the whip.

Nathalie was struggling to think because she was so tired and hungry, but she didn't think she wanted Grandma to hit her. It looked as if it hurt a great deal. She didn't want to be in pain.

'Don't be afraid,' Karl whispered to Nathalie. 'The pain passes. But the focus it gives you . . . I promise, you'll see the world in a whole new light after this.'

Ines continued to make her way along the row. The five people she had struck with the whip were embracing each other and laughing and crying interchangeably. All Nathalie knew was that if she let go of the plank of wood, she would probably topple over from exhaustion. The others all seemed so happy. She wanted to be with them too.

The whip whistled through the air beside her and she heard Karl draw breath just before it hit his hands with a crack like a gunshot. Then Ines turned to her. Karl hung his head, breathing heavily. A droplet of blood emerged from the red line across his fingers.

'Hello, my sweet,' said Ines, brushing a strand of hair from Nathalie's face. 'Welcome to the truth.'

When the riding crop hit her fingers, a part of her brain exploded. She screamed. It was as if someone had set fire to her hands, or shoved them inside a wasps' nest. Ines took her in her arms, making her leave her hands on the plank of wood.

'Don't fight it,' Ines whispered. 'Examine the pain. Embrace it. Look out through it.'

Nathalie tried to do as Ines said, but it was too much. It was too overwhelming. She wanted to get as far away from the pain as she could.

'You're in shock,' Ines said into her ear. 'But see the pain for what it is.'

She tried again. It hurt, so, so, much. But what did it really mean? What did the hurting mean? It was only signals in her brain. She tried to make out the constituent parts of the pain, in the same way she'd seen grown-ups analyse wine. Trying to find the different flavours, aromas and sensations. And all of a sudden, the pain was a little easier to bear. It still hurt terribly, but not quite as much as before. She inhaled through her teeth. Somewhere there was also a clarity: a sharpness formed by the adrenaline in her brain. She saw what was important and what wasn't. She understood what Grandma had meant by John's words.

Then Ines raised Nathalie's hands and placed them into a bucket of ice-cold water that someone had set down on the plank. The soothing water was one stimulus too many, and Nathalie began to cry uncontrollably. Grandma was right. Pain purified. And Nathalie was carrying so much pain – pain she hadn't even known about. Her grandmother pressed her head to her breast, and Nathalie sobbed.

'There, there,' Grandma comforted her. 'We'll always take care of you. I promise. You're one of us now.'

77

Peder leaned against the roughcast wall. He had hoped the dry dock's depth – some four metres – would offer a degree of protection from the sun, but it wasn't to be. There were three vessels in the dock that Peder guessed were there to undergo repairs – all of them propped up on metal trusses.

'Yes, that business last winter was deeply tragic,' said the man standing in front of him. 'With the boy, I mean.'

The man's name was Bengt, and he represented the Beckholmen Dock Association. It hadn't been Bengt who had found William, but he had phoned it in to the police.

'We have boats here year-round,' he continued, 'but most of them come in the summer and are only in for a week. Had it been any other time, the body would have been washed out to sea when we opened the lock. But the vessel that was here in the winter needed new planking, so she was in for a month or so. It was her crew that found him. It was just too awful. Imagine having to stay and carry out repairs in a place where you'd . . . Well, obviously they ended up being delayed since your lot at the police needed to check out whether the people working on the boat were suspects, so that wrecked our schedule for the rest of the year, but—'

'Planking?' Peder interrupted.

Bengt gave him a look clearly reserved for those who didn't know a jot about boats.

'Have you ever seen a wooden boat? You know, those planks on the side of the ship? That the whole hull is made of? Planking.'

Peder nodded. Then he pretended to catch sight of something further off and fled to join Mina, who had made her way to the corner of the dock where the rays of sunshine did not penetrate.

Vincent paced back and forth between the vessels, examining the surroundings with his hands clasped at his back. Peder could see the concentration writ on the mentalist's face despite the sunglasses. Vincent had those horn-rimmed sunglasses that had stopped being popular in the fifties. In some inconceivable way he made them work.

Peder had been surprised when he'd seen Vincent at the meeting – no one had mentioned that he was going to be involved in the case. Apparently it had been Mina's idea, but Julia had given it the OK. He had done a good job last time – there was no denying it. So long as Peder didn't have to sit through another lecture on sleep, it surely couldn't hurt for Vincent to take a look.

Not that Peder could wrap his head around what Vincent thought he might find. Each time the boats in the dock were swapped out, it was filled with water – as Bengt had pointed out. And according to Bengt, that happened as frequently as once a week. Any possible traces had long ago been washed away.

'Are you looking for anything in particular?' he called out, scratching his beard.

The struggle between him and Anette on whether to keep his beard or not rumbled on. On the one hand, she said it probably scratched her more than it did him – she said it was bringing her out in a rash. On the other hand, she had admitted it was very sexy – in photos. He supposed that henceforth he would have to appear at home only in photographs.

Vincent shook his head and came over to him and Mina.

'I just want to get a feel for the place,' he said. 'In case that in itself is a clue. But it's not going too well. I can't find any context. Nova's theory that the murders are related to water might still be true. We are, after all, standing in a dock. But I can't help thinking that statement is too . . . general. Too vague. In Stockholm there's water everywhere. It doesn't really make sense to mention it. Pfft, I suppose Ruben might be right that William isn't linked to the other cases. Perhaps it was his father who killed him and left him here to make it look like an accident. William isn't point B. We don't have a pattern.'

'Ruben would love to hear that,' said Mina.

'And that puts us back to square one,' Peder sighed.

'By the way – did you know there's a German study that

265

shows that women think men with full beards are more attractive?' said Vincent.

'Er, no. But that might explain . . .' Peder began before realizing he was scratching his beard again.

'By the by, did Amir have a beard?' said Vincent, casting a knowing look at Mina.

Peder had no idea what he was getting at, but Mina clearly did, given the murderous look she gave Vincent.

'Although on the other hand, most other studies have concluded the opposite,' Vincent added, unperturbed. 'For instance, Barnaby Dixson in New Zealand has done a plethora of beard studies, as have Nicke Neave and Kerry Shields in the UK. They conclude that some stubble works, but more than that and men cease to be attractive. Almost the funniest thing is the Germans' explanation for their anomalous result. They guessed it was because the beard hides so much of the face that women were free to fantasize about what the men actually looked like.'

Peder wondered whether Anette might have any German blood. That would explain parts of their relationship – and not just her attitude towards his beard. Vincent didn't seem to notice that he wasn't getting any answers. He had got started now and nothing could stop him.

'But given your role as a police officer, perhaps the most important thing to be aware of is Dixson's note that beards reinforce angry facial expressions,' said Vincent. 'If you ever want to come across as dangerous, you're on the right track.'

Mina smiled wryly as she stood in the shade.

'I think you're thinking of Ruben now,' she said.

Vincent turned to her and nodded before continuing.

'Of course, then there's a fascinating master's dissertation from the University of Twente in the Netherlands which notes that in job interviews, having a long beard has the same positive impact as being clean-shaven, while facial hair lengths in between have a more negative effect. So it's a good look if you're thinking about changing jobs, Peder. Assuming, of course, you're OK with the fact that a beard contains more human pathogenic bacteria than a really grubby dog's coat. We found that out a number of years ago when a group of radiologists in Switzerland—'

Vincent cut himself short. Mina's eyes had widened in horror when he'd mentioned bacteria. Just typical. Peder knew he wouldn't be allowed to sit next to her in any more conference room meetings. She would maintain a gap of at least two chairs between them until he shaved it off. The question was whether Bosse, Christer's dog, was even welcome following that observation. Just like bloody Vincent to mess things up. Now it was up to him to quickly divert Mina's thoughts before she outright demanded he visit the barber on the way back to police headquarters.

'Speaking of nothing in particular,' he said into the silence, 'have I shown you the video of the triplets singing along to Mellon? Well, not so much singing as . . .'

His mobile was already halfway out of his pocket before he caught sight of Mina's tormented expression. He sighed and put it back again. Beards were a reasonable topic of conversation, but not the video of his rays of sunshine? It was so typical of people who didn't have their own kids. They just didn't get it.

'You've showed us the video already this week,' said Mina. 'And the week before. And the week before that. Ruben really wasn't exaggerating – we've seen it rather a lot since Melodifestivalen took place last winter or whenever it was. If I'm being honest . . .'

So what? It wasn't as if you could ever get tired of the triplets. But he obeyed. It was a good thing he had plenty of other videos to show them that were at least as cute. Fortunately, Mina had stopped giving his beard pained looks.

The mentalist suddenly frowned and returned to the dry dock and the spot where William had been found, waving to Peder and Mina that they should follow.

'What is it?' said Mina.

'I realize that all the photos of the scene where William was found were taken from this angle,' said Vincent. 'Stand here and imagine you have a camera. Tell me what you see through the lens.'

'Why . . . ? OK then,' said Mina. 'I see . . . the concrete floor

267

where William was lying. A rock face a few metres away. The wall extends around four metres into the air. Car tyres hanging along it – I suppose they're to stop the boats scraping against the rocks when they enter the dock. Above the top edge there's a red balustrade. And a red-painted building.'

'Go down a bit,' said Vincent. 'To the point where the rock face meets the balustrade.'

'OK, I was careless. The last metre or so of wall is actually cast concrete. The top edge of the dock. People seem to have painted squares onto the concrete and written names inside them . . . *Altarskär. Sunbeam. Panama. Afrodite.*'

She turned to Vincent.

'The names of the vessels that have been docked here, I suppose.'

He nodded.

'What you just described is exactly what is visible in the police photographs. Now let's take a look at the picture we haven't seen. What was behind the camera when William was photographed?'

'I don't understand,' she said.

'Turn the other way, Mina. Now what do you see?'

Mina did as he said. Peder looked in the same direction. He felt as confused as Mina appeared to be.

'It looks the same,' she said. 'Concrete floor, rock wall, concrete, graffiti, balustrade. Although there's no building up there. And not as many boat names on the wall.'

'Good. Now let's say that William is lying here – at our feet. If you were to take a photo with him in the foreground, how many names on the wall do you think you'd get into the picture?'

Mina screened off her field of vision by making a square with her thumbs and forefingers.

'Two. *Jera* and *H* . . . something. The one starting with an H has been worn off by the water. I can't see what it says. But it ends in an O. Actually, no. *Jera* wouldn't be in the photo, since it would be taken in portrait to get the whole wall in. So it would probably only be the name with the H that was visible.'

Peder couldn't help but laugh.

268

'That's one hell of a name for a boat,' he said.

Mina and Vincent looked at him blankly. The fact that Vincent didn't understand was not unexpected, but he was surprised that the penny hadn't dropped for Mina.

'But surely you must see what it says?' he said. 'OK, so the water has taken some of it away, but it's not that hard to figure out. It's the name of a notorious armoured personnel carrier, used in South Africa in the seventies by the police and army – it was custom-built to deal with landmines. I say built, but really they were just pensioned-off British military trucks that they reinforced. These things were crazy heavy, you could barely see a thing while driving them, and they were more like tanks than people carriers. But they did the job. In several wars to boot. Just as long as you didn't shoot at them, of course. They might have been able to deal with mines, but they were less good with bullets. I hope the ship with that name wasn't as heavily armed. If it were, I expect it would sink.'

Mina and Vincent were still staring at him.

'What? Like you two don't have any personal interests? I do actually have a life beyond hanging out with the triplets. Just so you know.'

That last bit wasn't entirely truthful. He had been watching a Discovery Channel documentary on the war in South Africa because the triplets had fallen asleep in a heap on his stomach following a wrestling match that he had lost. He hadn't dared to move from the floor out of fear that they would wake up. The TV had been on inches away from him. The documentary had been an hour long. Then Anette had come home and saved him.

Vincent called to Bengt and pointed up to the semi-illegible ship's name.

'When was that ship here?'

Despite wearing a cap, Bengt shaded his eyes with his hand and paused for thought.

'Do you know what?' he said, doubt in his voice, 'I can't remember every boat that's been here, but I really don't think we've had a ship by that name pass through. Must be graffiti left by some adventurous teenagers.'

269

'I don't think so,' said Vincent, looking at Peder. 'Do you know whether the South African army were inspired by the Trojan War when they named their vehicle?'

Typical. He shouldn't have been so confident about his supposed military history expertise. They hadn't mentioned ancient Greek battles in the documentary.

'Troy?' he said in an attempt to buy time. 'Where they built that wooden thing to hide the soldiers inside?'

'Exactly. Because the name of your military vehicle – the name someone has painted right above the spot where William was found – is a Greek word. *Hippo.*'

Vincent waited a few seconds to give Mina time to make out the faded word on the concrete.

'*Hippo* means horse,' he said.

78

Ruben crossed the expanse outside the flats. The playground where William had last been seen alive lay empty. No one was out in the heat. People had either fled to the beach or were indoors with the comfort of their cooling fans.

'Surely you cope better with the heat, don't you?' said Ruben, wiping the sweat from his brow with the hem of his short-sleeved police shirt.

'Why would I?' said Adam, who was walking a few steps ahead of him.

They were making for the entrance to the stairwell where Lovis's neighbour lived.

'Well, because, uh . . . Oh, to hell with it.'

Ruben had to up his pace or be left behind. Either Adam was playing dumb or he was a moron. Surely that wasn't a strange thing to ask? After all, guys like him and his brethren were supposed to be able to withstand the sun and heat of Africa, while pasty types like him from northern latitudes were built to cope with long, cold winters. As far as he was concerned, there was nothing racist about that. It was pure biology.

A woman in her thirties came towards them with a pushchair. The parasol to one side of the pushchair shielded the child from the sun, but the woman looked very hot. She stopped bang in front of them, forcing Adam to come to a halt to avoid walking into the pushchair.

'I just need to say something,' said the woman.

'Of course,' said Ruben, stepping forward. 'What's it about?'

'Little Maximillian is starting nursery in a year's time,' she said, pointing down at the pushchair. 'We'd been looking forward to it. But not anymore.'

She pointed her index finger in Ruben's direction as if she were trying to impale him on it.

'Children are being kidnapped from nurseries and you're doing absolutely nothing about it,' she said, pressing her finger against the police crest sewn onto his breast pocket. 'Aren't you ashamed? If I were you, I'd change jobs. Or better yet, jump in front of a train. Ted Hansson is right. Maximillian shouldn't have to grow up in a world where immigrants can take our kids from under our noses without the police lifting a finger.' She looked at Adam through narrowed eyes.

'Although it's pretty obvious why,' she said.

'There's nothing to suggest that "immigrants" are involved in these crimes,' said Ruben with a smile that had frozen to ice on his lips.

'You tell yourself that,' snapped the woman, making to leave with the pushchair. 'When Ted wins, you and your darkie mate will be out of a job,' she shouted over her shoulder.

Ruben glanced at Adam, who watched the woman go until she had vanished around the corner on the far side of the playground.

'Wasn't it door B?' Adam said.

He turned towards the entrance to the nearest building.

Ruben nodded.

'Door B, seventh floor. But—'

'Forget about it,' said Adam. 'It's not the first time and it won't be the last.'

271

'Do you get used to it?'

'Would you?'

Ruben shook his head. They stepped through the door and felt the continued onslaught of the heat inside. A large hand-written note awaited them at the bottom of the stairwell. The lift was out of order.

'For fuck's sake,' said Ruben, looking up.

Seven flights of stairs. Seven fucking flights of stairs.

'We're going to have to see if we've got what it takes,' Adam said with unnecessary jauntiness. He began to briskly climb the stairs.

Ruben liked him even less than before, if that were possible. Seven storeys later, he was on the brink of a heart attack. Not a thread on his body was dry and he sounded like a broken set of bellows. But to his great satisfaction, Adam was just as sweaty and looked quite uncomfortable. A small victory. Still . . . a victory was a victory.

They rang the bell and after a while they heard shuffling inside. A small, dry-skinned woman of indeterminate age opened the door and peered at them from some way below the security chain.

'Yes? If you're selling something, then I'm not buying. And I'm not interested in Jesus, and the salvation of God's only begotten son.'

'We're from the police,' said Adam, presenting his identification.

Ruben wondered whether to produce his too, but he was all out of energy. Neither his arms nor legs would obey him following the climb up the stairs.

'The police? I see. Well, you'd better come in.'

The woman closed the door and took off the security chain before opening up again to admit them into the hallway. Ruben felt a pang in his heart. The flat smelled just like Granny's. And the clock ticking away somewhere sounded just like the clock he'd heard throughout his childhood. It was a sound that had always told him he was safe.

'Would you like coffee?'

The woman, who was called Viola Berg according to their files, walked slowly ahead of them to the kitchen. The ticking sound intensified the closer they got, and proved to emanate from a fine Gustavian Mora clock in the corner.

'Are you from Dalarna?' said Ruben. 'My grandmother comes from Älvdalen.'

'Älvdalen? Then you and I are neighbours, of a kind. Although that was years ago. I moved to Stockholm when I was nineteen. Not that I intend to disclose to two handsome lads like you which year that was in.'

She winked at them and turned to the coffee maker, which was already spluttering away.

'I take it you're here about the boy?' she said as she poured coffee into three Rörstrand cups covered in blue flowers.

After she'd hurried over to a cupboard in the far corner of the kitchen, biscuits also appeared on the table. Ruben hesitated. He knew he ought to consider his health. Now that he was a father and all. He didn't want to have a stroke when they had to go back down the seven flights of stairs. But when Adam helped himself liberally to the biscuits, he did the same. If Adam could have a six-pack and still put away biscuits, then surely he could treat himself too.

'The boy. Yes, that's right,' said Adam. 'We're aware that you've already given a statement about this on several occasions. And that it's now been some time since it happened. But we'd still like to ask you to go through what you saw on the day William disappeared one more time.'

'So you don't think it was the father anymore?' said Viola, peering at them. She inserted a sugar cube between her teeth and luxuriously drank a few sips of coffee through it. Just the way Ruben's grandmother did. He gulped.

'We can't comment on the investigation,' said Adam, reaching for another home-baked biscuit.

Ruben helped himself to another too.

'No, of course not,' said Viola. 'But I know Lovis has always claimed that it wasn't that layabout of hers who did it. Well, what do I know? Everyone who lives here knew the way he treated her and the child. The walls aren't that thick, after all. But I saw what I saw, even if none of you lot wanted to hear what I had to say.'

273

'So that morning . . .' said Adam, helping her to get started.

'Well, yes. It was early morning and I saw William out by the swings on his own. There was nothing strange about that – he was always up early at the weekend, playing in the playground all by himself. I suppose he got a bit of peace and quiet that way.'

'Do you know more precisely what time it was when you saw him?'

'I know exactly what the time was, and I've told you lot every time. I was sitting on my balcony and I was going to do the music quiz. They usually start at ten, or sometimes eleven, but that morning they were early. I'd only just turned on the radio. It was exactly half past nine. That was when I saw him come up to William and speak to him.'

'A man then? Was he alone?'

'Yes, it was just him. Young and handsome. Looked the part. There was nothing about him that stood out. Dark-coloured jacket. Short hair. Blond. He was too far away for me to see clearly what his face looked like. He looked like . . . well, anyone.'

'I don't mean to be impolite,' said Ruben. 'But can you really see all the way down to the playground from here?'

'Of course not – my eyesight isn't much to cheer about these days,' Viola laughed. 'That's why I've got binoculars. Those let me see all the way into the flats on the far side of the park.'

Ruben laughed and glanced at Adam.

'How long did the man talk to William?' he said.

He wetted his finger and gathered the crumbs that had fallen onto the checked waxcloth.

'Not that long. A minute, maybe two. I didn't give it much thought. The quiz had started on the radio and he . . . well, he didn't seem . . . dangerous. He had a nice smile, I could see that from all the way over here.'

'And then?'

Adam drank his coffee while observing Viola. The delicate cup seemed out of place in his big hand.

'Then he took William's hand and they left. Well, I assumed everything was as it was meant to be. That he was some relative or a friend of Lovis. Someone who was there to help. And God knows if there was one thing that family needed, it was someone to help them. A big strong bloke wouldn't have been a bad thing. So I guess I was hoping for that. That Lovis might have come to her senses.'

'And then you didn't see them again? William and the man, that is.'

'No. I didn't see them again. And I tried to tell the police this at the time – I tried to tell them that it wasn't the boy's father. But no one wanted to listen.'

Viola shook her head. She pushed over the tray of biscuits and pressed them to take one, but Ruben patted his belly.

'No thanks,' he said. 'I've probably had enough.'

'Same here,' said Adam, standing up. 'We have to make a move. Thank you for having us.'

'My pleasure,' she said, beginning to clear up. 'I don't get many visitors. It ends up like that after a while.'

When she closed the front door behind them, Ruben could still hear the clock ticking. He thought about the last thing Viola had said. He really ought to pay his grandmother an extra visit on the way home.

The Third Week

79

It was a new week. They'd ended the previous week by compiling the new information the team had gathered, which was honestly not much. Mina had tried to take some time off and get some rest over the weekend. She knew she needed it, but she had almost been climbing the walls before the weekend was out. She needed to be in motion – she needed to be working – to make sure her thoughts didn't get stuck on other things. So she took pleasure in returning to see Milda Hjort at the National Board of Forensic Medicine first thing on Monday, even if Milda had had to ask her to wait until she was done with her previous task.

Mina leaned forward curiously to see what Milda was doing. Her assistant Loke passed her an instrument and Milda began to examine the body on the autopsy table with intense concentration. It was a woman of around thirty-five years of age. Slim, blonde and with clear signs of old wounds on her body. Loke held a scalpel, which he used to slowly and steadily cut a deep, straight line from the throat down to the pubic bone. Then he switched to the rib shears to cut open the ribcage. Nothing about this process bothered Mina. And she knew why Milda had suggested they meet here instead of in her office. There were few places that Mina felt as comfortable in as this sterile autopsy room.

'What did she die of?' said Mina. 'Do you know yet?'

Milda waggled her head in a response that implied both yes and no. The ribcage was now completely open, the organs exposed.

'When she arrived in hospital, her husband claimed she'd fallen down the stairs,' said Milda. 'She died a few hours later, and there was plenty to suggest that the husband's account didn't stack up. Among other things, she's got heavy bruising to her neck. So what I want to do now is get the throat organs out whole.'

Loke had stepped back to allow Milda to take over. Mina knew that this was meant to be the assistant's task, but assumed they had reached a stage that Milda wanted to do herself.

'I don't get it . . . Why are you rooting around in her ribcage then?' she said. 'If it's the throat you're interested in?'

Seeing Milda in action was like watching an artist at work. An artist who, Mina knew, liked to screech along to schlager music as she worked when there were no outsiders present.

'You'll see,' said Milda, doing something with a knife. 'Now I'm loosening the muscles and ligaments that keep the organs in place.'

Milda moved her hands up towards the woman's head.

'This is the hardest part.'

Exercising infinite caution, Milda moved the knife gently in small movements.

'Now I'm loosening the skin from the throat muscles. Among other things. And obviously trying to avoid making any holes in the skin.'

'How can you see what you're doing?' Mina said in fascination.

'I can't. It's experience and feeling.'

Milda stood up, straightening her back. Then she put down the knife and placed her right hand below the woman's jaw. When she gently pulled, the tongue and throat came down into the ribcage where they could then be lifted out as a complete package along with the rest of the organs.

'*Et voilà!*'

Milda pulled off her plastic gloves with a triumphant snap and pointed down at the neat parcel of organs now lying beside the body on the shiny steel surface.

'I'll pick up again in five,' she told Loke. 'Why don't you take a break? I've got a few things to go over with Mina.'

The assistant discreetly slipped out of the room. Milda smiled as she watched him go. Then she shook her head.

'I'll tell you something – I really don't understand that man,' she said. 'Loke, that is. Did you know that he's financially independent? Even though he's so young. I think he inherited some legacy or something. He could while away the days playing video games for the rest of his life if he wanted. Yet he's the first to arrive here in the morning and last to leave at night. And he's incredibly good at what he does. Now that's what I call a calling. I'm not sure I would have done the same thing in his shoes.'

'Although I think you'd probably dream about autopsies if you weren't working,' Mina said, smiling at her. 'You're the best. You know that, don't you?'

'Thanks,' said Milda, nodding at the organs on the side. 'What do you see?'

Mina looked closely. 'Crushing injuries?'

'You've got a good eye. Yes, there are clear crushing injuries, and not only to the larynx, but also to the hyoid and the thyroid. Together with the previous injuries, I think I can conclude that the husband is in hot water.'

'Christ. But that brings us to William. As I'm sure you're aware, his father is inside for his murder.'

'Yes, given what we knew then, I can understand that,' said Milda, filling a paper cup with water. 'We can only work with the facts we have at any given moment.'

'No one's accusing anyone of anything. Like you say, we now have information that casts a different light on William's death. That's also why Ruben and Adam are going to interview the father today. Have you had time to take another look at the autopsy report?'

Milda swallowed her water and nodded. 'I've gone through it with a fine-tooth comb. And there are a few similarities between William's death and the deaths of both Lilly and Ossian.'

'Which are?' said Mina.

'Well, William has more external injuries than the other two. As the victim of prolonged abuse, it's also no surprise that he has marks on his lungs – suggesting compression of the ribs. But that's interesting in light of the fact that both Lilly and Ossian have the same marks on their lungs. I'm afraid I'm still unable to tie it in with a plausible cause.'

281

'Wait, what is it you're saying? Ossian had marks on his lungs too? Why didn't you mention that before?'

Milda looked at her in surprise. 'It's in my autopsy report.'

Mina swore to herself. This was a very important detail and they had missed it. *She* had missed it. Because she hadn't read the report about Ossian. Whichever one of her colleagues had taken care of it was in line for a telling-off. Never mind . . . The information was invaluable, even if it was arriving late.

'So what you're saying is that the three deaths are definitely connected?' said Mina. She didn't care whether Milda heard how accusatory she sounded.

'Had it only been the internal marks I wouldn't have been prepared to draw that conclusion,' said Milda. 'As I said, William would probably have had them anyway. But . . .'

She fell silent and looked at Mina.

'The fibres,' she said. 'There were fibres in William's throat. Just like there were in Lilly's and Ossian's airways. There's nothing unusual about that in itself. You have no idea how many microscopic fragments of different things end up in our throats over our lifetimes. But all three of them had exactly the same kind of woollen fibre inside them. That, combined with the odd internal bruising in the lungs . . .'

It wasn't a cast-iron connection. Not yet. It was always hard to know which details meant anything and which were random. But Mina could already feel it in her whole body. Milda had just found what they were searching for: a pattern.

Finally they had something.

'We need to take a closer look at what kind of fibres they are,' she said, trying to conceal her eagerness.

'I'm afraid that's beyond my expertise,' said Milda. 'But NFC should be able to help you out.'

Loke returned, together with the faint smell of cigarette smoke. He sang under his breath as he washed his hands.

Mina recognized the lyrics: it was a Sanna Nielsen song.

'That's what happens when you work here,' he said apologetically, clearly uncomfortable that Mina had noticed him doing it.

Breaktime was over.

'Just one more thing before I go,' said Mina. 'Is there anything else you can say about William?'

'Only that some people shouldn't be at large in society,' Milda said drily. 'Jörgen Carlsson should be left to rot.'

She pulled on a fresh pair of gloves from a box on the side.

'Thanks. I'll let you work in peace,' Mina said, nodding at Milda's assistant before taking her leave.

As the door slammed shut behind her, she noticed a buzzing in her pocket. She pulled out her phone and checked the display. Nathalie's father was trying to get hold of her again. The GPS was erratic but, given the message, she assumed that Nathalie still hadn't returned home yet. There were presumably mere seconds left until Nathalie's father jumped into a helicopter to go and fetch her.

80

Ruben took off his watch and put it into the grey plastic tray along with his mobile. After digging through his trouser pockets for a few moments, he managed to produce his keys, which he added to the mix. Then he stifled a yawn behind his hand. Mondays always seemed to demand a slightly longer run-up than the other days of the week. Yet he had spent the whole weekend waiting to get this visit over and done with.

'Magnus said you'd be coming straight after the weekend,' said the prison officer tasked with piloting them through the visitor access at Hall.

'Magnus?'

'Svensson. Our detective inspector here. Your boss Julia spoke to him on Friday. Service weapons? If so, they'll need to stay in the cabinet.'

He pointed to a cabinet with a large padlock on it fixed to the wall.

Ruben shook his head. No weapons.

They had considered going to Hall in full uniform, but reached the conclusion that a more relaxed visit in civilian attire would be better if they wanted to get Jörgen Carlsson to open up. As Ruben remembered him, he wasn't a man who was particularly impressed by the long arm of the law. Which wasn't surprising, given that he'd probably experienced a miscarriage of justice. Not that it made him any less of a scumbag, but it was never a good thing when the wheels of the justice system turned the wrong way.

Ruben and Adam were standing together with the prison officer in a small room that served as an airlock. The room contained lockers with precise instructions stating what was to be left there. Hall was a maximum-security prison, which meant nothing was left to chance.

'I haven't been notified of any other technical equipment,' said the prison officer. 'If you've got anything with you then it'll need my approval.'

'No weapons, no equipment,' said Adam. 'We're just here for a chat with him.'

The prison officer nodded and ushered them to the metal detector at the far end of the room. The last time Ruben had passed through one, he'd been heading off for a holiday in Palma.

'Go through one at a time,' they were instructed. 'Carlsson is waiting in the second visiting room on your right.'

'Bleakest package holiday of the year,' Adam muttered as he passed through the detector.

Ruben followed and they emerged into a corridor.

'Why is Jörgen here of all places?' he said, catching up with Adam. 'Last time I checked, Hall was for inmates with a taste for prison breaks and those where there's a risk they'll be broken out by others. Gang members and organized criminals. Jörgen Carlsson is the least organized person I've ever met.'

Adam shrugged.

'Jörgen tried to make a break for it while he was on remand,' he said. 'And given what he was charged with, I don't suppose anyone fancied giving him a second chance.'

They reached the room and opened the door. Jörgen Carlsson was waiting for them at the table inside. His mid-length hair was combed back and he had the slenderest moustache Ruben had ever seen. His arms were also slim, almost sinewy, and covered in tattoos. Ruben had a hard time understanding how someone so feeble-looking could terrorize his family in the way Jörgen had. But violence didn't necessarily require bulging biceps.

'What's this about?' said Jörgen, crossing his arms.

'My name's Adam and this is Ruben,' said Adam, taking a seat. 'We're from the police. But you know that. We want to talk to you about when your son disappeared.'

Jörgen sat up straighter and placed his hands on the table.

'Disappeared?' he said with a lopsided grin. 'OK, interesting choice of words, given you claim I beat the boy to death. Not that I'm complaining – the food here is better than any of that shit Lovis makes. Mind you, she knows how to fuck. But that just added a kid to the bargain.'

Jörgen was more obnoxious than Ruben remembered. He pictured himself standing up and sticking a fist into that smirking face. He took a deep breath in order to master himself. Jörgen probably knew exactly what he was doing. He was searching for the right buttons to press. *A kid added to the bargain*. Ruben had no intention of revealing to Jörgen that he'd recently found his own kid.

'The evidence against you doesn't stand up,' said Adam. 'So we're examining other explanations. But we need your help.' It was apparently Adam's turn to press buttons. He too had found the right ones.

Jörgen leaned forward, a glint in his eye.

'OK, so if I help you with this then they'll quash my conviction, and I'll get out of here, that how it works?' he said. 'I won't have to put up with this shit?'

'Thought you just said you liked it,' Ruben said coldly.

He hated that they were making this arsehole feel good. But they had no choice.

'I said the grub was all right, but I'd prefer to take my own shits without someone helping to wipe my arse afterwards, if you get my drift?'

Adam nodded and leaned forward as well. When he spoke,

his tone was almost conspiratorial. As if he and Jörgen were sharing a secret.

'If you help us, then the murder conviction will be torn up,' he said in a low voice. 'And I can't promise anything, but I dare say you'll be looking not only at getting your freedom back but also a healthy settlement.'

Ruben couldn't help but smile to himself. The low voice involuntarily drew the listener in to what was being said. And Adam wasn't actually lying. Not outright. Even if Jörgen would no longer be guilty of murder, the convictions for all the other assaults on William and Lovis would stick and ensure he was accompanied to the shitter for many years to come. Ruben could only hope that Jörgen's legal knowledge was drawn mainly from the television.

'So help us to get your conviction quashed,' Adam concluded, leaning back again. 'Tell us who picked up William from the playground if it wasn't you.'

Jörgen held out his arms and leaned back in his own chair again, in sync with Adam.

'I haven't got a clue,' he said.

'You've got to do better than that,' said Ruben. 'As far as we're concerned, it might well have been one of your mates who took William to Beckholmen where you then beat him to death together. I thought you were smarter than that.'

A bead of sweat appeared on Jörgen's upper lip. He ran his thumb and forefinger over the slim moustache. The air conditioning was no better here than at police headquarters. At least there was some justice in this world.

'I never beat the boy anywhere except at home, OK?' said Jörgen. 'I'm not a complete moron. But I wasn't there when William went missing, and I don't know who took him. I already said as much in every interrogation.'

Ruben firmly grasped the tabletop. How could this bastard sit here talking coldly about beating someone who presumably did nothing in return except love his father? Someone who was that little? And what was worse, he thought he was smart for confining the abuse to within the walls of his home? Making use of his fist was more tempting than ever.

'That's right. You said you were . . . "hanging around the shops", said Adam, glancing at Ruben. 'I'm afraid no one's been able to confirm that. Otherwise you wouldn't be here now.'

Jörgen's eyes darted from side to side, and he brushed his hair back with his hands. 'OK,' he said. 'OK. You win. I hadn't been planning to say anything for her sake, but six fucking months in here is enough. I was at Sussi's. I was at Sussi's and we were fucking like jackrabbits. All right? But I didn't want to get her involved, cos Sussi is Lovis's friend. Fuck's sake, more than that. She's Lovis's best friend. But Sussi would never say anything to the cops, cos she knows what would happen if she did. Anyway. When I got back from hers – heh, I really did stink of sex – well, William was gone.'

Ruben sighed. Even behind bars, Jörgen was convinced that he had others at his mercy. Adam produced a notepad and asked for Sussi's address, but Ruben could no longer hear properly – he was staring at Jörgen's narrow, now very sweaty moustache. He wanted nothing more than to rip it off. Adam said something else and then stood up. Ruben stood up too.

'I think we've got what we need,' he heard Adam say as he waved the notepad around.

Ruben already knew Sussi would give them nothing useful. Jörgen had been telling the truth. He had no idea who had taken his son.

'We'll be in touch as soon as we can.'

Ruben turned around to leave. The sooner he left that room the better.

'There's one thing you should know,' Jörgen suddenly said behind them. 'I loved William, all right? That lad was my everything.'

Ruben stopped with his hand on the door handle. He couldn't contain it any longer. Something exploded inside him.

In his mind's eye, he pictured the photos of William's body.

The bruises everywhere where they wouldn't be seen, under his clothing.

Jörgen's sinewy, tattooed arms, constantly raised in a threat of further beatings.

That lad was my everything.

287

Lovis's face contorted with terror, perhaps protecting the boy, but probably not.

And then suddenly: Astrid. His Astrid.

Only a few years older than William.

I'd prefer to take my own shits without someone helping to wipe my arse afterwards, if you get my drift?

William.

The beatings.

Astrid.

Ruben turned around, quickly advanced on Jörgen and grabbed his hair firmly.

'Ouch!' Jörgen exclaimed. 'What the fu—'

His words were interrupted as Ruben pounded Jörgen's face hard against the table. Jörgen screamed his head off, which Ruben thought was very fitting. He wiped off the grease from Jörgen's hair on his trousers and returned to Adam, who looked at him with a shocked expression.

Adam said nothing as they walked down the corridor. They passed through the metal detector and retrieved their things. Adam was still silent. Ruben took his keys and mobile phone.

'By the by,' Ruben said to the prison officer, 'I assume the visiting room has CCTV. If you watch back, you'll see that Jörgen Carlsson tripped and hit his head as we were about to leave. If you have audio then you'll hear why he hurt himself. He may need medical attention. But there's probably no rush.'

81

'A tip's come in!'

Mina was on her way back from the meeting with Milda and she almost tipped her cappuccino down her front when Ruben came running out of the main entrance to police headquarters. She managed to save the coffee, which was fortunate given how far she'd walked to buy coffee from the only person she trusted when it came to handling takeaway cups. She took a sip.

The coffee was actually better at the place around the corner where Julia had secured a staff discount for the whole team. But what use was that if Mina shuddered with discomfort every time he touched the cup containing the coffee, leaving her unable to drink from it? But Wille worked at Espresso House. He was well versed in her particular requirements and always opened a new pack of cups when she came in. If he wasn't there, then she would turn in the doorway and leave empty-handed. You couldn't take chances with takeaway cups. But today Wille had been on shift, which was why she was clutching a steaming hot cappuccino. A cappuccino that she had almost drenched herself in.

'What's all the commotion about?' she said, following Ruben. 'Aren't you supposed to be at Hall with Adam?'

A police car was parked outside the main entrance, and she spotted the keys to it in Ruben's hand.

'We just got back,' he said, heading towards the driver-side door with long strides. 'Adam is writing up the report now. But this is more important. I'll tell you in the car. Get in.'

Mina hesitated before opening the passenger-side door. It was only in her own car that she was afforded the luxury of plastic seat covers – situations like this were always a trial. But that was also the price she had to pay to have a functioning life. Or something bordering on that, at any rate. If she fully succumbed to her phobia, it would be impossible to hold down a job. And she loved her job. She also loved being paid a salary and paying her rent and not having to live under a bridge. She shuddered. But the thought that it could be worse made it easier to get into the car, and it was fortunately in a pretty tidy state for a police car.

'Like I said, a tip has come in,' Ruben said as they pulled away. 'A customer found children's clothes stashed in a toilet at Mauro Meyer's restaurant on Sveavägen.'

'Children's clothes?'

'Children's clothes in the same size as Ossian's.'

'That sounds a bit tenuous,' she said, taking a careful sip of coffee. 'Couldn't it just be another customer who changed a child's clothes after, I don't know, they spilled something on their original ones? Or maybe wet themselves, so they left the clothes there?'

Ruben shook his head and took a corner a little too tightly. After a second's hesitation, Mina grabbed hold of the handle above the door. She forced herself to breathe, taking slow, deep inhalations.

'We've sent a picture of the clothes to Ossian's parents,' he said. 'They've identified them as his. What's more, some of them have name tags.'

Mina clenched her jaw. She had a hard time making the information fit with her impression of Lilly's father. The Mauro she had met had been a loving man pouring ice into his pregnant wife's foot bath and tenderly massaging her shoulders. At the same time, she had seen enough in her years on the force to know that you could never tell what was going on inside someone from their exterior.

It was a truth she was reminded of every time she looked at her own reflection.

'But I don't understand how it can be Ossian's clothes,' she said, frowning. 'Ossian was dressed when he was found.'

'Well, I know you don't have kids, but at that age they often take spare clothes with them to nursery,' Ruben said sententiously. 'Josefin and Fredrik don't remember what he had with him as his change of clothes when he disappeared, but they think it may have been the clothes that have been found. And like I say, there are name tags. To make sure the kids don't mix them up.'

Mina stared at him. Since when had Ruben become an expert in children and nursery routines? She bit her lip to avoid offering the retort that she had more experience of children than he ever would.

They pulled over and parked behind another police car outside the restaurant. The restaurant patrons had been cleared and the venue cordoned off so that they could work in peace and quiet. An Italian flag on the facade indicated the culinary focus of the restaurant, and for anyone with doubts the scent of tomatoes and basil would have given away its origins as soon as they stepped across the threshold. Mina swallowed. She knew the statistics for how many restaurants in Stockholm were failed by the health inspectors every year. There were far too many for her to ever be comfortable in restaurants that she hadn't already pre-screened to check whether they adhered to the necessary standards of cleanliness. As luck had it, they weren't there to eat.

'In here,' said a uniformed female officer who met them as they entered.

Mina and Ruben followed her to two doors at the very back of the restaurant, with symbols on them indicating which door was for men and which for women. The discovery had been made in the ladies'. They peered into the room carefully without stepping inside. The forensics team were brushing for finger-prints and Mina noticed that the porcelain lid had been removed from the toilet cistern.

'Is that where they . . .?' she said, pointing to the toilet seat.

'As I understand it, a customer found the clothes in a bag inside the cistern,' said Ruben.

Mina stifled her nausea.

'Why on earth would a customer lift the lid off the cistern in the toilets at a restaurant?' she said. 'Were they trying to hide drugs?'

The mere thought of brushing against – let alone feeling about in – a restaurant toilet was enough to make her want to throw up. Ruben shook his head.

'No, not this time,' he said. 'It was a grandmother in her seventies who brought her grandchild in to use the toilet. She saw the lid wasn't on properly and thought she'd adjust it. Then she discovered that there was something in the water. Apparently she had read in the media about Mauro and the murders of Lilly and Ossian, so she called the police.'

'A proper Miss Marple,' said Mina, raising her eyebrows.

'No, I think she was Swedish,' said Ruben.

'Miss Marple is a character . . . Oh, forget it.'

She guessed that not even the author's name would mean anything to Ruben.

'What does Mauro say?' she said instead, nodding at Ruben to indicate that they should return to the restaurant area.

'The staff say he and his wife went to the maternity ward at Södersjukhuset, and that she went into labour an hour ago. We're standing by to send a car down there to pick him up.'

'I think we should hold off for a bit,' said Mina. 'If he's at his wife's bedside as she gives birth then he's not going to do a runner right away.' She went over to a young girl wearing a shirt emblazoned with the restaurant's logo. She was sitting at a table watching what was unfolding with wide eyes.

'Hello! My name's Mina Dabiri. Do you mind if I sit down?' Out of the corner of her eye, she saw Ruben approaching two other staff members who were skulking in a corner by the door to the kitchen.

'Sure,' said the young woman with a shrug. 'What's . . . what's this about?' She was sweet, but had that rather swollen look that was the fashion among the younger generation. Her lips were slightly too bursting for comfort, and Mina wondered whether she could even close them, or whether she was forced to assume a constant expression of mild surprise with her mouth half-open.

'Sorry, could I start by asking your name?'

'Paulina. Paulina Josefsson.'

'Thanks. I'm afraid I can't tell you much – it'll have to be me who asks the questions. I hope that's OK.'

'Sure.' Paulina shrugged again.

'When was your boss last in?' said Mina.

'Mauro? He was here this morning. He's always the first one in. And as a boss, he's the dog's bollocks. I just want to say that. Best boss I've ever had. He's so bloody nice.'

'I'm sure he is,' Mina said, nodding. 'When did he leave?' She was about to prop her elbows on the table but spotted the crumbs and smears of butter on the surface at the last moment. Paulina obviously hadn't had time to clean up following the lunch rush.

'About an hour ago. His wife called. She'd started having contractions, so he went home. Or to the hospital. I don't know. But either way, he left.'

'This may sound a bit of a cliché, but have you noticed anything unusual about Mauro lately? Has he been his usual self?'

'Well . . . he did get a little strange after the news about the boy who disappeared. But that's hardly surprising. Given Lilly, that is. It was only a year ago.'

'And when the news emerged that the boy had been found dead? How did he react then?'

'I think he called in sick that day. Which Mauro never does. But you can understand it. I'm so fucking sorry for him because of what happened to Lilly. And his ex is completely off her fucking rocker. She comes in here occasionally, starts yelling and bawling, and the customers wonder what the fuck it's all about. She's nuts. Fucking insane.'

Mina nodded. That tallied with the picture that Julia and Peder had painted for her of Jenny. At the same time, she knew that simply because someone cried and shouted didn't necessarily mean they were wrong.

'How often do you clean the toilets?' she asked, unsure whether she wanted to hear the answer.

'Daily. Mauro has a cleaning lady who comes in every day. He makes a fuss about that kind of thing.'

Every day. But that didn't have to mean anything. Not even the most zealous cleaner would clean under the lid of the cistern. On the other hand, it had to be of significance when analysing the fingerprints that forensics were collecting. Although it was usually a nightmare capturing fingerprints from public settings where a lot of people passed through.

Ruben came over and nodded to indicate it was time to leave.

'I've spoken to Julia,' he said. 'We're bringing him in.'

'Who are you bringing in?' said Paulina, looking worried for the first time. 'Surely not Mauro?'

'Like I said, I'm afraid we can't say much right now,' Mina said as she stood up. 'But thanks for your help.'

Outside the restaurant a cluster of curious onlookers had gathered. Human nature never denied itself the opportunity to rubberneck. Nowadays, police officers were always met by an ocean of mobile phones recording video. But she did recognize

293

one face in the crowd. What in Christ's name was *Expressen* doing there already? She saw that Ruben had spotted the same thing and they hurried towards the car. Something told her they were facing chaos. That this was the calm before the storm.

82

Vincent knocked on Benjamin's bedroom door and entered. He hadn't stopped being surprised that the fifteen square metres of room was pretty tidy these days. His son was slumped in front of his computer, studying figures.

'I didn't ever think you'd be studying stock prices instead of Warhammer manuals,' Vincent said with a smile. 'How do you have time between lectures?'

'I've got some positions I need to close,' Benjamin said, without looking away from the screen. 'Can you wait a few minutes?'

Vincent nodded and looked around. The bed was still unmade, so it wasn't a seating option. Instead, he leaned against the wall and waited for Benjamin to finish his share trading. It wasn't really that much of a surprise that his son had developed an interest in day trading. On the other hand, Vincent still wondered how Benjamin fitted it in alongside his law studies. But Benjamin was a grown-up – he could make his own decisions. Vincent would just have to bite his tongue and hope for the best.

'Did you want something?' said Benjamin, standing up.

'Yes. You know that police investigation I was involved in almost two years ago? I'm helping Mina again . . . helping them, I mean, with a new case. I've been there all day and I'll be heading back in again soon.'

Benjamin laughed.

'What? You've got more sisters then?' he said. 'Your family are totally crazy.'

Vincent shook his head as Benjamin went over to the bed and threw a bedspread across it. He glanced gratefully at his son and sat down.

'No siblings this time,' he said. 'Or any other family, for that matter. Promise. But just like last time, there are indications that there's a code – or at least a pattern – involved. The problem is that I don't know whether there really is, or whether it's just wishful thinking on my part. Do you know who Nova is?'

Benjamin sat back down on his chair and began to spin back and forth.

'Who doesn't?' he said. 'Her videos keep showing up on Instagram.'

'Well there we are. She seems to have got the police to believe that there's a cult involved, or at least an organization structured in the same way as a cult.'

He hadn't noticed it before, but even the painted figurines that had been lined up on their own shelf on the wall were gone. Instead, textbooks with incomprehensible legal titles jostled for space.

'Why does she think it's a cult?' Benjamin asked. 'That sounds extreme.'

'Probably because these are extreme acts carried out by different people. It may be that someone has told them to . . . do things they probably wouldn't otherwise. There are also certain ritualistic aspects to how the murders were carried out. According to Nova.'

'So it's murder again?' Benjamin said, turning pale.

That was stupid – he hadn't meant to say that. But he would at least refrain from mentioning that it involved children. That was a detail Benjamin did not need to know about.

'Yes, I'm afraid so,' he said. 'In the worst case, three of them. Three people kidnapped and then killed.'

'And what do you think? Do you think it's a cult too?'

Vincent mused. Then he shook his head.

'It's an unnecessarily complicated explanation,' he said. 'You're usually the one who bangs on about Occam's razor. Do I think the same person is behind the crimes? Yes, I do. But you don't need a cult leader for that. All it takes is someone with

295

arguments that are compelling enough to get people to perform seemingly innocent but devastating deeds. It's not all that difficult to give people different perceptions of reality which they then act upon. And the kidnappers might not even have known that the people they were abducting were going to die.'

'You mean they might have thought they were taking part in a practical joke or something?' said Benjamin.

Vincent nodded and shrugged.

'The scary thing about the cult theory is that it opens so many doors. When Shoko Asahara, who was leader of the Aum Shinrikyō doomsday cult, released sarin gas on the Tokyo subway and killed twelve people – thirteen including the one who died in hospital later – he claimed to be taking on the victims' karma and liberating them so they could achieve nirvana. According to that perception of reality, he wasn't doing anything wrong. And he was most definitely not a murderer – he was performing a good deed.'

'So members of a cult like that could be convinced that they weren't evil but were doing the victims a good turn by killing them,' Benjamin said, his eyes wide.

'Yes. And there are plenty of destructive cults in Sweden. But I've not heard of any that are destructive towards people outside their own enclave. So before we jump down that particular rabbit hole, I want to explore who or what might have staged these kidnappings without presupposing it was a crazy cult leader.'

Benjamin nodded and turned towards the computer.

'So what is this code or pattern?' he said, opening the spreadsheet that he had used last time.

'That's the thing,' said Vincent, trying to make himself more comfortable on the heaps of bedding concealed under the bedspread. 'Apart from the fact that the ones who've . . . been killed . . . were missing for seventy-two hours, there are really only two things. To start with, all of them were found in immediate proximity to water. Not such a surprise in a city built on water. But still, Nova thinks it's of symbolic relevance. She may be right. But I'm hesitant, to say the least. Personally, I've noted that a connection has been planted by the bodies . . . to horses.'

He had expected a laugh, but Benjamin merely noted the information on the computer without judgement. Vincent couldn't help feeling proud of how focused his son was when it came to problem-solving.

'Seventy-two hours, water,' said Benjamin. 'Horses. You mean live ones or gaming pieces?'

'Neither. Well, actually . . . What do you mean? What gaming pieces?'

'Like the ones in chess. After all, the knight is just a depiction of a horse, since knights who protected the king's castle usually did so on horseback. In Swedish, Danish, Norwegian, German and a number of other languages the piece takes its name from the way it "runs" across the board. But in plenty of other languages they just call it a horse – like *caballo* in Spanish and *cavallo* in Italian. I think it's the same in Russian. In Sicilian it's a donkey, if I'm not much mistaken. I think it's only in English that it's known as something not horse-related – knight.'

Vincent stared at his son.

'I've got a friend who sometimes tells me off for being Wikipedia,' he said. 'I've never quite understood what she was getting at until now. Why do you know this?'

'Because it's interesting,' Benjamin said. 'You know how it is.'

Vincent nodded. He really did know. Part of him was immensely proud of the fact that Benjamin was his son. But there was something about what Benjamin had said at the start . . . About gaming pieces . . . Oh, to hell with it.

'You could be on to something,' he said eagerly. 'About gaming pieces. There's a connection to extreme movements right there, even if you leave cults out of it.'

Benjamin looked up at him from the screen with an expression of surprise.

'Now you've completely lost me.'

'Do you know who Robert Jay Lifton is?'

Benjamin frowned for a second.

'I think so,' he said. 'The psychiatrist who researched brainwashing and fundamentalism?'

Vincent nodded. Most definitely his son. He refrained from mentioning that he had borrowed several techniques from

Lifton's observations on mind control in communist China for use in his own performances.

'He says that in fundamentalist movements, most members – sooner or later – end up realizing that the movement is perhaps not all they thought it was. But by then it is usually impossible to leave. They're stuck. To ensure they don't have a complete mental breakdown, many choose to shape their own personal will to align with that of the movement. Which naturally means they become model pupils when it comes to betraying and manipulating others – at the cost of erasing their own individual will all by themselves.'

'I don't see what this has to do with horses and gaming pieces? Or for that matter, these murders . . .'

Benjamin opened Spotify and began to search for a playlist. Vincent's time with his son was apparently about to come to an end.

'Lifton has a name for the strategy where you deliberately make yourself have no will at all,' he said. 'The Psychology of the Pawn. The pawn being a gaming piece you can sacrifice. In chess, for example. Which, as you pointed out in such detail, also includes horses.' Vincent tried to get a grip on all the associations being triggered in his head, but it was fruitless. He would have to go to his study and lie on the carpet to try and sort his thoughts out after this. With a little luck, the puzzle would begin to arrange itself in his own subconscious.

Benjamin had already googled *psychology of the pawn* and started reading.

'Listen to this . . . According to Lifton, you not only become a gaming piece,' Benjamin said, squinting at the display, 'you also become a professional at playing the game itself. So let's say it is a cult. Might this be to do with murdered members of the cult who didn't measure up? Who didn't play the game well enough? The murders and the horse might be a sign to the other pieces – that is, the members of the cult – to pull their weight. To make sure the same thing doesn't happen to them.'

Vincent closed his eyes and leaned his head against the wall.

'That's an interesting theory, but unfortunately it's not very plausible,' he said. 'For two reasons. Firstly, the horses at the murder scenes weren't gaming or chess pieces. Secondly . . .

298

secondly . . . Benjamin, the people who were murdered . . . They can't have been members of a cult.'

'How do you know that?'

It had been so close. But the pieces of the puzzle still wouldn't fit together. They had got nowhere. And out there was someone who didn't hesitate to do the most appalling thing Vincent could imagine. He drew breath.

'Because they were five years old,' he said.

83

To Mina it felt strange to pass through the door marked 'Maternity Ward'. It was like a vague memory from a distant time. The only thing that made it seem real was the smell. It made memories flash through her head – of pain mixed with joy in a combination that nothing else in life offered.

'Hear that screaming?' said Ruben, shivering with discomfort. 'Two of them screaming in time. Shouldn't they have more soundproofing in a place like this? It sounds like a fucking house of horrors. Jesus.'

Mina ignored him and went over to the reception desk. After a brief period of arguing and showing her police badge, they were admitted. She reluctantly conceded that Ruben had a point. It was eerie stepping into the long, clinical corridor with its closed doors while screams came from all directions, intermingling in a peculiar chorus of pain.

'Which room?' said Ruben.

'Five.'

'Here we are,' said Ruben, pressing down the handle of the door marked with a five.

The room was empty.

'Surely they haven't gone home already? Even if the kid has been born? Does it go that fast?'

'No, Ruben, it does not go that fast,' Mina said with a snort.

'That's some sharp analysis there. They've probably gone to the break room.'

'They have those here?' Ruben said in surprise.

'Yes, every maternity ward has its own Starbucks. They mostly target hospitals and airports.'

'For real?'

Ruben's eyes widened even more.

'Dear God, are you completely . . . Of course not. Have you never seen a maternity ward before? With the classic break room with some coffee and sandwiches and all that? Surely you've been to one at some point in the line of duty over the years?'

'I've never set foot in one,' said Ruben.

Mina suddenly thought she saw sadness of some kind in his expression.

'There,' she said, pointing to a slightly bigger room with a kitchenette, sofas and a TV.

Mauro and Cecilia were sitting on the sofas. Next to them was a plastic box on wheels.

'Hello,' said Mina, entering.

She immediately felt uncomfortable. Mauro and Cecilia had only just welcomed a new life into the world. Their existence was probably one of rose-tinted exhaustion. And now she and Ruben were here to barge in and smash it all up. She glanced down into the box. An infant of indistinguishable sex was sleeping on its back, wrapped in a blanket. A small plush elephant was lying next to it.

'Hello!' Mauro said in surprise. 'What are you doing here?'

She guessed that a visit from the police was the last thing he'd been expecting. Then his face darkened and he stood up.

'What's happened?' he said.

'Can we talk privately?' Mina said, glancing at Cecilia, who, despite the white hospital gown, looked unabashedly perky for someone who had just given birth.

'No. Whatever you have to say, you can say to both of us.'

Mina exchanged a glance with Ruben, who nodded. She opened her mouth but didn't have time to say anything before both Mauro and Cecilia turned as white as a sheet. They were staring at the TV behind her.

300

Mina turned around. There on the screen was Jenny. She was standing in front of Mauro's restaurant talking to the hack from *Expressen* that Mina had recognized.

'Turn it up!' Mauro shouted as he lunged for the remote control.

He found the button and Jenny's voice filled the room. She was staring angrily into the camera as she spoke. Her eyes were wild and black, her voice filled with so much hatred that Mina's skin crawled.

'I've known all along it was him,' she said, placing heavy emphasis on every syllable. 'I'm the only one who understood – who saw behind his facade. I knew what he did to our Lilly, and I hope she forgives me for not being able to protect her. And now his evil has hit another family. He's a wicked man. This time the whole world is going to know.'

Her gaze was triumphant. She didn't blink once. Mina could see Mauro had begun to shake. Ruben took a step forward and gripped his arm.

'I think you'd better come with us.'

In the plastic box, the baby began to whimper.

84

Nathalie was lying on the camp bed looking at the wooden beams that met on the ceiling a few metres above her. It was a structure she had helped to build. She felt weightless, as if she could float up towards the beams and build a nest among them. The constant hunger was no longer as bad – not that she had got more food to eat; she had simply started to get used to it. Her tummy didn't hurt as much now. Instead, she felt . . . lighter. More alert. As if all the food she had been stuffing herself with before had been weighing her down.

But not any longer.

Now she could soar.

Of course, it was difficult to cling to any bigger thought without it flying off and joining the other thoughts up among the wooden beams. She knew she used to be better at thinking things over. But why did she need to think complicated thoughts? She was with Ines. She was safe. That was all she needed to know. Big thoughts belonged to her previous life. To the world beyond.

But the world beyond no longer mattered. It was as if the world beyond no longer existed. All that existed was the here and now. This place. These people. Grandmother.

She looked at the gauze wrapped around her fingers. She wondered whether there was still a red line underneath it. She hoped so. If not, perhaps it was time for her grandmother to give her a new one. Or she could get one of those tight rubber bands that her grandmother had. Nathalie didn't want the others to dislike her or think that she wasn't pulling her weight. She belonged here. And they gave her so much love. The least she could do was give back.

She had spent her whole life in a protective bubble. It hadn't been reality. It hadn't been life. It had merely been existence. But here she was living. The edge of her field of vision flickered when she tried to sit up, and she felt dizzy. She sank back onto the bed and let her thoughts float up to the ceiling again. There was something she had been meaning to do – but she no longer remembered what. It didn't matter. Ines would tell her what she needed to know. Her grandmother knew what was best for her. Her grandmother possessed all the truths.

85

Vincent had taken care not to put on his clothes until just before he left to go and see Mina and the rest of the team, so that they didn't have time to get sweaty. He had noticed during his performances at the weekend that not even his stage clothes smelled particularly fresh any longer – he had been obliged to drop the lot off at the dry cleaners as soon as it had opened yesterday. And Mina was decidedly more sensitive than an audience of theatregoers. For half a second, he had considered slipping some washing powder into his pockets, in the hope the scent would have a positive impact. But he had immediately realized that sooner or later he would accidentally shove his hand into the pocket.

When Mina met him by the barriers in the foyer of police headquarters, she wore a more troubled expression than he had seen in a long time. She probably wouldn't even have noticed the scent of washing powder.

'Hello, Vincent,' she said grimly.

'What's the matter?'

'For the love of God,' she said, letting him in through the barriers. 'Can't you even pretend?'

'Sorry. I meant to say: so your padel training is going well?'

Mina smiled faintly.

'Better,' she said. 'Although of course you're right. Something is up. We detained a suspect in the Ossian murder case yesterday. He was also accused last summer of being involved in Lilly's murder.'

Vincent watched her, admiring how efficient her movements were as they walked down the corridor. Mina moved with the precision of someone who never hesitated. He guessed that it had taken a long time to hone.

'But that's great,' he said. 'What a start to the week! And it sounds as if you're not describing any of the kidnappers we knew about, so in other words Nova was right about it being organized? And now you've found the brains?'

'That's just it,' said Mina. 'The whole thing is problematic. Mauro Meyer can barely stumble his way through the world right now. If he is behind all of this, then he's the best actor I've ever seen. At the same time, the evidence against him is much stronger than anything you and I have found. I just want you to know that. Had you given this presentation to the team two days ago I think they would have listened. Now I have no idea how they'll react. Apparently, word is that the top brass think

303

we were wrong to bring in Nova. They want us to focus on Mauro.'

Once again he was going to be the whacky mentalist advancing his far-fetched theories. Plus ça change. But he realized he was OK with that. More than OK, actually. It wouldn't matter one bit if he was wrong or if it turned out that the connections he had spotted were a pattern that didn't exist.

But Mauro Meyer. The name seemed familiar. Vincent had encountered it recently. He had heard it mentioned . . . No, he had read it only a few days ago. But someone else's voice had been there. Mina's. He and Mina had been . . . His eyes widened.

'Mauro as in Lilly's father?' he said.

'I told you it was complicated. Come on, they're waiting. And don't forget to ask Christer for a fan.'

86

The heat in the room made the air shimmer. It was at its worst in the middle of the day. Mina was standing on the threshold, unsure whether she even wanted to share a room with the others. If it hadn't been for Vincent, she would probably have fabricated an excuse to get out of it.

A waspish buzzing was emanating from the battery-powered fan in Christer's hand. A bag containing another ten or so newly purchased mini fans lay on the table before him. His inventory required constant replenishment since they broke so quickly, but they did make a difference. He passed one to Vincent, who had adopted a look of torment when the heat of the room had struck him.

The sweat patches at Ruben's armpits had assumed enormous proportions on his pale shirt, and even Julia appeared to be having difficulties in the heat.

'Thank you for all the work you've done so quickly in the William case,' Julia said, turning to Ruben and Adam. 'By the by, it's lucky you visited Jörgen Carlsson first thing at Hall yesterday. Apparently, he had some sort of accident afterwards. He took a real tumble and they had to give him stitches. I didn't quite grasp what had happened, but they said that men who abuse their families often develop issues with their balance while in prison. Does that mean anything to you?'

She fell silent and looked searchingly at Ruben and Adam. Ruben coughed and Adam's gaze remained fixed on the ceiling.

Mina realized she was up. She and Vincent. But she no longer knew where to begin.

'We may have something else,' she said in the end, glancing at Vincent. 'We, as in . . . Vincent and I. I realize that the Mauro angle is a strong one. And that what we have is just circumstantial. As Vincent has pointed out to me, there's a balancing act between finding an existing pattern and creating one out of thin air because of our own wishful thinking. But we don't think there's a high degree of probability that what we're telling you is coincidence, although it could be.'

'You say "we"', said Ruben, 'but isn't this just Vincent? It definitely sounds like Vincent, and you haven't even said what it is yet.'

'As it happens, we both spotted the pattern,' said Mina. 'But Vincent has found more. Vincent . . . ?'

'Erm, yes,' the mentalist said, clearing his throat. 'I heard that you'd had Nova in and that she cast light on the ritualistic aspects of the murders: the three-day intervals and the differing kidnappers, all of which makes a serial killer unlikely, so it's more probably a group of people. Which in turn may indicate that this has been somehow organized. And we can see a pattern with the three bodies.'

'You say three bodies,' said Ruben. 'But there are only two. Let me remind you that while we may not know who murdered William, he doesn't belong in your supposed pattern. And we already know that it was most likely Mauro who killed Ossian and Lilly. On the other hand, he has zero connection to William.'

'In that case what I'm going to tell you will help in your case against Mauro,' said Vincent. 'Or it will point in a completely different direction. As Mina said, we only have circumstantial

305

evidence to go on. But the more we uncover, the more we can surmise that they are connected. And Mina and I have found another thing that ties together Ossian, Lilly and even William. We had already spotted it in the cases of Ossian and Lilly, but I didn't want to mention it until we had also found it in connection to William when we visited the dry dock last Friday. Peder saw it too when we were there. As a result, I'm sure we're on to something.'

'Well, out with it then,' said Ruben. 'What are you prattling on about?'

'Horses.'

Everyone in the team gaped like hungry baby birds. Then Ruben began to roar with laughter and Peder's beard bobbed as he suppressed giggles. Mina sighed to herself. He might have put it a little more convincingly. At the same time, it was hard to blame him – she wasn't even sure she dared to believe it herself.

'Not real horses,' said Vincent, clearing his throat. 'But Lilly had a bookmark on her body, probably planted there, that depicted a thoroughbred Arab. Ossian had a My Little Pony backpack that didn't belong to him. And at the scene where William was found, someone had written the Greek word "hippo" on the wall – which means horse. It's too strange to be a coincidence.'

'So someone is trying to say the kids are horses – is that what you're saying?' Ruben guffawed.

'Or we're looking for someone who loves horse stuff a bit too much?' said Peder.

'Well, well,' Christer chuckled. 'That means we'll need to question every single ten-year-old girl in the city to find our killer!'

Ruben suddenly stopped laughing.

'What kind of shitty generalization is that?' he hissed. 'Not all ten-year-old girls are nuts about horses.'

Christer stared at Ruben in surprise and didn't even notice the fan in his hand die. Mina had no idea what Ruben was talking about. He was so strange these days.

'It's not that simple,' Vincent continued.

He took a pen and began to write on the whiteboard.

'If Nova is correct in her assumption about the ritualistic elements, then the horse may be an important symbol to the perpetrators. There have been cults that worshipped horses ever since the Iron Age. The horse was considered a divine being – a king or a warrior. Horse worship is also found in more well-known religious mythology: the Greek god Poseidon was believed to have created the first horse, and we mustn't forget Loki in Norse mythology who transformed himself into a mare and gave birth to Sleipnir – the foremost of horses. But I don't know. That's something that . . .'

Vincent fell silent and stared into space. Mina followed his gaze. He seemed to be thinking at the same time as he was looking at the map on the wall where central Stockholm's neighbourhoods were accommodated in a perfect square. Then he returned to the moment.

'Horse worship is still with us today,' he said, 'including in South Asia. And that's surely no surprise – after all, the horse is a universal symbol for freedom without any obstacles.'

He paused, appearing to look at the map again. A slight crease appeared on his forehead. Vincent wasn't acting his usual self. She wanted to help him. But something was off.

'So . . . if we were to listen to you and Nova, we would be chasing a horse-worshipping water cult that murders little kids,' said Ruben sarcastically. 'Which sounds much more likely than Mauro Meyer. Can I get you a jumbo pack of tinfoil to reinforce that hat you're wearing, Vincent? My God. Seriously, if you just wanted to pop in for a coffee or to see Mina you could have said so. Instead of . . . all this.'

Mina felt her cheeks turning red. But she couldn't let Ruben upset her that easily. She looked up and straight into Adam's penetrating gaze. Which made her blush even more.

'What? No . . .' Vincent said absently. 'I in no way think that's what we're dealing with. I just mean that . . .'

He fell silent yet again and went over to the map of Stockholm. He ran his index finger across it in a cross-like motion.

'For once you're absolutely right,' said Ruben. 'That's not what we're dealing with. We're dealing with Mauro Meyer, accused by his ex-wife of killing their daughter, and who now appears to be mixed up in the murder of Ossian. As for William, there's no connection except in your imagination.'

'Mina, why did you wait to tell us about this?' said Julia. 'You visited the dry dock last Friday and it's now Tuesday. Didn't you think this information might be important?'

'I did, but I suspected we might get the reaction we've just witnessed,' said Mina. 'So I wanted to wait until I'd spoken to Milda about William's autopsy to find out whether there was anything else. And there is one more thing. Ossian, Lilly and William all had the same type of woollen fibres in their throats – and similar marks on their lungs. There's no explanation yet as to where the fibres came from, or how the marks came about. But overall, there are too many coincidences for them not to be connected.'

There was silence in the room.

'Bloody hell,' said Ruben. 'So William might be one of them after all. Mauro's a serial killer.'

'The Psychology of the Pawn,' Vincent muttered to himself over by the map. 'Hang on.'

The mentalist returned to the whiteboard and picked up one of the pens and a long ruler. Then he positioned a chair against the wall by the map and stood on it. Using the ruler and the pen, he quickly drew seven vertical lines across the overview of the city from one end to the other. Then seven horizontal lines.

'Was there something the matter with the map as it was before?' said Ruben.

Vincent didn't reply. Instead, he climbed off the chair and took a step back to better examine the grid he had created. Mina hoped he wasn't suffering from heatstroke. If he was then she'd be hearing about this fiasco for the next ten years. Likely on a daily basis. It really did look as if Vincent had completely lost it.

'Vincent, an explanation please . . .' said Julia.

Vincent turned around and looked at them in confusion, as if he had forgotten that he was not alone in the room.

'There was something that . . . a friend said. About horses

being game pieces. Just like members of a cult. So I was wondering which games include horses.'

Ruben sighed and held his hands out.

'Chess,' said Christer, who suddenly seemed interested. 'And harness racing, obviously. The latter is expensive, the former humiliating.'

Mina suddenly saw what Vincent had done. He had divided Stockholm's city centre into neat squares – eight by eight. Like a chessboard. The outer edge of his grid framed the whole of the heart of Stockholm.

'I thought the children might symbolize gaming pieces,' said Vincent, quickly numbering the rows one to eight from bottom to top. Then he labelled the columns a, b, c, d, e, f, g and h.

'Why aren't there other pieces in that case – like pawns or rooks?' said Christer. 'No one plays chess with just the horses. Er, knights, I mean.'

'Normally you'd be right. But . . .'

Vincent went over to the map and found the spot where Lilly had been found. It was in the bottom right-hand corner in the square marked h1. He wrote 'Lilly' in the box. Then he wrote 'William' in square g3 which covered Beckholmen – the penultimate square in the third row from the bottom. And finally he inserted 'Ossian' on Skeppsholmen, which was square f4 – the sixth square in the fourth row.

'There's a classic chess-based mathematical problem known as the knight's tour,' he said. 'One of the first mentions was in Sanskrit. Back then it was known as *turagapadabandha*. It literally means an "arrangement in the steps of a horse".'

Mina coughed discreetly into her hand. When Vincent looked at her questioningly, she shook her head imperceptibly. It would be a bad thing for him to lose their attention now that they were finally listening to him.

'I just wanted to clarify the horse connection,' he said, looking apologetically at the others. 'But perhaps you . . . Anyway. The problem is based on moving the horse – our knight – so that it visits every square on the chessboard once without ever returning to a square it's previously passed through. If we start with the spot where Lilly was found, that's in the bottom right-hand corner. From there we can see that there are only two possible moves that a knight can make if we adhere to the rules of chess.'

He added dots to two squares on the map.

'As you can see, one of these moves is to g3, where William was found six months later. From here there are five new possible moves.'

He added dots to the five possible squares.

'But none of them are where we found Ossian,' said Adam.

'True. But don't you see?'

The mentalist nodded meaningfully at the map. After a few seconds without any reaction, he sighed and pointed to one of the dots in square e2. In the centre of the square lay Fatbursparken.

'This is one of the possible moves from William. And from here you can move straight to Ossian in f4. As it happens, Fatbursparken is the only reasonable move from William if you don't want to back your knight into a corner.'

'OK, but that means your little theory doesn't stand up,' said Ruben. 'There was no kid who died in that park. Something like that would have been discovered right away, given how many people use the park. Cute idea for the kids to be pieces in a giant game of chess across the city. And I have to admit it was pretty advanced for the bookmark, the backpack and that graffiti to be associated with a . . . what did you call it? The knight's day?'

'Knight's tour.'

'But I don't know how many times I have to say this. There is no puzzle this time. There's just Mauro Meyer. And believe me, he's not capable of doing something like this. He's got his hands full changing nappies,' Ruben said in irritation.

'Mind you, there is a fountain in the middle of the park,' Peder muttered. 'Apropos water.'

'Jesus fucking Christ . . .' Ruben muttered.

'Have you checked under the fountain?' said Vincent.

'No, why would we have?' said Ruben. 'Because we had nothing better to do while we were picking up Mauro?'

Bosse panted, his tongue lolling out, as he lay on the floor beside Christer. The dog had been so quiet that Mina hadn't even realized he was there. The damn heat was slowly but surely working to finish them all off.

'A suggestion then,' said Vincent. 'Check out the park. If you don't find anything then I won't bother you again. You may not believe me, but I really do hope that Ruben is right and that you have your killer and that Nova and I are both on some wild goose chase. That we're spotting patterns that aren't there. There's nothing I want more. But if you do find something, that means my theory is right.'

Julia waved a folder in front of her face as a makeshift fan. The movement made them all look in her direction.

'It does entail considerable expense,' she said. 'Digging a park up like that. Cracking open a fountain. It's not something we can do on the spur of the moment just because you drew some lines on a map. Especially not when we already have a suspect in the cells. I would quite like this team to remain in existence, at least for a little longer. You've got to give us something else. And . . .'

She hesitated for a second.

'. . . I've received clear instructions from on high. They don't think the cult avenue of inquiry has any bearing on this. They would welcome closer scrutiny of Mauro. They've made themselves very clear on that front. This team's very existence may be threatened if we don't heed that. And I'm not going to say they're wrong. Rather unusually, I'm inclined to believe they may be right. This sounds too far-fetched.'

Vincent put the cap on the pen. Then he tapped it against the empty squares on the map.

'I hear what you're saying. But suppose they *are* wrong. Let's play with the idea that Mauro Meyer *isn't* behind all of this. That whoever it is remains at large. If Ossian, Lilly and William really are the beginning of a knight's tour, then there's a lot of moves left. In that case, every new move may result in a new murdered child. And there are another sixty-one squares to go on the chessboard after these three. Can you really afford to take chances?'

311

87

Vincent let the others leave the conference room first. As Peder passed him, something fell out of his pocket. It was a small slim red box. Vincent picked it up from the floor. He would recognize that box anywhere. It contained a deck of cards, but not just any deck – it was a 'Bicycle' branded deck of cards from the United States Playing Card Company. The deck featured red reverses in poker format, and the cards were slightly wider than the classic Swedish bridge decks.

Vincent only knew two kinds of people who used decks of cards like this. Poker players and magicians. Peder appeared to be neither.

'Peder, wait,' Vincent called out, hurrying after him and waving the deck of cards in his direction. 'You dropped something.'

Peder stopped and turned around. His eyes widened when he saw what Vincent was holding.

'Oh, thanks.'

'Poker players don't usually carry their decks around with them,' said Vincent, catching up with Peder. 'So why do you?'

Peder looked around the corridor. Then he gestured to Vincent to come with him into an adjacent room where he quickly shut the door behind them.

'I don't want the others to hear,' he explained in a low voice. 'But the triplets have a cousin. Casper. His mother is my wife Anette's sister. Casper is having his birthday party in just under three weeks and . . . Well. Anette and her sister have apparently decided I'm going to perform magic at the party. Casper was over the moon. So I'm desperately trying to learn a few card tricks.'

Peder looked so deeply unhappy that Vincent had to bite his lip to avoid laughing.

'And how old is Casper?' he said.

'Five.'

Vincent set down the deck of cards on the desk and pointed to a chair, indicating that Peder should sit down. He also sat down. 'In that case I fear you've started at the wrong end,' he said. 'Magic for kids is one of the hardest things out there.'

If at all possible, Peder looked even more unhappy.

'Why are so many people fascinated by magic tricks?' said Vincent. 'Because they break the rules that govern the world. We know people can't fly. That's why it challenges our imagination and our understanding of the world when someone suddenly flies on stage in Las Vegas. But children haven't had time to learn the rules. For them, the world remains unexplored. There's no reason why magic can't be for real.'

'Like the fairies in *Winx*,' Peder said gloomily. 'Their adventures are very real to the triplets.'

'I've no idea what you're talking about, but sure. My point is that children aren't impressed by a card changing places with another in your deck. Children have no reason to believe that it's impossible in the first place.'

Peder sighed and stroked his chin.

'So you're saying that it's impossible to do magic for children?' he said. 'Thanks. I'll raise it with Anette. Her sister is going to hate me. Do you mind if I give them your number?'

'You misunderstand,' said Vincent. 'Of course you can do magic for kids. You can surprise them. Engage them. Make them hold things. Make them laugh. If you make that your goal instead of learning tricks perfectly, then you'll be a hit. Just focus on the right thing.'

'Surprise and engage. I'm so dead.'

Vincent picked up the deck of cards and held it over the wastepaper basket.

'But please, forget about this,' he said, letting go.

88

'How do you think it went?'

Vincent had disappeared after the meeting – he'd apparently needed to discuss something with Peder. But then he'd sought her out and she wanted nothing more than to talk to him again. But not in police headquarters – the walls had ears. Not to mention her colleagues and their stares. She'd seen the way Ruben had rolled his eyes when Vincent outlined his theory.

That was why she had taken Vincent out of the building and up to Kronobergsparken, which was really nothing more than a tree-clad hill between the police building and Fridhemsplan. But the trees provided welcome shade from the sun. It was at least a few degrees cooler on the footpath through the trees than it had been in that meeting room.

'I'm grateful to you for granting me this audience in the woods, Queen Mina,' Vincent said, 'but I'm going to repeat my question. Do they think I'm mad?'

She looked at him with feigned surprise.

'Has there ever been any doubt about that?' she said. 'We all know you're off your rocker.'

'Ah. Well, then . . .'

Vincent picked up a stick and began to scrape something off his shoe.

'Remind me never to buy white trainers again,' he said.

'Yes, I was actually a little worried when I saw them,' she said. 'I thought you'd lost your old sense of style.'

Vincent prised out a small lump of mud and then waved it at her on the end of the stick in revenge for her comment. She gave him a look that could have set the twig alight.

'As long as you think I'm a genius, that's good enough for me,' he said, dropping the stick.

'Of course,' she said, kicking it away. 'You're so wise. And strong. Not to mention mysterious.'

'Don't forget how kind I am to children.'

Why hadn't she been able to talk to Amir this straightfor-wardly? Or to anyone, ever? There had been nothing the matter with Amir. She was the one at fault – she knew that. It had always been that way.

Until Vincent had turned up.

With Vincent, there was no longer anything wrong with her. And that was a problem in itself.

'Seriously, what you said in there . . .' she said. 'It was stretching things a bit. Mathematical chess? With knights?'

'I know.' Vincent turned to her. He looked unhappy.

'Since the whole business with Jane, something has happened to me,' he said. 'I can't always perceive patterns that I ought to spot. And I see patterns that sometimes aren't there. It's as if my brain and I are no longer friends. Part of me hopes that you're right – that you've found your killer and that it's all over. But at the same time, I think there are too many similarities for this to be nothing more than my fantasies.'

'Those must be quite some fantasies you have then,' she said.

Vincent blushed and averted his gaze.

'Why didn't you get in touch?' he said quietly.

It came so abruptly that it took a while for her to understand what he meant. 'Me?' she said. 'I thought you didn't want . . . You didn't get in touch either.'

'I know. I didn't know how . . . The case was solved. I thought of lots of other reasons, but none of them were true.' He still wasn't looking her way.

'So what *is* true then?' she said.

'I'm afraid I'm getting worse and worse at answering that question,' he said, finally looking at her.

She looked straight into his pale blue eyes. The mentalist's shoulders were more slumped than usual. His posture was usually straight-backed and confident. But not today. It was clear that something was troubling him. That was no surprise, given what he'd said previously about Maria, but it felt as if there was something else too. Something that was bothering him deep down in that place she had only glimpsed. The place where he was his true self. She laid a hand on his shoulder. 'Vincent . . .' she began.

315

'The date!' he suddenly exclaimed. 'Have you been on the date yet?'

'That's the end of our audience,' she said. 'Didn't you have a stick to be playing with?'

89

Ruben was standing outside the yellow terraced house, trying to pluck up courage. It was completely absurd that he was this nervous – he never usually was. But this was no ordinary situation. And things hadn't gone well last time. He took a deep breath and then rang the doorbell. The door was opened almost immediately. She was standing there before him. She had long brown hair and wore a T-shirt and jeans. And she looked just like her mother. But also like someone else. Someone he saw in the mirror every morning.

'Hi Astrid,' he said.

He suddenly had difficulty swallowing.

'Hi Ruben,' she said cheerily.

She moved back into the hallway and he followed. Was he supposed to take off his shoes and jacket, or was that too forward? It was best he didn't do anything too hastily. Astrid remained close with an expectant look, but she said nothing.

'So . . .' he said falteringly. 'How's school going?'

'It's the summer holidays.'

He wanted to slap his forehead. Was he a complete moron? Obviously, she was on her summer holidays. Fathers really were supposed to know these things.

'Oh hello, is that you?' said Ellinor, emerging from the kitchen. 'I didn't hear you ring the bell.'

She looked at her watch. She still didn't look altogether thrilled to see him, but the tone was at least a little softer than last time.

'Take your jacket off and come in.'

The small hall led to a dining room where a large oak table was covered with pencils and sheets of paper. Someone in the family was obviously a fan of drawing. The house was airy, with white walls and light furniture. This lightness accentuated the colourful paintings hanging on the walls. Over the years they'd been together, Ellinor had always talked about wanting to take up painting. It appeared she'd done so. And she showed real talent, he noted.

They sat down at the table. Ellinor didn't ask him whether he wanted anything, and the coffee maker in the kitchen appeared to be switched off. The signal was clear. He was not to stay any longer than necessary.

'It's good to see you again, Ellinor,' he said. 'I mean it. It's good to meet you both. Thanks for replying.'

He hadn't been wrong last time – Ellinor had a presence that was bigger than the room they were in. He'd been a total idiot to let go of her. But he wasn't going to make the mistake of dwelling on the past. That would only make things worse.

'I must admit I was surprised that you wanted to talk,' said Ellinor. 'But it's one thing you knowing, quite another to start trusting you again. How did you picture this exactly?'

'Well, I thought Astrid and I could hang out a bit,' he said. 'When she wants to. And can. And when you say it's OK, of course.'

Ellinor looked at him suspiciously.

'You're not exactly the most responsible person I know,' she said. 'You might well leave her in some night club.'

'Believe it or not, I'm not the same person today I was ten years ago,' he said. 'Or even a year ago. You'd be surprised.'

'Well, Astrid, what do you say?' she said. 'I know we've talked about this several times, but you're still allowed to change your mind. It doesn't make any difference that Ruben is your biological father – you still don't have to see him if you don't want to. How do you feel?'

'It's kinda weird,' Astrid replied. 'But I think it's going to be good. And I do have a phone, Mum.'

'OK. Two hours. To start with. Then you have to come home for your tea.'

317

Two hours. It wasn't quite what he'd had in mind. But it was better than nothing – after all, it was the afternoon. He had no idea when ten-year-olds ate their tea. Or when they went to bed at night. If he didn't make too many mistakes, then maybe it would be longer next time.

They went back into the hall. He pulled out the police cap he'd brought with him and set it on Astrid's head. It sank down to her ears. Was it cute, or would she be annoyed? He had no idea what to do with little girls. He remembered what he'd been like when he'd been ten years old. Surely there couldn't be that much of a difference?

'I thought we might take a ride in the police car,' he said. 'And go and say hi to the police dogs down at the station. I'm supposed to be working really, you see. Do you like dogs?'

Astrid nodded eagerly. He wondered whether he should add a visit to the firing range too, but decided that might be a bit much. He had to save something for next time.

'I really like dogs,' she said. 'But aren't police dogs big? And I thought they bite?'

'They can be a bit scary if you're a burglar,' Ruben laughed.

'Good,' said Astrid, adjusting the cap. 'Because I'm not one of them. Mum, Ruben and me are going now.'

Astrid skipped out through the front door. Ruben was about to follow, but Ellinor stopped him with a hand on his arm.

'If you screw this up then you'll never see her again,' she said, glaring at him. 'You get one chance. One.'

Ruben gulped. He wasn't used to being this uncertain. He didn't like it. He nodded silently and went outside. Astrid was already making her way towards the car park. Bloody hell. He hadn't even asked Ellinor whether Astrid was allowed an ice cream. But then he changed his mind. That was something he could decide for himself. He was her father, after all.

90

Vincent reread the email from Umberto yet again. It had arrived while he'd been in the park with Mina, but he hadn't seen it until he'd got home. The red logo of TV4 was emblazoned in the email signature next to the smiling woman in the logo of the Jarowskij production company. Umberto's only comment was 'Here we go, *amico mio!*' accompanied by a smiley with sunglasses. The rest of the copy came from the production company. Vincent felt himself slowly dying inside as he sat there on the kitchen chair.

The email set out the arrangements for his trip to a small island off the coast of France. More specifically the island where *Fortress Prisoners' Flight* was recorded. The production company had also sent a number of photos of the fort itself – probably to awaken his curiosity. However, the pictures of the distinctly militaristic stone building had the exact opposite effect. It was the last place on earth he wanted to go. When he zoomed in on the picture, he thought he could see the cannon. They would choose him for that. He knew it.

The email explained that he had to be there in around three weeks' time. Twenty-five days. That was probably enough time to find a lawyer and write his last will and testament. He was most concerned with ensuring that Umberto and ShowLife Productions would not receive a penny in the event of his demise.

'What's that?'

Rebecka had appeared at his shoulder and was peering over it at his phone.

'It's Fort Boyard! Dad,' she said, horrified, 'you're not going to be in *Fortress Prisoners' Flight*, are you?'

He turned to look at his daughter. She was clutching a sandwich that she appeared to have suddenly forgotten about. The horror on her face was not feigned.

'So what if I am?' he said.

'I won't be able to go to school the whole term. I'll have to move in with Denis and never leave the house again.'

'You can't,' he said. 'I'm going to take Dennis with me on the trip as my interpreter. After all, he is French. I've already printed T-shirts with that family photo from when we went to Liseberg. The one with you at the front of the roller coaster train looking terrified. Dennis and I will be wearing them constantly.' The horror in his daughter's eyes was replaced with pure hatred.

'He's name is *Denis*,' she snapped, pronouncing the name in French. 'And if that photo even comes close to him then you're dead.' A Lego car raced into the kitchen with Aston hot on its tail, humming along to what was undoubtedly another Queen song, even if it wasn't entirely audible. Rebecka's influence on Aston was both worrying and touching.

'Dad! Look!' said Aston. 'Road trip! We all fit in the car. I'm playing happy families. Just like you!'

'I think you mean nightmare family,' Rebecka said to Aston.

'Aston, just because Benjamin and Rebecka have a different mother doesn't mean that . . .' Vincent sighed and gave up.

Rebecka narrowed her eyes and looked at him.

'I hope they shoot you straight out of a cannon and forget to attach the safety rope,' she said in a low voice before heading to her room, the sandwich in a vicelike grip.

'Could you feed the fish while you're over there anyway?' he said.

'I'll feed *you* to the fish,' she hissed, slamming the door behind her. Aston had started singing again and now he reached the chorus. He bellowed out the only words he knew by heart, the song's title: 'The Show Must Go On'.

Vincent completely agreed. The show must go on. The only question was, for how much longer.

91

Mina woke up to a shrill sound. At first, she struggled to identify it; she was stuck in a dream sequence about horses, fibres, Milda holding a scalpel and chess pieces bigger than her threatening to crush her as they moved across a giant board.

She looked around in confusion. Some summer light entertainment show was under way on the television. She'd drifted off on the sofa. The shrill sound went off again and she realized it was her mobile. It was lying on the coffee table, glowing angrily.

'Hello . . .'

Her voice was hoarse and it cracked as she answered. She cleared her throat and made a fresh attempt.

'Hello?'

'I'm not going to wait any longer, Mina.'

His timing in calling and waking her was almost uncanny. As usual, she was overcome with a vague anxiety at the sound of his voice. Looking back, she could barely remember a time when that hadn't been the case. He had always made her feel inferior. As if she were the flawed one and he was the perfect specimen. He had always liked mending things. Putting them right. Perhaps that had been the case with her too. At any rate, it made him completely perfect for the role he now held.

'Today's Tuesday. It's been eleven days,' he said. 'And I've heard nothing. A responsible parent would have picked her up long ago.'

A responsible parent. She knew perfectly well what he was getting at.

'There's no point you going there and scaring the life out of them.' she said, checking her wristwatch. 'I'll go to the farm in the line of duty tomorrow morning. Ines will probably be more tractable if I come in uniform. I have a hard time believing she'll disclose who I am.'

'Why tomorrow?' he said impatiently. 'Why not now?'

'Because it's a quarter past eleven in the evening,' she said. 'And I don't think anything serious has happened. I spoke to Ines a few days ago and she confirmed that everything was fine.'

'And since when do you trust your mother? Make sure it's the first thing you do tomorrow. Call me as soon as you're back.'

He hung up without waiting for her reply and she felt her shoulders slump.

Her stomach growled loudly. Apparently she had forgotten to eat dinner.

She got up, went to the freezer and opened a drawer. She contemplated the selection for a while, vacillating between pasta alfredo and nasi goreng. She plumped for the alfredo. She carefully inspected the plastic covering the box. She held the packaging up to the kitchen light, searching for slits in the vacuum seal – cracks where bacteria might have got in. But the plastic looked intact. She carefully removed it and inserted the box into the microwave. She heated it on the maximum setting and for a little longer than she was supposed to. While it left the food overcooked, that was preferable to the alternative. Although she knew it was irrational, she was convinced that the more radio waves there were, the more effectively all living things in the food were killed.

In the end, she pressed the button to open the door and removed the food. The steam burned her fingers.

'Jesus!'

She dropped the container on the side and blew on her fingers. She only hoped they wouldn't blister. She pictured big, water-filled blisters forming on her fingertips. The thought was almost enough to make her vomit. She'd prefer to have them amputated. Maybe she should skip eating, it was very late after all. But her gut said otherwise.

Once the container had cooled down, she made a fresh attempt to pick it up. This time she was more successful. She took the box, a fork and some wet wipes with her back to the sofa. A veritable TV dinner. It was always TV dinner. She cleaned the fork carefully with a wipe, then she skewered some food on the fork and took a deep breath. There was a company that bragged about having live bacteria in their yogurt. How disgusting. She sincerely hoped that everything in the food in front of her was well and truly dead. On the TV, Benjamin Ingrosso was singing something or other about lost love. She closed her eyes and inserted the fork into her mouth.

92

'You do realize that this doesn't exactly support your theory, right?'

The fountain at the centre of Fatbursparken was only half a metre in height, the basin much too shallow for a body to be there without someone discovering it. Not even under the arched edges. Vincent walked around the fountain while Peder let its cool water bring respite to his hands.

'Julia did you a favour when she asked me to come here with you,' Peder continued, stifling a morning yawn. 'It was pretty hard to digest what you told us. By the by, I reckon you owe the force a new map. But we're here because Julia wants you to understand the absurdity of your chess game theory. And I hope you understand the high stakes she's facing herself, letting you stay on. She'll be in big trouble with the top brass if they catch wind of this. Which means that the team will be in trouble.'

'It's not a game,' Vincent muttered. 'The knight's tour is a mathematical problem: the challenge is to visit every square without visiting a square twice. Just like our killer, who always finds a new place for their victims.'

He surveyed the park, which was flat. It was small enough that he could easily see from one end to the other.

'But you can see for yourself,' said Peder. 'Except by the fountain, there's nowhere a body could be hidden in this park without being discovered immediately. In which case we would already have found it. If we had done, then maybe you would have been right. But we didn't. So you're not. More's the pity, if you ask me. It was an exciting theory – even if it was a little crazy.'

'Unless the body has been buried, that is,' said Vincent. 'Maybe you should do a little digging.'

Peder sighed and kicked the cobblestones set around the fountain.

'As Julia said – we can't cordon off a whole park and start digging it up at random just because you like the odd game of chess,' he said, splashing cold water from the fountain into his own face. 'We don't even know where we would start if we did. No, I actually think Nova's water theory is more believable.'

He sighed happily as the water cooled him.

Vincent began to walk around the fountain on the footpath.

'Nova is a shining light in her field,' he said. 'But her theory is useless. It just slows you down. Even if it were true, there are more places by water in this city than places that aren't. The symbolism of leaving someone by water isn't as powerful if it happens to be the easiest thing to do. Maybe it's as simple as being a murderer who arrives by boat.'

'And you reckon he just dumps the bodies ashore wherever he lands?' said Peder, looking thoughtful. 'As a matter of fact, that's not a bad idea. Much simpler than both her cult and your chess game.'

Drops of water glistened in his bushy beard. Mina would probably have had quite a bit to say about the cleanliness of the water now dripping off Peder's beard and onto his shirt.

'Trust me,' said Vincent. 'I'd really like to be wrong about the intellect I've ascribed to our killer. No one would be happier than me if it turned out it was someone who had never heard of the knight's tour and just owned a boat with an outboard. That person would probably be much easier to catch. Unfortunately, we have a small problem. William was found in the dry dock when it was drained. The only boats that would have been able to get close were already inside the dock.'

'On the other hand, your chess game theory is flawed because there's nowhere to hide a body in this park,' said Peder.

'Just because we can't see something doesn't mean it's not there,' Vincent said thoughtfully.

'Feels like we're going in circles here,' Peder said. 'Can we strike a deal? I have to pop home to Anette. I accidentally left the new nappies in the car this morning. But why don't you hang on here? If you find a spot where you think the body is and you can somehow convince us of it, then I promise to try and get Julia to agree to an excavation. But only in that exact spot. And only once. OK?'

Vincent surveyed the park with its lawns, trees and carefully laid out paths. The park where nothing could be hidden without it being discovered immediately.

The park where nothing had been found.

'Very reasonable,' he said.

93

Mina pulled up to the farm where Epicura ran its business. Just to be safe, she had called ahead earlier that morning to warn them she was coming, so that Ines and Nova were ready to maintain their facade in front of Nathalie. Mina would be there only as a police officer. Despite the whole matter with Nathalie, Nova might be useful to them in the investigation and Mina didn't want to allow personal circumstances to jeopardize Nova's relationship with the team. She would just have to keep the two things separate.

She raised her hand and waved when she saw Nova waiting for her in the courtyard. The heat was shimmering in the air despite the early hour, but Nova looked cool in her white silk outfit. Mina could feel the sweat beginning to drip down her back as soon as she got out of the car. What kind of sadist had decided the police should wear black? She fought the impulse to lunge back into the car, crank up the air conditioning as high as it went and propose that they chat in the car instead.

'Welcome!' Nova said, smiling broadly.

She came towards Mina but made no move to embrace her this time.

That was at least something.

'Come on, let's go inside,' Nova said, glancing at Mina's uniform. 'It's much too warm to be outdoors.'

Nova walked quickly ahead of her towards the main building. Mina followed, sweat now seeping out of every pore. She checked that she had her pack of wet wipes with her, and then she looked around curiously at her surroundings. She hadn't quite known what to expect of the farm, but she definitely hadn't anticipated that it would be quite so . . . serene.

The cool inside the heavy front door was a blessing. She closed her eyes and her pulse slowed gradually. Perhaps she ought to ask Vincent for help with some breathing exercises if it was going to carry on like this. The atmosphere in the reception hall was one of calm and peace. It had a high ceiling and was flooded by light which streamed through the masses of glass. She shivered as the beads of sweat turned cold on her skin.

'Are you cold? We always keep it very cool in here,' Nova said apologetically.

'No, it's lovely,' said Mina, with a shake of her head. 'I like the cold.'

'Let's go to my office,' Nova said with a smile. 'We can talk there undisturbed. Everyone always seems to want me for something or other. And you might prefer not to be seen . . . unnecessarily?'

She darted left into a long corridor and opened one of the doors at the far end. Mina followed her into the room, which was big and also very bright. The decor was sparse and simple, in light hues and with green plants the only dashes of colour. Nova sat down behind a large desk made from clear plastic that looked to have a designer price tag, and gestured to Mina to sit down in one of the two armchairs on the other side of the table. The wall to Nova's right was lined with well-filled bookshelves. Apart from books, there were also photographs in neatly polished silver frames.

'May I look?'

Mina went over to the bookcase to take a better look at the photos.

'Of course.'

Nova stood up and came over to the shelves too. She pointed to one of the photographs. It was a black-and-white photo of an elderly man with a stern countenance. Next to him was a teenage girl in a wheelchair, both her legs and one arm in casts and a big support collar around her neck. The girl's expression was serious and it took a while for Mina to recognize Nova.

'My grandfather. And me. After the accident.'

'What happened?' Mina said carefully. 'If I may ask?'

'A car accident. My father died – I pulled through but was seriously injured.'

'I'm sorry.'

Nova shrugged and smiled. 'It was a long time ago. In another life. And my grandfather took care of me. I was lucky.'

'Did you fully recover?'

Mina shifted her gaze to another photograph. A younger man. He had an open, happy face, his hair came down to his shoulders and his shirt was unbuttoned.

'Yes and no. Everything healed. But the pain remained. I've learned to see it as an asset. Much of what we do here is based on learning to handle pain, and turn it into something positive. Both physical and mental pain. If there is in fact a difference. Pain is pain, and the difference between body and soul isn't as big as we might sometimes think.'

Nova walked over to the desk and sat back down. Mina remained and pointed to the photo of the man.

'Your father?'

'Yes. My father.'

Nova said nothing more and Mina didn't feel it was appropriate to ask. She'd heard the grief in Nova's voice. She didn't want to dig too deeply into the emotions evoked by a dead parent in their child out of fear of what she would hear.

Instead, she sat down in one of the armchairs. Nova regarded her with her intense brown eyes.

'How are you getting on? Are you making any progress in the investigation?'

'We've got a few promising leads,' Mina said evasively.

Nova continued to contemplate her with such a penetrating gaze that she began to fidget in her seat.

327

It felt as if Nova could somehow see right through her. Only Vincent had ever made her feel like that before. But while Vincent's gaze had always been soft and gentle, Nova's drilled into her like laser beams. It was impossible to be anything but 100 per cent honest with her.

'We haven't ruled anything out yet,' said Mina. 'Including the idea that it might have been organized. But between us, it all sounds so . . .'

'It sounds so improbable,' Nova interjected. 'I know.'

She smiled. But it was a wry smile that seemed more inwardly directed than outward.

'That's exactly what allows cults to take root,' she said. 'No one thinks they can get caught up in a cult. No one really believes that cults actually exist, and definitely not in their immediate vicinity. No one sees themselves as impressionable. But we humans are herd animals. We want to follow the herd, and the herd wants a leader to follow. A cult does nothing more than exploit our most instinctive and deepest psychological programming.'

'I still want to believe in the individual's ability to think for themselves,' said Mina.

'Of course that exists too. But it's very much more limited than we like to think. People are sheep. And our very unwillingness to accept that means we don't see the webs spun by spiders that mean to harm us. And then we get stuck – carried on towards death, convinced of our own willpower.'

'That sounds harsh,' Mina said, looking at her in surprise.

Nova's face dissolved into a warm smile.

'Yes, I apologize. It sounded harsher than I intended. And the work we do at Epicura focuses on the strengthening of the self. We believe in the individual's inherent ability. The thing that drives people to groups is often fear, and all fears are the same when it comes down to it. The fear of trying new things comes from the fear of being judged, which comes from the fear of not being liked, which in turn comes from the fear of exclusion, which in turn comes from the fear of not getting to share in the group's resources, which is the result of a fear of death. All fears are really nothing more than a fear of death.

328

And the very essence of Epicureanism is to achieve not only ataraxia – calm in body and soul – but also aponia, the absence of pain. Thus we eliminate the fear of death. Only when you do not fear death are you wholly and completely free as a human being. We believe that everyone can achieve happiness and peace of mind. How many people nowadays can say that?'

'Powerful stuff,' said Mina, nodding thoughtfully. 'But I've no idea what it involves in practice. I mean, how does your philosophy govern daily operations here? What do people learn – in purely practical terms – on your courses?'

'I can sign you up for one. You'd be most welcome.'

'I think you've probably got enough members of my family here.'

Nova let out a peal of laughter.

'I'll try and explain,' she said. 'What my grandfather laid the foundations for, and what I chose to nurture, is the creation of a centre where we give people the tools to live in accordance with the founding principles of Epicureanism. When they come here, people can withdraw from everything that is troubling: politics, quarrels, conflicts. They can live in peace and simplicity, learning which things offer lasting happiness instead of imper-manent and instant gratification. Not all pleasure is good. Not all pain is bad. Pleasure in the short term can bring pain in the long term. And vice versa. But above all, we teach people to live in the moment.'

'How long do most people stay?'

Mina found herself reluctantly fascinated. In a way, she envied Nova's strong convictions, even if she still thought the whole thing sounded completely divorced from real life.

'We have everything from day courses with leadership teams to people who take a timeout from life and stay for longer,' said Nova. 'Some have been with us for years. Your mother, for instance.'

'Speaking of her,' said Mina. 'I'm also here on a private matter. Nathalie has to go home to her father. I hope that inner journey you mentioned has been rewarding for both her and Ines. But it ends now. It would be best if you put her on the bus this morning. Or if you prefer, she's welcome to come back in the

329

police car with me. Those are the choices you and Ines have. Unless you want her father to descend with a small army and take her back by force. His patience has been exhausted.'

'I'd love to,' said Nova. 'Of course she has to go home. The problem is that I haven't seen Nathalie or Ines in . . . well, I think it must be over a week.'

A cold and unpleasant sensation washed over Mina. She should have known better than to trust her mother.

'You mean they're not here? Where are they then?'

'It's not uncommon for our members to go hiking in the woods for a few days,' Nova said, smiling again. 'It's an effective way to get to know each other, and there are plenty of places to camp overnight around here. I would guess that Ines took Nathalie on an outing like that. That's the only possibility I can think of.'

'For over a week?'

'In this weather and with the right gear, you can be gone two weeks – no problem,' Nova said. 'We often go on hikes like that. Nothing beats sleeping under the stars in the summer and making your own meals with what nature has to offer. You should try it.'

She'd be happy to, just as soon as they asphalted the woods. The Ines that Mina had once known wouldn't even have known how to lace up her hiking boots. But her mother had changed – she had noticed it when they'd met. She had underestimated Ines's 'inner journey'. Of course it involved finding herself in nature . . . Her caffeine-addicted, boozing and chain-smoking mother was an outdoorswoman these days. And why not? It was no less likely than any of the rest of what had happened.

At the same time, she didn't like that Nathalie was – by chance – gone just as she herself had arrived. It was too much of a coincidence. She looked at Nova, who merely smiled back.

'There's nothing to worry about. I promise,' she said. 'Ines knows the woods well.'

'I'll contact Nathalie's father and explain,' said Mina. 'But I suggest you try to get hold of Ines. For her sake, I hope that they come back much sooner than you said. Otherwise I suspect it'll be the first and last time she meets her granddaughter.'

94

Mina left the meeting with Nova and went straight to Fatbursparken, where Vincent was waiting for her. But she intended to change her sweaty underwear as soon as she returned to police headquarters. She was going through at least two pairs of knickers a day now, although sometimes more depending on how much she overheated. She had even begun supplementing the bumper packs of pants with stacks of cheap vest tops shipped in packs of five, which were also thrown out after a single use. Over the summer, the stock she kept in her study at home had begun to resemble the storeroom of a small shop. Not that it mattered. She never had any visitors.

She glanced at Vincent when they met in the park. He managed to look handsome even when wearing a loose-fitting white T-shirt. She presumably looked a wreck. A sweaty wreck. Bloody Vincent.

Walking in parks with him was almost a habit by now. But Fatbursparken was too small for a proper walk. Instead, they sat down on a bench and looked around. Mina had brought a plastic seat cover with her, which she sat down on. There was no chance she was going to let that park bench touch her clothes, no matter how clean it looked. But she didn't want to sanitize it – not when Vincent was there.

She said nothing about what Nova had told her. Thus far, Vincent was the only person who knew she had a daughter, and even he didn't know any of the fine details. But Mina had no control over the situation at Epicura. It felt as if she was a short breath away from the whole world finding out everything. And then the questions would come. Questions she had no desire to answer.

Above all, she thought of Nathalie. She really longed for Nathalie not to find out the truth. At the very least, it ought to be Mina who told her. Perhaps she might be able to get her daughter to understand. But she wouldn't get that chance. Ines was guaranteed to tell her on that hike through the woods. What a load of rubbish that was! Finding yourself among the trees. The result would be that Nathalie wouldn't want to be acquainted with Mina after learning that her mother had been alive all this time.

'Thanks for coming here,' said Vincent, interrupting her train of thought. 'I think better this way.'

'You mean when I'm there?' she said, seeing that he had immediately begun to blush.

Vincent cleared his throat.

'How's the dating going, by the way?' he said.

'How are things going with Ulrika?' Mina said by way of rebuff. 'Any more spontaneous encounters in restaurants?'

'Ouch.'

Vincent looked hurt.

'I'm genuinely curious,' he said. 'My daughter has a boyfriend. Or so she claims. I've never laid eyes on him. He's called Denis. But apparently I'm the reason they never spend time in the house. Apparently I'm too embarrassing. Since I can't ask her annoying questions about her love life, I have to ask you about yours instead.'

She shifted her body, trying to find a more comfortable position. The plastic rustled beneath her. Vincent had sounded like he was joking, but his expression was one of honesty. He really did want to know. But what was she supposed to say? It was a very personal question – a private one. Yet there was no one she felt as comfortable with as Vincent. If she couldn't talk to him about this, who else would she be able to turn to? Anyway, he had probably already figured out how the date had ended.

'Let's put it this way: I've learned what it is I actually want,' she said. 'But let's change the subject. Fatbursparken – what's the deal? Do you really think there's a murder victim somewhere here?'

The change in tack felt almost embarrassingly clumsy, but it appeared she'd pressed the right button because Vincent beamed.

'Fatbursparken is most definitely one of Stockholm's more unusual parks,' he said. 'The southern half – opposite us – is, as you can see, a semi-circle with grass and paths laid out. The

332

northern half – where we are now – is concrete and straight lines. If I remember correctly, the park's architects wanted to illustrate the image of chaos versus order. Yin meets yang. Dionysus and Apollo.' He pointed to a bronze statue a couple of metres from their bench.

'Say hello to the Greek god Apollo,' he said. 'Dionysus is on the other side of the park. Although he was only allowed to be a drinking vessel. At least Apollo is a man – albeit one with horse-like thighs.'

'Tell me: what is it with you and statues in parks?' she said, laughing. 'This fixation doesn't strike me as entirely healthy.'

Vincent shrugged.

'Public statues relate to pagan and even occult symbolism far more often than you'd think. It fascinates me. The statues form a network throughout the city that no one sees or thinks about. If I were a mystic, I would regard it as supplying the city with occult energy. As it happens, I don't believe in that, but the statues can still have a psychological impact of sorts. In some cases, it's quite obvious.'

He pointed to the low fountain in the centre of the park. Mina couldn't decide whether it looked like an oversized bird bath or a plate split in two with its edges dented.

'What do you think it is Apollo and Dionysus are competing for in this park? I'll tell you: it's Aphrodite, the goddess of love. Obviously. And there she is. Or more accurately, her gaping vagina.'

'Vincent!'

But she saw exactly what he meant. There were clearly erotic shapes in the fountain, yet they weren't obvious unless someone pointed them out.

'The thing about all this symbolism is that it subconsciously affects our psyche,' said Vincent. 'How many people do you think walk past this fountain and suddenly feel slightly embarrassed, excited or upset without knowing why? Why do you think there are always so many people snogging in this park?'

She could indeed see multiple couples entwined on blankets on the far side of the park, absorbed in each other and seemingly unaware of the world around them.

333

'If there's a dead body in the park then I hope it's over there, under the grass,' said Vincent, standing up. 'It's much easier to dig up a lawn than it is to break up asphalt and concrete.'

Mina also stood up. She removed the sweaty seat cover using two fingertips and threw it away in a bin. Then she went over to the fountain. She suspected there was a dark stain on the back of her shorts. She positioned herself to ensure that Vincent couldn't see her rear, just to be on the safe side.

'Sounds as though you're jealous of those couples snogging on the grass,' she said.

She saw that it would be impossible to hide a body in the fountain – the basin was far too shallow for that. The cobblestones under her feet were also an unlikely burial site. Who would have the time and resources to break open and then replace a whole stone footpath simply to hide a body – even a small one?

She followed Vincent along the path towards the lawn. The southern semicircle of park was barely one hundred metres in width from one side to the other.

'If you were to bury a corpse here, where would you do it?' he said a little too loudly.

The closest infatuated couple – a man and a woman in their thirties on a yellow picnic blanket – shuddered and stared at him.

'Maybe at the edge of one of the paths,' Mina said, trying to maintain the same serious expression writ on Vincent's face.

The woman sat up and pulled her knees under her chin, looking unhappily at the grass around the blanket. The man was staring daggers at them.

Vincent nodded thoughtfully.

'The grass there is probably easier to lift and replace without it being visible,' he said.

The couple began to pack up their glasses, wine bottle and blanket. The date was definitely over.

'Naughty Vincent,' Mina said, poking him gently in the side.

He raised his eyebrows and looked at her innocently.

'I don't know what you mean.' Then he lowered his voice: 'But what do you make of the trees over there? They're planted close enough together that people avoid passing between them and no one can sit there. If you dug up the ground there and you were careful about it, it's likely no one would discover it before the grass had grown back again.'

They went over to the grove of trees. Suddenly Vincent grabbed her arm and pointed. Usually, he rarely touched her. He knew her too well to do that. He was probably unaware that he was holding her arm. Since she was wearing a vest top but no jacket, Vincent was clutching her bare arm. His skin against hers.

And she wasn't panicking.

Not yet, anyway.

She didn't intend to say anything until it was absolutely necessary. Instead, she tried to understand what he was pointing at. The grass between the trees was a darker shade of green than the lawn beyond.

Vincent bent down and pulled a few blades of grass loose.

'Why do you think it looks like this?' he said. 'Darker?'

'Don't know – but I can see it too. Maybe it's because the grass doesn't get as much sun in between the trees?'

'Maybe. It's definitely 125715 anyway.'

'What are you talking about?'

'The colour code for this shade of dark green. It spells out LEGO if you translate it into letters. Don't ask – it's all to do with *Fortress Prisoners' Flight*.'

She understood not one word of what he was saying and wasn't entirely sure whether he was joking with her or not. Probably not.

Vincent examined the leaves of the nearest trees, then he moved onto a tree that was further away and did the same thing. When he came back, he had a few leaves in his hand.

'Hmm . . . the trees at this spot also have greener leaves than the other ones. And there are more weeds growing here. That's pretty strange – the parks department are usually good at keeping that kind of thing under control.'

She merely stared at him.

'Do you have a plastic bag?'

He needn't have asked. Vincent knew very well that she always had one with her. She produced a small Ziploc bag.

335

Vincent inserted the leaves and a few blades of grass before sealing the bag.

'Did you just become a botanist?' she said. 'If you want to press them between the pages of a book like when you were fifteen then there are nicer leaves to choose. Maybe you should dry some roses and hang them on the wall too?'

'No need. Maria's birthday present to me this year was dried roses. They're hanging over the bed.' He pulled out his mobile. 'I don't know how long the leaves and grass will stay fresh, so maybe it's best I take photos too.'

He began by photographing the bag's contents and then did the same with the grass on the ground between the trees, as well as taking close-ups of the leaves on the trees.

'I'm not sure I want to know what you're up to,' she said. 'But as far as the case goes: do you really think a maniacal chess player has buried a body around here somewhere?'

Her phone suddenly buzzed. Vincent had sent her all the photos he had taken.

'Maybe it's nothing,' he said, handing her the bag containing the leaves and grass. 'I don't want to say anything until I'm absolutely certain. I'm already in your team's bad books after the meeting yesterday. And I've got a performance tonight to prepare for. Actually, the shows this weekend are my final ones for the season. But I think it might be a good idea if you gave these pictures and the bag to Milda. If what I believe is right, then it's probably for the best if you hear it from her.'

95

'You don't have time for this!'

His mother snorted and crossed her arms.

Adam merely smiled. 'Stop telling me what I don't have time for,' he said. 'Surely I can invite my mother to dinner as much as I like.'

'You know what I think,' Miriam said, critically examining the decor of his small studio flat with its adjacent kitchenette. 'This home needs a woman's touch.'

'I can get by just fine on my own.'

'I have a hard time believing that. Look!'

She pointed accusingly at a pot plant that had definitely seen better days. 'And I think *you* need a woman's touch too,' she said. 'No man should be without it.'

'Mum! Stop it! You're making me blush.'

'All I'm saying is that I won't always be here. You need someone to take care of you.'

They fell silent. The meaning of her words hung heavy in the air. He hadn't asked about the results of her most recent tests at the hospital as yet. He wasn't sure he wanted to know. Then Miriam cleared her throat and pulled a strained smile. He realized it was for his sake, and he loved her for it. But that didn't make it any easier.

'You said you've got new colleagues at work,' she said. 'Is there anyone there who might be a good fit?'

'Well, there is actually. Maybe. She's special.'

'Have you told her that?'

'No! Are you out of your mind? I've been very careful to avoid showing my interest. I don't think she . . . It would be complicated. Anyway, how am I supposed to fit a woman in *here*?' Adam surveyed the thirty square metres that comprised his small flat in Farsta as he drained the water from the spaghetti into the sink.

'Pah!' said Miriam, slapping him on the back of the head and making him miss the sink as he poured. 'You care about the wrong things! Begs questions about the way I raised you! And what do you mean? There's plenty of space for a woman and four children here. This is a palace compared to what your father and I had in Uganda. We lived in . . .'

'Sure, sure. No need to go over that again. You always make it sound as if you lived in a hut with an earthen floor.'

'Spoilt brat,' she muttered, slapping the back of his head again.

'Ouch! You do know that parents are banned from smacking their children in Sweden, don't you?'

337

'Nonsense. I birthed you. I can do what I like. And don't you think that you'll be spared a taste of the wooden spoon on your bum, even if you do think you're so big and grown-up . . .'

'So you were picturing four grandchildren in here,' he said. 'I heard enough.'

'At least to start with. So you'd better hurry up. You aren't getting any younger. But you'll have to take down those pictures you picked up in IKEA – no woman will want to set her foot in here as long as they're hanging on the walls.' She nodded towards a monochrome photograph of some construction workers eating their lunch while sitting on a joist hanging high above New York City.

'Sit down now!' Adam laughed as he put the saucepan filled with piping hot spaghetti on the table. He picked up the pan of mincemeat sauce and set it down beside it.

'Children's food,' Miriam said, but that didn't prevent her from helping herself to a hearty portion. 'It would seem that a woman's touch is needed in the kitchen too.'

They ate for a while in silence. Then Adam put down his cutlery.

'What did they say?'

She avoided his gaze. She reached for the pasta server and helped herself to more. Then she muttered: 'I start treatment tomorrow.'

In the silence that descended on the kitchen, the clatter of cutlery sounded like gunshots. Adam pushed his plate away. He could no longer eat.

96

Milda's heart always fluttered with happiness when she came home to Grandpa's. The red house in Enskede symbolized so much of what had been good about her childhood. The red house was Grandpa Mykolas personified.

He opened the door before she'd even had time to knock.

'Good morning!' he shouted. 'I've put the coffee on!'

She stepped into the hallway, which was full of dazzling geraniums and hydrangeas. She took off her shoes. She grimaced a little as she followed him into the kitchen. His loud voice was because his hearing had begun to deteriorate in the last year, an unwelcome reminder of his advancing age. She wanted to maintain the delusion that Grandpa would live forever. But she of all people had difficulty keeping that fantasy alive.

'Sit down – you look tired,' Grandpa yelled, setting down a cup of steaming hot coffee on the table.

'Grandpa, you're shouting,' she said loudly.

He laughed, making the dimples in his weather-beaten cheeks deepen.

'Deary me. Well, my hearing isn't quite what it was. But it could be worse! Might have been my eyesight!'

'I brought rolls,' she said, pulling the small bread rolls from a paper bag. Without any additional seasoning – just the way Grandpa liked them. She cut up the rolls and fetched butter and cheese from the middle shelf of the fridge. Then she sat down opposite him at the kitchen table.

Grandpa ignored the butter, took a slice of bread and bit into it with his eyes closed.

'Mmm,' he said. 'Freshly baked. This is the best life has to offer.' Then he turned serious. 'So. What's the matter? I can tell there's something.'

'No, no,' she said, waving her hand even though she knew from experience it was pointless. He wouldn't give in.

'Is it Adi?'

She sighed. He was far too good at putting his finger straight on the sore spot. She spread butter on her own roll and told him briefly about Adi's demand for the house.

Grandpa rolled his eyes and laid his gnarled hand on hers.

'Every family has a rotten apple,' he said. 'But you're a good apple. You're a Mio. Many say it's the best tasting apple out there. Fruity, juicy flesh, with a hint of strawberry about it. Its roots are Swedish and English, and it has taken the best aspects of its parents. Its beauty comes from the maternal variety – the

Worcester Pearmain – and the delicate flavour is from the paternal variety, the Oranie.'

'Is the name from the story? The one by Astrid Lindgren?' Milda smiled. She liked being compared to a beautiful apple.

'Yes, exactly.' Grandpa's eyes lit up. 'The golden apple. Yes. At least that's what they say.'

'What kind of apple does that make Adi then?'

He snorted. 'Adi is no apple. He's a codling moth. Its larvae burrow through the apple right to the core.'

'Come on, Grandpa, he's your grandson too.'

Grandpa Mykolas snorted again. 'Exactly. And this isn't the way you treat your family,' he muttered, his eyebrows drawing together into a frown. 'I really ought to give that codling moth a piece of my mind.'

She glanced at Grandpa. She had only ever seen him angry on a few occasions. But if his expression was anything to go by, Adi was in hot water.

Then he smiled again. 'But I assume that's not why you're here. You didn't just come to talk about Adi.'

She looked down at the table. She had promised herself that she would visit Grandpa sometime without having a specific reason. Soon. And she wouldn't only bring rolls – she'd bring Vera and Conrad too. But not today.

'It's OK,' said Grandpa. 'I'm glad that my expertise can be put to use in the world beyond my greenhouse. My only request is that you don't bring a bag of hair with you again. That was rather . . . unusual.'

Milda smiled and shook her head. Grandpa had the ability to make everything so easy for her. It had always been that way. Nothing was difficult when Grandpa was around. She dreaded to think what it would be like without him.

She pushed her breakfast aside and produced the photos and plastic bag that Mina had given her. She had enlarged and printed the pictures so that he would be able to see the details more easily.

'No hair,' she said. 'But I do have blades of grass. These leaves and blades come from Fatbursparken in Södermalm. As you can see in the pictures, the grass is a darker shade of green in one spot. And the darker leaves come from the trees that surround that spot. The rest of the trees and grass in the park are much lighter. What do you think this change in colour is the result of? Could it be to do with how the sun reaches the ground between the trees, or something like that?'

Grandpa Mykolas brushed crumbs of bread off the kitchen table and tipped the leaves out of the bag. He held two up to the light and inspected them. Then he gently massaged them by rolling them between his thumb and forefinger before sniffing them.

'The sun is undeniably a factor in all that grows,' he said. 'But plants are affected just as much – if not more – by what is below as they are by the sun. That is to say, the soil. Soil is different in different places. There are different amounts of minerals, different nutrients. More or less moisture. These blades of grass and leaves are darker because they have produced more chlorophyll than the others. Likely as not, this means there is more nitrogen in the earth where they are growing. There would also appear to be more nutrition in general, given the weeds visible in the photographs.'

'So we're talking about a very localized change to the chemical composition of the soil?' said Milda. 'What might cause that kind of increase in the nitrogen content of such a small area? Nearby power lines? Copper piping? Temperature differences?'

'I really don't know,' said Grandpa. 'I would have to take a soil sample to determine that.'

Grandpa carefully returned the leaves and blades of grass to the bag again before resealing it. 'Can you tell me why you're so interested in photosynthesis all of a sudden?' he said. 'Is Vera doing a school project?'

But Milda was no longer listening. She'd had a terrible thought. The human body contained some two kilograms of nitrogen. Admittedly much of it turned to ammonia during the putrefactive process, which was something she'd always had to be vigilant about when handling old corpses in a professional capacity. That wasn't the sort of stuff you wanted to breathe in unnecessarily. But even after that process, there would still be enough residual nitrogen in a buried human body to increase the levels in the soil in which it was buried by at least a multiple of fifty. That would be more than enough for the change in chlorophyll that Grandpa had mentioned.

She stared at the zoomed-out photo showing the full green patch between the trees. The spot was barely two square metres in area. About the right size for a child.

97

The police cap provided protection – the crown of Mina's head wasn't being fried in the sun – but on the other hand, the heat under the cap was beginning to reach unbearable levels. Julia had demanded that they all be in uniform today. They had to show themselves in public and let people see that they were working. But Mina already regretted agreeing to it. She went into the shadow of one of the trees in the park and took off her cap. That offered instant respite.

Vincent came and stood beside her.

'How come Julia managed to get this together so quickly?' he asked.

Julia was standing with some of the forensic specialists who were digging down layer-by-layer with the utmost caution through the grass a few metres in front of them.

The experts in ground-penetrating radar had been able to see that there was something in the ground that might be a body through the use of radio waves. Soon they would find out whether that was what was under the grass in Fatbursparken.

Before they had started digging, they had inserted long sticks into the ground to find out where the substratum changed in consistency. That had allowed them to establish the approximate contours of the space – their potential grave. The body – if there were one – was presumably unprotected.

Milda had explained to Mina that if it had been sealed inside

342

something like a plastic bag, then the nitrogen wouldn't have reached ground level. At any moment, forensics might encounter a body in some state of decay. Since they didn't want to damage the body, the whole affair was akin to an archaeological excavation, requiring considerable caution.

'I actually asked Julia to pull some strings on Tuesday as soon as you mentioned the park,' said Mina. 'When Milda called and told us her suspicions this morning, everyone was already standing by. It didn't take more than a few hours to mobilize the team.'

'So what are you saying? That when you and I were here yesterday, Julia had already applied for permission to excavate? And you didn't think to mention that?'

'Well, you didn't say anything about me having a damp patch on my rear end from that seat cover.'

'But that's not the same thing. Anyway, first things first, I wouldn't ever conceive of looking at your arse. And secondly, a gentleman never comments on anything like that, even if he does see it.'

'So you did see it? You're saying you did look at my arse?'

His face turned bright red and he coughed violently. 'I always study body language and don't you think they're taking an awfully long time over there in the grass?' he said. 'I should probably pop over.'

It was probably mean, but teasing Vincent had become one of her favourite pastimes. She suspected revenge would be gruesome when it arrived. But it was worth it.

'I think they need your help about as much as an architect needs a swimming instructor,' she said with a grin. 'But you're right. It's not the same thing. I didn't say anything because I was hoping you were wrong. And normally these kinds of permits take weeks to get. But apparently city hall weren't thrilled about the idea of some tourist stumbling across the corpse of a child in one of the city's parks. I think they would probably have supplied the shovels if Julia had asked. And I still hope you're wrong. I'm hoping against hope. Because the consequences if you're right . . .'

'I know,' he said. 'I'd prefer not to think about it.'

One of the forensics team suddenly began to wave his arm. 'Here!' he shouted. 'I've got something.'

Vincent stared at the flailing officer and once again took hold of Mina's arm, just like he had done on their previous visit to the park. And just like last time, he didn't seem aware of what he was doing. She felt his skin against hers. It didn't bother her.

Julia, who was standing with the huddle of forensic personnel, leaned forward to see what they had found and all the while the sharp smell of ammonia spread through the air.

Julia seemed to study the discovery closely. Perhaps it was taking her a while to process what she was seeing. Or she didn't want to process it. Then she came over to Mina and Vincent.

'This is going to have unwelcome consequences,' she told Mina. 'It may seem macabre to discuss politics at a juncture like this, but I'm afraid I must. Politics down at police head-quarters affects the very existence of our team. And this discovery is completely contrary to the wishes of the top brass. It doesn't fit into the jigsaw they wanted us to complete.'

She turned to the mentalist.

'It seems you were right, Vincent. Congratulations.'

98

Julia cleared her throat. There was a perceptible dichotomy between her private relationship with her father Östen and their professional one. Which was perhaps to be expected. After all, her father was the Stockholm police commissioner.

'I'm getting some troubling signals here, Julia. It seems as if you've once again been listening to this . . . magician person?'

'Dad, he's not a magician,' Julia sighed. 'He's a mentalist.'

She could tell from Östen's eyes that this distinction was in no way helpful.

'We have a very credible lead,' he said. 'A very credible suspect – Mauro Meyer. And I have a damn sight more experience in this line of work than you do. My experience is that the simplest solution is usually the likeliest. This second lead . . . I'm coming close to having to issue you with a direct order to drop it. I was already doubtful when you brought in Nova as a consultant. But at least she's . . . Well. But this is completely out of control. Swapping her for this . . . this . . .'

Julia took a deep breath. She felt as if she were seven years old again – being scolded by her father for forgetting to put the milk back in the fridge.

'I hear what you're saying. But it's also impossible to escape the fact that we found a body in Fatbursparken a few hours ago. Thanks to Vincent and his theories. So it's impossible to say that what he's pointed out isn't true.'

'I've never claimed that . . . Vincent . . . is wrong,' said Östen in the same voice that he'd used that time she'd forgotten to close the gate and the family's German shepherd had got out and knocked up the neighbour's Cavalier King Charles Spaniel. 'But one does not rule out the other. He may be right in his conclusions without it ruling out that Meyer is guilty. What you should be focusing on is getting Meyer to confess, and finding out who his accomplices are.'

'But what about motive?' said Julia, fidgeting on her chair.

'It'll work itself out. There's always a motive. Sometimes you get it out of them. Sometimes not. But you must start with the crime itself. Facts. Evidence. Things that are concrete and tangible. Like the boy's clothes being found concealed in his restaurant. Facts. From what I gather, his ex-wife has long been warning us about him. Facts. And do you know what? I sometimes wish our society was better at listening. But this is unfortunately the reality we have to deal with.'

Östen shook his head regretfully and Julia bit her tongue. She knew it was futile. Whenever her father clambered onto his high horse, there were no voices that could reach his lofty heights. He meant well. His heart was in the right place. But he belonged to a bygone generation of police officers who had been brought up to think inside the box. And if the box didn't fit, then you simply adjusted the contents – occasionally at the expense of the truth. And that was a game that she was still required to play at times. They were still the ones calling the shots and setting the rules. She had known what she was getting herself into when she became a cop. Possibly better than most.

'Don't spend any more time on that other nonsense. Do some proper police work instead.'

Her father's voice was dismissive and she knew that the audience and its inherent telling-off had come to a close. Then his face brightened.

'So when do we get to see our little nipper? It's been too long. Harry must be nearly ready to move out!'

He stood up and put his arm around her. For a moment, Julia allowed herself to lean against his shoulder, as she had done so many times during her childhood. Then she straightened up.

'We'll pop by as soon as this is all over,' she said, kissing her father on the cheek.

'Don't worry, Julia. We're close now! You've got him!'

Her father's words pursued her out of the door.

99

Vincent was on stage. He had performances tonight, tomorrow night and on Saturday. Then he was finally done. The show was nearly at the point where he strangled himself with the belt. It was lucky that he only had to do that number three more times. That would be quite enough. After the last show, he'd had to conceal the red marks on his neck with make-up. During recent performances, the number had also begun to be about something other than the supernatural. He no longer suggested he was in contact with the spirit world. It remained the same demonstration, but its framing had become more topical. Perhaps it was just a way for him to process the unpleasantness taking place around him at present. Regardless, it was even stronger like this. His new theme of cults was really hitting home.

He had arrived at the Oscar Theatre in Stockholm three hours before his show was due to start, so that he had ample time to prepare. Since they were onto the final shows, he had decided to go the whole hog. When the audience had arrived, they had been met in the foyer by his assistants, who had passed out free caps to anyone who wanted one. The caps were adorned with a decorative pattern comprising black dots against the white fabric.

At least fifty people in the auditorium were now wearing these hats. When Vincent appeared on stage after the interval, he had changed out of his shirt into a T-shirt with the same pattern.

'I'm pleased so many of you dared to take a cap even though you didn't know what it entailed,' he said, throwing out his arms and showing his top to everyone.

'I have proof that all of you – all 857 people in here – are among the smartest people in the population. The proof is the simple fact that you're here.'

The joke was a bit daft, but flattery also served the purpose of creating a sense of community in the audience. Indeed, most people were smiling contentedly. He was going to destroy this community.

'At the same time, some of you have made much more progress than others,' he said. 'Those of you who took caps are clearly more inquisitive than those that didn't. I'm passing no judgement on that – it's simply a fact. I would think that most of you with caps are interested in becoming your best selves – you will definitely have books on personal development at home in your bookcases and you might even have taken a course or two on it. Those of you with caps share a unique mindset that the rest of the audience haven't yet achieved.'

Several of the cap wearers nodded eagerly, while several people without caps began to look disappointed and crossed their arms. It was this easy to create a sense of us versus them. All he had done – just like before – was to use so-called Barnum statements. Comments that sounded personal and specific but which were actually almost universal. He had also ensured that he used a softened tone of voice and smiled more as he turned to the cap wearers. The effect was almost instantaneous.

'When you have a mind as unique and open as yours,' he said, 'it's also possible to communicate on a special level. You're sharing a unique mental sphere with me.'

More flattery. And total bollocks. Had he begun with a statement about 'unique mental spheres', no one in the audience would have swallowed it. But the lines he had just delivered were tailored to ensure that the audience were led to accept things they might not otherwise have agreed with. The scary thing was how rapid it was. That kind of transition rarely took more than the words he'd uttered.

'I know this may sound strange,' he said with an apologetic smile, 'but this is a quality that you can develop. It's about disconnecting your body from the mind. Let me show you.'

He steeled himself. Time for the belt. An assistant helped one of the cap wearers onto the stage and they sat down on a chair next to Vincent. Vincent pulled the belt around his neck, and as ever, a buzz rippled through the audience.

'This is to symbolically – as well as literally – disconnect my body,' he said in a strained voice.

He reached out his hand to the horrified man wearing his cap.

'Please would you take my pulse. And note when it starts to decrease. Then I will attempt to dive into our shared consciousness.' The bloody belt hurt just as much as always. After this weekend, never again. The rest of the routine proceeded more or less as usual. Vincent stopped his pulse in his arm and pretended to lose consciousness. Within minutes, he had recounted parts of the man's childhood and a number of personal memories, and he had revealed a couple of secrets that the man had told to nobody. It certainly seemed as if Vincent and the man shared the same thoughts.

In fact, Vincent had used a mixture of Barnum statements, pure guesses, conclusions drawn from the man's attire, manner of expression and body language, and statements that were sufficiently vague that the man was obliged to help him 'interpret' what they meant.

When things that Vincent claimed didn't add up, he apologized – offering the excuse that he must have picked it up from one of the other members of the unique group. There was always a cap wearer who gasped and muttered that it had been about them in particular.

When Vincent was done, he loosened the belt around his neck slightly and allowed the pulse to return to his arm.

'Thank you for your attention,' he said, addressing the cap wearers alone. 'But this ability is actually something that you all possess. In fact, I run a residential centre where I give courses on how to come into contact with our shared consciousness. The way it works is that you come and stay there with me for two weeks while I instruct you. But I must warn you: it is *very* expensive. And there are only ten places available. How many of you are interested?'

Twenty-five hands immediately flew into the air. Vincent nodded thoughtfully. He silently counted to ten to ensure he paused for as long as he could.

'And that's how you set up a cult,' he said slowly.

There was dead silence.

A surge of new emotions was rushing through the audience. Those that hadn't taken caps went from feeling rejected to elation thanks to *Schadenfreude* and vindication. The cap wearers went from being the chosen ones to feeling betrayed. They had trusted him. And he had pulled the carpet from under them. He had five seconds to activate the audience's rational mode of thought before their emotions took over completely. The trick was to get them to swallow their bitter medicine without starting to hate him.

'Sorry,' he said, doing his best to look ashamed. Of course, even that was acting.

'Before I explain what happened I want to make one thing clear. I really do believe that you are all intelligent people. Every single one of you. But there's no difference between those of you wearing caps and those of you who aren't. No group is smarter or stupider than the other. The only difference is that some of you were handed an item of clothing by my assistant. But the caps also created an immediate sense of belonging between those of you wearing them. That was a feeling that I reinforced. The caps also helped to remove your individual identity, which is very important when starting a cult. You became part of the collective. And the term "shared consciousness"? Total rubbish. But it's essential for cults to coin their own expressions to further strengthen that feeling of community.'

Most of the caps had by now been removed. Their former wearers were fidgeting unhappily.

'I'll say it again,' said Vincent. 'Anyone could have been given a cap. There is no difference between you and the others – regardless of what I said. Or between you and me, for that matter. What you then saw me do was nothing more than a couple of psychological feints and a carnival trick. But it was sufficiently convincing for you to want to pay dearly to come and stay with me. I guess my point is this – beware false prophets.'

He hadn't intended to transform the entire evening's entertainment into a lecture. But sometimes it couldn't be helped. The next number would have to be something colourful to make up for it.

'Does the symbol mean anything?' someone called out, waving their cap around. 'The black dots?'

'Oh, the dots,' said Vincent, winking mischievously. 'It's braille. It says I OBEY on all your heads.'

The entire audience exploded in redemptive laughter. He surveyed the stalls and smiled. They could think he'd taken it too far if they wanted to. But right now there were 857 people out there who would be far more difficult to dupe.

As the light shifted he suddenly caught sight of a face he recognized. He hadn't noticed her during the performance. Nova was sitting in the front row of the balcony. She wasn't laughing. She wasn't applauding. Instead, she had her arms crossed and she was looking at him.

Then she got up and left.

100

Someone was already in the green room when he got there. Vincent shuddered involuntarily when he saw the figure on the sofa. He hadn't expected anyone to be there. In fact, no one was meant to be there.

'Sorry, I didn't mean to scare you,' said Nova when she saw his reaction. 'But the security guy said I could wait here.'

It took a moment for him to collect himself before he replied. For a split second, he had thought it was Anna who had come back. Anna with the tattoos. Anna – his stalker. Even though Anna and Nova looked completely different. His gaze was drawn to the table. During the performance, someone had laid out a bowl of sweets and three bottles of water. It was almost as if they were trying to mess with him on purpose.

'Don't worry about it,' he said. 'But I had a stalker on my last tour who did everything she could to get backstage. Then I met her and . . . well, it didn't go well. She had a room full of pictures of me. And an altar. I'm still a bit jittery following that. And I'm usually alone back here.'

He glanced at the floor. The plan had been to lock the door and lie down for a bit. But Nova might think it odd if he did that. And he needed to do something about the trio of bottles. He sat down on the other sofa, opposite her, and steeled himself for a scathing critique of his cult number. He hadn't mentioned the Epicureans by name. But he'd come close.

'I didn't mean to intrude,' she said. 'I just wanted to pop in and say hello. And to thank you for such a fascinating performance. It was exciting.'

'You thought so? I thought you might be a little upset, given . . . well, what I said at the end. About gurus and cults. Water?'

Nova shook her head. Bloody hell. He'd hoped to get rid of a bottle. 'Why would I be upset?' she said. 'You're right. And I think it's an important distinction to make. Teaching people to distinguish between constructive and genuine movements, like

351

the one I work with, and harmful, manipulative cults can only be a good thing.'

Vincent wasn't entirely sure that this was the distinction he'd aimed to make, but he said nothing.

'By the way, should you be interested . . .' she said, opening her bag.

Vincent noted the Louis Vuitton label. Nova extracted a brochure with the Epicura logo on the cover and passed it to him.

'You might want to come out and see me some time,' she said.

Vincent flipped through the brochure. There was a quotation in italics on the first page.

Epicurus' guideline for the new age is same as for all ages: Allow only the anxiety passing like a comet a star. Fast and imperceptible. Life of stillness is life that purifies. Carefully avoid all kinds of pain and desire nothing, for a life without desire is a life fully freed from suffering, and instead allows you to enjoy great success in attaining Everything
John Wennhagen

'I saw that quote on your website,' he said. 'But I didn't know your father was also an Epicurean.'

'It was mostly my grandfather,' said Nova. 'Dad helped out now and then with texts and things, but he didn't fully share my grandfather's philosophy. That was the last thing he wrote before he . . . disappeared.'

'Disappeared? I thought he died in the accident?'

Nova turned pale and looked down.

Vincent bit his tongue. Insensitive. Apparently Nova didn't want to think about her father's death in such definitive terms. Now he had not only forced her to do so, he had also reminded her of the accident that was the cause of the chronic pain she still suffered from. Nicely done for someone who claimed to be able to read people.

'They dragged for two weeks after the accident,' she said. 'But they never found the body. Of course, I know he's gone really.

But a small part of me – the girl who was in that car – still hopes that he'll turn up one of these days. Unharmed, maybe his hair just a little damp.'

Vincent tried to shake off the image of a John Wennhagen who had risen from the dead, dishevelled and with seaweed in his hair, ringing Nova's doorbell. He knew that wasn't really what she had meant. Still . . .

'Your father was something of a poet,' said Vincent, pointing to the text in an attempt to steer the conversation in a different direction.

Nova laughed. Apparently it had worked.

'There's no need to be so polite,' she said. 'That passage borders on incomprehensible for any outsider. But he wrote it based on the rule that he could only use a certain number of words. No more and no fewer than he had decided in advance. He often set himself creative challenges like that. The result was rather . . . Well, we still use it to honour his legacy. And the address is on the back. If you do fancy popping by, that is. Do you mind if I change my mind and take that water after all?'

Nova pointed to one of the bottles on the table. Finally.

'Help yourself,' he said as casually as he could, setting aside the brochure.

Nova picked up the bottle opener lying in a bowl and opened one of the bottles. Vincent exhaled air he hadn't known he was holding inside him. Then he took an empty glass and filled it with water from the tap.

'By the way, I've been brought in on the same police investigation as you. The one with the murdered children,' he said, sitting down again. 'And I must say that it's an interesting thought you had – about there being an organized group behind it. But don't most extreme movements choose to remain out of the public eye? This one appears to be rather keen for us to see them.'

Nova drank straight from the bottle while she looked at him. Her perfectly applied lipstick didn't smudge even slightly.

'Maybe they don't want to be seen themselves,' she said, 'but want us to see their message?'

'What message is that? You mean your water theory? I'm

353

afraid it no longer makes sense. The police found another child's body in Fatbursparken earlier today. They haven't performed the autopsy yet as far as I know, but I'm convinced that the discovery is connected to the other murders. And Fatbursparken is rather a long way from any watercourses. Notwithstanding the fountain.'

Nova smiled, her eyes twinkling at him. Her presence seemed to fill the room. He couldn't help but be impressed. He also wanted to be that obviously . . . magnetic – for want of a better word. Frankly, it was a mystery that she hadn't bagged her own TV show long ago. Presumably she had turned down overtures. Nova didn't seem to seek out more attention than necessary, which was a rarity for those in the public-speaking game.

'I would say the discovery confirms my statement,' she said. 'You of all people ought to know that Fatbursparken was a lake. Around six centuries ago, there was a lake at the centre of Södermalm. It was very important to people – it was their source of water and they fished from it too.'

Of course Nova was right. The park was the remnant of one of Stockholm's most important bodies of water. He was ashamed not to have remembered that himself. Peder would probably have liked to know more about that.

'By the end of the seventeenth century, the lake was so full of rubbish and waste that they referred to it as the Fatbur-swamp,' Nova added. 'By all accounts smelled awful. Nevertheless, it took until the mid-nineteenth century, when they were building the area around the southern railway station, for them to drain the lake. But there was water there from the time the city was founded until barely two hundred years ago. Then it became a park. Where a body has now been found. Why are you smiling like that?'

Vincent laughed. He hadn't realized he was smiling. Nova laughed too and flashed her dazzling smile again. He was forced to consider the idea that it might be because she had been right, instead of him. But if that were true – if he had come to the wrong conclusion – then he had no idea what was going to happen next. If so, he was further from understanding the killer than he had been when he'd started.

Nova stood up and put her hand on his arm.

'We're more alike than you think,' she said. 'I'm just a little smarter. Why don't you stop by for a visit one of these days? You've got the address.'

101

Peder had made sure to be at the shop the moment Herman arrived that morning. Actually, the shop only opened at noon on Fridays since the morning was spent doing inventory of the week's new stock. But given what Herman had said on the phone, it was best to get it over with before the doors opened to the public.

Peder leaned forward over the glass counter and peered at the object lying on a piece of dark blue fabric.

'Thanks for your call yesterday,' he said.

'Not a problem. I recognized the watch immediately when your lot circulated the description. Pity it didn't arrive a day or so sooner. But I've been keeping an eye on it until you got here . . .' Herman patted his belly contentedly.

Peder had met Herman the pawnbroker many times over the years, and Herman was delighted on each occasion he could offer the police his assistance.

'And you say there's an inscription too?'

Herman smiled jovially and turned it over.

'*To Allan Walthersson on his 60th birthday,*' Peder read out.

Allan Walthersson. Ossian's grandfather. Fredrik's father.

Herman barely fitted behind the counter thanks to his huge belly, which only grew with the passing of the years. Peder and his colleagues used to joke that one fine day they would have to saw him free from that shop in Stockholm's old town.

'And this is all that came in?' Peder asked, examining the rest of the objects. 'Have you already sold any of it?'

In addition to the watch there was a gold ring, a pearl brooch and a matching pair of Bismarck necklaces.

'No, everything's here. I don't handle stolen goods. So I called the moment I realized what it was. You know, my old man was a copper. So I was raised to know that you should always help the Law.'

'And we thank you for that,' said Peder, patting his shoulder. 'So. Here's the sixty-four-thousand-dollar question: Who pawned this?'

'Ah, that would be an old mutual acquaintance of ours,' Herman chuckled. 'I suppose that's why I was slightly more vigilant than usual.' Then he paused.

Peder was more than familiar with this particular dance. Herman always wanted to get as much out of the situation as he could, and Peder was more than happy to let him. He looked around the small shop. Something about the medley of bits and pieces awakened a childlike joy within him. There was everything from an old-fashioned cathode-ray tube TV to jewellery, diving kit, dusty stamp collections and what looked like a stuffed badger.

'Don't you want to know who it was?' Herman said, casting him a sly look.

'Very much so,' Peder said with a nod. 'Herman, I really would like to know.'

'Then you'll have to answer my riddle first.'

'I wouldn't have it any other way,' said Peder, laughing. 'Well, what do you have up your sleeve today?'

Herman giggled. 'Here it is: where are you guaranteed to always find money?'

'Hmm, that's a tricky one,' said Peder.

He scratched his beard as he thought. He usually got them, but this time he couldn't think of the solution. He sighed.

'You're too clever, Herman. I give in.'

Herman paused for dramatic effect.

'THE DICTIONARY!' he howled, almost choking with laughter.

Peder smiled and shook his head.

'I've no idea where you get this all from. But look, won't you take pity on a dim-witted copper? Who are we talking about? One of the old guard?'

Herman nodded. 'Yep. One of our regulars. Rhymes with fatty . . .' He giggled again.

Peder frowned. He could get this one. Fatty . . . Then he perked up. 'Matte! Matte Skoglund!'

'Got it in one,' said Herman, patting his belly with satisfaction. He pointed at the objects on the piece of fabric.

'That's nice stuff. There no chance of a . . .'

'Sorry, Herman. I'll have to take it with me. You know that. But why don't you think up another riddle for next time?'

'Only if you have a shave!' Herman chortled as Peder made for the door. 'Have a good weekend!'

Peder pulled his phone out as soon as he was outside.

'Hi Adam, Peder here. I think we can write off any and all conspiracy theories relating to the break-in at Ossian's parents' at Bellmansgatan. It was the usual rabble. Matte Skoglund. Yes, exactly. I'll tell the lads on the streets to keep an eye out for him. But I've recovered what was taken. We can drop that.'

He hung up. Then he laughed to himself. The dictionary. That was bloody funny.

102

'Good job,' Milda said drily.

In the background, Mina could make out Charlotte Perrelli singing 'One Thousand and One Nights', and the medical examiner was humming along here and there, clearly unaware that she was doing so. As ever, Loke was skulking silently in the shadows, ready to follow Milda's instructions.

'I can't take all the credit – it was Vincent,' Mina said, glancing at the mentalist.

For some reason, there was a faint red line around his neck this morning. In fact, she had seen it on and off since he had become involved in the investigation. She would have to ask him about it – but at a better time.

Vincent was staring at the corpse on the table. She had asked him several times before they went in whether he thought he could handle it. Adult corpses were bad enough. Children were ten times worse. But he had insisted. Judging by his face, which was even paler than usual, he wasn't taking it particularly well.

'I've just stitched him back up,' said Milda, pulling off her gloves with a snap.

'What can you say? Are there the same injuries as on the others?'

Mina looked away from the anonymous boy on the table. It felt undignified that they didn't know who he was. He must have been missed somewhere, by someone, for a long time.

She heard Vincent gulping rhythmically as if the contents of his stomach were yo-yoing up and down his throat. Yet the fact that Mina was maintaining her composure did not mean she was dealing any better with the situation. Dead kids were always something that felt horribly wrong. And they now had a tally of four.

'Given that the body has been buried for some time, the circumstances are a little different,' said Milda, lowering the volume. 'One thing in our favour is that a body in the ground takes longer to decompose, partly because it's colder under-ground, and partly because there are no flies. But despite that, decomposition is well advanced. The skin has split into layers, which always makes my work a little harder, and the tissue has also started to turn into adipocere. But yes, there are a lot of similarities here with the other victims.'

She fell silent. In the background, Charlotte Perrelli faintly moved on to 'You Are in My Dreams'.

Vincent gulped again and opened his mouth.

'How similar?' he asked in a hoarse voice.

'Very similar I should say,' Milda replied. 'The same marks on the lungs. I've also found the same fibres in the throat as on the other victims.'

She nodded towards a steel trolley which held various samples to be sent off for analysis.

'Your assessment is that it's the same killer?'

'That's not for me to say – that's up to you. But like I said, my impression as a medical examiner is that there are significant similarities in the method.'

Mina nodded thoughtfully. She could see out of the corner of her eye that Vincent needed to get out of there. However, he opened his mouth before she could say it was time they were on their way.

'When?' he said. 'When do you think the murder took place?'

Milda looked at the body on the table and creased her forehead.

'It's very difficult to say. The best I can offer are my assumptions. I'm guessing the body hasn't been buried for more than two months. But take that estimate with a pinch of salt. It's not easy when you're dealing with bodies where the adipocere has begun to form. Well, actually, sometimes it can help, because if corpse wax forms quickly then it can preserve visual injuries. Unfortunately that hasn't been the case here. By the way, we also found this close to the body, but it doesn't help to determine a time of death since plastic doesn't degrade.'

Milda pointed to a transparent container on the side. It appeared to contain a red and blue toy.

Vincent went over to look at it. A little colour returned to his cheeks.

'Lego cars,' he said, pulling out his phone. 'May I . . . ?'

Mina nodded and he began to take snaps. Vincent's interest in the Lego seemed to be almost as great as Milda's in the dead body. 'Do you think the toys belonged to him?' said Mina.

'There's no reason to believe otherwise,' said Milda. 'Of course, it's a bit odd for them to have been buried with the body, but that's not the only strange thing about this whole business.'

Mina nodded. There was more truth in what Milda said than she wanted to admit. Vincent returned, engrossed in his newly taken pictures.

'Thanks, Milda,' said Mina. 'Get in touch as soon as those samples have been tested – and let me know about anything else that comes up. I'll take wild conjecture, if that's all you have. We need everything we can get at this stage.'

'Will do,' Milda said tautly, nodding to her assistant, who began to wheel the body away.

As Mina and Vincent headed for the door, they heard the volume being cranked up and Perrelli belting out a romantic ballad behind them.

As soon as the door slammed shut, Vincent took a few deep breaths with his chin tipped towards his chest. Then he looked up and met Mina's gaze.

'Four children,' he said. 'Kidnapped by different people, killed in the same way. I'll never be able to sleep again after this.'

'I know. But we have a problem. The body in there was supposed to prove your theory about the chess problem. Your supposed knight's tour. Well, we found the body in Fatbursparken, like you predicted. But without any horse connection, we can't be sure whether the body is connected to the chess pattern or just a coincidence. Your pattern depends on two things. The location of the bodies is one. The bookmark, backpack and graffiti are the other. But Lego cars have nothing to do with horses – at least, not so far as I know.'

Vincent nodded thoughtfully.

'I know,' he said. 'I also thought one of the toys looked vaguely familiar. There's something strange going on here.'

103

Vincent pressed the intercom button by the door at the address they'd been given in Birkastan. It buzzed immediately and the door clicked to indicate that it was unlocked.

'I'm not sure this is the right way for us to be spending our time,' Mina said sceptically.

'I know you've got a suspect in custody,' he said. 'But we still can't rule out that it's related to some kind of group. I mean, four murders? Of children? That's pretty heavy. I haven't wanted to use the word "cult" before, but I'm beginning to wonder whether that might not be the best description. It may turn out that Mauro is its leader – that's a question for later. But there is one person in Sweden who has a complete overview of which movements are established in the country. After this visit, we can hopefully determine whether we can write off the idea of an organized extremist group, just like your commissioner wants us to.'

'But we've had Mauro in the cells since Monday. It's now Friday. We ought to be concentrating more on him while we've got him.'

'Think about it like this: if it is Mauro who's behind all the murders, then you've already got him. That means you have all the time in the world to make this visit. But if it's not Mauro, then the clock is still ticking. In that case there may be a child somewhere who is in danger. We can't afford to miss something. Which means what we find out here may be incredibly important.'

Mina looked at him.

'If it were anyone else . . .' she said haltingly. 'But fine. I assume this will be meaningful.'

They had climbed the stairs to the second floor. The lift had looked like it could barely accommodate a grown adult, so there was no chance of Vincent getting into something that cramped. Fortunately for him, it appeared not to have been cleaned in an eternity, so Mina had also rejected it in a flash.

'Trust me,' Vincent said as he rang the doorbell by a plaque reading *Ljung* on it. 'Lunch is on me afterwards.'

A red-haired woman in her thirties opened the door and greeted them.

'Thanks for seeing me at home,' she said apologetically, stepping aside so that they could enter the flat. 'I keep most of my materials here.'

Vincent noticed how anxiously Mina was looking around. Presumably no one had a home that lived up to the standards she demanded in order to relax. Besides, he suspected that his 'trust me' hadn't been enough to stifle her conviction that they were about to waste their time.

Thank goodness Beata Ljung had a clean and tidy home.

Mina seemed to exhale in relief. Vincent looked at her questioningly and she nodded as if to indicate that she was OK.

'Come into my study.'

Beata showed them into a big bright room lined with shelves filled with books and folders in neat rows.

'From what I've gathered from Vincent, you're Sweden's greatest authority when it comes to research on and facts about cults?' Mina said, sitting down on a blue-and-white-striped armchair after first inspecting the fabric – presumably to check for stains.

'Oh goodness. It sounds so pompous when you put it like that,' Beata said, sitting down behind her desk.

It was a large, beautiful piece made from a dark wood. Vincent stood in the middle of the floor, unsure where to sit down.

'I'm afraid I've only got that to offer you,' said Beata, pointing to a grey beanbag chair.

Mina stifled a giggle as Vincent sank into the beanbag, trying to make himself comfortable. He was trying to find a position where he could still radiate some degree of professionalism. It was not going well. He guessed it didn't help that his grey linen suit was in the exact same shade as the beanbag. He supposed he looked like a floating head. The only things that stood out were his Cookie Monster socks in their violent shade of turquoise.

'I've read quite a few of your articles,' he said in a failed attempt to sound natural, 'and I'm impressed by your breadth and depth. Am I right in thinking that you not only have a journalism degree but another in psychology?'

'Yes, I had trouble making up my mind,' Beata laughed. 'At first I thought I wanted to be a psychologist, but then I realized upon graduation that I wanted to be a journalist instead. Having said that, I've been able to make a lot of use of my academic detour in my work, so I don't complain when they send the repayment demands for my student loans.'

'Hang on. Did you write the book about the Järvsö case?' said Mina, pointing to a book on the desk.

Vincent hadn't read it himself, but it had been a much-discussed title a few years previously. Apparently it described

362

in explicit detail what had happened in the village of Järvsö on a fateful January night when two families had been wiped out in the culmination of many years of cult-like activity in their small community. If he was not much mistaken, the book had been turned into a TV series, and he couldn't help but be impressed.

'Yes, that's right,' said Beata, looking at them expectantly. 'So . . . What do you want to know?'

'We're not actually sure,' he said, fidgeting on the beanbag, which rustled under his weight. 'We don't know what it is we're looking for, beyond a group of people who are currently behaving in a way that is . . . incomprehensible. So we need to get a handle on which cult-like organizations are to be found in Sweden. And which ones might potentially be dangerous.'

'I think I understand what you're getting at, even if you're being deliberately vague. As you may have gathered, this is a huge area. I'll only be able to scratch the surface. But I'll do my best to tell you all I can. My son is five years old, so I feel particularly affected.'

Beata nodded towards a photo on the wall of a sweet, red-haired boy with a big smile; he was missing a front tooth.

'OK, let's start in general terms with the concept of a cult,' she said. 'How much do you know?'

'We've talked to Nova, who has told us a bit,' said Mina.

'Nova's good. She's done a lot of work with defectors,' said Beata. 'In that case she may have mentioned that there are somewhere between three and four hundred cults and sects in Sweden. We reckon perhaps thirty or so are destructive.'

'Yes, she said something like that,' said Mina, nodding.

'To be honest, the word cult doesn't in itself mean that something is dangerous. It's like saying a knife is inherently dangerous. If it's used to hurt someone then it is, but if it's used to cut up ingredients for an incredible meal then a knife isn't a negative thing. It's the same with cults and sects. It's all about the purpose, the goal, and what they fill the movement with. There are also different types. Many people automatically assume that cults are religious, and perhaps that's the most common type. But there are also cults based on finance, philosophy, and even sales.'

363

'I've never thought about it in those terms,' said Mina.

'But regardless of focus,' Beata continued, 'most destructive cults are driven by power. The founders' need for power. It doesn't have to start like that, but power corrupts. It makes people rot from within. And money often goes hand in hand with this. But money isn't always necessary – sometimes power itself is the most important thing. Unfortunately, it often ends in tragedy. You've probably heard of mass suicides. More than nine hundred people died in Jonestown – most of them when they drank grape juice spiked with Valium and cyanide. Those who refused were shot. Almost forty people in the Heaven's Gate cult died when they drank vodka laced with sleeping pills. And there's a long list of similar examples.'

'That sounds terrible,' said Mina. 'But surely it's people with certain traits who end up in cults? People who are easily persuaded, uneducated or alone?'

She perched on the very edge of her armchair. This was obviously more interesting than she had expected. Vincent hoped that meant he was forgiven for having insisted on the meeting.

'That's a dangerous assumption,' said Beata. 'It's not just the socially excluded, lonely and other vulnerable people who seek out cults. There's an inherent desire in human beings to seek meaning in life. To find something that gives them purpose. You can be a seeker even if you come from a good background, have a stable life, family, friends. All that can be replaced quicker than you think by someone offering you a purpose. Well, I'm sure Vincent could tell you all about that.'

'If you grow up in chaos you come to detest it when you're older,' Vincent said, nodding. 'And you seek out an organization that exerts powerful control. But equally, you might have come from a strict family and therefore appreciate a movement with its own strict rules. Since control and chaos are both a part of growing up, there's the possibility that we are affected in ways we can't avoid. But I have a question. Which cults – other than the most obvious, like the Scientologists – do you think are most worthy of mention in this context?'

He shifted position on the beanbag again and it rustled. Beata frowned. She took an elastic band from a bowl on her desk and tied up her red hair. He noticed a somewhat envious look flash through Mina's eyes. There were so many daft prejudices about women with red hair – that they were more vivacious and wild. Perhaps something like that was passing through Mina's head. He suspected that in Mina's world redheads didn't sanitize their hands to the same extent that she did. They didn't allow themselves to be limited the same way she was. Or maybe she just thought Beata had nice hair.

He wanted to tell her that no matter what Samson might have thought, personality was not found in someone's hair. He also wanted to say that her own thick raven-black hair was fantastic. Both when long and when cut short. But how was he supposed to say something like that without sounding like an idiot?

'It depends on which angle you choose,' said Beata. 'The established ones? The ones we already have good knowledge of? The new ones? The ones we don't yet know much about? What I can do is give you a list that I've compiled. But I can't guarantee it's complete. I've built it by synthesizing other people's facts, my own interviews with defectors, and in some cases undercover journalism in cults themselves. There's many years' work in my research into cults in Sweden. But I still can't claim that it is in any way complete. Cults have a unique ability to conceal themselves behind normality. Well, obviously not all of them. Some are clearly totally crazy from the word go. But most don't come across that way. Sometimes they're the worst. And the man in the street has never heard of them, even though they're big both in terms of size and finances. For example, have you ever heard of Eastern Lightning?'

Both Vincent and Mina shook their heads.

'Its full name is the Church of Almighty God, and it was established in China in 1991. They have several million followers internationally. They have a history of murder, kidnapping and hijacking other congregations. The cornerstone of their faith is that God has returned to the world as a woman by the name of Miss Yang. They committed various acts in China that made their continued existence there impossible, and then they spread across the world. Now they're in Sweden. We also have the Plymouth Brethren. Sound familiar?'

Mina shook her head again. But Vincent recognized the name.

'They control a corporate empire in the world of manufacturing,' Beata said. 'There are thirty-eight Swedish companies with ties to them. They're an extremely closed religious sect with some four hundred members in Sweden. They're very conservative, with man superior to woman, and they are very isolated from the rest of society, which means they also have their own schools. As you can probably tell, I could keep going. I hope you can find something in my work that helps you, even if there are holes in it. I've had to put this puzzle together without a lot of the pieces.'

'We fully understand that,' said Vincent.

He tried to stand up from the beanbag but failed. Mina had to stifle another giggle. He glowered at her and made a renewed attempt, this time accompanied by involuntary grunting precipitated by the effort. Mina couldn't contain herself. She laughed loudly and Beata joined in. Then they both took pity on him, got up and grabbed an arm each before pulling him out of the rustling bag.

'Good grief,' he said. 'Middle-aged men shouldn't sit on furniture designed for teenagers. I thought I might end up spending the night on that thing.'

He brushed a hand over his trousers and jacket to check whether they had creased. In reality, he was trying to avoid Mina's gaze. He had been very conscious of her proximity and warmth when she had helped him to stand up.

Mina seemed just as keen to avoid looking at him – she was already making for the door.

'Thank you, Beata. Would you mind emailing the document to me?' she asked over her shoulder.

'Not a problem,' said Beata.

Vincent and Beata shook hands as Mina led the way out.

When Vincent emerged from the flat, Mina was already on the floor below. As he walked down the stairs, he idly scrolled through the notifications on his phone. One of them made him gasp. Then he upped his pace. 'Wait!' he called out. 'Mina, wait!'

He caught up with her just inside the door to the street. He held up his mobile.

'I think we'll have to skip that lunch. Look!'

'What?' Mina moved closer to get a better look. Then she swore loudly.

'Bloody hell. Mauro.'

104

The headline was emblazoned across the monitor in big black lettering.

SUSPECT IN CHILD MURDERS HAS PRIOR CHILD ABUSE CONVICTION

Mina drummed her fingers on the table in annoyance. She and Vincent had gone straight to police headquarters and her stomach felt like an empty, hungry void. She probably ought to have let him buy her that lunch en route after all, because now she was so angry she was ready to burst.

'Why didn't we know this?' she said.

'Because he was seventeen years old when it happened,' said Julia. 'A minor. It was expunged from his criminal record long ago.'

'But how on earth do the papers even find this stuff out?' said Mina. 'How are they allowed to publish this?'

'I don't suppose that matters much right now,' said Ruben, who sounded just as annoyed as she felt. 'The main thing is that it's true. And that it's logical. Stuff like that doesn't start in adulthood – it starts much earlier.'

'But there's too much that doesn't make sense!' said Mina,

glaring at her colleagues around the table in frustration. 'He also continues to deny all involvement.'

'Of course he does!' Ruben snorted.

'Even with this information, I think we're going to struggle to hold him for much longer,' said Peder.

'The fact remains that Ossian's clothing was found in his restaurant,' said Julia. 'And hidden, at that. Now we've got a past conviction. No, I'm inclined to agree with Ruben.'

'The clothes were in a toilet cistern,' said Mina. 'If it's meant to be some kind of trophy, then I've never heard of anyone who was so careless in storing their loot.'

'Just how much experience do you have of murderers and their trophies?' Ruben said snidely. 'What, in your view, would be a sufficiently murderer-like way to store them?'

Julia glared at him and Ruben ostentatiously rolled his eyes. The heat seemed to be making everyone irritable. What was more, the media had been like sharks in bloodied water even before the latest revelation. Mauro's remand had been leaked to them, which hadn't done anything to dissipate the tension. Ted Hansson, leader of Sweden's Future, hadn't wasted the opportunity to repeat over and over on social media and to anyone that would listen that Mauro hadn't been born in Sweden. Now he'd have even more support for his cause. Mina didn't dare think what would happen if the media caught wind of the fact that there were now four children involved.

'I'm only saying there's a lot that doesn't add up,' she sighed. 'The way Ossian's clothes were being kept. And how did Mauro manage to remove the spare clothes from the nursery without anyone spotting him? They must have been in Ossian's box in the cloakroom inside the nursery building. And what about the girl's witness statement to the effect that it was a woman? Jenny claimed that Mauro had an accomplice, but no one in his family matches the description. Yet we've treated the girl's testimony as credible to date – there's no reason to start doubting it simply because we'd like to square the circle. I also don't understand what Mauro's connection to Ossian and William is. Not to mention the victim we found in Fatbursparken on Tuesday. Milda has confirmed that she found the same fibres and marks inside that body. Why would he go after them? To throw people off the scent? That seems extreme. Or do you think he started with his own daughter and then carried on with other, randomly selected children? You've all met Mauro by now. Do you really think that seems likely? And we need to find out more about the past conviction. You know as well as I do that there are cases that aren't black and white. Vincent, say something!'

She turned to the mentalist, who had thus far remained silent during the meeting.

'I can't offer any comment,' he said, shifting awkwardly. 'Sorry. I've got nothing to go on as regards Mauro. I haven't met him. But based on what I'm hearing, I agree with you. These pieces really don't fit together.'

'Obviously you agree with Mina,' Ruben said with a sigh.

'If it's not Mauro,' Peder said, tugging at his beard, 'then we need to explain certain odd coincidences in relation to him. There are more pieces, after all. Like the thing with the horses that Vincent mentioned.'

'What do you mean?' said Mina.

Peder pointed to that day's copy of *Aftonbladet* on the table, its front page visible.

EQUESTRIAN REMANDED ON SUSPICION OF CHILD KILLINGS, read the headline. There was a photo of Mauro with anonymity provided by a black box over his eyes.

Mina jumped. An equestrian. The trophies on Mauro's shelf came back to her. He'd even said so himself. 'I was very active in my youth,' he'd said. 'Everything from riding to fencing.'

She had been there. She had seen his past up close. The riding trophies with engraved pictures of horses on them. She ought to have made the connection days ago. How could she have missed it? On the other hand, that had been in Mauro's youth – decades ago. And it had been nothing more than a passing comment in a residential hallway. Mauro wasn't the only person on the planet with an interest in horses. It was no wonder she hadn't put two and two together.

Peder looked searchingly around the table.

'I mean, it is a bit strange,' he said. 'That our suspect comes from a horse background at the same time as we have these . . . horses . . . constantly turning up. If we're to believe you, Mina and Vincent. Do you think it's a coincidence? Because I think it's basically the opposite – it strengthens our case against Mauro.'

'Lots of people in this country have spent time with horses at some point in their life,' said Mina, holding out her hands. 'Half the girls in my class at school were riders.'

'Yeah, but still,' said Peder, clearly uncomfortable that for once his perspective differed from hers.

'You're right,' said Vincent. 'There's a clear connection between Mauro and horses. And there's a clear connection between horses and the murders. Both through chess and the objects that have been recovered. But Mina is also right. The Swedish Equestrian Federation has 155,000 members. Mauro is just one of many with a connection to horses.'

Julia raised her eyebrows.

'I checked earlier,' Vincent said apologetically.

'Mauro also has an alibi,' said Mina.

'Sure, but the alibi is his wife,' said Julia. 'So we can neither assume she is telling the truth nor that she is lying.'

Bosse padded over from his water bowl in the corner and Christer scratched the dog behind the ears.

'I think Mina may have a point . . .' Christer said hesitantly.

Julia turned to Adam, who was standing leaning against the wall, his arms crossed.

'What do you think?'

He didn't reply immediately – seemingly pausing for thought.

'I see both sides,' he said eventually. 'I agree with Mina that there are a lot of question marks. But then again, physical evidence is physical evidence. What other reasonable explanation is there for Mauro having Ossian's clothing in his possession? As for the odd place they were found, there might be a logical explanation for that. He might have hidden them elsewhere where someone had come close to finding them, so he temporarily stashed them in the loo while in a panic.'

'I want to talk to Mauro,' said Mina, looking questioningly at Julia. 'And I want to take Vincent with me.'

After a moment's hesitation, her boss nodded.

'The horse connection and the clothes are good enough for me,' Ruben said grumpily, idly thumbing through a copy of *Expressen*. 'Not to mention a previous conviction for child abuse. Open-and-shut. We've got him.'

105

'I don't understand any of this.' Mauro looked tired and drawn after spending several days in the cells. The fluorescent tubes cast long shadows from their chairs in the small, bare room, and the green prison uniform gave his face a greyish tinge. Mina was sitting at the table with Mauro. Vincent had positioned himself on a chair by the wall in order to better observe the conversation.

'Someone must have planted the clothes,' Mauro continued. 'Jenny. It must have been Jenny.'

'She has an alibi and no connection to Ossian,' said Mina. 'There are also other aggravating circumstances relating to the discovery at your restaurant.'

She was careful not to touch the table. Pulling out her wet wipes was not an indulgence she could afford while in the middle of an interrogation. She clasped her hands on her lap and tried not to think about the chair she was sitting on – the one she hadn't been able to clean.

'Huh? There can't be more. I haven't done anything. I would never—'

'When you were seventeen,' she interrupted. 'What happened then?'

Mauro's face fell.

'Huh? That . . . that was . . .'

'You must realize that we're wondering why you refrained from mentioning your previous conviction? I've reviewed the transcripts of your interviews this week. It's not mentioned anywhere.'

'Nobody asked,' Mauro said, holding his hands out.

'Don't play dumb. You knew full well that it would be highly relevant in this context. Didn't it come up in the custody dispute? Wasn't Jenny aware of it?'

'No,' Mauro said quietly. 'No, she didn't know about it. If she had, then she would have used it against me. But it's . . . it's not what it looks like.'

'Then what is it?' Mina said.

'There wasn't any abuse,' Mauro said. 'We were together. I was seventeen, she was fourteen. It was mutual and voluntary. She was a member of the same riding club as me. But her parents wouldn't accept it. I wasn't posh enough, or Swedish enough, for that matter . . .'

'You're saying she told the court that? That it was consensual?'

Mauro flashed a wry smile.

'No. Her parents promised her a new horse if she changed her story. She'd been wanting that horse for a long time.'

Mauro fell silent. He crossed his arms tightly against his chest and tucked his hands into his armpits. Then he stared down at the table in dejection. Mina glanced at Vincent, who nodded imperceptibly. Mauro appeared to be telling the truth.

They sat in silence for a while. The whirr of the fan was the only thing audible in the room.

'The thing about horses is something we need to discuss,' she said.

'Horses?'

'Yes. There's a lead linking all the children that relates to . . . horses. As you can imagine, it's not a point in your favour that you have an equestrian background.'

'I'm not the only person to have a background in horses.'

'I know. You and one hundred and fifty-five thousand others.'

Out of the corner of her eye she saw Vincent smile faintly over by the wall.

'But how did you get into riding? Isn't it still quite unusual for guys?'

Mauro hesitated.

'Unusual is an understatement,' he said at last. 'Ninety per cent of riders are girls. But my mum wanted me to. She grew

372

up on an equestrian farm in Italy and she loved horses – so she sent me to riding camp one summer. I suspect the ulterior motive was to show me something other than asphalt and concrete. And I loved it from the word go. Anyway, I had an aptitude for it. So that's how I got into it. My parents not only put time and commitment, but also every spare krona they had, into my eventing.'

It was hard to hear Mauro speak so movingly about his parents. It hadn't been like that for her. And she hadn't been that kind of parent. She got up. 'You're probably going to be in here for a while longer. But I promise to check out what you've told us.'

'Thanks,' said Mauro.

'Just one question,' said Vincent, who had also stood up. 'E-four e-five. The Italian game. How would you defend against it?'

Mauro looked confused. His eyes darted between Vincent and Mina. 'Defend? Who am I . . .? Sorry, I don't know a thing about football. Why do you ask?'

'Forget it,' said Vincent. 'My mistake.'

Mina opened the door and Vincent exited the room.

'He doesn't know a thing about chess,' Vincent whispered as she passed him. The last thing she noticed about Mauro was that his eyes had clouded over again.

In that bare room, the fan continued to whirr.

106

Ruben contemplated Ted Hansson's triumphant face on the conference room TV with distaste. The earlier press conference had been a success – multiple clips featuring the leader of Sweden's Future had gone viral. So now that Ted had announced that he had something new to say, the media weren't hesitating to pounce. This time a TV4 news crew were on the scene to interview him in a live broadcast.

Ruben could swear that it was going to be about Mauro. He hadn't bothered to summon the others – they were busy and he had difficulty believing that Hansson would say anything that was of interest to them. If necessary, they could always watch it afterwards. The fact was that their work would probably be affected by the new TV segment whether they liked it or not.

On this occasion, Lilly's mother Jenny was present again, standing side by side with the party leader. They were in Mynttorget square, outside parliament. Ted had presumably concluded that he seemed more personable if he was outdoors. The glee on their faces was unmistakable.

Ruben leafed through the day's *Aftonbladet* while keeping an eye on what was happening on screen. It wasn't that he doubted Mauro's guilt – unlike Mina, he reckoned that if you could hear the sound of hooves then it was probably a horse and not a zebra. But there was still something about the way that Ted Hansson and Jenny Holmgren were eagerly revelling in what was happening that left him with a deep sense of unease.

'We are relieved and grateful that the truth has now been exposed to the public. Mauro Meyer is a criminal. Just as Lilly's mother Jenny has always said – without being listened to – he is a man who abuses innocent children. He is a predator who should not be allowed to walk free on Sweden's streets. We now look forward to justice being served and Jenny getting the redress for her daughter that she has battled for so long to secure.'

Ted put an arm around Jenny, who wiped an invisible tear from the corner of her eye. Ruben snorted. He really couldn't understand how the media could give this spectacle airtime.

'Yes, I'd like to offer my thanks to everyone for the outpouring of support I've received since the truth came out,' said Jenny. 'I look forward to Mauro getting the sentence he deserves. I know that somewhere in heaven my Lilly is smiling and that she's happy and grateful that I never stopped fighting for her.'

Jenny wiped another invisible tear away and Ted's hand squeezed her shoulder in a way that made it look like he was

374

a claw gripping her. Ruben averted his gaze and began to thumb through the newspaper again. The sound of their voices was bad enough – he couldn't bear to see more.

He stopped at the centrefold where the paper had featured a big interview with Jenny. They'd taken a photograph of her at home to make the story seem more personal. In one shot, she was sitting on the sofa clutching a picture of Lilly on her lap while other family photos were on display on the dresser behind her.

Ruben suddenly leaned forward. He brought his face close to the photo and scrutinized it intently. Then he swore.

'Fuck. Fuckety fuckety fuck. Mina's right. It's not Mauro.'

He was looking at a big framed photo behind Jenny. It was a portrait of her alongside a familiar face. Ruben turned towards the TV and smirked. Ted Hansson's *Schadenfreude* would soon be nought but a distant memory.

107

Vincent tried to appear unfazed in the lift. He had left police headquarters to think. The talk of horses had reminded him that they still didn't have a connection in that respect to the most recent body found. He hadn't solved the mystery involving the Lego either. So he had strolled to city hall to gain some new perspective – quite literally.

He closed his eyes and pretended he was in the queue for the checkouts in the supermarket instead of in the claustrophobic lift rising up the tower. The bodies pressed against him helped to add to the illusion. When the doors parted and the tourists poured out, he was able to breathe again.

He was the last to exit, and stopped to look around. He was only halfway up the tower attached to city hall – the lift had brought them to what was meant to be a small museum.

'*Entschuldigung!*'

A German family, the sons were wearing propeller hats emblazoned with the Swedish flag, squeezed past him.

'*Bitte,*' he muttered, scouting around for the door to the stairs that would take him up to the viewing point.

He thought better when he had a bit of perspective. Distance. Seeing the city from above always helped when he was trying to find new patterns. He could lose himself in the network of streets, the locations of parks and public buildings. It allowed him to see bigger connections and relationships that were hidden to those walking below.

It was impossible to see a pattern in its entirety while moving between the pieces of it. The brain needed help to zoom out.

He found the stairs and glanced up. The staircase wound its way up inside the narrow tower. The similarity to the stairs in Alfred Hitchcock's 'Vertigo' was striking. The lift was one thing, but this . . . And it was full of people too. He didn't know whether he'd be able to cope.

But city hall was an easy stroll from police headquarters. And he didn't dare go back to his usual vantage point at the Gondolen restaurant. He hadn't been there in two years. Not since he'd kept an appointment with his ex-wife Ulrika there. When they had . . . No, he didn't want to think about it. He would probably need to wait until they had replaced all their staff before he dared to set foot in the place again.

He raised one shoe to the first step, trying not to think about how close the walls were. Then he began to climb. There were a total of 365 steps in the tower. As many steps as there were days in the year. The tower was 106 metres tall, and the lift had taken them around halfway – 54 metres. That left 52 metres to go. As many metres as there were weeks in a year. Was it coincidence that the number of steps and the height in metres both symbolized a calendar year? Of course it wasn't.

To distract himself as he slowly climbed, he pulled out his mobile and found the photos of the two Lego toys they had found at Fatbursparken. The mystery he had come here to solve. Because Milda might be wrong. He wasn't as sure as she was that the toys belonged to the victim.

A blue racing car and a red tow truck. So innocent. So full of meaning.

Unless he was once again seeing meaning where there was none. It was something he had started to do more and more, he thought to himself as his ascent slowly continued. Because what were the odds that only a few days earlier he had thought about Lego and a mossy shade of dark green in the same breath, and then the police had found Lego under moss-green grass in a location he had specified? It was almost as if he had deposited the toys there himself. Which it went without saying he had not. Sometimes crazy things happened by pure chance, but when they did he hated it.

He stopped to catch his breath. There were still a lot of steps to go to the top.

He had recognized the blue Lego car. He'd thought he would realize why, but as yet he hadn't succeeded. He looked at the pictures again. A faded sticker had been applied to one side of the car. He zoomed in as much as he could and was able to make out the letters *drif*.

As he began to climb again, he searched for 'Lego drift' on Google. It was a reasonable guess, given it was a car. The search yielded several Lego cars, but not the right one. He looked at the sticker again. He spotted that the word didn't actually start with a d – there was a letter in front of it that had been rubbed out. He couldn't see what it was, but there couldn't be that many options. He took a chance and googled 'Lego adrift'. This time he struck gold. His phone display filled with pictures of the car they had found in the park. Not only were there adverts for the model in question, but there were also assembly instructions and article numbers.

All of a sudden, he realized why it was so familiar. It was part of a series – Lego Racers – that had come out in miniature when Benjamin had been little. His son had been given a blue racing car just like it together with the box of bricks he'd been thinking of lately.

Vincent finally reached the top and stepped out onto the viewing platform. Stockholm lay below in all her summery glory, but he could no longer concentrate on the city. The pieces had already started to come together in his mind. He quickly took out a pen but realized he had nothing to write on – he would have to make do with the back of his hand. He wrote down what he knew so far.

Lego Classic. 6116. Brick box.
Lego Racers. 8151. Lego adrift.

He paused for a moment's thought, then struck the bottom row through. Benjamin's box of bricks couldn't have anything to do with this. But the red car they had found was the same size as the blue one. It was presumably from the same series. He examined the photo on his mobile up close and spotted that there was a sticker on that too. It said *Tow t.* Googling for 'Lego Racers Tow truck' turned up assembly instructions for the red vehicle in the first hit. Finally a bit of movement. He wrote down the new information.

Lego Racers. 8151. Lego adrift.
~~Lego Classic. 6116. Brick box.~~
Lego Racers. 8195. Tow truck.

Now it was just a matter of finding the pattern.

He stared out across the water towards the island of Södermalm. To the east, he could see the verdant trees on Långholmen – the island that housed the former prison that was now a hotel. Water everywhere he looked. Water and dead children.

Adrift. Truck.

At least the link to Benjamin's Lego told him one thing. The red car was a little newer than the blue one, but they were both Lego models that hadn't been on sale for over ten years. And those kinds of small models rarely came up on the second-hand market. If he assumed it was a message from the killer, then someone had been planning the murder of the child found in Fatbursparken for a very long time. Longer than the child had

378

been alive, he realized. What did that mean? How could one plot to kill someone who didn't even exist? It was probably an important question. But not one that he needed to answer this very moment.

Without a connection to the knight's tour, the child found in Fatbursparken was nothing more than a tragic murder victim. Maybe the Lego cars weren't cunning clues left behind by a murderer who liked to play games. He hadn't identified anything unusual about their appearance. They seemed to have been built fully in accordance with their instructions. It was possible that Milda had been right – that the child might have been holding them when he was killed.

But it didn't feel that way.

The children in the propeller hats ran past him hooting away in German. He pressed himself against the balustrade to make room. Far below him there were people sprawled across the grass sunbathing. If the clue wasn't to be found in the objects themselves, then perhaps it was in their names? The words gave him nothing. But he tried translating the article numbers to letters in the order that the models had been released. The numbers 8 1 5 1 8 1 9 5 gave the letters H A E A H A I E. Which was nonsense.

But then again, the alphabet featured more than the first nine letters. In order to get to the later ones, he would have to group the numbers into twos. He started again. The first two numbers were 81. That couldn't be a letter. So the first number had to be the 8 – which would be an H. The next two were 15. That could translate to a letter – an O. Likewise 18, which equated to R. And 19 was S. That left only a 5, which meant it was E.

He stared at the letters he had written on his hand.

H O R S E.

Turagapadabandha. An arrangement in the steps of a horse. Knight's tour.

He had been right all along.

The Germans were making more of a racket than ever.

108

'Do you realize what you've done?' Ruben's voice trembled with suppressed rage. He was usually able to keep his emotions in check when on duty. But this was stupidity surpassing almost any that he had previously encountered. He and Julia had gone down to Mynttorget as soon as they could. They had arrived just as the TV4 interview was wrapping up. When they had asked to speak to Jenny Holmgren, Ted Hansson had made himself scarce pretty quickly. Ruben suspected that he preferred not to be seen in the vicinity of the police. Especially when the TV cameras had attracted an audience. A little Friday fun for the tourists.

He'd asked Jenny to come with them to police headquarters, and had made it clear to her that she had no choice in the matter. Jenny had been smart enough not to cause a scene.

But when they'd shown her into the interview room, Jenny's nonchalance had been replaced by obvious irritation.

'I've no idea what you're talking about,' she said. 'And I can't fathom how you could be so insensitive as to pick me up in a police car in front of all those people. I've half a mind to sue. I've got my reputation to think of. And poor old Ted. What will people think? But I suppose Mauro has managed to get to you with his lies. He's always got by on his charm – that bloody facade of his. My God, you lot are gullible . . .'

Ruben exchanged glances with Julia, who was sitting beside him. The red tinge at her ears disclosed that she was just as furious as he was. They could do without morons wasting their time. Matte Skoglund had already been arrested for the burglary at Ossian's parents' flat. He hadn't even mustered a denial when they'd picked him up.

'I want you to think carefully before you dig that hole any deeper than it already is,' Julia said, her voice silken.

For the first time since they'd brought her in, there was a glimmer of anxiety in Jenny's eyes.

'A colleague of ours has already spoken to your brother Matte,' Julia added, maintaining the same smooth voice. 'He's currently about to sit down in one of our interrogation rooms. I wonder what he might have to say? Especially if a reduced sentence gets thrown into the bargain.'

Jenny's eyes flashed equal parts anger and fear. They had her. And she knew it.

'You can't believe anything Matte tells you,' she said, waving her hand. 'You probably already know about his background. Prison. Drugs. Theft. Assault. Well, you tell me what Matte hasn't done.'

'We know about all that,' said Ruben. 'Above all, that theft has always been something of a specialism for him. Like you said.'

He pushed a few photos over to Jenny.

'These are items he pawned. Would you like to guess where they're from?'

Jenny swore.

'I told that fucking moron to ditch them.'

'I take it then that we can dispense with the pretence,' said Julia. 'You know these things come from the home of Ossian's parents. We asked them to take a look at Ossian's clothes and they realized that some were missing. The description of them was an exact match to those we found in a toilet cistern at your ex-husband's restaurant.'

'Er, well, Mauro must have taken the kid's clothes when he snatched him from that nursery.'

'Yes, that's what we thought too. But Ossian's spare clothes were still in his backpack at home. The clothes at the restaurant went missing from Ossian's home at the same time as the break-in. Are you telling us that's a coincidence?'

Jenny stared at the table without replying.

'We've absolved Mauro of all suspicion,' Ruben said, unable to conceal his glee. 'He's already been released and is on the way home to his family. Did you know they'd had another little one?'

'On the other hand, we will be holding both you and your brother,' Julia added, before standing up. 'On a real pick-and-mix of charges. Everything from theft and handling stolen goods to obstructing a police investigation.'

'You can't do this. I've got powerful friends. They'll—'

'You mean your mate Ted Hansson?' Julia interrupted. 'The leader of Sweden's Future? He won't touch you with a bargepole when he hears about this. The media are going to eat him alive thanks to you. I'm afraid that your fifteen minutes of fame are over.'

'Fuck you, cunt,' Jenny hissed.

Julia stopped. She leaned over the table and put her face close to Jenny's.

'You're addressing a mother. Say that again. *One. More. Time.*'

Jenny avoided Julia's stare.

'Thought as much,' said Julia. 'Have a good weekend.'

As Ruben and Julia left the room, Jenny sat there staring sullenly into space.

'Nice job, Ruben,' said Julia.

He was so dumbfounded he could only nod.

109

Nathalie's grandmother looked worried as she sat on the suite of furniture they had built and positioned in the shade of some trees. She was reading and rereading a piece of paper over and over again.

'Is something wrong?' Nathalie said anxiously.

'We're running out of money,' Ines said, putting down the sheet of paper, which Nathalie saw was a bill. 'Renovations are costing us more than we expected. And we have more mouths to feed. I really don't know whether we'll be able to stay on this farm.'

Her words were like a slap to the face. Nathalie flopped heavily onto the chair beside her grandmother.

'Can't stay?' she said. 'But . . . but . . . where will I go?'

Grandma shrugged dejectedly.

'Most people here have been generous and given whatever money they could spare. But it's not enough. And I don't want to ask you – you're too young for that. Not that it would really make much difference. We need rather a lot.'

Nathalie felt ashamed. How could she have been so selfish? She had been living off the others without knowing it. But she should have realized, because the money had to be coming from somewhere. She wanted to explain to Grandma that she wasn't just a kid – she cared as much as the others. But words wouldn't be enough. She had to help them. And she knew how.

'My dad and I have got some money at home,' she said. 'There's a miniature pirate chest in my bedroom. When I get birthday money, I put the cash in there. And occasionally my dad puts some money in there too. Once there's enough we're going to use our pirate booty to go on holiday. There must be ten thousand kronor in there. We could go and pick it up.'

Grandma looked at her with wide eyes. Then she smiled.

'Are you sure?' she said. 'It would mean a lot, and you'd really be showing your worth to the others. But it is a lot of money. *Your* money.'

'What do you mean by "showing my worth"?'

'Sorry, I shouldn't have said that,' Ines said, taking her hand. 'But sometimes the others ask questions. They think you're getting special treatment because I'm your grandmother.'

If Nathalie hadn't already made up her mind, she would have done now.

'I want you to have the money,' she said. 'I think we should go and get it right away.'

Grandma smiled again – that warm, embracing smile that proved to her that all was well in the world.

'Let's wait until Karl can join us,' she said. 'You never know when a Karl can come in handy. After all, we do have your father to deal with.'

110

Christer wiped a little sweat from his brow as he stepped into the Ulla Winbladh restaurant. He had been coming here every Saturday in recent months, but for the last two weeks there had been too much going on around the Ossian investigation for him to make it. He looked around anxiously as he entered the grand historic venue on the island of Djurgården. On just his second visit he had decided that the little table for two in the left-hand corner was his spot. On one occasion, a young couple had managed to bag it ahead of him and he had reluctantly taken the table next to them. He had spent his lunch casting grumpy sidelong glances at them – albeit discreetly enough that they wouldn't notice. It was more for his own satisfaction – they couldn't very well have known it was his table.

'Well, who do we have here? The prodigal son returns!'

The maître d' beamed when he saw Christer come in, and Christer felt warmth spreading through his chest. Hoping he wasn't about to start sweating again, he regarded the maître d' and was struck – as always – by the fact that his hair was just as blond as he remembered it. There wasn't a strand of grey to be found, and there was no hint that it was dyed.

'I was beginning to worry you'd decided you didn't like us anymore,' the maître d' said, winking at him. 'Your table is free.'

He grabbed a menu as he passed by, and then led Christer to the table. It was beautifully laid with a white tablecloth, silver cutlery and a burning candle.

This time he was going to do it. He was going to introduce himself. Tell him who he was. It was going to happen. Today. For sure. Definitely.

'Oh well, y'know, there's been a lot on at work,' Christer muttered.

'Would you like to see the menu? I fear it's just the same old same old. Will we be having the usual?'

The maître d' proffered the menu and Christer took it while

he sat down with his back to the wall. *Will we be having the usual?* Which *we* was he getting at? Christer wondered whether the maître d' had recognized him from way back when after all. He both hoped he had and desperately hoped not. Not yet. He needed to collect himself a little more first.

The view from the window was magnificent. The pavements were thronging with people out for a stroll, many of them with their dogs on leads. He missed Bosse. The dog accompanied him everywhere, but the restaurant didn't permit pets and he didn't want to leave him in a hot car, so Bosse had to be a good boy and wait at home. The first time it had cost Christer his favourite pair of patent leather shoes. A week later it had been the left armrest on his upholstered TV armchair. But it was worth it.

'I'll take a look,' he muttered, making an effort not to look at the man holding out the menu.

His pulse was pounding so hard that it was surely audible to all. Soon. Soon he would say something.

'Take your time – it's quiet today. I suppose people have gone to their places in the country, or out to the archipelago.'

Christer mumbled a response and pretended to be deeply engrossed in the menu. He had already made up his mind. It would be the usual: Baltic herring. But he wanted to prolong the moment and give himself another few seconds to find that perfect opening. Three months and it still hadn't presented itself. Or perhaps it had been and gone, and he had missed it. He was no longer sure.

'By the way . . .' the blond man in the white coat said.

He'd been moving away in the direction of the kitchen, but then he had stopped and turned around. Christer looked up from the menu and met his gaze. Even his eyes were as blue as he remembered.

'I've been meaning to ask several times,' the maître d' said, 'but it's usually so busy that I haven't got round to it. I was just wondering . . . have we met before? You seem somehow very familiar.'

A slight crease of worry appeared between his eyebrows. The blue of his eyes was amplified by the sunlight as it caught his face at a perfect angle. Christer's pulse was pounding so hard that he thought it must surely be resounding throughout the restaurant, making every other patron turn around to see what was going on over by the small table in the corner. But no one turned around. No one seemed to hear the thundering sound in Christer's ears. He took a deep breath. There was the opening he had been looking for. Finally.

But . . .

'No, I don't think we've met,' he heard his own voice say. 'And I think I'll have the herring. With a pilsner, if you please.'

He closed the menu and handed it back to the maître d', who shrugged and departed for the kitchen to pass on his order. Christer watched the man's back until he disappeared from sight. Then he sighed heavily.

Next time. It would have to be then.

That would be when he said something.

111

Surely a day off wasn't too much to ask for? Besides, it was Sunday. And they had done a good job on Friday bringing in Jenny and Matte, and releasing Mauro. Ruben thought he deserved a little rest.

But apparently not.

He drove as fast as he dared. Admittedly he had requisitioned a police car for Astrid's benefit, which meant he needn't bother with the speed limits. But if someone spotted a little girl in the front passenger seat as he blasted past them on the motorway they might be puzzled. He would just have to hope that the police cap on Astrid's head would provide at least a little bit of disguise. Ruben thought she was beginning to grow into it.

It was typical of Vincent to summon everyone to a meeting just minutes after Ruben had picked up Astrid from Ellinor's for the second time. 'Drop everything and be here fifteen minutes ago,' he had said. Who did he think he fucking was? On a Sunday to boot. Although the last time Vincent had called a meeting had been in the summer two years ago. On that occasion, the mentalist had managed to make himself the prime suspect in the space of half an hour. Ruben was tense with anticipation about what Vincent might come up with this time.

'You're driving really fast!' Astrid said, laughing at his side. 'Are we chasing a burglar?'

'Something like that,' said Ruben. 'We're off to meet a mind reader. He can steal your thoughts, you know.'

Astrid fell silent, as if ruminating on what Ruben had said.

'Could we have the sirens on then?' she said at last.

Ruben's insides felt warm. To hell with the rules. His daughter wanted sirens. She was going to have sirens. He turned on both the sirens and the blue lights and put his foot down a little harder. Astrid howled with delight.

When they arrived at police headquarters, Astrid urbanely greeted the staff in reception. Then they took the lift upstairs and jogged to the conference room. Astrid kept up with him every step of the way. When he entered the room, he didn't initially understand why everyone else looked surprised. That was until he spotted that they weren't looking at him but at his daughter.

'Oh, yes. This is Astrid,' he said. 'She's meant to be with me today.'

There was silence in the room.

'I don't know whether it's all that appropriate for . . .' Julia began, before merely shaking her head.

'Is she . . .' Peder muttered through his beard. 'I mean . . . how did you . . . ?'

Then he too fell silent.

Vincent was standing by the far wall where the now che-quered map of Stockholm was pinned up. Pictures representing Lilly, William, the body in Fatbursparken and Ossian had been attached to the locations they had been found in. Someone – Vincent presumably – had drawn a line between them so that the murderer's path was easy to follow.

387

'Hello Astrid,' said Vincent, smiling at Ruben's daughter. 'A pleasure to meet you. Golly, don't you and your dad look alike! Even without that police cap, I'd wager.'

'Your *dad*?' Christer said, his jaw dropping as if he were waiting for birds to start building nests inside his mouth.

'What?' Ruben snapped, pulling out a chair for him and another for Astrid. 'Surely you can see that she's my daughter? Are you lot stupid or what? Vincent's right. Surely you can see how alike we are! Who else is handsome enough to be her dad?'

He pushed the plate of biscuits over to Astrid and ignored the undisguised grins that began to spread around the table. Even Mina had something resembling softness in her eyes.

There were only a few jam-filled biscuits from the day before left on the plate. Astrid didn't mind. She happily nibbled on them. The corners of Julia's mouth were twitching.

'I know a boy called Aston who I think must be about your age,' Vincent said to Astrid. 'And that's a very similar name to Astrid.'

'Is he here?' Astrid said hopefully. 'Can we play?'

Christer, who had been about to put his coffee mug to his lips, began to chuckle.

'There you have it, Ruben,' he said. 'Playdates at Vincent's from now. That's your future!'

The prospect held no appeal for Ruben. Suppressing a shudder, he cleared his throat loudly. 'What was so urgent?' he said. 'Astrid and I have other plans today.'

'Quite right,' said Julia. 'We need to make a start. What do you have for us, Vincent? Er, Ruben, you may want to cover Astrid's ears if this becomes too much.'

'She'll be fine,' he said, adjusting Astrid's cap while his daughter reached out for another biscuit.

'You're all aware of the . . . discovery . . . that we made in Fatbursparken,' Vincent said cautiously, glancing at Astrid. 'We also found a horse there. Not a real horse, Astrid. It was actually some Lego. But it contained a message. The word *horse*. It confirms my theory about the knight's tour. However, as has been pointed out to me, the discovery doesn't contradict Nova's water theory. I think her point about our killer and their

accomplices resembling a cult-like group is also valid. Too many
. . . victims . . . have been kidnapped by completely different
people for it to be anything but organized.'

'As for the victim in Fatbursparken, we don't have any idea
which person or persons were the kidnappers,' Christer pointed
out.

Vincent nodded. 'True. That still remains to be seen. But
what we can note is that there are other factors at play that
show it's the same murderer.'

Astrid's eyes widened when Vincent said the word *murderer*.
It was typical of him to be so careless. But she didn't say anything
– instead she just grasped Ruben's hand tightly in hers. If he
hadn't been proud of his daughter before, he was now. She wasn't
unnecessarily afraid. Astrid was going to be the best copper
ever.

'The problem is that Nova's theory can't be used to make any
predictions. If there's another . . . crime . . . then all we know
is that it will take place near water. Or indeed where there has
been water. Which means pretty much the whole city. But the
knight's tour at least gives us somewhere to search. So if it's OK
with you, Julia, I would like to propose that you continue to
work off my basic idea until you find something better.'

Vincent didn't wait for an answer, instead putting his finger
on Lilly's square on the map. Then he traced the line over to
William, then on to Fatbursparken, from there to Skeppsholmen
where they had found Ossian, and then on to the next position
on the map. 'According to this route on the map, the next . . .
discovery . . . will be made in Djurgårdsbrunnsviken bay,' he
said.

'That's basically a whole canal,' Peder said. 'Apropos water.'

Vincent gave him a dark look.

'This won't do,' said Julia. 'What you're telling us, Vincent,
is where to search if we fail again. But we need to prevent the
abduction itself. We need to put every nursery on alert. We
should ask them to exercise particular caution during pick-ups
and not to let any children out of their sight.'

'For how long?' said Peder. 'There was six months between
Lilly and William. But the interval between William and the

discovery in Fatbursparken was much shorter, and to Ossian too, for that matter. There doesn't seem to be a pattern to when this happens. How long should we be asking all parents to live in fear?'

'Parents have already grown weary,' Ruben said, remembering the woman he and Adam had met outside Lovis's building. 'Ted Hansson is climbing in the polls with every passing day. With or without Jenny Holmgren.'

'I don't think warnings will help,' Christer said gloomily. 'The kidnappers have outwitted both parents and neighbours so far.'

Ruben looked at Astrid. She was only a few years older than the children they were talking about. Vincent and Nova claimed that it was a whole organization. He struggled to understand how so much wickedness could be concentrated in one single place. In his city.

He suddenly had difficulty swallowing and once again adjusted the cap on Astrid's head. Any bastard who got close to her would have him to deal with.

112

The others left the room. Vincent alone remained, examining the map. He ran his hand over it, following the knight's path across the board. The killer's journey through Stockholm's neighbourhoods. They were missing something. He could feel it.

Mina said something from over by the door.

The thing that Peder had pointed out was gnawing away at him. The intervals between the kidnappings being different. Someone going to as much trouble as their murderer wouldn't leave something like that to chance. Everything that happened in the world happened in time and space – at a special time in a specific place. There was always a when and a where. The pattern on the map was extremely clear about the where. But that was only one piece of the puzzle. They were missing the second half of the pattern. They didn't have the when.

'Vincent.'

He turned around. Mina was standing in the doorway, looking as if she was awaiting a reply.

'Sorry,' he said. 'What did you say?'

'I asked whether you were coming.'

He rewound his memory, trying to recollect what Mina had said. But the sound of her voice had been drowned out by his own thoughts. There was no memory there for him to find. He lowered his gaze, afraid to reveal that he hadn't been listening.

'Don't worry, I know you didn't hear me,' said Mina. 'Which is kind of my point. I think you need to think about something else for a while. Come along now.'

Not daring to ask where they were going, he meekly passed through the door that she held open for him. They went to the lift. He felt uneasy.

'You need to let Maria know that you'll be home late,' she said as the doors slid open. 'The police meeting got dragged out or something.'

'OK, but may I ask where we're going?'

'We both need to clear our heads for a bit,' Mina said, pressing the button for the car park in the basement. 'So that we can function better later. Surely that's something you know all about.'

When the doors opened, Vincent waited a moment before emerging from the lift. He didn't like lifts, much less underground car parks. The ceiling was always much too close. At the same time, he supposed he ought to be happy that Mina hadn't parked in the street. That would have meant them driving around in a sauna on wheels. To wherever it was they were going.

When they got into Mina's car, he noticed that there was no plastic cover on the passenger seat, and he took this to mean that she hadn't had anyone else in the car for some time.

'Are you sure this is OK?' he said.

'The cover's in the glovebox,' she said, starting the engine. 'Lay it out yourself.'

'You really know how to make a guy feel welcome,' he said, but he obeyed.

She drove across the Sankt Eriksbron bridge and then on to

Odenplan. Just before the city library, she pulled into a side street and then drove into a multistorey car park.

'It's a fair way from work,' she said. 'But that's the whole point.'

When they emerged from the car park, he saw the sign on the adjacent door. The letters ROQ were inscribed next to a skull. If it were possible, he was now even more in the dark. What was this place?

'I know,' Mina said when she saw him looking at the sign. 'I try to come here when there's not a band playing. I don't mind the music, but have you any idea how many particles a drummer kicks up into the air? They ought to be put in a glass box when they play.'

He followed Mina through the door. It took a few seconds for his eyes to adjust from the blazing sunshine outside to the dim light within. Then he saw that they were in a large room with row upon row of deserted pool tables.

'I did say I was good at pool,' Mina said. 'So I thought I'd give you a lesson in humility by beating you. That way you won't have to feel smug. For a change.'

Vincent stared at her. He had no idea where to start. Pool?

He had a hard time placing the policewoman, who didn't like other people, who panicked if someone so much as spelled the word *bacteria* to her, in a pool hall. At the same time, he could see that the place was basically empty. It was still the afternoon. The premises also appeared to be well-cleaned. And Mina had indeed said she liked pool, even if it had been forever ago.

'We aren't going to make any progress with the kids right now,' Mina said. 'We won't solve anything by bashing our heads against the wall. We'll be better at what we have to do if we let ourselves focus on something else for a while.'

'Hi Mina!' said a woman behind the bar.

'Hello Alice, how are things?'

The woman named Alice wore a black vest on top of a white one with the venue's logo printed across her chest, and her hair was worn up in a carefully styled messy look. She shrugged.

'Oh, you know,' she said. 'Sometimes he's stubborn. You just have to take a deep breath. Table eight is reserved for you like usual.'

Alice bent down behind the bar and produced a tray on which there was a bottle of sanitizer and a wire basket filled with wet wipes.

'Give me a shout if your worse half gets to be too much,' Mina said. 'I've got a few colleagues who will be able to talk some sense into him.'

She took the tray and began to head for the pool tables. Vincent had no choice but to follow her.

'So, how's this going to work?' he said. 'I don't want to be that guy, but do we clean all the balls first? Do we wrap the table in plastic? Do you have your own collapsible, antiseptic pool cue with you in your bag? I don't mean to pry, but I can't see how you're going to do this. Thousands of people must have touched these things. People who have drunk beer, had tobacco on their fingers, sweating along to the live music . . .'

'That's quite enough, thank you,' said Mina.

'Is this some kind of aggressive cognitive behavioural therapy?'

'Being in your company necessitates therapy,' she said. 'Since I quit AA, I've been coming here every week. Sometimes several times a week. It's far enough from work that no one will recognize me. I get left alone here. In a way, it's helped me more than AA did. Alice at the bar always cleans the table before I arrive. The cue and balls too. And yes: I have asked her to wear plastic gloves while she does that. She doesn't think it's strange at all. It's completely normal compared with what her husband asks her to do. He's . . . an exhibitionist, as they call them.'

Vincent watched as she placed the pool balls into a plastic triangle and adjusted them.

'You mean someone who gets off on having sex in public places? Preferably where they will be caught?' he said. 'That must be tiring.'

He tested the pool table to see how stable it was. It was all too easy to imagine what had happened on that table.

'Numbskull,' she said when she saw his expression. 'Obviously that was the first thing I asked her.'

393

She gave him a cue and removed the plastic triangle.

'Your break.'

The pool game went just as Mina had predicted. She was merciless. But Vincent was also magnificently terrible. The thoughts about time hadn't completely disappeared from his brain; they lingered there, gnawing away, disrupting his concentration.

Mina took careful aim, lining up a pot. She struck one ball which then hit another. Several balls knocked into each other in a chain reaction until the last one dropped into the pocket.

Vincent stopped himself. He tried to replay the sequence like a film in his head. There was something about the way that the balls hit each other at ever-shorter distances. Time. Events where one thing led to another. Over time. Time getting shorter at each stage of the reaction as the balls hit each other . . .

'Mina,' he said.

She was bending over her pool cue, but she raised her gaze to look at him.

'Do you think we'll be able to get everyone back to police headquarters tonight?' he said.

'Well, that's today's fun over,' she said, standing up and leaning the cue against the table. 'Don't you ever relax?'

'Well, I do remember it happening once when I was nine,' he said. 'It was super boring. But what do you think? Can we . . . ?'

'Peder's wife is likely to tear you to shreds,' she said. 'And Julia's husband will be right behind him in the queue. But I don't think there will be any problems otherwise. Why?'

'I'll tell you on the way.'

'And you're sure this isn't just because I'm thrashing you so magnificently?' she said, peering at him suspiciously.

'Promise.'

Mina sighed and gathered up her things. They went back to the bar and returned the tray with its cleaning supplies to a surprised-looking Alice.

'That was a quickie,' she said.

'Something came up,' Mina said. 'But see you next week.'

Vincent waited until they were outside and on the way back to Mina's car. 'Did you see the way she kept glancing at the table

394

while we were playing?' he said. 'She and her husband have *definitely* used that table.'

113

Mina was able to gather the team together quickly since everyone except Ruben was still in the building. The tired, grim expressions around the table indicated that Vincent was most definitely in their bad books. Of course, she had made it clear that it was his idea to reconvene. Not even Peder managed to look enthusiastic. Mina understood why. She had threatened to force Vincent to walk back to police headquarters from the pool hall as a punishment for his comment. Because of him, she would have to ask Alice to change tables next week.

'Sorry to drag you all back again,' said Vincent. 'But it would have been too complicated to do it over the phone. I've been thinking about something that Peder said . . .'

He checked his wristwatch.

'. . . two hours ago.'

'And what have the two of you been up to since then, eh?' Ruben said in a suggestive tone.

He no longer had Astrid with him and was clearly back to his usual self.

'That's none of your business,' said Mina. 'But I can tell you that the balls were freshly polished and that Vincent knows how to play hard.'

Christer and Peder burst into raucous laughter. But Ruben turned an angry shade of red and looked like he didn't know what to say. It was wonderful. Finally she'd got the chance to push back. After all those years of Ruben's looks, comments and insinuations, she'd made him blush like a schoolboy.

'May I be so bold as to ask whether you were at the billiards table?' Adam said hesitantly.

Christer laughed even louder.

'Now, now. Settle down, class,' Julia sighed. 'Much as I'd like to stay here bickering with a bunch of primary schoolers, I've got someone more important to get home to. His conversation is also a tad more mature.' Mina noted that Julia had referred to one person, not two. Torkel was clearly still out of favour.

'So what's this about?' Julia said, looking at Mina.

Mina took a step back and waved her hand in Vincent's direction.

'It's all yours,' she said.

Vincent cleared his throat and positioned himself by the map on the wall as he had done in the previous meeting.

'As I pointed out this afternoon, my theory suggests that the next body will be found here – somewhere around the Djurgårdsbrunnsviken bay. What we haven't known is when the killer – or the organization or cult – intends to strike. But I think I've worked it out. Peder was right. The murder dates are like pool balls knocking into each other, but their acceleration is increasing rather than decreasing.'

All the detectives stared at him with expressions of confusion.

'And you're telling me I just drove all the way in from Vallentuna for this?' said Ruben.

But this was Vincent the way Mina liked him most. When he was engrossed in his thoughts and forgot everyone else in the room. His body language changed when he was thinking, becoming more casual. Assured. As if he were always on guard, except for times like this. Now he was the Vincent she had let down her defences for.

'I couldn't see the pattern before,' Vincent said, apparently having missed Ruben's tetchy comment. 'Even when Milda suggested that the body from Fatbursparken was no more than two months old, I failed to see it. But it's too neat to be a coincidence.'

'What's neat?' Ruben said, even more annoyed.

Adam and Julia were watching Vincent, waiting to see what came next, while Christer furrowed his brow as if he were trying very hard to get to grips with what the mentalist was saying. Peder was staring disconsolately at the empty plate. Ruben appeared to have bagged the last few biscuits for Astrid.

'The rate of acceleration,' said Vincent, going to the white-board.

He picked up a pen and began to write.

'Look. The use of the knight's tour shows that we're dealing with individuals who approach their actions on strictly mathematical terms. There's no reason to believe that they wouldn't use the same approach in terms of the frequency of their acts. Lilly disappeared in early June last year. William at the end of January this year. That's a gap of seven months. If the body in the park has been there no more than two months, like Milda says, that means he disappeared in mid-May. Three and a half months after William. And Ossian disappeared eight weeks after that. Don't you see?'

Vincent pointed to what he had written.

Lilly → William, 7 months

William → Fatbursparken, 3.5 months

Fatbursparken → Ossian, 1.75 months (8 weeks)

'They're halving the time between each killing,' he said.

He waited until everyone in the room could see what he'd already spotted.

'Jesus Christ,' Christer muttered.

'That means that the next disappearance will be four weeks after Ossian's,' said Julia.

'Exactly,' said Vincent with a nod.

'Hang on a second,' said Christer. 'Didn't you say that it would happen sixty-four times if we didn't stop them? As many times as there are squares on the chessboard? It doesn't feel like this divide-in-half approach will allow for many more murders.'

'You're right,' said Vincent. 'Well spotted. If the interval between each killing is halved, the murderers can – at most – carry out another four. After that, they would be resorting to kidnapping a child a day, and before long they'd be on one an hour, which is completely unfeasible. So there's a natural stopping point after eight kidnappings. I'm not saying it's going to be eight – just that it might be. But for now we need to concentrate on preventing the fifth one from happening.'

No one in the room said anything. Everyone seemed to be taking Vincent seriously. Even Ruben appeared to be pondering what he had said.

'So what are you saying, Vincent?' Julia said slowly. 'How long do we have until the next one happens?'

'Like you said,' the mentalist said, tapping the whiteboard. 'The next kidnapping will be four weeks after Ossian was abducted. It's Sunday afternoon now. This Wednesday it will have been three weeks since Ossian was taken. If we don't solve this, a new child will disappear – somewhere in Stockholm – in ten days' time.'

The Fourth Week

114

'Hello.'

The voice made Ruben jump. He hadn't noticed anyone approaching.

'Hello,' he said, automatically raising his hand to brush back his fringe.

On this particular Tuesday morning, his hair seemed to have a will of its own.

'How's it going?' said Sara from Analysis.

Sara, who was assigned to help them to sort through all the data, and who for some reason didn't like him. She sat down next to him and he caught a whiff of perfume mixed with fabric softener. Sara looked cool and untroubled despite the heat in the room, and Ruben resisted the impulse to sniff his armpits. Instead, he focused on the task at hand.

'Our job has got infinitely more difficult,' he sighed, pointing at the computer display. 'Now that the murders are getting so much more media coverage, parents have started reporting their kids missing after fifteen minutes. We're drowning in reports. What's more, people are furious. They think we're not doing our jobs. And they're scared. Parents are barely letting their kids out of their sight.'

'Better to have one report too many than one too few,' Sara said, squinting at the screen.

'As if that wasn't bad enough, we found out at the weekend that the murderer might strike again next Wednesday,' he said with a sigh. 'And after the Mauro fiasco, we're back to square one. I'm ashamed to say it, but we've got nothing to go on. We spent all of yesterday going through the notes from the interviews relating to Ossian's disappearance, but it gave us squat.

No new leads, nothing we didn't already know. Our killer is like a ghost.'

'Is there anything I can do?' Sara said, reaching for the full mug of coffee she'd set down on the desk.

'Thanks for the offer, but I don't know what that would be right now. And let me issue a fair warning to you if that coffee's from the vending machine. It's pure rotgut.'

Sara laughed. She had a resonant and melodious laugh. Funny he hadn't noticed that before.

'I'm used to piss-poor weak American coffee,' she said, taking a gulp. 'Even the worst coffee in Sweden tastes divine by comparison.'

'OK. How's that going, by the way? America, I mean. I heard on the grapevine that your move back here was being made permanent?'

'You mean you heard I'm getting divorced.' Sara sighed.

He tried not to sneak glances at her curves, which were undeniably in the right places. Her husband was surely an idiot.

'It turned out that we had slightly different perspectives on life,' she said. 'He thought I should become a housewife and generally keep my trap shut. And I thought . . . well, not that.'

'Got it,' said Ruben, continuing to scroll through the missing persons reports on the computer. 'Sorry if this is overly personal, but how's it going to work with the kids? If you're living on different continents?'

Sara looked at him in surprise. 'This is a new side to you. I didn't think you even knew I had kids?'

Ruben blushed, but then he straightened his back. She was right. There was a new side to him. Well, new and new. He'd always been a caring and considerate person, even if he said so himself. There just hadn't been that many people that he'd had to care about. Or there had been, but he hadn't seen it. Bloody hell – things were getting messy again. But mess was good, as Amanda the shrink had always told him. Mess meant progress. Even if it was exhausting at times.

'I've discovered that I have a daughter,' he said. 'Her name's Astrid and she's ten years old.'

'Oh wow. Congratulations!' Sara looked at him with even more surprise. 'What . . . How does that feel?'

'It feels amazing,' he said, and he could feel how true that was.

Because it was. He really did think it was amazing. She was amazing. 'It's obviously a shame that I've missed so much of her childhood. But things are the way they are. And I don't know if I would have been much use. Her mother's got it together. Deep down, I think I recognize that she made the right call to kick me out. But now I want to make the best of it. Be the best dad I can.'

Sara shook her head, raised the mug, looked at her coffee and put it down again.

'You take a few days' leave and wouldn't you know, you come back and stuff has happened,' she said. 'But I'm thrilled for you. And to answer your question about the kids, it's . . . tricky. I want to stay here, close to my family, and I want the children to grow up here. He doesn't want that. American law isn't great when it comes to maternal rights – at least not when mothers come from foreign countries. If the kids go to see him, then I'm worried he'll keep them. So for the time being I've said he'll have to come here if he wants to see them. And our lawyers are "in discussion".'

She formed air quotes with her fingers.

'Bloody hell,' Ruben blurted out, and Sara nodded.

She took another sip of the coffee and grimaced. 'You were right. This stuff is rotgut.'

'Told you so,' he said. 'Do you fancy helping me go over the reports of missing children from the last few weeks? Most of the kids will already have been found or come home by themselves without the parents letting us know, so I suggest we start calling people. Not that we're going to find our kidnapper, if the theory that he's going to wait until next week is true. But this job has to be done anyway.'

'Sensible,' Sara said, sitting down next to him and pulling out her phone. 'And who knows, maybe we'll turn up something interesting. The age of miracles doesn't necessarily have to be over.'

403

He peered at her surreptitiously. Why had he never talked to her before? She was both on the ball and funny. Age of miracles indeed . . . To top it off, she still looked cool. He cautiously checked his armpit with his hand. Fuck's sake. Soaking. *And* he was wearing a pale grey T-shirt. He knew he should have picked the black one instead.

115

Peder reluctantly had to admit that his beard was now itchy to a degree that exceeded the aesthetic advantage he felt it offered him. Granted, he seemed to be more or less alone in feeling that he looked damn cool with the beard. Even Anette had now defected to the enemy. Had it not been for the constant itching, he might have been able to fend off the peer pressure, but right now he felt as if he was faltering miserably.

Peder scratched himself as he scrutinized the lists with his customary thoroughness. This was where he felt most at home – when he could dive into heaps of data and spot correlations and anomalies in the statistics. He loved the challenge of trying to find that tiny needle in the middle of the haystack – the nugget of gold that might advance the investigation towards a conclusion. But this list was different. The list of missing children couldn't be boiled down to anonymous data. Ruben and Sara had already done a first pass and weeded out the ones who were no longer missing. Which was most of them. But there were still several left. Too many.

For every face and every report containing details of the child that came up, he was unable to stop himself from picturing the triplets. Since their arrival into the world, it was as if his whole body – his whole life support system – had been directly connected to them. For him, they were Yggdrasil – the tree of life. They were the veins and capillaries in his body, they were the lungs that made him breathe. Each child he saw in the police database had at least one parent who could no longer breathe.

There were plausible explanations for the disappearance of most of the children. A relative who had fled abroad with the child. A refugee family in hiding to avoid deportation. A child who had, by their own volition and for a thousand different reasons – all equally awful – run away from their parents, their foster home or their residential care unit.

But then there were the remaining ones. The ones for which there was no plausible explanation. The ones who had inexplicably disappeared. They were the ones he was interested in. One by one, he compared them with what Milda had reported about the body found in Fatbursparken. While there wasn't much to go on due to the state of the corpse, they still had something. And Milda was good at pulling together the details that might be helpful.

Peder checked Milda's notes again and summarized what he had. Height: 120 centimetres. Age: around six years old. Hair colour: brown. Sex: male. The little boy had also broken his right femur at some point in his life. Milda had estimated that the injury had occurred some two years ago based on the degree of healing. Obviously that had to be taken with a pinch of salt, but it was still an important indication.

Peder scrolled on slowly and carefully through all the documents on the computer. Sometimes he came to a halt, thinking he had found the right one – but there was always a factor that didn't fit.

Finally, he stopped. He read the text on the display, compared it with his list, double-checked, and then pushed his chair back.

They desperately needed a new lead. Something to take them a step closer to the killer. And Peder had just found it. He knew who the boy in Fatbursparken was.

116

'Dad, what's this?' Rebecka was flipping through the Epicura brochure on the coffee table, a look of distaste on her face. 'This doesn't seem like you. "Epicurus' four cornerstones"?'

Vincent looked up from his book. He had been completely absorbed in volume 1 of Michel de Certeau's *L'invention du quotidien* – more specifically a fascinating essay on the difference between how a city was perceived from a high vantage point and from down on the streets. He'd had the very same thought standing at the top of the tower at city hall.

'Epicureanism is a philosophy,' he said, closing the book. 'A colleague of mine – Nova – runs a rural retreat where they teach that kind of stuff. We're at home tonight, are we? Is everything OK with Denis?'

'Nova's hot,' Benjamin said from his corner of the sofa. 'Loads of my course mates follow her on Insta.'

'Denis is visiting relatives,' Rebecka said. 'And that's disgusting, Benjamin. Nova is, like, twice your age.'

'So what? Doesn't mean she can't be hot . . .'

Aston emerged from his bedroom dancing to music that only he could hear. He had added twerking while singing to his repertoire. Some day Vincent would ask him where on earth he'd learned that.

'Sooooo hoooottt,' Aston sang to the melody of Queen's 'The Show Must Go On'.

Apparently it had toppled 'Radio Ga Ga' from the top of his personal chart.

'Sooooo hoooottt!'

Vincent reflected that the older his children got, the less he understood them.

Maria was slumped over her phone. It didn't take a mentalist to guess who she was messaging. But now she looked up.

'And you're saying you know this Nova who's so hot?' she said. 'Just how well?'

'I already said,' he said. 'She's an old colleague. We bump into each other every now and then. She happens to be involved in the same police investigation . . .'

He promptly cut himself off when he realized his mistake.

Too late.

Maria's face had become ashen.

'The same one as you and that cop?' she said. 'Mina? And now this woman too? Honestly, Vincent, have you no shame? A police investigation? Whatever you say.'

She stood up, looking completely furious. Texting Kevin appeared to have been completely forgotten about.

'Gangbang more like,' she spat.

'Maria!' Benjamin and Rebecka both exclaimed in chorus.

'Gaaannngggbaaaannngg,' Aston sang, twerking merrily in front of the fish tank in the living room.

Vincent buried his face in his hands. Traumatized fish were the last thing he needed. He checked his watch. Blast – he was late for the train that he had to catch to give his lecture in Gävle. He had managed to forget all about it because he had been so pleased that his shows were over. After all, a lecture was easier. There was no belt involved.

'That's not a word that . . .' he said. 'Hmm . . . your mother can explain. I have to go now. But I'll be back on the ten o'clock train tonight and here when you wake up, Aston.'

He grabbed his computer bag and headed into the hallway. Maria followed him. He readied himself for a final telling-off, but instead she surprised him.

'Good luck at the lecture tonight,' she said in a low voice. 'Don't forget about me.'

Startled, he looked at her. He had assumed she was being sarcastic. Or that there must be a hidden dollop of reproach in there. But Maria's eyes were wide open and glistening slightly. She probably meant exactly what she had said. She even looked a little sad.

'Is that . . . what you think I do when I'm not at home?' he said. 'That I forget about you?' This was brand new. He tried to think what it might entail. They hadn't even come close to this in therapy. But it explained a lot. Maria's aggressive attacks, her mocking attitude. He had naturally assumed that it was a defensive mechanism. But he'd never heard her say as much. And it hurt him that she felt that way.

'Vincent Walder, the Master Mentalist,' she said, removing an invisible strand of hair from his shirt. 'The man everyone wants. It's very hard to measure up to you – you know that, don't you?'

'You ought to come to some of my shows or lectures,' he said. 'Then you'd see that I'm the man everyone wants to watch from a safe distance. There's a difference.'

He put his bag down on the floor and took her face in his hands.

'As for forgetting,' he said, 'it's the very opposite. I thought that was obvious. The only thing that makes me feel at least a little normal when I'm out at work is knowing that you're all here. That no matter what happens, I have you to come home to. Without you and the kids, I'm nobody.'

She blinked her eyes a few times and smiled faintly. Then a shadow crossed her face.

'You mean when you don't have Mina.'

He sighed and retrieved his bag from the floor. They had been so close. Maybe next time. In the living room, Aston was still belting out his gangbang song as Vincent left through the front door.

117

'I don't understand . . . How did he end up in Fatbursparken? Is Vendela there too?'

Thomas Jonsmark shooed away the make-up artist's hand and turned to Ruben. It had taken several days for the police to arrange a meeting with the great actor. But Ruben and Peder had been unwilling to provide any details about the case to Jonsmark's agent. They felt Thomas ought to be the first to know.

'They want you ready in ten,' the assistant pointed out timidly to him.

'They'll have to wait,' Thomas said brusquely, running a hand through his thick dark hair. 'Would you leave us, please?'

Ruben regarded the trademark mane of hair with envy. If he'd considered himself a ladies' man down the years, then he paled into insignificance when lined up against Thomas Jonsmark. Not only was he the superstar of the Swedish television and film world, but he was every single Swedish woman's wet dream.

The gossip magazines had been able to fill their pages for decades thanks to his romances with a string of women – some celebrities, others not. And Dexter was his child. Had been his only child, Ruben corrected himself. For a brief moment, he felt a pang in his heart.

He pictured Astrid's face before him, and in those seconds when he was suddenly consumed by a feeling that something might happen to her, it felt as if he were in freefall. He shook himself to get rid of the sensation. This was an abyss he had been ignorant of. He really had no idea how to handle it.

'I'm afraid we haven't found your ex-wife yet,' said Peder. 'And you weren't exactly easy to get hold of.'

'Ex-girlfriend,' Thomas corrected him, and Ruben saw him staring at Peder's beard. 'Vendela and I never married. Dexter was . . . Vendela and I had a pretty brief fling, to be perfectly honest. Dexter was an accident. At least on my part.'

He let the insinuation hang in the air. It wasn't an unfamiliar topic, Ruben reflected, recalling a plethora of headlines in the tabloids and gossip rags. Relations between Thomas and Vendela seemed to have been bitter from the start, with harsh accusations levelled against both parties. And it had been complicated by Vendela's mental health struggles, which had also been highly public.

'We met on a film set. She was a consultant and was meant to be helping me out with my role in *Blood at Twilight*. You know, the one I won my Guldbagge award for.'

Thomas ran his hand through his hair again. Ruben nodded, but knew nothing about either the film or any awards it might have won. If Bruce Willis, Tom Hardy or Dwayne 'The Rock' Johnson weren't in the movie, he probably hadn't seen it.

'She was very, *very* beautiful. And strong. In that fragile way. I fell for her the moment I met her.'

A young girl in a headset poked her head around the door. 'They need you on stage soon.'

Thomas waved his hand and she hastily closed the door.

'Can you tell us about Vendela's and Dexter's disappearance?' said Peder. 'Or at least what you know about it.'

'Well, we obviously don't live together. Never have done. And when Vendela was sectioned, Dexter went to her mother's. But Vendela had recently been discharged.'

'Were you worried?' Ruben interjected.

Thomas thought about the question for a while as he fiddled with something on his cuticle.

'No, I don't suppose I was. Vendela has always had a taste for the dramatic. She'd had her fair share of suicide attempts over the years, but it was always more . . . for show, not the real thing.'

'Had she made any threats this time?' said Ruben. 'To take her own life?'

'Well, yes, I guess there'd been a text message or whatever. She'd seen an article about my new girlfriend. A glamour model from Brazil. As usual, she went through the roof. But I've learned over the years that it's best to ignore that.'

He held his hands out in resignation. A lock fell across his brow, and Ruben thought he could see what the ladies fell for.

'Was there anything different about the day they disappeared?' said Peder, scratching his beard.

Ruben pondered how bluntly he could tell him that it was time to shave that creature off his face immediately.

'No. It was only when Vendela's mother called and said that Dexter hadn't arrived at nursery and that she couldn't get hold of Vendela that I began to worry. That was unusual.'

'And then you found the letter in the apartment?' said Peder.

'Yeah, Vendela's mother has a key, so we went around together. The letter was lying on the kitchen table. Well, you say a letter. All it said was "goodbye". Nothing else.'

410

'Did you take it seriously?'

An urgent knock at the door made Ruben jump. An older woman with a stern face opened the door as soon as she'd finished her rapping.

'You need to come now!'

'It's the police. They've found Dexter,' Thomas retorted.

The woman's face turned white. She nodded.

'Take all the time you need,' she said, closing the door. 'I'll let the team know.'

'To answer your question, no. We didn't take it seriously at the time.'

For the first time, the actor's mask slipped a little and Ruben saw something resembling genuine sadness. Then the mask was back again. As if life were nothing more than a role to be played.

'It was only when she didn't come home that night that we realized something might actually have happened. That was when we called the police. And the rest, you know. She was last seen getting on the ferry to Tallinn. And witnesses said they'd seen her with a boy even though she'd only bought an adult ticket. But they didn't get off the ferry in Tallinn.'

He fiddled with his cuticle again.

'We spoke to those witnesses again before we came to speak to you. They're no longer certain that the boy they saw was with her. We believe Vendela boarded the ferry alone. And that she most likely jumped. But Dexter wasn't with her.'

Peder looked pityingly at Thomas, who seemed to be sinking deeper and deeper into his make-up chair with the arrival of each new piece of information. His make-up had been almost done, and Ruben could see close-up that his skin was covered in powder and his eyebrows had been accentuated with a pencil. The kinds of things that you never noticed when you saw him on the box.

'What? How? And why was he found in Fatbursparken?'

'We don't know yet,' said Ruben. 'I'm afraid we have to tell you that he was murdered, but we don't yet know by whom. We can't rule out that it was Vendela, but for reasons that we can't elaborate on, we don't believe it was your ex-wi— your ex-girlfriend who killed your son.'

411

'The kids,' Thomas said flatly, his skin turning white under the layer of beige concealer. 'The kids on the news.'

'Like I said, we can't say any more right now,' said Peder.

Both detectives stood up.

'If you think of anything – anything at all – that might be relevant, please don't hesitate to get in touch.'

Peder placed a hand on his shoulder. As they left, Ruben saw out of the corner of his eye Thomas spin the chair around to turn his face to the mirror.

118

'Stop here,' said Nathalie. 'We shouldn't get too close.' Karl nodded, pulled over to the kerb and parked up. They were on Karlavägen, two blocks from Nathalie's father's apartment on Linnégatan. At that distance, they would surely be beyond the range of his watchful eye.

'Do you want me to come with you?' said Ines.

'I don't think that's a good idea. Better I do it myself. You guys wait here.'

She put on her rucksack, got out of the car and went around the corner onto Jungfrugatan. The question was, how much did Dad's bodyguards know? Had he mentioned that she was missing? If so, they would very likely call him the moment they clapped eyes on her. But there was nothing to be done about that. She would have to cross that bridge when she came to it. She walked onto Linnégatan. A black car was parked opposite the doorway to the stairs – possibly just a regular car, but it could be one of Dad's entourage. She had no way of knowing. But no one was visible as she slipped off the street and through the door.

She climbed the four flights of stairs instead of taking the lift. The lattice gate across the lift door made a distinctive sound that was audible inside the apartment, and she didn't want Dad to notice anything. She stopped outside the huge front door to the apartment and listened. She heard the distinctive clatter of Dad in the kitchen. He was presumably preparing some unnecessarily intricate meal even though he was at home alone. She couldn't understand why he always went nuts when cooking.

She slowly inserted the key into the lock, turned it and slipped inside. From the hallway, she caught a glimpse of her father's back. He was standing there with a towel slung over his shoulder, tasting a sauce, which he had probably made using four different types of fresh chilli. He would probably also check the temperature of the smoked meat as he chose from his homegrown tomatoes. She could never understand why he hadn't just opened a restaurant, if food was that much fun.

Nathalie stole away to her room. The small casket was on top of her chest of drawers. It was made from black ceramic and had a silver skull and crossbones on the lid. She opened it and looked inside. There was probably considerably more than the ten thousand she had told Grandma about. She felt proud, thinking how happy her grandmother would be as she slid the chest into her backpack. Then she opened the top drawer and took out all the clean knickers and socks she owned. She considered taking a pair of jeans too, but they weren't necessary – Ines provided her with all the clothes she needed, except for underwear. What she did remember to do was to find her mobile charger. Then she made for the bathroom, where she retrieved her toiletry bag, and finally she put it all in her rucksack.

She retreated back through the hall as quietly as she had come. The frying pans in the kitchen were sizzling, and her stomach ached with hunger. She stopped in the doorway to the kitchen. Dad was only a few metres away from her. She could just go over to him. He would be overjoyed to see her. And she would get as much food as she wanted.

She looked down at her hands, where a tender pink line ran across her fingers. It really did smell wonderful in the kitchen. She could so easily return to how things had been before. All it would take was one step across the threshold.

But then she would probably never see her grandmother

413

again. And Ines needed her. The others needed her. They were her family now. Not the man in the kitchen.

She tiptoed out of the front door and it closed behind her with a soft click.

119

'Aha! What an honour! I'd just started wondering if you'd be in today. After all, it is a Saturday.'

The maître d' smiled broadly and Christer gulped. This was probably a bad idea. A really, really bad idea. It wasn't too late to change his mind. He could turn on his heel and leave.

But . . . he was already there. He might as well have some herring and a pilsner. Then he could go.

'Follow me – your table's free. Do we just want to go for the usual?'

The maître d' walked ahead of him through the large room. Lunching patrons murmured quietly around them. The Ulla Winbladh restaurant was a place where you used your quiet inside voice, as his mother had called it.

The thought of his mother made him gasp for breath. She hadn't accepted the thoughts that were a constant, whirling presence in his head. Night and day. Round and round. Mother hadn't accepted any of that. But she wasn't around anymore, Christer reminded himself. Mother could keep her views to herself. He was fully entitled to live his life however he pleased.

He just had to be brave enough.

Christer took a step back and gazed through a window. Bosse had come with him today – Christer would be bankrupted if he had to sacrifice any more furniture to this endeavour. The dog was tied to a bike rack outside in the shade. He had a water bowl they'd brought with them. Still . . . It was probably too hot for him. He really ought to . . .

'Here we are. Already laid and all yours. Do we need a menu?'

The maître d's smile lit up the already-sunny room as Christer sat down clumsily at the table.

'Herring,' he muttered, his gaze glued to the tablecloth. 'And a pilsner.'

'The usual it is. If you ask me, it's the best thing on the menu. Why risk anything else? Leave that to the young.'

Some young people, at any rate, Christer thought to himself. The maître d's laughter bounced off the walls and formed a knot in Christer's stomach. It was as if he could read Christer's mind. Christer looked up. Then he spoke in a voice that trembled slightly:

'Speaking of young people, you were right. Last week, I mean.'

The maître d' squinted at him with an expression that Christer remembered well. His whole body felt warm and he took a deep breath.

'You did ask. And yes, we have met before. More than that, actually.'

He got no further before he was overcome by panic. What was he playing at? He suddenly stood up and almost knocked over the table and chair in doing so.

'Oh, sorry. I have to take this,' he said, waving around his clearly-switched-off mobile phone. 'Police business.'

He made his excuses again and hurried outside, feeling the maître d's eyes drilling into his back.

120

Peder was sweating profusely under the tall hat. It was Sunday afternoon and Casper's birthday party was in full swing. Ten pairs of children's eyes – of whom the triplets at two and a half years old were the youngest and their cousin Casper, who was turning five, was the eldest – were watching him doubtfully.

After the children had eaten cake, he had made his entrance in a tall hat and with his beard dyed blue. He had insisted that

415

he was not, in fact, Peder, but Pedro – Peder's secret brother. The kids thought that was hilarious. The more they bellowed that he was Peder, the more he protested that he wasn't, and the triplets were laughing so hard at his blue beard that they were almost choking.

The sound of their joy filled him with so much love that he thought he might burst. At the same time, it also filled him with anxiety. Vincent's declaration that there would probably be another kidnapping had been ringing in his ears ever since the meeting a week ago. He, Peder, had identified the child in Fatbursparken, which had been an important step forward. They had also reviewed all the lists of missing children to double- and triple-check that they hadn't missed anything. Adam had scrutinized all the information they had from Skeppsholmen with a critical eye. They had spent the week getting as prepared as they could be.

At the same time, they had no idea what to expect on Wednesday. Or where to search. The police obviously lacked the manpower to post someone at every nursery in the city. Issuing a public warning was out of the question too. It would only increase the already rampant panic among parents of small children. Sooner or later, someone would get hurt.

It felt as if the team were caught between a rock and a hard place. There was no direction in which they could move. Yet if they did nothing, a child would disappear in three days' time.

It might be Casper. Or one of the triplets. Or one of the other kids at the party. There was as much chance it would be them as anyone else. So he needed to save them all. It was just that he had no idea how.

And now he was standing here.

Doing magic.

He'd started by disappearing a red ball. That trick had been received with half-hearted enthusiasm. Then he'd folded a piece of paper into a hat for Casper. Then the triplets had started telling the other kids what had happened to the fairies in *Winx*. And the paper hat had been too small to fit on Casper's head.

He had only a few seconds before chaos ensued and a cake fight erupted. This called for his secret weapon. The magic trick that Vincent had given him. He hadn't had time to test it – he would just have to follow the instructions. But that couldn't be helped.

'And now for my final and most dangerous trick,' he said in a voice loud enough to be heard over the *Winx* discussion. 'The trick that turned my beard blue the first time I did it.'

The children fell silent when they heard the word 'dangerous'. He had them. For a short while. He glanced at the instructions and then produced two yellow handkerchiefs that he knotted together.

'Two big hankies,' he announced. 'Which Peder – er, I mean Pedro – has now tied together by the corners with a tight knot. It's important that we put these somewhere where no one can get up to any mischief with them. Luckily, I have the ideal hiding place.'

He scrunched up the knotted part and abruptly inserted it into his trousers, leaving the two hankies hanging out of the sides of his waistband.

'Ewww, he put them in his trousers,' someone shouted, and the other children whooped with laughter.

He could suddenly feel how much fun he was having. This was what Vincent had meant by entertaining rather than doing magic. He checked the instructions again and produced a third, red, handkerchief that he displayed to the audience as dramatically as he could. The older children giggled. Then he put the red hankie inside the big hat and replaced it on his head.

'Now, I need you all to shout "Abracadabra!" and then the red handkerchief will vanish from the hat and appear tied between the yellow ones,' he said solemnly. 'In my trousers!'

The children laughed again.

'Abracadabra! All at once now!'

'Abracadabra!' the kids yelled raucously.

Peder gave them the most exaggerated smile of confidence and pride he could muster, grabbed the yellow edges of the hankies and tugged them out of his waistband while simultaneously separating them.

'Ta-daaaaa!' he sang out.

There was dead silence. Then the room exploded into

417

laughter. Casper was bent double, laughing so hard tears were pouring from his eyes.

'Peder!' Anette said in horror. Although she too was grinning and her sister next to her was beaming at him.

That Vincent knew his stuff. Peder looked at the hankies with mock surprise. Hanging between the two yellow handkerchiefs was a pair of faded underpants.

He supposed he'd have to offer an explanation to the staff at the triplets' nursery since they were guaranteed to tell everyone about the time their dad had taken off his pants at a children's party. But it was all worth it. He was their hero. And in that moment, there was no evil in the world. He – Peder – had vanquished it.

The kids' laughter continued to resound in his ears long after the party had drawn to a close.

The Fifth Week

121

Benjamin had been outside to retrieve the post. The small heap on the kitchen table comprised Aston's magazine from the Lego club, a few bills for Maria, and an envelope addressed to Vincent. Not much for a Monday. The holidays were clearly well and truly under way.

He knew immediately what the envelope was. Even though it had arrived six months early. He removed the Santa sticker sealing it and emptied the Tetris-style pieces of paper onto the table. The anxiety he'd felt when he'd received the other puzzles returned at lightning speed when he saw the pieces. This time the feeling was stronger too. Why had it arrived now – in the middle of summer? What was different?

He was startled when he opened the enclosed Christmas card. Unlike the previous ones, it was not blank. This time there was a handwritten message.

It seems that you don't learn. I'm tired of waiting.
Ossian shall be omega. (A vulgar alliteration but there is poetry to its meaning.)
   And remember that there is no one to blame but you. You could have chosen a different path. But you didn't.
   So we have reached your omega.
   The beginning of your end.

PS If you're wondering why you've received the puzzle now, it's because omega is, as you know, the 24th letter of the Greek alphabet. 24 divided by two – you and I – makes 12, which gives us 24/12: Christmas Eve. Wishing you an early Merry Christmas.

The nape of his neck itched, as if there were an insect crawling around at his hairline. Omega. It was unpleasantly similar to the thought he'd had when Julia had talked about Ossian at the press conference. He had thought to himself that omega was doomsday. The end of everything. And then there was that Christmas calculation at the end. Exactly the sort of thing he liked to distract himself with. Someone was much too familiar with the way his mind worked. Not only that, it was as if someone was living in his head with direct access to his thoughts. *You and I.* He shivered.

The worry had awakened the shadow within. That was the last thing he needed. If he embraced the darkness, then he would be of no use. Instead, he focused on solving the puzzle – an activity that activated the frontal lobes and kept his emotional amygdala in check. He couldn't afford to be overwhelmed. Not now.

The Tetris pieces were harder to assemble this time. That was presumably a warning sign that he was being filled with stress hormones and adrenaline, which inhibited the ability to think rationally. He swallowed. His throat was so dry.

In the end, he managed to assemble an irregular shape. Like the others, it was full of holes. And like the others, it contained a message:

Damn cage dying rites!

Rites.
Rituals.
Nova had mentioned the ritualistic aspects of the murders. And the knight's tour motif was definitely a ritualized behaviour. Were the puzzles from the killer?
A *damn cage*?
Was the murderer laying down a challenge to Vincent to ensnare him? Had that challenge always been there – from the very first puzzle? A puzzle that had arrived in his letterbox six months before Lilly – the first murder victim – had been found.
He was overcome by a terrible thought. Lilly, William, Dexter, Ossian . . . What if they were all just a challenge directed at

him? What if the killer was one of his admirers, who had read about him in the papers and decided to create the ultimate conundrum for him to solve? Perhaps he, Vincent, was the reason why four children were dead. Simply because he hadn't taken any of the Christmas greetings seriously.

The very idea of it was too hideous to contemplate.

The message in the card felt deeply personal. *And remember that there is no one to blame but you. You could have chosen a different path.* This was someone who was disappointed in him.

He looked at the writing again. A graphologist would have said that the pointy letters indicated an intense, highly intelligent individual, and that the slant of the lettering revealed powerful emotions verging on aggression. The closed o's also revealed that the person was an introvert, while the slim l's indicated conscious self-restraint.

The conclusion was a hyper-smart, introverted person trying to control themselves but on the brink of an emotional outburst.

He fetched a glass of water and looked at the four words in the puzzle again. *Damn cage dying rites!* This time he would solve it. After finding a roll of tape, he carefully stuck together the pieces so that they wouldn't move. Then he fetched the other two Tetris puzzles from the desk drawer in his study, assembled those and taped them together too. He laid out all three cryptic messages next to each other.

Tim scared deny ageing.

Maria dinged cygnets.

Damn cage dying rites!

He drank a big mouthful of water. The liquid was cool and made him breathe more easily. Eighteen letters in each message. Exactly the same number of letters in each message. He exhaled through his nose. Now there was no doubt. The anagrams mattered. They were the key. The only question was what the true message was. It was right in front of him – somewhere among those letters – but he couldn't see it.

He drank more of the water and glanced at the time. Maria was with Kevin. Rebecka, Benjamin and Aston had gone swimming. Well, Aston was probably swimming. He found it hard to believe that Benjamin was in the water, given that Rebecka's two good-looking friends were also with them. But it would be at least an hour before anyone came home and asked Vincent to explain what he was up to.

He went into Aston's bedroom and retrieved his son's copy of Scrabble. Then he laid out all the letters on the kitchen table and selected the ones that appeared in the messages. Eighteen letters. That yielded 6,402,373,705,728,000 possible combinations.

He had started to calculate it in his head, but it had hurt his brain. In the end he'd used an online app to find out the number. Then he'd had to google how to read it out. Six thousand four hundred and two trillion. All from just eighteen Scrabble pieces. It was enough to make the brain boil.

Fortunately, there weren't nearly as many possible combinations of the letters that could form intelligible words. But there were still a few hundred thousand. Although there were slightly fewer if all the words had to come from a single language – Swedish. Even fewer if they had to form meaningful syntax. And yet fewer if they were words that had to mean something to him personally. Which he thought these did. So there was a decent chance he might solve it. Theoretically speaking.

He began to lay out the eighteen letters at random. He started with short, simple words.

GAME

ANGRY

END

END TIMES

'End times' was eight letters long – not bad at all. Unfortunately, only worth eleven points in a game of Scrabble. Besides, he had a gut feeling it wasn't the right combination. He went back to trying shorter words again.

MANIAC

MAGNET

MAGIC

That was something. 'Magic'. That might be a connection to him. Perhaps it could be combined with one of the other short words?

MAGIC

ENDS

He stared at those letters, struggling to swallow. He suddenly realized what the rest would say. But it couldn't be. He didn't want it to be that.

All the same, he knew. He'd been right – the solution was to make it entirely personal to him. Out of more than six thousand trillion possible solutions, there was only one possibility. Just one that was about him. The shadow within rose from the lake of his boyhood and loomed above him, filling the horizon. It threatened to crash down over him at any moment. He wanted to throw the taped-together puzzles in the bin – he wanted to pretend they didn't exist. But he had to know. He went back to his study and found the pale brown A4 envelope that Ruben had given him almost two years ago. The one that contained the clipping from *Hallandsposten* about his mother's death.

Vincent had assumed that it had been Jane who had sent it to Ruben, in an attempt to cast suspicion onto him, but she hadn't known what he was talking about when he'd mentioned the article to her. Now he understood why.

The roar of the shadow on the horizon was deafening.

The feeling of dread in the pit of his stomach was resonating in chorus.

He pulled out the piece of newspaper and put it next to the Scrabble pieces. Then he laid out the letters one at a time on top of the bold headline spanning the page. His hand trembled as he did so. It was a perfect match. The three puzzles were anagrams of a sentence he had hoped never to see again.

MAGIC ENDS IN TRAGEDY!

There was zero chance this was a coincidence. The person who had sent the puzzles to him over the last Christmases and now in the middle of a baking hot summer was the same person who had sent the old newspaper clipping to Ruben two years previously. It was someone who had known far more about him than most people did, even back then.

It was someone who wasn't Jane.

But he had no idea who it might be. Vincent examined the handwritten message again.

We have reached your omega. The beginning of your end.

His end to what? An omega always had an alpha – a beginning. If this was his omega, then what was his alpha? What had he begun that the murderer now wanted to end? He would be unable to protect himself while he didn't know. The darkness within him told him that he didn't have much time.

122

For a change, he ate lunch in the canteen at police headquarters. The air conditioning trumped the need to stroll down to the neighbourhood bar through the heat. Anyway, it was a Tuesday which meant the lunch special was potato pancakes – something Ruben ranked second in his personal gastronomic preferences. As long as they were served with bacon and lingonberry preserve. Perhaps an apple compote too. But definitely no prawns or any other stupid add-ons like some places insisted on. Why improve something that was already perfect?

Everyone in the team was on tenterhooks ahead of the next day. Tomorrow, the kidnapper would strike again. Unless they prevented it. He fervently hoped that Vincent was wrong on this occasion, and that it was all over.

Lunch represented a welcome break from the frustration of making no progress, but the feeling of breathing more freely for a few seconds vanished when he spotted Gunnar and the lads from the flying squad. They were sitting at a table further back in the canteen. The possibility of ignoring them evaporated when Gunnar gestured him over. He swore silently, headed over and set down his tray on their table.

'I hear you have a daughter,' Gunnar chuckled once he'd sat down. 'Who would've thought it?'

Gossip really did travel around this place like wildfire. It was probably Peder who had mentioned it – delighted to have another dad on the team.

'Yeah, her name's Astrid,' Ruben said. 'She's ten.'

He cut into his potato pancake, listening to see how crispy it was. A little on the soft side, but it would do. The alternative was a walk in the thirty-degree heat. Better a soft potato pancake.

'Bloody hell, Ruben. A kid,' said Gunnar. 'I thought you took precautions. Then again, who wants to eat a banana with the peel on?'

Ruben quickly shovelled a big piece of bacon into his mouth to avoid answering. A small dollop of lingonberries fell off his fork and landed on his white shirt breast. Fuck's sake. Apparently Gunnar wasn't done.

'Ten, eh,' he chortled. 'Just you wait until she brings her friends home in five years' time. You're going to have some right tasty morsels in the house.'

Ruben swallowed his bacon and smiled patiently.

'You mean like your son?' he said.

'What?' said Gunnar, looking confused.

'Well, Filip is sixteen, isn't he?' Ruben continued as he carefully nudged preserve onto his fork. 'Why don't you bring him

427

and his mates down here? I reckon we've probably got plenty of female colleagues who would lick their lips at him, or whatever it was you said. Men too, I suppose. Sexual orientation isn't the big deal it once was.'

Gunnar's smile stiffened and disappeared.

'What the fuck do you mean?!'

Gunnar's face began to turn a bright shade of red. Out of the corner of his eye, Ruben noticed that the other officers had stopped eating. Presumably everyone was wishing they'd brought popcorn. Ruben gave Gunnar a blank look.

'What?' he said innocently. 'I thought I just said the same thing as you?'

'That wasn't the same fucking thing! Filip is . . . he's . . .'

'It's exactly the same thing,' said Ruben, standing up and picking up his tray. 'Go to hell, Gunnar.' He turned and left. The silence behind him was deafening.

Astrid would probably be wise to take a self-defence course. Maybe Krav Maga. There were far too many Gunnars in the world.

123

I hit him and try to get free, but I can't. First he covers my mouth so that I can't scream, but then I bite him as hard as I can. He says some really bad words, so it must hurt. Serves him right.

But no one runs after me when he picks me up. Or maybe they do – there's a lot of people there. Lots of people see it. But he runs fast. I kick my legs, but he keeps running. He puts me in the car.

In the car, I'm scared to hit too hard because what happens if he drives off the road? We might die . . . So I scream instead. All the time. He can't cover my mouth while he's driving. But he doesn't stop. I'm almost hoarse, but I keep screaming anyway.

I'm not supposed to be in his car. I'm meant to be buying ice cream. I've got Mummy's money in my hand. I have to give her the change when I get back home with the ice cream. After a while, my throat is too sore to keep screaming – so I'm silent for a while.

'Don't be scared, Wilma,' he says.

'I know who you are,' I say back to him.

He shudders.

'You . . . know?'

'Yes. You're one of those people who steals kids. A peffer-dile.'

'What? No, no, definitely not,' he says, looking almost scared. 'I don't want to hurt you. Just the opposite, in fact. You're going to be reborn.'

'But I don't want to be,' I shout. 'It was boring being a baby. Take me home right now.'

I get so angry that I start hitting him. I start hitting the steering wheel, his arms and his head. All of a sudden, he yells at me. Really loud. It scares me so much that I start crying, and I fill my pants with wee.

124

Julia was pacing back and forth along the corridor. It was Wednesday – the day that Vincent had predicted they would see another kidnapping, and it felt as if everyone was holding their breath. As usual, she was embroiled in a mobile phone call in a low voice using the firm tone she reserved for Torkel alone.

'Let me get this straight,' she said. 'The problem right now is that Harry is finally asleep, but you can't get to sleep yourself? If you're really, really quiet, I think you should just be able to make out the world's tiniest violin playing for you.'

'Julia, I—'

'No. I told you to be quiet. Listen to the violin.'

Mina came running down the corridor, sufficiently out of

429

breath for Julia to realize that she must have run up the stairs instead of taking the lift. It had to be urgent. Julia hung up without saying goodbye.

'I had a call from Sara in Analysis,' Mina panted, waving her notepad around. 'It's happened again. Just like Vincent said.'

'Is she sure?' said Julia. 'We're receiving a hundred reports a day about kids supposedly being abducted by strangers. It usually turns out to be someone who saw a child out with their granddad.'

'And some of them are pure fantasy,' Mina added. 'From attention seekers hoping to get their names in the paper. I know. But Sara is the best of the bunch at Analysis. She's been going through the files and she knows her thing. She says she's convinced this is relevant. According to witness testimony, a blond man with a moustache wearing sunglasses was seen lifting a child from the pavement outside the Fältöversten shopping mall in Östermalm before running to a car with her and driving off. The girl was screaming and protesting, but the man was fast. There were lots of other adults nearby, but before they realized that it wasn't a dad carrying off an angry daughter, they were already gone.'

Julia stared at Mina. She reflected on the fact that her husband's biggest problem in life was that he wasn't able to synchronize his sleeping patterns with their baby son's. He was more than welcome to come in and do a placement with her one of these days.

'Weren't the parents there?' she said.

'That was what sealed it for Sara,' said Mina. 'A report came in just after the one I mentioned. From a couple: Jens and Janina Josefsson. I know, that's a lot of J's. They live by Fältöversten – right on top of the mall, actually. Their daughter had been allowed to go out and buy ice cream on her own for the first time ever. They thought it was safe. The shop is literally ten metres from their main door. But she never came back. Her parents thought she'd lost track of time and sat down on a bench by the shop, or that she'd got lost in the mall – so they went out to find her. But they couldn't. Timewise, it fits precisely with the man seen running away with a child.'

Julia felt dizzy. The kidnapper must have been lying in wait. Lurking. Biding his time. How on earth could there be sickos like this on the planet?

'We've got a description of the car – a red Renault Clio,' said Mina. 'But since the man didn't seem worried about being seen, we can probably assume that the hair and moustache were fake. And the car has likely been dumped somewhere.'

Julia sank to the floor. She leaned her head against the wall and closed her eyes.

'And you say this was half an hour ago?' she said. 'Why didn't we react more quickly? We should have been out there running down that car twenty-eight minutes ago, given how much of a priority this is.'

'Like you said, emergency dispatch and the police switch-board have been bombarded with calls,' Mina said, sitting down beside her. 'We can't respond to every report the second it arrives – we don't have the resources. I realize this is a nightmare situation. And the perp exploited that. The kidnappers might even have made a number of those calls themselves in order to distract us.'

Julia nodded slowly.

'I'll issue a general alert,' she said. 'This time we're going to get the bastard. He won't be able to hide from us.'

'I'll ask Christer to run the description against the databases,' Mina said, making to stand up. 'Like I said, it was probably a disguise, but you never know.'

'Would you ask Adam and Ruben to go and talk to the parents too?'

'Of course.'

Julia put a hand on Mina's arm.

'The child,' she said. 'What's the child's name?'

'Her name is Wilma.'

125

Vincent hated that he hadn't been of more use. He had found the pattern with the children being positioned as if they were performing a knight's tour on a chessboard. He had even foreseen when and where the next body would be found. But what use was that when they needed to stop the perpetrator – not just clean up after him? He still had no idea who the leader was – he didn't know why they were killing children or how the different elements linked to each other.

And that was why Wilma had been missing since the preceding afternoon – because he hadn't found enough information.

It was his fault.

It was Mina who had called to tell him about the disappearance. But Julia hadn't asked him to come in. And he could understand why. They had been counting on him to figure it out. Mina had trusted him. And he had let her down.

Benjamin came into the kitchen. He was clutching the brochure that Vincent had been given by Nova. Benjamin's eyes were unfocused, as if he were engaged in feverish thought.

'Dad, you have a minute?' he said in a low voice, glancing over at Maria.

Vincent nodded.

Benjamin cocked his head towards his room and made for the door.

Maria was sucking distractedly at the end of a pencil. She was engrossed in creating a new logo for her online store and was on a completely different planet. She didn't even notice Vincent getting up to follow his son.

He entered the bedroom and Benjamin closed the door behind him.

'What's up?' said Vincent. 'Why are you being so secretive? And aren't you going to have any breakfast?'

'I had mine earlier,' said Benjamin. 'But you look like you haven't slept all night. Has something happened?'

Vincent nodded. 'We'll get to that,' he said.

'OK. Anyway . . . I know Maria doesn't like us talking about Nova. But read this.' He pointed to the quote in the brochure – the one that Vincent must have read a hundred times, with Epicura's explanation of Epicureanism.

Epicurus' guideline for the new age is same as for all ages: Allow only the anxiety passing like a comet a star. Fast and imperceptible. Life of stillness is life that purifies. Carefully avoid all kinds of pain and desire nothing, for a life without desire is a life fully freed from suffering, and instead allows you to enjoy great success in attaining Everything

John Wennhagen

Vincent suspected that John had crafted the text on purpose so that it seemed deeper than it was. Not that there was anything fundamentally wrong with Epicureanism, but it was hardly mysterious.

'I agree it's unnecessarily vague,' he said. 'But the more self-interpretation people are required to employ with the message, the bigger the chance that they agree with it. Can't say I'm a fan of the sales technique, even if it is a classic.'

'No, but look at the text itself,' Benjamin said, pointing again. 'Forget about the meaning. Do you see the capital E used in the last word? And how there's no full stop after it? I've always thought there was something strange about that.'

Vincent shifted a book called *How to Make Money in Stocks* off Benjamin's desk chair and sat down.

'Brochures like this are rarely properly proofread,' he said. 'What's more, that's quoting Nova's father – something he wrote in the nineties. I'm guessing they've included it as some kind of tribute to him, typos and all.'

'Perhaps,' said Benjamin. 'Since it looks exactly the same on their website. Anyway, I began to take a closer look at the text. You know that . . . chess problem . . . you're working on? How many squares does a chessboard have?'

Vincent began to leaf through the book on beating the markets. He was curious to know which paragraphs Benjamin had marked as important. The stock exchange had always been a complete mystery to him.

'You know just as well as I do,' he said as he browsed the book. 'A chessboard has sixty-four squares.'

'Exactly. And this text has sixty-four words.'

Vincent closed the book and looked at his son.

'Let's rewind a bit,' he said. 'For starters, I'm not working on a chess problem. I'm trying to understand a serial killer with a taste for children. It's true that it seems the murderer is applying a strategy derived from chess. With an emphasis on *seems*. But it doesn't automatically follow that anything chess-related is linked to the murders.'

Vincent was already on thin ice with the police, thanks to his theories. They knew his theories were based on circum-stantial evidence – little more than assumptions. If he allowed himself to go any further down that rabbit hole, he would emerge on the other side with a massive tinfoil hat on his head and without all his wits accounted for. Not to mention the fact that Mina would never speak to him again.

'I could probably go to the freezer and find sixty-four ice cubes,' he added. 'Or a show on TV featuring a king and queen. That doesn't mean they're related to the murders.'

'I hear you,' said Benjamin, sitting down on the bed with his laptop. 'Correlation and causation aren't the same thing. I know that.'

'Exactly. Remember a few years ago when people were claiming that 5G masts made us sick and it was "proven" with maps clearly showing that the places in the country where people were the most ill were also the places with the most 5G masts?'

Benjamin nodded.

'Which also happened to be the places with the most dogs, the most cars, and also the most healthy people. Which was because they were the places where the most people lived,' he said. 'Yes, I remember. But can't we pretend they're connected – at least for a little while? Think of it as one of your shows.'

Benjamin's eyes sparkled. There was no stopping him. Vincent sighed and held his arms out. Might as well indulge his son for a while. As long as he knew it wasn't for real, where was the harm.

He watched as Benjamin opened Google on his computer.

'Since John Wennhagen wrote the text, we might as well start by searching for him,' said Vincent, and Benjamin typed in the name.

Benjamin angled his laptop so that Vincent could see it. 'John Wennhagen' turned up around 71,000 hits. Then he tried 'John Wennhagen Epicura' but that only scored a few hits for various blogs and self-help websites that shared details of Epicura or mentioned Nova's book. None of this helped them to find John himself.

'Try "John Wennhagen Stockholm" instead,' said Vincent. This turned up 50,700 results.

'Better, but not good,' said Benjamin. 'Didn't he have some sort of place in the country? Do you know what it was called?'

Vincent shook his head. He really knew very little about Nova's childhood apart from what had been in the papers, and as a rule, he tried not to rely on that.

'If you want to go all the way down the rabbit hole – something, by the way, that I don't recommend,' he said, 'then what about this? Just as an exercise. Nothing more. We have a text written by Nova's father – sixty-four words long. We have four murders positioned on a chessboard that has sixty-four squares. So . . .'

Benjamin typed 'John Wennhagen chess'.

Pictures of magazines and newsletters from various local chess clubs appeared. Among these was one called *The Swedish Journal of Chess*. It appeared to be a national publication.

The cover of the issue chosen by Google had a smiling man with an ample moustache on it. The man was clutching a trophy. JOHN WENNHAGEN NEW REGIONAL CHAMPION, said the headline.

'That proves my point,' said Vincent. 'Search for long enough and it all seems connected. Just because you've found someone with the same name as Nova's father who happens to play chess doesn't mean that . . .'

He stopped speaking.

He stared at the picture.

John Wennhagen was holding the trophy in one hand, while his other was holding a child.

A girl with black hair and eyes that were already enchanting.

There was no doubt about it.

It was Jessica Wennhagen.

Latterly known as Nova.

'That's her father,' Vincent said almost inaudibly. 'Nova's father. Bloody hell. He really did play chess. And apparently he was good at it too. Mind you, that doesn't prove anything. Still . . . Welcome to the hole, little white rabbit.'

Benjamin laughed. 'I'd rather be Alice, thanks,' he said. 'I think the stressed-out rabbit is more your style. Why don't we have a look at that text too?'

Vincent could only nod.

It was all so far-fetched. Or rather, he wanted it to be. He wanted them to have been lucky in finding an unlikely co-incidence which was nothing more than that. A coincidence. There were plenty of those – more than people imagined. Although every unlikely coincidence had extremely low odds of happening, the statistics said that some unlikely coincidences simply had to happen. Quite a few, in fact. He sincerely hoped this was one of them.

But then he remembered what Nova had said at the Oscar Theatre when they had met in the green room and she had explained that her father had written the text according to the rule that he could only use a certain number of words.

Chess-playing John Wennhagen had chosen sixty-four words. No more, no less. Like a chessboard.

Benjamin was right.

The text was key.

A feeling that something was terribly wrong began to simmer within Vincent. And he knew that the feeling would get much worse before it went away.

He took the laptop, opened a new document and set out the text in eight rows, assigning eight words to each row.

Epicurus'	guideline	for	the	new	age	is	same
as	for	all	ages:	Allow	only	the	anxiety
passing	like	a	comet	a	star.	Fast	and
imperceptible.	Life	of	stillness	is	life	that	purifies.
Carefully	avoid	all	kinds	of	pain	and	desire
nothing,	for	a	life	without	desire	is	a
life	fully	freed	from	suffering,	and	instead	allows
you	to	enjoy	great	success	in	attaining	Everything

'So every word in the text represents a square on a chess-board,' Benjamin said thoughtfully. 'Eight by eight. What's next?'

'The knight's tour.'

'Shit. OK, which words – or rather, which squares on the board – correspond to the locations where you found . . . the kids?'

It was to his son's credit that he was almost unable to say that last word.

'On a chessboard it's h1, g3, e2 and f4,' Vincent said.

His throat had suddenly gone dry. Much too dry. He needed to get a glass of water from the kitchen, but he also knew that it would be nothing more than a psychological escape from the unpleasantness that might at any moment take shape on Benjamin's computer. He forced himself to focus.

'If you continue with that move then the next square is h5,' he added. 'On a map of Stockholm that's at Djurgårdsbrunnsviken bay. It's somewhere around there that we'll find Wilma's dead body in two days' time unless we solve this.'

'OK. Let's start with h1 in the bottom corner,' Benjamin said, finding the five words that corresponded to Vincent's chess positions and making them bold.

Epicurus'	guideline	for	the	new	age	is	same
as	for	all	ages:	Allow	only	the	anxiety
passing	like	a	comet	a	star.	Fast	and
imperceptible.	Life	of	stillness	is	life	that	**purifies.**
Carefully	avoid	all	kinds	of	**pain**	and	desire
nothing,	for	a	life	without	desire	**is**	a
life	fully	freed	from	**suffering,**	and	instead	allows
you	to	enjoy	great	success	in	attaining	**Everything**

'Purifies, pain, is, suffering, Everything,' Benjamin said. 'Hmm. For a second I thought . . . Oh well. Maybe the rabbit hole wasn't that deep after all.'

Vincent was staring at the words on the screen.

'On the contrary,' he said, putting a hand on Benjamin's shoulder for support. 'The capital E isn't a typo. "Everything" isn't the end of a sentence. It's the beginning of one. Read the words in the same order as the positions I gave you – the order in which the children were killed.'

Benjamin ran his finger between the words on the screen.

'Everything . . . is . . . suffering . . . pain . . . purifies. My God.'

'Everything is suffering, pain purifies,' said Vincent, nodding. 'The famous quotation from Nova's father. Right down to a capital letter at the beginning and a full stop at the end. It couldn't be clearer. It wasn't even complicated. Five steps was all it took. I've got to call Mina.'

John Wennhagen continued to beam at them from the cover of the chess magazine. All of a sudden, Vincent thought the hand holding the little girl didn't look so loving. It was a hand holding her in an iron grip.

126

Mina ended the call. Vincent had sounded strange. He had apologized umpteen times for being – as he put it – 'cognitively incomplete for the last few weeks'. He'd said something about his show and depriving himself of oxygen slightly too often and not being able to think clearly. Then there had been something important he wanted to show her this morning before she went to work. It was too complicated to do on the phone, he said. And now he was on his way. To her.

Mina looked around the apartment. The only difference from when Vincent had last visited some two years ago was that the walls had been given a new coat of pale grey paint. The same shade as before, of course, but cleaner. He would probably be rather taken aback by the stocks of knickers, vests and cleaning supplies in her study. She had sufficient supplies to get her through a minor world war or a pandemic. But there was no need for him to see that, and the study door could be locked.

On the other hand, she wasn't sure that she was ready herself. She liked hanging out with Vincent, but it was an entirely different matter having him in her home again. Here – in her fortress against the world. Not that he'd given her the opportunity to say no.

She checked the time. He would be there in ten minutes. At least she had time for a quick shower. Normally she showered in water as hot as it went – she liked to imagine the bacteria being burned off her skin. But the hot summer made any further warmth intolerable. Instead, she took an ice-cold shower. Hopefully she wouldn't have started sweating again before Vincent arrived.

After the shower, she fetched a fresh vest top and knickers from the study. She put on the rest of her clothes slowly to retain the coolness in her body for as long as possible. Then she got a bottle of sanitizer and wiped down all the door handles, chair backs and tables in the flat.

When she brushed a hand across her brow, it was slightly moist. Bloody hell. She checked the time. She didn't have time to shower again – not if she wanted to avoid being found by Vincent in nothing but her underwear.

What on earth . . .

She bit her lip. Why had she put Vincent and herself in her underwear into the same thought? She squirted a dollop of sanitizer onto her hands and cleaned them. Then she took another dollop and rubbed it against her forehead and under her arms. Her armpits stung – but that couldn't be helped. She would just have to take another shower later.

The doorbell rang and the sound made her jump. She had to stop being so daft. After all, it was only Vincent. She reminded herself that she actually wanted to see him.

She gave the flat a final, hasty glance and then she opened the front door to the mentalist.

'Hello,' he said, stepping inside.

He took care to put both his feet on the small doormat and

stay there as he removed his shoes. There was something strange about his trousers. They were unusually loose and fluttery.

'Vincent,' she said. 'Are you . . . wearing pyjama bottoms?'

Vincent looked down and his face turned bright red.

'I, uh, gosh . . . I was in a bit of a hurry,' he stammered. 'I was having breakfast when Benjamin . . .'

He looked at her, his gaze one of deep unhappiness.

'Would you mind changing into pyjamas too?' he said. 'So that it's less embarrassing . . .'

There it was again. Vincent and underwear. Much too close together. She hadn't even properly let him into the flat. That thought must have been visible on her face, because Vincent took a step back on the small doormat and held his hands out.

'Sorry,' he said. 'I didn't think. Luckily I'm not here to show you my trousers. Perhaps you could imagine that they're part of a linen suit or something. Just be grateful I'm not a shorts guy. Hand sanitizer?'

She pointed towards the bathroom where she had left the bottle.

Vincent went off to clean his hands.

He had never hinted that he found her rituals peculiar. Instead he had simply adapted to them. He was pretty much alone in that. And she had adapted to Vincent in much the same way. Even if that mostly entailed trying to understand the mentalist's winding train of thought. She guessed there weren't many who did that either – not properly – no matter how much applause he received on stage.

Vincent emerged with the bottle in his hand.

'It's very chilly in there,' he said. 'You taking cold showers these days?'

She nodded, trying not to tear up when she saw him casually clean the inside front door handle that he had just touched.

'The cold showers thing is an interesting one,' he continued. 'Wim Hof has really become popular. And there are lots of documented physiological and mental benefits to it – everything from making you more resistant to stress to improving your concentration. But in reality those effects are the result of you shocking your body with an act it doesn't like. The increased

441

levels of cortisol – that's the stress hormone – caused by being cooled down naturally mean that you'll develop an enhanced tolerance to it. And extreme cold makes you take deeper breaths, which oxygenates the blood more, and the brain too. Which for a short while, at least, improves the brain's activities. Such as your concentration. And the fact that it can also affect your decisiveness is simply because it takes quite a lot of that to continue subjecting the body to a shock even when it tells you not to. So it's not really the act itself that has these magical properties. It's the way you react to it. It's a bit like a nail through your foot. What's your goal with it? Taking cold showers, I mean.'

She took the bottle of sanitizer from him.

'Two things, Vincent. Firstly. Way too much information. Again. I thought I'd taught you to zip it by now. And secondly – I take cold showers because it's hot out. Simple as. What was so urgent?'

Vincent smiled grimly.

'I've got something you need to see. I wanted to show you before I show everyone else in the group. You get to decide whether I'm crazy. But before I do, have you found anything else on Wilma?'

Mina shook her head. She led him into the living room. 'Adam and Ruben visited the parents yesterday,' she said. 'Same story as with Ossian. Shocked parents, no previous threats, no angry relatives, not a clue who might have done it. And no leads. At least we got a photograph. But I don't think we dare hold a press conference this time. We'd be lynched by the media. So show whatever it is to me – this investigation needs something good. Even if you are crazy.'

She sank onto the sofa and Vincent sat next to her. He pulled out a brochure, a map of Stockholm, a black-and-white print-out of a magazine cover, and a handwritten text on a transparent plastic sheet.

'This is the brochure from Epicura,' he said. 'It contains the same quote that I've written by hand on the plastic. The only thing I've changed are the line breaks. Nova's father wrote this shortly before the accident. He was also a talented chess player.'

Vincent jabbed at the magazine cover where a smiling man with a moustache was holding a trophy. The headline mentioned John Wennhagen. She realized it must be Nova's father. Vincent took a pen and began to apply dots to the map, which had been covered in a grid like the map at police headquarters.

'Lilly, William, Dexter and Ossian were found here, here, here and here on the map. And according to the knight's tour, Wilma is going to turn up over here – by Djurgårdsbrunnsviken bay.'

He placed the transparent sheet over the map so that the text covered it, but the dots were visible through the plastic. Then he circled the words that were on the same squares of the chessboard as the dots. Finally, he drew a line between the words so she could read them more easily.

'Everything is suffering, pain purifies,' she read aloud. 'What the . . . ?'

'That's the right reaction. John Wennhagen wrote that for the Epicureans at least thirty years ago. He deliberately wrote it using sixty-four words, and hid that message in it at the time. An invisible message that precisely matches our murder scenes. I know it sounds crazy, but Nova's father is our killer. He's been planning the whole thing for a very long time.'

Mina didn't know what to say. She usually complained that Vincent gave too much information, but in that moment it felt as if he had nudged a door ajar without her being able to see what was behind it. She didn't like the feeling. Besides, Vincent couldn't possibly be right.

She stared into the eyes in the black-and-white photo as if she could demand an answer from them. John Wennhagen merely smiled back.

'Don't take this the wrong way, but I really do hope that you're just a bit overworked,' said Mina. 'If I've got the right end of the stick, the bodies have been positioned to form John's hidden motto from a text he wrote thirty years ago, which you can only find if you're as good at chess as he was. It's pretty convincing. Except that it's not possible. The murders are happening here and now. And Nova's father died soon after that message was written.'

'Are you sure? His body was never found. Nova told me they looked but that it never turned up. There might be a reason for that. I think this is a pretty good indication that John Wennhagen is rather more alive than we imagined.'

She stared at him, her body suddenly icy cold. She needn't have bothered with that cold shower. She had been too little at the time to remember it, but she had read about it later on when she had been at police college. About the tragic incident when a farm had been set on fire and the subsequent car accident where only a girl had been rescued from the wreckage of a sinking car. The driver had never been found. It had been assumed that he'd drowned and been swept away by the current. But as Vincent said, there might be another reason that no body had been found: he had survived and lain low. Biding his time. It fitted with Vincent's conclusion far too neatly.

'Oh my God,' she said, nodding. 'You were right. John Wennhagen is alive. Do you . . . do you think Nova knows?'

'Not necessarily,' he said. 'He may have been staying away from her too. That would be the smartest thing to do, given that she's involved in the case. And given what her role at Epicura involves, I don't think she would approve of his actions.'

Mina exhaled. That had to be it. But Nathalie was there. She needed to get hold of her. Needed to know that everything was fine. The easiest thing to do would be to call Nathalie's father. But she had asked him to back off. That meant it was up to her to find their daughter, who might just be off on a camping trip with her grandmother.

'How has John been able to stay under the radar for all these years?' she said.

'I dare say it's pretty straightforward for a man with the resources John has – or at least the ones his father had. It's easy being invisible if people think you're dead.'

Mina shook her head. She was still struggling to digest this information.

'We need to tell the others about this,' she said, and Vincent nodded.

'We still have a chance to rescue Wilma,' he said. 'We finally know who it is. All we have to figure out now is *where* he is.'

127

We've been in the car for ages. We've driven out of the city and into the woods. I almost fall asleep. But then we arrive at what I think must be a barn. We get out of the car and I try to run but someone catches me. I bite into the hand holding me as hard as I can. Someone screams and the hand lets go. But someone else grabs me before I have time to run. I kick and punch until they shut me up in a room. Try to kick them down the ladder but fail. Then I have to climb down by myself.

This morning, they ask me whether I want breakfast. I'm starving. But I don't want their disgusting food.

They tell me to calm down.

They say they know my mummy and daddy.

But I know that's not true.

'You're lying!' I yell every time they say something. 'I hate you! I want to go home!'

They stop coming close to me. I'm so angry. And scared. But I have to be angry. Because otherwise I'll get sad and be even more scared. I don't want that.

I sleep on a mattress on the floor. It doesn't look soft. But it is.

I hurl myself onto the mattress and cry into the pillow. There's something hard under me. I stick my hand under the pillow and pull out an iPad. Oh yes – the guy who brought me here said something about that. He said I could use it as much as I wanted. I throw it at the wall but it doesn't break. I slam it against the floor until the screen cracks.

'Serves you right!' I shout. 'Let me go home NOW or I'll kill you!'

If I scream loud enough, perhaps they'll hear me.

Daddy might come and save me with his angriest voice. On his fast bike.

Or Mummy.

But no one is coming.

No one.

128

The team were staring at the wall as if they refused to grasp any of what Vincent had told them. Nevertheless, he thought he had been beyond clear. He had prepared his props with even more diligence than he had done for Mina. Christer had helped him to track down an old overhead projector in a store cupboard in police headquarters. Ruben had started laughing out loud when he had trundled the contraption into the room.

But now that he had told them everything about John's message and then demonstrated his discovery by projecting the text on the plastic sheet over the large map of Stockholm on the wall, they were silent. Their eye movements revealed that every single one of them was following the lines on the map as they assembled John's message. Over and over again. As if it might be different if only they read it one more time.

'Fuck me,' Ruben said at last.

'John Wennhagen, you say,' Christer muttered. 'If he's really alive then he's had decades to build up his old cult. No one has been looking for him. He's probably not even called John these days.'

'What do you mean "old cult"?' said Ruben.

'Don't you remember the rumours about what was going on?' said Christer. 'They all lived out there together – a bunch of them. The place is about halfway to Nynäshamn. There was talk of a cult-like movement, but no one knew for definite. And after the accident, they all dispersed into the wind. I gather that Nova dropped her surname as soon as she could. When she says she has extensive experience of cults, she means on a personal level. Why do you think she's so committed to deprogramming nowadays?'

'Good God,' said Peder, stroking his beard, which today appeared to have big blue stains in it for some reason. 'If John ran a cult back then and has remained covertly active all this time . . . He's had decades to brainwash new members.'

They turned back towards Vincent. Every one of them had deep creases on their foreheads. Except Mina – but she'd heard it all before.

'Shit,' Christer muttered.

He heaved a plastic bag onto the table and began to issue miniature fans to everyone. Vincent gratefully accepted one. Only then did he notice that Bosse wasn't with them.

'He's at home today,' said Christer when he saw Vincent's gaze fixed on the empty food bowl. 'It's a bit cooler at home. If I know that dog at all, he'll have run himself a cold bath too.'

Vincent grinned at the image that appeared in his mind's eye of a large golden retriever happily splashing about in a bathtub. It was probably filled with fragrant bubble bath.

'We need to find out as much as we can about John Wennhagen,' Julia said tersely. 'And quickly.'

'I've already started,' said Peder, opening his laptop.

'Someone has to tell Nova that we're on the hunt for her old man,' said Christer.

Then he stopped himself.

'You don't think . . . you don't think she's in on it do you? Or that Epicura is mixed up in this?'

There was silence around the table. Mina looked to Vincent, but he was staring intently at his phone, scrolling through Google search results, no doubt pursuing some new train of thought that had just occurred to him and completely oblivious to their discussion.

Mina shook her head.

'Her sadness when she told me about losing her father sounded genuine,' she said. 'Besides, I may not know much about Epicureanism, but I do know that it has nothing to do with killing children. The Epicureans mostly seem to be focused on maintaining calm and – how did she put it? – living in still-ness. This is going to be a bitter blow for Nova. I'll tell her.'

Julia raised her eyebrows but said nothing.

'The only question is why John has done all this,' said Adam, who didn't seem to have managed to get his fan working.

'No, that's not the question,' Julia said firmly. 'We can find that out later. The only question now is where we should be

447

looking. We only have today and tomorrow to find Wilma. Assuming that John sticks to seventy-two hours this time too. Peder, I must ask: Why is your beard blue?'

Peder blushed and looked down at the table. 'Erm, children's party,' he muttered. 'But the dye won't rinse out. I don't—'

He was cut off by Milda bursting through the door. She came to a halt when she saw the team.

'Oh, hello. Everyone's here, are they?' she said in surprise. 'I was actually looking for you, Mina, but you weren't in your office. I've got an update on the kids – or more specifically what we found inside them.'

'You mean the fibres?' said Mina.

Christer lobbed a fan to Milda, who caught it with a practised hand. Vincent suspected Milda had played a lot of rounders while growing up.

'Thanks,' she said. 'Spot on. We weren't able to identify the fibres at first – beyond them being some kind of wool. But we kept looking and we found a bacterium – Dermatophilus congolensis – on all the fibres. This reinforces the theory that the fibres came from the same place.'

'What sort of bacteria is that?' said Julia.

'As the name implies, it causes a form of dermatosis in various animals including horses, cattle and sheep. It's known as strep-tothricosis – or more commonly rain rot. Moisture cracks the skin, allowing bacteria to get in and form a crust. On occasion – albeit rarely – streptothricosis has been transmitted from animals to humans, making it a zoonotic agent. It's spread through direct contact or as a result of the crusts getting wet and releasing zoospores that get stuck to grooming brushes and horse blankets.'

Milda paused while she started her fan.

Vincent wasn't sure he followed. The children had all had the bacteria inside their throats. But it came from the skin of animals? It felt like he was missing something.

'So why was the bacteria on the woollen fibres?' he said.

Milda smiled. That was apparently the question she'd been hoping for.

Her fan began to spin with a slight whining sound.

'The wool that the fibres came from must have been in direct contact with infected animals,' she said. 'At the same time, the wool must have been big enough to cover a child's face – perhaps even their whole head – so that they inhaled the fibres. We didn't find any signs of material having been forced into their mouths. My best guess – and I must add this is pure speculation at this—'

'Yes?' Julia said impatiently.

'I believe these fibres come from horse blankets.'

Vincent's thoughts were coiling themselves into a perfect circle and biting their own tails. Horses. It all began and ended with these ubiquitous, enigmatic horses.

'Er, guys . . .' said Peder. He'd had his head bent over his laptop while Milda had been talking. 'You know the farm that John had in the nineties – the one someone burnt down?'

'Yes, wasn't that the one full of animals that burned alive?' said Julia. 'I seem to recollect something along those lines. It was quite a tragedy.'

'They weren't just any animals,' said Peder, turning the laptop to show the others the pictures he had found.

A smiling man with a moustache was standing by a paddock. The animals beside him were muscular and imposing.

'Horses,' said Peder. 'John Wennhagen owned one of the most popular horse farms in the country. It was only some fifty kilometres from here – in Sorunda. And do you know what? On Google Earth, it looks like it's been partially refurbished since then.'

Everyone in the room stared at each other. Then the entire team leapt to their feet.

129

Julia asked Christer to man the fort at police headquarters and see what he could find out about John Wennhagen, while the others all rushed to get into cars. Most of the team climbed into police cars, while Mina took her own car. Julia said she would call out the flying squad while they were en route.

Mina put her foot down. Vincent was sitting beside her, holding on for dear life as they drove down Nynäsvägen heading for Sorunda. At least the car had decent air conditioning. Despite all the thoughts careering around inside her head about John Wennhagen and what they might find at his farm, she temporarily enjoyed the coolness.

'You're very quiet,' said Vincent.

'Concentrating,' she said, without taking her eyes off the road.

'Did you know that Sorunda is known for Sorunda tart?' he said. 'It's very symbolic, as baked goods go. The tart is decorated with symbols of eternity and fertility, and while it generally contains apples and prunes, you're only allowed the prunes if it's being served at a funeral, so that it has a darker colour. But the eternity symbolism goes hand in hand with Nova's idea of water which symbolizes life and unity, and—'

'Vincent.'

'What?'

'You're rambling.'

Vincent fell silent.

She understood his need to talk – he was just as nervous as she was. Nervous about what they would find at the farm. Would they discover more dead children? Would they find John himself? But if his defence was to talk then hers was silence. And she needed to share it with him. Especially now.

Fortunately, he seemed to understand. 'You're right,' he said, looking out of the side window. 'Sorry. We aren't on the hunt for a baker.' He was silent for a few seconds before he began speaking again. 'On the other hand,' he said, 'did you know that the Swedish Transport Administration removed all signs directing people to Sorunda a few years ago? Now it just says Spångbro. Originally, they had—'

She silenced him with a grim look. He smiled wryly.

'Got you,' he said.

She punched him on the shoulder.

'So you want to get me – is that what you're saying?' she said.

'Huh? I, uh . . . it wasn't . . .' he stammered, fidgeting in his seat.

'I thought we'd discussed the blokeyness before, Vincent?' She could almost feel the temperature in the car rising as Vincent blushed to the roots of his hair. She let him agonize for a few eternal seconds.

'Got you!' she said at last.

Vincent exhaled enough air to fill a hot air balloon and then laughed as she overtook a Škoda.

'Touché,' he said. 'But if I'm honest . . . you're not wrong.'

Vincent took a deep breath before continuing. Whatever he was about to say, it was apparently not entirely straightforward for him.

'While a lot of terrible things happened two years ago,' he said, 'I don't think I've ever felt so alive as I did then. That was mostly thanks to you. Then I tried to forget and move on, but . . . well, it's not gone very well.'

Mina quickly glanced at him before returning her eyes to the road.

'Are we really talking about this now?' she said.

'I think we have to,' said Vincent. 'We're on our way to catch a killer. This might be over soon. But I . . . I need you in my life, Mina. Simple as that. I don't know anything about your life except that you've started dating and presumably don't have any time at all for me. But once this is over, would you have anything against carrying on . . . seeing me? If you have room for another friend?'

Another friend. As if she had any others. She wanted to scream and pummel the steering wheel. Oh Vincent. He knew her so well and yet not at all. Why did he have to come back and destroy the shield she had so carefully built up? She didn't want to need anyone. But she needed him too – damn him. That was just how it was.

She turned onto the road to Spångbro so hard that Vincent was thrown to one side in his seat.

'You're sure you wouldn't prefer to hang out with Nova?' she said.

'With Nova? Why on earth would I . . . I mean, I admire

451

Nova's depth of knowledge and expertise. I'm impressed by how hard she's worked to get to where she is. She's a distinguished colleague on the public-speaking circuit. But that's it. A colleague. She's not . . . She's not you.'

Mina nodded silently.

'I can always teach you to play pool,' she said.

He nodded as well.

'Did you see?' he said, sounding much more chipper. 'It said Spångbro at the exit. Not Sorunda. I told you so.'

130

I have a really sore throat. I've been screaming too much. But I'm allowed to be angry. As soon as someone turns up, I hit them. Or kick them. Serves them right. I hate them and I hate all grown-ups. And I hate being in the woods.

If they're not going to take me home then I'll just have to walk home myself. Right now there's no one here. I hurry out but no one sees me. I can hear noise from inside the barn. Everyone is in there. They must think I won't leave. It smells like animals. But it mostly smells like animal poo. It's the most disgusting smell in the world.

I stand in front of the barn. None of the others come out. Good. That means I can go home. I start to walk down the gravel track away from the building. Something – maybe a door – squeaks behind me, but I'm not going to look. I just keep walking.

'Wilma?'

It's him shouting. The one who brought me here. The peffer-dile. He's somewhere behind me. I don't care about him.

'Wilma – where are you going?'

I start running. The gravel under my feet crunches. But I can still hear the sound of him when he starts running too. I run even faster. As fast as I can.

452

'Wilma! Wait!'

The peffer-dile sounds as if he's struggling to talk and run at the same time. Serves him right for being so fat. But he has long legs. I don't. I jump over a ditch and run towards the trees. He might not be able to find me in the woods. Just as I reach the first tree, someone picks me up from behind. I kick as much as I can. But I'm tired.

'Wilma,' *he says.*

He's out of breath, but still laughing. 'You don't have to run – you're going to get to leave here,' *he says. I don't believe him, but this time it almost sounds true. I stop kicking.*

We go to the barn and he puts a blanket over my shoulders even though it's so hot out. The blanket smells of disgusting horse. All the others are there. But I can tell that they're on their way back to the ladder into the ground. It feels as if something is going to happen. Something I don't like.

'How are you feeling, Wilma?' *says the peffer-dile.* 'Do you remember when you were born?'

131

The asphalt on the road petered out and gave way to gravel. They were in the middle of the forest. Vincent couldn't understand how Mina dared drive so fast down the narrow track when they might meet something around the next bend. On the other hand, Adam, Ruben, Julia and Peder were in the cars ahead. If something happened on the road, then it would happen to them first.

The gravel track continued for a kilometre or so through the trees before the forest suddenly cleared. To the right there was a large pasture. To the left was John Wennhagen's farm. Or what remained of it. Vincent guessed that the nearest part had been the dwelling. It was impossible to tell what the house must have looked like before – it had been burnt almost to the ground and what remained of the walls was overgrown in vegetation. The forest had spent the last few decades reclaiming its territory. Had it not been for the large building behind it, he would probably have missed the ruin.

The bigger building, which he assumed was the old stable, was in almost as bad a state. Unlike the house, the stable appeared to have retained parts of its roof and walls, but the roof had caved in and the walls comprised blackened wooden uprights that looked like spillikins sticks. It was free from vegetation, which made the black beams look even more ghostly against the verdant backdrop of trees. He looked around for what Peder had spotted on the satellite images but saw only ruins.

'There,' said Mina pointing to the grove of trees behind the stable.

She was right. Bright red and white was visible between the trees. The gravel track went around the copse and they arrived at a relatively new stable building. In front of it, there were two parked cars. One was a red Renault Clio. The same car that Wilma had been abducted in.

'They've not been here long,' said Mina.

'How do you know that? Those cars could have been here six months.'

'Look at them. No leaves or needles. No bird poo. No dust. They're way too clean to have been out in the open for any length of time. Aren't you meant to be the one who's an expert at observation?'

Adam pulled in behind the parked cars and Julia parked immediately behind him so that they were fully blocking the cars in.

'It's more fun when you do it,' said Vincent. 'What happens now?'

The others were already out of their cars and heading for the stable. Mina parked behind Julia's car.

'Now we get him,' she said.

They set off after the others, with Vincent lagging behind, taking in his surroundings. The silence of the forest was almost deafening. It was as if even the birds were holding their breath, awaiting what would happen next.

Ruben went first. Mina shaded her eyes with her hand and frowned.

'What is it?' Vincent said behind her.

'I don't know. I thought I saw something over in the gravel . . .'

The stable door suddenly opened and a man appeared, a big smile on his lips. He was blond, and he had a distinctive moustache. A precise match for the description they'd been given of Wilma's kidnapper. He hadn't even bothered to change or disguise his appearance. That said something about how confident John's followers were that they wouldn't be found.

When the man spotted the police, his smile vanished in a flash and his face turned ashen. He had obviously been expecting someone else.

The man spun on his heel and ran back into the stable. Only then did they see the girl standing behind him. A rug was draped over her shoulders and she was looking at them in confusion.

It was Wilma.

'Stop!' Ruben shouted, running after the man.

Peder was on Ruben's tail, as was Julia after first pointing to Wilma and indicating to Adam that he should attend to her. He went over to the little girl in her dungarees and crouched down beside her.

'We're from the police,' he said. 'We're here to take you home to your mummy and daddy. Would you like that?'

Wilma nodded eagerly.

'Has he hurt you at all? Did he do anything you didn't like?'

'No,' said Wilma. 'But he lied. There aren't any horses here. He said I'd get to pet horses. But all I got was this icky blanket.'

Then she started crying and wrapped her arms around Adam, who picked her up off the ground and carried her over to the car.

'Mina, a little help here,' Adam called out, nodding to the police car.

As Mina ran over to assist, six people were led out of the stable by Ruben, Julia and Peder. Vincent saw the blond man, a middle-aged woman, an elderly man and three women who

455

looked to be in their mid-twenties. All of them were looking down at the ground and didn't seem to be showing any sign of resisting. Vincent wasn't certain, but he would have bet a considerable sum that they had just found the kidnappers of Lilly, William, Dexter, Ossian and Wilma.

'That's everybody,' said Ruben. 'John isn't here. But these muppets look like they're getting ready for some sort of ritual in there, so I'm guessing he'll show up at any moment.'

The sound of a car coming around the copse of trees made them turn around. A blue Audi skidded to a halt as a cloud of dust rose off the gravel some hundred metres away.

'Jesus, there he is!' said Ruben.

Vincent wanted to see what John looked like these days – thirty years after the photo had appeared on the cover of the chess magazine – but the sun was reflecting off the windscreen, making it hard to see.

Ruben barely managed two steps towards the car before John spun the Audi 180 degrees, throwing up a cloud of gravel and dust. Then he was on his way out of there just as quickly as he'd arrived.

'Bloody hell!' Ruben snapped as he kicked the gravel. 'I don't suppose anyone caught the registration. Vincent – aren't you good at remembering numbers and stuff like that?'

'Not from a hundred metres.'

'Don't sweat it,' said Peder, stroking his beard.

He smiled at the six people, who were still staring down at the ground. 'Our new friends here are going to tell us where he is.'

'We don't know who you're talking about,' said one of the women. 'We did everything of our own free will.'

'I'm sure you did,' said Julia.

132

'Great job everyone,' Julia said, smiling broadly. 'Wilma seems to be unharmed and in good health, but very angry about not being allowed to go home yet. She's been taken to Karolinska for a full medical examination and her parents will meet her there. If it weren't for you, this might have ended very differently. And badly.'

She gazed around the room, pausing to look at each of them. Everyone appeared utterly spent. It was often like that when a case reached a resolution. The tension and adrenaline dissipated. Fatigue settled like a wet blanket across all those who had worked so hard and tirelessly. Mina felt like a punctured balloon. That was normally a welcome sensation since it indicated that the danger had passed. But this time they could only relax for a brief moment. Wilma had been saved. But John Wennhagen was still at large. And Nathalie hadn't come home.

'Christer, you've pulled together some details of John's background. I think it might be worthwhile if you took the rest of us through what you've found. As yet, we have no way of knowing which aspects of his life might be relevant.'

Christer nodded at Julia and produced a sheaf of papers.

'Yes, we've got a real player here. He's the son of a wealthy man – Baltzar Wennhagen – who made his fortune in real estate. He grew up with ripe plums falling into his mouth, as the old saying goes, wanted for nothing. Beyond that, there's not much information about his childhood, but we do know his father was involved in this Epi . . . Epi . . .'

'Epicureanism,' said Mina.

Christer ignored her and continued.

'At some point in his early twenties, John went abroad. To India. While he was there, he joined some sort of cult . . .'

He squinted at the paper.

'The Rajneesh movement. And he went with them to Oregon,

where they started up with a vengeance. Lots of murder and other shit.'

'Isn't that the cult Ted Gärdestad joined?' Peder interjected.

'Ted Gärdestad was in a cult?' Ruben said in surprise. 'The Eurovision guy with the amazing voice?'

'Yep, that's the one,' said Peder. 'It's too bad really; he was so incredibly gifted. But he's still received a lot of acclaim as an artist, so I guess . . .'

'Focus,' Julia said wearily, pointing at Christer to continue.

'What seems to have happened is that John did a bunk just before the shit hit the fan in Oregon. And he brought a bunch of them home to Sweden with him. He bought that farm and established some little cult of his own.'

'How did they support themselves?' Ruben asked.

'They ran a horse farm for a number of years. The very one you just visited. Nova was born on the farm, and her mother was one of the women who accompanied John from Rajneesh. But there's very little documentation from back then. They kept to themselves and the only contact they had with outsiders was with the pupils who came to the farm to take riding lessons. All I've been able to find are some angry letters in the local paper from people who lived nearby and were aware of their cult background. The riding lessons were very popular with the children, as far as I can tell. I'm guessing it wasn't viewed kindly. Which is rather confirmed by what happened.'

'The fire?' said Mina.

'Exactly. There's not much in the way of forensics. But one night a fire broke out at the farm. The forensic investigation afterwards suggested it was arson.'

'I remember seeing that in the paper,' said Ruben.

'It was big news at the time. Several members of the group died in the fire. Both adults and children. The horses also died in the fire. John and Nova were the only ones to escape. And until now we've all believed that John died too – in the car crash that happened while they were fleeing the farm.'

Christer pulled out a copy of an article from an old issue of *Expressen* and passed it around.

'It's surprising that this hasn't come up in the media more often, given Nova's celebrity status,' Mina said thoughtfully.

'It's not exactly a secret,' Vincent said. 'I just don't think anyone has wanted to cause her unnecessary pain by bringing it up again. There's nothing new to add, and she was only a child when it happened.'

'How has he managed to stay under the radar all these years?' Peder said, scratching his beard.

'That's what we need to start finding out now,' said Julia. 'If we manage to find out what he's done, who he's been, where's he been, then that'll be our best indication of where he's hiding out.'

'It's not all that easy to get a fake ID in Sweden,' Christer said.

'He may have been living without an identity altogether,' Ruben said, scribbling thoughtfully on a notepad in front of him.

Mina could see that it was nothing but pointless doodling. Some of the shapes looked like hearts, but that was obviously her mind playing tricks.

Ruben cleared his throat and continued.

'If he's had people around him – loyal followers who also survived and have been taking care of him – then he may not have needed to interact with society. That's the only time we actually have to identify ourselves: when we come into contact with the authorities. If he's had a roof over his head and help putting food on the table, then he may have been able to go completely off grid. Especially since no one was looking for him because we all thought he was dead.'

'We've issued an alert with John's description,' Julia said. 'And we're considering whether to release the information to the media. The problem is that we don't have any current pictures of John – the most recent ones are thirty years old. But we've initiated the process of producing a picture showing how he might have aged and what he might look like now.'

'You mean an artist's impression? What a load of fucking twaddle,' Christer said, looking around the table for support.

'On the contrary,' Adam said with a shake of his head. 'It's been scientifically proven. And they do it with computers these days instead of drawing them by hand like they used to. My God, there are even mobile apps out there to do it for the man in the street. Try to keep up, Christer.'

'Twaddle,' Christer repeated huffily. 'That's all I'm saying.'

'We've also put out an alert on the blue Audi,' said Julia, 'but there's no trace of it yet. However, it'll only be a matter of time. Every car on duty is on the lookout.'

'What about the members of the cult?' said Ruben, scribbling yet more psychedelic doodles in his notebook. 'Surely we can make them talk? They must know where John is.'

'I think Vincent should have a try,' said Mina. 'He's been helpful in those situations before – like with Lenore Silver. In fact, he's spotted things that none of the rest of us did.'

Julia looked at the mentalist, who had hitherto remained quiet.

'Well, Vincent? What do you say? Can you help?'

Mina noticed that Julia had big patches of sweat around her armpits. She discreetly raised her own arms. So far, her deodorant seemed to be keeping the sweat at bay. She had applied more following the visit to the farm, and she had tried to dry her body using wet wipes as best as she could. Not that she had touched anything dirty – but the stench of horses and the insalubrious situation at the farm had seeped their way into every pore of her body.

'I'll be happy to help if needed,' said Vincent. 'But Adam is a trained negotiator. I think he'll do just fine. John's followers may be a little fanatical, but they don't have the same experience of police interview techniques that Lenore did. At most, I think they'll try to keep quiet for a bit. But that'll end when they realize they've been used.'

'I agree,' said Adam. 'We'll just have to crack them through boredom. Which ought to be easier without their saviour around.'

'Sounds like it's time for me to head home,' said Vincent. 'But thanks for an eventful afternoon.'

'It's us who should be thanking you,' said Julia. 'We wouldn't have found John without you. Everyone in the team has made important contributions. So another pat on the back for everyone and well done on the good work. Then let's gird our loins and find John Wennhagen. Do we all know what we should be doing?'

Everyone murmured in the affirmative and nodded at Julia, who stood up and left.

Mina, however, stayed seated at the table even after everyone else had left the room. Something was bothering her. Something she ought to remember.

A couple of hours later, Mina was still troubled. Things weren't adding up. The others had their hands full looking for John Wennhagen. A man resurrected from the dead. During the afternoon, they had spoken to Nova, who had confessed that she had always suspected her father wasn't dead. But that was as far as they had got. Nova had asserted very firmly that she and John had not been in contact at any time. She hadn't even set foot at the farm since the disaster. Of course, they were double-checking her statement. The police would have to review call logs and probably search the premises at Epicura. Paperwork would have to be completed, warrants sought. But Mina had difficulty focusing on what she was meant to be doing.

She had seen something at the farm.

It had been so fleeting that she hadn't managed to remember it with everything else happening. But she knew it was important.

The people who had been holding Wilma captive were in interrogation. Vincent had been right – they were all keeping schtum. So far. Adam hadn't even managed to get their names out of them. If their fingerprints weren't on file, then it would be verging on impossible to identify them. They would probably have to resort to the media and enlist the assistance of Detective Inspector Public.

Wilma was still in hospital. As soon as the doctors were done examining her and were sure that she was in a state to answer questions, Julia and Peder were going to talk to her. But for now they would just have to keep waiting.

Mina got up and paced back and forth between the desk and

461

the wall. It was so hard to focus. She had spent a couple of hours digging up what little there was on John Wennhagen in the records. Perhaps something in his past might lead her to him in the present. She had also searched the land registry in case he owned any properties other than the farm, but she had come up empty-handed.

But she knew that whatever she was looking for wasn't in any database. It was buried in her subconscious, just out of reach. It was eluding her. Teasing her. She wanted to kick something hard out of pure frustration. All of a sudden, she stopped. Maybe she couldn't force her brain to produce an answer. But she knew someone who could. She had seen him do it.

A phone call later, he was on his way.

133

Vincent let Mina show him into one of the relaxation rooms at police headquarters.

'Sorry you had to come back so soon,' she said. 'Does your family hate me now?'

The room contained a bed, a small table and a chair.

'Yep, I take back everything I said in the car about being friends,' he said. 'No, it's fine. Maria wasn't home. Rebecka was supposed to be at her boyfriend's, but I bribed her and Benjamin to watch a movie with Aston until I'm back.'

Vincent noticed Mina stiffen when she saw the bed in the room. She was presumably already grappling in her mind with how many people had lain there and rested, slept or whatever else they did in this corner of the building without the mattress having been cleaned even once.

'I left *Solaris* on Blu-ray,' he said. 'Tarkovsky's that is, even if a documentary said that Stanislaw Lem was interested in what Soderbergh and George Clooney could achieve. But the Russian original from 1972 will always be the original. Benjamin promised to pop some popcorn.'

Mina stared at him.

'Isn't Aston nine years old?' she said. 'You think he'd rather watch . . . what you just mentioned, over, say, *Despicable Me*?'

'I saw *Solaris* for the first time when I was his age,' he said with a shrug. 'And I turned out just fine. Anyway, it's almost three hours long. In case we need time.'

Mina shook her head. But at least she didn't look like she was tempted to cellophane the whole room anymore. The distraction had worked, for the time being. He sat down on the edge of the bed so that she could take the chair.

'Talk,' he said. 'What are we doing here, in this room? What was so urgent?'

'You hypnotized Lenore,' she said. 'Didn't you? When you asked her your questions.'

He hesitated for a second. Hypnosis was a controversial topic, with as many ideas about what it actually was as there were people who did it. No matter how you looked at it, it probably wasn't something the police would encourage. But if Mina was going to tell him off, she had chosen an odd time and place for it.

'I . . . spoke to Lenore,' he said. 'I used certain verbal and physical techniques to help her access a particular mental state where she was relaxed and attentive, but didn't want to question or analyse what was said.'

'So you hypnotized her.'

'If that's what you want to call it.'

'Could you . . . can you hypnotize me?'

This came as a complete surprise. Regardless of where he'd thought the conversation was going, it hadn't been here. Mina, with her lofty walls built around her self, Mina with her defensive shield a mile thick – that same Mina had just asked whether he could climb into the most vulnerable and innermost part of her.

'Are you asking as a challenge to me, because you don't think it can be done?' he said. 'Or do you mean that you'd really like me to try?'

463

'Look, when we were at the farm earlier today, there was something there,' she said. 'I can almost remember it. But there was so much going on at once that I didn't have time to reflect on it then. At least not consciously. And now I don't remember it. But I think it's important. Can you hypnotize me and help me to remember?'

He swallowed. Had it been someone else, the question wouldn't have been strange. He'd been asked it hundreds of times before. But coming from Mina it meant something else. It meant she trusted him completely. That she was prepared to let him see whatever he wanted in her head. At the same time, she trusted him not to look any further than was necessary. All of a sudden, the room felt too small. Or too big. He tried to find a better position on the bed. He wanted to reciprocate this declaration of trust. Mina grimaced when the bed squeaked under him.

'Firstly,' he said seriously, 'if we do this then you don't need to lie down. It's fine to sit on the chair.'

Mina looked visibly relieved. At the same time, the hint of a frown between her eyebrows that had appeared when she had first mentioned hypnosis was still there. She was very clearly not altogether comfortable with the concept.

'Secondly, I don't think hypnosis will be necessary,' he said swiftly. 'I can help you remember without it. There are other techniques for that.'

The frown disappeared. He'd been right. If he had continued with something that she thought was hypnosis, the results would not have been good. It was incredibly courageous of her to ask for it, but in reality she was scared, which created roadblocks. He would have to use a different approach.

'But you still need to close your eyes and relax,' he said. 'Try it out now.'

Mina closed her eyes and he heard her breathing grow slower.

'Good. Now open your eyes again. We haven't started yet.'

Mina's eyes fluttered open with a slightly confused look in them.

'But when we do it next, I want you to be conscious of how your hands feel against your knees. Close your eyes again and try it.'

Mina closed her eyes and this time her head tilted forward a little. He counted silently to five.

'Excellent. Open your eyes again. We haven't started yet.'

This time it took longer for her to open her eyes. She looked almost sleepy.

'In a minute, I'm going to help you to remember, and when I do, you need to do everything I ask of you and you'll be transported back to the farm and you can do that and close your eyes now . . . and relax more than ever before.'

Mina shut her eyes immediately and her head hung forward.

'And deeper . . . and deeper . . . sink into your subconscious and everything that you experienced at the farm,' he said in a soft and monotonous voice. 'Sense the smells there, hear the sounds, see what you saw.'

He took her wrist and raised her hand above her knee. When he let go, the hand stayed in mid-air.

He didn't really like this method. It was partly based on what was known as fractionation, where you began to put someone into a hypnotic state several times before immediately bringing them out of it – a change that was sufficiently physiologically demanding for the brain to want to remain in the state of hypnosis of its own accord. And partly it was based on a sheer overload of instructions. It was a truth as old as the hills in hypnosis that if you confused someone enough, they would follow the first clear instruction given to them. In this case, it was to relax more than ever before. He didn't like the method because it felt so manipulative. But it undeniably paid dividends. Mina had already entered a deep hypnotic state.

He put his index finger on Mina's hovering hand and pressed it carefully down, back towards her knee.

'The further down the hand goes, the clearer your memories become,' he said. 'The sharper your vision is. And when you're ready, tell me what you can see.'

Mina was silent for a few seconds.

'We're parking,' she said at last. 'Outside the stable. Getting out of the car. Ruben is heading for the stable door. I'm looking around.'

'What do you see?'

'The new building. Trees. Cars. Our and theirs. Bushes. Gravel.'

'But there's something that's caught your attention,' he said. 'Is it a sound?'

Mina shook her head.

'There something glittering on the ground,' she said. 'There shouldn't be anything there. It's just gravel. But there's something sparkling in the sun. It might be glass, or a piece of rubbish, but it looks symmetrical. I can't see it properly – I have to shade my eyes with my hand. And then Ruben calls out . . .'

'Stop there,' he said. 'You've seen the object once – it's in your memory. Now you have laser vision. You can see everything from a mile off. Stop time, look at the object again and tell me what it is.'

Mina nodded. He watched as she strained to see her memory. Suddenly she opened her eyes and looked into his. She had leapt straight out of her hypnosis, as if it had never happened.

'I know what it is,' she said. 'We have to go back to the farm.'

134

'Are you aware that you're driving rather fast?' Vincent said in a terrified voice. 'Again.'

Mina kept her eyes on the road. They were almost there. She had headed straight for the car without checking in with the other members of the team. She wanted to be sure before she did. There was no one left at the farm, and she had Vincent with her. But he almost looked as if he regretted that, given how tightly he was clutching the handle above the passenger-side door.

She turned right towards Spångbro without indicating and saw the long straight stretch leading towards the Wennhagen horse farm. She steeled herself. The feeling of dirt was already settling on her, seeking its way under her clothing and into her pores. But the need to confirm her suspicions was more powerful.

'It's a long shot,' said Vincent. 'It might be nothing at all.'

'I know,' said Mina, putting her foot down even harder.

A stone shot up from the road and hit the windscreen with a loud crack.

'Jesus fucking Christ!'

'Apparently we're cursing like a pagan now,' Vincent said drily while still clinging on to the handle.

'Are you working on sounding like a pensioner by your fiftieth birthday or something?' she said.

'Right now I have some concerns about whether I'm even going to experience it.'

Mina ignored him as she passed the ruins of the house and then skidded to a halt in front of the stable. There was an eerie silence as they got out of the car – the only sign of life was a bird cawing somewhere nearby in a tree. The gravel kicked up dust as they quickly crossed the yard.

They passed by the burned-down building, continuing on to the new stable. She stopped and contemplated the ruins. She didn't want to miss anything. 'Ugh,' she said when she spotted the collapsed roof. 'It almost feels as if I can hear the people screaming. It must have been horrendous. The fire. The sound of everything crashing down. And the horses. All the horses . . .'

'I can hear them too,' Vincent said quietly. 'More clearly than I'd like.'

They studied the devastation for a while. She had read about overgrown ruins in the woods that have become peaceful and semi-mysterious over the years. This was not the case here. John's burnt-down stable was still a big black scar on the land-scape. As if what had happened there was so awful that even nature had taken a detour to avoid it.

She began to walk quickly around the copse of trees towards the new stable. She shaded her eyes with her hand just as she had the last time, even though they now had the sun on their backs and it wasn't really necessary.

'There,' she said, pointing to a spot further away in the gravel.

She got closer, Vincent behind her.

'Look.'

She squatted and pointed to a piece of metal on the ground. Vincent crouched down too.

'A horseshoe,' he said, nodding.

'That isn't strange in itself,' said Mina. 'After all, it was a horse farm. And while there aren't any horses in the new part, John may have had them here before. There are probably used horse-shoes all over the place. But if so, shouldn't they be dirty and rusty – or at least a little worn? This one is completely clean and shiny. Why is it lying here?'

She tried to lift the horseshoe to take a closer look, but couldn't get it off the ground.

'It's stuck,' Mina said in bafflement.

Vincent leaned forward to look. He was so close that she could feel his breathing by her ear.

'Do you see the hoop it's attached to?' he said. 'It's not just a horseshoe. It's a handle.'

Mina turned towards him in amazement. Far away, a bird's cawing was again audible.

135

Mina tried to pull the horseshoe one more time, but it was stuck.

'Wait. There's a spring-loaded bolt there,' Vincent said. 'Do you see?' He brushed away some gravel and revealed a bolt with a spring coiled around it almost immediately adjacent to the horseshoe. Vincent pushed the spring aside and inserted a small stone to hold it in place.

'Right. Let's give it another try together.'

He stood behind Mina, put his arms either side of her and positioned his hands by hers at the horseshoe.

The horseshoe was so small that his hands needed to partially cover hers when grabbing hold of it. He was still, waiting for her to say something about the skin contact – perhaps to withdraw her hands.

Instead, she leaned back a few centimetres so that her upper body was pressed against his. The warmth from her back spread through his ribcage and permeated throughout his body. He barely dared to breathe.

'Vincent,' she said.

'Yes?'

'Get on with it and pull.'

They pulled together, and slowly a crack began to appear in the gravel. Someone had carefully covered a hatch with gravel to make it invisible, but when they opened the cover it revealed a gaping hole with a ladder that went straight down into the dark. The spring-loaded bolt on the frame of the hatch meant that it would automatically lock when closed.

'And now we go down into the rabbit hole . . .' Mina said fatalistically.

The rabbit hole. Sometime, when this was over, he would have to ask whether Mina had been eavesdropping on his conversations with Benjamin.

'Are you up to this?' he said.

'Honestly, the mere thought of what might be down there makes me want to vomit,' she said. 'But you can forget about going down there on your own.'

'OK,' he said. 'I think we've found John's shelter.' He crouched on his knees in the gravel to try and see further down into the hole, but it was deep enough not to reveal any secrets.

'Shelter?'

'Yes, that's the likeliest thing. Cults often come with a dash of doomsday expectation. Doom becomes a common threat that unites and terrifies the members, which makes them more susceptible to influence. Building a shelter is a very tangible way of increasing the sense of impending disaster. Of course, it's not only cults that think like that. Eschatology is a feature in the majority of religions. Even the big ones. Another option is that John is paranoid and believes he needs a shelter for his own protection.'

'Scatology?' said Mina. 'Just what do you think we're going to find down there?'

She looked at him with an expression of sheer horror.

'Eschatology,' he said, turning his back to the hole and crouching near the edge. 'It comes from the Greek *eschatos*, which means last, and *logos*, which means doctrine. "The last", or the *eschato*, can be interpreted as the end of an individual's life, or as the end of the world. The end of time. In Christianity, it's tied to the resurrection of Jesus and the final showdown between God and Satan.'

His heart was pounding hard in his breast as he glanced behind him and down into the hole. It wasn't necessarily claustrophobia-inducing. But it was dark. And who knew what it was like further down? He might very well be climbing into his own coffin.

'The Bahá'i faith, however, does not believe that *eschato* is about destruction – they believe the peoples of the world will create a new world order of peace in the shadow of God's goodness,' he said quickly, in order to distract himself as he inserted a foot into the hole and found the top rung of the ladder. 'A slightly brighter message, in other words. But Christianity has always been a trailblazer when it comes to scaring the shit out of people.'

He could hear how strained his voice sounded. Too bad; that would just have to be the way it was. He concentrated on his breathing while slowly climbing downwards.

In. Out.

In. Out.

The panic was so close by. It might spill over at any moment, sending him spinning into an anxiety so deep and bottomless that he was afraid he would never find his way back to the surface.

136

Mina watched Vincent's blond head disappear further and further into the dark hole.

'There's quite a lot of it,' she heard him say.

She didn't reply. It would be so horribly dirty down there. She just knew it. The mere sight of the rusty rungs made her shiver.

'You can come down.'

The voice was fainter than before. Vincent must have descended even further.

'It's as clean as it can be down here. Don't touch the walls and you'll be fine.'

Mina swore silently and climbed down, rung by rung. She tried not to think about how many pairs of grubby shoes had trodden on the rungs she was holding, and she was almost grateful when the darkness made it impossible for her to see the dirt. But only almost. For the darkness was not her friend either. In the dark, you might not be able to see the bacteria-ridden dirt, but that didn't mean it wasn't there.

Finally, she reached the bottom. He was right. It was probably as clean as it could be, given that she had entered a subterranean concrete bunker. It felt as if they were in a hellhole. Even if you dragged the whole burning sun down here, there would still not be enough light.

'This must be where they had the kids,' she said.

'Yes. It never seemed likely that they would have kept them in the stable above. Sure, it was out of the way. But it was too unsafe – too hard to defend if something were to happen.'

'We were lucky to find Wilma,' she said, while searching the small space. 'Something must have made them bring her out of the bunker just before we arrived.'

There wasn't much here. A stack of mattresses. Some blankets. Scraps of food packaging. Sweet wrappers. A bucket.

'Jesus Christ,' Vincent said, looking down. He was standing

in the centre of the circle of light formed by the opening at ground level, pointing down at the mattresses.

'Looks like horse blankets,' he said. 'These must be the ones that the fibre traces in the children's throats came from. Although I still don't understand how the fibres got into them. Or how those marks on their lungs that the reports mentioned got there. There's so much we still don't know. What's John's motive? Why these kids? And this way? John and his followers must have been living an extremely quiet life to have managed to stay under the radar for so many years. Why did they choose to act now?'

Vincent fell silent and stared at the mattresses. And at the blankets. For once, he seemed unable to find any pattern. She couldn't imagine what that must feel like for someone who saw patterns even when he didn't want to. But down here, there were no patterns. Just darkness. Even the circle of light he was standing in had shrunk to a crescent. Vincent's light hair shone in the sunshine. She followed his gaze.

The mattresses.

The blankets.

The marks – as if the lungs had been subjected to strong pressure.

Fibres in the throat.

And then an old memory began to slowly come to life. Something she had read before she'd become a police officer. One of the cases that had made her decide she wanted to stand up to evil.

'A girl died in America,' she said slowly. 'Back in 2000, I think it was. Her name was . . . Candace. Candace Newmaker, I think. Her adoptive mother took her to a psychiatrist because she felt the girl wasn't behaving normally . . .'

Her skin was crawling. She wanted to get out of here. Up into the sunshine, so she could call Julia, get a team from forensics out here to go over the place millimetre by millimetre. The circle of light shrank even more around Vincent.

'When the medication didn't help,' she continued, 'the mother took her to see a therapist so that Candace could have attachment therapy. One of the techniques that the therapist used was known as rebirth. Candace died in the second week of therapy.'

472

'Rebirth? What?'

She pointed to the mattresses and blankets.

'Candace was rolled into a blanket. Then they put mattresses on top of her to simulate a birth canal and she was told to fight her way out. The idea was that she would somehow bond with her adoptive mother. I don't know. Anyway. While she was fighting to get out, the adults applied pressure with their body weight. She cried, vomited and screamed several times that she was dying. But no one listened. The next day she was declared brain-dead due to oxygen starvation and she died. It was all on video.'

'My God,' said Vincent. 'That's alarmingly close to Milda's reports. We have to contact Julia.'

It wasn't as warm in the bunker when the sunlight was no longer shining straight down. The circle of light was now much smaller than a crescent.

The light.

The light was disappearing.

Her gaze went from the shrinking semi-circle of light on the floor up to the opening.

'Vincent,' she said. 'The hatch. We didn't attach it properly. It's closing.'

Vincent looked up at the hatch, then hastily at Mina before lunging for the ladder. As he set his foot on the lowest rung, the final shard of moon-shaped light disappeared and the hatch fell shut above them with a heavy thud. She didn't hear the click as the spring-loaded bolt locked them in. But she felt it throughout her body.

137

'Might someone have locked us in?' Mina felt the walls closing in. Closing in on *her*. Her breathing had become laboured: it was fast and shallow. Suddenly there was a hand on her arm.

This would not usually have helped her anxiety in the slightest – on the contrary. But it was Vincent's hand.

'I'm afraid this can probably only be blamed on the human factor,' he said. 'Our own stupidity. We should have thought to secure the hatch properly. How did we fail to do that? It's just fallen shut.'

'Go and open it, please,' she said through gritted teeth.

Silence. A silence that lasted a little too long. Mina pulled out her phone and switched on the torch so she could see Vincent properly. His facial muscles were tauter than she would have liked.

'The lock is designed to prevent it from being opened from inside,' he said.

'What? How does that make sense? This is a shelter – it's supposed to protect people from the outside. Not the inside. Why would John build a shelter without the ability to get out?'

'You can't apply standard logic to a doomsday prophet,' said Vincent. 'In John's world, the day they would need to use the shelter was the end of everything.'

'But that's even less logical. Why go to the trouble of building a shelter if they're going to die anyway? They might just as well face their final day above ground . . .'

Vincent sat down heavily on the mattresses in the corner. He didn't reply. Mina saw that he was thinking, and she let him think in peace. She checked her phone. No reception. Admittedly, she hadn't been expecting any. She climbed up the ladder and held her phone to the hatch. No difference. The phone was unusable.

'People with John's personality type will often regard them-selves as indispensable,' Vincent said when she had climbed back down the ladder. 'And somewhat superior to the others. He's the one with the answers and it's up to him to share them. He has the responsibility to . . . to live on. I think . . . I think John's idea was that the others would die. But not him. This was a death trap. He probably kept some kind of poison in here to kill them. You know, just like Beata Ljung told us about Jonestown and Heaven's Gate. Of course, now I'm speculating, but John's plan may have been to lock himself in with the members down here and tell them that the world outside was gone. The only option remaining would be to step into the void themselves. As he used to say: everything is suffering; pain purifies. Except for John. He intended to survive.'

Vincent looked around thoughtfully. Mina did the same, holding up the phone to provide light. She contemplated the bare concrete walls as panic continued to rise within her.

'How?' she said. 'There's no way out.'

Her mobile battery was at 9 per cent. And the battery always ran down quickly when she used the torch.

'Do you have your phone with you? My battery is running low.'

Vincent shook his head.

'It's still in the car.'

He stood up. Then he walked along the walls. He asked her to shine the light on him as he felt them with his hands. A spider quickly scuttled out of the light, and Mina almost dropped the phone. Vincent turned around.

'Are you OK?'

'I'll be fine. Keep searching.'

Down to 8 per cent.

'Turn off the torch,' Vincent said.

'Sorry, but what the hell?' Mina said, staring at him. 'No, I will not.'

'I know it's uncomfortable. But my sensory system and the feeling in my fingers is heightened if my vision isn't disturbing them. I need to feel my way around without the obstacle of my eyesight.'

'You'd better bloody hope you find a way out,' Mina hissed, switching off the torch with her fingers trembling.

It became pitch-dark. Impenetrable. No light came from anywhere. There was nothing that could help her eyes to adjust. The darkness was bottomless. She stood still and heard Vincent moving around the chamber. She closed her eyes. Even that didn't make a difference. But the familiar darkness behind her eyelids was more comforting than staring into nothing with her eyes wide open.

'Mina! Shine the light here!'

Vincent was behind her. She jumped and then spun around. Her hands still shaking, she managed to turn the torch back on and shone it in the direction she'd heard his voice coming from. Vincent was standing with both his hands against the wall. He fumbled in his pocket and produced a bunch of keys. He took one of them and began to draw it along the wall. Dust from the concrete fell onto his shoes as Mina watched what he was doing with fascination. Slowly but surely, a straight notch in the concrete began to appear. Vincent followed the notch and then ran the key horizontally from the first vertical line. After a while, he'd traced a square in the concrete.

A hatch.

'I think I've found it,' he said calmly. 'John's secret way out.'

He pressed the panel. There was a click as it came loose. Vincent lifted the panel off and set it on the floor.

Mina's throat contracted as she shone the light into the opening.

'No chance,' she said, recoiling away. She stumbled on the mattresses and fell over.

She quickly leapt to her feet. The thought of the dirty, disgusting mattress that had touched her made panic bloom inside her. And it didn't help that the dirty hole next to Vincent was their only way out.

'I can't . . .'

'Mina! There won't be enough air for us down here. We're using up the oxygen with every breath we take. Anyway, you said yourself that your battery is running out. Wouldn't you rather have light on your way out?'

Mina stared at the dark hole in the wall.

'What is it? A tunnel?'

Part of her wanted to get closer to take a look. But another part of her didn't want to take a single step towards the horror that had opened up before her in the wall. She could both see and hear Vincent's hesitation before he replied.

'My best guess is that it's an old sewage pipe,' he said. 'Probably from a previous building that was here before they built the bunker.'

'You're kidding.' Mina backed away. This time she carefully

476

avoided the mattresses. She looked at her phone: 5 per cent. Damn it – she knew she should have got a new one with a better battery ages ago. But she'd always kept putting it off. Now its juice was seeping away at a steady pace. Soon she would have to crawl through that pipe in complete darkness. Or die in here.

The choice wasn't as obvious to her as she supposed it was to others. She thought she'd be able to accept the alternative of dying of suffocation in the room before the unknown awaiting her in that much too small pipe.

'We'll do this together,' said Vincent. 'I'll be with you all the way. Do you want to go first or last?'

That question made her ears roar. First or last? Plague or cholera?

Breathe.

But she knew he was right. After all, she didn't really want to die.

'Last,' she said.

'Let's roll,' Vincent said with a nod. 'You can do this.'

'Before I change my mind,' Mina said grimly, handing the phone to Vincent.

He crawled headfirst into the pipe and wriggled forward on his elbows, shining Mina's phone ahead of him. She tried to imagine his linen suit absorbing all the grime and leaving the pipe clean for her, but she didn't get very far with it. The stench when she crawled in behind him was stomach-churning. She sobbed, and then she gagged. She swallowed the acidic bile. Throwing up in the pipe wouldn't make things any better.

'It can't be far,' she heard Vincent's voice say in a muffled echo ahead of her. 'Seven hundred and one, seven hundred and nine, seven hundred and nineteen . . .'

She wasn't going to ask what he was counting. But it sounded like odd numbers only. It couldn't be good, given what she knew about Vincent.

Centimetre by centimetre, she wriggled forward, trying to breathe through her mouth so that she couldn't smell the stench of excrement through her nostrils. The taste of vomit was still pungent in her mouth. When she spotted deposits on the walls

477

of the pipe out of the corner of her eye and she realized what they were, she could no longer hold it in. She threw up. It splashed Vincent's shoes ahead of her.

'Oh dear – are you OK?' Vincent said, his voice still muffled and echoey. 'Seven hundred and fifty-one, seven hundred and fifty-seven, seven hundred and sixty-one.'

She spat and hissed, trying to get rid of the last of it from her mouth.

'It didn't exactly smell good before,' he said. 'Seven hundred and sixty-nine, seven hundred and seventy-three . . .'

Vincent's voice died away. With growing horror, Mina realized that her hands were covered in stomach acid and vomited chunks of food – a vile concoction that she now had to crawl through on her elbows. In a tunnel smelling of shit.

'Crawl faster!' she shouted in panic, beginning to wriggle forward while the smell forced its way into her nostrils.

The gastric juices were warm and stuck to her chest and stomach. She spat out yet more bile and began to breathe through her mouth instead. Something suddenly moved next to her. She screamed, and one arm slipped in all the slime, so that she hit her shoulder. A huge spider scuttled away in the beam of light that flickered ahead of her. Her heart was racing so hard it felt like it might burst in her ribs.

'We must almost be there,' said Vincent. 'Or at least I hope so. Eight hundred and fifty-three.'

The thought of an exit made her crawl a little faster. Now her trousers were also sticking to her legs. Most of all, she wanted to overtake Vincent and hurl herself into the fresh air – but the pipe didn't allow for that.

Something fell into her hair and she screamed again. The scream resounded through the pipe, was amplified and bounced back to her like a horror-stricken chorus. She could feel something crawling in her hair, but there wasn't space to raise her arms to swat it away. She began to hyperventilate.

'What's happening?' Vincent said, stopping. 'Do you need help?'

'Keep going,' she panted, struggling to get her breathing under control.

Suddenly she realized that his voice wasn't just being warped by the acoustics in the pipe. He was talking through a clenched jaw. She had been so focused on herself that she had forgotten about Vincent's issues. He couldn't stand confined spaces. It must be taking a considerable amount of effort for him to remain as calm and supportive as he was. He was in fact in just as much of a state of panic as she. The thought gave her strength. If he could do it, then so could she.

The phone's torch went out and the tunnel became pitch-black. The battery must have finally died.

She wanted to cry. She wanted to scream and thrash about wildly. For a moment, she forgot to breathe through her mouth and the smell hit her again. The sour, bitter smell of vomit and excrement. Tears burned her eyes, but she carried on, centimetre by centimetre, through the darkness. Hoping he was somewhere ahead of her.

'Mina?'

Vincent's voice penetrated through the darkness.

'Yes?'

'I think I see light. One thousand two hundred and ninety-seven. We've reached the exit. One thousand three hundred and one.'

Tears – this time of relief – ran down Mina's cheeks while something continued to move in her hair. She followed the sound of Vincent crawling towards freedom.

138

When Vincent saw Mina tumble out of the pipe, he wanted to embrace her. But he knew that would probably be the worst thing he could do. Especially given how rank she smelled and the filthy clothes clinging to her. Anyway, he didn't know whether he had it in him. Keeping the panic at bay in the confined space had drained him of all his energy. Mina raked her hair madly and three enormous spiders fell out and disappeared on the ground. Vincent followed their example and lay down on his back in the tall grass, staring up at the clear blue sky.

The light hurt his eyes after the darkness, but that didn't matter. He could breathe again. He had air and space around him. He turned his head. Mina had also dropped onto her back with her arms extended from her body as if she wanted to make a snow angel in the grass. The fact that she had voluntarily lain down on the ground said a great deal about what she had just experienced. Her brain was probably overloaded with adrenaline – it had permitted nothing but a primal survival instinct so that she could get through that pipe, and now it was protecting her from the world around her. But it wouldn't last much longer. Tears were already glistening on her cheeks. He saw that they had cut a path through the grime. She smelled truly awful. And he had never seen her look more beautiful.

'Fucking. Hell,' she said in a spluttering voice.

He supposed she wanted nothing more than to tear off all her clothes. But she appeared to have as little strength as he did.

'What kind of sick fuck is he?' she said in the end, her gaze fixed on the same blue sky as his. 'If you're right, then he was planning to kill everyone around him while he got away and saved his own skin. Do you think he was planning to take Nova with him? Or was she supposed to die there too? Isn't it meant to be in a parent's nature not to abandon their child?'

Vincent watched a cloud slowly passing over the big blue expanse. He pondered before answering. He realized that the question was about much more than just John Wennhagen. And he wanted to proceed with caution. Mina had never shown a crack in her armour, or a desire to talk about what must be an open wound inside her. So he hadn't wanted to ask. It hadn't been for him to pick the time.

'I don't think . . .' he began hesitantly. 'I don't think it's possible to look at it as simply as many people want to. My view is that a parent's love of their child is among the most powerful forces in the world. And I could explain why on scientific, psychological

480

and evolutionary grounds. But I think there's something else there too – something that can't be explained through biology and survival of the species. I would call it a gift, but that kind of interpretation leads to unnecessary questions about who gave us the gift.'

He paused and hesitated. He was operating in the outermost peripheries of his own beliefs about the state of things. And he didn't want to insult Mina with what he intended to say next.

'That love bridges all divides,' he said. 'Do you know the story of King Solomon? Two women come to the king, who is known for his wisdom. Both claim a small child is theirs. Neither of them will give in. The king draws his sword and declares that he will cleave the child in two so that they may have half each. One woman thinks it's a splendid idea, while the other says the first woman can have the child rather than let it die. Solomon identifies the second woman as the true mother since she was the only one prepared to sacrifice her own happiness for the sake of the child.'

Mina was quiet for a long time.

'It was the hardest thing I've ever done,' she said at last. 'Giving her up. But I knew it was for the best. Or I thought I knew, anyway. I didn't want her to grow up like I did. With a mother who couldn't be relied on. Who was consumed by addiction. I had nothing to give her. Nothing. I was nobody. I was a shell. And I didn't think I would ever be anything else. I didn't think I had anything to give her.'

'Are you talking about Nathalie?'

'Yes. Nathalie.' Mina let out a sob, but then she gathered herself. A new cloud passed over her. She continued in a low, fragile voice.

'He was so hurt, Vincent. Hurt that I left him. But he was most hurt that I left Nathalie. So he issued an ultimatum. If I left, I left for good. Out of her life. Out of his life. And I think . . . no, I *know* that he meant nothing bad by it. He doesn't think like that. He believed at the time – and he still does – that the best thing for Nathalie is strict consistency. He has his own reasons for that. His own baggage. Like all of us. But I know that he only had her best interests at heart when he issued

481

that ultimatum. And part of me couldn't blame him. I chose to leave. She was five years old and I chose to leave her.'

The cloud had passed and the sun was pleasantly warm. But it did nothing to stifle the smell emanating from Mina's clothes. Vincent lay on his side so that he could see her. He supposed he had grass stains all over his suit by now – not to mention shit from the tunnel. He didn't smell too good either.

'The beauty of being human,' he said, 'is that everything – or at least most things – can change. You're not the same person as you were then. Not a single cell in your body is the same as then. And neither are your thoughts. You can face Nathalie today in a way that you couldn't before.'

'But what if she doesn't want to know me?'

The utterance rose like an unhappy scream up to the sky. Vincent wanted to touch her, to reassure her that she was wrong, but he left his hand in the grass. At this moment, she was out of reach.

'I didn't say it would be easy. But you've got an opening. Her father has let you in through the door. That has to mean something.'

'It's not like he had any choice,' said Mina. 'If it had been up to him, I would still be out in the cold.'

'Don't say that. Sometimes people only do things that they really want to when circumstances force them to.'

Mina didn't reply. A new cloud appeared and began to pursue the first clump of cotton wool across the sky.

'What were you counting, back in the pipe?' she said after a while.

'Prime numbers. I needed to keep my hippocampus calm so that I could keep crawling.'

'Hmm.' They lay in silence for a while.

'I have to ask something,' she said. 'That red mark that's around your neck sometimes – is it something I need to worry about?'

'What do you mean?' he said, looking at her. 'Oh that. I didn't think it showed. It's from my show. But I've stopped doing that number.'

'So . . . it's not erotic asphyxiation then?'

He couldn't help it – a big, booming laugh welled up inside him, erupted and bounced between the trees. The sound was incredibly liberating. Mina smiled next to him. He wiped away tears of laughter from his eyes before he was able to compose himself again.

'Do you know how atoms are formed?' he asked.

'Atoms?'

'Yes, atoms. They're created inside stars.'

'Like the sun?' she said, squinting at its rays.

He nodded and looked up at the sky too. Far away beyond the blue was where the stars were. In the dark.

'Stars are really just atom factories,' he said. 'At their very hearts, where they're warmest, is where the building blocks for the rest of the universe are made. Those atoms are hurled into space and end up all over the place. Such as here, on Earth. Everything you see around you – all the people and objects – are made from atoms from thousands – perhaps millions – of stars.'

Mina began to tug at her blouse. Apparently her internal alarm system had finally decided that the danger had passed and the adrenaline had begun to dissipate. And with that came the realization of what was on her clothes.

'That fabric too,' he said. 'And the ground we're lying on. And you and me. To say that we come from the stars isn't romantic poetry – it's just science. Everything is made from star atoms.' He fell silent for a moment, no longer sure how to continue.

'Why are we talking about atoms?' she said, no longer tugging at her top.

'Because when I'm with you . . .' he said, before cutting himself off.

He swallowed once. He looked her in the eyes. Those big, clear eyes that contained everything that she was. All that was Mina. The eyes that saw him. He had to look away. Then he looked her in the eyes again.

Time to bend or break. 'I know how lame this sounds. But when I'm with you, I get the feeling that you and I are made from atoms from the same star. One that's so far away that when the building blocks reached Earth there was perhaps only enough for you and me. Star atoms that no one else got. Because I'm . . . it's as if I . . .'

What was the right word? Know you? Understand you? No. They weren't good enough.

'I think I know you, Mina,' he said. 'In here.'

First he pointed to his head, then he changed his mind and pointed to his chest.

'And in that case I've never known anyone else. I can't explain it any better. But with you I feel for the first time . . . as if I'm the same.'

She nodded slowly without answering. He'd probably just made a complete fool of himself. He sat up laboriously.

'Time for us to get back?' he said.

'If I don't get out of these clothes in the next thirty seconds, I'm going to scream,' she said, prising the car keys out of her trouser pocket. 'But I've got fresh underwear in the car. For me, anyway. You'll have to make do with wet wipes.'

Vincent examined his filthy, tattered suit. He would have some explaining to do when he got home.

139

For only the fourth time in his life, Vincent was on his way to a police interview room. That was four more times than he had ever expected to experience. But this time it had been Adam who had asked him whether he wanted to sit in and talk to one of the cult members. This made him curious. After all, Adam was a trained negotiator. But what use was that if John's followers opted to remain silent?

Adam was waiting for him in the foyer at police headquarters. Vincent definitely preferred it when Mina met him by the barriers. But following their escapade in the bunker the day before, she was at home. He had called but she hadn't picked up. He guessed she'd spent the last twelve hours in the shower.

'Thanks for coming,' Adam said, proffering his hand. 'I heard about what happened to you and Mina yesterday. You're still looking a bit knackered. Are you sure you want to do this?'

Vincent smiled weakly.

'I think this is the best thing I could be doing right now,' he said. 'Anything to distract me.'

'I get it. But I wouldn't blame you if you didn't want to set foot in this place ever again. Anyway, you're better at this than I am. And it would be nice to get this cleared up before the weekend.'

'Complicity through praise?' Vincent said, passing through the barrier. 'I didn't think you of all people would deploy that.'

'Was just checking,' Adam said with a laugh. 'But I really do have a problem here. They're refusing to talk.'

In other words, it was exactly as Vincent had guessed.

They went down the corridor towards the interrogation rooms.

'Can't you just wait them out?' he said.

Adam shook his head. 'We can't hold them indefinitely. And we don't know whether this is over until we have John. We may not have caught them all. There was an elderly couple seen at Lilly's abduction – the woman in a purple coat – but we haven't got a couple matching that description here. Just an older man. What if it happens again while we're here trying to get them to talk? I thought you might be able to pick up some unconscious signals while I question him.'

'I've got a better idea,' said Vincent. 'If we're doing this anyway. Let me talk to him alone, but leave your phone in the room and have it recording everything that's said.'

Adam looked at Vincent. He seemed to be considering it. Then he nodded and opened a door to a room identical to the ones in which Vincent had met Lenore and Mauro. But this time it accommodated a man in his sixties. His grey hair was wavy, and the laughter lines around his eyes made him look like everyone's favourite granddad. If it hadn't been for his presumed participation in a child-killing, that was . . .

The man watched them intently as they entered. That was,

in itself, interesting behaviour. Vincent had thought he would encounter measured or hostile conduct. He had also thought that John's followers would be tired – perhaps even afraid after a night in the custody suite. After all, they weren't career criminals. But the man was . . . alert. Present. He didn't give the impression of being someone who didn't want to talk. It was merely a case of finding out what he wanted to talk about. Vincent had a pretty good idea of what it might be, given the glowing embers in the man's eyes. Those who had seen the light were generally eager to convince those still awaiting salvation.

Adam paused just inside the door and set something down on a small shelf. His mobile, Vincent assumed, as he proceeded into the room.

'Hello,' he said. 'My name is Vincent and I've been very much looking forward to meeting you.'

The man didn't reply.

'I'm not a police officer,' Vincent added, tilting his head in Adam's direction. 'So this isn't a formal interview. But I am interested in moral philosophy and Epicurus is my favourite philosopher. That's why I've been given permission to talk to you. Do you mind if I sit down? I'm a bit peckish as it happens. What about you? Do you fancy something to eat? I was going to ask for some coffee and biscuits or something. If you'd like some . . .'

Vincent turned towards Adam as if he were about to place an order with the waiter in a cafe. The less Vincent acted like a cop, the better. Right now, he needed to form a bond with the man and find something that united them. Feigned disinterest in the power of the police was a good start. Even if Adam didn't look like he appreciated that.

'Biscuits would be good,' the man replied. 'Coffee too, if you're going anyway.'

One-nil.

Vincent glanced at Adam, who slipped out of the room. The tactic had worked. But the man's answer also contained other critical information. People who were ashamed of their actions rarely accepted gifts or services from others, since they subconsciously didn't think they deserved them. The fact that the man wanted biscuits was a measure of just how deep John's claws were in him. There was no shame there. It also meant that it would be harder to interpret whatever Vincent hopefully found out, because the man was presumably living in a fantasy world constructed by John. A world that allowed him to abduct and even kill children without feeling any concern.

'Everything is suffering; pain purifies,' Vincent said. 'John Wennhagen's magnificent addition to the four grounding rules of Epicureanism.'

The man's eyes shone even more brightly.

'Can you help me to understand what "pain purifies" means? Given that Epicurus actually said we should avoid pain.'

'I can see you're well-read,' the man said. 'Not like the others here. As you well know, when Epicurus said that you should avoid pain, he was really talking about suffering. The suffering that life in the modern world entails when we are seduced by all that is transient. It's the same thing the Buddhists think. But John understood that some pain – physical or emotional – also gives you a useful perspective on the world. When you live with pain, it gives you razor-sharp laser sight that cuts through the unnecessary. Pain is necessary in order to achieve an absence of it. I'm Gustav, by the way.'

The man offered his hand and Vincent took it. It was a warm and self-assured handshake. Most definitely a favourite granddad.

'I've never thought of it like that,' said Vincent. 'So it's a good thing to feel pain then?'

'I can tell you've never been in real pain,' said Gustav.

A kaleidoscope of recollections flashed through Vincent's mind. His mother in his magic box. His mother, who died because of him. Himself, trapped in a water tank with Mina. Water filling his mouth and nostrils as he drowned. And then Mina. Mina whom he couldn't live without. He screwed his eyes shut to vanquish those images and then shook his head. No pain at all.

'Until you've experienced something that actually hurts, you won't understand what I'm talking about,' said Gustav. 'I suffer from whiplash. My wife and I were in the car when someone else hit us. They said I'd be better after a week on medication and some rehabilitation. It's been fifteen years. Every time I move, I risk the sensation of daggers in my whole back. My fingers are numb. I get dizzy. And my wife has had surgery on her hip five times, but it only gets worse. Don't get me wrong – I'm not complaining. The pain helps us to prioritize correctly. It's given us a different perspective on life.'

'I've never thought about it like that. So John's inner circle is made up of people who understand how pain purifies since they live with it themselves?'

Gustav nodded.

'Exactly. We're the only ones who are able to see the world for what it is.'

Vincent didn't dare turn around to look at Adam's phone on the shelf. He would just have to hope it was still recording.

'Where's your wife now?' he said.

Gustav pursed his lips. Bloody hell. That was far too similar to a question asked in interrogation. Vincent needed to back off.

'I just meant is she OK?' he said, and Gustav appeared to relax a bit again. 'What was it you were trying to give the children then? Pain?'

The man furrowed his brow. The favourite granddad was suddenly gone.

'You haven't understood a thing,' he said. 'Why would we want to do that? No one wants to hurt a child. Are you sure you're not a cop?'

'Sorry, I just have trouble understanding how John justifies the killing of children.'

He knew it was clumsy, but he had to bring it up somehow. He'd come very close to saying 'justifying you killing children', but he'd gone for a more neutral option. The last thing he wanted was for Gustav to feel personally implicated, no matter how much he actually was. His chances of continuing to get answers were much greater if he let Gustav retain an outsider's perspective.

'We don't kill anyone,' Gustav snorted. 'That's far too narrow a way of looking at what we do. Thanks to our guiding star, we save the children from the suffering that life on this earth will entail for them. We merely convey them into the next existence. One without suffering. Our sacrifice is to stay here and help to liberate others.'

'How many more children do you need to "liberate" before you are done? And why these children in particular?'

Gustav narrowed his eyes and folded his arms tightly across his chest.

'I thought you had been initiated,' he said. 'I thought you understood something about pain and suffering. But it seems as if John's words have not yet awakened in you. We're done here. I don't need that coffee.'

140

Mina wiped the steam off the mirror with a cloth and looked at her reflection. Droplets of water were running from her hair and the tip of her nose. She examined the skin on her face and then her teeth to see whether she could find anything that shouldn't be there. Even though she knew it was impossible.

As soon as she had got home on Thursday, she had got into the shower. She had scrubbed every square inch of her body. She had cleaned with particular care under her nails, between her toes and anywhere else something might cling. She had also brushed her teeth four times while in the shower, and she'd gone through a litre of mouthwash. But it hadn't helped. What she would have liked would have been to wash her mouth and throat with chlorine.

She cupped her hand in front of her mouth and smelled her own breath. In her head, it still stank.

At the same time, she was improving a little. On Thursday, she had spent three hours in the shower. She'd had it turned up as hot as it went, and in the end her skin had been red and stinging unbearably. Then she had scoured the flat with a dish brush and hot, soapy water. Including the walls. Then she'd showered again. For an hour. She had also showered multiple times yesterday, but today she had only been in the shower for half an hour. Although she'd kept it just as hot as before. Her skin, however, was no longer quite so red.

In hindsight, she couldn't conceive how she had managed to lie in the long grass with Vincent. It was as if her brain had been overloaded in that awful sewage pipe and had shut down her anxieties for a few minutes to ensure she survived. Or perhaps she was stronger than she thought.

But the feelings of disgust had come back before they'd even reached the car. She had torn off her blouse, trousers, shoes and socks and dropped them on the ground. She had yanked a fresh vest out of the bag in the car. She would have preferred a fresh pair of knickers too. Then her teeth had begun to chatter and she'd started shaking uncontrollably, meaning Vincent had to drive. With her sitting next to him, shaking like a leaf in her vest top and pants. As if she were in the worst sort of chauvinistic detective novel. The strong, resourceful man bringing the fragile woman to safety. Half-naked too, as if things weren't already bad enough. It might as well have been a Brian De Palma movie. She hated it. Hated that she had been weak.

It was lucky for Vincent that he'd spent the entire journey talking about the body's nervous system and had refrained from any attempts to be macho. He had explained that both the shaking and the inexplicable fits of crying, as well as the feelings of guilt, were physical and psychological reactions that they could both expect. After all, they had experienced a traumatic event.

Then he'd had to be her lookout so that she could run up to the flat without being seen by anyone in the street.

She thought about Nathalie and suddenly she burst into tears. Fits of crying . . . She had told Vincent about the unforgivable thing she had done. Her biggest sin. How she had let addiction ruin her family and how she had left it. Left Nathalie. Her own child. The thing a mother could never do. And what had Vincent said? He'd talked about atoms.

She looked at her reflection again. Her hair looked like a magpie's nest. She had used washing-up liquid instead of shampoo to make absolutely sure that she got rid of everything. It was that or shear it all off again.

He hadn't been disgusted by her. Or the shameful act she had revealed. Instead, he'd said . . . What was the expression he'd used? That he knew her.

Bloody Vincent.

141

This was a stupid idea. It was a really fucking stupid idea. And he was sweaty to boot. Christer pulled a handkerchief from his pocket and mopped his brow. Bosse was panting at his side, but the dog seemed much more positive about the walk than Christer did. Djurgården was as beautiful as ever, but Christer had trouble appreciating it. The white building with its orange tiled roof and lush garden hove into view ahead of him.

It had been a week since he'd last been. Last Saturday, his visit to the Ulla Winbladh restaurant had ended in disaster. It had all started so well – he had finally dared to tell Lasse, the maître d', that they knew each other. But then he had immediately been overcome by panic. He had pretended to take an urgent call and stumbled out of the place in a rush.

And now he was on his way back again. He might as well have hurled himself off a cliff. He silently prayed to some unspecified divine being that Lasse wouldn't have worked out who he was. That way he could start again. Because good gracious, if only his mother could see him now. She would have had a thing or two to say.

When Bosse recognized the restaurant, he ran over to the bike rack where he had waited last time. Christer guessed he was looking for the water bowl. That was one smart puppy.

'You can wait here,' he said, ruffling the dog's coat. 'I won't be long.'

He entered the restaurant and wondered what to say. He realized that he ought perhaps to have thought that over beforehand. But Lasse caught sight of him almost immediately, removing any possibility of planning.

'Oh,' Lasse said curtly. 'It's you.'

His voice was devoid of emotion. Christer looked down at the floor. It was already going worse than his worst-case scenario.

'Yes, um, I wanted to apologize,' he said, clearing his throat. 'About last time. I . . . was silly. There wasn't really a call. You probably knew that. I didn't mean to cause a scene.'

'I think you owe me an apology, Christer,' said Lasse.

Christer looked up at him in surprise.

'When you legged it, it suddenly became obvious who you were. Same propensity for escape as ever. I waited a long time for an apology for what happened thirty-five years ago. I trusted you, and you let me down completely. It took me a long time to get over that, let me tell you. But after a while I realized I'd never get that apology, so I moved on.'

This was not the direction Christer had intended for the conversation. He was going to apologize, they would laugh at how stupid he'd been, he would reveal who he was, Lasse would be pleased and they would share happy memories. But that idea felt increasingly utopian. He mopped his brow with his handkerchief again.

'What happened . . . How do you mean?' said Christer. 'I don't really know what . . . I only came here because I wanted to . . .'

He fumbled for words.

'Look,' he ended up saying. 'Could we talk in private somewhere? When you're not working?'

Lasse surveyed the restaurant, which had begun to fill with lunching patrons. A few were waiting impatiently to be seated by him.

'I don't think that's necessary,' he said, gesturing to the customers that he was coming.

'Please.'

A pained expression crossed Lasse's face for a split second. Then he looked Christer in the eye.

'OK,' he said. 'Next Saturday. I'm off then. Twelve o'clock in Vasaparken. By the cafe. Don't be late.'

A small butterfly fluttered through Christer's considerable belly – a butterfly that would have horrified his mother. He watched Lasse hurry away to look after his guests. Then Christer returned to Bosse and strolled back towards town. The butterfly stayed with him all the way.

142

Vincent had spread out the various sections of *Dagens Nyheter* on the kitchen table. He was still wearing his dressing gown and couldn't concentrate on the headlines. He had been completely listless all day. His thoughts kept circling back to when he and Mina had been crawling through the pipe. He hadn't known whether they would get out. The only way not to panic completely in the dark had been to suppress his emotions more than he ever had done before. He had shut down that part of his brain. Become a robot. But then – afterwards – the emotions had come back. All at once.

He hadn't been overcome by the shakes like Mina had been in the car. But he kept returning to the realization that they might have died in that sewage pipe. The fantasy in which he suddenly hit his head when the pipe reached a dead end and they were helplessly trapped far below ground wasn't one that would leave him. Every time it appeared, he began to sob uncontrollably. Fortunately, he had thus far managed to avoid doing so in front of the family.

He guessed that the exhaustion he felt was a defence mechanism. His body was doling out the trauma at a pace he could cope with. Last Friday, he had felt fine heading to police headquarters to talk to Gustav, but after that the heavy fatigue had descended on him. Now he was trying to help his body to handle the trauma by activating his rational thoughts again – at least a little. He blew on his coffee. The old coffee maker had been pressed back into service and the coffee was as piping hot as he remembered it.

A good start would be to go through what they had established over the last few weeks. First of all, the four murdered children. Located according to the knight's tour, a classic chess problem by the old cult leader and champion chess player John Wennhagen. The children had been killed in order to spare them earthly suffering – at least according to Gustav.

Everything is suffering; pain purifies. A philosophy of life so drummed into John Wennhagen that he had coded it not only into the Epicura creed, but also his own chess problem. Thus John had come full circle somehow, or so Vincent assumed. He shivered. It was insane. Even to him – and he usually liked patterns. But there was a limit.

He looked around the kitchen to try and reground himself in some degree of normality. Aston had already gone out on his bicycle before it got too hot, and Benjamin was doing something share-related in his room. Rebecka, however, was still at the breakfast table and had started reading the paper. He loved that the kids had nothing against reading the news in print every now and then, and he enjoyed the rustle as she turned the page. Not that he was going to make a show of it . . . If he did, it would probably be the last time she read a newspaper ever. Their relationship wasn't the simplest one at present.

Everything is suffering; pain purifies.

Disgusting. And the police still hadn't caught up with John. He was still out there somewhere. John Wennhagen might start over at any time.

They still hadn't reached checkmate.

Maria was in the garage going through yet more newly arrived orders of ceramic figurines and hand-painted wooden signs. Her business was now doing well enough that she no longer had space for everything in the living room. Maria and Kevin had apparently grasped something about their fellow human beings that Vincent never would.

Kevin.

It had been a while since Maria's entrepreneurial coach had

been in touch. Or at least, as far as Vincent had noticed. On the other hand, Maria was frequently engrossed in her mobile with a permanent smile on her lips. When she was home at all, that was.

He saw that her mobile was lying on the kitchen table, picked it up and spun it around. He had never told Maria about what had happened between him and Ulrika two summers ago. You didn't always have to share everything. Perhaps neither he nor Maria did.

His mind wandered back to John Wennhagen. He seemed to do everything with mathematical precision. And he clearly loved showing off how smart he was. Perhaps it was possible to figure out where he was hiding by going back through John's life?

Something else Vincent needed to figure out was why John had committed these gruesome crimes. Why had he murdered four innocent children? Vincent couldn't understand what drove someone who had seemed fully normal – at least before – to do something like that. There had to be almost incredible levels of conviction, or blind hatred, underpinning it all.

A conviction that would not be subdued by almost being caught. John would probably only grow more careful in future.

Vincent drank his coffee and looked at the phone in his hand. Maria loathed all things technological, and hadn't bothered to set up facial recognition on hers. Purely reflexively, he contemplated what PIN she was likely to have. She had probably gone with an easy one. The most common four-digit PIN codes in the world were 1234, 1111 and 0000. People really ought to know better. Maria had probably gone to more effort than that – if nothing else, in order to avoid a gibe from him. But she wouldn't have tried so hard that the code wouldn't be easy to recall. He entered the number 1. Then he took a stab at 00. And then 4, since it was just below 1.

The display unlocked.

At that moment, a notification of a new text from Kevin flashed up. Vincent's thumb hovered over the message symbol. With one single tap he would have access to everything that his wife and Kevin had written to each other. If he were so inclined, he could also check Messenger and WhatsApp before she returned.

But . . . Hmm. He had asked her to take his word for it when it came to Mina. What kind of person would he be if he didn't do the same thing for her – didn't trust his wife's word?

'What are you doing with Maria's phone?' said Rebecka, who had looked up from her newspaper.

'Nothing,' he said, setting it down. 'Nothing at all.'

He hadn't actually asked Maria about Kevin to her face. He might have hinted. Insinuated. Which she was fully entitled to ignore. But if he decided to ask the question, he had to believe she would tell the truth. Anything else would be devastating to their relationship.

As if Maria could read his mind, she returned from the garage at that very moment clutching a box in her arms. She gave him a look that was difficult to interpret. 'What is it?' she said. 'You look like you're thinking about something.'

He opened his mouth and then closed it.

'No, not a thing,' he said. 'But you really must set a better PIN code for your phone.'

143

Nathalie had been back at Epicura's residential centre since picking up the cash from her father's apartment the Friday before. They hadn't gone back to the horse farm where she had been staying before. Instead, Ines had taken her to Nova. At first, Nathalie had been disappointed since she had helped to renovate the farm and get it spick and span. It had started to feel like home. But really, Nova's retreat was the height of luxury compared with the rather more shabby farm, so she wasn't complaining. It felt like a reward to be there. And the more she thought about it, the more clearly she realized that perhaps that was precisely what it was. After all, she had proven that she was one of them.

When she returned from brushing her teeth in the evening, there was a white cloth bundle waiting for her on the bed. On top of it there was a note.

Change and meet me in the assembly hall
Grandma

Nathalie unfolded the bundle. It was a robe, similar to the one she had once seen Ines wearing. Maybe it was for sleeping in? It was pretty late, after all. But it felt . . . fancier somehow. She took off her trousers and top and pulled the robe over her head. It felt clean. And important. As if something big was about to happen.

She was unsure where the hall was, so it took her a few minutes to find her way through the complex. However eventually she reached a big white room.

Ines was standing in the centre of it next to a stack of mattresses and blankets. Some dozen or so people were standing in a semicircle behind her. Nathalie recognized a few of them, but most were new faces. She couldn't see any of her friends from the horse farm. There was no one with bandages around their hands.

'Welcome, Nathalie!' Ines declared solemnly, extending her arms. 'Today is a special day. You are already one of us. Now it is time for you to shed your skin. Today is the day you step out of the dead shell of your former, discarded life and into a new one. A consummate and colourful life. When you look back on this day, you will regard it as the day when you were truly born.'

Nathalie had no idea how to reply to this. But it sounded important. Stars were dancing around the periphery of her vision – as was often the case nowadays – and they made Grandma glitter.

'Thank you,' Nathalie said in a low voice. 'I would love to be as colourful as you.'

A smile flashed across Ines's face. She took Nathalie's hand and led her to the heap of mattresses. They sat down.

'You've heard me quote our great leader John Wennhagen

497

on many occasions,' said Ines. 'Everything is suffering; pain purifies. But I haven't fully explained what it means. The first part comes from Buddhism. When they say that everything is suffering, they mean that we are suffering unnecessarily because of our wants and desires. We want to buy things we can't afford. We think we'll be happy if we move to a bigger, nicer home. Everyone else on Instagram is having more fun than we are. Each unrealistic dream, each thing that we want but don't need . . . all that creates suffering. The Buddhists believe that in order to dispense with suffering, we must dispense with desire. Are you with me so far?'

Nathalie nodded. This sounded like one of Nova's lectures. Hadn't she been to one of those once? It felt like an eternity ago.

'Here, we do it by creating perspective,' Grandma continued. 'Or as John puts it, pain purifies. You've already experienced what that means. But what do you think the most painful experience in your life was?'

What was she supposed to choose? Once upon a time, she might have said it was the first time her dad's bodyguards scared off a boy she liked. Or when she broke her leg skateboarding. Or when she realized what her mother being dead meant. But now? She shrugged.

'It was when you were born,' said Ines. 'Before that, pain wasn't something that existed in your world. You were safe, warm and cared for. You knew nothing else. But suddenly, out of the blue, you were forced to experience hours of being pushed through a tight canal with heavy pressure from all sides before emerging into a world of light, cold and unfamiliar smells where you could no longer hear your mother's heartbeat. Dreadful. And you had nothing to compare it to – no way to understand your experience. Nothing can compare with the initial pain. So what we are going to do is recreate that memory to enable you to understand who you truly are. Nathalie – you are going to be born again. Please undress.'

498

144

Maria was sitting on the living room floor, packaging ceramic figurines. Vincent wasn't quite sure how the weekend had got away from him – he seemed to have been wandering around in a daze for two days without achieving anything meaningful. It was now half past ten on Sunday evening and the dusk gave Maria's figurines a rather wizard-like appearance. In the golden evening sunshine, they didn't seem so bad after all. Vincent looked at his wife. She had a small smile at the corners of her mouth and her cheeks were slightly rosy. It even sounded as if she were singing to herself.

He needed to ask someone where his wife had gone and who was sitting there on the floor. Unfortunately, it was pretty obvious who had that answer. He had told Mina that he didn't want to know. But that was no longer true.

'Darling,' he said. 'We really must talk about Kevin.'

'You do harp on,' said Maria, sealing a box in tasteful shades of pink and lime green.

She turned around and looked at him.

'Why don't we talk about that Mina instead?' she said. 'That feels much more important.'

'Can't you give that up?' said Vincent, holding out his hands. 'Remember what the therapist said. That's just in your head. And blaming me doesn't change anything. I still want to talk to you about Kevin.'

'Well, he is much easier to get along with than you,' Maria muttered.

Vincent caught sight of Benjamin and interrupted his train of thought. Benjamin was holding an iPad that Vincent assumed showed the latest stock market figures. But his son's brow was deeply furrowed. Apparently none of his investments were going the way he had expected them to.

'Dad, do you have a second?'

Maria pursed her lips and began to pointedly package another ceramic figurine.

'Can it wait a while?' said Vincent. 'Maria and I are talking about Ke— . . . her business.'

But something about his son's body language made him change his mind. Whatever it was, it looked like it couldn't wait. Benjamin angled the iPad so that Vincent could see the display. It wasn't share listings at all – it was Epicura's website.

Vincent glanced towards his son's bedroom and raised an eyebrow along with two fingers in a silent question. Two minutes. He needed two minutes. Benjamin nodded briefly and vanished towards his room.

'Maria,' he said. 'No matter what happens, there's something I want you to know. Can you look at me when I talk to you?'

Maria turned her gaze up from the box. Her eyes were full of reproach and anger, but also tears and sadness.

'I want you to be happy,' he said. 'I'm sorry if I ask too many questions. It's only because I want to understand. But the only thing that matters is that you're . . . if not happy, at least well. Nothing else matters. OK?'

Maria looked at him for a long time. Then she nodded slowly.

'Good,' he said. 'Now I have to go and be a father to a twenty-one-year-old.'

He went to Benjamin's room and closed the door behind him. Benjamin was sitting at his desk staring at the iPad.

'What's so urgent?' said Vincent, sitting down on the bed, which had been made for a change – and not in the usual way by chucking a bedspread across anything and everything on the bed. It had been made properly. Vincent was going to ask whether he ought to be worried, but suddenly he noted how pale Benjamin was.

'I don't know,' said Benjamin with a nod towards the screen. 'It's just . . . a feeling. I spend my days processing figures and statistics from the exchange. I weigh up risks and probabilities against each other and make decisions about investments without having all the necessary information to hand. In the beginning, I read loads of books. Like David Tennant says in *Doctor Who*, books are the best weapons in the world.'

'I didn't know you watched *Doctor Who*.'

Benjamin stared at him.

'I'm your son. Why on earth wouldn't I? And David Tennant is the best actor to have played the role. You know that too. But that wasn't what I wanted to talk about. What was . . .? Yes. My investment decisions. Often I have to go on intuition. I trust my subconscious to capture patterns that it doesn't have time to explain to my conscious mind – instead it just gives me a feeling of what is right.'

Vincent smiled. Benjamin was becoming more and more like him with each passing day. Not that it was something he wanted for his son. Far from it. But as a father, he couldn't help but feel immoderately proud of Benjamin's analytical capabilities.

'That's exactly how it works,' said Vincent. 'You can train your subconscious to make complicated decisions quicker than stopping to think about it. Of course, it requires you to be in similar situations on a regular basis and to get immediate feedback on whether you made the right or the wrong decision. There are so many unknowns when it comes to the markets that the majority of patterns that you think you spot are probably illusions. But I suspect you didn't call me in here to talk about your share portfolio?'

Benjamin shook his head and pointed at the tablet showing Epicura's website.

'I'm trying to say that what we found doesn't feel right. Obviously it all fits together perfectly. You realized that the five victims matched the positions of a knight's tour on a chessboard. The same positions that led us to five words and a hidden message from Nova's father, who was a dab hand at chess. It all fits. And yet . . . there's no way my gut would have let me invest in this on the markets.'

'But in that case, I don't know that . . .' Vincent began before stopping himself.

He realized what Benjamin had said. His insides went cold when he realized the mistake he had made. Five victims. Five words. Their conclusion hadn't been wrong. He had just stopped looking too soon. It wasn't supposed to be five.

He'd had them chasing the wrong murderer.

145

She couldn't breathe. The pressure was too great from all sides for her to be able to defend herself. She couldn't move her arms and legs – she wasn't even sure which way was up and which was down anymore. All she knew was that it was dark and her oxygen was running out.

Ines had begun by wrapping her in blankets so that she felt like a stuffed cabbage roll. At that stage, Nathalie had mostly been giggling – the whole thing felt a bit daft. Then Grandma had explained that Nathalie should lie down on three of the mattresses. The other mattresses would be laid across her so that she was encased between them – like a human hamburger, Nathalie had thought to herself. Or a hot dog.

All she had to do was wriggle out of the mattresses and blankets to symbolize her rebirth. She didn't really understand the point of it. But she didn't feel up to disagreeing.

What Ines hadn't warned her was that after Nathalie was inserted between the mattresses, all the other people in the room would get on top of the pile. Ten adult bodies had suddenly been pressing her downwards into the mattresses.

It had happened quickly and almost squeezed the air out of her. All the fatigue and dizziness had been vanquished, and instead she was filled with adrenaline. The mattress stuffing distributed some of the weight, but it still felt like she was going to be squashed to death. For real.

She realized that she might actually suffocate between these mattresses. She didn't have enough air to scream, and who would hear her? She must not lose consciousness, no matter what happened.

At least if she could get her hands free and claw her way out . . . But the blankets that had been wrapped around her made all such movements impossible. All light had disappeared when the mattresses had been sandwiched together, so she couldn't see anything either.

It was hard to know where her body ended and the blankets began. All she could do was twist her body back and forth and hope that it was enough to move herself – a few millimetres at a time. Or at least she thought she was twisting her body – but she couldn't be sure.

Ines had said something about her finding out who she was between these mattresses. But right now she was just a sensation. Tangible thoughts vanished in the heat and darkness. That sensation was . . . panic. But also . . . resignation.

The adrenaline wasn't going far enough.

She had way too little energy.

And no air.

She was inhaling the same air she had just exhaled. That was when she was able to breathe – her lungs were being flattened by the pressure from on top. She was close to drifting off. Unconsciousness was trying to take her away from there – to make her relax. To make her give up. Perhaps that was OK. She usually gave up, didn't she? When it came to school and friends, she never took the initiative. She just went with the flow of whatever was happening. Why put up a fight? Life was hard enough anyway. So perhaps it didn't matter if she gave up now too. Was that the kind of person she was?

She didn't know.

But it didn't feel quite right.

Because she was . . . she was Nathalie. Nathalie, who lived in Östermalm with her dad and came from a totally deranged family but had decided she was going to be a policewoman when she grew up. Nathalie, who had bodyguards on a day-to-day basis, yet had briefly managed to have a secret boyfriend at school without her dad finding out. Admittedly, all that had been before, but still . . . That had been her too. More than anything, she was Nathalie who knew that pain purified. But you got through it. Sure, she gave up sometimes. But who didn't?

She searched for the outer boundaries of her body, trying to feel where it began and ended between the blankets. It was not straightforward; her thoughts flickered back and forth but she refused to relent. And in the end, she found the contours.

There were her feet, her legs, her tummy, her breasts. Her hands, her arms, her back, her throat, her head.

There was Nathalie.

The one who was going to get out. Nothing else mattered. Not what Dad thought, not what Grandma was doing, not her friends at school. Nothing else mattered anymore.

There was only one thing that really mattered.

She was Nathalie and she was going to get out.

Somewhere she found a strength she hadn't known she possessed.

She screamed with rage in the darkness. The blankets became damp against her lips. And she writhed. She felt herself moving. She screamed and writhed again. Moved. She was going to make it. She was going to win.

A dull sound was audible from beyond. It sounded like voices arguing with each other. At least there was an outside. An outside she was going to reach.

A tendril of light in the darkness above her head. A crack between the mattresses. That meant there was air coming in. She tried to fill her lungs, but the pressure on her body was too much. She tried anyway. The gap was just there.

There was a voice audible through it – clearer now.

'Are you out of your minds? We need her! Have you forgotten why she's here?'

Nathalie growled through gritted teeth and writhed yet again. Her nose and half her face jutted out of the gap. She had been intending to swear at them. But she was beyond all such rational thoughts. She was nothing but pure emotion – pure rage. She used her final strength to explode into a primal howl that would not end.

The pressure against her body eased.

She fell onto the cold concrete floor. Someone sat down next to her and raised her head into their lap. Someone caressed her cheek, gave her love. Showed that everything was fine. She carefully opened her eyes and looked into Nova's.

'Sorry,' Nova said softly. 'I didn't know that Ines was going to do this to you. If I had, I would have forbidden it. I don't want to put you in any danger.'

Nathalie was taking deep breaths. She felt the oxygen pouring into her lungs and spreading through her bloodstream. The dazzling light in the room filled her eyes with tears. She was alive. Newly born into a world she had previously taken for granted. Oh, she was so very, very much alive. She had been so naive before. But not anymore.

'It's OK,' she coughed. Because Grandma had been right. She finally knew who she was. She was Nathalie. Nathalie, who at this very moment felt loved and safe. Received by someone who cared about her, who wouldn't leave her this time.

And that was the only thing that mattered.

'I wish we had more time, but I'm afraid it's run out,' said Nova. 'It's time you knew the truth about your mother.'

146

Vincent could have hit himself. The link to Nova's father had been so well hidden that when they had found the connection he had been content with it. Yet he had stood there at police headquarters exactly two weeks ago explaining the correct lead without understanding it himself.

He wanted to blame the fact that they had been in a hurry – that a child's life had been at stake. But that was no excuse. He was the Master Mentalist. He wasn't allowed to make mistakes like this. If he was going to start being human, then it would have to be some other time.

Vincent went to fetch his notepad from the study.

On the way from Benjamin's room, he passed Maria, who had switched to wrapping pieces of soap. The living room had taken on an unmistakable lavender scent.

She didn't look up as he walked past.

'You say five murders,' he said to Benjamin when he returned. 'And five words.'

'Yes, the fifth "murder" – the one you prevented – completes the quote,' said Benjamin. 'Everything is suffering, pain purifies. There's even a full stop at the end.'

Vincent thumbed through his notepad until he found the beginning of his knight's tour. To the uninitiated, it would have looked like the world's strangest embroidery pattern. But the pattern was a mathematical feat of its own.

Not only was a knight's tour a challenge from the very beginning but Vincent had realized that the murderer's version probably also contained what were known as magical mathematical properties.

The mathematics came with an extra dose of complexity and meant that the killer's knight's tour was symmetrical. The knight moved in such a way that the moves on the chessboard's left-hand side were mirrored in the moves on the right in a pattern of almost perfect regularity and harmony. A pattern like that was incredibly complicated to create. He had only found the first ten steps.

Psychologically, this meant that the killer not only allowed their behaviour to be governed by strict rules, but that those rules had in turn to be governed by their own rules. He suspected the murderer had such a strong need for control that it required medication.

'Dad? Helloooo?' said Benjamin. 'Where did you disappear to in there? We were talking about five murders.'

Vincent blinked hard to bring himself back to reality.

'So we were,' he said. 'Except that there never were five murders. We never knew the exact number. I noted that there was capacity for a maximum of eight murders given the halving intervals between them. That didn't necessarily mean there would be eight – just that there was a ceiling. Obviously we were hoping for fewer. Wilma would have been the fifth. And since we had found a full sentence consisting of five words, everything suggested that Wilma was the last.'

'So . . .' said Benjamin. 'If it wasn't just five . . . Then eight murders also means eight positions on the map.'

Vincent nodded.

'Eight positions on the map. And eight words in the message.'

Benjamin pulled up the Epicurean creed on the computer,

where they had laid out the words in a grid that was eight by eight.

'We never looked at the last three,' said Vincent. 'Because we thought it was over.'

'So, where does the knight go after position number five on the board?' said Benjamin. 'After Wilma?'

Vincent cleared his throat and read from the notebook:

'After position h5 and the word "purifies", we have . . . g7. Second row from the top, penultimate square.'

Benjamin bolded the corresponding word on the grid.

'Then e8 followed by f6.'

Epicurus'	guideline	for	the	**new**	age	is	same
as	for	all	ages:	Allow	only	**the**	anxiety
passing	like	a	comet	a	**star.**	Fast	and
imperceptible.	Life	of	stillness	is	life	that	**purifies.**
Carefully	avoid	all	kinds	of	**pain**	and	desire
nothing,	for	a	life	without	desire	**is**	a
life	fully	freed	from	**suffering,**	and	instead	allows
you	to	enjoy	great	success	in	attaining	**Everything**

'Bloody hell,' said Benjamin, moving out of the way to let Vincent see the screen.

Three new words had been bolded in Epicura's text.

'In the order you gave, that gives us "the new star",' said Benjamin. 'Everything is suffering; pain purifies. The new star.'

Vincent was overcome by a slight dizziness and he held onto the edge of the bed with both hands.

He knew full well what 'the new star' was in Latin. And he guessed that Benjamin did too.

'The message isn't from John,' Vincent murmured.

Just a few weeks ago, he had heard her explain on TV that she lived her life as a Hamiltonian path, never visiting the same point twice. And what was a knight's tour if not such a path?

The old man he had spoken to in custody had even said as much. *Our guiding star*, he had said. Someone who lived with physical pain. Vincent hadn't been listening. He had to say it out loud to himself to make the words true. But he had to stop himself shouting as soon as he opened his mouth.

'A new star,' he said. 'Stella Nova.'

Benjamin looked, if it were possible, even paler.

'It's been Nova all along.'

The Sixth Week

147

Mina found Vincent sitting on one of the benches close to the fountain in Kungsträdgården. The fountain comprised a recessed basin into which blossoms from the surrounding trees had fallen and were floating about along with ice-cream wrappers and discarded napkins. No matter how much the city's sanitation department tried to keep the pool clean, it was a losing battle. She suspected that there was probably the odd used needle at the bottom too. Despite all that, Kungsträdgården was a beautiful place. Above all, the benches under the trees were shaded.

The wooden seat next to Vincent was somewhat darker than the rest of the bench, and smelled faintly of antiseptic. He must have wiped it down just before she arrived. Not that he would ever mention that, of course. Vincent wore a jellyfish print short-sleeved shirt and shorts. He looked like a tourist.

'Have you changed your style?' she said in surprise, taking a seat. 'I thought you weren't a shorts guy?'

'That pipe we crawled through made me revise my fashion choices,' he said. 'I felt I needed something a little . . . looser. I've had enough of tight things for . . . some time to come. But don't you like the shorts? Maybe you're right.'

He glanced at the jellyfish on his chest.

'Perhaps not one of my finest ideas. I'll have to do it your way instead – just a vest top.'

'Absolutely not,' she said. 'Men aren't allowed to wear vests in the city. Anyway, a nod to a formal style suits you.'

Vincent looked sidelong at her.

'Lucky you qualified your statement there. Otherwise I would have been obliged to disclose that I cleaned the bench using water from the fountain.'

She resisted the impulse to stand up. He must be joking. He

would never do such a thing. Right? The effort of remaining in her seat made her sweat at the armpits, which was the worst thing in the world. Not until she saw that the bin next to the bench was stuffed with wet wipes did her breathing return to normal.

'So, what did we need to talk about?' she said, trying to sound unaffected, and failing completely.

The corners of Vincent's mouth twitched.

She was going to give it to him good. The bit about the water from the fountain definitely merited revenge. Preferably when he was least expecting it.

'Maybe I should have called you last night,' he said, immediately turning serious. 'But it was late. And I don't think there would have been anything we could do.'

'I honestly have no idea what you're talking about. Have you found another Lego model by some water? Is that why we're here? By the fountain?'

Vincent shook his head and rummaged around in his bag.

'Nova's water theory was a red herring,' he said. 'It was a thought she planted in order to get you to devote your energy to the wrong things. It's my fault. I've made a terrible mistake.'

He pulled out a folded piece of paper and handed it to her.

'You know the hidden quote from Nova's father?' he said. 'The one found in the Epicurean creed? We assumed he was the killer because he'd written it.'

'But?'

'I stopped looking too soon. There was more. As it happens, I don't think John wrote that text. It was another red herring. Misdirection, as we call it in the magic business.'

She unfolded the paper. It was the Epicura statement with the words divided across sixty-four squares, with eight words marked in bold.

'We only read the first five words of the knight's tour,' he said. 'As far as the kidnapping of Wilma. But there has to be eight for it to be complete.'

'Yes, you said something about the killer only being able to make it to eight because of the time between each murder,' Mina said with a nod.

He pointed to the last three words.

'The . . . new . . . star,' she read.

It took a second. Then she understood.

'Nova,' she said, staring at Vincent.

'Exactly. Nova,' he said, confirming her suspicions. 'She's been the brains behind it all.'

A howl of disappointment came from the far side of the basin where a parent had managed to catch a child on its way into the water at the very last moment.

'Not just Nova,' she said. 'She's had the whole of Epicura at her beck and call.'

Vincent nodded.

'I would imagine that not everyone there is involved,' he said. 'The majority of the people who have joined her have probably done nothing worse than give her their cash. But she presumably has an inner circle. Probably the same people that you've had in the cells since you freed Wilma. No wonder they're not saying anything. These are people who have been with Nova from the very start. They trust her, just as much as she trusts them to do what she needs them to.'

Mina slumped on the bench. Nova's innermost circle. She had heard about that from far too close up.

'Like my mother,' she said. 'Like Ines.'

But Ines hadn't been there with the others at the horse farm when they'd picked up Wilma. There was a chance that her mother didn't know anything. Albeit a microscopic chance.

'We almost had her,' said Mina. 'At the stable. It must have been Nova in that car when we thought it was John. Fucking hell. So what do we do now? Head out to Epicura's residential centre to bring her in?'

'I don't think she's there anymore,' said Vincent. 'John Wennhagen was a red herring, but Nova must have realized it wouldn't take long for us to realize it was her. After all, she did sign the message. If it had been me, I would have got the hell out of that place the second I could. But there's something else, too. You know how I've said that the killer – Nova, I mean – was halving the time between each abduction? If we hadn't stopped her then it would have been two weeks between Wilma and the next murder, which would have been the sixth. After that it would only have been a week until the seventh, and just half a week before the eighth and final killing. But like I said, we stopped them. You've apprehended the members who were able to help her out with the kids. That's why I think she's going to go straight to the finale. The eighth move on the chessboard. And according to her own rules, that will be in half a week.'

The child on the far side of the fountain was heading into the water again, and howled yet again when prevented from doing so by its parents. Mina was tempted to shout at them to let the child have its swim so she could think in peace and quiet.

'Hang on,' she said. 'We saved Wilma last Thursday. Today's Monday. It's been over seventy-two hours.'

'Exactly,' Vincent said, turning to her.

She had never seen him so grave.

'Nova's finale will take place this afternoon,' he said.

The panic galloped through her whole body.

'Nathalie,' she said. 'I have to fetch Nathalie.'

Her hand was shaking so much that she was almost unable to pull her phone from her pocket. Then she dialled the number for Nathalie's father. It couldn't be helped.

'Hi, it's me,' she said, interrupting him as soon as he picked up. 'You have to go to Epicura and pick up Nathalie. And you have to do it now. I'll send you the address. I could go there with blue flashing lights, but by the time I get down to the station and requisition a car it will have been too long. It's time we don't have. Break every law of the road. Or take a helicopter. But she has to be brought to safety.'

She hung up before he had time to reply.

She had never dared to talk to him like that before. Never. Not in all the years they had lived together had she told him what to do. Let alone given him orders. It would presumably have consequences. But what choice did she have?

She opened the GPS tracker app and bit her lower lip hard as it searched for the transmitter in Nathalie's backpack. It was taking a long time for the app to find where Nathalie was. Much too long. In the end, it gave up. Transmitter inactive, it said. Please check batteries.

148

Vincent was rummaging through his bag again. He pulled out his map and unfolded it on his lap. Using a ruler, he had drawn the eight steps of Nova's knight's tour onto the map of Stockholm. It led to the end of her message.

'Look,' he said to Mina, pointing. 'The word "star" has the same position as this square on the chess board, f6. It's the eighth and final move. On the map, it's in the centre of Östermalm. There's nothing there but buildings – there aren't any parks or watercourses. But somewhere in that neighbourhood is where Nova's finale is going to take place.'

Mina scrutinized the map while clutching her phone so that she could see it constantly. The sun had begun to climb high into the sky, forcing her to shade the screen with her hand.

'Östermalmstorg is in the same square,' she said. 'I suppose it's not a park, but it is a big open area. And the church right by it is also in the same square. Seems to me that a cemetery would suit Nova down to the ground.'

Vincent glanced at Mina. She was apparently doing her best to be calm and collected, and he admired her for it. But she was blinking a little too hard and a little too often. Her movements had also become jerky in that slightly strained way that gave away that the diaphragm had contracted. Mina was close to breaking point. He so desperately wanted to help her, but he didn't know how.

'I'm not sure that Nova wants to be quite as visible as she would be in a square or at a church,' he said. 'She presumably knows that we're on her trail. If I were Nova, I'd want to be discreet. Almost all the other buildings in this square are residential. So it's possible she's at the home of an Epicura member. We may need to start knocking on doors. But there's also . . . this.'

In the top corner of the square there was a building that was a different shape from all the others. 'Östra Real upper secondary school,' said Mina, running a finger across the square of the map. 'That's where I spent my sixth form years.'

'A happy time?'

'If you really must know, I wasn't quite so . . . sensitive back then. Albeit sensitive enough to be the class weirdo. I remember one time in my first year there when the lads amused themselves by sticking a bunch of Post-its with a circle on them all over my locker and on the lock itself. I didn't get it at first. Then someone explained that it meant that someone had rubbed their dick against the lock.'

Vincent laughed. Then he saw how unhappy Mina looked.

'Sorry,' he said. 'It was a little unexpected, that's all.'

'They were probably just kidding,' she said. 'They wouldn't have dared to do it for real. But after that, I always wore plastic gloves when opening my locker.'

She met his gaze, almost defiantly. He saw the sparkle of tears in her eyes. But he also saw the struggle in them – her refusal to give in to anyone. It was probably what had made her classmates play such a coarse joke on her. She might have been the weird one, but she couldn't be put down. Because she was Mina. Always sincere, with fire in her eyes and chapped hands.

'Anyway, the school will be closed for the summer,' she said. 'So Nova is unlikely to be there. We'll have to call Julia and see how many people she can round up to start doing door-to-doors around there.'

'I hope your tormentors all failed their final assessments,' he said. 'But you're probably right about the school. The only times that schools open in the summer are when – like Aston's school – they earn a little extra cash by hosting conferences while the pupils are . . .'

He stopped speaking.

They stared at each other.

Mina still had her phone in her hand. She quickly called Christer and put him on speakerphone. Christer picked up almost immediately. He sounded slightly out of breath.

'Christer, are you there?' said Mina.

'Just a second,' said Christer. 'Bosse and I are just, we're . . . wait . . . Bosse, leave that lady's dog alone!'

'Christer,' Mina said.

'I must apologize,' said Christer, clearly not speaking to Mina. 'He only wanted to say hello, he doesn't usually . . . Certainly. Not a bitch you say? No, no, I understand . . .'

'Christer,' Mina said, a little louder.

'I'm here.'

'I just needed to check something.'

'What's that?'

'Please can you find out whether Östra Real has any conference bookings this week?' said Vincent. 'Preferably right away . . .'

'And Vincent's there too. Hello, hello. No problem – as soon as I get back to base and fill Bosse's bowl.'

'This is more important,' said Mina. 'Östra Real first, then Bosse.'

Silence descended. Vincent could have sworn that both Christer and Bosse were glaring at them down the line.

'Sorry, Bosse,' Vincent said. 'Your master will get you some extra tasty water after. Christer, we wouldn't ask if it wasn't urgent. You know that.'

'I'm on it,' said Christer. 'I'll call you straight back.'

Mina ended the call and started up the GPS tracking app again. The transmitter hadn't given up the ghost completely. The circle on the map that the app was searching was now smaller, but it still lacked focus. The only thing they could see was that Nathalie didn't seem to be at the Epicura farm any longer. Just as Vincent had suspected.

'Do you think Nova is going to carry out the final act herself?' she said. 'We've brought in everyone we think was behind the previous abductions, so she may not have anyone left to help her.'

Vincent surveyed the fountain. The tourists in Kungsträdgården were eating ice cream, taking selfies and swigging soft drinks. Groups of teenagers were sitting on the ground doing the things teenagers did when on their summer holidays. In a few years' time, Aston might be one of them. But Lilly, William, Dexter and Ossian would never experience that. For them, everything was already over. And what for? He still didn't understand what Nova was trying to achieve. But he was certain that she wasn't done.

'I don't think the eighth square on the chessboard is as simple as a kidnapping,' he said. 'After all, she's put her own name to it. It will be something else. The final position. The endgame. I think she'll be there in the flesh.'

Mina's phone rang and she put it on speakerphone again.

'I don't know why you didn't call them yourself,' Christer said on the line. 'It was easy to get hold of them. They've only got one booking this week – it's today.'

A notification appeared on screen as Christer spoke. The GPS transmitter had apparently started working again. The app had located Mina's daughter. She held up her phone so that Vincent could see the map on the display. Nathalie was in central Stockholm.

'Funnily enough, we know the outfit hiring the place,' Christer added as Mina zoomed in on the map. 'Epicura are holding a full-day course there: eighty people. Right, I really must see to Bosse, whatever you say.'

Christer hung up. At the same time, Vincent shaded the phone with his hand to get a better view. Mina had zoomed in the map in the tracking app so close that every building was visible. There was no doubt about it. Nathalie was at Östra Real.

Despite the fact that the sun had climbed even higher into the sky and it had to be at least twenty-seven degrees Celsius, Vincent felt a chill down his spine. He hugged himself.

'Everything is suffering; pain purifies,' he said. 'My God. You know how John built that bunker as a death trap? And what Beata Ljung told us about destructive cults? I think Nova is going to follow her father's words to their logical conclusion. Her finale isn't just one murder. There are eighty people. And Nathalie. Nova's going to kill them all.'

149

Vincent feels more powerless than ever before. He wants to help Mina – part of him has to get help for her. But he doesn't know what he should do. Right now, he is utterly useless. Mina gets up from the bench and at the same moment a message arrives on her phone.

'Is that Christer again?' he asks.

Mina stops mid-movement, half-standing. She stares at the screen. The colour has drained from her face.

'Nova,' she says, handing him the phone so he can read it.

Hello Mina

I look forward to seeing you today.

However, I'm afraid you have a small problem.

You can either save your mother or your daughter. But you won't have time to save both.

What do you choose? What's your next move?

See you soon.

Nova

'What should I do?' says Mina. 'I don't even understand what she means. What does she mean by "choose" and "next move"?'

Vincent rereads the message. Something about it bothers him. But there's no time to go into that.

'Forget about it,' he says. 'She just wants to buy time by confusing you. The best thing for her is if she can make you hesitate, so don't do that. Go to Östra Real and find Nathalie. Save them all. When it comes to dealing with Epicura and catching Nova, you don't need me. You need your colleagues. People who know what the procedure is. I'll only be in the way.

It's better for me to focus on understanding Nova's message. You're right that it's hiding something. She's never this straight-forward. But be careful. She'll be there. And we don't know what surprises she will have in store.'

'I'll try and get hold of Nathalie's father again,' says Mina. 'He has resources.'

Vincent nods.

'Go now.'

'This is going to be exciting,' says Nova.

Nathalie can't remember having seen Nova's gaze look so fierce before. She looks around the room. Resplendent is a word that springs to mind, although she's not quite sure what it means.

'Why are we here?' she says. 'Instead of with the others?'

She can't really understand why they had to split up. She would have preferred them to all be together, the others and Nova. Together with the people who actually understand her.

'They're going on their own journey,' says Nova with a smile. 'I was planning to go with them, but I've changed my mind. I've realized I'm not at all done. They'll have to go ahead of me.'

'OK, but why are we in this room?'

'We're here because I've given your mother a chance to pick you up before it's time for me to . . . start over.'

The words are not altogether comprehensible, but Nathalie has grown accustomed to this. That's just how Nova is – a little mysterious. She looks at the wooden door as if she might be able to force it open. Her mother. She still hasn't got over the fact that her mother is alive. A month ago, she didn't even know that she had a grandmother, and yesterday Nova told her that she had a mother. A mother who clearly hadn't wanted to contact her throughout her childhood. Even though she was apparently a cop.

That was Nathalie's plans for the future up in smoke.

She tries to recollect the memories she thinks she has of her mother. The memories that she isn't even certain are real . . . Perhaps they are nothing but dreams. The smell, the voice, the laughter. She doesn't want her mother to come and get her.

Right now, she hates her mother more than anything else. And her dad can go to hell – how dare he not tell her anything about her mother? Nova is the only one to have taken care of her properly and seen her for who she is. Nova is the only one who has never lied to her – unlike the rest of the world. If it was up to Nathalie, she would stay with Nova forever. Nova is the only mother she needs.

Mina walks quickly towards the nearest palatial brown-brick building. She hasn't been there in years. It's a building she hoped she would never have cause to visit again. There is no one to be seen in the large space in front of Östra Real. She glances down at her phone. The signal from Nathalie's GPS tracker is still coming in loud and clear. She is inside the school building. Mina doesn't give a damn what Ines is playing at, but Nathalie . . . She has to find her daughter.

Adam and Peder are on her tail in full police gear. There is still a faint blue tinge to Peder's beard. She called the team en route and Adam and Peder reached the school at the same time she did. Julia and Ruben aren't far behind, but Mina doesn't have time to wait for them. And Nathalie's father still isn't picking up. There just isn't time.

You won't have time to save both.

'Here,' says Adam, chucking a radio to her. 'So that we can stay in contact.'

Aware that she is acting out every cinematic cliché in world history, she runs up the steps to the big main door, alone. Without adequate backup. But if Vincent is right, Epicura's worst enemies are themselves.

She opens the light brown wooden door, her two colleagues behind her.

'Where are they? Which room?' she asks.

Beyond the door they find a broad black stone staircase. It's all too familiar. On too many occasions she stood at its foot wondering whether to turn on her heel and go home. The air is static; the place is as hot as a sauna. Peder mops sweat from his brow. Then he quickly checks the information board inside the door showing where all the halls and rooms are located.

'They've booked the assembly hall,' he says, pointing upstairs. 'Two storeys up.'

Mina checks the app again.

'Nathalie isn't there,' she says. 'She's in a classroom.' Without waiting to hear what Peder or Adam have to say, she runs up the stairs and down a corridor – checking her phone constantly. Nathalie is in the room at the far end. The old wooden classroom doors look sturdy. She won't be able to get in if the people on the other side don't want her to. But hopefully Nova doesn't know they're already there. She runs faster.

Nova is standing by the window. She frowns.

'What's the matter?' says Nathalie.

'I thought I'd be able to see the main entrance from here,' says Nova. 'But the room's at the wrong angle. It would have been good to see how many of them are coming.'

Nova sits down with Nathalie again and beams her warm smile. She strokes Nathalie's hair.

'I'm sorry you have to wait like this,' she says. 'I know you would have preferred to stay at the farm. But you know what Epicureanism says: live your life so that you don't cause waves. Anyway, we won't be here long.'

Nathalie needs something to eat. Or drink. She's so hungry that her tummy aches. Her tongue is sticking to the top of her mouth. It's hard to think when she's this hungry. But Nova's gaze is warm, and Nathalie can tell everything is good. Even though she doesn't understand what's going on, she knows that she can trust Nova – that Nova will take care of her.

'If you're going somewhere then can't I come with you?' says Nathalie. 'There's no one but you who cares about me.'

Nova smiles and pulls a bottle out of a cool bag.

'You'll be joining your friends from Epicura soon,' she says, setting down the bottle and a glass on the table. 'Monica, Karl, everyone you know. And Ines, of course. You'll soon be with them again.'

The bottle looks like it contains iced tea, or maybe a cordial. Finally – something to drink. Nathalie reaches gratefully for the bottle, but Nova pushes her hand away.

'We'll save this for in a little bit,' she says.

That fierce look is back in her eyes.

'If it turns out it's not your mother who shows up.'

Vincent can't let go of Nova's message to Mina. There's something strange about the choice of words. Obviously it's intentional and in order to confuse them, but it's better for him to ponder that rather than Mina. The situation at Östra Real requires her full attention. After all, it is her daughter. He isn't at all sure he'd be able to maintain the same focus as Mina has if Aston were in danger like this.

What is it about that text message? If there's one thing he's learned, it's that Nova likes to leave clues. Fake ones *and* real ones. He needs to get to the bottom of which kind this message is.

You won't have time to save both, she wrote. *What do you choose? What's your next move?*

At first glance, Nova's question seems to relate to whom Mina will choose to save. Nathalie or Ines. But purely grammatically, that isn't what Nova is asking. 'What do you choose?' is really referring to the next question posed – what Mina's 'next move' will be. That's the choice that Nova is offering.

To make a move – or not.

Two possibilities.

Two people to save.

Make a move – don't make a move.

Nathalie – Ines.

He stands up straight when he realizes what it means.

'How long do we have to wait?' Nathalie says with a sigh.

Nova checks her wristwatch.

'Not much longer,' she says. 'They should have figured it out by now. I made the booking in Epicura's name. Some of them are likely to be in the building already. I would guess your mother is hunting for the room as we speak. So either someone is about to turn up – or they won't at all.'

As usual, Nathalie understands nothing. But she can no longer bring herself to ask. In addition to being hungry and thirsty, she's also bored. Having Nova to herself for this long is unique – she knows that. It almost feels like a sin not to treasure every last second of it. But truth be told, she'd prefer to take a nap. That might make her tummy hurt less. Surely she can at least have a drink? She reaches for the juice again, but again Nova moves it beyond her reach.

'I'm parched,' Nathalie says, standing up.

'Then I'll go and get you some water instead. I'm afraid you'll have to stay here,' Nova says, her gaze making Nathalie sit back down.

Nova's eyes are no longer warm and smiling. They are made of cold steel. The love that Nathalie felt before is suddenly gone.

Nathalie doesn't want to be here any longer. She really doesn't want to be here. But she knows that she doesn't have enough strength to stand up again.

'You're my insurance policy,' says Nova. 'If anything goes wrong. And you'll get your juice soon – don't you worry about that.'

Nathalie fidgets. Suddenly, she's no longer thirsty. It sounds as if there's someone running beneath them. The footsteps get close, then they turn and disappear.

'What do you mean insurance?' she says. 'What's happening?'

Nova merely smiles in reply. But the smile no longer reaches her eyes. Nathalie pushes her chair backwards and away from Nova.

Mina reaches the end of the corridor. She suddenly feels very, very alone with her fear. Vincent isn't there with her, and her febrile calls to Nathalie's father have remained unanswered. Eventually, she leaves him a voicemail message. Now she has to focus. Now she has to save her daughter.

The doors don't match with the location of the GPS pin in the app. Shit, shit, shit. Her daughter isn't on this floor. She runs back to the stairs, where Adam seems to be talking to Julia on speakerphone.

Sweat drips from Mina's nose but she doesn't have time to worry about that. Why on earth did they build these fucking stupid long corridors?

'Just how far away are you?' Adam says into the phone while

exchanging a glance with Peder, who is standing impatiently at his side. 'We need you guys here, *now*.'

She passes them, climbs another flight of stairs and ducks into the corridor on the next floor. She runs more quietly than last time. Nova is probably in the assembly hall with the others, but it's not certain. At the far end of the corridor is classroom A311. The famous one with the mural by Georg Pauli. She reaches the classroom and puts her hand on the wooden door as she catches her breath.

She checks the app. It's a match. She's in the right place.

Nathalie is on the other side of the door.

She's about to see her daughter. A daughter who has no idea who Mina is. She can't screw things up now.

Suddenly her communications radio crackles. She quickly backs away from the door and hopes that whoever is on the other side didn't hear anything.

'Mina, we just took a look through the door,' Adam says on the radio. 'They all seem to be here. Must be everyone in Epicura. And it really does look like they're having a conference.'

She frowns. Everyone from Epicura. That means Ines must be here too. Odd that it was so easy to find her. Mina thought it would be hard, given Nova's text message.

You won't have time to save both.

Something must be wrong.

She can feel it in her whole body. But she has no idea what it might be.

'What are they doing right now?' she asks.

'Coffee break. But I can't see any thermoses. Looks like they're pouring some juice or something into glasses. Real clean-living people.'

Ice-cold sweat pours down Mina's spine. The chill of it makes her gasp. She knows what's wrong.

Nova is pacing back and forth across the room. This is not a Nova that Nathalie has seen before. Nova usually reminds her of a doe. But right now she is a she-wolf.

'I'm getting sick of this,' Nova says. 'Am I really the only one who is prepared to play this game to its conclusion?'

525

She turns towards Nathalie, her gaze thunderously dark. Nathalie backs away.

'Your mother interrupted me,' she says. 'I had three to go. Four with Wilma. Only once that was done would I have respite from all pain. But I only managed to do half. So now I have to start over. Well, not immediately. I have to stay under the radar until people have tired of this and forgotten. But then.'

Quick footsteps are audible in the corridor outside. There is a crackle and then the footsteps disappear again.

'And it's your mother's fault,' Nova continues. 'Hers and Vincent Walder's. I tried to trip Vincent up, but it didn't work. Which is why we're here. But I'm tired of this. We've been here an hour and no one has come. We're done. You're going to join Epicura. You did say you were thirsty.'

Mina presses the radio to her lips so that she can whisper into it. A part of her registers that she is pressing her mouth to the same surface that was just in Adam's warm hand. The thought makes her nauseous. But they mustn't hear her on the other side of the door.

'You've got to stop them from drinking,' she whispers into the radio. 'Tip over the table. Anything. Vincent said Nova's going to kill them all. It's not juice. It's poison. I'll be there as soon as I can.'

'Shit,' Adam says. 'Something's happening. We're going in.'

They're cut off. She puts the radio down on the floor and takes another look at the app. Whatever is happening in the hall, she is too far away to be able to help.

No one has moved behind the door. Hopefully, they haven't heard Mina. She takes a deep breath, opens the door to classroom A311 and goes in to her daughter.

What's your next move?

Vincent understands. Nathalie and Ines are in two different places. That is what the message means.

Nova is someone who picks and chooses every one of her words. Everything means something. It is no coincidence that she uses the word 'way'.

And he knows exactly which way she is referring to.

He closes his eyes and tries to picture the chat show with Tilde de Paula Eby. It feels like an eternity since he watched it. He can't recall the memory at once – clearly he didn't classify it as sufficiently important when storing it in his memory. He switches strategy and starts with the sensation of sitting on the sofa at home in his living room. He can feel its soft velvet against his back. Then he combines that feeling with the aural memory of Maria's voice saying 'woo-woo' next to him.

This is enough to activate his visual memory of the TV programme. It becomes almost as clear as if he were watching the show again.

Nova and Ines are there, sitting on the studio sofa. They're talking about pain. Tilde asks what Nova does to avoid bitterness after the accident that has left its mark on her for life.

'Hamiltonian paths,' Nova replies. 'It's a mathematical concept that refers to a way of moving between points in a geometric shape in such a way that you only visit each point once. I try to live my life the same way.'

He heard the words, but he didn't understand that Nova meant several different things at the same time. She wasn't just referring to the fact that she didn't want to dwell on old memories. She was also quite literal in her statement that she moved along a specific, mathematical path.

Vincent unfolds the map on the park bench again. The sun is reflected from the paper, almost blinding him. He has already drawn in the first eight points in the knight's tour, leading to Östra Real. For each new move of the knight, there are several possible squares on the board it may reach, but only one that is the right one. That is true for every move. No wonder people use computers to calculate this kind of thing.

He puts his finger on the eighth position. Östra Real. The word 'star'. He's already worked out ten positions, but he may as well be certain. He applies Warnsdorff's rule of going to the position with the least possible new positions to move to. That takes him to square e8 at the KTH Royal Institute of Technology. He tries not to let the adrenaline coursing through his body affect him. All it does is negatively impact his rational thinking.

527

This is going to take time. Each new step he takes on the map may lead him to a dead end one, five or even ten moves later. Each time that happens, he has to back up and start over. But time is something Mina doesn't have.

What's your next move?

There are still fifty-five squares left on the map before Nova's knight's tour reaches its conclusion. Before Nova stops moving between the points. One of the squares is the last one. One of them is the end of the path.

He just has to find out which one.

The classroom looks exactly as Mina remembers it. The white desks and chairs look almost ghostly in the sunlight streaming through the windows. The figures in the greenery of the mural are in the same poses she remembers them being in.

The room is also completely deserted.

At first, she thinks Nathalie is hiding somewhere, but there is nowhere to hide. There's something lying on one of the desks. It is the only thing that shows someone has been here.

A backpack.

Mina hasn't seen that particular bag in two years, but there is no doubt that it is Nathalie's.

She runs over to it. A folded sheet of A4 is positioned on top of it. When she reads what it says, she stops breathing.

Hello again, Mina. Smart move putting a tracker in the rucksack. All it needed were new batteries. I guessed you would choose your daughter over your mother. Right choice. That's exactly what my father did too. Unfortunately it didn't help then, and it won't help this time either. While you are reading this, your mother is drinking poison downstairs. And you are much too far away to be able to help Nathalie, just as you have been for many years. Check and mate. She's mine now.

Nova

She gasps for air, but panic means she's unable to draw any

into her lungs. Her arms and legs no longer feel like hers. Nathalie. The periphery of her vision begins to flicker as the room starts to spin. She has to save Nathalie. But she can't go anywhere. She tries to support herself against the table, but it seems to be a mile off. She needs to be there for Natti. And she knows she's failed.

The fireworks in front of her eyes take over and she can feel herself falling. There's sudden pain in her arm. She must have hit herself on one of the chairs on her way down. Then she lands on the floor and room A311 disappears along with the rest of the world.

Adam can hear a host of agitated voices from inside the assembly hall. Whatever Nova has planned, it doesn't seem to be going completely painlessly. Julia and Ruben are still not there, but there's no time to wait for them. He needs to act. He nods to Peder to make sure his colleague is on board, then they burst through the doors.

'Police!' he shouts at the crowd inside. 'Stop this minute! Whatever you're doing! Nobody moves!'

He sees two things at once. The first is that there appears to be a fight going on between members of Epicura. They don't care about him and Peder. Or they haven't noticed them amid the shouting and chaos. A young woman is on her knees by the table crying hysterically. Next to her there is a man lying on the floor, his body shaking with convulsions. There is an incredibly pungent smell in the room. Urine?

'We won't drink it!' bellows a man standing in a group of seven or eight.

A young man, barely more than a teenager, steps forward and strikes a blow to the knees of the nearest person using a baseball bat. The man screams and falls down over several other bodies already prostrate on the floor. He roars with pain, clutching his knees. The bodies underneath him don't move.

'You will drink,' says the young man, waving the bat at the group. 'Everybody will drink. Pain purifies.'

By the table there is a row of people intoning something in low voices.

529

'Everything is suffering; pain purifies,' he hears them saying over and over again as they receive plastic cups and pass them on to others.

The crying woman gets to her feet and tries to swipe away their cups, but she staggers and they manage to put a cup to her mouth.

The second thing that Adam sees is the pistol in the hand of a stocky woman in her sixties wearing a purple coat. The gun is aimed at a group who have refused to take cups, but now it swings around to point at him and Peder. She, at any rate, seems to have spotted them.

'No, *you* are the ones who should not move,' she says.

Adam stops, his hand just above his service weapon. He dare not draw it. From the corner of his eye, he sees that Peder is in the same situation.

'Nova said you might show up,' she says. 'So this is loaded. Place your weapons on the floor. Slowly. You first.'

She nods at Peder.

Adam notices two of the people by the table fall to the floor, clawing at their throats. One man who has refused to drink shouts the name of one of them and tries to make his way over to them, but others grab him by the arms and bring a cup to his mouth.

The older woman doesn't take her eyes off Adam and Peder. She nods at Peder again and he pulls out his gun using three fingers, keeping his movements clear as he lays it down.

'Your turn,' she says, waving her gun at Adam.

Adam uses the same three-fingered grip as Peder did. The woman is calm and collected. She's hardly going to fire her weapon out of nervousness, but he doesn't want her to misinterpret any of his movements so he slowly lays the pistol on the floor next to him.

The pungent smell intensifies as more people wet themselves as they lie on the floor twitching spasmodically. Adam tries to breathe through his mouth. The woman mentioned Nova, but he can't see her anywhere.

'Stand over there by the wall,' says the woman, gesturing with the muzzle of her gun. 'Where you won't get in our way until we're done.'

She raises her voice and shouts to someone further back in the room.

'Monica! Are you going to deal with the rest?'

'Of course,' a woman by the refreshments table replies. 'It's going to take a while, but we shouldn't have any problems. Karl?'

A tall, blond-haired man who looks very fit steps up to the woman's side and hands her a spring baton, a huge smile across his face.

'Remember Nova's promise,' Monica says loudly to the assembled Epicureans. 'You'll finally be freed from your pain. You'll finally get your reward. And in the next existence *we* will be kings and queens as thanks for what we have endured here. I can understand if you are frightened. But fear is an illusion. Come and drink; there is enough for everyone.'

Some of the members glance at the baton. And at Karl. Then at the gun being pointed at Adam. And then they make for the refreshments table.

'Don't do this,' Peder says to the woman in the purple coat. 'You're wrong! Life isn't just suffering.'

'You two are a nuisance,' says the woman, waving the gun around slightly. 'The plans for this have been in place for many years. But we had to rush it all because of you. It's not ideal, but it will have to do.'

'But you can't just kill everyone,' says Peder, taking a step forward. 'It's absolutely insane.'

Adam stares at the patches of blue in Peder's beard. The periphery of his vision flickers. Adrenaline is starting to give him tunnel vision. That won't do. He screws his eyes up tightly a few times. He has to be alert – has to be ready for anything. Peder takes another step forward and Adam tenses his whole body.

'We're not killing anyone,' says the short woman, taking a step back as she raises the pistol towards Peder's face. 'We're just taking the next step. Everyone is here of their own free will, but they're a little confused by it all. And you can understand that – this is an important decision.'

She extends the arm not brandishing the gun.

531

'Everything is suffering; pain purifies!' she cries out.

'Everything is suffering; pain purifies,' comes the resounding response from everyone in the room.

The woman smiles.

'Don't make the mistake of thinking I won't use this,' she says, nodding at the weapon. 'I'll do whatever it takes. I'm only going to be in this existence for another minute or so.'

'But there's so much you'll miss out on,' says Peder.

His voice sounds desperate now. Adam can understand – Peder wants to save them all. Peder with his blue beard who wants the best for everyone. But it won't work. In fact, it's already too late. There must be twenty people on the floor. Adam knows he'll never forget this moment – when they were forced to watch Nova murder all who believed in her.

'I'll show you what I mean,' says Peder.

Amazingly, he is smiling in the midst of all this horror.

'I've got a video of the triplets singing along to Mellon,' he says, a smile still on his face.

His hand moves towards his back pocket.

'With Anis Don Demina. If you see them, you'll understand—'

The woman fires the gun. In the hall, the shot sounds like a star exploding.

Peder recoils backwards as if attached to an elastic band.

His body smashes against the wall.

Someone screams loudly.

It may be Adam.

150

Mina jumped. She knew exactly what sound had roused her. A gunshot. She got to her feet, the reality of what Nova had written in her note beginning to penetrate her consciousness. She ran out of the classroom but she was still unsteady on her feet, hitting a couple of chairs as she went.

Downstairs, Nova had written. Her mother was downstairs. In the assembly hall. Was Natti there too? Nova's approach to the game was confusing and Mina didn't understand everything.

The corridor seemed to extend to an infinite length before she reached the stairs. She ran down, taking big leaps. Halfway down she almost fell, but managed to stop herself by grabbing hold of the banister. Her heart was pounding hard in her breast, and she forced herself to take the final steps with more composure.

As she approached the hall, she heard screams and raised voices through the half-closed door. She carefully nudged the door open to peek inside and took in the situation. It smelled terrible – like the world's biggest cat litter tray. Adam had his service weapon drawn and aimed at a group of people with their hands in the air. Others were lying on the floor. Most of them weren't moving. Some seemed to be in pain and were writhing. But whatever it was they had done in there, it seemed to have hit the buffers. An old woman in a purple coat was sitting on the floor with her arms behind her back. Someone – Adam or Peder – had put handcuffs on her. Further away, she spotted Ines among the others on the floor.

She shouted to avoid being accidentally shot by her colleague. 'Adam! It's Mina! I'm coming in!'

She slowly drew her service weapon while awaiting Adam's 'OK'. When it came, she opened the door fully and rushed across the room to Ines. Her mother was struggling to keep her eyes open. There was an empty paper cup beside her.

'What have you done? Mum! Where's Nathalie?'

Ines looked at her, extending her hand with painful slowness. After a moment's hesitation, Mina took it. The feeling of her mother's hand in hers was strange and familiar all at once. Back then, it had been her mother holding her hand tightly in hers. Now she was holding her mother's hand. It felt brittle and fragile, as if it would break under the slightest pressure from Mina. She was furious with her mother. It couldn't be like this. They had so much to talk about – so many questions that needed answers. But one question mattered more than all the others. Mina looked into her mother's eyes and pleaded.

'Nathalie, Mum. Where is she?'

'I tricked her, Mina,' Ines said, her voice rasping. 'I actually did it. I tricked Nova. Sorry. I didn't understand . . . until just before the end. I didn't know what she was doing. What the others were doing. But once I realized, I did what I could. For you. For Nathalie. She was going to kill Nathalie. I realized that before it was too late. So I told Nova she would buy herself time if she took Nathalie with her. That she needed more time to complete her work. That Nova was too important to leave with us now. I knew her narcissism would kick in . . .'

'Where has she taken her?'

Ines coughed and Mina saw how laboriously she was forcing out each word. Mina didn't want to leave her. But the thought of Nathalie made her begin to stand up. Ines clung even more tightly to her hand.

'Sorry. For everything. Sorry.'

Then Ines let go of her daughter's hand and closed her eyes.

151

Vincent's phone was ringing. Mina. Perfect timing.

'I know what Nova meant,' was the first thing he said. 'Nathalie and Ines are in different places.'

'I know,' Mina said loudly in his ear. 'Mum made sure Nathalie was kept away from here. But I don't think we've got much time left. And I don't know where she is. Fuck it, I don't know where she is! So much has happened here. They drank poison and Ines . . . she . . . oh my God, she . . .'

Something was wrong. Very wrong. Mina's voice was fading in and out as if she were unable to hold it together. He heard Adam shout something in the background, but there was no time to ask what had happened. First Nathalie. Then everything else. That was the order he would have to tackle this in if he were to be of any use whatsoever.

'I know where she is,' he said, running across the street towards his parked car. 'Nova wrote it in the message to you – she told you that you had to make your next move to find her. Do you remember? So I did. I figured out the rest of her knight's tour. It took a while, but now I'm absolutely certain. If she's going to maintain a mathematically symmetrical pattern then there's only one square on the board – sorry, the map – where she can finish. It includes both Reimersholme and Långholmen. But Reimersholme doesn't feel right. Given Nova's dramatic tendencies, I'd bet she's in the old prison on Långholmen – the one that's now a hotel and hostel.'

He reached the car and dug into his pocket for the keys.

'But that's on the other side of town,' Mina exclaimed in despair. 'It'll take forever for me to get there. And Ines . . .'

'I'm already on my way,' said Vincent, finding the key and unlocking the car.

'Vincent?'

'Yes,' he said, pausing halfway into the car.

'Drive faster.'

152

'My daughter and Nova are on Långholmen. I have to get there,' Mina said as she moved away from Ines's body.

Adam's voice was muffled behind her. He was saying something repeatedly, but she was unable to listen. The thought of Nathalie was too dominant in her head.

'Mina!' he shouted again.

She jumped and then spun around.

'Mina, there's something you need to know.'

The sound of sirens outside intensified. The cavalry were on the way. She looked around. Adam seemed to have the situation under control – she didn't need to stay and wait for her colleagues.

'And tell me what your daughter is doing with Nova – I didn't even know you had kids.'

'I don't have time! I've got to find Nathalie,' she said impatiently, making for the door.

'Mina!'

Adam still had his weapon trained on the group of members, but they didn't seem at all inclined to challenge him. He nodded towards the floor by the door. She had missed it earlier, but now she spotted a pair of shoes protruding from behind some chairs. Her first assumption was that it was another cult member who had drunk their poison. Then she recognized the socks. His favourite Bart Simpson socks. She took a couple of steps towards them.

Didn't want to.

Didn't want to see.

Didn't want to know.

But she had to. She took a few more steps. And then she was unable to stifle a scream. A throat-scouring, wounded scream. Lying on his back behind the chairs was Peder. Blue-stained beard and eyes wide open. A small red circle on his cheek was the only thing that revealed anything was amiss. The circle and the blood that had spattered onto the wall behind them and was now pouring freely from the big hole in the back of Peder's head.

'She shot him,' said Adam, nodding towards the old woman sitting on the floor in handcuffs without looking at her.

His voice was a monotone – as if he had run out of emotion.

It was too much. Mina couldn't cope with any more death.

Her eyes clouded with tears, then she turned around and ran towards the exit. There was nothing she could do for Peder, but she could – she had to – save Nathalie.

153

Vincent drove along Söder Mälarstrand heading for Långholmen. The water to his right was glittering, but there was no time to admire the view. For once, he was happy that it was a roasting hot Monday in the middle of the summer holidays. The road was practically deserted. He did as Mina had asked and drove as fast as he dared.

'Vincent,' Christer boomed from the car's speakers via hands-free.

Vincent had called him as soon as he was in the car.

'I've got all the details now, like you asked – all the bookings for the hotel and the hostel. It's almost fully booked, given it's peak season for them.'

Vincent pulled onto the small bridge to Långholmen – the island that boasted one of Stockholm's oldest prison buildings.

'But the hotel received an odd booking last night,' said Christer. 'Room 121. She only needed it for three hours. That's why they were able to accept the booking. You can guess who it was.'

'Nova,' Vincent said as he pulled into the car park. 'Thanks.'

He quickly parked and ran towards the former prison, which now served as a hotel.

He had to focus his thoughts. He couldn't think about what he might encounter. Couldn't let his emotions take over. He liked the symmetry of the room number: 121. It started as it ended. Doubling in the middle. A normal distribution curve.

But nothing about this was normal. Nathalie was essentially the same age as Rebecka. If he didn't make it in time . . . No, that was out of the question. Focus.

He looked up at the yellow stone building. He knew that the prison had been completed in 1880. It had taken 6 years to build; 18 plus 80 was 98. Minus 6 years was 92. They had begun to decommission the prison in 1972. 1972 minus 1880 was also 92. Hmm. Odd. Perhaps there was some mathematical relationship, but he couldn't find it, and he didn't like it when chance was that symmetrical but he was unable to see why. But 92 plus 92 was 184 – 18 4. The eighteenth of April. David Tennant's birthday, if he was not much mistaken. David Tennant – Benjamin's favourite actor to have played Doctor Who.

As Vincent opened the door into the hotel lobby, he visualized the alphabet in his mind's eye. He concluded that the letters D O C T O R W H O were found in positions 4, 15, 3, 20, 15, 18, 23, 8 and 15 in the alphabet. The sum of those numbers was . . . 121.

A normal distribution curve.

The room where Nova was waiting with Nathalie.

He couldn't be late.

In reception, they explained where he could find the room. It was on the first floor. For some reason, there were three people behind the low reception desk. Three sides to a triangle. Mum's toasted sandwiches. Why couldn't they make do with two people behind reception?

He ran upstairs and past a row of old prison cells as he reminded himself that 2 times 3 was 6. A fine even number.

He stopped in front of cell number 121 and realized that he had no plan. But there was no time. He tried the handle and the door swung open. It wasn't locked.

Nova was sitting at a table inside the small room. She was about to pour something from a bottle into a small glass.

'Hello, Vincent,' she said, smiling, as she put down the bottle. 'I was beginning to despair.'

'Sorry, I got caught in traffic,' he said, looking around quickly.

There was nothing threatening in the room – nothing that hinted at impending violence. All he could see was the glass and the bottle on the table in front of Nova, who was impeccably turned out in an elegant blue trouser suit. A young woman

– presumably Nathalie – sat on the bed opposite. She wore a white T-shirt and white trousers. She appeared to be there without coercion.

'Hi Nathalie,' he said. 'My name's Vincent, as you'll have gathered. I'm friends with . . .'

'With your mother,' Nova said, finishing his sentence.

Nathalie's posture changed when she heard that. She crossed her arms and slouched, glowering down at the bed.

'So . . . what happens now?' he said.

'It's very simple,' said Nova. 'My freedom for Nathalie's. I give her to you, and you convince the police to stop looking for me.'

'How do you know the police don't already have the place surrounded?'

Nova smiled her beautiful smile at him.

'Vincent, please! I know they've got their hands full over at the school. It's going to be a while before they can get away from there. And I also know they're not as smart as you and I. No one but you could have concluded that I was here. I suspect you probably came as soon as you realized. Which means you're here alone.'

Vincent sat down on the only vacant chair in the room. Nova was right – there was no point pretending otherwise.

'Nathalie, I'm sorry about all this,' he said, looking at the teenage girl. 'None of us realized what your grandmother was up to.'

'Don't inflate Ines's importance in all this,' Nova snorted. 'The very moment I found out that Ines's daughter was involved in the police inquiry and that she had a daughter of her own called Nathalie, I ordered Ines to find her granddaughter. You can never hold too many trump cards.'

'What do you mean?' Nathalie said from the bed. 'Grandma . . .'

'Your grandmother did what I told her to do,' said Nova. 'I already knew a month ago that you would be useful sooner or later. Did you really think it was a coincidence that Ines happened to be on that metro train?'

Nathalie curled up into a small ball, as if she were trying to disappear.

'So, your freedom in exchange for Nathalie's?' said Vincent. 'You must realize that I'll call the police as soon as you leave? They'll never stop chasing you.'

'It's in your best interests for you to persuade them to do just that,' she said. 'I'll let them know where they can pick Nathalie up once I'm convinced I'm in the clear. It's up to the police to decide when – or if – they see Nathalie again.'

'What makes you think I won't just take Nathalie with me and turn you over to the police?' Vincent said, pulling out his mobile. 'I don't really see how you could stop me.'

'Maybe not me. But what makes you think I'm alone? I can promise you now that you won't even make it across the car park if you try to leave the hotel alone with Nathalie.'

It was perfectly plausible that Nova would have backup in place. Yet she kept touching her throat as she spoke. Increased physical touch was common in times of severe anxiety, since it inhibited the secretion of stress hormones. Was it possible that she was lying? After all, the decision to bring everything forward to today had to have been a hasty one, and Nova being separated from the others could hardly have been part of the original plan. Had she really had time to muster her own personal bodyguards?

Vincent looked out of the window. Three men in white jackets were roving aimlessly around the car park outside. The jackets looked out of place in the summer heat. They might be tourists – or Nova might be telling the truth, in which case they were her henchmen. He had no idea how to determine which was the case.

On the other hand, he didn't believe for one second that Nova intended to let Nathalie go. She had far too many lives on her conscience for one more to make any difference. She had begun to dig Nathalie's grave the very second the girl had arrived at Epicura. And he had told Mina that Nova was harmless. If it hadn't been for him, Nathalie would have been picked up by her father long ago. This was his fault. It was his mess to clean up. He peered out of the window again. The men were still there.

The likelihood that they were associated with Nova wasn't

substantial, given how little time she'd had and the fact that she was emitting unconscious-but-powerful stress signals. But he couldn't ignore the possibility that she was telling the truth.

He rated the probability of them being Nova's bodyguards at 30 per cent. That meant there was a 70 per cent chance that they weren't. If they were, how likely was it that they would manage to overpower him and Nathalie? There were multiple exits from the hotel. They had a relatively good chance of escaping via a route that the men wouldn't have eyes on, so they wouldn't be seen until it was too late. The probability that they would make it through something like that was only 20 per cent; 20 per cent of 30 was 6. So they had a 6 per cent chance of getting out if those men were hired heavies. If not, it was a 70 per cent chance. That meant that he and Nathalie had a 76 per cent chance of pulling through if they overpowered Nova and got out of there – guards or no guards.

But they also had a 24 per cent chance of failure. And the probability that one of them – or both – might pay with their lives in a situation like that was verging on 100 per cent.

He couldn't take that risk.

'OK, you win,' he said, putting down his phone. 'But I still don't understand why we're here. If you just want to use Nathalie for blackmail purposes, then you might as well have phoned in from an undisclosed location. You're risking a lot by being here yourself.'

'No,' Nova said, frowning. 'My Hamiltonian path ends here. I have to be here, because this is where the final move takes place. You've seen for yourself. I have to follow the path to the end. The next place I reach will be the start of a brand-new path. I don't yet know where that path will take me. But I have to finish this one first.'

He stared at Nova. He had assumed that the killer was a slave to their own mathematical rules. But Nova was more than that. She was mad. Brilliant, but mad. And he probably had mere seconds before she left, taking Nathalie with her. Seconds before he might lose Mina's daughter for good. He needed to get Nova to stay put until he thought of a plan. But what?

What?

What?

What?

There was something in what she had said. That she had to follow the path to the end. The final move.

That was it.

He had it.

A chance for her to show that she was smarter than him. Nova was a dyed-in-the-wool narcissist – she wouldn't be able to resist.

'Like you said, this is your last square,' he said. 'Your endgame. But your last move can't be blackmail. It's too . . . sloppy for you.'

Nova's smile no longer reached her eyes.

'And while we're talking about games,' he continued, 'I really don't understand the puzzles you sent me. Were they intended to divert my attention from the investigation if I got brought into it? I applaud your ambition in sending the newspaper article to Ruben two years ago – a whole year before you kidnapped Lilly. But I'm afraid the puzzle didn't have the desired effect. I'm still here, aren't I?'

It was a gamble. But Nova was probably proud of her meticulous planning. Hearing that she had been careless or that something she had devised hadn't worked would hopefully provoke her into acceding to what he was going to propose – out of sheer pride.

'I didn't send any puzzles or articles,' she said.

The smile was completely gone now.

That wasn't what he had expected. Admittedly, she might be lying, but he didn't get the impression she was. She was too proud of her work for that. But if it wasn't Nova, then who was it? He frowned. There was no time to ruminate on that now. It would have to keep for later.

He smiled at Nova and picked up the bottle on the table. Mina had said there was poison at the school. The liquid in the bottle was presumably more of the same – set aside for Nathalie.

It was time. He had pushed Nova mentally as far as he could. Now it all hinged on her reacting in the way he hoped she would and accepting the challenge he laid down.

542

'You've been playing chess with yourself,' he said, 'and you've reached the end of the road. Literally. By the way, it's an incredibly beautiful pattern you've created across the city. When I saw that it was also symmetrical . . . Well, that was really quite something. So now that we're at the last square, let's play the game the way it ought to be played. Because what's the point in a game of chess if there's nothing at stake? What's the point of starting on a new path tomorrow if you can't end this one in the right way? Not with this improvised blackmail attempt . . . You and I both know you're too good for that. Let's play for checkmate. I take it you have more glasses?'

Nova stared at him. Then she smiled again and extracted two glasses from her Louis Vuitton bag, along with another bottle.

'No poison in that one, I hope?' said Vincent.

'Pear juice,' Nova said with a nod.

She set down the new bottle beside the first. The contents looked identical. But one was deadly. The other fruit-flavoured. Nova looked him in the eyes.

'If I win and you drink the poison, I get Nathalie,' he said. 'The last thing you do in life will be to tell your goons not to touch us. But you'll also be liberated from your chronic pain. If you win, and I die, then you get Nathalie and you can continue your plan. I know there were four squares you never got to visit. Four kids you never killed. So it's really a win-win for you.'

Nathalie's eyes widened.

'What kids?' she said, looking at Nova in horror. 'What's he talking about?'

Nova didn't meet Nathalie's gaze – she continued to stare at Vincent. If he had seen a glow in Gustav's eyes, then Nova's were like a fiery volcano.

'I don't understand,' Nathalie said, her voice filled with panic. 'What poison? Are you guys going to play for me like I'm some chess piece? I won't go along with this! Nova, say something. Explain to him that he's misunderstood – that you don't want to hurt anyone.'

Nova didn't reply.

'I think the alternative that Nova intended was for you to

play yourself,' said Vincent. 'And with just the one bottle instead of two. She was going to poison you when you got out of here, Nathalie. It was never about playing you off against the police. She was going to kill you and then disappear. At least this way you have a fifty per cent chance of getting out. If it goes wrong, at least you can't say we didn't try.'

He continued to look at Nova as he spoke. If he turned to Nathalie, he was afraid he wouldn't be able to do what he had to do. This was his fault – he hadn't spotted the warning signs in time. He had to do it for Nathalie. She reminded him so much of Mina. He realized that he would do anything for her.

'I'm sorry, Nathalie,' he said. 'I know it's not much. But it's the best I can do.'

He unscrewed the cap on the bottle of poison, poured it into one of the glasses and tapped the final drops out against the edge of the glass. Then he put down the bottle and screwed the top back on. Nova didn't let his hands out of her sight. Vincent picked up the next bottle and began to pour it into the other glass.

'Are you sure you picked the right bottle?' Nova said, smiling.

'I really do hope so,' Vincent said, returning her smile. 'Otherwise I've accidentally poured poison into both glasses. That would be stupid of me.'

Nova's smile disappeared.

'Nathalie,' Vincent said. 'Nova and I are going to turn around and count to ten. While we do that, you're going to swap the glasses around a few times so that we don't know which is which.'

'I don't want to,' Nathalie said wretchedly.

'Nor do I,' said Vincent. 'But we're going to do it anyway. One . . .'

He gestured to Nova to turn away from the table and began to do likewise. While counting to ten out loud, he heard the scraping of the glasses as they were moved around behind him.

'. . . and ten.' He turned back at the same time as Nova. The glasses were in the same positions as before. They were identical.

'We'll drink at the same time,' he said, picking up one of the glasses.

544

154

Nova downs her glass at the same time as Vincent. She watches the mentalist. It tastes of pear. Not that it means anything – the poison tastes the same as the juice.

She feels the liquid making its way to her stomach. She tries to detect nausea, a burning sensation, or her throat contracting. Nothing. Time stands still.

Nova sniffs her glass. Still nothing but pear.

Then she scrutinizes Vincent's face.

The mentalist has stopped – his hand in mid-air. His pupils are slowly dilating.

His hand begins to move down before falling slackly to the table. The empty glass hits it with a clatter and falls from his hand. It rolls across the tabletop, leaving behind a trail of fluid.

Vincent is still looking at her, but his eyes are unfocused – it's clear his gaze is on something not in the room.

Then Vincent begins to lean to one side. His upper body tilts more and more until he tumbles off his chair and onto the floor. His head strikes the floor of the cell with a thud.

Nova waits a few more seconds. Nathalie has curled up into a ball on the bed. She has buried her head between her knees and is rocking back and forth. It's probably for the best that she doesn't see it.

Nova didn't think it would be this easy. But pride comes before a fall. And Vincent was so very proud.

She gets up and goes over to where the mentalist is lying on the floor. His eyes are half-closed. His ribcage is rising and falling in rapid, shallow breaths. This continues for a few seconds. Then it stops completely.

Nova crouches by the body on the floor and checks for his pulse.

Nothing.

'Check and mate,' she says, standing up again. She brushes down her suit and fetches her bag before turning to Nathalie.

'I have to go and check that Vincent really was alone and

that there's no one waiting for us down there,' she says. 'Don't you dare move. If you do, you'll be having the same drink Vincent had.'

Nova hopes the brat is sufficiently intimidated to do as she's told. It seems to have had an effect, given the look of terror on Nathalie's face as she looks at her.

She opens the door and emerges into the hallway.

She won.

She can barely believe it, but she has actually won. She's finally free to continue her plan. Of course, Nova needs to disappear, which is tragic given everything she's built up. Epicura is over. But she can always go back to being Jessica.

She puts a hand on the wall and catches her breath. It's been a more trying day than she thought. Nathalie will be useful for keeping the cops at bay while she gets away to safety. Then Nathalie can . . . disappear. After that, all she has to do is wait a year or two before she can start over. There are still four to go.

Four more kids until John is vindicated.

She begins walking again and trips over her own feet. What on earth? She needs to act naturally in case anyone sees her.

Her thoughts return to the four. The police never understood who the children were or why they were dying. So they won't be able to stop her next time either. She has all the time in the world.

Suddenly she is struggling to breathe. A wave of dizziness sweeps over her. It's more than just fatigue.

She looks back towards the open door to room 121. Vincent is still lying lifeless on the floor.

Oh no!

She pictures him pouring the poison. First into the one glass, then . . . The idiot really did do it. He joked about it, but he actually meant it. There was only one guaranteed way for him to stop Nova, and he did it.

He sacrificed himself for Nathalie. He poured poison into both glasses.

Nova sinks to the floor as her throat swells. She claws at her own throat as someone sets fire to her lungs. She was wrong. She doesn't want to get rid of the pain anymore. She wants to live – that's worth all the pain in the world. Yet at the same

546

time, another part of her welcomes what is happening. She has always been the one to survive – at the cost of those who matter dying. Her father chose to save her instead of her mother. All that led to was her losing both her parents, while she lived on.

For once, perhaps this is fair.

But she still wants to keep going.

Keep living.

With the guilt. With the pain.

She lies in the hallway, still able to see Vincent on the floor of the cell. Stars – perhaps they're new stars, her stars – are dancing across her field of vision, telling her that her oxygen has run out and that her heart is about to give up. She reaches out with her hand towards Vincent. She tries to reach him across that starry abyss. She wants to ask if he too has lived a life in pain. How he handled it. Whether he now feels free.

But then it's time.

155

'Nathalie!'

Mina shouted as loudly as she could as she ran up the stairs inside the hotel. When she reached the first floor, she almost tripped over Nova, who was lying in the hallway.

'I'm here!' a girl's voice called out.

Nathalie. Somewhere ahead of her.

'Wait there, I'm coming,' Mina yelled.

She bent over Nova, checking for signs of life. She couldn't cope with more death. Not after Peder, not after Ines. Not after Epicura. It was all so horribly meaningless. She had seen more death in the last hour than she wanted to see in the rest of her life. If there was any chance of saving Nova then she would take it, no matter how much she hated her for all that she had done. But Nova seemed to be a lost cause. And beyond her was Nathalie.

Julia and Ruben were right behind her – they would have to call an ambulance for Nova if it wasn't already too late. She stood up and ran towards the open door that the voice had come from.

Before Mina even reached the room, she saw that someone was lying on the floor and all she could think was that it mustn't be her daughter.

She ran in, surprising Nathalie, who was huddled up on the bed.

'You?!' Nathalie said. 'I recognize you.'

Mina nodded. They'd had coffee together in Kungsträdgården that summer two years ago, but Mina hadn't told her who she was. Not then. She hadn't been sure whether Nathalie would even remember the encounter.

'So you're my mum? I don't get any of this.'

But Mina was no longer listening – because she had seen who was lying on the floor. She didn't want to take it in. She refused to accept it was Vincent. Her Vincent. The one who had got inside her defences. The only one she had let in. Now he was lying there as if he hadn't given a thought to what it would do to her.

'What have you done?' she whispered, looking at the mentalist. 'Vincent, what have you done?'

She fell to her knees and checked for signs of life, just as she had done with Nova. And just like with Nova, she found none.

'We've called an ambulance,' said Julia, bursting into the room, 'but I'm pretty sure that Nova's dead, so we . . .'

She fell silent when she caught sight of Vincent.

'Bloody hell. Mina . . .'

'So you're my mum . . . ?' Nathalie said again.

Mina couldn't bring herself to answer. She had just got her daughter back. She ought to be overjoyed. But when she got up from the floor, when she got up from beside Vincent, when she got up to continue with her day and the day after that and the months and years that followed them and the rest of her life – without him, without Vincent – there was nothing left in the world except sorrow.

156

Christer contemplated the black and white squares on his computer monitor with distaste. He had lost all inclination to play chess. John Wennhagen's daughter, Jessica – better known as Nova – had ruined it for him once and for all. What a sick human being she was! Because of her, Mina had lost her mother. But thanks to Vincent, she had at least regained her daughter. Christer hadn't heard anything since they'd told him they'd taken Nathalie straight to hospital from Långholmen the day before. He hoped she was OK. It was a funny thing – a few days ago he hadn't even known that Mina had a family.

He glanced at the chessboard on the screen again. He would finish the game he'd had on the go for the last week, then that would be that.

He knew that humiliation was imminent. Any move now, the game would be over. He had tried to postpone the inevitable for as long as he could. But he might as well get it over and done with.

Christer highlighted the current game in the list of possible games and brought it up on the display. The pieces were set out on the board exactly where he had left them. He examined the configuration, trying to remember whether he'd had a plan and if so what it had been.

It definitely didn't look like a plan.

He had no chance.

He played a few lacklustre moves to shorten the suffering. However, there weren't many pieces left on the board. Apparently this game had been going better than usual before he'd paused it. He moved his remaining knight. All of a sudden, he heard Vincent's voice in his head, rattling off all the things he'd talked about in the last few weeks.

'Knight.'

'Horse.'

'Hippo.'

'HORSE.'

'Arabian thoroughbred.'

'My Little Pony.'

'The Psychology of the Pawn.'

'Knight's tour.'

'Turagapadabandha.'

Bloody chess. The computer made its move and Christer moved the knight again. Suddenly the chess app made a sound he'd never heard before.

'WINNER: WHITE!' was emblazoned across the screen.

He had been playing white. Well he'd be damned. He had won. After all these months.

Christer let the realization sink in for a moment. Then he quit the program, found the files for it on his computer and dragged them all to the trash can. Then he clicked on 'Empty trash' and heard the associated rustling sound as the app was deleted forever.

157

'Would you like a cup of coffee and something sweet before you go?'

Ruben tried to discern whether the question was the beginning of a telling-off, or whether Ellinor was wearing that expression she'd always had when it was time for them to 'have a serious talk'.

When Ellinor had found out that a week earlier Astrid had been to a meeting about murdered children, she had not overflowed with exuberant praise. Bloody Vincent. Although he probably ought not to think about the mentalist like that any longer. Not after what had happened at Långholmen.

This time, however, Ruben couldn't think of anything he'd done wrong. Indeed, Ellinor didn't look angry. Still, she was a past master at crushing other people with facts. A cup of coffee might entail a polite conversation that resulted in him never getting to see Astrid again.

He glanced at his daughter. She was still wearing her white martial arts suit. From what he'd heard, it was hard to get her to wear anything else at home.

'Yes please,' he said cautiously. 'If it's not too much trouble?'

'Come on, Ruben,' Astrid said, taking him by the hand. 'We can have another snack. Anyway, I want to show Mum my choke hold.'

'*Another* snack?' Ellinor said, raising an eyebrow.

'There may have been an ice cream after training,' he said, clearing his throat. 'Or two.'

He had tried to keep his spirits up when collecting Astrid, rather than thinking too much about Peder. Or Anette and the triplets. Or Vincent's sacrifice for Mina's daughter. It had only been two days since it had all happened. He hadn't even begun to process it. But he didn't want Astrid to have to deal with a sad dad when they did see each other. He supposed he had been hoping that Astrid would be a kind of therapy for him. But keeping everything at bay hadn't been an unqualified success. It was all too much. So he had masked it with ice cream instead. It seemed to have worked.

He followed Ellinor into the kitchen. Astrid had already settled down and was drawing with her colouring pencils. She had clearly inherited her mother's talent. Ellinor set out a coffee cup for him on the kitchen table.

'Would you like some juice?' she asked Astrid, who got up and did her best to grab her mother in a hold.

'Yes, sensei!' Astrid said, releasing her mother and bowing.

Ellinor laughed. It was a sound he hadn't heard for more than a decade. Not until he heard it did he realize just how much he had missed it.

'I haven't said it before,' Ellinor said, pouring coffee, 'but thanks for everything you've been doing for Astrid. I thought she might be more hesitant towards you to start with – after all, she doesn't know you – but it's been the exact opposite. I really don't know how you've done it. But I'm glad that you have.'

551

Ruben laughed, feeling slightly embarrassed. He barely dared look at Ellinor. Even after a year of conversations with Amanda, it was still uncomfortable talking about certain topics. Instead, he sipped his coffee. It was strong. Just the way he remembered she liked it.

'Hanging out with Astrid is nothing but fun,' he said. 'I mean, she likes the same stuff as me.'

Ellinor looked at him for a long time. Then she nodded.

'You might have been a worthless boyfriend,' she said, glancing at her daughter, who was preoccupied with mixing cordial in a huge jug. 'But you're a good dad. I want you to know that.'

Ruben merely nodded. He was afraid that his voice might sound strange if he replied.

'I've got something for you,' Ellinor said, passing him a thick photo album. 'This is Astrid: from birth to the present day. I thought you might like to know what she's been up to for the last ten years.'

He nodded again. If he couldn't answer before, he most definitely couldn't now. His eyes filled with tears and a big lump formed in his throat. He thought of Peder again. But then all of a sudden Sara appeared in his thoughts. He remembered how warm her voice had sounded each time she mentioned her kids. He understood why. He felt that same warmth within every time he looked at Astrid. He would bet anything that Sara was a good mum – just like Ellinor. And Sara's husband was quite obviously a moron.

Astrid sat down next to him with a glass of juice. Then she downed the lot and burped loudly.

'Astrid!' Ellinor laughed.

'Ruben, can you stay for tea?' his daughter said. 'Dad, I mean. Please?'

Ruben gave Ellinor a sidelong look. He still didn't dare say anything.

158

The conference room was deadly silent. No one knew what to say. And none of them could bring themselves to look at Peder's empty chair.

All except Bosse, who gazed unhappily at the chair and then gloomily laid his head in Christer's lap. The chair was like an elephant in the room. In the end, Ruben stood up, went over to the chair and shoved it into a corner. Everyone jumped. But Mina understood that it wasn't an act of anger – merely one of frustration. She, too, wanted to smash something to pieces.

It was all so terribly unfair.

And nothing they did would change any of it.

Bosse whimpered gently and Christer reassured him. Mina looked at the map of Stockholm on the wall. The one that Vincent had carved up into a chessboard and then drawn a route across. A route that led to nothing but death. Far too much death.

Julia stepped up to the whiteboard that they had used to make sense of the case. It was all still there. Pictures, words, arrows, photographs.

'We mourn our colleague,' she said in a low voice. 'He was a friend and one of the finest people that those of us in this room have ever met. We will make the time for it because we will be grieving for a long time. But right now, we need to do what Peder would have wanted us to do. We have to make sure that there's nothing we've missed. That we know – without any doubt – that this is all over.'

Julia's voice cracked and she cleared her throat.

Mina's throat was filled with sobs – sobs that had not yet been uttered. After she had seen Nathalie and confirmed that she was safe and sound, Mina had briefly allowed herself to rejoice that her daughter was OK. But it had been a brief respite.

Now the grief had struck her with such force that she didn't know how to cope with it. Or how they would move on as a team. With his cheerful humour, his kindness and his energy drinks, Peder had been what cemented them together. She would have given anything to see another video of the triplets.

And then there was Vincent.

Good God, there was Vincent. She still hadn't forgiven him.

She looked at the mentalist, who was sitting beside her. He had put his crutches on the floor.

'But first, perhaps Vincent can tell us all why Mina thought he was dead,' Julia said sharply.

Vincent looked extremely self-conscious. It served him right.

'Well, I can stop the blood flow in my arm for a while,' he said. 'It's a trick I do in my shows to make it seem as if I don't have a pulse. That's how I fooled Nova into thinking I'd drunk the poison. I hoped she'd leave Nathalie alone if she thought I was dead. But it's pretty dangerous – I wouldn't recommend it.'

'For a while, you say?' said Adam. 'But you still had no pulse when Mina showed up. Who do you think you are? Lazarus?'

Vincent looked even more embarrassed. He glanced at Mina, but when he saw her eyes he quickly looked away again.

'I heard the tumult and thought it might be Nova coming back,' he said. 'I was having a hard time thinking straight because of how painful my foot was. So I stopped my pulse – well my blood flow – again. Just to be sure.'

'Stupid idiot,' Mina muttered. 'You deserve a broken foot. Anyway, who ever heard of someone breaking their foot falling from a chair?'

She had been so dreadfully frightened when she had found him. And she had been even more frightened when he suddenly opened his eyes and began talking to her. She'd barely exchanged a word with him since then. Vincent's apparent death, the panic about what would happen to Nathalie, and Peder's death – it had all fed into the same maelstrom of overwhelming emotions. All she wanted to do was retreat into her own apartment, curl up in the foetal position and shut out everything that was clawing away at her insides.

'Sorry,' he said quietly. 'It was for Nathalie. By the way, did you pick up the three guys in the car park? Were they with Nova?'

Mina felt a hand on her arm and looked into Vincent's blue

eyes. She knew she would forgive him. At least he was alive. As was Nathalie. 'The ones in the white jackets?' she said. 'They were Japanese tourists.'

'I still don't get why Nova did all this,' Christer said. 'What was her motive? And why the hell did she pretend to help us? She took a huge risk cooperating with the police.'

He swallowed hard, as if holding back tears.

'May I?' Vincent said, looking to Julia for confirmation.

She nodded, and he went over to the whiteboard while she took her seat.

'I've spoken to a few of the surviving cult members,' he said. 'They're rather more talkative now that Nova is dead. The explanation I've been given is a bit limp, but I think it gives us some answers. As you know, Nova experienced an incredibly traumatic event in her childhood. She was seriously injured in a car crash and her father most likely died that night, despite the fact that we were led to believe otherwise. After the accident, which left her with permanent injuries, she was cared for by her grandfather – Baltzar Wennhagen – who raised her on the teachings of Epicureanism. But I think she brought a lot to the table that she had learned from her father while he was alive. These things were all mixed up together, creating a distorted version of Epicureanism where the physical pain that was a constant presence in her life took centre stage. Nova had to find meaning in her pain. That search made it easy for her to draw others to her who also had pain – people searching for meaning. Searching for something that might make the suffering a little easier to bear. Don't forget that Nova's pain was both physical and mental. It was a combination that turned out to be ill-fated and destructive. It saw rationality and logic replaced by fanaticism and desperation.'

For a moment, Vincent's tone and choice of words made it easier to parse all the awfulness. When he talked as if he were giving a lecture, it made it possible to adopt an outside perspective – to set aside all the emotion.

Mina noted how intently he was looking at each and every one of them as he spoke, and she realized that he was probably offering them emotional distance from what had happened on purpose. The mentalist was doing his thing the only way he knew how, so that the grief was at least temporarily a little easier to handle.

'I still don't understand why she got involved in the investigation,' Christer said. 'Surely she had nothing to gain by that?'

'It probably gave her a feeling of control in that she was able to find out more about what we knew, while also steering the inquiry in the wrong direction,' said Vincent. 'But above all, it was about Nova's strongest character trait. Narcissism. It's not uncommon for criminals with narcissistic personalities to try and interfere in police investigations into themselves. She's in no way unique in that respect.'

'Did everyone in Epicura know what they were doing with the children?' asked Julia.

'No, I gather they didn't,' said Vincent, folding his arms. 'Most often, not all members of a cult are equally informed about what's going on. It's like the layers of an onion. The further in you get, the more information you have access to. It's the same way Scientology works. But there you buy courses in order to gradually work your way up to a higher level of knowledge. At Epicura, it was about proving your worth to Nova. Bearing enough of your own pain.'

'Did Ines know?' said Mina.

She knew she was laying herself bare by asking – by now, everyone around the table knew of her connection to both Ines and Nathalie. She was waiting for the first comment to be made.

'Not according to the members I've spoken to,' said Vincent.

Mina nodded, but she wasn't convinced. She didn't know who her mother had really been or what role she had played. But just before she had died, Ines had said she hadn't known what Nova was doing. Mina clung on to those words, wanting to believe them at any cost.

'Nova claimed the children were the way to a new life without pain,' Vincent said. 'Children have always been the ultimate symbol of innocence and have often been regarded as guides in religious contexts. The inner circle in Epicura believed they were liberating the children from pain by allowing them to be reborn as pure, new beings. They were going to go ahead into a new age – Epicura's version of the thousand-year reign.'

'What a load of cobblers,' Ruben muttered.

'I don't know that it's any stranger than millions of people believing that God's son died and was resurrected on the third day,' said Adam. 'Every religion and every faith has its myths.'

'Nova was a strong leader,' said Vincent. 'Convincing. And she offered the thing her followers wanted more than anything else: deliverance from pain.'

'But why these kids in particular?' Julia said thoughtfully. 'That's one of the things I still don't understand.'

'I haven't been able to make any headway on that point either,' said Vincent. 'The people I spoke to had no idea. Nova only told them what they needed to know, and they obeyed orders. The children may have been chosen at random. Perhaps based on how easy they would be to abduct. That's the likeliest explanation. If Nova chose them based on other criteria, it wasn't something she disclosed to anyone else.'

He fell silent and looked at them. Mina followed his gaze. Adam, who was for once wearing a T-shirt instead of a button-up shirt. Ruben, whose face turned to thunder as soon as children were mentioned. Christer, whose expression was dour as he scratched Bosse between the ears. And Julia, with the hint of a frown that had been ever-present since her return from maternity leave. She was the last of them to meet Vincent's blue eyes. He looked tired. So very, very tired.

'But if there's one thing to take out of all of this,' he said, 'it's that if Nova hadn't been stopped, more families would have been hit. She wasn't finished – we know that much. You almost certainly saved the lives of another three children in addition to Wilma. We'll never find out who they are. But they're out there somewhere, and their lives are no longer in danger.'

No one answered. Vincent's words ought to have been encouraging, but it was hard to find any solace in them.

Ruben stood up and retrieved Peder's chair from the corner. He righted it, carried it back to its spot and carefully pushed it under the table. Then he left the room. But not before Mina had seen his lower lip trembling uncontrollably.

As the door slammed behind him, the silence became deafening. The only thing to speak was Peder's empty chair.

159

Adam was sitting at his desk browsing flat listings. His mother was right. He couldn't live like a bachelor anymore. He needed to sort out a better apartment and then find someone to share it with. No one would take him seriously if they saw the way he lived.

Perhaps it was time he took a cookery course as well. You couldn't serve spaghetti and mincemeat sauce on a date. Well, you could . . . It was securing the next date that became the problem. His repertoire was rather limited. Work had always come ahead of any possible personal interests. But it was time to change that.

The online adverts drifted before his eyes. What about a one-bedder in the city centre? Actually, make that a two-bed. That would look better. Although could he *really* afford that on his own?

He reclined in his chair and sighed. Maybe he'd approached this from the wrong angle. Perhaps he should download Tinder instead? Or sign up for that cookery course.

He pictured his mother chasing four chortling children. He smiled at the picture and felt warm inside. She would be so happy. Although maybe not four kids . . . She would have to settle for three.

There was a knock at the door and Julia popped her head around it.

'Hello,' he said.

'Hello,' she said. 'I was only going to say . . . Good job all around. And welcome to the team. It's not always this intense – just so you know.'

'I really hope it isn't,' he said, laughing.

His mobile began to buzz on the table. Number withheld. He didn't usually pick up if he didn't know who was calling.

'Aren't you going to get that?' said Julia.

He shrugged, tapped the green phone button and answered. Then he gasped. 'I'm on my way.' He hung up.

'Has something happened?'

'Yes. It's my mum.' Adam rushed out of the office and down the corridor. Julia shouted something at his receding back but he could no longer hear what she was saying.

160

Christer regretted not choosing a better-looking shirt. Exactly what had he been thinking when he'd put on the brown and beige striped viscose job? He would have preferred his wool waistcoat too, but that was out of the question in the heat, and he supposed it wasn't that exciting either. At the same time, it almost felt like a sin to care about something as superficial as his appearance.

He and Anette had spoken to the triplets on Thursday. Children were so special – they understood while at the same time they didn't. And they were so little. It was just words to them. They had been sad. He and Anette had been sad too, but it was still just words. Not today, not tomorrow, but soon the realization would hit them properly. When their dad didn't come home, day after day. That would be when Anette's real job began.

And life would move on. Life. Bloody hell.

Christer pulled out a handkerchief and wiped the sweat from his brow. At the same moment Bosse caught sight of another golden retriever in the distance and began to bark merrily.

'No, Bosse, stay here,' he said, yanking at the lead.

He had a sinking feeling that this was all a big mistake. And why had he brought the dog along? When Lasse had suggested they meet in Vasaparken, Christer had automatically thought to himself that it would be perfect for Bosse. But it was one thing leaving him tied up outside a restaurant, and quite another to bring someone into close contact with him. After all, Lasse might be allergic to dogs.

Damn it.

He mopped his brow with his handkerchief again.

A little distance away, he could see the cafe where they were due to meet. He had thought he'd arrive early so that he could be sitting there when Lasse arrived, looking like an urbane detective with the responsibilities of the whole world on his shoulders. Perhaps he'd be making notes on a case or reading the newspaper while nursing a double espresso. He wanted to look like his favourite character, Harry Bosch. But right now he wasn't even sure Harry Bosch was on the same planet.

The sinking sensation spread from his stomach into his legs. He stopped. Looked at the cafe. He couldn't do this. He needed to go home. Now. He was about to turn around when he heard a resounding laugh behind him. The voice it belonged to had got deeper since their younger days. But just as it had done then, it warmed his insides.

'So you're pulling the old dog trick on me?' said Lasse, laughing again as Christer turned around.

Lasse crouched down and let Bosse greet him.

'Hello friend, yeeess, helllllooo friend. Who's a good boy?'

Lasse ruffled Bosse's fur and the dog began to boisterously wag his tail, a remarkable quantity of drool leaking out of his mouth.

'The dog trick?' Christer stuttered. 'No, I, uh . . . I mean . . . it wasn't . . .'

What must Lasse be thinking? He was utterly pathetic. It felt as if Lasse had caught him by surprise with his trousers down. Well, that was a highly inappropriate metaphor. Exposed. That was the word he was looking for. He felt exposed.

Lasse stood up.

'Because if you are, then I've got to say it's the lousiest dog trick I've ever seen,' he said, grinning. 'An overweight man in his sixties with a flea-bitten mongrel sidekick.'

Christer remembered that smile from when they had been

560

young. He had always liked it. He tried to smile back. It probably looked totally false.

'You know I'm actually angry with you,' said Lasse. 'We've got some stuff to sort out. But I must say the two of you look absolutely divine. Why don't we get that coffee?'

161

Mina crept into the hospital room. She guessed it was more than just luck that her daughter had managed to bag a room of her own. But in this case, Mina was perfectly happy that Nathalie's father had thrown his weight around.

Her daughter was sleeping peacefully. She had no visible injuries, but they had wanted to keep her in for observation. Mina stifled the impulse to go over to her and stroke her hair. It had been so long since she had touched her. She was afraid she wouldn't know how to do it anymore. How did a mother touch her child?

She carefully pulled a chair close to the bed and sat down. She wanted to gaze at Nathalie's sleeping face. Although Mina had been following her at a distance for years, it was still a strange feeling to examine every detail of her up close. So familiar, yet so alien. Her daughter had been a cute, spirited five-year-old when Mina had left her. Some of the features and gestures from back then were gone, erased by the passing years. But others remained. The slight twitch in her upper lip as she slept. The dark, long lashes resting on her cheek like a fan.

Mina could not get enough of the sight of her. But she quivered at the thought of what their journey would be like in future. There was so much baggage to unpack. So much guilt wrapped up in excuses and idiotic reasons that no longer felt anything like as logical as they once had.

Nathalie's eyelids fluttered. Then she very slowly opened her eyes. For a moment, Mina felt as if she wanted to escape. To run out of the room, to leave her without having to answer the questions that she knew would follow.

'You . . .' Nathalie said in a strained voice while she slowly swam to the surface of consciousness.

Her gaze became clearer as she woke up. Mina's hand had been close to Nathalie's – right by it without quite touching it. Nathalie snatched her hand away and averted her gaze. She looked pointedly at the window instead.

'What are you doing here?' she said coldly.

'I wanted to see that you were OK,' said Mina. Her voice trembled.

'I'm OK,' said Nathalie. 'You can go now.'

Mina was silent at first, not moving.

'I know I've got a lot of explaining to do,' she said at last. 'And a lot to apologize for. But I hope that you'll at least listen.'

'Me and Dad have been just fine without you. I don't need you.' Nathalie's voice was defiant and chilly, but there was a crack in it that suggested emotions were simmering away below the surface.

'I know you've been fine,' said Mina. 'That *you* have been fine. I hope . . . I just hope that there's some way forward for us both?'

'I told you to get lost!' Nathalie sobbed, no longer able to sustain her chilly exterior. 'Why won't you listen to me? Leave!'

Mina stood up. Behind her, she heard someone come into the room. When she turned around, Nathalie's father was standing there.

'It's going to take time,' he said with surprising gentleness. 'It's all so new. But I've begun to realize that breaking off all contact was maybe not the best solution. There would have been no need for this to happen if we hadn't. Come for dinner once she's home. We'll take it from there.'

'I don't want her to come for fucking dinner!' Nathalie roared from her hospital bed.

Mina stifled a sob. Nathalie's father placed a hand on her shoulder. That too felt strangely familiar and yet alien.

'It'll be OK. I'll be in touch. But for now it's best that you go. And . . . sorry that I didn't answer when you called and asked me to pick Nathalie up. I had a . . . crisis . . . at work.'

'Yes, I saw the headlines,' Mina said with a nod.

He bowed his head, unable to meet her gaze.

'My job . . . Look, she's my top priority, she always has been; I want you to know that. But my damn job . . .'

Mina simply nodded. She wanted to make it into the corridor before the tears came. She didn't want him to see her cry. She had no right to cry. And he had no reason whatsoever to feel ashamed in her presence. She was the one who had spent her whole life prioritizing other things. Making other choices.

As she left, she turned around in the doorway. Nathalie had her arms around her father's neck and was hugging him tight.

Once Mina had taken a few steps down the corridor, the tears came.

162

'Torkel! What's happened? How's he doing?'

Julia rushed into the small room to which she had been directed when she'd arrived at the Astrid Lindgren children's hospital.

Torkel stood up from a chair by the far wall and came towards her. He hugged her tightly – so tightly she could hardly breathe. She yanked herself free and looked at Harry, who was being examined on a counter. A woman in a white coat was leaning over him.

'Harry?'

Julia rushed over.

Harry's big blue eyes met hers and he gurgled happily at the sight of her. The relief almost made her legs give way.

'Well, it seems this young man caused quite a drama at home,' said the doctor, smiling reassuringly. 'He put something he shouldn't have in his mouth, but Dad seems to have been resourceful and the ambulance arrived quickly. It appears there's no harm done except that he almost gave his dad a heart attack.'

The doctor picked Harry up and passed him to Julia. She held him close. Then she met Torkel's gaze.

'Thanks.'

Torkel merely nodded and she saw that there were tears in his eyes. It was the first time she had ever seen him cry. Not even when Harry had been born had he cried. Instead, he'd jumped for joy like a hyped-up Duracell bunny.

'Can we take him home?' Julia asked.

The doctor nodded.

Torkel gathered his things and followed Julia out of the door. When he put an arm around her, she could feel him trembling.

'I'll drive if you sit in the back with Harry,' she said firmly as they made for the car.

'OK,' said Torkel without any protest.

Once they had strapped in Harry – who was still babbling away happily – Julia walked around the car and got into the driver's seat while Torkel buckled his seatbelt in the back seat. Just as she was about to start the car, she felt his hand on her shoulder.

'Wait. There's something I want to say.'

Julia met Torkel's gaze in the rear-view mirror. He swallowed.

'I've been a complete arse,' he said.

'Torkel . . .' she began to say, but he interrupted.

'No, let me say this. I've never been as damn scared as I was today. I thought he was going to die, Julia. I really thought he was going to die. Only then did I realize what it is you do at work. Those parents . . .'

His voice trailed off.

'I can't imagine how they can even survive the loss of a child. And you go to work every day to help them find answers – to prevent more parents having to experience it. While I'm at home whining like a brat. Sorry. I'm so ashamed of myself. And I promise that from now on I'll be Mister Mum. You won't hear a single complaint out of me.'

He zipped his lips using his fingers, before turning and throwing away an invisible key.

564

Julia turned around. She looked him straight in the eyes.

'You're right. You have been a total arse. But you're *my* total arse. And you're the best dad Harry could have wished for. You were just a bit unfortunate in your thinking for a while . . . So here's my suggestion: we forget all about this and start over. And do you know what? I've got three weeks' leave I was planning to use to give you a bit of space. I know I've only just gone back, but after this case not even my dad is going to say anything if I want a bit of time off. So you can go back to work tomorrow. Or play golf. Or do whatever you want. I'll take him.'

'You know I hate golf,' Torkel said, laughing. 'And work is doing fine without me. It was just me who wanted to convince myself that I'm indispensable. But time off sounds good. Why don't we do those weeks together? Every other night? Every other nappy? Both of us at home? Then I'll take over again when you head back to the office. How does that sound?'

Julia smiled and started the engine. Then she met his gaze in the rear-view mirror again. 'Sounds good to me,' she said.

163

Mina was taking a walk around Rålambshovsparken, trying to gather her thoughts. Her ex-husband was right, of course. She had to give Nathalie time. As luck would have it, that was something she had plenty of. Her thoughts wandered to Vincent. She only had one child, but he had three. Had he had a hard time with them too? Probably. She supposed it was part of the whole experience of being an active parent.

Vincent.

Unlike last time, she and Vincent hadn't said farewell after the meeting at police headquarters. They hadn't even said goodbye. Just an evasive 'see you'. The problem was that they hadn't said where they would see each other. Of course, they would see each other at Peder's funeral, but that didn't really count. At the very least, she was going to make sure that they didn't leave it twenty months this time. After all, he had broken his foot for Nathalie's sake. Not to mention that he'd saved her life.

Perhaps that was apology enough from him.

She pulled out her phone, on the brink of calling him. An app icon, a white flame against a red background, made her stop. Tinder.

It struck her that she had done it. She had really done it – the way other people did it. She had followed their rules. She'd met a regular person the regular way. She'd gone on a normal date. Conducted herself like a mostly normal person. Laughed when she was supposed to. If there was anyone who doubted that she could be like everyone else, she had shown them.

And she was never going to do it again.

She held her finger on the app until it was deleted. Then she began to walk alongside the water.

The last two times she had walked along here she had been with Vincent. Once in the winter, and once just a few weeks ago. The park felt somewhat uninteresting without him there. He would probably have been able to tell her about the psychological effect of bridges crossing high above the park, or to explain the mathematical relationship between the jetties and the position of the cycle lane.

She ran her hand through her hair. This time she had resisted the temptation to cut it off after emerging from the bunker. Vincent's broken foot would have to suffice in the war damage tally.

Vincent, whom she had believed, for a brief but seemingly never-ending moment, to be dead. She still hadn't forgiven him for that. He was really going to get it when she took her revenge – both for that and the joke about the water in Kungsträdgården. When he was least expecting it . . . She would have to make a list of possibilities.

She put her hand in her pocket and felt a piece of plastic. Damn it. She had forgotten to give it to him. She pulled out the plastic object and looked at it. With Milda's help, she'd preserved two of the blades of grass that Vincent had picked in

566

Fatbursparken in acrylic. One light, one dark, side by side and sealed into a small plastic block. Like a piece of Lego.

It was supposed to be a gift. A souvenir of what they had gone through. But perhaps it was for the best that she'd forgotten to give it to him. It was probably overly morbid. She sometimes had trouble judging that kind of thing. At the same time, the strands of grass were more than just a reminder of a murder.

They were her.

And they were Vincent.

They were everything that needed a light and a dark side in order to exist. There beside one another, the strands might even represent her and Vincent together.

She returned the plastic cube to her pocket and adjusted her sunglasses. The park was full of people, but no one seemed to pay her any attention. That was fortunate, because it was eminently possible that she had just begun to blush.

164

Vincent hopped along the path through the Tantolunden park on his crutches. He remembered another warm day when he had walked here. On that occasion, Mina had been with him. It was far too long ago. He decided they ought to recreate the moment before the end of the summer. Although only if she wanted to . . . He suspected he was still in her bad books.

But that didn't matter. He had time to make it up to her.

He hadn't told anyone how close he'd come to selecting the wrong glass in the hotel room with Nova. The trick with the bottles was done on purpose to plant the idea in Nova's head that he might have poured poison into both. Even if she didn't really believe that he had done, the thought would still be there, which would help with the credibility when he pretended to die.

Tapping the poison bottle against the rim of the glass had

been with the intent of adding a nick – a common tool in the arsenal of a conjurer. It created a mark invisible to anyone who didn't know it was there, but which would help him know which glass was the right one. It was an old technique that was sometimes used by mediums on the make when holding séances for multiple people simultaneously. A classic routine was for each participant to write down a personal question on a slip of paper. The slips would be checked to ensure they were identical in order to guarantee the questioners' anonymity. But when the medium's assistant gathered together the questions, he or she would add a tiny nick to the edge of the paper using their fingernail. By feeling the position of the nick, the medium would know which question belonged to whom, and be able to pretend that the spirits were guiding her to the right person.

But no mark had been left on the glass. He should have tapped the rim harder. After Nathalie had moved the glasses around, he'd had no clue which one contained the poison.

In the end he'd taken a gamble.

And it had worked out. Well, discounting his foot. After the last meeting with the team at police headquarters, both he and Mina had been offered therapy for what they'd been through, but both of them had declined. The only police employee he needed to talk to was Mina.

He wasn't going to make the same mistake as last time and not get in touch. In retrospect, that had been an unnecessarily stupid move. What on earth had he been playing at? Withdrawing like that . . . Maria would just have to get it into her head that he had friends nowadays. And if she didn't, then they'd have to book some more couples therapy sessions. Because Mina lived inside him – in his innermost self. That was just how it was. He needed her in order to be whole. Sometimes Mina was the only person who was actually real to him. Not that he would ever say that aloud. He didn't want to seem completely insane.

In fact, he could call her to suggest a walk right now. Why not? The summer wouldn't last forever. He was jolly well going to do it. He just had one call to get through first.

568

He inserted his AirPods into his ear to enable him to talk on the phone while hobbling along on his crutches. Then he found the number in his contacts.

'Hi, it's me,' he said when Umberto at ShowLife Productions picked up.

'Vincent! Hello!' Umberto bellowed cheerfully. 'I haven't heard from you in a while. All ready for your trip to Fort Boyard tomorrow?'

It was lucky they weren't on FaceTime so that Umberto couldn't see Vincent's grin.

'That's what I'm calling about,' he said, trying to sound upset. 'I'm afraid I've got bad news. I've broken my foot. I've got to use crutches for at least another week. So I won't be able to appear on *Fortress Prisoners' Flight*.'

There was silence on the line for a while.

'But Vincent, didn't you receive the last update . . . ack, it doesn't matter. You're crazy lucky, you know that? It doesn't matter that you can't walk properly. The production team decided you are going to be put in the cell with all the creepy crawlies. You know, that narrow passage that's full of eight-legged things and other delights. So you don't have to use your feet. You just wriggle along and let your arms do the work. Talk about fluke.'

Vincent drew breath. Umberto's definition of 'crazy lucky' clearly needed to be reviewed. The last thing he was going to do was what Umberto had just outlined. Never, ever. He pondered whether the production team would release him if he broke both his feet instead of just one. Or had them amputated . . . It felt like a reasonable solution compared to the alternative.

'By the way, I spoke to the recording assistant,' Umberto added. 'She was over the moon when she heard you were going to be on the show. Anna, I think her name was. Said you guys had met before. You probably know who she is, and fine, this may be a little crazy, but word on the street is that she has a tattoo of you on her back. She'll take good care of you.'

Vincent closed his eyes and leaned on the crutches. He pictured himself in a close-fitting tracksuit, being cheered on by an over-exuberant TV presenter while his stalker Anna screamed at him to seize the day.

Mina was going to laugh so hard she'd wet herself.

165

Fredrik Walthersson parked on the gravel track outside the small summer cottage on the island of Djurö. Judging by the number of cars already there, he and Josefin were the last to arrive. They crossed the grass, making for the brown wooden house. The lush garden was in full bloom, with a hammock suspended between two apple trees. There was no finer Swedish summer's day than this. But Fredrik was struggling to appreciate it. A few days had passed since the police had notified them who had abducted Ossian, and that she had died by suicide.

After that, he and Josefin had waited for the call.

And now they were here.

Mauro Meyer emerged from the house and came to them across the grass, shaking their hands.

'Everyone is already here,' he said in a low voice. 'Come in and we'll make a start.'

He showed them inside. The hallway was full of shoes and Fredrik automatically took off his own. It was funny how some routines stuck regardless of the circumstances.

When they came into the living room, it took a few seconds to recognize the others. Everyone had grown so much older. And age had treated them very differently. Some, like Mauro, had blossomed. His forties suited him. For others, like Lovis Carlsson, age seemed a burden that merely served to remind her of her impending death.

Fredrik offered a silent greeting to Jens and Janina Josefsson, who were sitting quietly on the sofa. Hugo and Karin were there too, next to Henry and Tobias. Just like Jens and Janina, their children were still alive. There was a clear difference in the atmosphere where they were sitting compared with the part of the room where he and Josefin were standing alongside Mauro and Lovis, who were seated.

Fredrik and Josefin sat down at the dining table. Mauro had laid out coffee and buns, but they looked untouched.

'I suppose I ought to be serving something much stronger,' Mauro said when he spotted Fredrik looking at the table. 'But you all need to be able to drive your cars when you leave.'

He cleared his throat and continued.

'I suppose we should make a start. We're all here except for our beloved Vendela. As you know, she chose to take her own life in the spring, and everyone believed that she had taken Dexter with her, since he went missing at the same time. But a few days ago, a thread appeared on the Flashback forums saying that Thomas Jonsmark's son had been found in a park in Stockholm. So we must assume that was Nova's . . . that is to say, Jessica's handiwork.'

Jens and Janina looked at each other.

Josefin was removing pearls of sugar from one of the buns. Fredrik suspected she didn't even know she was doing it.

'Does Thomas know anything?' said Henry.

Henry and Tobias had a son called Alfons. Fredrik had never met Alfons, and he didn't want to either – unlike Ossian, Alfons was still alive. He was ashamed at the thought, but he would happily have swapped. A life for a life. Just like Jessica had done. Or Nova, as she had begun to call herself later on.

'No, I don't think Thomas knows,' said Mauro. 'I haven't told Jenny anything, and things went really badly when she tried to frame me for the murders. But I didn't say anything then and I haven't said anything now. Cecilia doesn't know either. In a way, it might have been a fair cop if I had been convicted.'

'Don't think like that,' said Josefin, placing a hand on Mauro's arm. 'It was a long time ago. And it was an accident. We had no idea what would happen. We were kids. We were stupid, tattling kids.'

'It wasn't an accident,' Mauro said bitterly. 'We were the ones who lied. John never did a thing. He was innocent. But we made up stories about him and the others. I can't even remember why. For kicks? Revenge because he said something we didn't like? Because we'd heard they were weird? The crucial thing was that our parents believed our lies. And it all went off the rails – catastrophically. It was never supposed . . . We never meant . . . None of us thought our own parents would . . .'

He fell silent.

No one else said anything. The guilt hung heavy over the room.

'I've never told Jörgen anything either,' Lovis said at last, her voice rasping. 'He's in Hall for William's murder, and may he rot there for eternity. Even if the bastard didn't do it.'

There was silence in the room. Most people were staring at the floor.

Once they would have walked through fire for each other. But then life had happened. Some of them had become – or still were – couples. Some had carved out incredible careers. Others had lived the quiet life. The only one for whom things had gone really badly was Lovis. Well, and Vendela . . . Poor Vendela. But how could any of them have known that it would end in such tragedy for her?

They had sworn never to contact each other. Even when Josefin had shown Fredrik the article in the newspaper the summer before about a girl called Lilly Meyer who had been found dead, he hadn't got in touch with Mauro.

'What's happened is awful in a way that can't be described,' Mauro said. 'But it's over now. Jessica is dead. So I just want to check that our promise to each other is still in force. None of us will say anything. Or has anyone changed their minds? Has anyone been tempted to talk to the cops about the past? Or the media, for that matter?'

Everyone in the room shook their heads firmly.

'Good,' said Mauro. 'That's settled then. Those of you who are in contact with each other – be careful. Only use WhatsApp and don't use your real names. But like we said back then, it's best we cut all contact. This is ours to carry together. In silence. And those of you who still have parents alive – do not let them find anything out. Our guilt is hard enough to cope with alone.

They should not have to share it. If we hadn't lied, then none of this would ever have happened. At least that's how I see it. Let sleeping dogs lie.'

The others nodded. Then they all stood up and left without any words of farewell.

166

It was evening. Most of the family had started getting ready for bed, but Vincent was too restless to do that. An unexpected summer storm had drawn in and the wind was tugging at the trees outside the house. The trunks were creaking and the leaves were rustling as if they wanted to break free.

Vincent was in the study looking at the newspaper clipping that he had read so many times before.

MAGIC ENDS IN TRAGEDY!

On a farm near Kvibille, a playful illusion
suddenly became deadly reality.

Vincent had lost count of the number of times he'd seen that headline.

But since getting the article out of the bookcase a week before, he had been unable to put it back. He had read it over and over again, trying to remember the encounter with the inquisitive reporter. But it was just blurry. So long ago. And he hadn't been all . . . there.

He remembered a kind policeman and a peevish woman, but it was impossible to know which of his memories were genuine and which were figments of his imagination, crafted in a child's mind from things seen on TV, read in books and experienced in reality. The truth, of course, was somewhere in between. He knew that very few of his memories – if any – had happened just the way he remembered them. And the sad seven-year-old eyes staring back at him from the newspaper were a memory he had done his best to filter out.

But the three puzzles on the desk spoke their own clear message. Someone wanted to remind him about what had happened when he was little. And whoever it was, it was neither Jane nor Nova. He had assumed the puzzles were from her, intended either as a way of confusing him and distracting him from the investigation, or given Nova's narcissism, perhaps containing vital clues. It wasn't uncommon for people who thought highly of themselves to want to share their perception of their own brilliance with those they regarded as smart enough to understand it too.

But it hadn't been that at all. It hadn't been Nova who had sent the puzzles to him. Nor had she sent the clipping to Ruben.

Someone out there was playing an unpleasant game with him, and he had no idea who it was.

'What are you doing?' Maria said from the doorway. 'The record you were playing in the living room ended ages ago. Comfort Module – what kind of name is that for a band anyway?'

She looked at him anxiously.

'Are you feeling unwell?'

He couldn't answer. He really didn't know. In a reflex action, he put his hands over the newspaper article on the desk. It was a childish thing to do, but he couldn't stand the thought of the questions it would elicit. Maria saw the newspaper, as he knew she would, and glanced at him – but she chose not to say anything.

'You really look dreadful,' she said. 'Come on, I'll help you get to bed. You're supposed to be off to Fort Boyard tomorrow – you've got to rest. I'll tidy things up for you and we can go to bed.'

She gathered together the three taped-together puzzles from the desk by placing them on top of each other. Fortunately, she didn't seem to take in their strange messages.

'Where do you want these?' she said, waving the bundle of papers around under the desk lamp.

He rubbed his eyes. Perhaps Maria was right. He shouldn't

be sitting here alone with his thoughts. He appreciated her spontaneous thoughtfulness. He realized he had missed it.

Suddenly, there were letters flickering across the desk. They were dancing in the lamplight, in and out of focus. Were his eyes deceiving him because he'd rubbed them too hard? No, the letters were most certainly real. A distant crack outside told him that the wind had just snapped a branch off a tree somewhere. 'Wait,' he said, taking the puzzles back from Maria.

She shrugged.

'At least I tried,' she said. 'Don't stay down here too long. You really don't look well.' She left as he examined the pile carefully.

The holes.

The three taped-together puzzles each had irregular holes between the Tetris pieces, holes that were too big and irregular to mean anything. The holes were in roughly the same place in each puzzle, but had different shapes. When they were overlaid, the holes created new, more defined contours.

Letters.

The holes formed letters.

He shifted the newspaper article out of the way and held the puzzles under the lamp just as Maria had done. The light that reached the desk through the holes clearly formed a word.

GUILTY

The shadow within him began to murmur, and his eyes filled with tears. He had to blink hard to see.

This wasn't fair. He had done everything he could. Why couldn't he be free? He blinked hard again, his gaze falling on the photo accompanying the newspaper article. The photo of the boy he had been.

His tears made the picture swim out of focus, and he suddenly saw certain lines on the photo more clearly than the others. He wiped his eyes with the back of his hand and looked again. Someone had drawn on the picture in pen. He had sometimes done the same when he was little and had nothing better to do. Even in adulthood, he often drew around the contours of people or things in the newspaper while thinking. He always finished with a moustache.

He hadn't given the doodle any thought when he had read the article previously – it was hard to see it since the ink had faded, and the lines did nothing more than follow the outlines of the magic box visible in the background of the shot.

The box where Mum . . . He cut that thought off and focused on the picture again. The shadow within grew in size and intensity.

The doodle on the photo comprised three lines. One line followed the upper edge of the magic box and connected to another line going down its side. The third line joined the other two.

He suddenly realized what he was looking at.

It was a letter A. A, as in alpha. As in the beginning.

He grabbed the card that had come with the third puzzle and read it.

> And remember that there is no one to blame but you.
> You could have chosen a different path. But you didn't.
> So we have reached your omega.
> The beginning of your end.

He had thought that if he found what was supposed to be the beginning then he would more easily understand what the puzzle maker meant. Whatever it was that was going to come to an end. And now he had found it. The puzzle maker had marked the beginning for him the day that Ruben had received that article two years ago, but Vincent hadn't looked. The beginning was when he had been seven years old and his mother had died. When he had become Vincent Walder, who counted even numbers and created intricate patterns to avoid feeling anything. When the shadow had moved in.

That was his alpha.

He had thought he had moved on in life, but the message in the puzzles was clear. He was not permitted to leave anything behind. It had all started there – on the farm in Kvibille. And now it was catching up with him.

So we have reached your omega.
The beginning of your end.

The wind was whistling around the house, rattling the windows violently, as if it were trying to get inside. He would be held accountable. More than forty years after his mother's death, his punishment was going to be meted out to him. He didn't know by whom. Or when. All he knew was that it was coming. The roar of the shadow within him was so deafening that he put his hands to his ears.

167

Sorunda Horse Farm 1996

Jessica had been dreaming. She wasn't sure what it had been about – but it had been a good dream. She had been with the big kids. That was how she knew it was a dream. She never got to be with them otherwise – except at a distance. They thought she was too little. And too weird. The little thing she understood, although she wasn't that much smaller than them, but she didn't get the weird thing. There was nothing weird about her family. Only that it was a big one and she could never quite get to grips with how they were all related. She knew Mum and Dad. After all, they were her mum and dad. All the others were just . . . family.

She rolled over in bed and buried her face in the pillow. She wanted to go back to the dream – where no one was teasing her. When she could still go to school in Ösmo without people talking about her behind her back. The big kids were just jealous, she knew that. Dad didn't let them come to the farm anymore. He said they needed to grow up and learn some manners first. They were welcome to visit the horses when they stopped badmouthing other people.

It wasn't often she heard Dad say things like that. He was always so kind. Kinder than anyone else in the universe.

Obviously Mum was kind too, but she could be strict. Dad was special. Sometimes when she tried to describe how much she loved him, she found words weren't enough. Dad used to say he loved her to the moon and back. But the moon was too close. She loved him so much that it was impossible to describe using anything that could be seen.

There was a funny smell. She cast the covers aside and put her feet on the floor. She was barefoot because it was the summer, but tonight it was warmer than usual. She thought she could hear voices. Agitated voices. Grown-up voices. But she wasn't sure whether it was a dream or reality.

She opened the door and padded quietly out of her room. The smell grew stronger, stinging her nostrils and making her cough violently. She cautiously crept down the stairs, keeping her hand over her mouth. She took care to avoid the steps that creaked. Mum wouldn't be happy to be woken.

When she got downstairs, she saw the fire right away. The smell was so overpowering that her eyes filled with tears. The hallway was on fire and the door was ajar. Had someone been here?

Through the door, she could see the stable. There were flames coming from it too, and she could faintly hear the horses screaming.

Without thinking, she rushed straight through the fire and out of the front door. The flames reached out for her but they didn't take hold. Her heart pounding, she ran across the courtyard towards the stable.

As she got closer, she could hear Star screaming. Star was her favourite horse, a small white pony with grey patches and a pink muzzle. She loved Star. Almost more than she loved Dad. She had been there when Star had been born. She had seen her first tottering steps. She'd bottle-fed her. And Dad had told her that this was the very first horse of her own.

Star was screaming more loudly, as if trying to get her starry sisters in the sky to help her. The screams of the other horses mingled with hers. But the door was closed. They couldn't get out. The flames were now several metres high and licking their way up the exterior walls towards the night sky.

The stable door was bolted. Tears streaming down her cheeks, Jessica tried to lift the bolt. Star's terrified cries grew even louder, but the bar was too high up and too heavy – she couldn't budge it.

She felt the heat of the fire approaching her at breakneck speed. But she didn't care. All she cared about was Star. She roared out her impotence and fear at the heavens – prayed like she had never prayed before – but the bolt wouldn't move even a millimetre.

Then she felt someone pulling her away from the door.

'No, no, no,' she shouted, flailing wildly with her arms to try and get loose, but the person holding her was too strong.

'Shh . . . shhh . . . It's too late. You can't save them.'

Dad's voice in her ear – his strong arms around her. She sobbed, screamed and pummelled his chest, but all he did was hold her more tightly. Then she lifted her head. The heat from the fire behind her was fierce on her back.

'Mum?' she said, only now looking back at the main building. There was no longer a small fire in the hall – the whole house was engulfed in flames and the sound of the fire rumbled into the summer night.

'It's too late,' Dad said. 'I didn't wake up soon enough. But the two of us can still save ourselves.'

He pressed his face into her hair. Then he lifted her into his arms and ran across the courtyard. She had lost all strength – any ability to get free. It was all gone. Dad's embrace was all she had.

'It was probably an accident,' he said. 'They didn't mean it – the petrol was only supposed to be a threat. But they were so angry. They said their children had said . . . I don't understand. But it must have been an accident . . .'

She could tell that he didn't believe his own words.

He gently put her in the passenger seat of the car but didn't buckle her in. Instead, he quickly shut the door, ran around to the other side, got into the driver's seat and started the engine.

Human silhouettes were standing by the roadside in the darkness. The flames haunted their faces, but it was hard to make out how many there were. They withdrew into the shadows, standing still as the car passed.

The car bounced on the gravel track and for a brief moment the headlights illuminated the silhouettes' faces. Jessica saw them all in the light as clearly as if it had been day. Their mouths were gaping, their gazes filled with fascination, as they surveyed the inferno they had created. She recognized them from when they had dropped off and picked up their children from riding lessons.

And suddenly she understood it all. She knew it was the adults who had set the fire she could see in the rear window, blazing high into the sky. But she had heard the whispers at school, the gossip going around about her family. And she knew that it was really the children who had started the fire with their spite and their lies. She even knew their names. Fredrik. Lovis. Josefin. Mauro. Vendela. Henry. Karin. Tobias. Hugo. Jens. Janina.

'I promise,' she said quietly to herself.

She thought of Star burning in the stable.

And she thought of Mum.

It was as if her own insides were also on fire.

'I promise that one day I will take the most beautiful thing you have away from you,' she said through gritted teeth. Then she looked forward again. That thought had bestowed calm on her. It was going to be OK.

She had a purpose.

Travelling through the darkness was like travelling through a tunnel where there was only a small speck of light ahead of them. But she wasn't afraid. She was with Dad. It was going to be OK.

He was driving fast. Faster than he'd ever driven before. She wound down the window on her side, closing her eyes as the wind blew into her face. The wind was warm, caressing her skin as they tore along the track. She could still hear the fire behind them. They would soon reach the bridge. She loved the bridge and the water gushing fiercely under it. Sometimes Dad stopped the car in the middle of the bridge just to let her look.

She loved the way the water was free to do as it pleased – it went where it could, always took the best path, lived in freedom. Just like fire – but the other way around. Water gave life. She hoped Dad would stop on the bridge this time too, so that she could drown out Star's screams with the sound of the water. But Dad wasn't slowing down. Instead, he was going even faster. Then they were no longer on the bridge – they were flying freely through the air. Then her ears were filled with the sound of water. But that didn't help. She could still hear Star's screams.

And she knew she would never stop hearing them.

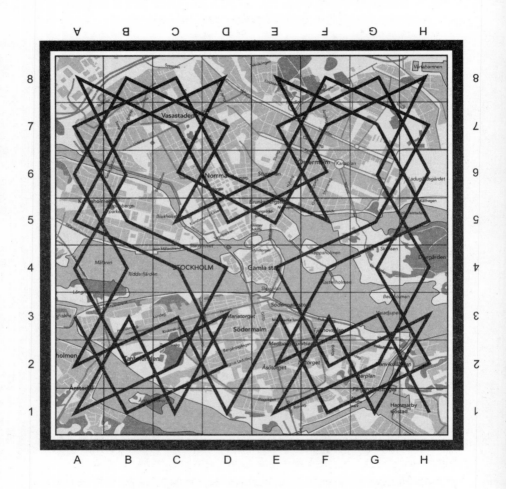

Acknowledgements

It has been pointed out before and is worth pointing out again: you cannot write a book alone. Not even if you have two authors, it turns out. We owe a debt of gratitude to a large number of people who have helped us to keep this book on an even keel.

For starters, there is everyone who has assisted us with the content:

Kelda Stagg MSc, a crime scene investigator with the Stockholm Region Police Authority has continued to explain to us (in almost unpalatable detail) what happens to a body after death – for instance, if it has been buried under grass – and how to open it up properly. With her expertise in microbiology, she has also corrected our mistakes about which bacteria can spread from horses to humans, which is an area far more complex than we could ever have guessed.

(Kelda Stagg is also one of the three brains behind the Instagram handle @liket_efter_doden which explores what happens to the body in death – if you're as fascinated by this as we are, then give it a follow!)

We have also received invaluable assistance from people with insight into the police force's negotiation work who closely scrutinized our new character, Adam, and ensured that he behaved plausibly in high-pressure situations, and that our police officers all conducted themselves appropriately in raids. Naturally Adam has his own shortcomings, but we are full of admiration for real-life negotiators and their extraordinary skills. Due to their profession, they have requested anonymity, but you should know that these individuals frequently tiptoe along a tightrope that is much too slack.

Detective Inspector Magnus Svensson at Hall Prison has

replied with the utmost patience to far more emails than he probably expected to receive regarding visiting procedures at his facility. It may seem trivial, but you know what they say about the details – they're what matter.

Eline Dinnetz has a mathematical brain far bigger than our two put together; she has tenderly guided us as we have tried to work out the permutations of anagrams and other things which are obvious to her, but which have left our frontal lobes in knots when we have tried to tackle them ourselves.

We would also like to thank all those of you who have selflessly fielded cryptic emails and phone calls about murals, hotel rooms and everything else we needed to know about – or who have otherwise contributed information and inspiration.

As ever, we have taken liberties with reality, both in terms of details around police work (to our knowledge, pawnbrokers do not receive lists of stolen 'commonplace jewellery') and the world as a whole (there is no Backens nursery school or Epicura residential training centre). We hope this has solely enhanced the story.

However, it took more than just the people above to make this content into a proper book. Without the following people, *CULT* would still be nothing more than a very long Word document.

To begin with, there is the indefatigable team at our Swedish publishing house Bokförlaget Forum. There are many people involved, but spearheading them are two of the best. We solemnly promised our publisher Ebba Östberg that this book would not be longer than the last one. We lied. Sorry. Our editor Kerstin Ödeen has by now checked that more than one million letters and commas are where they should be, as well as fact-checking our many hundreds of statements about all manner of things. Big thank-you hugs to you both, and once again, sorry.

Three cheers for our ingenious designer Marcell Bandicksson, whose covers for the Swedish editions have interpreted our peculiar brains with pinpoint accuracy – his work has ensured these are the finest volumes in the history of the printed book.

Joakim Hansson, Anna Frankl, Signe Lundgren and the rest

of the gang at Nordin Agency, as well as Lili Assefa and Paulina Bånge and their crew at Assefa Kommunikation, have all done an incredible job around the world – their efforts continue to leave us speechless. If you find yourself on a remote Japanese island or high in the Himalayas in Nepal and you happen upon a book in your hostel about Vincent and Mina, translated to the local language, this is all thanks to these superstars.

However, the biggest thanks of all goes to you, dear reader, for choosing to make this journey together with us, and with Vincent and Mina. A story only really comes into being when someone enjoys it. So thank you for bringing Vincent and Mina to life. We hope you have become firm friends and that you will join them for their next instalment.

Camilla's personal acknowledgements:

Without the people close to me in my personal life I would never be able to write books. Their support, encouragement and love carries me through the many pages. Heartfelt thanks to my husband Simon, and my children Wille, Meja, Charlie and Polly. I would also like to applaud my support team, who make daily life and my work possible: thanks to Mathilda Norman, Natasa Maric and Johan Hultman. And to all my friends – where would I be without you? None mentioned, none forgotten, but I hope you all know what you mean to me.

Henrik's personal acknowledgements:

Writing a book during a pandemic is an unusual experience. *CULT* came into existence during a period when my family and I saw more of each other than we had ever believed possible. I must therefore award medals to Linda, Sebastian, Nemo and Milo for the great feat of refraining from assassinating me in my sleep thus far. Thanks also to all my friends who continue to offer their encouragement and support. Finally, special thanks to mentalist and pal Anthony Heads for our lengthy discussions over good whisky and bad cocktails.